Acclaim for *The Interpreter*

"Few writers chronicle the Korean-American experience, and even fewer are as talented as Kim . . . A good eye for detail, an excellent prose style, and the ability to create compelling characters . . . luminous . . . hypnotic . . . an intriguing, tortured portrait of a second-generation Korean-American by a promising young writer."
—*Publishers Weekly*

"Kim zeroes in on the debilitating tensions of interpreting between languages, countries, childhood and adulthood, lies and secrets, sex and hurt, anger and love."
—*Daily News* (New York)

"Utterly absorbing . . . stylish and elegant psychological mystery."
—*Toronto Globe and Mail*

"Kim is a precise, patient observer. . . . A sleek, nearly hypnotic glimpse into the world of a Korean family ruptured in translation to America."
—*Kirkus Reviews*

"Riveting . . . No mere whodunit, Kim's debut also examines the myth of the 'model minority' and what it's like to live in cultural limbo."
—*Glamour*

"Kim has come up with one of the most original and disturbing motives for murder that this reader has ever encountered. It brings into play loyalty, cultural differences, and the sometimes lonely existence of our nation's many immigrants."
—*USA Today*

"Outstanding . . . Most admirably, Kim avoids identity politics entirely. She is not interested in ghettoizing her protagonist. Suzy is a character first, a representation of human psychology, one that Kim has studied too carefully to label simply as Korean, or Depressed."
—Max Watman, *The New Criterion*

"*The Interpreter* is a melancholy study of a young Korean-American woman's alienation from both her Asian roots and her American environment. It's also a murder mystery. That Kim makes these two aspects of the novel work together suggests that she's a writer to keep an eye on."
—*San Jose Mercury News*

"Amazing . . . The author's a master tease, surrendering details so slowly that you'll find yourself in such a frenzy to get to the next chapter that you'll skim the one you're on."
—*Jane*

"In Suzy Park, Kim has fashioned a moody, memorable misfit who both captures our heart and twists our guts in one of the new year's more complex and rewarding novels."
—*The News-Press*

"To readers of this compelling, cryptic novel—[Kim's heroine] Suzy is a gorgeous enigma, simultaneously sophisticated and naïve, corrupt and pure."
—*Shout*

"Part murder mystery, part psychological thriller, the novel grippingly explores damaging trade-offs made by people desperate to survive in a strange new place . . . *The Interpreter* opens out into vistas of human complexity that will captivate readers from any culture."
—*The Tennessean*

THE
INTERPRETER

THE
INTERPRETER

SUKI KIM

PICADOR

FARRAR, STRAUS AND GIROUX
NEW YORK

www.picadorusa.com

For information on Picador Reading Group Guides, as well as ordering, please contact the Trade Marketing department at St. Martin's Press.
Phone: 1-800-221-7945 extension 763
Fax: 212-677-7456
E-mail: trademarketing@stmartins.com

Designed by Abby Kagan

Library of Congress Cataloging-in-Publication Data

Kim, Suki, 1970–
      The interpreter / Suki Kim.
          p.   cm.
      ISBN 0-312-42224-5
      1. Korean Americans—Fiction. 2. Women interpreters—Fiction.
    3. Parents—Death—Fiction. 4. New York (N.Y.)—Fiction. I. Title.

PS3611.I457 I58 2003
813'.6—dc21

                                                2002072120

First published in the United States by Farrar, Straus and Giroux

10   9   8   7   6   5   4   3

For my parents

THE
INTERPRETER

1.

CIGARETTE AT 9 A.M. is a sure sign of desperation. Doesn't happen to her often, except on mornings like this, November, rain, overcrowded McDonald's in the South Bronx off the 6 train. Like a block party, this place, with those dopey eight-year-olds who should be in school, and their single mothers sick of shouting, and the bored men at each table still not at work. Morning is full here. Everyone's in it together, a communal experience, this day, this life. It is not her life, though. She does not know this. She does not want this. She looks up, instead, at a huge sign for the breakfast special across the window. Not much mystery there, food is plenty. Ninety-nine cents for hash browns, an English muffin with microwaved egg yolks, and a miniature Tropicana. Too good to be true, such abundance for barely a dollar. This is a generous neighborhood.

She is twenty-nine, and it is November. She is overdressed, as usual. The black cashmere coat that costs double her rent, and the pin-striped pants are sleek enough for any Hollywood starlet. Across her shoulder is a navy tote bag that matches the steel shine of her leather boots. Her face bears no trace of makeup. She is morose in black and blue. These are power colors.

November, and she stands facing the entrance of McDonald's on Burnside Avenue. In her left hand is a black vinyl umbrella, and in her right, a half-smoked cigarette she barely sucks on. Five minutes past nine. She is too early. The subway was unexpectedly fast. Only when she is running ahead of schedule should this happen, should the local suddenly reroute to express and drop her off at the Bronx stop within minutes. Fifty-five minutes to hang outside McDonald's in this part of town, a world away from her apartment back in downtown Manhattan. Fifty-four minutes and counting; she is stuck in this wilderness and peeks at her watch again.

But a rescue is handy, a cup of fresh coffee, a slab of butter on a toasted muffin. All she has to do is walk through that door and wave a dollar. A long drag on a cigarette, longer than necessary. She is stalling. She has not yet bought into this place.

Rain keeps on, halfhearted, barely soaking. She is Cinderella-at-midnight, and her chic ensemble a pumpkin dream ready to pop. There is no glass slipper in this part of town, no Prince Charming in search of a princess. The crossover is final. Beyond that door is the wrong track, whose morning begins with a dollar and a jaded appetite.

Looking in is easy, to stand out in rain and take note of what unfurls from a distance.

Instead, she is inside now. There are several lines, which all reach several faces taking orders. The line in which she stands moves fast enough, but she has time, enough time to stand and wait. Oh, but time is plenty here. People sit around in all corners. No one dashes out to a merger meeting at the head office. No one screams double espresso with a touch of skim milk. No one fumbles with a tray balancing a Motorola on their right ear.

None of that happens here. This is a place of leisure. She's in no rush.

What do you want after all, do you want me to tell you? Damian had lunged at her in his final message, as if he were pushing himself into her once more.

"What do you want, miss?"

She did not hear the man the first time. Such mishaps keep happening to her lately. She keeps missing the cue. She sets an alarm for eight and bolts out of bed at seven, or she presses "3" in the elevator and finds herself on the second floor, or she runs to answer the phone only to realize it is not ringing. Here she is dumbstruck before a man in a brown uniform who is shaking his head now, repeating for the third time, "What do you want, miss?"

"Coffee, a medium-sized cup of coffee, please." She thought she had said it. She thought he knew what she wanted. The big-haired teenager behind her is popping her pink gum, visibly annoyed. The man in the brown uniform snatches the dollar from her, shaking his head once more. The coffee costs seventy-nine cents. Twenty more cents, she could have a complete breakfast; what's she thinking? She can sense the man's disapproval. Bitch, he must think. A cup of coffee for seventy-nine cents when a whole tray comes for a dollar, Miss Too-Good-for-a-Discounted-Meal, Miss Stuck-Up-Coat, Miss Can't-Hear-for-Shit!

Bitch it is, this 9 a.m. Marlboro high. She needs to sit down, but the place is jam-packed, and no one is leaving anytime soon. But a miracle, it must be. There is someone waving at her, pointing at the empty seat across from him. Once she plops herself down and takes a hot sip of coffee, she notices that the man is in fact the only other Asian present.

He is reading the paper. *Hangukilbo*—the *Korea Daily*—she recognizes the bold type. Beneath the thick Walgreens reading lenses, his eyes appear puffy and reddish. Lacking a good night's sleep, she thinks. They all do, these immigrant men. He wiggles his nose, which is too small for his spacious face, before glancing up at her for a second. She smiles, grateful for the seat. He does not return the smile but continues to stare at her awhile before turning back to his paper. He knows, she thinks. They always do. It's one of those things, the unspoken recognition among the same kind. She can tell who's Korean from miles away. Of course, she's been wrong before, though only a handful of times, mistaking a Japanese person for Korean. She is not sure why, perhaps something in the history, a possible side effect of the sick affinity between the colonizer and the colonized—Japan had once ruled Korea for thirty-six years, her father never forgot to remind her. Or it might simply be the way their facial bones are shaped, Koreans and Japanese more oval while Chinese seem flatter. All she knows is that she can always tell, and he can tell, and they both know that they are the same kind, sitting so close amidst a roomful of the rest of the world.

He is not interested in conversation, and she is glad. He does not harangue her with "Were you born in the States?," "What do your parents do?," or "Why is a good Korean girl like you not yet married?"—the prying questions that fellow immigrants often feel entitled to ask. Buried behind his newspaper now, he is no longer visible to her. It's almost noble of him, she thinks, to offer her a seat and leave her alone.

Nothing comes for free, look closer, you always find a tag, Damian had whispered into her ear while pulling at the last button on her dress. Then he took five steps backward and stood gazing at her first nakedness as if he were an artist before a muse. His eyes had appeared awfully blue then, bluer than they justifiably were, almost aqua, the ocean color, so different from her own black eyes that she looked away in a sudden wave of embarrassment, thinking the whole time, "Even this has a price, even his lips on my skin, even his bluest eyes on me."

Rain this morning is an accomplice. Even at the edge of the city through a cloudy window across which hangs a ninety-nine-cent-breakfast banner. The coffee is cooling. The waiting is not so bad after all. This might be her break. No one will find her here. A perfect hideout.

Then the man across from her shuts his newspaper. He picks up his tray without meeting her eyes. She watches him walk away. It is the shrunken walk of one who had once been a young man but is no longer, who has not spoken his language for longer than he can bear, who no longer believes that he will ever see his homeland. She can feel the weight of each step. She wants to look away. Yet she is relieved when he stops outside and lights a cigarette under the orange awning.

He is not gone. He is not yet gone from her. He stands with his back turned to the window, which she is facing now. The back of his hair is thinning. He is older than his actual age, perhaps. She notes the wrinkled seams of his gabardine pants and the shiny leather of his dress shoes, which are long out of style. He is awkward in his clothes, she thinks. Those are not his everyday shoes. When was the last time he put those shoes on, what was he like then, what was the rest of his life? But this is a terrible habit, to wonder upon a past, to dig into a history of anything, anyone, even a passing stranger at a fast-food joint in a neighborhood that is not hers. A lack of reserve, or boundary. Yet she still cannot look away. She knows men like him. She imagines how he might have fumbled through the back of his closet to pull out those black leather shoes, which might have sat in the dirt of his buried past for as long as a decade, or even longer, depending on when he had moved to this country, and how he might have shined them all morning with a bit of paper towel and wax, thinking to himself, "Ah they are fine still, they fit still, I am not such an old man after all, this mute delivery guy from Queens whom no one ever looks at, including my own wife, who hasn't had a day of smiles since she made that bad slip of following me so far, as far as this McDonald's land in the middle of nowhere, to this bad-food, bad-mannered country where I am nothing but a frail old man, smoking the last butt of a Marlboro in the November rain, as if my life depended on it, as if this life were a thing I could have known when I last wore these shoes."

She knows men like him. She knows what his days are like, the home he might return to at night, the daughters to whom he no longer reaches out.

She glances at her watch again. Quarter to ten, time's almost up. Didn't take so long after all. They must all be waiting for her. The case is nothing without her. She looks up and notices that the man outside is gone.

2.

FORTY-FOUR BURNSIDE AVENUE is a three-story concrete building east of McDonald's, the sort of place where an insurance agent or an accountant keeps an office, filled with ancient filing cabinets and dubious clientele. The elevator has not worked in months. The "Broken" sign is ripped halfway across, and a tiny scribble in red ink proclaims not so shyly "Your Ass." The staircase to the basement leads to a chunky wooden door adorned with a musty gold plaque that reads DIAMOND COURT REPORTING.

Inside, a Hispanic receptionist with bright-pink lips is screaming something into the phone. Then she looks up for a second and snaps, "You here for *Kim* versus *Santos*?," pointing her matching pink-manicured index finger toward the room marked "3" without waiting for an answer.

"Your name?"

Name is always the first thing they ask, not out of personal interest, but because everything has to be recorded here, stamped and witnessed. This is a mini-court. A place of honor, justice, and underpaid lawyers who didn't make the grade at hundred-thousand-dollar firms.

"Suzy Park," she answers automatically.

The stenographer scribbles the name in her note and adds, "Love that name Suzy, with 'z-y,' right?" Stenographers are always such chatty characters, mostly women from south-shore Long Island, mid-thirties with blond highlights. This one is no exception, although the blond streaks on her head appear almost natural against her blue-shadowed eyes. "As in Suzy Wong?" one of the lawyers blurts out with a chuckle, quickly realizes that no one is laughing, and tries hard not to blush. He is the young one, freshly out of law school and awkward in his crisp tan suit and the awful green tie with tiny boats on it that must have come from Macy's sale rack. "You mean the Chinese prostitute in that Hollywood classic?" Suzy is tempted to throw back at him, but she ignores him, grabbing the seat next to the one reserved for the defendant, who is still not here.

"Oh, Mr. Kim just went to make a phone call, but he'll be right back. Nice fella. Too bad about the union mess, though." The stenographer nudges, as if any of this is Suzy's business, as if the details of the case matter to anybody in the room at all. "Poor guy, he really doesn't speak a word of English. I don't know how they carry on. Amazing, don't you think?" The stenographer addresses the young lawyer, who is still blushing and is now glad at the chance to redeem himself. "Well, he does know a word or two. A smart man, though. Just because he doesn't speak the language, it doesn't mean he's dumb." With this declaration he is quite proud of himself, and turns to Suzy, grinning.

The other lawyer glances at his wristwatch with the insolence of a student ready for the bell. He is older, perhaps in his late forties. He is not interested in the Ping-Pongy chat across the table. He's heard it all, and he is not having it today. He is worried that he might have parked his car in the wrong spot. What the hell, if he gets a ticket, he'll just bill Santos. But where's Santos anyway? Should be outside waiting for his line of questioning, even if he doesn't want to sit face-to-face with this Kim guy! But he's not sure he turned the headlights off before getting out of his car. Damn rain, shouldn't have brought his brand-new Honda Accord to this pissy neighborhood. Then he remembers what his wife said to him this morning, about the loan on the car and how she's not going to help pay a penny of it if he doesn't pitch in for their Florida vacation this Christmas. And he thinks, Florida. They've gone every winter, dragging the kids, well, not really kids anymore, but brooding trench-coated teenagers who'd much rather stay online in their chat rooms than follow their mom and pop to the package hotel where they lie around the pool arguing over loans that seem to tag along with everything they own, from their Forest Hills house to the kids' prep-school tuition to the brand-new Honda, which is possibly sitting on the wrong street corner with sparkling headlights calling to any thugs who watch from McDonald's across the street, killing time.

With a mumbling moan, he rushes out. The stenographer, raising an eyebrow, is about to say something and then changes her mind. The young lawyer appears nonchalant, as if this sort of thing happens all the time at a deposition. "Oh well," he says, "we're gonna have to start a bit late. Why don't you ladies take a little break?" Then he excuses himself and walks out also. "A cigarette?" the stenographer suggests, grabbing her white leather bag to head outside, and Suzy declines. They smoke like high-school girls, these Long Island women, usually Virginia Slims or Capri, menthol if they are over thirty-five and newly divorced.

So it's Suzy all alone in the windowless room, staring at the stenograph mounted on a tripod, which is the only object other than the oversized conference table. The pay is by the hour, so it hardly matters if the case is delayed. Depositions never start on time anyway. Witnesses are rarely the problem. In fact, they usually show up early, nervous and guilty by association. The confusion begins with the whole arrangement of such interested, or disinterested, parties. Lawyers behave like children at a playground. Some are bullies flying on a verbal roller coaster like kids on speed; and others, bored and sullen, reluctantly finish up homework under supervision. Stenographers are jesters, butting in with needless commentaries and inevitably running out of ink or paper right at the crunch of a testimony. The interpreter, however, is the shadow. The key is to be invisible. She is the only one in the room who hears the truth, a keeper of secrets.

In fact, that is why Suzy has stuck with the job thus far. She has never before held a job for more than six months. She's done what college dropouts do—lie and get on with what she can scrape together. Waitressing required too much smile, although she did give it a shot for a few weeks at a sushi restaurant on Bleecker Street, only to get fired for refusing to pretend to be Japanese. Nightclub hostessing was a disaster, and she hated sleeping through the day and missing the sun. Internet sales made her head spin, as if her life were being gambled on fictitious credits. An artist's model meant being grabbed in the wrong places by the wrong hands. Copyediting ruined her eyesight. Copywriting was a hoax. The latest gig was a fact-checking stint at a literary magazine. She lasted barely four months. She only got there through the connections of an old college roommate who was an editor and declared Suzy's career phobia to be "so nineties." "Get over it," Jen told Suzy over the phone. "Damian must've fucked with your brains." It was Jen who begged her to reconsider when Suzy packed her bag in the spring semester of their senior year. "Everyone will forget soon, it'll soon blow over." Jen had always been the sensible one. She never seemed to suffer from hangovers or PMS. Jen was right, of course. Except forgetting came with its price, as Damian had said. Was it a premonition? How did he know?

It wasn't that the fact-checking job was necessarily boring. Suzy didn't mind reading the copy all day. She could pretend that her cubicle was a waiting room at a doctor's office or an airport lounge as she scanned articles about the President's latest run-ins with that big-haired intern, or Philip Roth's ex-wife's tell-all book about Philip Roth, or the usual groundbreaking news, most of which she forgot instantly. Every day she had to call the New York Public Library and ask them to verify the year of publication of *The Bell Jar* or *The Crying of Lot 49* or the exact number of literary texts mentioned in Harold Bloom's monstrous canon book. The line was always busy, and she had to keep redialing. She thought it was kind of a miracle, that someone somewhere across the city was looking up all the gritty facts for her, as if it mattered to anyone, except Mr. Bloom, whether the magazine should print 100 texts or 101. What she did mind, and could not stand, in fact, was the voice of the researcher who came on the phone in the third month. It was a new person; by then, Suzy could recognize all voices on the other end. There was a shy, whispery girl-voice that answered in the morning, which Suzy imagined might actually belong to a tall woman in her fifties with wavy silver hair and a pleated skirt. Another was a husky male who often answered during lunchtime, whose intonation of words like "chiaroscuro" and "serendipitous" made Suzy swallow hard before saying thank you. But the new voice was without much character: monotone, matter-of-fact, flat. Suzy cringed when he answered, and was not sure why. She would forget the question and mumble whatever came into her mind, or, worse, she would hang up instantly. But it bothered her, this ominous voice she had to hear every day, almost every hour on busy days. Finally, in her fourth month, she quit. She did not explain why, and she was never asked. Fact-checkers are a dime a dozen. They come and go. Some get real jobs at the women's magazines around town, and a few actually sell the novel they've been slaving away at for years. But most move back home to Wichita or Baltimore, swearing never to return to New York. Jen laughed when Suzy told her later and said, "Damian, he must've been some fuck." Sure, something about the researcher's dark drone reminded her of Damian, but that was almost an afterthought.

Interpreting, Suzy finds, is somehow simpler, freer to be exact. The agency calls her when there is a job, and she shows up wherever the deposition happens to take place. Most cases are banal: automobile accidents, slip-and-falls, medical malpractice, basically any misfortune that might generate cash. The details are almost always predictable. The plaintiff wasn't really hurt at the time of the accident, but now, six months later, cannot move his head. Or the plaintiff had surgery and is now suffering from complications. Suzy never finds out what happens to these cases, whether they actually end up in trial or settle out of court or lead to another set of depositions. Her job is just to show up and translate into English verbatim what the witness testifies in Korean. She often feels like the buxom communication officer in *Star Trek*, the one who repeats exactly what the computer says. Except Suzy's role is neither so fleshy nor so comical. The contract, which the agency made her sign, included a clause never to engage in small talk with witnesses. The interpreter is always hired by the law firm on the side opposing the witness. It is they who need the testimony translated. The witness, summoned to testify without any knowledge of English, inevitably views the interpreter as his savior. But the interpreter, as much as her heart might commiserate with her fellow native speaker, is always working for the other side. It is this idiosyncrasy Suzy likes. Both sides need her desperately, but she, in fact, belongs to neither. One of the job requirements was no involvement: Shut up and get the work done. That's fine with her.

Except it doesn't go as smoothly as that. Suzy often finds herself cheating. Sometimes the witness falters and reveals devastating, self-incriminating information. The opposing counsel might ask how much he makes a week, and the witness turns to Suzy and asks what he should say. Should he tell him five hundred dollars, although he usually makes more money on the side? Suzy knows that the immigrant life follows different rules—no taxes, no benefits, sometimes not even Social Security or green cards. And she also knows that he should never tell lawyers that. So she might fudge the answer. She might turn to the lawyer innocently and translate, "My income is private information; approximately five hundred dollars, I would say, but I cannot be exact." Or the opposing side might try to make a case out of the fact that the plaintiff, when struck by a car, told the police that he was feeling fine and refused an ambulance. "Surely," the lawyer insists, "the injury must not have been severe if you even refused medical attention!" But Suzy knows that it is a cultural misunderstanding. It is the Korean way always to underplay the situation, to declare one is fine even when suffering from pain or ravenous hunger. This might stem from their Confucian or even Buddhist tradition, but the lawyers don't care about that. "Why did you say you were fine at the time of the accident if you weren't? Were you lying then, or are you lying now?" the lawyer presses once more, and Suzy winces, decides that she hates him. The witness gets all nervous and stammers something about how he's not a liar, and Suzy puts on a steel face to hide her anger and translates, "I was in shock, and the pain was not obvious to me until I got home and collapsed." Then the lawyer looks stumped and moves on to the next question. Suzy knows it is wrong, to embellish truth according to how she sees fit. In fact, she will be fired on the spot if anyone discovers that her translation harbors a bias. But truth, she has learned, comes in different shades, different languages at times, and lawyers with a propensity for Suzy Wong movies may not always see that. The job comes naturally to her. Neither of her parents had spoken much English. Interpreting is almost a habit.

Suddenly a light tap on her right shoulder. Suzy turns around to find a man standing there. It is the Korean man from McDonald's, the one with the freshly polished shoes, with a tired wife and unreachable daughters. "Mr. Kim?" She is delighted at such a coincidence. Breaking into a shy smile, he nods. He looks meek and timid now, no longer the grave man sitting across from her buried in his newspaper. "*An-nyung-ha-sae-yo.*" She makes a slight bow, the way Koreans do when addressing the elderly. Then he stares at Suzy's face intently, as he had done earlier this morning, and says in the unfamiliar midregional Korean accent, "You remind me of someone I used to know, a good woman, too young to be killed like that." Before she can ask what he means, the stenographer and two lawyers charge in as if they have been hanging outside together the whole time. "Shit, a ticket." The older lawyer shakes his head, waving a piece of paper. The younger one frowns, trying to appear sympathetic. The stenographer ignores both and adjusts the paper into her machine with the efficiency of a pro, turning to Suzy.

"Raise your right hand. Do you solemnly swear that you will translate from Korean to English and from English to Korean to the best of your ability, so help you God?"

"I do," Suzy answers, thinking to herself, *Yes, please help me, God.*

On the way home, Suzy calls Jen from Grand Central, which is just a few blocks from Jen's office.

"Do they always let you out this early?" Jen smiles when she greets Suzy at the Starbucks counter in the north wing of the station, sipping a Frappuccino. She is impressed that Suzy has stuck with interpreting for eight months, but she also makes it clear that she is not fooled.

"You're hiding," Jen says after ordering a chocolate-dipped biscotti with her decaf. "This is your little revenge, to make him find you, but you know Damian's far too decadent for that."

Suzy pretends to not hear and blows the foam on top of her Frappuccino into a little bubble, which makes a perfect round circle for a blinking second, then pops.

"The witness today said that I looked like someone he knew," Suzy says almost in passing.

"Another married asshole with a midlife crisis?" Jen rolls her eyes.

"No, he looked sad. He reminded me of Dad."

"Why, was he . . ."

"No, not angry, just sad."

"*Suzy . . .*"

"I've gotta go," Suzy says, sucking on the straw to get the last taste of the sugary bit at the bottom. "Michael's calling me at three."

"Where's he this time?" Jen asks with a smirk, creasing her perfectly powdered face.

"London. He loves calling me from there. He says that his cell connects clearest from Heathrow. I don't know. He might be right. Last week, he called from Lisbon and I could barely make out a word."

"Why doesn't the big guy just call you from a regular phone?"

"Because he thinks anything's traceable, and at least with his cell, he's on top of it."

They both burst out laughing then, like two coy college girls picking on the cutest boy in the room.

3.

THE PHONE CONTINUES for four rings and stops as Suzy reaches the fifth floor and stands at the door looking for the key. It rings again as she inserts the key into the hole, and stops at the fourth ring. Then it begins again. Whoever it is does not want to leave a message. Whoever it is does not know that she never picks up the phone, a habit that started the year she left school and moved in with Damian. He always let the machine take the call. It was from neither arrogance nor aloofness. During the first few months, it was a necessity. There were too many people hot on their trail, acquaintances with too much spare time who would call periodically to alert them to exactly what other people were saying about this "terrible situation," which they would repeat in a conspiring whisper as though it were not they who thought it "terrible" but everyone else. "New Yorkers aren't busy," Damian mused. "They just don't have enough time for themselves." Then there was the family. Damian's one sister lived in Lake Forest, Illinois, and had rarely been in touch over the years; Professor Tamiko would only speak to him through the lawyers. What Suzy feared was hearing her father's silence on the other end of the line. But it soon became clear that her parents would not try to contact her. Grace left a message a few weeks after the eruption of the scandal: "Suzy, you must get out of there. God will only forgive the ones who forgive themselves."

God had become Grace's answer by then, although she had been the bad one all through their growing up. Grace was the one who got grounded for being found naked with that Keller boy in the back of his dad's Toyota when she was fourteen. Grace was the one who hid her marijuana pouch inside her tampon case, which she nicknamed her "best friend, Mariana," and then, to Suzy's surprise, declared so boldly at the dinner table, "May I be excused? I promised my friend Mariana that we'll do our homework together." It had also been Grace who told Suzy that the only reason she applied to Smith College on early decision was that no decent Korean boy would want her now, because everyone knew Smith was for sluts and lesbians. But somehow, during her four years away, God found his way into Grace's untamable spirit, and Suzy could no longer recognize her older sister, who left such an inappropriate message on her machine, as though salvation lay somewhere on the stoop of a Presbyterian church on Sunday mornings. Suzy began to dread the phone. Damian said that if he could help it he would live without the damn thing. He was distrustful of people anyway. The thought of Damian being stuck on the phone with any of her young friends—although, after a few months, Jen was the only one who called with any consistency—was almost painful.

When Suzy enters the apartment, the phone begins ringing again. She waits for the click at the fourth ring, but instead the machine takes it.

"Babe, it's me, pick up!"

The voice is cheery and confident.

"Suzy, I know you're there."

She is not sure why she does not pick up immediately, but there is an unmistakable moment of hesitation. For a second, she is tempted to leave Michael at Heathrow, sliding down the moving sidewalk, shouting into his Motorola. For a second, that seems to be the most obvious thing to do, the only thing to do—to leave him there.

"Hi, I just walked in." The hesitation is over.

"See, I knew." Michael is all happy.

"London?"

"Yeah, it's fab, brilliant. Those Brits just ate it up, man. They fucking love the whole crap. They've got it all mixed up. They think Java's some coffee from the Caribbean, and HTML a code name for the newest hip-hop nation. They're sure I'm their Bill Gates, and I told them, 'Bill and me, we're like brothers.' "

"Good," Suzy agrees, as she always does when Michael's had a shot of whiskey or two.

"I sent Sandy out to Harrods to get you some stuff, some slinky things here and there, for my pretty girl back home, I told her. I'm sure she thinks I'm a pig, so I told her to get some sexy stuff for herself too, although you make sure my girl gets the best of the pile, I said."

Suzy smiles, imagining Michael's curt, crisp, forty-something-and-single secretary lingerie-shopping for her boss's mistress. Sandy often calls for Michael when he is stuck in a meeting or on the plane. Sandy is efficient and excessively private. Although, Michael has said, the minute she finds a man, she will quit in a flash. He is sticking with her, he has claimed, just to see that happen.

"Babe, you listening?"

"Michael, I miss you." Suzy is surprised at this sudden confession and thinks that it must be true.

"Meet me in Frankfurt. Sandy will arrange the ticket."

"I can't. I don't have a passport." In fact, she has never been out of the country, not since she followed her parents to America as a child. At twenty-nine, Suzy has never been abroad. Partly for fear of flying, and partly because she can no longer leave New York.

"Suzy, I'm being serious." Michael does not believe her. Why should he? He knows practically nothing about her.

"I really can't. Family business."

"What family? Babe, you haven't got any . . ." Michael is good at dodging serious conversation. "Except for me," he adds almost peevishly.

You're hiding. That is what Jen said this afternoon.

"When are you boarding?" Suzy asks, trying to shake off Jen's voice.

"Right now. Gotta go, call you tomorrow!"

Michael is gone before she can ask if it was he who kept hanging up at the fourth ring.

Suzy's apartment on St. Marks Place is at the hub of downtown. It was the first place she saw when she moved back to the city five years ago. She had been in such a rush then that she just grabbed the first thing offered, although there had been a few more apartments to check out. Apartment hunters in Manhattan are truly desperate. At 7 p.m. on Tuesdays, they line up outside Astor Place Stationery, where the first batch of *The Village Voice* is delivered upon printing. That is where the apartment war begins, everyone grabbing the first issue and running to the nearest phone booth to call the handful of landlords who fill the ad space with "No broker, low rent!"

For three consecutive Tuesdays, Suzy stood in line with no

luck. Although she had been worried that such a collective panic would make her so nauseous she would run straight back into Damian's arms, she actually found it comforting to see that she was not the only one looking for a new home or new life in the streets of New York. Mostly they were college graduates fresh from Middle America who had watched too much MTV and decided to try their luck the minute they could scrape up some money to get to the city. They often appeared even hipper than the city kids. Clad in vintage velvet and leather, they looked everything they said they were. "We need a loft where me and my girlfriend can both paint; our paintings are huge, bigger than the stuff Pollock used to do," one goateed boy declared, so loudly that everyone in line turned to him, as though he and his girlfriend were the newly crowned postmodern Abstract Expressionist royalty. Then others chimed in competitively: "New York rocks, man. I wrote like two hundred songs about it," or "I'll take anything on Avenue A; how could you be a poet and not follow Ginsberg?," or "This casting agent says that I look just like Monica from *Friends*, and I'm, like, no way would I ever do TV!" Suzy would listen and wonder how many of them, if any, would attain their dreams, and she would realize that she, in fact, envied them all, these buoyant kids for whom life was just offering its first mysterious glimpse, while she, at twenty-five, had already given up. Then, one day, a boy who stood behind her tapped on her shoulder and asked if she needed a roommate. He was the first true redhead she had seen in a long time, and he wore a sky-blue bowling jacket that had "Vince" stitched above its right pocket. He could not afford to live alone, he said, and did not trust strangers to share an apartment, but she looked nice and he'd always wanted to live in Asia, and perhaps she was the closest thing he'd come to the continent. Then he held out his multi-ringed hand and said, "Hi, I am Caleb, I'm twenty-one, a philosopher and a performance artist." She tried not to laugh as she shook his hand with "Suzy, twenty-five and unemployed."

She liked Caleb. He was honest and surprisingly shy. He also brought her luck, because on that very night they found the apartment on St. Marks Place. She was amazed that it had been so easy, considering that she was unemployed, and as far as she could tell, his day job of working at a vegan restaurant on the Lower East Side did not quite fulfill the criterion of a desirable tenant. Then Caleb told her that his doctor parents who lived in Scarsdale co-signed the lease. When she asked if they knew that the beneficiary of their generosity was an unemployed stranger their son had met outside Astor Place Stationery, Caleb winked. "Darling, I told them that I had a mad crush on you. They would've bought the apartment for us if they thought we were actually doing it."

The apartment was a typical East Village walk-up railroad, an elongated stretch of three connecting rooms. Suzy had to pass through Caleb's bedroom to get to the kitchen, which led to the bathroom that was missing a sink. Neither noticed the missing sink until they finally moved in, when Caleb walked out into the kitchen with a seriously distraught look on his face and exclaimed, "There's no place to put a toothbrush!" Suzy thought it could have been worse. Better a sink than a tub. She could not imagine surviving New York winters without the relief of a hot bath.

Caleb often brought home leftover tofu pancakes and non-dairy crème brûlée from the restaurant. The only edible things there, he explained. The rest tasted so depressingly dull that it was simply cruel to put his taste buds through such an uninspiring challenge. A cleverly concocted diet plan, he claimed. Imagine working at a restaurant where the food is actually good! The philosopher-and-performance-artist bit was hard to figure out, though. Caleb never read books and was certainly too cynical to perform in front of a crowd. When Suzy finally approached the subject without wanting to sound either dismissive or disrespectful, he burst out laughing. "Oh, it's a private joke with myself. My dad once said that homosexuality is for philosophers or performance artists. How could you grow up in Westchester and end up fucking boys? He wept when I came out at my high-school graduation, really. Imagine this Jewish optometrist in his fifties with tears streaming down his face. He didn't use the f-word, of course."

Suzy found it almost comforting to hear about Caleb's unending drama with his parents, who phoned every Sunday and yet always managed to avoid addressing her directly. Soon they stopped calling. Caleb's therapist, whom his parents hired and paid for, thought it was unwise for them to keep up with this weekly communication, which only encouraged resentment in both parties. "Once the homosexual issue is 'solved,' Dr. Siegel told them, then they can call!" Caleb exclaimed with the cheeky smile of a kid who has just pushed the bully off the merry-go-round.

"What about your parents? Do they know that you never get laid?" Caleb asked one night after three months of living together. It must have been Thursday, the crème brûlée night, which they often celebrated with an Australian Chardonnay from the "Deal of the Week" shelf at First Avenue Liquor.

"They're both dead. But, no, I guess they never knew, or never wanted to know at least," Suzy answered in the most matter-of-fact tone she could muster, which she hoped would make him feel less sorry about asking.

"Gee, I'm sorry, Suz, I didn't know . . ."

"Don't worry about it. It's been a while. Besides, we never talked much when they were alive anyway."

With that, Suzy polished off the last scoop. Caleb sat still, waiting for her to say more. But she didn't. It was the first time she had said aloud that they were dead. It came out just like that, almost naturally. She had not talked to anyone she knew since the funeral. She had not seen anyone, except for Jen. She certainly did not plan on finding herself in an East Village walk-through kitchen with a twenty-one-year-old boy whom she'd met three months ago and casually saying, while picking at a bowl of crème brûlée, that her parents were dead.

Suzy never mentioned her parents again, and Caleb never asked. Instead, she asked him about his. She inquired after his progress with Dr. Siegel, and if his father still occasionally cried, if his mother was curious at all about the supposed girlfriend who lived with her son. Suzy asked to see their photograph, which Caleb then stuck on the refrigerator door with a magnet that said "From Here to Eternity." They looked almost exactly as Suzy had imagined, with Caleb's red hair and extra-long eyelashes, posing before their unmistakable Stanford White house and the nougat-colored Mercedes Benz. Caleb would tell her all about his father's glass-walled office in the center of Scarsdale, and his mother's book club, which included other doctors' wives from the better part of Westchester County. "Whatever's on the *Times* best-seller list they'd read, especially the lewd ones, you know, books like *Hollywood Madam*, which I'm sure they took home to pore over only the dirty parts." Caleb would steal a glance at Suzy as if he knew that she kept prodding him with questions so that she would not have to talk.

Then, three months later, Caleb started dating an older man who one day walked into the restaurant and fell in love with him, and three weeks later, he packed his bag and moved into the man's spacious one-bedroom apartment in the West Village. "He has a real sink, with gold faucets and everything. I feel like I'm back in Scarsdale," Caleb said, chuckling into the phone on his first night away.

Suzy did not bother looking for a new roommate. There was still some money left over in the savings account that Damian had set up for her during the later stage of their escapade. It occurred to her that she should send it back to him, but she knew that he also expected her to. It was Damian's way. It was his hook, his excuse to keep her in his tow, and she knew that he waited patiently for a day when she would throw the money back at him with a letter, a memo, a phone call, so Suzy would not do it. She kept it instead, and paid her landlord $966 each month with Damian's money. She thought this ensured her as his kept woman, as everyone had believed, including Professor Tamiko and their mutual colleagues, including her parents and Grace, including Damian himself, although Suzy was the last one to find out.

Suzy spent the first year back in New York doing nothing. She lay around the apartment all day and called no one. Caleb dropped by once in a while, after his day shift at the restaurant. They would walk around the neighborhood on sticky evenings and sit on a bench at Tompkins Square Park munching on crème brûlée wrapped in tinfoil. Caleb would buy her a Starbucks Frappuccino, which he said was her Jappiest habit and that if she ever met a decent boy, she should keep it a secret from him until he was well hooked on her Asian charm, and she would laugh, realizing that her own laughter sounded almost foreign to her. Caleb would tell her all about his new boyfriend and the incredible sex they were having: "Three courses a night, darling. I tell you, you ain't seen nothing yet until you fucked someone your dad's age."

But everything comes with a price, Suzy thought. She was twenty-five then, unemployed, goal-less, an orphan.

At the funeral, Grace avoided Suzy. They sat next to each other and did not exchange a word. No one spoke to Suzy, not her parents' acquaintances, not the man with gold-rimmed glasses who had helped Grace out of a car, not Mr. and Mrs. Lim, whom Suzy grew up next door to when they lived in Flushing years ago. It was as if they considered her also dead, as if respecting the wishes of her parents, who had disowned her the minute she ran off with Damian in her senior year. Quite a crowd had gathered at the Korean church in Fort Lee, New Jersey, where Grace now lived. There were no relatives, because they did not have any except for a few aunts back in Korea whom neither Suzy nor Grace had ever met. Her parents barely had any friends, never liked people much, but their death had been shocking, scandalous, tragic, and people, especially church-going immigrants, loved tragedies. The only thing Grace said when Suzy went up to her to say goodbye was, *Don't bother showing up for the ashes, they are with God now. Do me a favor, Suzy; leave us alone.*

The phone starts ringing again. Whoever it is does not want to leave the evidence. Whoever it is is desperately looking for her. The Caller ID says "private." But she knew that without even looking at it. Suzy finally takes off her coat, throwing it on a silk hanger from the pricey Madison Avenue shop. Took Sandy all afternoon to find it, Michael claimed. Michael wants Suzy in the latest fashion. He wants the latest of anything. Often she stands in front a mirror, clad in what strikes her as carefully sewn and stitched money, lots of it. She hardly recognizes herself. A bona fide mistress, whose clothing shields her from herself. Suzy brushes her fingers across the array of silk shirts and cashmere sweaters. They come in every shade of black. "To match your hair, Suzy," Michael said. She imagines his wife in the most flamboyant pitch of red and green, a blonde surely, once-upon-a-sorority, maybe a book club or two, that would suit him. Michael never discusses his family. It is taboo, and

Suzy prefers it that way. She knows how to be a kept woman. She got her start early. She even sacrificed her own parents to be one, so she had better be damn good at it. The phone starts again, and Suzy stares at it without turning off the ringer. Then she walks to the end of the railroad and turns the hot water on to the fullest.

4.

THE VOICE ON THE OTHER END shouts, "Delivery." Suzy presses the intercom button, standing at the door in her bathrobe with her hair wrapped in a towel. The deliveryman smiles, as if her wetness suggests a private promise. In his arms is a bouquet of white irises. "Sign the receipt, please," he says, and she asks, "From whom?" although she already knows the answer. No sender's name, nothing. No note, no miniature card with a happy smile, no heart-shaped balloon with a double I-love-you's. A bunch of white irises, a rarity in November, but only in November, always in November. Almost exactly four years ago, a man first appeared at her doorstep with a bunch of white irises much like these. It occurred to her that they might be from Damian, but this was not Damian's style, and delicate white irises definitely not his thing. Then who? Not Michael, because she did not even know him then, and not a secret admirer, Caleb said he hoped, because the joke was too old and she was not so young anymore. They were always delivered right around

the anniversary of her parents' death. She wonders if they were
sent to Grace also. But why irises, why such insistence? Mom
had liked them, Suzy vaguely recalls. Her parents used to sell
them at their store. Mom said that, among all garden flowers,
irises needed the most care, because they withered quickly and
had virtually no smell. Her mother was not one of those softies
whose hearts melt at the sight of long-stemmed roses or tulips,
and neither was Suzy. They were pleasing to look at, she
thought, but why not leave them wherever they came from, either the perennial fields of the Netherlands or the sloping valleys
of northern California, anywhere at all but primped like a poo-
dle and squeezed into a glass vase on a now-satisfied girlfriend's
mantel in order to reassure her that somebody loved her on this
Valentine's Day or birthday or anniversary? A bouquet reminded
Suzy of a Hallmark card from a corner stationery store, whose
price was preprinted and whose purpose was long prescribed.
Only once she thought that flowers served a purpose, and that
was at the funeral. Grace must have arranged it, which surprised
Suzy, but one could never tell how a sibling might react to one's
parents' death, which sort of coffin, open casket or not, a chorus
of hymns even if they had never believed in Christ. There were
white flowers everywhere around both coffins, either lilies or
chrysanthemums, although Suzy cannot recall if she saw irises
among them. Dad would have thrown a fit, she thought then.
"Frivolous!" he would've screamed. "What a waste! In Korea, no
one would dare to throw away so much for nothing!" And that
must be exactly why Grace chose to do it. Everyone thought
that the flowers were appropriate. But Suzy knew that they were
the last things her parents would have wanted at their final moment.

Grabbing the nearly empty Evian bottle from the refrigerator, Suzy cuts open the top part and sticks the flowers in it. She
is not sure where to put it, although she must have found a spot

for it each year. On the dining table, there, she places the bottle
on the corner as if putting it away. Irises are sad flowers, she
thinks, neither as glamorous as roses nor as graceful as lilies, just
a run-of-the-mill sort. Each flower stalk stands perfectly straight,
with slivers of drooping falls. White ones are the worst. Such
petals, signaling perpetual mourning. Mom was right. It is eerie
how they carry no scent, no trace.

Suzy told no one about the flowers. Somehow she thought
that she was not supposed to, that it was meant to be a secret between her and whoever sent them, and that if she were to break
this code something bad was bound to happen. Caleb was the
only one who knew, because the first delivery came while he was
over. "An acquaintance of your parents, probably," he said.
"Maybe he owed them money, maybe he cheated your parents a
little and feels sorry, who knows, but whoever it is sure isn't very
original!"

November is a strange month anyway, not quite the winter,
not quite the end of a year, and Suzy not quite thirty. She is
happy to be almost done with her twenties. The whole youth
thing escaped her. While other girls fretted about noncommittal
boyfriends, maniacal bosses, or aimless Friday nights, Suzy was
always looking to see who might be lashing at her from behind.
It is impossible to insist on youth when your own parents call
you a whore. But one cannot blame the dead. Whatever mean-
ness is forgotten, washed away, gone with the ashes. It is their
privilege. And here's Suzy, five years since the funeral, still looking over her shoulder, or looking at the screeching phone, which
will not leave her alone.

Perhaps it is the last echo of Dad's anger, the way he muttered "*yang-gal-bo*" under his breath, or perhaps the faraway
look on Mom, who would not meet Suzy's eyes, but Suzy continues to stare at the phone without turning off the ringer. Each
ring is a slash, a slap, a shot or two.

Two shots only; the gun had fired exactly twice and pierced their hearts.

Too precise for a random shooting, too perfectly executed, too clean. There wasn't much bleeding, she was told. The bullets stopped their hearts.

A cold murder, a professional's job, miss, your parents died instantly.

Suzy knows nothing further, and Grace will not speak to her. The Bronx Homicide Unit did the usual investigation, but there was no witness, no evidence, no suspect. There had been several similar shootings around the neighborhood, all unsolved. The case was quite typical, Detective Lester told Suzy: a useless killing by useless thugs. The victims were almost always immigrants, but there were no outstanding conflicts between specific immigrant groups, just the usual squabble. "Don't worry," he said. "We'll get them; these thugs end up in jail anyway, if not for this, then something equally horrendous sooner or later." And that was that. Grace took care of the store, the funeral, and their Queens brownstone. She contacted Suzy only once, through the accountant, about a small sum of money Suzy was entitled to from the sale of her parents' possessions, but Suzy quietly declined. What right did she have? When Dad called her a whore, she stood up and said, *I wish I wasn't your daughter!* That was her farewell to him.

Nine years now, almost ten. She had just turned twenty when she ran off with Damian. Four years later, her parents were shot at their store. Five years have passed since their death. Once you start counting years, the numbers drive you crazy. A decade since she's seen her parents alive, which should make her a credible orphan, and yet one never gets used to being alone. A bouquet of flowers arrives, and she cannot imagine who could've sent it, who would know that irises were her mother's favorite flowers, who would mark each November to commemorate her parents' death, who would care whom she loves, who would cry because she will never marry him because he is already married, who would call her a whore, hoping it would stop her from plunging onto the wrong track, who would lose sleep at night because she is all alone in her railroad apartment afraid to answer the phone.

I wish I wasn't your daughter.

She had meant it, and they knew it. There are words one cannot take back, intentions that are permanent.

It is useless going back to bathe now. The moment is gone, the shock of hot water running over her body has had its fill. She stands in her towel and lights a cigarette instead. She barely inhales before putting it out. The ashtray is filled with half-smoked cigarettes. Lately, cigarettes have begun to taste bitter. She has heard that it happens when one stops longing. Each time one of those righteous ladies comes up to her on the street and clicks her tongue with the cigarettes-are-so-bad-for-you speech, she wants to spit back something equally rude, like "So is your corduroy dress for your sex life." But instead, she throws them the coldest stare, which usually wipes the benevolent smile right off their faces. Damian used to tease her for it. He used to say that Philip Morris should give her a medal for being one of the last true militants. He himself never touched them. He said that cigarettes were for the young, and it would be embarrassing for him at forty-nine to be sucking on something so obviously seductive. But he liked watching her smoke. "Take off your bra." He would surprise her with an order so abrupt, and she would hold on to the cigarette between her lips while unhooking the strap with both her hands. "Take off your stockings," he'd say. And before the end of the cigarette, she would be ready, and Damian would finally reach over and take the cigarette from her lips and stub it out.

Still she refuses to quit, although she can no longer smoke a whole cigarette. Still it is the one thing she recognizes in herself. It's like a line from a Leonard Cohen song, a girl who's been left with nothing but a pack of cigarettes. Nothing is familiar any longer, nothing sinks. Since Caleb left, the apartment became bare. Hardly any furniture except for a futon and a mahogany dining table with two chairs. No posters lighten up the walls, no pretty fabrics cover the cracks in the corner. The only obvious electronic items are the Sony boom box and a fourteen-inch television set. The table and the TV belong to Caleb. "Turns out that a married life needs something more than Ikea," he sighed when she asked him if he wanted his stuff back.

During her first year back in New York, Suzy watched TV all day. It was a new thing for her. Her parents never had time to sit around, because they were always working, and when they did watch, for an hour or two on rare weekends, they would put on Channel 47, which was the East Coast's only Korean programming, whose jokes were lost on her. Grace had no tolerance for it either. It bored the hell out of her, she said, turning back to the book in her hands; the only thing she did with any enthusiasm was read. And when Suzy lived with Damian, of course there was no TV. Despicable, he grunted. American culture is the gutter, worse than drugs, definitely worse than cigarettes! Damian would have turned away in disgust if he saw how Suzy started the day now with *Good Morning America* and continued with *Regis and Kathy Lee* until midday, when the wildly convoluted sagas of daytime soaps unfolded. They had fabulous titles like *All My Children* and *Days of Our Lives.* There was one called *The Bold and the Beautiful,* which she thought was a more appropriate name for a body shampoo or a cologne. She welcomed the whole ritual, to lean back in her futon with a bowl of microwaved popcorn and lose herself in the entangled lives of Yasmina or Desiree or Katharina, who all seemed to have popped out of the Ms. Clairol box, and the occasional black or Asian ones, who looked even more Ms. Clairol–like with their perfectly coifed hair, which, even though they were definitely not blonde, still carried the just-walked-out-of-a-salon essence as they bobbed along with the saccharine smile of the golden girl's best friend. Her favorite was *One Life to Live.* She tried not to miss it, only because she found out while watching *Regis and Kathy Lee* one morning that it was the least popular among the soaps. She thought this was unfair, since they were basically interchangeable. In fact, even the actors seemed to skip around. She was sure that she had seen one particular actor in the two o'clock soap as a handsome but evil doctor, and then, a week later, she would find him at three o'clock on another channel as a self-made millionaire. Then, of course, she would quickly discover that he had been killed in a plane crash in one soap but smoothly popped into another with a newer and nicer character. She envied their resurrecting lives. They never died, not completely. There seemed to be always a way out, a second, even a third chance. People did not just disappear without proper explanation. Tragedies came with namable causes and retribution. Their fate was a puzzle but an easy one, and days, months would fly by as she watched and toyed with the missing bits.

She stopped watching TV when she got her first job. Or maybe she got the job in order to stop watching it. No matter how frequently and closely she watched, she was never sure what really went on, who had supposedly died only to return with amnesia, who was cheating on whom with whose husbands and wives, who was kidnapped on the day of the wedding by the priest who turned out to be a spy. She thought these dramas required specific minds that could keep up with all the details. Yet what made her finally turn the TV off had nothing to do with its mind-numbing spell, but the gunshot. At least one or two characters were killed on TV each day. Almost always in daytime soaps, the victims came back alive, and the actual shooting scene

was skipped over. But there were the odd ones that would show
the entire gruesome sequence in detail—the index finger on the
trigger, the horrified victim shuddering, the squinting of the
killer's vengeful eyes, the slow falling of the body as the final ray
of blood spurts out. The first time she saw a scene like that, Suzy
was fixated. She could not stop thinking about it and wanted to
record it to watch again and again. But the second time it happened, she felt sick and lay still on the futon and did not move
for hours. And the third time, she shut it off and moved the TV
set to the farthest corner of the apartment. She never went near
it again.

"You're waiting for a whistle to blow; it'd take you less than
five minutes to grab your stuff and run," said Jen when she
stopped by a few months ago, which she rarely did. "Deadline,"
she claimed. "Drop by the office, we'll go to the Royalton for
lunch on the company's account." But Suzy knew that Jen did
not want to meet at home. When lounging at each other's apartments, they naturally fell into the familiar ways of former roommates. One would get up to pour coffee before the other even
asked for a refill, or bring the ashtray before the other took out a
cigarette. Yet somehow, sitting on the futon with the coffee
brewing, they could not help remembering the way Suzy had
quit and left an irreparable hole in their college days. Jen was
right, though. The apartment resembles a temporary shelter.
There is no sweetness here, no flowery sheets, no matching du-
vet cover, no framed childhood photos. In fact, Suzy cannot say
if she is attached to anything anymore. A jade ring that once
belonged to her mother? An album filled with her childhood
photos? A videotape of her seventh-birthday party? No such
memorabilia in her apartment. Sure, Grace might have retrieved
a few items from the Queens house where their parents had
lived in their final years—their family having moved frequently
through their growing up—but how important were such things

if she had rarely missed them all these years? In college, Suzy envied Jen, who went home every few months to her parents' Connecticut mansion, where her childhood bedroom was intact with her Barbie and her tattered Cure poster and a bulletin board filled with the snapshots from her high-school excursion to St. Petersburg. The shrine of such a lovely American past, to Suzy, suggested an emblem, a reference to what Jen would become, what Jen could only become—a successful editor, the one-bedroom apartment on Central Park West, a summer share in the Hamptons, a boyfriend of her own age in his final year of residency at Johns Hopkins. They were all the right, correct things in life, which a smart, ambitious young woman such as Jen, upon finishing an Ivy League education, was expected to find in such a scintillatingly possible ground as New York City.

But those *things* were not what differentiated Jen from Suzy. Two girls of the same age, the same education, the same earnest propensity for Brontë's *Villette*, and yet their makeups were different from the start. It was neither because Suzy spent her early years moving constantly from Flushing to the Bronx to the inner parts of Queens, as new immigrants often did, nor because Suzy's inner-city public-school education suffered next to Jen's suburban private-school history, a deficit that Suzy was bright enough to overcome. But there was something else, something markedly different, something more fundamental, ingrained, almost inborn. Jen seemed to float about their mutual college life with the brightest sunlight, whereas Suzy, no matter how she tried to hide it, was stuck somewhere cold and brooding. And Damian was the first one to notice, and was not afraid to tell her about it.

On their first date, sitting on the bench in Riverside Park—although "date" might be a misnomer, since they had just slept together for the first time that day—Damian gazed at her awhile and said, "Stop looking at me for an answer; you're not going to be happier." Suzy knew that he was telling the truth and kept silent, because she still did not know what she wanted, and could still feel the pain between her legs, and felt no regrets. She looked away instead at the afternoon calm of the Hudson River, across which New Jersey loomed with not much promise, and remembered that she had missed language lab that afternoon. Damian was forty-nine then, a married scholar whose picture she had seen framed at Professor Tamiko's office. Suzy had just turned twenty, a comparative-literature major, a virgin, which strangely did not matter at all. Neither discussed it. Suzy's virginity was the last thing on their minds. From the first meeting, there was no doubt that they would make love. What bothered them was the darkness they sensed in each other, which pulled them together, which let them know almost instantly that their union was not a good thing, was doomed, was bound to hurt people and leave scars that might not go away no matter how much time passed, how they reorganized their lives so that one might forget that the other had ever happened at all.

The phone is persistent, and Suzy is not sure what makes her finally answer it. Perhaps she hopes it is Damian after all, perhaps she imagines that he has gotten softer with years and will break down just once. She tightens the towel grip and walks over to the end of the room and picks up the receiver before its fourth ring. She does not say hello. She waits for a voice, a signal. But instead, a pause, a drawn-out silence. She will not speak. She will not give up easily. Then, finally, comes the click—she knew it—a smooth, intentional hang-up. Must've been a wrong number, surely a prank call. And yet, for a quick second, she cannot help looking to make sure that the blinds on both windows are drawn.

5.

NO MATTER WHAT TIME OF DAY, it seems, the north wing of Penn Station is packed. Eight a.m., and a horde of men and women in suits and briefcases pour out of Long Island Rail Road trains and rush into the subway to reach their cubicles on Wall Street or the Avenue of the Americas by nine o'clock sharp. The commute costs them the better part of the day, the better mood of their lives. But a small sacrifice for a two-story house with a basketball hoop in the backyard and a cozy public school whose PTA meets for a monthly picnic in the town park. It's worth one and a half hours each way, three hours combined. Who would want to raise kids in the city, who could afford it? So they recline in their seats with *The Wall Street Journal*, the *Long Island Weekly*, or the *Times*. The clever ones make the best of the lull by balancing their checkbooks, or reading over contracts or invoices, whatever they do all day at work and still take home extra of because there never is enough time, because time is what such commutes are all about. And amidst crowds who reappear from the LIRR each morning like ants out of mounds, Suzy stands waiting for her 8:25 to Montauk, glad to be going in the opposite direction.

Montauk is the final stop. Suzy finds a seat easily enough. The train leaves exactly on time. She will have to make the connection in Jamaica, which is about twenty minutes away. Leaning back, she looks out the window, although the view is nothing, just the outskirts of the city, impossible to place. And yet she keeps on staring, because she is sitting by the window and there is nothing to do except follow this motion and let the barren scenery pass like a dull movie.

Outside is a mess of twisting highways and cement buildings. Some bits seem familiar. The train passed by Long Island City, where they had once lived, many years ago, when her father got a job at a Korean deli for a few months. It was an ugly, depressed part of Queens, and she was glad when he finally quit, or was he fired? Suzy is not sure anymore, but she recalls the fiercely unpleasant drive through the neighborhood and the oversized man with the overlapping front teeth named Mr. Yang who owned the store, who tossed a dollar at eight-year-old Suzy to run along and get him a slice of pizza from across the street, and how Dad had put a hand on the man's right shoulder and said in a quiet but menacing voice, "Don't tell my daughter what to do."

The memory seems slightly skewed. What had she been doing with him at work? Why wasn't she at school on that day? Did he really say those exact words? Perhaps he mumbled with an awkward slouch to his shoulders, "Please don't order my daughter around," or lashed with a stone in his voice, "Who do you think you are, ordering my daughter about?" Or is it possible that he did not say anything at all? It's been so long, over twenty years. Hard to remember now how it had really been between a father and a daughter, how he might have taken her small hand and stormed out of the store with the parting spit at the rotund man, "Don't you *dare* tell *my* daughter what to do!"

Outside, the familiar streets are gone now. The train is moving swiftly, almost gliding. She cannot recall the last time she was inside a moving vehicle in such tranquillity. Perhaps Dad's Oldsmobile had felt this safe, pure. All you had to do was just hop in and let him take you. Mom never drove, although she kept saying that she should learn, since she could not get anywhere on her own. But she never did, because they had only one car anyway and she had gotten used to being driven around. Dad was the best driver, never got a ticket, never got into an accident, never drove in the wrong lane. Later on, Suzy expected the same when she first rode in Damian's Volvo, and was shocked to discover that she had to check her seat belt several times before settling down. Luckily, she rarely found herself riding in cars. New Yorkers don't drive. The city is all about smelly subways and screaming taxis. Subways often get stuck in the middle of dark tunnels, and cabs, of course, are driven by a breed of wild men who zoom through the grids with a certain unexplained rage. The train remains ancient, Suzy thinks, like Dad's Oldsmobile. It sticks to the right course, from here to whatever its destination.

The first time she went to Montauk was for the ashes. She did not know that her parents had ever been there. Like most immigrants, they never took a vacation. Long Island for them ended in Bayshore, a seedy town where a few Koreans owned dry cleaners and fish markets. Dad once mentioned in passing that the business was not bad over there and the schools were better than the ones in Queens. But both Mom and Grace were fiercely against the idea. Mom could not imagine having to take a car to the nearest supermarket, which meant having to learn to drive immediately, and Grace said she would rather die than divulge that she was from Long Island. Suzy did not care one way or the other. They moved so often that it did not seem to matter where they went, for she was sure that they would move again before the year was up. Besides, she did not feel that she came from one particular place. When someone asked where she was from, she would pause and run through her mind the various apartment complexes in Flushing, the Bronx, the inner parts of Queens, even Jersey City, where they had lived for a few years when Mom got a job at a nail salon during their first years in America. None of them fit the bill, she thought. Korea, she would ponder, but that also seemed far away, for they immigrated when she turned five, and Grace six. Suzy could hardly remember the place. They had lived in a tiny apartment complex on the outskirts of Seoul, she was told. Oddly enough, the only detail she remembered about this childhood home was the elevator. Their apartment was on the fifth floor, which was the uppermost floor, according to her parents, because the top-floor units usually cost less; most young families did not trust the elevator and feared that kids might fall from the windows, which had happened in some buildings. What Suzy remembered vividly was the tiny box of the elevator, which was not so tiny in her child's eyes, and the mirror that had hung on its wall. She always wanted to look at the mirror, but it hung so high that she could never reach it. She would ask Mom to hoist her up on her shoulders, but Mom was always carrying bags of groceries and was busily pressing the numbered buttons, because the elevator would never respond to the first try. Sometimes Dad would give her a lift—although this happened rarely, for he came home long after the kids went to sleep—but then she was too high up on his shoulders, and the mirror reflected only her dangling feet. Suzy was not sure why this mirror should stick so distinctly in her mind, but almost always she would look for a mirror upon entering elevators and would immediately feel a lack, or a pang of something distant and impossible to name.

They never did move to Bayshore, and Long Island remained a distant place she never thought much about until shortly before the funeral, when she was told that the ashes would be scattered over the Atlantic from the Montauk Lighthouse. She thought it was a bizarre idea; there had been no will, and she had not realized that her parents had ever been to Montauk. Grace would not explain, and everyone assumed that it was fully discussed and understood between the two daughters. When Suzy pressed the matter, Grace cut her off in mid-sentence and snapped, "That's what they wanted; since when do you care about their wishes?" Suzy took the LIRR to Montauk three days later and watched Grace scatter the ashes. Suzy merely walked alongside Grace and let her conduct everything, as the older child, which was what her parents would have wanted, she thought. There were only a few people who seemed to have known her parents through work, and a reporter from the *Korea Daily* who showed up uninvited. It was exactly five years ago. November, rain, and her entire world had just ended.

Why Montauk? No one told her anything. Maybe Mom had mentioned something about it to Grace, or Dad had left a diary somewhere in the back of filing cabinets, or Grace knew things about their parents that Suzy did not—but it was a mystery, and there was no one Suzy could ask other than Grace, who, even five years later, would not speak to her. The one thing Suzy knew was that Grace disapproved. Grace was a fervent Christian, and burning the body was unacceptable. If Grace had had her way, they would have been buried in a sunny lot somewhere in New Jersey, preferably near her own church, where the funeral was held, as though her parents had ever believed in Christ.

Her parents had been floaters. They went to churches on a whim. Good for business, Suzy thought. They always had a specific reason for each visit. Either a job connection from one of the elders or trade gossip or market information. A church was where most Koreans gathered on Sundays, and it would have been foolish to ignore its usefulness. But they were atheists at heart. More than once, she overheard Dad cursing off Christians. "Bastards," he'd say. "They'd even give up their own mother if they thought it would guarantee a spot in that nonsense called heaven." Sometimes Mom would say a prayer to Buddha when Suzy or Grace got sick, or Dad would say something about the ethics of Confucius at the dinner table, which all seemed confusing somehow, but the message was clear: Jesus was not for Koreans. One night, Suzy walked into the kitchen to find her father in a heated argument with someone on the phone and overheard only the last bit before her mother pointed to her to get back in her room. He was screaming into the phone, "Your ancestors would weep if they knew you were pushing this Christ shit on your countrymen!"

"Ancestors"—that was a familiar word. Suzy heard it again and again while growing up. If she got a B instead of an A on a test, the shame lay on her ancestors, who watched from their graves. If Suzy and Grace fought and did not speak for days, it was again the ancestors, who lamented over these descendants who were not only girls but bad-mannered as well. And of course it was due to the watchful eyes of the ancestors that Suzy and Grace were forbidden to speak English at home. "You must never forget your language; once you do, you no longer have a home," Dad told them. It was not easy to keep on speaking Korean when English came so naturally, and Suzy and Grace often cheated, falling into English when their parents were not around. But in the end, Dad got his way. Ancestors or no ancestors, the girls never forgot Korean. They were even sent to a Korean-language school every Sunday afternoon, though there was almost no need. The girls spoke Korean with near-fluency.

. . .

The train is slowing down again. Everyone is getting up at once. Outside, the sign reads "Jamaica," a stopover station with several platforms. The morning started out overcast, and now the sky is turning black. Each time she comes out here, the rain follows. Or perhaps she has come only when it was raining. With each year, she can bear the rain even less. It makes her terribly aware of being alone. Her father had said that remembering one's own language ensures home, but was that true? She wonders if her parents would approve of her coming out to see them so often. Suzy at twenty-nine, still single, still careerless, still stuck with a married man—would they turn away in shame?

From here on, it is a smooth ride. Two hours and fifty minutes, and the train will arrive in Montauk.

Once she boards the second train, she shuts her eyes and pretends that this ride will continue forever. She is on her way to see Mom and Dad. She imagines their new home, a pastel oceanfront house they have just moved into. Dad's newest whim, the beach, the lighthouse, the moonlight, the edge of New York. "Oh, who would've ever thought," Mom would say, laughing, picking up Suzy at the train station in her brand-new Jeep. Mom behind the wheel in her Christian Dior sunglasses and a sky-blue tank top with tan lines showing through its straps despite the November rain, while Dad is out fishing for fluke, which he would then get the local fishermen to fillet for sushi later. Suzy would present them with a bag of Korean groceries, which her parents would delight in opening; Montauk is not Flushing, definitely not Woodside or Jackson Heights, no Oriental goods within miles. They would gloat over a jar of *kim-chi*, dried squid, salted pollack eggs. They would laugh like children, and Suzy would squint from so much sun in their faces. But then, always, Suzy remembers that she is nineteen still, and college is not easy at all, and she's come home to tell them: *Dear Mom and Dad, I don't want to stay in school anymore, I'm afraid of the rules and of breaking them all, I'm afraid of the boys who want me and the men I desire in return, I'm afraid of being stuck out there and not finding my way back unless I hide with you for a while, stay in the bedroom upstairs, and let you take care of me, I will wait for you all day while you fish, while you sunbathe, I will mop the floor and vacuum the living room and even fillet the fish if I can stay just a few nights or weeks or years until I am okay, until I can stand on my own and chase her away who stands in dark with wet hair and a cigarette, afraid of the phone that keeps ringing, until her fingers turn red from the ashes.*

The screeching of the engine signals a stop, and Suzy looks out through the rain-streaked windowpane to find one of the Hampton towns. Even in November, she can spot the white-and-khaki ensemble on the platform. This part of Long Island has nothing to do with Bayshore and its Korean immigrants. This is Ralph Lauren land, the *crème de la crème* of Madison Avenue. "Why call this a country? Disneyland would be more accurate!" Damian ranted as they drove across the entire coastline one summer in search of the antique shop where the missing Edo print was found. It was a research trip for the book he was working on. Suzy thought he was overreacting, but she liked that about Damian, his refusal to forgive the tiniest flaw or weakness. She believed that it was a sign of honesty, his unwillingness to compromise, his search for the ideal. She admired his intrepid pursuit of beauty, which she thought was his faith in love, the very essence of what she lacked.

The first time they made love, Damian began with her hands.

I've always believed that a woman's hands should tell me nothing, to keep me from the rest of her, but you, yours surprise me, a sign of temper, tenacity, such long, angry fingers.

He was running his index finger across her face. He was whispering the whole time. He kept talking, not so much to her as to himself, as though it was he who needed convincing.

I would've recognized you anywhere, your sad eyes, the ones marked for tragedy, your nose is emotional, the angle tells me so, your forehead is high like mine, you're ambitious like me, your lips are too small for your face, so imperfect and afraid, you're a beauty full of holes.

Suzy lay still and watched the peeling of her skin with wonder. She had just turned twenty. It seemed miraculously natural, and Damian the wrong man for the job. Afterward, she shuddered at the possible consequence of this love, if that is what it really was. She was not sure if she was frightened or excited at the prospect. Their lovemaking was an escape. It was passionate certainly, not in the usual lusty way, but with a fierce current of sadness, for they both knew that they would be alone at the end of each other.

People later said that Suzy was the precocious thing who ruined the most celebrated marriage of academia. Damian Brisco, the foremost expert on East Asian art, and his wife, Yuki Tamiko, the renowned translator of the newest edition of *The Tale of Genji*. Some blamed a midlife crisis, how Damian, at forty-nine, seemed to have lost his head over a mere student at the expense of his career, which had been crucial for everyone, including himself and his marriage. The couple had collaborated on many groundbreaking studies. They were the authors of the three volumes of *East Asian Art and Literature*, which was the main text for every university's Asian-civilization course. Most agreed that their marriage catapulted the field of East Asian studies, which up until their prolific partnership had been in a vacuum. Although it was Yuki Tamiko who held the chair position in the East Asian Department at Columbia University while Damian Brisco took an extended leave to work on the

IRONIC!!

fourth and final volume of the text, it was clear that any major decision had to pass through both. Their names were forever linked together, always in the context of "edited, researched, compiled, translated, written by Brisco and Tamiko." Their joint lecture series on "Trekking Buddhist Art Through East Asia" was immensely popular, and their marriage admired by those in the field as the perfect union between East and West.

But Suzy knew otherwise. She had been one of Professor Tamiko's advisees since the beginning of her junior year. Yet it was nearly impossible to get Professor Tamiko in person. Twice a semester, Suzy was supposed to meet with her to discuss her impending thesis, but so far, she had been greeted by a different TA each time, someone who seemed merely a few years older than Suzy herself, and rather flustered at having to advise anyone at all when his own dissertation lay forgotten somewhere between the hands of the university's bureaucratic committees. She saw her in lectures, of course. Postwar Japanese Fiction was one of the few standing-room-only classes on campus, and even though Suzy had actually registered for the class whereas half the attendees seemed to be auditors, she was always stuck at the farthest distance from the podium, on which stood Professor Tamiko, whose profile seemed almost ethereal.

It was true that she was beautiful. Yuki Tamiko was stunning. At forty-nine, she had retained much of the delicate-boned, high-cheeked, ultra-slender, and immensely haughty girl whom Damian Brisco had met at Harvard when they were both freshmen. The coy-girl beauty might have long passed the woman, but there was something regal in its place, something strikingly soft and compassionate and yet impenetrable, edged by the vastness of her knowledge as she stood before the hundreds of eager minds and recited lines from Mishima's *The Sea of Fertility* as though Western scholars had done the most unthinkable injustice by declaring *Ulysses* the ultimate fiction when the real thing lay shrouded in this Japanese tetralogy, which cast its spell over everyone in the auditorium while she, Yuki Tamiko, towered from her highest ground, suddenly demure and fiercely competent. Everyone was at her mercy. The boys looked up at her with awe and admiration—Yuki Tamiko was not the sort of woman one dared to have a crush on—and the girls marked her every word in their spiral notebooks in red ink with double exclamation points, as though everything would be different now that they knew what they had not realized merely fifty minutes ago, when their literary scope lacked the passionate breadth of that remarkable woman up on the podium. Suzy, however, remained untouched. The lecture was perfect, and Professor Tamiko's seductive banter mesmerizing, but Suzy felt somehow left out. There was a twinge of coldness that Suzy sensed in the older woman's face, guarded by the finest words of Japanese literature. Suzy felt claustrophobic and was struck by a distinct desire to get up and walk out. It was during one of these rash walkouts that she saw Damian for the first time.

She had slipped out the door and skipped down the steps facing Dodge Hall when she sensed that she was not alone, that another person had just taken the same steps and was walking behind her. Resisting the temptation to turn around and look, Suzy kept on walking. It must have been April. The first two weeks of April were always deadly. Finals were just on the way, the summer was around the corner, and a strange mix of excitement and panic spread through the campus as students crammed for exams. It had rained for a week straight, and the afternoon looked unnaturally bright. And it was during these nervous hours that Suzy, instead of returning to her dorm room, turned right onto Amsterdam Avenue. Now a few more people were on the street, mostly campus people still, but a bit older, because beyond the actual gates of the campus, yet still within the ten-block radius of 116th Street, most passersby were graduate students or school employees or faculty family. All seemed to be hurrying, although it was Friday afternoon, and the rain had finally ceased. Suzy ambled with not much feeling at all, or with so much feeling that she felt breathless. This extreme ennui came upon her with no warning, a dark hand moving onto her heart. Sometimes she would suddenly get up and leave, even though Professor Tamiko's lecture was faultless and there was no reason for such an impatient exit.

Along Amsterdam Avenue there were two usual stops for wandering, restless undergraduates—St. John the Divine and the Hungarian Pastry Shop. The former was more a construction site than a cathedral, under renovation for as long as anyone could remember. Although it was one of the largest cathedrals in the world, its imperfection, Suzy thought, was really what soothed and attracted visitors. There was something oddly comforting about a cathedral whose façade was forever being repainted or repositioned. She liked sitting on a pew while listening to the usual banging of hammers and drills coming through the stained-glass windows. She hoped that the cathedral would never get done, that it would always remain half finished with steel wires sticking out. God had problems too, Suzy thought, and his cavernous sanctuary was a mess. God belonged more in the café across the street. It was the typical underground hangout often found in college neighborhoods, where goateed boys and hand-knit-sweatered girls sipped their refills of double Hungarian, which was a shot of espresso with a squirt of amaretto, and discussed the usual suspects—Derrida, Kierkegaard, Wittgenstein, even Said—although for a break they might bring up Woody Allen, whose latest film had been shot in this very café only a few weeks ago; they agreed that it sounded rather dull—a middle-aged professor falling for one of his students—so typical, so jaded, so hopelessly redundant that they all got tired of talking about it, and the conversation shifted right back to Derrida.

But Suzy entered neither that day. She was about to, and then something stopped her. She had climbed the steps to St. John the Divine when she became aware of the man next to her. He had been walking behind her; although she could not see his face, she knew he was there all along. And then, suddenly, he was on her right, almost directly parallel, facing the entrance of the cathedral. The entrance was wide enough for two people to pass without having to impose on each other, and she feared it was an aggressive gesture from a stranger who seemed to have followed her all the way from the lecture. She was cornered, and was left with no choice but to turn and face him.

His eyes are unhappy—that was her first thought. Deep, penetrating blue eyes that did not appear exactly hard, but somehow absent, even heartless. The rest of him she noticed much later: that he was considerably older, stood quite a bit taller than her five-foot-five frame, had a faint dimple on his left cheek that seemed out of place, and a face marked by permanent stubble that would graze against her thighs when finally opening her up into complete honesty. But in that initial second when she saw him standing so near that she could almost feel his fine-lined, insistent fingers on her, she thought, *I must seem so terribly young.*

Certainly an odd reaction to a stranger, as he was to her then, an older man, neither particularly handsome nor striking, a passerby possibly her father's age, although her father always seemed older than those around him, whose conviction was the absolute law by which everyone must abide, because he was the sort of man no one in the family disobeyed. But when Suzy saw Damian that first time, she felt hopelessly young, almost silly, naked, as though she knew that he could see through her own flaring vulnerability as she stood there in her brown suede jacket and faded Levi's, looking so lovely and tortured the way nineteen-year-olds can look on wet April days, staring up at this older man who seemed to have appeared from nowhere.

In fact, Suzy had never really known men. The boys around her age never showed much interest in her. It did not help that her father forbade dating. "School dances? Whatever for? Schools are not for dancing around!" In Korea, he said, girls did not frolic like these American ones. In Korea, he said again, girls stayed clean, as girls should. Under Dad's "Korean girl" rules, nothing was allowed: no lipstick, no eye shadow, no hair dye, no perm, no perfume, no miniskirts, no cigarettes, and absolutely no boys, especially American boys. The family's frequent moving seemed to guarantee all that. The girls never stayed in one school long enough to develop a crush. No time to get attached to sinful American habits, Dad used to say. Suzy thought he was justifying all the years of moving his family around. He might have even been trying to blame them. There never was a doubt that, when the time was right, Suzy and Grace would marry decent Korean men. Once, during a drive to a church on Sunday, they nearly hit a puppy, a curious mix of terrier and chow. It looked strange as it whimpered away, a hybrid with pointy ears and a moon face. Dad declared, laughing, "See what happens when you mix blood? Even dogs turn out a mess, stupid and ugly!"

Grace somehow managed to sneak around with boys behind Dad's back. She would make up excuses about the yearbook committee or student-council meetings and tumble in long after the nine o'clock curfew, and Suzy knew where she had been just by looking at her rumpled skirt and tangled hair. Grace had always been the daring one until she found God and moved to New Jersey. Suzy, on the other hand, never even kissed a boy until her freshman year in college, when she moved out of her parents' house into the dorm. His name was Brad. Suzy never even knew his last name. He was her first roommate Liz's boyfriend and stayed over every weekend; each time Suzy turned to the wall to sleep, she would hear moans and giggles from the other bed. Then, one day, Suzy came back from class and found him waiting for Liz. It was awkward to be puttering about with him sitting on Liz's bed. The silence hung heavy as Suzy sat facing the desk, still feeling his eyes on her. It was when she decided that she'd had enough and began gathering her books that she felt his hands on her shoulders. He said nothing at all, and Suzy just froze. He slowly turned her around and kissed her without hesitation, not the sweet and soft kind, but the forceful probing of a tongue that was confident and mechanical. Then he walked away from her and lit a cigarette and asked when Liz was coming back. "Any minute now," Suzy answered without looking at him, and threw the books in her bag and walked out. He never kissed her again, and Liz never knew.

Later, Suzy would recall that first kiss as if it were an omen. *What was it about her that marked her as the other woman? What did he see?*

What Suzy never forgot was the smell. It was a sick smell, like something dying almost, like instant powdered milk, non-dairy creamer, the milky-baby smell but fake. It leaped into her throat and would not wash away, no matter how fiercely she rinsed her mouth afterward. Each time she kissed boys after that, she looked for the smell. She pretended to kiss them and looked for the smell. Sometimes she would sniff the awful smell and would push the boy away violently and never speak to him afterward. But when the smell wasn't there, she would be curiously disappointed. It was as if nothing quite erased the initial shock of being kissed by someone who was not hers, a kiss that was stolen, claimed from her flippantly, a kiss so abrasively illicit that she seemed to deserve it, as though she was not worth much to begin with. It stuck with her, the shame, the smell, and came back at odd moments, such as when she stood on the steps of St. John the Divine and saw in the older man's eyes a clear reflection of herself, terribly young and terribly dissatisfied.

Damian would later confess that he had indeed followed her from the lecture hall. What made him do it? He would never say. He might have been bored, or simply tempted by a young woman who seemed as unmoved as he was by his wife's lecture, or, more likely, he really had nowhere he wanted to be on that afternoon. Perhaps he wanted Yuki Tamiko to notice him following the girl; that Suzy reminded him of Yuki at nineteen was a minor detail he would have preferred not to see. But he did follow her, which was embarrassingly impulsive for someone so much older and supposedly more sensible. He followed her all the way down the College Walk and along Amsterdam Avenue, to stand before her finally with an awkward smile, which only accentuated his lone dimple, and seemed to her somehow heart-breakingly sad. His stare did not waver, and she stared back, because she thought it might make her appear less young. Finally, one of them burst out laughing—Suzy is not sure which—and soon both were laughing like kids who had cut class and gotten away with it.

Ten years since, and it seems impossible now that she should be alone, no parents, no Damian. She thought that the choice was one or the other, and it was up to her to decide. It never occurred to her then that she would lose both, that she would not be able to keep the one even after sacrificing the other, and that the choice was never really there from the beginning.

All around her, people are gathering their things. 11:37 a.m., Montauk. Outside is the November beach town, empty and forlorn. Between the rain streaks on the windowpane are her parents buried at sea, half rising to meet their daughter here at last.

6.

NOTHING IS AS DESOLATE as a late-autumn beach. The motels with "Vacancy" signs wear the dejected face of the abandoned. The fish-and-chips stands have pulled down their shutters, closed for the winter. Fickle and selfish, the rest of the world has skipped out. Gone are the flirtatious smiles, the bronzed bodies, the neon beach balls flopping down on the bluest water. Girls with names like Tracy and Cindy and Judy no longer hang out at McSwiggin's, which is the only bar near the train station still open for business.

Even at this early hour, a few men are stooping at the bar, nursing pints. They glance at Suzy but soon look away with the stolid faces of small-town men. Most fishermen hang out at the dock, on the other side of the town, where many bars remain open, lobster and swordfish being their prime catch this season. But the nonfishing locals, mostly Irish descendants, prefer the bars in town, where the grime and sweat of the fishing crowd remain far away, where they might hang on to their Montauk as a sort of Hawaii for Long Island's working class.

It is lunchtime when Suzy enters. "Catch of the Day = $4.99" seems underpriced, and Suzy points to it immediately upon settling on a stool. The bartender is a grinning man in his mid-forties. She has seen him before, the same time last year, when she peeked in for a cup of coffee. Suzy remembers thinking how perfect that he should be called Bob, such a compact guy with a barrel chest and permanently tanned forearms.

"You want that poached, right?" he asks with a good-natured hearty smile.

"Pardon?"

"Lady, I told you we don't poach our fish, just fried, plain and good!" He is still smiling, so he is not annoyed, perhaps teasing a bit.

"Fried, yes, that's fine."

He must be confusing her with someone else. He thinks she's been here before, which she has, but a year ago, just for coffee, could he remember that?

"And coffee, right?" He is already pouring a cup. He then brings her packets of cream and sugar and says, "Oh, I forgot, you want Sweet'n Low, sorry, we're out."

Suzy stares at him awhile before reaching for the mug. She takes a sip and winces at its burnt aftertaste. The coffee's been brewed for much too long. Black, which is the only way she takes her coffee.

"No seltzer with a straw today?" Bob taunts with a wink.

Grace it must be. Grace must have been here recently. Grace, who never touches fried food and never takes sugar, who never drinks anything without a straw—he must be confusing her with Grace. When was she here? Does she come here often?

The sisters look fairly alike. When they were young, they often passed for twins. "Stupid fucks," Grace fumed, "they think all Asian girls look alike!" But Suzy was secretly happy, for she knew her sister was a beauty. They had similar features, but Grace had longer eyelashes, a finer complexion, sleeker cheekbones, poutier lips, and blacker, straighter hair. At first sight, there was no doubt that they were sisters, perhaps even twins to those who did not have an eye for beauty. But upon a closer inspection, it was clear that Grace had far superior features, the sort of face a man might die for, as Suzy thought and often witnessed through high school, when the boys would steal glances at her older sister, who remained aloof and haughty, as though her beauty were reserved for far better things than a mere boy with his dad's Toyota. The odd thing was that Grace had a reputation for being easy, but only with the older boys, the sort of boys who had cut out of school long ago, who hung in front of the local pool hall on their motorbikes, which probably did not even belong to them to begin with, who waited for Grace outside the school gate with helmets on, not for the sake of safety but to remain faceless, Suzy thought. Grace managed to hide it all from their parents. This must have been because the family moved so often. Before Grace could settle in with any of her troubled boys, they moved again, and Grace would find yet another pool hall, to which she would disappear on evenings when her parents worked overtime. Even more impressive was that Grace kept up her grades. Grace would sit by herself in the corner of the cafeteria and study furiously, while Suzy was cozily tucked in with her set of meek friends. Grace would never sit with Suzy. She said that it was embarrassing. She said that Suzy with her geeky friends embarrassed her. Everyone called Grace a stuck-up bitch, especially the girls who could not stand how their boyfriends kept looking at the new girl in the corner. All Suzy felt was distance. They must have been close once, but that seemed impossibly far away.

"So how about it, one order of fried cod!" Bob is all smiley, as though he is proud of having initiated this young woman into the art of fried cuisine. Suzy peers at the oversized piece of fish drenched in grease. She takes a bite while eager Bob dotes on her for approval. She gives him the sort of satisfied smile that makes him happy, then takes a long look around the bar. It is a typical beach-town dive, with a jukebox and a pool table. Against the wall is a laminated poster of a buxom blonde holding up a can of Budweiser. A few stools away from her are a couple of older men whose eyes are fixed on the sports updates on the TV screen suspended from the ceiling.

"So did you find what you were looking for?" Bob pretends to be nonchalant, but Suzy can tell that he is curious. She is not sure what to say. Is it really Grace he is taking her to be? What had Grace been looking for? She is tempted to tell him that he's got the wrong girl, but it seems too late now, and Bob looks too earnest. So, instead, Suzy drops her gaze at the plate of fish before her.

"Thought you went back to the city. Twice in one week in this lousy weather—whatever it is, lady, you've gotta find it fast, so you don't get that pretty head of yours wet again." He pours more coffee into her mug, although she does not want a refill. Suzy runs her fingers through her wet hair, realizing only now that she left her umbrella on the train. Perhaps it is not Grace he takes her to be, but another Asian girl who had wandered in one rainy afternoon. Perhaps Grace was right after all, white men can't tell one Asian girl from another. The fish is good. They all taste the same once fried like this. She did not realize she was hungry. She left the apartment in a hurry this morning, barely time for coffee, definitely no breakfast. The alarm did not go off again, and she woke up panicking, certain that she had missed her 8:25 train. It wasn't until she wiped the sweat off her face and took a sip of cold water and glanced at the clock again that she

realized she had more than an hour to kill. So she lay there recalling the strange phone rings and the bouquet of irises that
had come accompanied by a drill or a hissing noise, which she
failed to identify, which grew louder and louder until she could
not stand it anymore and finally bolted out of bed, only to realize that the deadly shrill had, in fact, been the alarm chiming
seven.

"See, nothing like a good piece of fish on a day like this!"

Bob is dying for her to say something, anything, so that he
can say to his regulars, "That girl over there, she's from the city,
after something, she won't say what," or "See that Asian girl? She
wanted cod poached until I told her, no, miss, we won't have
that here, not in Montauk, not at Bob McSwiggin's place!" But
all Suzy is capable of is another vague smile, a nice-girl smile so
that he knows there is nothing personal as to why she won't let
him in on what she's looking for. It would not take much to give
him the one-line answer, a simple acknowledgment: "Yes, the
fish's good; yes, I'm glad you talked me into it; yes, nothing like
a plate of fried fish on such a dreary afternoon." But even that
she cannot manage, for she is suddenly dying to get out of here.
It is as if her parents know that she has arrived, that she is here
to see them, and that not a day goes by when she does not wonder who shot them, who wanted them dead, who knew exactly
how to pierce their hearts.

The numbers on the TV screen flip with a dizzying speed:
Knicks 88 Bulls 70 Lakers 102 Spurs 99 Giants 21 Saints 10. The
coffee is tepid now and tastes somewhat less burnt.

"Did I leave an umbrella here last time?" Suzy ventures cautiously, hoping the question might bring light to when Grace, if
it was indeed Grace, was here. Something inside Suzy cannot resist. Become Grace for a moment. Embrace Grace's trace, which
might lead to Grace.

"Beats me. I keep whatever people forget in that bin." Bob

points to the plastic crate by the entrance. "You were here when, on Friday? Should still be there, but if you don't see it, just take any umbrella you find."

Suzy walks over and makes a pretense of looking through the crate before picking out the only umbrella among the torn jackets, chipped pocket knives, soiled bandannas, and baseball caps, the sort of leftovers no one wants. Friday, just three days ago. Did Grace come to see Mom and Dad early so that she wouldn't run into Suzy? Does she still hate her so? *Leave us alone,* Grace told her at the funeral, without once meeting her eyes. Hasn't Suzy done exactly that, hasn't she stayed away all these years as though she had no family left in the world?

The umbrella is a weapon. She can leave now, out into the torrential sea where her parents wait. Bob looks happy with his five-dollar tip, almost as much as the whole bill. But today is not a day for calculating the 20 percent, and Suzy is holding on to the nameless umbrella left by a drunkard on a rainy night.

"Oh, I knew I forgot something," Bob hollers after Suzy. "Kelly's back, tell him Bob sent you and he'll give you a deal. Make sure you tell him you can't even swim."

Crazy to hit the beach in this rain. The lighthouse is on Montauk Point, the easternmost tip of New York. From here, Suzy can either follow the shore for about six miles or just hop in a taxi. An impossibly long pilgrimage, but Suzy cannot bring herself to call a cab, not now, not on her way to see her parents. One of the wires of the umbrella hangs loose, through which the precarious sky threatens to break. It seems almost perfect, that the rain should follow each step and erase the trace of this mourning.

So it had been Grace after all. On Friday, while Suzy was interpreting in the Bronx, Grace had shown up at McSwiggin's looking for something. Neither Grace nor Suzy can swim. Their bodies simply will not float. Suzy tried to learn a few times, but her body would tense immediately upon hitting the water. Grace is terrified of the water—as far as Suzy knows, possibly the only thing she is afraid of. So it had to be Grace: poached cod, Sweet'n Low, seltzer with a straw, can't swim . . . Then who's Kelly? Three days ago, Grace may have stood on this very path. She may have continued up the shore holding the umbrella with a broken frame. She may have cried a little, praying for a miracle.

Suzy has a hard time picturing her. She has not set her eyes on her sister for five years. In fact, she has barely seen her since they both left for college at seventeen. Grace came home only twice during the four years. Suzy saw her just once, during the Christmas break one year. Suzy was struck by how thin her sister looked. Even Dad commented on it, telling Mom to give her an extra scoop of rice at dinner. Grace mostly kept to herself during the four days she stayed. A few phone calls came for her from the same husky-voiced guy, who would only identify himself as a "friend," to whom Suzy had to lie each time and say that Grace was not home. Grace seemed somehow subdued, a bit nicer. The only time Suzy glimpsed the familiar cynicism was when she expressed her surprise at Grace's choice of major, which was religion. Grace smiled faintly, as though it were a private joke that Suzy did not understand, and muttered, "What does it matter?" Although the visit went smoothly, without much commotion, Suzy was relieved when Grace took the bus back to Northampton.

Grace is thirty now. She will turn thirty-one at the end of this month, only two days after Suzy's birthday. Suzy the 24th, and Grace the 26th. Grace always resented their birthdays' falling so close together. She said it took all the steam out of her day. To appease both, Mom used to make them *miyukguk*, the traditional birthday seaweed soup, on the 25th. Kill two birds with one stone, Grace would grunt as she slurped her soup with a vengeance. What Grace really could not stand, Suzy suspected, was that they were the same age for those two days. They were equals suddenly, neither younger nor older. Grace no longer had the upper hand. Last year, for Grace's thirtieth birthday, Suzy bought a card for the first time in years. She stood for a while before the Hallmark section of the stationery store and looked through the ones with the gold-engraved "To Dear Sister." She chose instead a plain white one, but she never sent it.

The walk is not easy, increasingly rocky. On Suzy's left is the dramatic formation of eroded cliffs, the land broken by years of water. To her right is the ocean. No one is around. One o'clock on a rainy November afternoon, who in their right mind would be out here?

Except someone is. Far in the distance, Suzy can see a figure walking ahead. Either a man or a woman under the umbrella, but a tinge of familiarity in the shape, in the way each step is dragged. Where did the person come from? Had he or she been walking ahead the whole time?

For a second, Suzy imagines that it might be Grace, and that she will run and catch up until finally the two will be joined, holding hands, together to see their parents, a family as they had never been, as they should have been—Mom and Dad, Grace and Suzy. *Since when do you care about their wishes?* Grace will never let her forget. It was Suzy who had cut out first, the first escape, the first hole in the foursome. It was Suzy who had ruined it all, Suzy who ran off with her professor's husband and left everyone back home in shame, Suzy who disappeared for four years, until the day the police tracked her down at Damian's Berkshire house with the news that her parents were dead. Grace never forgave Suzy for ditching Mom and Dad in their final years. Jen found Grace's resentment toward Suzy un-

fair. "I thought your sister never came home either when she was
at Smith. Why is she suddenly the good daughter?"

But of course it cannot be Grace walking ahead. Grace must
be tucked safely back in her Godly New Jersey home. What
happened at Smith? What happens at her church, where Grace
must spend all her time now? In the spring of 1991, over nine
years ago, when Suzy chose Damian over everything, Grace had
just moved back home from Northampton, where she had tried
a few jobs with not much luck. Suzy was surprised when she
learned that Grace was home. Suzy thought that Grace, more
than anyone she knew, would have some grand plan waiting for
her upon finishing college. Moving back to her parents' house
seemed like a desperate decision. Grace was living in New Jersey
when her parents were shot in their Bronx store in November
1995. She taught ESL at Fort Lee High School. Most of her students were Korean kids who had recently landed in America,
whose parents were often gone, working overtime. The same
kids also attended Fort Lee New Joy Fellowship Church, where
Grace was in charge of the Bible study Wednesday nights and
Sunday afternoons. Grace was a good teacher supposedly, excep-
tionally competent and quick with her lessons. That was her
style, never sentimental, never messy. Suzy overheard all this on
the bus after the funeral. The older women who sat opposite
Suzy must have been the parents of Grace's students. "So what
about the other daughter?" one of them asked. "Shhhh." The
second woman made a hush motion with her finger on her lips,
glancing at Suzy.

Definitely not Grace up ahead. Someone entirely different, a
stranger with his back toward Suzy. Quite a distance separates
the two, and with the rain and all, Suzy can barely make out the
shape of the other. The rocks are getting sharper, and from here
on, there is no choice but to follow the steps to the road, which

continues for a few more miles parallel to the shore. The path is uphill, slippery. Whoever's ahead must be heading in the same direction. Whoever's ahead keeps an even distance without once turning around, or perhaps it is Suzy making sure that she keeps up. Perhaps there are other ashes scattered from the lighthouse; perhaps it is the locals' favorite burial spot. Why scatter the ashes from the lighthouse? Whose romantic notion was that? Suzy, of course, had been left out of the decision. It seemed like a good idea, a comforting idea, but definitely not her parents'. But, then again, what did Suzy know about her parents?

Barely two in the afternoon; the darkness is menacing. When she first came here five years ago, she saw nothing. All she could focus on was the urn Grace was carrying, in which her parents' ashes were mixed together. Dome-shaped, wrapped in stiff white linen, the way the dead were kept in Korea. Suzy could not stand looking at the thing that held her parents, and was relieved when Grace assumed all responsibilities for handling it. Neither cried. Suzy was still in shock, and Grace, being in charge, seemed unable to cry. Suzy had no doubt that once they found themselves finally alone in their respective apartments each would burst into tears. Afterward, Grace must have gone straight to church; Suzy packed her bag and left Damian's house immediately. He was not around when she left. During their final six months, she had stayed at his Berkshire house while he spent much of his time abroad. She left without a note, and he did not try to find her. She went straight to Jen's apartment and slept for several weeks. When she was finally able to get up and walk outside, she wandered into the East Village and found the apartment on St. Marks Place. And still Suzy had not cried.

The path cuts into the main road, where the sign reads "Montauk Highway." Definitely not the smartest thing to walk along the highway, not in this rain, not alone, not dreaming of tears. But Suzy is determined; so is the person ahead. Hardly any cars pass. The road may continue this way, and Suzy will have circled the edge of New York, down to its rocky bottom.

Then, suddenly, without warning, emerges the lighthouse, up there in the distance, beaming into the brooding sky. The white tower is forlorn and majestic, fenced in from all sides. Its silence seems so repressive that for a second Suzy is afraid for her parents, who lie beneath the cliff. Even in this rain, the flag hangs from the pole on its left. The gray colonial house has been turned into a museum with a gold plaque at its entrance which reads "Montauk Historical Society." She soon finds the spot where Grace stood five years ago, holding on to the urn before finally opening its lid. Nothing there now except a lone bench behind a rusty viewfinder.

Tell me what happened, Mom, Dad, what really happened to you?

One thing Suzy has learned in the last five years is that nothing follows death, no revelation comes into play. Death is silent, heartless, heart-wrenchingly unfair. Each time Suzy comes here, sometimes twice, three times a year, she realizes how stock-still everything is, how immutable the lighthouse, how infinite the Montauk sky, how constant the rain, how absolutely unforgiving the water appears from where she stands. Each time Suzy stands here, she cringes at the way the watchtower looms over everything, as if it suggested man's ultimate power over nature, and the star-spangled banner at the edge of the eastern coast, as if this very cliff were the helm of the American dream. And each time, she becomes certain that time has played tricks on her, and those five years—during which Suzy floated from job to job, from one married man to another—happened only so that she might stand and wait for someone, anyone, to step in and say, Look what you've done, look what you've been left with, look what you are, is this what you wanted?

What do you want after all, do you want me to tell you? Damian had pleaded in his final message.

But she is not alone. Someone else is here, over in the distance by the drenched flag, now facing her direction. It is hard to see the face buried beneath the hooded raincoat under the black umbrella, and so much rain between them. It is a man, she can tell that much. She takes a step toward him. An Asian man. Something about him strikes her as being familiar, the way he stands with his head tilted slightly to his right. She takes another hesitant step. She wants to shout something, say hello, excuse me, anything, but she seems to be choking and no words will come out. He stands there watching her, or perhaps watching beyond, toward the ocean. She follows his gaze and finds the angry sea gaping at her and wonders if it is a signal from her parents, a sign, a code she cannot understand. The sky is burning gray, almost red at its edges. Suddenly frightfully cold, Suzy tightens the opening of her coat. This overly chic trench coat—Michael had brought it from his last trip to London. Michael, whom she never thinks about when he is not around, which he never is. Odd that she should recall him now, so inappropriate, almost irreverent to her parents, who would weep for their daughter, who, after all these years, is hiding with another man who will never be hers. *My dear Suzy, my girl, my poor daughter, where have we gone wrong, where did we go wrong with you?* Mom might plead, which cannot be true, since she would never say anything so self-deprecating, would play dumb instead, avoid Suzy's eyes, turn to Dad, who would take one final look at Suzy with a disgust, an anger that should never be directed by a father toward his daughter, words that should be swallowed instead, erased, so Suzy will not stand here five years later, five long, grueling years that brand her with the echo—*Whore, you whore to a white man, a white married man, don't ever come back.*

But death is silent. Suzy shuts her eyes to the lashing waves.

She still cannot cry, nothing will make her cry. Then, turning back, she notices that the man in the distance is no longer there.

The train back to Penn Station departs at 5 p.m. No time for a drink at McSwiggin's. Twice in one day, Bob might become too familiar with her face, Grace's face, whichever he takes her to be. The taxi pulls up exactly at four-thirty. The driver, with a bright-yellow T-shirt that says "Montauk Taxi," looks no more than sixteen, and she wonders if the kid even has the proper license to be driving a commercial vehicle. He speeds on Montauk Highway along Napeague Bay, passing the dock with its fishing boats and a few bars with rooms upstairs where the fishermen blow the last of their sea-winded dollars. It takes less than ten minutes to get to the train station, and Suzy hands the driver the fourteen dollars before turning around and trying, for the hell of it, "Hey, happen to know who Kelly is?" The kid gingerly counts the dollar bills before replying in the thickest Irish lilt, "Sure, everyone knows Kelly, he rents boats out over at the dock, tiny sloops, two-person max. Why, you need a boat?"

7.

THIRST IS WHAT GETS HER. The clock points to 4 a.m., which is inevitably the hour when she is awoken, breathless. She lingers in bed for a while before dragging herself to the refrigerator. The water is cool, a clean break from sleep. She fell asleep with the light on again. It is hard to believe that she slept at all under such brightness. There was no dream. The night was a black, soundless tunnel. Nothing interrupted her, no crying girl by the shore, no unknown hand shaking her home.

It is a terrible habit, to wake up in the middle of the night and reach for a cigarette. But the world is claustrophobic at 4 a.m., nothing comes to the rescue. The irises on the table still look serenely white, even if there's a hint of wither, the writhing of petals. Averting her eyes, she notices the blinking red light on the answering machine. Several messages. Must be Michael. Suzy wonders why he calls her constantly, if he calls his wife also. The conversation is most often one-sided. He runs through everything he has accomplished that day, most of which Suzy does not really understand. He needs to report to someone, to anyone, to any ear that will listen. He talks about the conference calls with Germany, the merger meeting that busted, the additional clauses in the newest contract. Each feverish rant ends with the inevitable chuckle, "All it means, babe, is that they're suckers and I've got you for love." She wonders if he is lonely, if he ever thinks about being lonely.

The first time she slept with Michael, he got up at five in the morning to catch his train home. His wife and their five-month-old son lived in Westport, Connecticut. He had not seen them in two weeks, and Suzy could tell that he missed them. When he turned on the light to dress, Suzy pretended to be asleep. It was easier that way, and she preferred waking alone in the hotel room. She enjoyed lounging in the strange surroundings, which would become no longer strange, since Michael had a habit of always returning to the same room, 755 at the Waldorf-Astoria. The checkout was at twelve, and Suzy would take a long bath in the marble tub, whose enormous size seemed right out of a fairy tale. Afterward, she would wrap her body in the luscious terry-cloth robe and wait for the room service that Michael had ordered for her before leaving—the poached eggs with hollandaise sauce, a basket of freshly baked scones and croissants, and a tall glass of fresh carrot juice. The ritual seemed to be a good one; it had nothing to do with what she knew.

Except Michael was married, which seemed crucial. Jen, when Suzy told her about the affair, looked at her aghast. "Why?" asked Jen. "You know your parents are no longer watching, there's no audience anymore." Jen said nothing further and stopped introducing Suzy to those hopelessly Ivy League, defensively arrogant, devoutly bookish young men who passed through the magazine where she worked. None of them took to Suzy anyway. They would come along for a drink with Jen, which Suzy knew was all for her benefit, and ramble on about another young author on the verge of fame. Their tales of the author's propensity for run-on sentences and waify poet girls bored her. Most of all, she could not stand the tinge of jealousy in the bookish man's voice as he repeated, with a vengeance, the exact numbers of the six figures that the author's first book had garnered. Suzy remained silent, trying her best to suppress a yawn, and Jen would play the moderator by cracking jokes, which was not her style. Suzy was relieved when Jen stopped her matchmaking gestures.

"Getting older, Suzy, means just getting more selfish all the time. Does my heart break anymore because you're fucking another Damian? What if you're hiding with another asshole? What can I do really, how does that change my life?" Jen cried one night when they had emptied half a bottle of Jack Daniel's that had been sitting on Suzy's kitchen shelf for several months. *But nothing changes my life either, nothing touches me.* Suzy may have mumbled in a drunken stupor. The night was vague and easily forgotten.

No Jack Daniel's tonight, nothing at all but this empty kitchen and the Evian bottle of wilting irises. Why did Grace want a boat? Did she sail out into the shallow sea to mourn their parents? Has Grace become lonely over the years? For a second, Suzy is tempted to reach for the phone and dial Grace's New Jersey number. Over the years, Suzy tried calling Grace a few times during afternoons when she was sure Grace wouldn't be home. Each time, she secretly hoped that Grace might have stayed home from school by some sisterly telepathy and would pick up the phone. Instead, the machine clicked on with no outgoing message whatsoever, just a plain, long beep, and Suzy would hang up immediately. Perhaps Grace never answers her phone either; perhaps the sisters have that in common.

Sleep is impossible. Not quite the night, and interminably far from the morning. But Suzy is used to this sort of wait, a meander, a break with no end in sight. The ring of smoke casts a mournful veil around the flowers. A perfect white on white, but death over life really, as if the smoke is seeping through each pore of the iris.

The sisters wore white *hanbok* on that day in Montauk. They gathered their hair back with white cloth pins, following the Korean tradition for immediate mourners. *White is the color of sadness, the color of remembering, of home,* Mom had told Suzy when she asked why she wore a white cloth pin in her hair on each anniversary of her own parents' death. The delicate silk of their dresses appeared almost transparent against the lighthouse towering above. They must have looked hopelessly small on that day, two newly orphaned girls in white carrying the urn, their blackest hair rippling in the wind, suddenly alone amidst a vast country. Watching Grace scattering the ashes, Suzy thought that her sister seemed more Asian than she had ever remembered. Had it rained that day also? Did her parents disappear into the Atlantic, which kept calling her through that day and each day after?

To an insomniac, night crawls in secret. Suzy can hear each second tick so loudly that the anticipation of the next second makes her heart beat even louder. Sleep eludes her. It comes either all at once or not at all. During her first year in this apartment, Suzy slept all the time. She would watch TV and sleep. She had no trouble at all. She would close her eyes, and then, upon waking, she would realize that it was the next day. And then she would turn on the TV again, the continuation of programs from the previous day, and then, so naturally, a soft, smooth sleep would engulf her. Day by day, month by month, in fact, that whole year went by with a blink, as if she were not there at all, as if it were not she who slept and ate and watched TV with such mechanical efficiency. And then, at some point, almost overnight, she found that nothing would happen when she shut her eyes. Just as she could not bear to watch TV one day, sleep also failed her. No matter how hard she tried, as now she had to make a conscious effort to will herself to sleep, nothing came. And soon sleep missed her at all hours. It would come suddenly and grip her. She would collapse onto bed, often fully dressed, as though she were under a spell, a forgetting spell that would wipe her out. Such flickering, intensely invasive sleep never lasted long, never sank into her, and here she sits at 4 a.m. wide awake at a kitchen table, making herself smoke a cigarette because there is nothing else to do.

Michael helps. Sex helps. Suzy wonders if that is why she so willingly accepted his suggestion of a date when she first met him. Even he seemed taken aback when she said yes without a glimpse of hesitation. Suzy served as the interpreter at one of his joint-venture meetings with the executives from a giant Korean corporation. The Korean side brought their own translator, but Michael's firm had hired Suzy as a backup. It was one of Suzy's first interpreting jobs, and she masked her nervousness with cool detachment. During the lunch break, Michael turned to her and asked, "Ms. Park, are you not allowed to smile on duty?" Suzy looked at him for the first time then and noticed that he was attractive, the way men are when they are successful, late-thirties, and obviously married. His angular, almost square face was deeply tanned, as though he had just returned from a weeklong vacation somewhere tropical, and his sandy-blond hair set off his mischievous green eyes, which made him seem younger than he actually was. He was much shorter than he had appeared sitting down, about five feet nine perhaps, which might make him feel self-conscious, because he had a very tall air about him, which Suzy could not help but find endearing as she stared back at him without an answer, still with no smile. At the end of the meeting, Michael tossed his card at Suzy with, "Call me if you wanna show me your other face," which was not exactly romantically inspired, as he admitted later, but more like a dare, a brutish proposition, to see if this rigid, aloof girl would break rules for him, on whose fourth finger a wedding ring shone like a big fat warning sign. Instead, Suzy shot back at him with, "Forget the call, how about tonight?" She might have been waiting for someone like him, so bold, so crudely unseductive, so unlike Damian, that love never came into the question.

Michael found Suzy's acquiescence intriguing. He took her to the "21" Club that night, not the sort of place a married man should take a girl whom he had just picked up on a job. He gazed at her over the preposterously priced salmon zapped with mint-flavored sauce and said, "You've got issues, but I don't wanna know about them, not because I'm an asshole, but because you think I am." Suzy reached over and kissed him then, a light, fleeting kiss, and remembered that it had been years since she had kissed a man. He broke into laughter as if to cover his embarrassment. "You're a funny girl, Suzy Park; that clears it, we're not gonna fuck tonight." Michael was a romantic in his own way, Suzy thought. She went along with whatever he wanted, and it bothered him, she could tell. It took a few more dinners before they finally slept together. He wanted a bit of resistance, something befitting a mistress, some temper, some tears, but Suzy gave none, and he turned to her afterward and said, "That was like fucking a ghost, a very sexy one, but a ghost nonetheless." He kept coming back, though. He liked her. He admired her, even. He was a generous lover, and Suzy slept well afterward.

Yet here she sits still, listening to the radiator tap again, as it always does at this hour, an ambulance siren, a train engine, an evenly paced knock that will not stop, which she has gotten used to through the years, which comforts her on winter nights, as though its hissing noise were the only sign familiar to her, the closest thing to a home. The heat comes on slowly, and she is no longer sure if it is Michael she craves or the kind of warmth only another body can offer, the embrace afterward as his hands curl into her arms, as his breath caresses her neck, as his thighs are wrapped into her own. It is sleep she wants, perhaps, the sleep of a spent body, sleep buried in the body of another who's been so close, who's entered so far, who's moved back and forth with such insistence, emptying her of anything she might still remember.

Of course, Michael never holds her like that. He always rushes off afterward, to a meeting, to an airport, to his family. On the rare occasions when he dozes next to her, he will kiss her once with a note of finality, then turn to the wall and be fast asleep. Theirs is not that kind of intimacy. She knows that it would be false for them to cling to each other afterward. She knows that she would leave him if he ever reached out that way. She knows this because she lies next to him recalling another's hands, which had held her afterward, which had stroked her face so precisely, as though making sure that her eyes were closed now, that her lips were smiling with the sated ripple of what had just occurred, and her fingers still following his as if reluctant to let him go, as if her body had finally found the right angle, the right corner where it might rest until she would awake again and again find him whose hands had held her no matter how often she tried to leave, how far she ran, as far as this 4 a.m. apartment where she sits alone with a dying cigarette, wanting Michael instead, wanting Michael again and again, as though dispelling the dream of another's hands.

Four a.m. is a haunted hour. *Suzy, come back to bed,* Damian would plead upon finding her on the porch. She often did that then too. She would awake at this exact hour and retreat so easily into where Damian could not enter. He hated it. He hated seeing Suzy lost in what he dismissed as a "purgatorial suspension of guilt," for neither he nor she should suffer for what they had to do. *Suzy, I need you back in my bed.* He claimed her, the way she sought him above anything else in the world, above her parents, her college, her youth, and it was this desperate claim that made her feel uneasy, almost doomed. *Suzy, enough.* He was never afraid to say what he wanted. He was fearless. Most of all, he was fearless with her, which she thought could only be love.

The same unending night, the same uncertain hour in which Suzy sat in the wicker chair on Damian's porch many years ago, afraid of the ghosts who were living then, who had such short lives left before them, who have now returned as though they've been waiting inside her all day, watching her along the Montauk shore, riding beside her on the Long Island Rail Road, fighting through the evening crowd of Penn Station, hailing a cab to downtown, following her up the steps back to her apartment, and finally settling into this repose where nothing seems familiar except their darling daughter and a bouquet of white irises.

Suzy climbs between cold sheets, back in her futon, which floats like a tiny boat burying her inside the room. Is this what Grace sought? Out there in the sea? A burial for her who cannot swim?

Two shots only; the gun had fired exactly twice and pierced their hearts.

What happens when a bullet pierces a heart? What happens in that eternal second? What happens to a body falling so instantly, as a perfect answer to a perfect finger that pulled the trigger as if counting one, two, first the man, then the wife, or the woman, then the husband, whichever order, for it is all the same who goes first, they will fall together, the bullet never misses, a clean shot, two clean shots, no messy stuff, no pool of blood, no heart-wrenching cries, no crying daughter whose body lies five years later still hoping for the third bullet, which was surely fired, which will reach her heart with dead certainty, as it did once, twice, so easily, so conclusively, two shots only, exactly twice, and how Detective Lester turned to Suzy afterward with a sorry face and informed her, "Miss, your parents died instantly," as if to say, *Miss, your bullet is on the way; miss, be patient, your time will come; miss, we're sure of it, whoever never misses, whoever is a professional, the shot is a sure thing.*

The silence is deceiving. The hissing of the radiator has stopped. The night is a perfect calm. Soon the dawn will break. Already there is a faint light smudging the black sky. Already the next day is a possibility. She thinks she hears the shrill of the phone, the rings, the four desperate rings, though she cannot be sure, though she must be dreaming, this must be the hour when no one calls, no one listens, except for her who follows the sea in piercing rain, who craves a warm body despite love, who lies in the dark pretending to live.

8.

"THIS IS THE INTERPRETER HOTLINE SERVICES for the Korean interpreter Suzy Park. Client, Bronx DA's Office at the Criminal Court on 215 East 161st Street. Time, twelve-thirty p.m. tomorrow. Take Number 4 to 161st Street. Call back in one hour if there's a scheduling conflict."

The message on the machine sounds as if it belongs to one of those computerized answering services. The details vary, but the voice is always the same. Suzy has never met the one giving orders. She was hired over the phone after a forty-minute mock trial in Korean. She sent them the signed freelancer's contract and began working immediately. The procedure is always the same. They tell her where to go, and she shows up at the designated location. After each job, she faxes them the details of the case, including the file number and the contact information of the attorneys and witnesses present at the deposition, and they send her a check every two weeks. Unlike a fact-checking job, which can last through nights, depositions are over in just a few

like fact checking job—no dialogue in book?

hours—longer if the case involves a serious medical-malpractice suit, for which both the doctor and the hospital dispatch their individual lawyers, whose redundant questionings can make the whole thing tedious. Then there are the occasional cases where an interpreter is hired as part of a legal strategy even though the witness speaks English. When such a witness is caught lying, he can always point a finger at the interpreter and claim that it is she who translated incorrectly. Or the witness might double-talk and confuse the interpreter, thus making the testimony impossible to translate. These types of depositions can drag on for days, at which point it is no longer the truth the interpreter delivers but a game of greed, in which she has become a pawn. Luckily, such cases are rare, and almost always she walks out of a job within an hour or two.

At first, the agency recommended that Suzy get a beeper or a cellular phone, but she told them that it would be unnecessary. She was always home, she admitted to a mere voice, a stranger with a tab on her life. The message was left yesterday. While Suzy walked along the shore in Montauk, the subpoena was drawn, the witness summoned, the investigation scheduled. A little after midday, an odd time to start a job.

The machine is still blinking. The second message is from Michael. He groans about his dump of a hotel in Frankfurt, the food is glorified grub, and there're too many Germans everywhere. It is Michael's way of filling up the silence. When he cannot think of anything else to say, he complains. It is easy to find a man endearing when one's heart is not at stake. "I'll call you tomorrow, around four p.m. your time, after my meeting. Be home." Michael always volunteers his exact whereabouts to Suzy, as though he is afraid of disappearing between the airport runways somewhere in the world. He might do that with his wife also, and she might never suspect him. Suzy has no idea what he tells his wife on those nights he stays at the Waldorf.

Suzy never asks. It is an unspoken rule. She imagines Michael to be a good husband and father. He probably arrives at the front door of his Westport home with an armful of presents each time. On his wife's dressing table is surely an array of duty-free perfume bottles in every color and shape. She probably laughs and tells him to stop, a cute joke between the two, she refusing to wear the airline-sponsored scent and he promising never to buy another, and then, upon reaching home after a whirlwind of flights, with a cheeky smile, he takes out another crystal bottle from his coat pocket. The baby, now almost a year old, is on the lap of their nanny while the handsome couple in their late thirties kiss.

But his white-picket-fenced Westport house, his blonde wife in her primary-color outfits, and his baby boy who so resembles Michael have nothing to do with Suzy. Connecticut is a long train ride away, and her cell-phoning lover remains her secret through the cool winds of November. Oddly, no guilt, no sleep lost over his family, who really have nothing to worry about. Suzy is only happy to send Michael home. She has no intention of keeping him, as she had with Damian.

They didn't see each other until seven months after meeting on the steps of St. John the Divine. It happened in the third week of November of that same year. There were only a few weeks left in the first semester, and Suzy was anxious, still unsure about her senior thesis, which focused, of all things, on Shakespeare. The comparative aspect had to do with the Eastern treatment of *King Lear*, as adapted by Akira Kurosawa in his minimalist film *Ran*. Suzy had been intrigued by the fundamentally opposite viewpoints expressed in the two interpretations of the same plot, which supported her central argument of the impossibility of harmony between the East and the West. It seemed a militant way of analyzing the problematic relationship, and Suzy was not sure how much of it was really her idea, or if it had been Professor Tamiko who encouraged such a position. Suzy had met her only once privately, for half an hour. The scheduled twice-a-semester meetings never worked out. Back in September, soon after the senior year began, Suzy sat before Professor Tamiko, feeling awkward, if not slightly terrified. It was the first time she saw her up close. Of course Professor Tamiko showed up late and offered no apology.

"So you believe that Shakespeare was exhibiting a secret Zen desire through Cordelia's insistence on 'nothing,' or by declaring so boldly, which is really to negate the premise of 'nothing,' he was illustrating the very Western ideal of negative space?"

No warm-up chitchat, no polite hellos; Professor Tamiko liked to get straight to the point. Suzy was not sure if she expected her to say anything in reply. Besides, she really did not know what she thought about the whole thing, if she had any concrete position. Certainly, it was her thesis. She was still brewing with thoughts, some interesting, some absurdly minor, and yet, sitting before this woman who was now spewing infinite possibilities, Suzy felt dumb, as if she became Cordelia herself, who could declare nothing over and over as if it were the only conceivable cry against all that had brought her there, to this ground-floor office whose window revealed the sunny autumn outside, which seemed suddenly impossible to believe. Professor Tamiko was now saying something about Kurosawa's use of the scene depicting a tree as the Eastern answer to Cordelia's verbal filial piety. The tree, yes, Suzy liked that scene in the movie, how the younger son stands holding up the bony branch that casts a soft shadow over the old king's sleeping face. It was a heartbreaking scene, the son's last gesture of love for his aging father, the old immutable tyrant on whose face death has begun its menacing grip.

It felt unbearably hot suddenly, and Suzy took out a tissue from her bag to wipe the sweat off her face.

"Yours is quite an interesting thesis, but anything can be interesting if you just put your mind to it, even Shakespeare. Let's take it one step further . . . How effective is Cordelia's 'nothing'? How pure is Shakespeare's intent? Or perhaps have we all been fooled by Shakespeare, could he be the biggest con man of the world's literature? Why is it always the white man?"

The sudden tightness in Professor Tamiko's tone surprised her. No one uttered the words "white man" with such contempt, except perhaps her father. Suzy thought she had seen the fleeting anger across the older woman's pale face, whose violet lipstick shone so brightly against the cream silk blouse and the matching cardigan, and the afternoon sun almost too faint against her piercing black eyes.

"Don't look so timid, now; it won't get you very far, not with me, and definitely not with them."

Suzy realized that she was being dismissed. What did she mean by "them"? Her father often said things like that. He would say "us" and "them" as though there were always a line between the family and the rest of the world. The implication was clear. The guilt lay with "white men," as he never forgot to tell her: "Don't ever trust them, don't you ever let them touch you."

Suzy got up to leave. The meeting seemed to have nothing to do with her thesis. Shakespeare and Kurosawa seemed to have so little bearing on what had just been confessed in the office; she would be glad never to return. And it was then that Suzy saw the black-and-white photo of Damian on the corner of the bookshelf. He appeared very young, his chestnut hair down to his shoulders, the flared collar of his flannel shirt so unmistakably seventies. Next to him was Professor Tamiko, girlish with clean bangs and no lipstick. She looked happy, her head leaning against his shoulder, shockingly youthful, and clearly in love.

"It's from a long time ago. I should've put it away."

Professor Tamiko muttered as though she were excusing her-self, as though she thought Suzy had already left the room.

The next meeting was not scheduled until November, which was when Suzy saw him. She had been waiting in front of Pro-fessor Tamiko's office. The thesis was going nowhere, and she was seriously considering dropping the whole topic. Their meet-ing was supposed to be at two o'clock, but upon arriving she found the door locked. Suzy crouched on the floor with her bag at her feet, hoping that someone would show up eventually, per-haps one of the TAs who usually answered the door during her office hours. But half an hour passed, and no one came, and Suzy began to feel hungry and sleepy. She had not slept for days, sitting up all night before the blank computer screen, glancing at the familiar tree scene from *Ran*, which was now on her VCR permanently with its sound muted. She was beginning to get sick of it. Filial piety or not, what did it matter to her, who re-ally cared if Shakespeare was a con man or not, why lose sleep over something so abstract and ancient? Suzy was never a rebel, never imagined herself as one, and now was certainly not the time for her to behave as such, when her college degree was down to just one more semester.

Suzy must have dozed off, for she suddenly opened her eyes to furious knockings nearby. He did not seem to notice her crouching on the floor against the right wall. He was banging on the door repeatedly, stamping his feet, muttering something un-der his breath resembling a curse, though Suzy could barely make it out. A few minutes went by before he stopped.

"She's not there," Suzy volunteered hesitantly. He looked down at her as if he could not understand where she might have come from. His face lacked any discernible expression. But there again—she could not help noticing it—the hollowness in his eyes, the sort of loneliness collected for years, why should it seem so familiar to her? Even back in April, when she first saw him on the steps of St. John the Divine, even as they both burst out laughing, she found, in his shockingly blue eyes, the mark of something absent, akin to resignation, irrevocably past innocence. And now, sitting here, gazing up at him with her arms hugging her bent knees, she wanted to get up and take his hand and lead him away from this dark hallway, this locked office to which she had hoped she would never return. So, instead, Suzy fired a shot, with a boldness that surprised her: "I hope you didn't follow me again."

He stared at her intently, as though he had not recognized her until then. Of course, it had only been a chance encounter. He had once followed her out of his wife's lecture on a whim, on a silly, crazy, shiny April whim. Call it spring fever, call it the aging scholar's midlife confusion. The girl had caught him then, red-handed and guilty, and the two had laughed with an understanding that neither could really explain, and continued on their separate ways, innocent and strangely rejuvenated. And here was the girl again, sitting in front of his wife's office, watching him lose his temper with such sweet tenderness on a face frighteningly young. He was embarrassed, but not terribly.

Suzy watched his face soften, and took a chance: "I'm starving."

When they sat across from each other at Tom's Diner at 112th Street and Broadway, they were both silent. Gone were her smooth Lolita talk and his seething discomfort. There was nothing more to say. Whatever should be was happening. Damian sat before his tea, watching Suzy biting into a cheeseburger with the sated face of a child.

"I'll be twenty in one week," she told him when she cleaned off the plate, now toying with the last fry that remained free of the pool of ketchup surrounding it.

Will you make love to me then, I have never done it before.

Surely she could not have said it. She had never been so reck

less. She did not even want him in that way. He did not fill her
with lust, as she later learned to feel after learning his body as if
it were her own. But that afternoon, leaning on the orange
Formica table at Tom's Diner, she invited him to imagine her. It
seemed necessary, almost understood between the two, that it
should take place, that a part of him should pour inside her, a
significant part of him, not that fresh-faced, long-haired guy he
might have once been to Professor Tamiko, but instead this
much older, visibly distraught man nearing fifty, bad-mannered
enough to kick his wife's door open, who now sat opposite, un-
dressing her silently, wishing he were not doing so.

Certainly she seduced him, but he encouraged her with silence. He gazed at her, not laughing, not making light of her
suggestion, not saying anything to distract her maneuver. He
simply watched her eat and waited patiently until she stumbled
on her words. Once the waiter took the empty plate away, Suzy
felt a slight panic, not knowing what to do with her hands or
where to rest her eyes. She thought of taking out a cigarette
from her pocket, but she could not decide if that would make
her seem even younger. She was afraid that he might get up and
leave, although she knew, on some basic level, that he wouldn't.

"What is your name?" he asked, matter-of-factly, as though
he was finally beginning to see whatever lay between them,
which had been quite unspoken, quite imagined, which was yet
to be convinced or confessed, and the only thing left to do was
to say her name, the first uttering of her name, which might be
the first decision on his part.

She hesitated. She did not want him to say her name yet. She
was afraid of its permanence. She dropped her gaze as if to hide
her blushing face from him.

"I'm terrified."

Later that night, when she lay back in her dormitory bed
counting the creeping clock, she wondered what had pushed her

so far. Later, much later, when he did say her name once, twice, and again, she shut her eyes and thought that everything was different now, everything had changed permanently: the hollowness she had seen in his eyes at their first meeting, the passing of innocence she had so aptly sensed might have been the premonition of the escape.

What do you want after all, do you want me to tell you?

He might have said before touching her face, before gathering her in his arms. But that happened a week later, on November 24th, her twentieth birthday, when she stood before him like a small, trembling bride and let the white cotton slip off her body.

This body, as he had known so completely, remains now with no vestige of such nights, such hands, coyly innocent in her white terry-cloth robe, which Suzy pulls over any exposed skin as though she cannot bear such a glimpse.

She plays the final message as she steps into the kitchen and scoops coffee into the filter.

"Ms. Suzy Park, is this Ms. Park's residence? Detective Lester here, from the Forty-first Precinct. How're you? Listen, could you come on up to the station later this week? Nothing urgent, just a few questions. I'm out on a case but will be back by Thursday. Extension 111 if you wanna call before coming in."

It has been years since she last heard from Detective Lester, not since the case was filed away unsolved, which he never admitted. He kept assuring her that these "thugs" would sooner or later be caught. But she has not kept in touch with him either. There was no point. If any new development occurred, she was sure he would find her. Why such faith? She stares at the brewing steam of the gurgling Mr. Coffee machine. Why does he want to see her suddenly? Has he also contacted Grace?

Mr. Coffee lets out a big sigh. The pot is ready. Suzy leans over the boom box and presses the knob marked AM. "1010-

WINS!" the announcer is shouting at the morning audience. "The most listened to station in the nation!" It must be true. Every time Suzy hops in a taxi, she is sure that she hears the same greeting on the radio. "The time at the tone will be ten-thirty." The announcer is a pickup artist. "You give us twenty-two minutes, we'll give you the *world*!"

She had lain awake well into the morning. It must have been around seven o'clock when she drifted off to a second round of sleep, which always leaves her feeling groggy and oddly anxious. Suzy pours herself a cup of coffee. The morning is familiar: black coffee, the 1010-WINS cheers, the traffic watch every ten minutes.

Except for Detective Lester. What could he possibly tell her?

Criminal courts are not fun. Just getting past the security is a big hassle. They might as well strip-search you. It's even worse than downtown clubs on Friday nights, the way those biceps-heavy security guards block the door and make everyone wait in line. Pockets are emptied. Bags are scrutinized. Bodies are felt up and down. It is useless explaining that she is hired by the court, or that the assistant DA is waiting for her inside. It is useless fighting through the crowd. She is easily the only Asian person here. Everyone around her seems to be black, including the security guards, the guys in handcuffs being led by officers, and the rest in line, whose purpose for being here God only knows. Attorneys, though, often are not black. Judges, almost never. None of them are here. They must use a separate entrance, hidden in the back. The power structure is pretty clear. Between those who get locked up and those who do the locking is a colored matter. There are no two ways about it.

She has been to the Bronx Criminal Court once during the last eight months of interpreting. This past summer, she was hired for the investigation of a Korean deli in Hunts Point that burned down overnight. For some reason, there had been no insurance, and the poor guy who owned it was out on the street. He'd lodged a complaint against the Albanian landlord, who, now that the neighborhood had picked up and could fetch a higher rent, had been trying to force him out for years. The case had all the makings of a racial conflict. The store owner claimed that the landlord had brought in the neighborhood's Albanian gangs to threaten him physically and set fire to his store. Suzy never found out what eventually happened to the case, but it appeared serious, one of those racially charged incidents that, with a bit of brutality from the NYPD, could end up on the cover of the *New York Post*. For a few weeks afterward, she glanced at the *Post* whenever she passed newsstands, but she found nothing.

Once past security, Suzy is told to wait in the windowless reception area on the third floor. People pace about. Something urgent is in the air. She sits in the corner until finally a small, slouching man with a drooping mustache peeks out from the door behind the reception desk and waves her in.

"Hi, I'm Marcos," he says. "Interpreter? So young. We never get young ones like you for Korean." Given the way no one pays attention to him, he is clearly not the assistant DA. "Follow me; we're running a little late." Marcos points to the long hallway beyond the door. On both sides are rows of identical doors marked only by double-digit numbers. Inside, there must be different investigations under way. Burglary, murder, kidnapping, random shooting, all collected behind each door. It would be impossible to find her way back, she thinks, suddenly glad that Marcos is leading her through the labyrinth. After taking a few turns, he stops before a door that is missing its number. "Wait inside; the ADA's on his way with the witness." A quick pat on her shoulder. Marcos scurries into the abyss.

The austerity of the room suggests a typical municipal agency. The lack of windows is intentional. This must be what a prison feels like, she thinks. The walls are sealed in off-white paint. The table and chairs are so generic that they appear to have been hauled right out of a Kmart window. Curiously, it reminds her of her own apartment, the bareness, the chilling stillness, the unspecified waiting. It could be 4 a.m. still, and Suzy, alone, wishing for sleep.

"Ms. Suzy Park? James Richards, Assistant DA." He is tall, somber, in a dark suit that matches the furniture. He hands her his card and points to the man standing next to him. "You'll be interpreting for Mr. Lee here."

Against the ADA, whose six-foot-four frame seems unsettling under the low ceiling, Mr. Lee looks timid, although he is not small for a Korean man. In a stiff black suit and a starched white shirt, he could almost pass for a lawyer, or an undertaker. Koreans tend to overdress at depositions. Lawyers and judges, in fact, anyone to do with the law, are taken ultra-seriously, and witnesses put on their cleanest, smartest outfits, as though these meetings were Sunday mass. It is their way of showing courtesy before the law, although such effort might mislead the opposing council to assume that the witness's claim of economic hardship must be a fabrication. But a deposition is an event for these immigrant workers. A brush with the American law does not happen every day, never mind the summons from the Office of the Attorney General. For those who labor seven days a week at groceries, nail salons, dry cleaners, when, if not now, would they ever get a chance to don their fake Gucci, Armani, Rolex?

His face looks too tanned for a dry cleaner. Deli or grocery, maybe. But his hands have seen too much dirt and sun, which could only mean fruits and vegetables. The mystery does not last long, for the ADA sets down the folder he's been carrying: "Case 404: Office of the Attorney General Labor Bureau in the

Matter of the Investigation of Lee Market, Inc. of Grand Concourse, New York."

Mr. Lee nods slightly, the way Koreans greet each other in formal settings. Suzy nods back, a bit more deeply, since he is obviously older and requires more respect.

"Ms. Park, this is just a preliminary questioning, so no stenographer will be present. Will you ask him if he understands that he has the right to be represented by a lawyer under the law?"

James Richards has a kind voice, and Suzy is glad for Mr. Lee, who looks nervous, almost rigid, the way he knits his eyebrows as if trying to understand the flow of language that escapes him.

It's okay, she tells him. *Don't worry too much,* she says before translating what has been uttered by the ADA.

He answers, "Yes, I understand, I cannot afford a lawyer, I have no time to find a lawyer, I work twelve hours a day, I work seven days a week, I barely have time to sleep, I've done nothing wrong."

Suzy translates his answer, and the ADA nods eagerly, as if to acknowledge the man's concern.

"Mr. Lee, no one's accusing you of wrongdoing. You've been summoned here for a few questions in response to the complaints we've received, the source of which I cannot reveal to you due to the laws of confidentiality. The investigation has only just begun. This might lead to depositions and hearings, but for now all we are here to do is to ask you some questions, and to have you tell the truth."

Suzy scribbles a few key words into her notepad while the ADA speaks. No matter how long a sentence, she must not leave out a single word in her translation. An interpreter is like a mathematician. She approaches language as if it were an equation. Each word is instantly matched with its equivalent. To ar-

rive at a correct answer, she must be exact. Suzy, unbeknownst
to herself, has always been skilled at this. It cannot be due to her
bilingual upbringing, since not all immigrant kids make excellent interpreters. What she possesses is an ability to be at two
places at once. She can hear a word and separate its literal meaning from its connotation. This is necessary, since the verbatim
translation often leads to confusion. Languages are not logical.
Thus an interpreter must translate word for word and yet somehow manipulate the breadth of language to bridge the gap.
While one part of her brain does automatic conversion, the
other part examines the linguistic void that results from such
transference. It is an art that requires a precise and yet creative
mind. Only the true solver knows that two plus two can suggest
a lot of things before ending up at four.

But she is being more flexible than usual when she turns to
the witness and repeats the ADA's words, adding at the end, *You
should really bring a lawyer next time; in fact, if you want, you can
stop this right now and request one.*

Mr. Lee meets her eyes and says, "No, I will be fine, I will tell
it as it is, tell this guy here I don't lie."

From the way the ADA twirls the pen between his thumb
and his index finger, Suzy can tell that the real questioning is
about to begin.

"What is your full name?"

"Lee Sung Shik."

Koreans put their last names first. It is the last name that
matters. The last name determines the status, the family history,
the origin. Older people often refer to each other by last names
only. All last names come from different roots. There might be
twenty separate sects of Lee, or fifty divisions among Kim. Lee
of the Junju sect bears no relation to Lee of the Junuh sect. Each
sect carries its own registry of thousands of years, which documents the class status. Americans love to say that all Koreans are

named Kim, but Koreans do not look at it that way. To them, all Kims are not the same. In fact, there is often a world of class difference between two sects of Kim. For example, Kim of the Kyungju line descends from noble blood, whereas another sect of Kim might trace its ancestry among the commoners. It is all in the last name. So it is not unusual for Koreans to skip first names altogether. Many deposition transcripts get mixed up because of this switch of the name order. Lawyers who often handle Korean cases immediately ask Suzy at the beginning of a deposition please to put last names last in her translation. Do it in the American way, they say.

"Mr. Lee, what, if any, is your involvement with the store located at 458 Grand Concourse?"

"I am the owner," Mr. Lee answers.

"How long have you been the owner of the store located at 458 Grand Concourse?"

"Four years."

"Before that, where did you work?"

"I was unemployed."

"For how long?"

"For approximately a year."

"Before that, did you work at all?"

"I was employed at a fruit-and-vegetable store."

"By whom?"

"They are dead now."

"What were their names?"

This is where Suzy falters. This is where Suzy is afraid she will know the answer.

What were their names?

It takes her a second longer to translate the question, so easy, although the answer is even easier. She really should not be here.

"Mr. Park and his wife, over in the South Bronx; I never knew their first names."

So he had known her parents. He'd worked for them five years ago, which must have been right around the time of their death. This man here, with stubby fingers and swarthy face, had seen Mom and Dad every day. It should not surprise her. The Korean community is not big, after all. Many workers passed through the store in the South Bronx during the eight years in which her parents owned it. Turnovers seemed unusually frequent. When Suzy asked Dad why, she was told to stay out of their business. They had bought the store the year Grace went away to college. Before that, they kept changing jobs almost every year. Neither of her parents stuck to one job for long. One of them always got fired for one reason or another. With each new job came a move. Sometimes the relocation made the commute easier for her parents. But more often, they moved for no reason whatsoever. The family never stayed in one address for longer than a year. It was as if they were on the run. From what, Suzy had no clue. Once they bought the store, things calmed down a bit. They moved less often, although by then both girls had moved into dorms at Smith and Columbia. Suzy was surprised that her parents had saved enough money to buy a store finally, and was even more shocked when Mom told her about the brownstone in Woodside, Queens. They closed on the house soon after she ran off with Damian. Suzy never got to see it.

Now the questions have moved on to the store Mr. Lee currently owns. Suzy translates with mechanical efficiency, as though each question simply filters through her, each word automatically switching from English to Korean.

"How many employees are there in your store total, including both day and night shift?"

The ADA is looking through his notes. Suzy wonders why he asks such questions, when the answer must be right at his fingertips.

"Seven, including myself."

Mr. Lee is no longer thinking about Suzy's parents. He's back in his own fruit-and-vegetable store on Grand Concourse, where the underpaid illegal immigrant workers must be slaving away twelve hours a day, seven days a week, much the way he has been doing since he arrived in this country.

"Can you name the workers and their responsibilities, along with their salaries, weekly or bimonthly, however they are paid?"

So the issue at hand must be the violation of the minimum-wage law, for which countless Korean store-owners have come under scrutiny lately. Some have been forced to shut down, some so bombarded with back payments that they deteriorate into bankruptcy. Suzy has served in several depositions brought on by the union. She once overheard the lawyers gossiping about how the Labor Department has been tightening its watch, something about the elections coming up and the mayor needing a new shakedown. "Get them behind bars or back in their own country," one lawyer chortled, imitating the mayor, known for his tough-man act.

Mr. Lee is rounding up the names now. Jorge, Luis, Roberto, inevitably Hispanic names. The hierarchy becomes even more marked. The white prosecutors, the Korean store-owners, the Hispanic workers, and Suzy stuck in between with language as her only shield. He is now producing the record of all payments, scrawled in ink, for workers are always paid in cash. Of course they are. How many of them actually have working papers or even bank accounts? How many are legal in this country anyway?

Suzy is desperately hoping that the questions will go back to five years ago, back to when this man had worked for her parents, while they were still alive, while they were still swearing to disown her. But the ADA is zeroing in now. This is the moment the investigation has been leading up to.

"No benefits, no sufficient evidence of pay, no adequate vacation or sick days. Have you, Mr. Lee, been exploiting these illegal immigrant workers?"

The questions become more accusatory as they drag on, well into the late afternoon. When the assignment lasts this long, which must mean something serious, it is the interpreter who tires the most. The ADA only asks, and the witness answers accordingly, but the interpreter must do both, must keep her ears open at all times. Mr. Lee says nothing in return, and James Richards lets out a deep sigh, twirling the pen faster. Each question takes her a bit longer to translate. She is beginning to slow her words. They have been doing this for over three hours.

"Can you describe to me again the ways in which you hire and fire your workers?"

He has asked that before. The answer could only be just as tedious. Through word of mouth, Mr. Lee will say, through acquaintances I find them, and I let the worker go when he's not good. How predictable, such a question, such an answer. So, instead, Suzy makes up her own question, surprised even as the words escape her lips.

Five years ago, you said, you worked for people who are now dead. Can you describe to me what happened to them?

Mr. Lee casts a quick glance at the ADA's face, as if slightly confounded by such a turn of questioning. But he appears unsuspecting and gazes at the wall as if reaching back to five years ago, which is exactly what Suzy wants to see.

"They were killed. I had stopped working for them by then, been fired, actually. I only heard about it later. It was all over the Korean news."

Turning to the ADA, Suzy repeats the same response Mr. Lee had given previously. Her heart is pounding. She cannot stop herself. She is being guided by an impulse that is beyond her. James Richards nods, as though he's been expecting such an answer. Undeterred, he continues. "Mr. Lee, when a new employee is hired, do you offer him a set amount of time for training?"

Training, what a useless question. These jobs don't require sophisticated skills. Just strong muscles and a willingness to sweat for a bit of cash.

Instead, Suzy asks, *What was the nature of the murder?*

Mr. Lee answers grumpily, "They said that it was some sort of a random shooting. But I wouldn't be surprised if it wasn't. I shouldn't talk this way about the dead. But that Park guy, he had it coming to him."

Mr. Lee does not notice Suzy's face turning pale at his last words. She needs to register this information quickly, discreetly. She faces the other and gives him what's been answered before. Yes, she tells him. Yes, for about a week, all the new worker does is watch how the work gets done and do whatever the others tell him to do.

James Richards sees nothing. He is setting up the next question. He seems to be moving toward his mission: get them behind bars or back in their own country. The evidence is all right here in this terrible man who cheats on those illegals who should be sent back to their country immediately. What's the INS doing?

"Mr. Lee, can you describe the manner in which a worker is fired at your store? Do you offer him unemployment benefits?"

What does he think a fruit-and-vegetable market is? A Wall Street office? A nine-to-five, suit-and-tie job? Does he actually assume that working twelve hours a day, seven days a week, comes with that kind of privilege? Does he believe that the same rules apply to those who don't have the right papers, don't speak a word of English? Does he believe that the American dream is that easy? Unemployment and health benefits? They were never designed with these immigrant workers in mind. No one, not even the owners, have those!

So, instead, Suzy asks, *What do you mean? What makes you believe that the shooting was not random?*

Mr. Lee spits out the answer, as though the whole business is distasteful to him: "He had friends in all sorts of places. He and his wife, they were up to something."

It is clear that the man is not enjoying these questions. What had her parents done to evoke such strong feelings?

James Richards is patient. He keeps on. He wants evidence. Not those scribbled notes the man has brought with him, but a record, a receipt, an invoice, none of which seem to exist.

"Mr. Lee, how would you notify your worker when he is being fired?"

But Suzy barely hears his question as she asks instead, *Why did they fire you?*

Mr. Lee's face reddens a little, as if he cannot control the sudden rage as he recalls, "That Park guy had it all planned. He owed me two months' pay, so he decided to throw me out instead. He looked as though he could kill, the way he screamed what a lazy lout I was, so I walked out. I took off my apron, which they made me wear for the work around the salad bar, and just walked out. Of course he never paid me, and I didn't pursue it. I knew I didn't want to mess with him. I'd seen what happens to guys who stand up to him, like this delivery guy out in Queens, Kim Yong Su I think his name was. Man, was he really screwed by that Park guy! Let me tell you, half the Korean community didn't exactly shed tears when they heard about his death!"

It is hard to keep her composure, but Suzy must try, improvising an answer as long as the heated monologue. She repeats what Mr. Lee had said earlier, about firing a worker when he's not good. She repeats it a few times to make up for the length. It actually works, this repetition, and discourages the ADA from poking into what is quite simple and obvious.

"I understand," the ADA is pleading now. "I can see how you fire your workers, but tell me again about the hiring process; is there any contract which you or your employee enter into, a written contract, I mean?"

A written contract? Has he forgotten that no one, neither the one who does the hiring nor the one who is hired, speaks, never mind reads, a word of English?

Suzy turns to Mr. Lee without meeting him in the eyes. She is afraid that he will see the resemblance, find her father's face in her lowering gaze. She is afraid to ask further.

Tell me, who do you think was responsible for their death?

Mr. Lee snickers as he barks, "The brave one. Someone so righteous that eliminating them would've been a necessity. Even the police wouldn't touch the case. Random shooting, my ass; what idiot would believe that?"

Suzy believed, and Grace. Or maybe they wanted to believe.

Turning to the ADA, she tells him no, no written contract, no such thing. It is shocking how she manages to maintain her calm through all this. It is shocking how easily she lies.

James Richards appears exasperated at last. The questioning is going nowhere, or going so smoothly that his answers will haunt the trial as falsifying evidence.

"I am asking you one final time, Mr. Lee, are you claiming that you have always paid your workers the minimum wage?"

Suzy translates the last question quickly, wanting to be done with this.

"Yes," Mr. Lee shouts back with a vengeance. "You can see from all the record."

He's lying. He has clearly broken the minimum-wage law. It's her instinct. An interpreter knows almost instantly when a witness is lying. She is the most astute listener in the world. She listens between the lines, between the words. Nothing goes unnoticed. The first time Suzy interpreted for a lying witness, she was surprised how much it hurt. It happened at a trial, before a judge and a jury. Suzy stumbled, causing the entire room to stare at her. An interpreter must be neutral, and anonymous. It is not up to her to make judgment. Except the bitterness was on her tongue, and Suzy was not sure if she would be spared with her heart intact. Afterward, she could not help noticing that it was the lying party that won.

But now Suzy wonders how much of her averse reaction might be due to his confession about her parents. She repeats his answer, which fools no one.

Shaking his head, James Richards declares that the questioning is over. Closing his file, he tells her what a great job she did. Knowing two languages so well, that cannot be easy, he says. You need to interpret not only the words, but every nuance, don't you? Yes, every nuance, Suzy replies. *Every goddamn nuance, so I might know much more than I was meant to.*

It is Marcos who leads them out at last. The corridor is a maze. Suzy wants to lose Mr. Lee in its tangles. He'd hated her parents, although, according to him, there are more, many more people out there, who hated her parents even more passionately than he did, who hated them enough to risk everything in their bravery, their righteousness, whatever he declared was the motive for wanting them dead. She is dying to get out of here. When Mr. Lee calls after her "Thank you," she runs past the door without looking back.

Kim Yong Su, the guy from Queens. Where has she heard that name before? Where has she met him?

9.

"SUZY, MY DARLING, you're looking way too ravishing for an old maid!"

Caleb is grinning when she opens the door. She has not seen him in a few months, not since he started his first nine-to-five job at a gallery in Chelsea. "A bitch shopping mall," he whispered on the phone after the first week of working there. Caleb at twenty-six, much changed from the shy art-school graduate Suzy met outside Astor Place Stationery. He's let his hair grow out, gentle ginger waves down to his shoulders. "It's the Botticelli look," he tells her with a wink. "The curator adores it, and those Eurotrash buyers keep saying 'divine' in their phony accents." She pours him a glass of red wine while he looks around the apartment as if expecting to find an improvement since the last time he was here. "Suzy, my God, we need to get you a subscription to Martha Stewart, fast!" Suzy laughs and gives him the warning look, which he once said reminded him of his great-aunt, if he had one. When he finally sits down before her,

Suzy remembers how nice it is to have someone here. Another person sitting with her, listening to her voice, to her breath, to her silent walks around the kitchen. It's been so long since anyone's stepped into her apartment. She has almost gotten used to being alone.

"So the admirer strikes again!" Caleb points to the irises in the Evian bottle.

"It's that time of the year, remember?" Glancing at the drooping petals, Suzy realizes that she should throw them out.

"No, I didn't remember, but obviously *somebody* has." He takes a sip of wine from the glass, still looking at the irises. "So any idea who's the anniversary freak? I mean, it's grossly old-fashioned, and getting a bit creepy too."

"Maybe I'll never know, maybe I'm not meant to."

Suzy opens the plastic bag he handed her upon entering. Inside are small yellow balls with glimmering surfaces. The bag is filled with all kinds of cheese wrapped in cellophane. Blue cheese, goat cheese, Brie, Gouda, Swiss, Stilton, even fresh mozzarella. "What's all this?" Suzy turns to him, her black eyes wide.

"Call me the cheese fairy; oh no, that sounds *so fag.*" Caleb chuckles, happy to see Suzy's face brighten. "I would've gotten you crème brûlée, but gallery openings don't do desserts, since you know the art groupies don't eat, and there's nothing close to a pastry shop on Tenth Avenue."

Leaning over, she kisses him on the cheek and then begins unwrapping the cheeses onto a plate, one by one. "Blue cheese is good," she says without looking up. "It's sad somehow, almost melancholy. I can never eat it, really."

"Darling, I don't think you're getting laid enough. When a piece of cheese in Saran Wrap makes you cry, you know it's time."

"Michael's coming back soon."

"When?"

"I don't know. I never know until the day before. He doesn't know himself usually."

"Oh, *please*, let him feed that one to his wife."

It is true. Michael never knows his schedule. Suzy has no doubt about it. But she does not protest when Caleb rolls his eyes. It is more fun that way, to pretend that the man who is cheating on his wife is also cheating on his mistress. Michael left three messages today. He sounded irritated, impatient, the way he gets when she is not where she is supposed to be.

Hey, pick up the phone, I know you're there.

Then, *Suzy, pick up the fucking phone, where the fuck are you?*

Finally, *Suzy, babe.*

She'd left the court by four, but did not arrive home until half past six. She had not planned it. It was an impulse. She was on the Number 4 train, a downtown express from the Bronx, forty minutes maximum. The familiar drone announced Grand Central. Change here for the 5, 6, 7, and the shuttle to Times Square. Watch out for the closing door! It was the Number 7 that stuck out at her. Flushing-bound, passing through inner Queens, which she used to take to visit home from college. She got out almost automatically. Grand Central. A little past five in the afternoon. Its crowd heading to Metro North instead of the Long Island Rail Road, to upstate New York, the mountains and rivers instead of the ocean. Grand Central was more civilized, its corporate-sponsored orchestra playing Bach, Beethoven, Mozart. The fresco of constellations on its vaulted ceiling shone in lime green with freckles all over, as though these comings and goings made sense, a divine sense. It must make the commuters feel better, to rush along with the universe hovering above. That's why Suzy preferred the drab Penn Station, where a commute remained a commute, a train a train, nothing more, nothing even remotely artistic or celestial.

Soon she was back on the platform, the Number 7 train

platform this time. She could get out at different stops on the Number 7, which would lead to the various neighborhoods where she grew up. Queensboro Plaza, 46th Street, Jackson Heights, Junction Boulevard, and Woodside, although she had never seen the house there. The Number 7 line is for immigrants, the newly arrived immigrants, the ones they call FOB, fresh-off-the-boat, the ones who have to seek out their own kind for a job, a house, everything foreign in this new land. Hardly any whites on the Number 7 except for their seasonal outings to Shea Stadium, and blacks favor the 2, 3, 4, 5, the lines bound for the Bronx and Brooklyn. The Asians rule on the Number 7, mostly Chinese, many Koreans, some Indians, few Hispanics. Even the subway regulations on the steel door are written in Chinese.

When Suzy hopped into the last carriage, there weren't many people at all, despite rush hour. Immigrants keep different hours. Nine-to-five is a luxury. Rush hour is only relevant to the commuters with desk jobs. Suzy slouched in the empty seat in the middle, not knowing where she planned to go, why she got on to begin with. There was a couple sitting opposite her. A pair of high-school sweethearts, a willowy Chinese girl with shiny braces and bell-bottom jeans leaning in the arms of a Hispanic boy with a pimply face and a diamond stud in his left ear. Times were different now. You rarely saw couples like that when Suzy was growing up. Hispanic boys never looked at her. They might have checked out Grace, but they still wouldn't ask Grace out— not because they thought she was a bitch, which they might have, but because they just didn't do that. Different racial groups didn't mix. In fact, a war was often declared between rival groups. One school would be dominated by the Chinese kids. In another, Puerto Ricans were the bad and popular ones. The mood was multicultural, certainly, but all it meant was that there were fewer white kids, and the rest just stuck to their own.

Suzy and Grace moved schools too frequently to really grasp any of it; Grace often broke the taboo, although, for the sort of boys she hung out with, nothing was much of a taboo.

Once the train glided out of Manhattan, it emerged into the open, no more tunnels, no more underground darkness. The sudden sunlight was ruthless. The sallow faces of the passengers became too visible, and the faded graffiti on the walls appeared sad and past its glory. Outside revealed the uneven surface of Jackson Avenue, the first stop in Queens. The gray buildings crammed against the pale-blue sky, and the interweaving highways jutted forth in confused directions. The first stop she recognized as one of her past neighborhoods was Queensboro Plaza, but it was merely a stop, a place where they had lived for less than a year, like all the others. She barely remembered it. Soon the train passed another. But there was no reason to get out, no real recognition that sank into her heart. Woodside was next, where her parents spent their last days. But this was no homecoming. Homecoming didn't happen on the Number 7 train. When it pulled into its final stop in Flushing and all passengers scattered out, she noticed a man still sitting opposite her. His hand was pointing at his open fly. She quickly averted her eyes while he got up and walked sluggishly to the next car. Suzy sat motionless in her seat, dreading the long return trip back to the city.

"He's only thirty, a baby really."

Caleb is now telling her about his new boyfriend, whom he met two months ago. He left the man from the West Village last year. "It just fizzled out. We were like roommates after the first year. He spent all his time trading stocks on the Internet, and I got sick of crying for his dick, which wasn't much to begin with, really." Suzy admires Caleb's way of downplaying everything. She knows that he suffered after the breakup. She knows it was his first love.

"I'm thinking of bringing Rick home for Thanksgiving. I mentioned it to Mom the last time I called her. You know what she said? The phone goes dead for like five minutes, and then she comes back in this super-snotty tone, 'Must you do that?' Can you believe it? *Must you do that!* Sounds almost British, doesn't it? My mom, the queen of the Japs! She suddenly turns British 'cause she might have to meet her son's gay lover!"

Suzy stares at Caleb as he chatters away. His parents have finally come around, not fully still, but trying. It's taken years, but he is talking with them—not every Sunday, not as his therapist had once suggested, but talking. She enjoys Caleb's stories about his parents. She pretends that it is she who is fighting with her parents, who insists on bringing Damian home for Thanksgiving, who sits here telling whoever how ridiculous, how silly her parents are.

She sips the wine. It's tart. It tastes of half-ripe raspberries.

"So have you found out if your sister gets a bouquet also?"

Caleb changes the topic, as if sensing Suzy's mood. He pours more into his glass and also into hers, although she has barely taken a sip.

"No."

"Does she not talk to you still?"

Suzy shakes her head. Grace, she meant to call Grace today. She wanted to check if Grace had also heard from Detective Lester, if she was also summoned. But Suzy has changed her mind. She has decided to wait until tomorrow morning, when Grace will be gone to school, when she can safely leave a message without having to confront her on the phone. Suzy is afraid of the chilly silence. She is afraid that Grace may just hang up on her. Right after the funeral, right after Suzy moved out of Damian's house, she had tried calling Grace a few times. She wanted to explain, although there was really nothing to explain. She wanted to talk about their parents, anything that might have happened during the past four years of her absence. Anything at all. But Grace hung up each time. Soon Grace stopped picking up the phone altogether. The message was clear: Grace did not want to speak to Suzy. With each year, it became clearer that Grace intended *never* to speak to Suzy.

"She's family. This will pass. It can only pass."

Suzy is comforted by Caleb's optimism, although she does not believe it. The thing about newer friends is that they have so little reference. You might give them the synopsis of the life you've led up until the point when they met you. But it doesn't quite sink in, not really. How could it? Your past is only a story for them.

"I don't think she's ever liked me."

She did not mean to say it. Why say it? The truth might even stick and become truer.

"Why do you think that?"

"I just do," Suzy whispers, sharpening the end of the cigarette against the edge of the ashtray. The ashes fall, and the flame comes alive. Suddenly the orange-red tip of the cigarette looks almost transparent.

With Mom and Dad gone most of the day—sometimes through the night, depending on their job of the moment—the only one Suzy had was Grace. Yet they were never close, never comrades. It is impossible to tell why. It wasn't even jealousy. Sure, Grace was better in many ways, prettier, smarter, and often wiser. But jealousy would only happen if the sisters were willing to engage with each other. No, their distance has had nothing to do with jealousy. There has never been any room for warmth between the two. They had different friends. Grace knew boys; Suzy didn't. Grace's favorite book was *Moby-Dick*, which Suzy gave up after trying the first few pages, bored and confused. Grace had a life outside school. Suzy could not even fathom where she would go. They shared bunk beds always. Grace on top, because she said that she didn't want anyone seeing her when she was asleep. When she was not whispering into the phone with one of her many secret boyfriends, she would disappear up there and read. Grace was always reading. Even when Dad got drunk one night and ripped down her posters of Adam Ant and Siouxie and the Banshees, Grace did not flinch but climbed up to her bed with a book. When she was grounded for being found naked with a boy in the back of a car, she repeated, "Sorry, I'll never do it again," with not a hint of regret on her face, and read for a month straight. She read just about anything. Novels, newspapers, sometimes even the Sears catalog or a copy of the neighbor's *TV Guide.* She would flip through them for hours, which seemed unfathomable. Suzy once made the mistake of buying her a book and spent most of her allowance of twenty dollars for a new edition of *Anna Karenina.* Suzy could not decide what to pick at first, but she thought that the cover looked mature and that Grace might like the fact that it had originally been banned in Russia. It also looked promising that the volume was impossibly thick, like *Moby-Dick.* Grace, though, was hardly grateful. She handed it back to Suzy without a word. When Suzy began protesting, Grace said quietly, "I don't want you choosing my books." They were only about fourteen or fifteen then. That was the first time Suzy suspected that it wasn't about books after all. Grace's obsessive reading might not have had anything to do with books. It didn't matter what she read, as long as she was left alone. Reading was a refuge, a shield, an excuse to avoid facing the family, and Grace would not let Suzy be an accomplice.

The only regular interaction between the sisters concerned chores, as though they were two strangers with one thing in common—the house rules. Grace, being older, was in charge of most housework, while Suzy helped with whatever was left unfinished: vacuuming, dusting, taking out trash, preparing rice.

Grace was quick with everything. The house was spotlessly clean by the time she stood at the door in a skirt too short for a fifteen-year-old, telling Suzy, "The rice is rinsed. Stick it in the cooker in ten minutes. The rooms are vacuumed; make sure you put away the vacuum cleaner in the broom closet. Tell them that I've gone to the AP-English study group." That was the extent of their conversation. Sometimes, in the morning, Suzy would ask her where she had gone on the previous evening. "The study group," Grace would snap before walking out the door.

Then there was the interpreting. Neither of her parents had spoken much English, which meant that they relied on the girls to break the language barrier. But almost always the job fell on Grace, because she was the older one, and smarter. Grace, since she was little, had to pore over a letter from the bank trying to make sense of words like "APR" or "Balance Transfers," or call Con Edison's 800 number for a payment extension. Suzy would sit by her side, scared and anxious. There was something daunting about undertaking what should have been delegated to an adult. Not only was it nearly impossible to understand the customer-service representatives, but often they would not release information unless it was the account holder calling. Grace would plead, to no avail, that her parents were at work and that they did not speak the language. Sometimes Mom and Dad would sit by the phone, dictating exactly what Grace should say. But often such demands did not work, because their request was so anachronistic that it defied translation. After all, their understanding of such transactions was steeped in Korean ways. Finally, Dad would scream at Grace, "Tell them no late fee, they'll get their money by next week!" Then Grace would look helpless as she repeated, "But he said that the balance was due last week, so next week will be considered late!" At those times, Dad never seemed grateful for Grace's instant interpreting service. He seemed frustrated, even suspicious. He was certain that if he could speak the language he would resolve all matters with a quick phone call. He seemed to resent Grace for relating to him what he did not want to hear, that the debts must be paid instantly, because that's what most of those calls were about— money owed in one form or another. But most of all, he seemed angry at his own powerlessness. The ordeal of having to rely on his young daughter for such basic functions humiliated him. He never seemed to forget that humiliation.

Their parents' lack of English and the family's constant relocation only made things worse. There were always red-stamped notices in their mailbox. Once or twice a month, Grace skipped school to accompany Mom and Dad to the Department of Motor Vehicles or an insurance company or some other bureaucratic nightmare. They were often gone all day. Afterward, their parents went back to work while Grace returned home alone. Suzy would often notice the red in Grace's eyes, as though she'd cried all the way. Almost always, upon arriving home, Grace would confine herself to the upper bunk without speaking to Suzy. Or she would stay out and come home much later. Curiously, on those nights, Dad never said anything. He pretended not to notice that Grace was missing at the dinner table. Suzy never asked Grace about the exact nature of those interpreting tasks—because they seemed so scary to little Suzy, and because Suzy felt guilty for letting Grace do all the work.

"You know, I sometimes wonder . . ." Caleb's voice turns suddenly low, almost flat, the way it gets when he is serious.

Suzy keeps her eyes on the cigarette burning in the ashtray. The red wine, the plate of cheese, the smoke slowly rising.

"I wonder . . . why you never talk about your parents." Caleb is cautious, uncertain if he should bring it up at all.

She had told him about her parents once, briefly. But that was it. Nothing more. No heartfelt anecdotes, no tearful monologues. Suzy avoided the topic, and he had never asked. Instead,

Caleb would chatter on about his parents, his lovers, his uncertain careers, and Suzy would laugh. They have grown comfortable with that.

"*My parents*—I never think about them."

Suzy holds the cigarette between her index and middle fingers without actually bringing it to her mouth. She is hesitant. She is not sure what else to say, although Caleb is quiet, listening.

She recalls how she had abandoned them in their final years. She recalls the last time she saw them and how Dad had called her a whore, just once, but it was enough to slash her. She makes up little stories in her head about how happy the family would have been had she not run off with Damian, had her parents not been at the store on that final morning, had her sister forgiven her. Yet she cannot remember the sound of Dad's laugh. She never longs for Mom's Nina Ricci perfume. She never craves the empty late afternoons when Grace had gone out and her parents were still not home from work. She can barely picture her parents' faces in daylight; she rarely saw them before dark.

"Strange, isn't it?" Suzy lets out a small sigh, so thin that it sounds like a gasp. "I can't stand myself for letting them go that way. I blame Damian. I blame myself for choosing Damian. But at the end of it all, they're not here. I can't stop thinking about it. That they're gone, that they disappeared while I wasn't even looking, while I hadn't yet had a chance to solve anything, solve me, solve Damian, solve why I had to run away all those years. I thought I was the one leaving them, but parents, they always have the last word, don't they? Still, I never think about them. Not really. What I'm not sure of is if I miss them. I'm not sure if I can honestly say that. I'm not sure if guilt has much to do with love." Suzy is glad that there is a cigarette. She is glad that she is not here alone. "I'm a horrible person, aren't I?"

Caleb does not respond. He is playing with the plate of

cheese, separating the mozzarella into little braids, making the holes in the Swiss bigger. Finally, he piles the bits of blue cheese into a little heart shape before pushing the plate toward Suzy.

"Sagittarius? In two weeks, the 24th?" Caleb's eyes are on her now. Soft eyes. He wants to say something clever, something that will ease the moment. "The stars are in your favor, darling, you can't be horrible. Nope, they won't let you."

The night is deeper. The wine bottle is nearly empty. The heart-shaped blue cheese looks ruffled and strange, like the map of the universe on the Grand Central ceiling. It feels good to be with Caleb.

"So you think Michael's lying to me?"

"Absolutely."

"What a scum."

"What a two-timing bastard!"

They both start laughing when the phone starts ringing. Four times. Exactly. Then the click. Suzy is almost relieved. Whoever has been waiting. Whoever is still watching. Whoever is not letting go.

10.

MICHAEL, IT CAN ONLY BE MICHAEL at this time of the morning. The phone is an alarm. Seven a.m. Probably lunchtime wherever he is. A miracle that he's even waited until now. He probably thought to let her sleep a little. He is being considerate.

"So where were you yesterday?"

He is not happy, Suzy can tell. His voice is tight. Something's up. He never gets so tense unless it has to do with his work, the nature of which Suzy barely understands.

"The case took longer than usual. I was stuck at the DA's office." Balancing the receiver between her right ear and her shoulder, Suzy opens the refrigerator and takes out the Brita pitcher to fill a glass. Her head sways with pins and needles. The wine last night took its toll. They had opened another bottle after the first one. She vaguely recalls Caleb urging, *Why not, drink it up before thirty!* He kept pouring more, and Suzy kept giggling, emptying each glass much more quickly than she should have.

"I called the whole fucking day!" He is fuming now.

"*Michael*, it's early." Her head is caving in. She is not up for this battle.

"I'm tempted to just get on the next fucking flight to see you."

He can be such a child, so wildly different from Damian. Is this what Jen meant by "hiding"?

"So why don't you?"

Suzy is good at handling his moods. That must be why he calls three times in a row. He knows she will never humor him. He knows she will never let him in.

"Four-point-three million, Suzy. Four-point-three fucking million on the line. Germans are fucking snakes. Everything's all ready to go, and, boom, they need another fucking meeting, another fucking review, another big fucking waste of my time. And I'm fucking stuck here rather than fucking you, tell me the logic."

Michael hates Germany. He hates almost everything, but he hates Germany more than most things. He thinks all Germans are Nazis and penny-pinchers. Suzy has no idea where his resentment stems from; she's never quite bothered to ask. He is stuck in Frankfurt and can't bear it. Thus his petulant mood. Suzy could see Michael lounging at a hotel lobby, a cell phone in one hand, with the other stirring two sugar cubes into his espresso. The top button of his shirt would be undone. No tie, since he would have taken it off immediately upon storming out of the meeting earlier. His feet up on the table. His eyes glancing at the *Herald Tribune* as he rants into the phone. Suzy suddenly misses him.

"I've got my period. We can't do it anyway."

That gets the abrupt silence, and then a chuckle. He's already better, she can tell.

"*Christ*, Suzy, is that all you can say?"

"No, there's more. I also have a pounding headache." She pops two tablets of Advil into her mouth.

"A hangover?" He sounds doubtful. A bit suspicious, a bit jealous. But all an act, Suzy knows. Jealousy is not a part of their arrangement.

"Umm. I celebrated my twenties, the passing of it, I mean, or that's what Caleb said at least." Suzy is grinning. She might still be a little drunk.

"But your birthday is not for another two weeks?"

Of course he would remember. He would probably send her a dozen long-stemmed roses, boxed. He would make a reservation at the Rainbow Room. He would slide across the table a blue Tiffany case in which there would be a set of sparkling diamond earrings. He would do everything so that she would feel the weight of a mistress.

"I began celebrating early. I wanted to be happy yesterday."

Maybe that's what Suzy wanted. Maybe that's why she circled on the Number 7 train for two hours. Maybe she was doing everything she could to stop the gushing sadness. *Half the Korean community didn't exactly shed tears when they heard about his death!* Mr. Lee did not spare his words. So many people had hated her parents. One of them might have hated them enough to want them dead.

"Babe, you listening to me?" Michael is shouting. He's forgotten about her headache.

"Sorry, what did you say?"

"I said, save your celebration for me. I said, wait."

It is a game for Michael, to pretend to claim her. Suzy goes along with it because she knows what happens when it isn't a game, when the claim is for real, when the claim takes over and plays out. Damian would never have asked her to wait. He would have taken it for granted. He would have expected nothing less. And she would have, almost indefinitely, if he had asked.

"I'll wait, I promise."

"*Christ*, I'm really fucking dying to see you."

When Suzy puts the phone down, it is still early, too early for anything. But Grace would be up. She would be getting ready for school. A little after seven. Suzy cannot remember anymore when high school starts, probably eight, or maybe eight-thirty. Teachers always come in before students, or at least they should, although, as Suzy recalls from the schools she attended in Queens and the Bronx, kids were often made to wait for teachers who sometimes didn't show up at all. Grace wouldn't be like that. Grace would show up on time. Her lessons would be well prepared, all set to go. Her hair would be neatly trimmed and coifed, and her dark-navy two-piece suit freshly pressed and buttoned. Or at least that's how Suzy pictures her.

Grown-up Grace, born-again Grace, thirty, the ESL teacher at Fort Lee High School—her only family.

It must be an impulse. Or last night's alcohol still in her blood. There is no other explanation for such courage, such longing to hear her voice. Suzy begins dialing the number. 7:15 a.m., what is she thinking? There's the ringing, once, twice. Something lurches inside her. Her heart seems to be made up of tiny wings which all begin to flap at once. The sudden ocean inside. The waves breaking. She can feel the tightening in her throat. They have not spoken in years, not since the funeral, not since she was twenty-four and Grace twenty-five. Suzy keeps counting age, as though each year pushes her farther away from her parents.

The voice that comes on is unexpected.

The computerized operator.

"The number you have dialed is no longer in service. Please check the number and dial again."

So Grace has moved once more. Like their parents, she never stays at one address long. Each time Suzy has tried calling her, the operator would come on instead with the new number, which Suzy imagines is a sign, a message from Grace telling her that she has not completely given up on Suzy. Although Suzy also knows that Grace, as a teacher at a public school and a church, needs to have her number listed. But this time, Grace didn't. Nothing, no further information available. Suzy dials the operator. Grace Park, she insists. I need a number for Grace Park. Yes, the area code 201, Fort Lee, her last name is Park, my sister. The operator tells her, no, nothing; there's Grace Park in Edgewater, Grace Park in North Bergen, but not in Fort Lee, no one under such a name. Maybe Grace has moved to a town nearby. Maybe she has found a deal in one of those riverfront rentals along the Hudson. 7:30 a.m., not a good time for a wrong number, not surprising that they would hang up: Grace Park? I am Grace Park. I don't have a sister; you've got the wrong person; do you know what time it is? The school, then, she must try the school. Fort Lee High School. Surely the school must be listed. Surely there would be a secretary who would take the call and deliver the message. It is then that the thought flashes across her mind—*why not go?* Why not just go there, why not tell Grace in person that there might be more to their parents' death, that it might not have been random after all, that a guy named Lee had known their parents, that another guy named Kim out in Queens might know even more, and that Detective Lester, he called for the first time in five years, he might know something, he might even have found a clue?

But then Suzy is not so sure. Grace would surely just walk away. She would pretend not to have seen Suzy and hop into a car with one of her colleagues. Who's she? the colleague would ask. No one I know, Grace would answer without once glancing in Suzy's direction. Worse yet, she might get mad, furious. She might drive off after telling Suzy never to come near her. *Do me a favor, Suzy; leave us alone.* Those were Grace's parting words at the funeral.

Suzy throws her coat on anyway. It has not occurred to her that Grace would move without leaving a number, or that Grace might one day become unreachable. It is as if the phone number, or just having the phone number, or the possibility of the phone number, affirms Grace's presence in Suzy's life.

The headache seems to be getting worse. A bit of fresh air might not be such a bad idea. Fresh air, who's she kidding? Fort Lee, a half-hour bus ride from the Port Authority, not the freshest outing. Before she loses courage, she is out on First Avenue, waving down a cab to Port Authority, where the Number 156 departs every twenty minutes.

It takes all her concentration not to get sick on the bus. The constant lurchings, the reek of gasoline, the jammed traffic in the Lincoln Tunnel—none of it helps. It does not seem to matter that the bus is moving in the opposite direction from the Manhattan-bound traffic. The tunnel keeps spinning. Suzy holds her breath, thinking that it might keep her stomach from rising up again. Two bottles of wine, not so smart to get on an interstate bus the first thing in the morning. A man on the other side of the aisle keeps fumbling with the paper bag in his lap. He takes something out and begins nibbling it, exuding a distinctly crunchy noise. Hash browns, wrapped in the McDonald's cover. Soon he takes another out. Suzy wonders how many are in there. How many hash browns can a person eat at once? The sudden pungent smell of its microwaved, fried grease rushes up her nose, and Suzy swallows hard, pressing her forehead on the cold windowpane to push the nausea away.

The hard surface against her skin seems to help a little, but then a gigantic billboard emerges on which lies a striking blonde in a neon-green bikini that looks electric against her implausibly copper tan. WELCOME TO NEW JERSEY, it says across the top of the blonde. It is impossible to tell what the advertisement is for exactly, but the bus swerves past before Suzy can study more closely. Suddenly it is not clear if the chill in the air signals the winter's coming or leaving. Could the summer be just around the corner?

She hasn't had enough water. She wonders if Hash Brown Man has some spare water in his paper bag. She wonders if he will share it, although she can't decide if she wants water that has been stuck in there with all of his other fried snacks. She is thirsty, shivering. The summer is definitely nowhere near, she thinks, huddled in her coat with her face pressed back against the window.

It is impossible for her to raise her head. When the driver tells her that this is Fort Lee High School, this is where she should get off, Suzy inhales once before running out, holding her face in her hands. Then she is not exactly clear how she pushes through the main entrance, bypasses the security, makes it up the stairs, finds her way down the corridor, and finally, bending over a toilet bowl in the first-floor ladies' room, heaves up the contents of her stomach, her hair stuck on her wet face.

Her mouth tastes sour—that is the first thing she remembers thinking. After flushing the toilet, she staggers out of the stall, turns on the tap, and dunks her face in the cold water. Something gives inside her, a horrible knot, a twisted froth. She swallows the water, and it is surprisingly refreshing, this tap water in the ladies' room at Fort Lee High School. Then Suzy lifts her face with water dripping from her wet hair, only to see that she is surrounded by a roomful of young faces peering at her.

"You okay?" One of the girls steps forward, offering her a piece of brown paper towel from the dispenser.

"Yes, fine now, I'm fine. Thank you." Suzy wipes her face, and feels suddenly wide awake. The first period must not have begun yet. Around her are a group of girls, now scattering back to their corners to wait in line for a stall, to stand before mirrors holding aluminum cans of spray to their highlighted hair or applying another layer of lipstick, mascara, eyeliner on such youthful faces. A commotion. Teenage girls all getting ready at once. Suzy had been like that, long ago, so impossibly long ago. And Grace. Of course Grace. What would Grace say if she knew, if she saw her right now? The thought alarms Suzy, and she quickly rinses her mouth again and smooths her hair. It is better now. The sick feeling has passed. And most of all, she is finally here, at the Fort Lee High School, where her sister must be standing before a class, before a roomful of boys and girls who are now rushing out at the loud thud of a bell.

"Wait, please!" Suzy calls after the one who offered her the towel. The girl turns around, the glitter on her eyelids twinkling under the fluorescent gleam. "Do you know where I can find Miss Grace Park? She teaches ESL."

The girl turns to the group around her as if to say, Do you know? No one seems to know; their faces are blank. Of course, ESL, only for the kids whose English is not fluent. Then a tiny voice pops out of nowhere and volunteers in Korean, "I do."

Suzy turns around to find a small, round girl to her right, who seems to have been standing there all along. She is curiously short, barely over four feet tall. She is alone, unlike the other girls, who all seem to be traveling in groups.

"Are you one of her students?" Suzy stoops a little to face her.

"No, not anymore," the girl answers, lowering her gaze as though she is not used to making eye contact with an adult. Her jeans are belted too high, definitely no hip-huggers. No piercing in her ears. No makeup whatsoever. A true FOB. There were girls like this even back in Suzy's school days. They spoke very little English and only hung out with each other. They carried Hello Kitty bags and kept photos of Korean pop stars in their wallets. They looked frightened when white boys spoke to them and avoided girls like Suzy and Grace, whom they secretly called Twinkie.

"But you know where she might be?"

The girl nods, still without looking up. She seems suspicious of Suzy. Why wouldn't she be? Here's an adult who spent the better part of the morning throwing up in the school toilet. In the world of teenagers, just being an adult is reason enough for suspicion. To appease her, Suzy asks softly, "So is Miss Park a good teacher? Do students like her?" She is not sure why she wants to know, but she does. Grace's life. This bashful teenager in front of her. This first-floor ladies' room. This concrete building filled with ebullient sixteen-year-olds. This suburban town half an hour away from Port Authority.

"Yes," the girl answers with surprising eagerness. Then, as if suddenly aware of her own voice, she drops her gaze and mumbles, "They said I'm ready to quit ESL, but Ms. Park lets me sit in her class sometimes. She says it'll get rid of my headache."

"A headache?"

"Ms. Park says that so much English all day is what's giving me a headache."

A strange thing for an ESL teacher to say. Suzy has never quite thought of it that way—the English language being a headache-inducer. She wonders if such a reaction might also happen at depositions. She wonders if her translation sometimes sends the witness home with a migraine. Then she realizes that her own headache has faded. She probably threw up all the alcohol. Her stomach must be spotlessly clean, emptied.

"Can you show me to her class?"

The girl nods again, leading the way. The classroom is on the third floor. The stairs are steep and wide, the way they often are in old buildings. The students obviously get enough exercise, walking up and down between classes. The second bell must not have rung yet. Kids are rushing from lockers to classes, some grumpy and morose, some clapping high fives with dramatic facial expressions. Those are the popular kids, Suzy can tell. The ones who are not afraid to be seen, the ones used to being seen.

Neither Suzy nor Grace had known such teenage years. Theirs was the darkness surrounding home, the brooding silence before a storm. Suzy is not sure if her parents had always been so uninterested in each other, or if they just ran out of things to say over the years. It did not help that they were always tired. By the time they came home, around nine or ten, they had been working for over twelve hours. By rule, Suzy and Grace would have to sit at the table while they ate, although almost always both girls had already eaten. Often Dad burst into a rage, the violent, vicious thrashing of words. He would lash out at whoever happened to be near. Sometimes he would grumble about the *kimchi* being too sour, the rice not cooked enough, the anchovies too salty. He would take a bite and make a face, and then storm out of the kitchen, slamming the door behind him. Sometimes he would scream at both Suzy and Grace for sitting there like idiots while he slaved all day to put food on the table. Mom would never say anything back. She would sit there and finish her rice to the bottom of the bowl, and then get up to clear the dishes. She would never ask Suzy or Grace for help. She would never apologize for Dad's moods. She would pretend that nothing had happened. Then, finally, she would turn to both and say, "Go finish your homework and get to bed, it's a school night." Suzy can still hear Mom. *It's a school night.* She would say it sometimes even on weekends. Both her parents often worked seven days a week. They rarely had weekends.

With each job, with each endless hour they labored at dry cleaners, liquor stores, fruit-and-vegetable markets, nail salons, delis, truck-delivery service, car service, they seemed to have lost something of themselves, a sort of language with which they had communicated with each other and their daughters. Sure, it could have been the claustrophobia of immigrant life, being stuck in Korean enclaves that remained ignorant of English-speaking America. But there was something deeper. Something terrible that seemed to have haunted both. Something resembling fear that stirred Dad's rage and Mom's pointed absence, and always the two girls were made to sit and watch. Everything always came to the same end. The reason was Korea. The final answer was Korea. All of their discontent, their misery, their endless wanderings through the slums of outer New York happened only because they had left their country. The girls were bad girls because they spoke English, rather than their native Korean. The houses they kept moving through were temporary shelters with torn mattresses on the floor, because America could never be home. But of course her parents had no intention of returning to Korea. It was an excuse, Suzy thought. Korea was a crutch. It was what they used to keep the girls on their own terms.

Yet the one thing both Suzy and Grace so desperately wanted was to be American girls, full-fledged American darlings, more golden than the girl next door, even cheerier than the prom queen, definitely sweeter than all-American sweethearts. Far, far away from their parents' Korea, which stuck to them like an ugly tattoo.

How misguided such a dream: neither even made it to the prom. Dad would never have allowed it, but it did not matter really, for the girls were always new in their high school and had hardly any friends. No boy would have asked Suzy, and the ones Grace knew would have laughed at the idea. Besides, a prom was a luxury at the sort of schools to which they transferred. Most kids came from immigrant homes. No boy could dish out a hundred bucks for a night. No girl looked good in ruffled dresses. Pink satin was for white girls. A limousine? Why hire one when your father's the cabbie? A prom belonged in those Molly Ringwald movies, in which the prettiest girl, pretending to be a geek, ends up winning the rich, handsome, sensitive football captain for the last dance. High schools, as Suzy knew, had nothing to do with sweet sixteen. You were lucky if you didn't get mugged on the way to the locker. You were lucky if you didn't get frisked by the policeman at the gate ready to crack down on drug gangs. The golden girl, the girl next door, the all-American sweetheart didn't get made in the gutters of Queens.

"Here we are." The girl turns around, stopping abruptly in the middle of the hallway.

"The prom . . . when's your prom?" Suzy blurts out, then quickly regrets it, realizing that this might be too far-fetched for the girl.

"Prom?" asks the girl, her eyes widening.

"No, never mind," mutters Suzy, finding herself before Grace's classroom.

It is hard to believe that Grace must be inside. It suddenly occurs to Suzy that she might be too early. 8:50 a.m., not the best time for a surprise visit. But, then, it might even work to her advantage. Grace would have to greet her politely, first thing in the morning, showing up before her entire class. But it would not be fair to walk in on her like that, nor would it be wise. Instead, Suzy suggests, "Could you ask Miss Park to come outside? Tell her someone's here to see her." The girl is still vexed by Suzy's question about the prom but seems relieved that the subject is being dropped. Before disappearing inside, she turns around once, as if making sure Suzy is still there.

A few minutes later, the door opens to reveal the girl, followed by an older woman. Short-waisted and blotchy-skinned, she reminds Suzy of Michael's secretary, Sandy. Although Suzy has never seen Sandy in person, she imagines Sandy to have a similar look, the nervous look of a woman who's been on her own too long.

"May I help you? I'm Ms. Goldman," she says, peering at Suzy as if searching for a clue.

"I'm here to see . . . Grace Park. Is she not available?" Suzy stammers, barely hiding her disappointment, and a tinge of relief.

"Miss Park, well, she's not here today." Ms. Goldman glares at the little girl, as if shooing her away. The girl turns bright red, embarrassed for overstaying her welcome. Then she makes a slight bow in Suzy's direction and slouches down the hall, glancing back a few times.

"I'm a family member. Is she ill?" Strange that she should say "family member" instead of "sister." But Suzy cannot bring up the word "sister" with this woman who seems irrelevant, too irrelevant to be standing in Grace's place.

"Family? I didn't realize Miss Park had any family." Ms. Goldman raises an eyebrow, sizing up Suzy. "She's not ill. She's gone on vacation." Obviously Ms. Goldman does not notice the resemblance, unlike Bob out in Montauk. Perhaps Grace was right. Perhaps it is only white men who can't tell one Asian girl from another. But Suzy is used to this look, this subtle look of disappointment. Often it came from other Korean women. *Sisters?* They would repeat, scanning Suzy once more, as if they felt sorry for the sibling who fared so poorly, by comparison, in looks.

"A vacation? Did she say for how long?" It is as if Grace knew Suzy was coming, and had slipped away just in time.

"Two weeks, although . . . well . . ." Ms. Goldman is about to say something but quickly changes her mind.

"I've sort of fallen out of touch with her because . . . I've been away. Do you know where I can find her?" Suzy puts on an apologetic smile. People are suckers for family values. They don't like to hear about a sibling falling-out. They want reconciliation, and if it takes a slight breach of promise, oh well, it's all for the good of getting a family back together.

But Ms. Goldman is not so easy. She is not moved by Suzy's smile, and instead dismisses her with a firm note: "No, I have no idea. I must go back inside now. I'm sorry, I can't help you."

And just like that, Suzy is left standing alone in the hallway. Teachers, that's what she remembers about them. Never answer questions that matter; never give anything away unless they have to. Perhaps Grace had warned her. Perhaps the whole school is hiding Grace from Suzy.

With students gone, the hallway is endless. Eerily quiet, except for the occasional murmur and laughter from classrooms. She would now have to try the administrative office, which is located at the east end of the first floor. Its formidable door opens to a reception area, and another door farther back which leads to the principal's office. The haphazard state of the desk indicates that someone has only just stepped out. The carpeted sofa feels more plushy than it looks. Suzy is tempted to stretch out, eyeing the stack of newspapers and magazines on the table. *The Jersey Journal, Education Today, Child Psychology*, some of them dating back to the previous summer. There couldn't be a duller selection. Resting her head on the cushion, she is about to recline when she notices an odd one sticking out. It is barely a newspaper. A slim volume entitled *1.5 Generation*, which is just a bunch of legal-sized sheets stapled together. The first page reveals "A letter from the editor" that ends with an exaggerated signature. Across the top runs, "A Quarterly of News, Arts, Ideas and Colleges: published by the Asian American Student Union." It is an amateurish rendition of an alternative weekly. Its format is familiar, down to the last page filled with ads from local Korean restaurants and tuxedo rentals—not surprising, considering more than 30 percent of the student body is Korean. The 1.5 generation—the immigrants caught between the first and the second generations. They used to call Suzy that too. But it never sounded right. "1.5" still meant real Koreans, she thought. Ones who were born and raised in Korea long enough; ones whose fluent English will never forget its Korean accent; ones who, without a second thought, would root for the Korean team if the two countries were to ever meet for the World Cup. It's these kids who proudly call themselves 1.5 and brandish the word "multicultural" with the surest sense of allegiance. Definitely not Suzy, who has never even made the proper minority.

It is then that her eyes stop at the photo under a column called "Locker Talk," whose caption reads, "Check it out, BMW M5! Is this dude rich enough for Miss Park?" A gossip page in which recognizable names are highlighted with photos to match. The photo reveals a car parked in a lot; if there's a man inside, it is impossible to tell. Suzy quickly scans the article, searching for the corresponding paragraph, but the rest is the student stuff: who's going out with whom, who was at whose slumber party, who's likely to end up at Harvard on early decision. No more mention of Grace. No explanation of the car or the man.

"May I help you?"

Behind the reception desk sits a thirty-something redhead in a pink sweater set, holding a cup of coffee. Odd that Suzy did not even hear her come in. Which door did she appear from?

"Hi, I'm here to inquire about Miss Park," says Suzy, rising from the sofa while discreetly shoving the quarterly in her bag.

"Yes?" Her lips curl up in a simper. She is a natural. The sort of face any school would be glad to have.

"Miss Grace Park, she teaches ESL."

"Yes?" The parrot smile. The woman is custom-made.

"Do you have a number where she can be reached?"

"Have you tried her class?"

"Excuse me?"

"All teachers are in their classes now."

"But she isn't. I just checked."

"That's strange, I swore no teacher's absent today." The redhead punches a few keys on her computer and says, "Oops, sorry, our systems are down. Let me see, Ms. Gibney told me there's a list somewhere on this desk . . . Oh, here it is. Park, you said her last name was . . . Oh, here it is, try Room 302!"

"I've tried and was told she's not in."

"I'm sure there's been some mistake. You must've gone to the wrong room. Try Room 302." Then, with a toss of her fiery locks, she chirps, "Sorry, I have to take this call," picking up the receiver with "Fort Lee High School, may I help you?"

Useless; the redhead knows nothing. Suzy is not even convinced that she punched in the right keys before. Obviously a temp filling in for the real secretary. Room 302, exactly where Suzy just came from. What does it mean that no teacher's absent? What is Ms. Goldman not telling her? What about the car in the photo?

Reluctantly, Suzy climbs back to the third floor. Being sent around in circles—that's what she remembers about high schools. She was always the new girl, and the first day of a school happened too often. Soon she would be transferred to another school much like the one before. And through each step, each loop, each journey, Grace was her witness. And now this third-floor hallway of Grace's school seems no longer unfamiliar. That's what happens to people who keep moving homes. Everything becomes familiar; yet nothing is. It is possible that Suzy might also have attended this school at some point, somewhere between Jersey City, Jackson Heights, Jamaica, Junction Boulevard, and how many others were there? It is also possible that Grace might have chosen a school, any school, so that she could finally put a name, a face to their childhood, which seems to have gone missing in the vertigo of repetitions. Is it, then, fair to say that all of this, all that lies before Suzy—the hallway, the ESL class, the screaming sixteen-year-olds inside each classroom—might signal Grace's mourning?

Suddenly a bell. Doors crack open and happy faces begin pouring out. They are elated. The end of a class is always cause for celebration. The end of the first period. Three more to go until lunchtime. The last one to emerge is Ms. Goldman, whose face stiffens at seeing Suzy.

"Miss, I told you I have no idea where she is, and if you'll excuse me, I must get ready for my next class." Ms. Goldman walks briskly, heading for the elevator marked "Staff Only."

"Why isn't the school notified? How come you're teaching her class and the office knows nothing?" Suzy follows in quick steps, afraid that Ms. Goldman will disappear into the elevator without her.

Pressing the "Down" button, Ms. Goldman heaves a sigh and says impatiently, "Ms. Gibney, the school secretary, is out on maternity leave, so it's all chaos there. But that's not my problem."

"Why does the secretary downstairs seem to think Grace is in today?"

"Well, I don't know anything about that."

"Does any of this have to do with the guy she's seeing?" Suzy is tempted to pull out the quarterly and show it to the woman, but she decides it's better to let the question hang.

Ms. Goldman skips a minute or two, then says wearily, "May I ask how you are related to Miss Park?"

"She's my sister."

Just then the elevator arrives. Ms. Goldman motions Suzy to get in and snaps, "Fifteen minutes, but that's it, I have papers to grade."

The door opens to a cafeteria. Empty except for the kitchen staff and a few students at the far end, either waiting for a class or just killing time. Ms. Goldman returns to the table carrying two mugs on a tray. When Suzy declines the packets of cream and sugar, she dumps all into hers and stirs quickly. She knows Suzy's eyes are on her. She lets the coffee sit without taking a sip. Finally, she looks up and says, "It was Miss Park who asked me to keep quiet. Without Ms. Gibney keeping track, no one has to know she's gone as long as her class is covered. She didn't want the absence on record, 'cause, you see, she's used up all her vacation and sick days. She was afraid she might lose the job. Don't get me wrong. Miss Park is very conscientious. I don't know if I should even be telling you this, since you say you haven't seen her in a while, but she hasn't been herself lately, not since that guy started coming around, I guess for about a month. She's been missing classes. Then, a few days ago, this past Sunday night, she called me out of the blue.

"She was quite upset. She sounded frantic. She said that she couldn't come in for a while, and could I cover for her? You see, with ESL, the school doesn't provide substitutes. It's just not in our budget. So, when she's sick or something, we're all supposed to cover for her, the English teachers, depending on whose schedule works best with her class. So it was not a problem, except that she said 'for a while.' You see, I have my own class to teach, and it wouldn't be fair for me to teach someone else's class 'for a while.' So I asked her, for how long? She said two weeks. She'll be back by Thanksgiving. I told her flat out that it was impossible, it just wouldn't work. I told her to try Mr. Myers from English III, or Mr. Peters, who teaches remedial English. She's got her ways with men; I don't mean that in a strange way, I just mean that she has her ways."

Ms. Goldman talks fast, in nervous bursts, as though she is glad finally to be getting it all out.

"That's when she started crying, which surprised me. You know what she's like, she's always polite and proper, but I've always found her to be, well, a bit cold. But here she was, crying into my phone on a Sunday night. I'm a woman, I can hear it when there's trouble. She said that she didn't want to ask the other teachers 'cause she didn't want them to talk, and that she was calling me 'cause she respected me more than others. Well, I never knew she'd felt that way about me, although I guess I've always treated her with respect, much more respect than either Mr. Myers or Mr. Peters, who both look at her in ways not exactly decent, if you know what I mean. Besides, at large schools like this, students gossip, and especially with Miss Park—you know how she is—she's rather, well, much talked about, let's say." Ms. Goldman will not say it. She will not say that Grace is popular because she is beautiful. She is a woman, after all. She will not let herself go there.

"Then she told me she was getting married. She said that it was a secret from everyone, more like eloping, because they wanted to do it quietly, especially with her parents gone. Of course, everyone remembers about her parents. I asked her then whom she was marrying, although I've heard about the guy picking her up in a fancy car lately, which I have to say I found inappropriate, these young people showing off money, especially on public-school grounds. She told me not to worry, 'cause he was like a new family for her. I asked her if he had a proper job, which concerned me, you know, since he'd been coming around in the middle of afternoons. She said that he was in the music business, which I found odd. I can't remember why I found it odd, but I did. She then said that she was planning to announce it when she came back, but until then I was the only one she was telling. Poor girl, she was still crying. My heart just went out to her, a single girl getting married finally, without a family to help her, it must be overwhelming." Ms. Goldman's eyes flicker at Suzy, as if she blames her for Grace's tears, as if asking, *Where the hell were you when she needed you?* Then she quickly adds, "So I felt sorry for her and told her that I'd take over her class, just for two weeks, though, not any longer!"

Grace.

Married.

It never occurred to Suzy.

Surely one of them would marry first, someday with someone. Yet Suzy never thought of it. Suzy never imagined that Grace would one day start a new family. But why go away to do it? Why in secret? Why would Grace suddenly confide in this woman?

"Did she leave any contact address or number? His phone number, or his name, anything about him?" Suzy can just about muster the question. There's the sudden loosening, the hollowness inside.

"No, I thought of getting an emergency number, but then I thought it would be better to leave the girl alone through this. Let her have this moment, I said to myself." Ms. Goldman lifts her chest a little, as though she is touched by her own magnanimity, and then she whispers, as if she just remembered, "I know nothing about him, although, when I asked her if his family minded the wedding being so sudden, she told me that he was alone too. What a lonely wedding, I thought, and asked her how come he was so alone, and she said that he was an orphan, just like her."

Ms. Goldman is now studying Suzy a bit closer, contemplating her hair, all stringy from the sink water, and her overcoat still wrinkled from the bus. *Too bad*, her eyes seem to be saying. *A sister? You don't quite measure up to Grace Park, do you?*

Before Suzy thanks the woman, she writes down her own phone number and hands it to her. "Just in case Grace gets in touch," she tells her. "She's all I've got."

Although she is the one who insisted on sparing no more than fifteen minutes, Ms. Goldman appears to be in no hurry to end their conversation. It's probably been the biggest drama in this whole week of her otherwise single, paper-grading teacher's life. As though still jittery from all the excitement, Ms. Goldman knocks over the mug while getting up from her seat. Instantly there's brown liquid everywhere, spilling over Ms. Goldman's tan PBS tote bag and the piles of papers. Suzy immediately reaches over and pushes the papers off the table.

"Oh my God, I'm so sorry, did it get to your coat? Let me go find some tissues." Ms. Goldman scowls, running to the kitchen.

Too bad the mug was full. Ms. Goldman never even touched it.

Squatting on the ground, Suzy begins picking up the papers. Essays for the ESL class. Each cover sheet bears the student's name followed by "Miss Grace Park," underlined. Strange to see Grace's name typed so neatly. Then "*Assignment #3*" in italics, many with a single "s," which seems to be the common spelling error. It is then that Suzy notices their titles. "MY PERFECT HOUSE," says one. "MY SWEET FAMILY," says another. Slowly, Suzy surveys the papers strewn around her. They are all about one thing. The glorifying, larger-than-life capital letters celebrating home. "MY AMAZING FATHER." "MY BEAUTIFUL MOTHER." Then, finally, "MY GOOD SISTER."

11.

THE WATER looks burnt again. The color of weak coffee, twice run through a filter. It's not good for a bath. She should not be lying in it.

On some days, the water turns strange. Something about the rusted pipes and the clogged drain. When it first happened, Suzy called the super in panic. Wait a few hours, he told her, groggy from a nap. The clear water did come back, about seven hours later. Suzy waited, eyeing the pile of dishes in the sink and the empty pitcher of Brita on the table. It kept happening, though, every few months, only just as she's stepping into the shower or about to rinse the toothpaste out of her mouth. She has never gotten used to the burnt water, which has become a source of mystery. Why should it happen? What's going on inside the pipes? She asked Michael about it once. He had no idea. He'd never lived in an old tenement. Pipes? he asked. What do you mean by "burnt"? Suzy changed the subject. She didn't want to get into it. She would have to invite him over if she wanted to explain better. But that seemed wrong, Michael in her apartment. He would look awkward. He wouldn't fit.

She sinks lower. The tub is so small that she has to bend her knees to get her shoulders wet. Her body looks almost tanned under this water, like the bikini-clad blonde from this morning's billboard. From the minute she got out of the bus at Port Authority and into the taxi downtown, she was desperate to reach her apartment. She ran up the stairs. She was trembling when she stepped inside. But the water that trickled out of the tap was hazy brown. She jumped into it anyway. She lay in it. It seemed necessary.

Already, Fort Lee feels distant. Not even noon yet. The whole day before her.

Grace.

Detective Lester.

Mr. Lee.

Kim Yong Su, the guy out in Queens, as if half the Koreans do not live in Queens. Where has she heard that name before?

The water is cushiony, almost velvet. She must be imagining it. Her headache is lurking. She recalls the girl who thought that English was a headache-inducer. Why would Grace tell her that? Where did Grace go? Did she stop in Montauk to see her parents one final time before the wedding? Did she sail out into the sea for their permission? Would Grace fill her wedding with white flowers, as she had the funeral? Would she stand tall and make a vow, not once breaking into tears?

Suzy has never imagined herself married. By the time Damian's divorce was finalized, it was too late. They never brought up marriage. For Damian, it reminded him of Yuki Tamiko and the life he'd left. Suzy felt it was wrong. She kept hearing her father's last words. Whore, hers was the life of a whore. Marriage was never an option, which might have been why she chose Damian.

Suzy saw Professor Tamiko just once more, at the Greenwich Village apartment that belonged to Damian's friend who was out of town on sabbatical. It was Suzy's first day there. She had not quite intended to move in, although she arrived with a suitcase. Now it occurs to her that he might have set it up. She had thought then that it must be chance. An awful, unfortunate chance. Yuki Tamiko had known, though. She had seen it coming. She might have wanted to warn Suzy, but she also knew that the younger woman would never listen. It was the end of January. It had all happened too fast.

They had slept together once. Back in November. Then, right afterward, he was gone. A research trip to Asia. She only found out from reading the *Spectator*, which ran a small article on the upcoming expansion of the East Asian Wing at the Metropolitan Museum, for which a few experts had been selected to form a research committee. That is where she saw his name. Damian Brisco—Former Chairman of the East Asian Department at Columbia University, Professor of East Asian Art, on leave for the past three years. He was gone, somewhere, some city in China, Japan, even Korea. She could not stand it. He had told her nothing. He had held her afterward. She had lain in his arms, thinking about the blood, thinking it might have stained Professor Tamiko's sheets. Dusk was setting when they walked to Riverside Park. They didn't speak much. She was no longer a virgin.

She had no idea when he would be back. No postcard, no phone call. Somehow she knew that he would not get in touch, but she still waited. With each day, she was becoming less certain whether he had indeed made love to her, whether any of it had actually happened. But then she would recall how he had kissed her, in such quiet steps, until he was sure she was ready. It was embarrassing, how clearly the picture came back to her. She could recall his every breath. Her body held him intact. It was all in her body. She threw herself into her thesis instead. She would stare at the computer screen without seeing a word. She would replay *Ran* without remembering a scene. "First-class asshole," Jen said, wincing, when she finally told her. "But, Suzy, you're not any better."

Two months later, in January, Suzy ran into him on Broadway. She was on her way to buy books for the new semester. It was the first time she had left her dormitory room in days. She was wearing a sweatshirt and jeans. An oversized blue hooded sweatshirt with "Columbia Crew" on its front. It had belonged to Jen. Suzy had thrown it on because it was the first thing she saw hanging across the chair. She was turning the corner at 114th Street. He was leaning over a stall of books outside the shop. It was him. She knew even before she saw his face. She felt something slip inside her. Her breath caught in her throat. She thought of her silly sweatshirt.

"Hi," she said first. His eyes looked pained, she thought, neither surprised nor overjoyed by this chance. "Looking for books?" She tried to smile, although her face felt stuck, every muscle suddenly locked. She was afraid that she looked obvious.

He continued to gaze at her. His eyes still cold. She wished she had worn something else. "You look thinner," he said finally, his right hand moving up slightly, as though it was about to reach her face.

"The thesis . . ." she stammered, unable to think of anything else to say. There were silver sparkles in his dark-brown hair which she had not noticed before. Neither spoke, although neither looked away. She wanted him to say something. She wanted him to explain why he had gone away so abruptly, why he had not been in touch. But she also knew that he had promised her nothing. He owed her no explanation.

"Come," he said then. He took out a piece of paper and

wrote something on it and handed it to her. His hand barely touched hers. It was an address. A downtown address. He was already hailing a cab. "Come stay with me for a while," she thought she heard him say, but the cab was already speeding away. He did not turn around once.

Three days later, when Suzy rang the buzzer of the three-story brownstone on Hudson Street, it was Professor Tamiko who answered. Neither had expected the other. It was Yuki Tamiko who broke the awkward silence. "May I help you?"

Suzy just stood there, not knowing how to respond. She wanted to turn back. She felt caught, guilty, humiliated, all at once. She had never expected this.

"Here to see Damian?" Professor Tamiko asked, with an edged smile, as if she finally understood. This girl. This young girl in front of her.

Suzy nodded, feeling stupid more than anything.

"Come in; he won't be back for a while." Professor Tamiko moved away from the door, her eyes quickly taking in the suitcase in Suzy's right hand.

"I am . . . I didn't . . . I can come back another time." Suzy had never expected to see her. She simply never thought about her. Here she stood with a suitcase that contained her life, and yet she never considered Professor Tamiko in relation to Damian. She had made the first move. It was she who had asked him to make love to her. She had even lost her virginity on this woman's bed.

"Don't look so frightened. You're obviously not a child if you've come this far." Professor Tamiko sat on the sofa, crossing her legs, her long slim legs, shimmering in off-black silk tights. Suzy stood still. She felt confused. She was not sure what she should do, or say.

"Come in, for God's sake." Professor Tamiko shot a quick glance at Suzy at the door. "I'll be leaving soon anyway."

Suzy put her suitcase down at the door and walked in. She did not know where to sit, although she did not want to keep on standing either. Her legs felt as if they would collapse any minute, as did the rest of her. She finally slouched in the love seat, which was farthest from where Professor Tamiko was sitting.

"A drink?" Professor Tamiko got up and walked toward the kitchen. She seemed to be familiar with the place. She seemed to be wanting to move away from the younger woman.

"No, thank you," Suzy answered in a near whisper.

Professor Tamiko poured herself a glass of water. For a second, Suzy was afraid that the older woman would offer her something heavy. Whiskey would make sense.

"How's your Cordelia?"

The question caught her by surprise. Suzy had hoped that she wouldn't remember—Professor Tamiko had over a hundred students. But women like Yuki Tamiko remembered everything. Suzy remained silent. She had made virtually no progress on her thesis.

"I guess you've been busy." Professor Tamiko took a quick sip, as though she regretted the remark, which came off sounding almost bitter. Then she asked, facing Suzy from across the room, "Tell me one thing, why do you think he asked you here?"

Suzy avoided her eyes, uncertain what she was driving at. He had asked her to come. He had not told her when. He had not even given her the phone number. She had assumed that the downtown address was his own, a sort of place apart from his wife, where Suzy could drop in without calling ahead or making a special arrangement. Such an illicit suggestion, strangely, did not scare her. She had been dying to see him. She could not think of anything other than wanting to see him. She had waited so long. *Come stay with me for a while.* It was an open invitation.

"Or did he make you think that it was you who chose him?" A smile formed around her dark-rouged lips, a sardonic smile.

Certainly she made the first move. She came here of her own will. Was that not her own decision? Did he somehow will her here? Was Professor Tamiko hinting at some kind of manipulation that had escaped Suzy?

"Don't think so hard. You're not breaking up a marriage. This has nothing to do with you." Yuki Tamiko took her gaze away, as though she had finally lost interest. Then she finished the glass of water and grabbed the cream leather handbag that had been sitting on the counter. She stopped at the door. She seemed to hesitate. When she turned around, her eyes were no longer cold. Almost apologetic, Suzy thought.

"Damian's not capable. He cannot love an Asian woman."

The water is getting cold now. She climbs out of the bath and wraps herself in a towel. The mirror is her own face staring out at her, oddly unfamiliar. The lines have crept under her eyes, tiny threads of years which have not been there until recently. Her chin appears sharper, almost angular, no longer innocent. Her breasts are looser, facing downward slightly, a note of gravity. She's become a woman suddenly. She will turn thirty in less than two weeks. Her mother had never warned her. "Asian girls don't age, do they?" a painter for whom she had posed once told her, moving into her face a bit too closely. He was wrong. He implied that being Asian was a different destiny. He thought that it bought her time.

Suzy stares at her own reflection. Ms. Goldman seemed to think that she looked nothing like Grace. Bob had mistaken her for Grace. How could two people think so differently? Then it comes back to her.

You remind me of someone I used to know, a good woman, too young to be killed like that.

The witness from the other day.

The deposition in the Bronx.

Diamond Court Reporting.

Forty-four Burnside Avenue.

The man who had saved a seat for her at McDonald's, whose gabardine pants and shiny shoes had reminded her of Dad, whose name, if she is remembering correctly, was . . .

Suzy runs to the kitchen table, where she had dropped her bag upon entering. She unzips the side pocket and pulls out the yellow legal notepad. She flips through the pages. November 10th. Last Friday, November 10th. Five days ago.

Case name.

File number.

Witness information.

Kim Yong Su. Born: 6/10/36. Address: 98-44 Woodhaven Boulevard, Apt. 8F, Queens, NY 00707

12.

THE BUILDING NUMBERED 98-44 is a red brick co-op. Built in the 1950s, probably. Solid and grim, although here, among the residential complexes called Lefrak City, it is just one of many identical blocks. Two o'clock in the afternoon. Kids running here and there who should really be watched by parents. Old women's faces at windows who spend their days looking out. Distant howls of stray cats, although in this chill they've all gone hiding. From across the street, Suzy counts up to sixteen, roughly. A sixteen-story building. His is situated right in the middle, on the eighth floor. Better there, she thinks. Not too close to the ground floor, where bored hands loiter with not enough cash. But not too high up, for one can never trust the elevator.

She is used to buildings like this. Two-room holes for the entire family. Her parents in the bedroom, and the bunk bed in the living room for Suzy and Grace. Who needs a living room? her parents claimed. They might have had a point. How much living could one do when working seven days a week? Suzy had just started sixth grade when they moved to a real two-bedroom for the first time. From then on, their two-room days were over. Her parents must have been doing better.

It was also around then that Grace began to change. Grace had always been quiet. She had been one of those shy kids, at her happiest when left alone in a corner with a book. But it was in that year, when Suzy and Grace finally got a real bedroom, that Grace began to show signs of withdrawal. The change did not occur overnight, but she became increasingly dark and sullen. Suzy did not understand why, nor did she question. She just got used to her sister's prickly moods. Later, Suzy thought that it must have been teenage angst, the heightened adolescent sensitivity, which must have hit upon Grace much more severely than it had Suzy.

Once, Suzy tried to draw her out. It was when Grace was getting ready to choose a college. Smith was an odd choice for Grace, who could have gotten into any college she wanted. Although they had moved through countless schools, both girls had always maintained top grades. In fact, it did not take much effort to be the best in class when most students either spoke no English or lacked proper teachers. Smith was certainly good enough, but why not look into other schools before making the early decision? Grace was not interested. She said that she'd had enough of men, which might have been true. But she also mentioned that Smith offered her a full private scholarship. Grace would not accept any other aid. No federal grant. No financial aid. No support from parents. Suzy failed to understand the reason. They were more than eligible for financial aid. Who really cared whether the scholarship came from a government agency or a private donor? What difference did it make, Suzy thought, as she herself went off to Columbia a year later with a good enough aid package to cover her entire tuition and dorm fee.

But Grace was adamant. When Suzy tried to point out the absurdity of her insistence, Grace lashed out, "You're so fucking stupid, Suzy, you wouldn't care what kind of money it is as long as it puts food before you, would you!"

During her first year away, Grace phoned only once, to say that she wouldn't be coming home during the breaks. Oddly, her parents did not seem too upset. If they were worried about her, they did not show it. In fact, they avoided mentioning her name altogether. Once, Suzy remarked casually at dinner, "I wonder how Grace is settling in." They just ignored the comment. They seemed almost relieved that she was gone. For the final few months, Grace had barely spoken to the rest of the family. She seemed ready to leave home forever. Suzy did not think that her sister would ever come back, certainly not move back home, the way she did a few years later.

Without Grace, the house became unbearable. Although Grace had never been a source of warmth for Suzy, her absence made Suzy feel strangely alone. Her parents had just bought the shop on Tremont Avenue. Both had been working at different fruit-and-vegetable stores for a few years, Mom as a cashier and Dad doing delivery. None of the other jobs had panned out. Dry cleaning didn't bring in enough cash; fish markets smelled nasty; clothing repair was taxing to the eye; nail salons were toxic; liquor stores got robbed too often; car services were too prone to accidents. Miraculously, they seemed to have saved enough to buy a store, which also meant that they came home even later.

Running their own business made them perpetually anxious. There were nights when they did not come home at all, because the store was open twenty-four hours. Suzy never got to see it. The less she knew, the better, Dad said. A fruit-and-vegetable market, nothing to see, nothing to learn. When Mom mentioned how other kids helped out, Dad balked: "I'm not slaving

away in this goddamn country to have my kids cut up melons!"
And that put an end to that. Suzy was secretly relieved. She'd
seen Korean markets. They were familiar sights around the city.
While the rest of the country had 7-Elevens and Pathmarks,
New York City had Korean markets, where one could find almost anything at any hour, fresh and cheap. They all had the basic setup of fruits and vegetables, bunches of flowers in buckets,
stacks of groceries on shelves, and salad bars and fruit cups. But
the key was that almost all the food items were fresh; nothing
was ready-made. They even sold freshly squeezed carrot juice.

The thought of seeing her parents at work made her uneasy. The twenty-four-hour market. The sleep-deprived wife behind the cash register. The bossy husband in a baseball cap hauling boxes in the back. The confused customers gesturing to
workers, none of whom speak English. Such an absolute immigrant portrait terrified her. And she knew that the only one who
would understand such fear was Grace. Grace had been her
American ally. Grace had always been there as a shield. Without
Grace, her home became a refuge for two overworked immigrants and Suzy, the interpreter of their forsaken lives.

And then there were those bills to sort out. Grace had always
taken care of them. Suzy was suddenly lost without her. She had
never had to calculate deductibles from the balance due or fill
out loan applications. Luckily, by then her parents had learned
to operate within the Korean community. There were people
whom they could consult in Korean, an accountant or an insurance agent. When they absolutely needed to communicate in
English, they got by in their broken English. Her parents never
relied on Suzy the way they had with Grace. Because Grace was
older, Suzy assumed. Grace knew how to get things done. But
sometimes it almost felt as if it was Grace who wouldn't let her.
All those times when Grace was stuck having to translate for
Mom and Dad, she never once asked Suzy for help. When Mom

suggested Suzy take a turn, Grace snapped, "Leave her alone," and then said loudly, so Suzy could hear, "She's too slow, she'll never figure it out." That did it. Suzy never offered to help. Let *her* deal with the mess, she thought sulkingly. But now that Grace was gone, Suzy thought perhaps Grace had been right after all. On the rare occasions when Suzy had to read over a confounding notice from creditors, she wondered how Grace had managed, gone all day as Mom and Dad's personal interpreter.

The elevator reeks of urine and sweat. The floor appears not to have been swept in years. The loud bass line from a boom box vibrates through each floor, accompanied by the occasional shrill of a woman, either joyous or dying. Suzy pauses before the door marked 8F.

Kim Yong Su is a truck deliveryman, which means that he should be home now. A deliveryman's day begins around 10 p.m., when he drives his truck to the wholesalers in the Bronx Terminal Market or the Hunts Point Market and purchases the goods that have been ordered by his client stores. He then loads the boxes of fruits and vegetables onto a truck and starts making deliveries through the early-morning hours. On average, one driver has five or six stores on his roster. A regular truck won't hold more than six stores' worth of goods. He is the middleman. All deliveries must be made by at least 9 or 10 a.m., when the stores finish stocking inventories. By noon, he must rush home, eat quickly, and go straight to bed, so that he can rise again at sunset.

Suzy rings the bell once. Nothing happens. No sound comes from the inside. Maybe he is not home yet. Maybe he is already asleep. She rings again. Somewhere from the end of the corridor comes a hissing noise. A kid up to mischief. A curious neighbor looking on. Finally, a shuffling sound against the door and an eye through the peephole. "Who is it?" the voice asks in Korean. "Suzy Park." She brings her face close to the door. "I met you the other day at the deposition, I was your interpreter." Then a clatter of bolts, and a face emerges, the same face that beckoned her at McDonald's only five days ago.

He looks surprised, if not wary. He does not invite her in. Not yet anyway. His face seems to be asking, What are you doing here? Do interpreters make house calls now? Did my lawyer send you? Did the court? Am I in trouble for something I am unaware of? Whose side are you on?

"I would've called, but I had no phone number for you," she says finally. It is hard to know where to begin. She hopes that she is not imposing too much on his sleep time.

He appears even more puzzled. He is not sure if he should let her in. Why is she here?

"I think you knew my parents," she comes straight out. "They had a store on Tremont Avenue in the Bronx. They were killed five years ago."

A flicker of something in his eyes. A flash of recognition. He looks her over once, lingering on her face, and says, "I've got nothing to say." He is about to shut the door when Suzy blurts out, "Mr. Lee from Grand Concourse sent me. He told me that you know things, that you were wronged by my parents." It is not true, of course. No one sent her here, only her own suspicion, and poor Mr. Lee, he will never know what exactly ensued from his testimony. The man behind the door pauses mid-step, his eyes boring into her once more. Then he moves aside, reluctantly.

Inside is a small studio with a bed against one wall, along with a table and a tattered brown sofa. On the other wall is a kitchenette barely wide enough for one person. It is a shabby place, but not without a semblance of order. Obviously he lives alone. But of course that must have been in his testimony; she never recalls details afterward, one witness's life often blurring with another.

He motions for her to sit on the sofa before bringing a chair from the foot of the bed. He then sits opposite her with a table between them.

"I would offer you something, but all I've got is water."

"I'm fine," she tells him. "I'm not thirsty."

From the lack of expression on his face, it is impossible to tell what he is thinking. If he is still wary of her, he no longer lets it show.

"I didn't know when I met you at the deposition. I didn't know that you'd known them. I guess I don't know many people who knew my parents," she says, choosing her words carefully.

He takes out a pack of Marlboros from his shirt pocket and grabs the blue plastic lighter from the table. When he inhales, there is a hint of a gurgling sound from his throat. He has a weak heart, Suzy thinks. Weak lungs. This man should not be smoking.

"The police claim it was a random shooting. But the murder was professional. It was precisely executed. It was obvious. It made no sense that no one was getting to the bottom of it." Suzy raises her eyes, fixing him with a clear, steady gaze. "I'm not sure what I'm asking you to tell me. But I know you might've had reasons to hate my parents."

He is looking down at the black plastic ashtray on the table, the kind that belongs in a bar, not in the solitary home of a man well past sixty. When he exhales, the smoke casts a fog between them.

"So you think I had something to do with your parents' murder?"

The question comes so abruptly that Suzy does not know how to respond, except to continue staring at him. He does not return her gaze. He looks tired. Of course, he must have just come home from work. A man of his age should not be hauling boxes all night.

"Your father . . ." He pauses, as if just a mention, the uttering of the name, brings up memories he'd rather do without. "He'd worked with me many years ago. About eight years before he was killed, so I guess thirteen years now. A fruit-and-vegetable store, the only kind of work I know how to do."

He takes a deep breath, as though it is not easy for him to talk at length. Suzy wishes now she had asked him for that water. Her throat feels dry suddenly. She swallows hard, looking across at the red glow of his cigarette.

"Whatever you've heard is your business. It's been thirteen years, a long time. Nothing left now, nothing left to say." When he says "nothing" in Korean, the word leaves an echo, the peal of hollowness. Looking around, Suzy is again struck by the austerity she observed upon entering. It is obvious that he is not attached to his living quarters. Nothing gives a clue, nothing personal here. Except for a photograph framed by his bedside. A snapshot of a middle-aged woman with a short permed hair and pursed lips. Koreans rarely smile before a camera. It makes them uneasy, such a mechanical documentation of history.

"Is that your wife?" she asks, hoping to engage him, who seems determined to end this talk.

"*Was* . . . She's been dead for thirteen years," he mutters. Suzy cannot tell if he is annoyed by her interest.

"I'm sorry," says Suzy, vaguely recalling something about it from his testimony. A suicide, it was. The plaintiff's lawyer, the older one with a brand-new Honda Accord, brought it up a few times, only to back away when pummeled by objections from Mr. Kim's attorney. Nasty ones do that. Any tragedy in your past can be used to bring down your case. The more tragic, the easier it is to paint a bad character. A man who cannot be trusted, a man who's driven his wife to death.

"Thirteen years . . . seems like yesterday," he adds, contradicting what he said earlier. Suzy cannot help noting the coincidence. Thirteen years ago, he'd known her parents. Thirteen years ago, his wife committed suicide. Suzy was sixteen then. A junior in high school. They were living in either Jackson Heights or Astoria.

"I understand," she says softly, surprised at her own confession. Sometimes tragedy throws people together, even when they must stand on opposing sides and guard their ground.

He glances at her for a while and then lowers his eyes again. He taps the cigarette against the edge of the ashtray. Not because he really needs to, but because it gives him something to do, a slight motion of fingers, a scatter of ashes.

Suzy takes note of his every move. It is a habit. An interpreter must listen always, even when no words are being spoken. Language comes in all forms. A witness's sighs and hesitations might determine the tone in which she interprets his claim.

"A brave woman, but not brave enough maybe," he says as if to himself. It is obvious that just the mention of his wife brings him home, if only for a moment. Suzy says nothing. She knows that this is his moment, that his mind has drifted far from here.

"Some guy once told me that the airport is where the American dream begins. It's all up to whoever picks you up there. If it's your cousin who owns a dry cleaner, you go there and learn that business. If it's your brother who fillets fish for a living, you follow him and do that too. With me, it was my wife who'd come before me and found a cashier job at a fruit-and-vegetable store. Women are harder than men. The only thing I thought she knew how to do was be a housewife. She was eighteen when we got married right after I was released from the army. I never doubted that we'd grow old together. People who marry that early, they often do."

In his mind, he is a young soldier stationed at a remote

country near the 38th Parallel. Every night, before falling asleep in his barracks, he takes out his wallet to steal a glimpse at a photograph. Even in the wrinkled black-and-white photo, he can tell that her lips are the shade of a cherry blossom, the ribbon in her hair is a matching pink. A bashful girl smile. Anticipating her lover's gaze, she forgets the usual reserve before a camera.

"It was always the two of us, from the beginning, all the way until . . ." His voice is a bit shaky now, as though he is overwhelmed by the rushing memory. "We'd never had any children. She couldn't conceive. Neither of us knew when we got married, and later, when we found out, my wife was more terrified than me. She thought it was a sin. She even said that I should divorce her. In Korea then, and maybe even now, those things mattered a lot, having kids, carrying on a family name. Sure, I was upset. I never thought that I'd be without a son, or even a daughter. That was what one did, get married, have children. But then, once I accepted the fact, I wasn't so bothered. I even told my wife that it worked out better, imagine dragging children through the pain of it all, of leaving Korea and getting here. My wife, I don't think she ever got over it. She felt forever like a sinner. She thought she'd wronged me by not producing a son. Sometimes I think that might've been why we left Korea. Leaving a homeland, it cuts into you like nothing else. It's like an illness, haunting generations. But I wonder if we hadn't also hoped that America might make us forget, that in this new country a tradition wouldn't shun you because you're a middle-aged couple with no children.

"I'd been a manager at a small trucking company in Korea. I was forty-one when they went bankrupt overnight and left me with nothing, no severance pay, no workers' compensation. Jobs were scarce then. It was the late seventies. They say that it was our economy-building era, but I tell you, the only economy that was building was for the rich, Samsung, Hyundai, Daewoo, the megacorporations, *chebul*, you know. It was the rest of us, the working people, who paid for it. No small company survived. Bank loans, mortgage rates, trade regulations—everything worked against you. It was the time. There wasn't much any of us could do, except wait for a better time, or get out, which is what I did.

"I'd heard of a guy who'd moved to a place called Brooklyn in America and made a good life. Korea is a small country; once you lose your chance, there's nowhere you can run to and start over. So we looked for ways of getting to America. Not legally, of course, because obtaining the American visa was even harder than finding a job. We found a broker who hooked my wife up with this church group whose yearly choir tour to New York was due in just a few months. I followed, about a year later. The same broker got me in through the Canadian border. Fake papers, fake names, it's a miracle what those immigration brokers can fix. I landed at JFK in the fall of 1980. My wife wept at the airport. I couldn't believe how much older she looked in just one year. Those first years were hard, the things I saw and did when I first got here, this country called America, this number-one country in the world, it had nothing to do with home.

"I started out as a setup guy at the Bronx store where my wife was working. The owner was a good man, hiring me when he could've gotten anyone much younger. It was a favor to my wife. She was an honest worker, and he knew that. In a few years, I was basically managing the store. A tiny store, just my wife and I, and a few Mexican kids. The work was hard, but we were happy. We were building something together, finally a new life in a new land. I wonder sometimes if that wasn't the happiest time of my life. She and I, starting a life together for the second time, like newlyweds almost . . ." He pauses suddenly, as if struck by the image of the two together. An early morning, and the sun gloriously shining upon the stalls of fruit. The ripe yellow of plantains, the green hills of Hass avocados, the firm blush of McIntosh apples. Fruits were a sign of home then. A different kind of home from what he had known before, from what he knows now, not this studio apartment he crawls into for sleep.

All Suzy can do is listen. She is afraid of breaking his spell, although she cannot quite make sense of his story. Was that why his wife committed suicide? Because she could not conceive? But why thirteen years ago? The woman must have been in her late forties by then. What does this have to do with her parents?

"Sometimes I think maybe she was right. If we'd been able to have children, she might not have been so rash, or so heartless," he mutters as if to himself, as if he's reached the limit of his memory. He never talks this much. He never gets visitors. He is sucking on his Marlboro as though it is the only life left in him. He then says without looking up, "But that didn't help your parents, did it, to have you and your sister."

Suzy is startled by this sudden turn. She stares at him, although she cannot see his eyes. Finally, she asks, "What makes you say that?"

"Because you wouldn't be here otherwise. You wouldn't be so sure they'd wronged me."

It only occurs to her now how odd it is for her to be here, to show up at the house of someone who might have had reasons to hurt her parents. Why did she come to him instead of notifying the police? Why was she so quick to believe Mr. Lee's claim? Why didn't she give her parents the benefit of the doubt? By showing up here, by asking this strange man for an explanation, she seems to have already made up her mind. Behind the murder, the guilt lay with her parents.

Whose side is she on?

The air feels stuck. Its lumpy clouds surround her, and she can barely breathe. She walks over to the sink. She takes two glasses from the shelf and fills them with water. She puts one glass in front of him before sitting down.

"Thank you," he says, reaching for the glass. He looks exhausted. Aged, she thinks. It is clear that he is done talking. Almost three o'clock, long past his bedtime. Although, today, it does not seem likely that he would be able to fall asleep. The cigarette has burned itself out, the ashes drooping limp and long, still hanging on to the filter. The room has gotten much darker, as though the sun outside has given up. And the two mourners in their devastated corners.

Neither will speak. He won't speak anymore. He is waiting for her to leave.

Why is she here?

She suddenly becomes aware of her parents gazing at her from all corners. She can almost hear them, feel their eyes on her. She rises abruptly, as if fleeing. With her right hand, she brushes back a strand of her hair falling in her face.

"I should've recognized you right away," he says, walking her to the door. "You take after your mother, more than your sister does."

Suzy pauses, turning to face him.

"Has Grace been here too?"

"Yes, several years ago, a few months before your parents' deaths maybe. She wasn't like you, though."

"What do you mean?"

"She had only one question." He smiles faintly, his hand around the doorknob. "She asked where my wife was buried. Montauk, I told her."

13.

IT IS AFTER FOUR O'CLOCK when Suzy finds herself sitting on a bench at Bryant Park, on 42nd Street. The wind is cold against her skin, crisp, refreshing. Darkness sneaks in with a tinge of green, the way it does when autumn turns to winter overnight. The trees are drained of color. Suzy prefers the parks in winter. Their bareness comforts her.

It's been a long day, from the morning bus ride to New Jersey to the trip to Queens. She would have been happy to go straight home. But while waiting for the R train at Rego Park Station, she noticed Mr. Lim on the opposite platform, their next-door neighbor when they lived in Flushing many years ago. He and his wife had shown up at her parents' funeral, which surprised Suzy because she vaguely recalled a sort of falling-out between him and Dad. He did not exactly acknowledge her then. He seemed aware of the circumstances in which she had shamed her parents. Korean elders never look kindly at daughters whose filial piety is in question. His wife tried to meet her eyes a few times, but Suzy pretended not to notice, not feeling up to polite greetings.

Mr. Lim had also been a truck deliveryman. During his early years of delivery work, Dad used to call him for tips. The selection of fruits and vegetables depends on the neighborhood. Harlem stores needed more bananas than others. The ones in the Hispanic neighborhoods couldn't do without yucca roots and plantains. And the Manhattan stores, the Upper East Side especially, carried the most expensive fruits, like mangoes and raspberries and papayas. The trick is to figure out which wholesalers carry the best grapes, and which ones to avoid for melons. It was Mr. Lim who showed Dad where to go for half-priced bananas on Friday mornings, and whom to enlist for extra help during Thanksgiving seasons. But then, at some point, Mr. Lim bought a store on Lexington Avenue. Manhattan, Dad exclaimed, where rents are steep and employees cost a fortune! After visiting his store, Dad couldn't stop talking about his impeccable salad bar. From grape leaves to California rolls to vegetable tempura to *kimchi*, imagine charging as much as $4.99 per pound! Whoever knew Americans would develop such continental taste buds? You'd think they had never lived without salmon maki or chicken tandoori! Koreans are responsible for that, you know, the craze over world cuisine at your fingertips, it all started with our salad bars! But then, soon afterward, Dad stopped calling Mr. Lim. In fact, the mere mention of his name made Dad twitch in anger. Something to do with money. Dad needed a loan, and Mr. Lim seemed to have refused.

Suzy was about to wave at him across the track when she noticed something strange. A group of boys and girls were straggling around him, as though a nearby school had just let out for the day. Amidst the giddy teenagers in oversized parkas and baggy jeans, he cut a lonely figure, huddled in a dark overcoat, facing the black tunnel from which a train might come hurtling any minute. He hadn't seen her yet, or if he had, he was pretending not to have. She had been only nine or ten when she last saw him in Flushing, and at the funeral she barely paid him any attention. But now, in the dimness of the underground, she noticed something oddly familiar about the way he stood with his head cocked to one side, about thirty degrees to his right. What was he doing here anyway, on a subway platform in the middle of the day? Why wasn't he at work? Has he moved to this part of Queens now? At that very moment, the R train flew down the track with a roar, landing at her feet. She jumped in automatically, quickly turning to the window to find him still on the other platform. She thought she saw him turn to stare directly at her as the train gained speed. And it was not until a few stops later—between Elmhurst and Jackson Heights, where the train got stuck for fifteen minutes—that it dawned on her that Mr. Lim's peculiar posture had reminded her of the man who'd stood by the Montauk lighthouse in the rain.

Montauk, I told her.

Kim Yong Su's last words, circling in her head. What could it mean? A few months before their death . . . did her parents send Grace there?

Montauk.

Where her parents' ashes are scattered.

Where Kim Yong Su's wife is buried.

Where Suzy two days ago walked to its lighthouse, where a strange man had stood watching, a man resembling Mr. Lim, the next-door neighbor from her childhood.

Where Grace had shown up last Friday to rent a boat. Kelly's boat, over at the dock. A tiny sloop. Two-person, max. And Grace can't even swim. And the secret wedding. Somehow Suzy is not convinced. Just a gut feeling. No evidence to the contrary, no reason to disbelieve . . .

"Sorry, have you been waiting long? What a dreary day!"

Jen stands before Suzy, carrying a brown paper bag in her arms. She's gotten older, Suzy notices for the first time, but in just the right way. Her blond hair is pulled back in a simple ponytail; the light-mauve lipstick complements her creamy glow. Looking at Jen bundled in a knee-length camel coat, Suzy can see a woman reaching her prime in her thirties. Jen has never looked more radiant, Suzy thinks. So confident, so knowing, so perfectly compassionate. The same does not apply to Suzy herself, of course. Linear age eludes her. With her parents' sudden death, Suzy skipped her youth entirely.

"Thank God, I was worried you might've gotten us coffee too." Jen slides by Suzy's side and takes out two large cups from the bag. "Decaf. I didn't think you'd want the caffeine kick so late in the day."

Suzy recalls how they had both been such fervent coffee-drinkers in college. They spent most of their junior year huddled in the dark corner of the Hungarian Pastry Shop, sipping double espresso while writing their Eighteenth-Century Novel papers. They were both literature majors. Back then, they would have sniffed at the mention of decaf, as though caffeine were the sign of a true soul. And now nothing is that absolute, nothing evokes such a conviction. Must be the years. Comforting to know that they are gaining in years together.

"Soooo nice to be outside!" Jen takes a deep breath, handing Suzy one of the paper cups. "I didn't know that I'd end up wasting all of my twenties in a cubicle."

Earlier, when Suzy called from the subway station, Jen sounded flustered, even slightly panicked. Meet you at the park in twenty minutes; any excuse to leave the office for a bit, Jen groaned. The writer for the cover story was a total control freak, which explained the painful late hours this week. But that could not be the reason for her panic, Suzy thought, detecting a slight tremor in Jen's voice, which suggested trouble.

"You love it. You'll say the same thing when you turn forty," predicts Suzy, taking the hot cup with both hands. The heat is nice. Half the fun of hot coffee is holding the mug.

"Maybe not . . ." Jen looks away at the pair of musty pigeons tottering along the green patch nearby. "So how was your day?"

Suzy can tell that something is wrong. Jen always defers the subject to another when something is bothering her.

"I went to see Grace today." Suzy does not elaborate. It is obvious that Jen has a load on her mind.

"And did you see her?" Jen looks surprised, and intrigued. She has never met Grace, but she has never approved of Grace's hostility toward Suzy.

"She wasn't there. She's gone off to get married, supposedly."

"And you don't believe that anyone would want to marry her?" Jen is being cynical. It is a sign that something is definitely wrong.

"I don't know what I believe. I haven't seen her in five years. More like ten, if you count those years she was at Smith and I . . . took off. Ten years, then—I guess people must change a lot, no?" Opening the lid, Suzy blows on the coffee once before taking a sip. The hot liquid trickles down her throat, warming the inside. The park is a good place at this time of the day. The late-autumn sun is setting.

"Have we changed in ten years? Am I different now than I was in college?" Jen asks without taking her eyes off the pigeons.

"No, I guess not, because you still can't hide anything. What's the matter?"

"Is it that obvious?" Jen gives up pretending. "Nothing too serious. Just a job thing." Jen smiles, trying to appear nonchalant. Suzy remains quiet. This job means a lot to Jen. Suzy knows from having worked there herself, although for just a few months.

"There have been reports about me. The insider report, because only the insider could know the stuff, even though they're a bunch of silly lies really. How I purposefully leaked the Baryshinikov feature to the Sunday *Times*. How I've been assigning articles to one particular writer since his wild book party last April. How I've been ripping off the story ideas from freelancers. They all sound just absurd enough to get me weird looks. I don't know who's making these up, but I don't like it. It makes me feel . . . trapped." Jen pauses, taking a sip of her coffee. "I mean, the magazine world isn't innocent. Editors fuck writers, and writers fuck their subjects. That's the way mass journalism works. But these rumors about me, I'm not sure. Actual e-mails were sent to the editor-in-chief's private address, although no one knows from whom. At least that's what I was told by my assistant, who's up on office gossip. Who knows, maybe everyone knows who it is and is not telling me. Maybe no one's telling me the truth. Sure, someone could be jealous, someone could want me out." Jen turns to Suzy with a tight smile. "But I'm no longer sure who's on my side."

Whose side is she on?

When Mr. Lee testified that her parents' death was not random, that someone must have had a reason to plan and execute the killing, she did not doubt him. When he claimed that half the Korean community didn't mourn their deaths, it did not surprise her. When he swore that her father had had it coming to him, she did not defend her father. Instead, she sought out Kim Yong Su, as if to confirm her suspicion.

"Funny how life turned out much simpler than it promised to be in college," says Jen, smoothing the wrinkled end of the white silk scarf which wraps around her neck a few times to drape down to her lap. It is a dramatic sort of look, not quite Jen's style. Suzy wonders if that is why she suddenly noticed Jen's beauty, not because of the scarf itself, but because of such a subtle change, which seems no longer so subtle. "It was never about

Faulkner or Joyce or even Derrida or whatever they jammed into our brains for four years. What a superb con job, feeding us a fantasy for our hundred thousand dollars' tuition! Literature and semantics don't make us cry. It all comes down to such basic fights, like holding on to a job despite an infantile enemy, sucking up to the editor-in-chief for a higher profile. The survival has nothing to do with your brain. It's about who has the thicker skin. It's about shedding all the ethics and righteousness that we learned in college. It's about the resilience of your needs and fulfilling them even if it costs all your moral conviction.

"You might've been smarter after all, Suzy. To cut out when you did, when you followed your asshole Damian to the ends of the earth. At least you stuck to your heart. You did what you wanted to do, no matter how you reproached yourself afterward. Who's to say what's right and wrong? Who's to say the right path is so right after all?"

Suzy stops biting the rim of the paper cup and stares at Jen. It is unlike Jen to be so filled with doubt. Jen has always been confident, and right. She has always been the image of what Suzy was not, what Suzy could never be—the ultimate emblem of the American dream. It was Jen who begged her to stay when Suzy packed her bag in her senior year. "This isn't love," Jen repeated with unflinching certainty. "You don't love him; love shouldn't make you run." Four years later, when the escapade with Damian was over, it was also Jen who took her in without asking any question. She cleared her study so that Suzy could sleep through those unfathomable weeks following her parents' murder. Jen always knew exactly what to do. It is not fair, Suzy thinks, for Jen to retreat like this suddenly. It is not fair for Jen to break down before her.

What do you want after all, do you want me to tell you?

Damian had struck the right chord. The impossibility of desire might have been at the core of their union. The escape with

Damian, why did it happen? Did he manipulate her into their reckless affair, as Professor Tamiko had once suggested? Did he claim nineteen-year-old Suzy in order to punish his wife, whom he failed to love? Would he have wanted her still had she not been Asian, so much younger than Yuki Tamiko, and definitely less fierce? What Suzy had wanted in return is still not clear. Neither an act of courage nor mindless passion. In fact, it was very mindful, each step measured. It had to be Damian. It could only have been Damian. No one would have claimed her with such absolute disregard.

"But I had no choice." Suzy is not sure how to continue this, how to explain the inevitability of the past. "The difference between you and me is that you've always been on the right side. You say that you're not sure anymore. But you are. Because you're outraged still. Because you're sad, not for fear of losing your job but for its injustice. You search for explanation. You won't give up until you find the way. You have the eye to discern what is good and what isn't. You can point a finger and tell me where and when and why. You're confident in that knowledge. You're secure. No one can take that away from you." Suzy draws a quick breath and glances at Jen, who is quietly listening. Jen has one thing Suzy could never have: a sense of entitlement, the certainty of belonging. It was not a quality Suzy could learn to adopt, or even pretend to assume. Jen belonged, Suzy didn't. It was as simple as that. If Suzy had resented Jen for it, she would have hated herself, because it was easier to blame the one who lacked. And such resentment would have been so lonely that Suzy could not have borne it. Jen, Suzy knows, would understand this.

"Me, I'm not sure if I ever had it in me. For a long time, for as far back as I can remember, something was amiss, something fundamental. It's as if I've never had a home, as if I've never known what it is to have faith, as if I was never taught what's right from wrong, or if I was, then somehow the difference didn't matter. Why is it that I never felt guilty toward Professor Tamiko? Or Michael's wife? Why did I choose Michael? Why did I run with Damian? Why did I run from my parents?"

She did not mean to bring up her parents. Kim Yong Su. His dead wife out in Montauk. Her poor, sad parents. Missing Grace.

Jen stares at Suzy, meeting her eyes for the first time. She is about to say something, but she looks away instead at the empty green patch of grass where pigeons had flocked only minutes ago. The late-autumn breeze is sharper now. The bare branches have formed hard shadows. The lamps along the fenced path appear bright, giving off a warm glow when everything else is shutting down. Finally, without turning her face, Jen asks, "Do you still hate your parents, Suzy?"

It is useless to pretend with an old friend. Yet there are things one should never say aloud, never admit. So, instead, Suzy says with forced clarity, "But they're both dead; it's been five years."

"Five years, but you're still hiding," Jen mutters slowly.

"Not any more than what you're doing here with me," says Suzy, changing the subject.

Jen is smiling now. The first real smile since she got here. "Decaf sucks, doesn't it?"

"It was your idea." Suzy puts down the cup, which has gotten tepid too quickly. "So you still have to go back to the office?"

"Yeah. The issue ships tomorrow, and Harrison still hasn't faxed in his corrections."

"The control-freak writer?"

"More like the pain-in-the-ass writer. If he didn't have such a stunning mind, we would've severed our ties with his last piece, which came in three months late."

"What's this one about?"

"Nabokov. The pre-*Lolita* years, when he was teaching at Cornell. Harrison was one of his students then and makes a case about how Nabokov had hated America, and, even worse, how he despised writing in English. Harrison claims that Lolita was really a metaphor for how Nabokov felt toward the English language. The strange mix of desire, subjugation, remorse. It's an interesting theory, although I'm not sure how much of it I really buy. Nabokov wrote in English almost exclusively, you know. Once he moved here in the forties, he dropped his native Russian, which was a peculiar decision. But he'd been raised trilingual—English, French, and of course Russian. As far as I can tell, he was at ease with all three languages. The man ended up retiring to Switzerland, of all places, talk about neutral ground! They only okayed this article because it's controversial, and of course because it's Harrison. He even claims that Nabokov's decision to adopt American citizenship was little more than a pretext, that it gave him cover for his anti-Americanism. It happened in 1945, not exactly an innocent year. It offers a totally new reading of *Lolita*. I'm not convinced, though." Jen turns to her, knitting her eyebrows. "Does it mean all that much? What does it mean to adopt a new citizenship?"

American citizenship. Of course, Suzy, having come to America at five, had to have become a naturalized citizen at some point. The question rarely came up. She has never even applied for a passport. The idea of flying seized her with vertigo, but in reality, the opportunity never arose. Damian talked about their taking a trip together, since his research often took him to Asia. But it soon became obvious that he did not want her along on his trips. Without a passport, nothing proves her citizenship. She has always checked off the "citizen" box on financial-aid forms, because she once asked Mom and was told that she was a citizen. Since she herself was a citizen, wouldn't her parents and Grace be as well? When did they all become citizens? How did it happen? She was told that they had left Korea in 1975. They had followed a family member who had been living in the United States, a cousin on Mom's side, who must have applied for their visa. When Suzy asked the whereabouts of this cousin, Mom said that she died soon after their arrival. Suzy remembers feeling bad about it. Since they had no relatives in America and had not kept in touch with anyone from Korea, an aunt nearby would've been nice. But as it turned out, the family had no one. When other kids boasted about visiting a grandmother or a cousin or an aunt, Suzy just shrugged. She had never had any, so she felt no terrible loss.

Contrary to their insistence on everything Korean, her parents rarely discussed their life back home. Dad had been an orphan. A war orphan, a leftover from the 38th Parallel, he used to say. He'd been all alone from birth, and yet he'd managed to get himself to the richest country in the world, so how about that!—Dad would grunt at little Suzy and Grace on nights when he downed a whole bottle of *soju*. On those nights, Dad seemed to forget that they were there at all. The rage they often witnessed was gone too. He seemed to be fighting the urge to remember and yet could not stop recalling the demons from his Korean past, which had nothing to do with his daughters or his wife or this faraway land, as far as the ocean, as far as the length of a decade or two decades or however long it took to call it a home, a place called Queens, a place called the Bronx, a place called America, none of which assuaged whatever stuck in his heart unturned. What Suzy saw was a kind of sorrow, so raw that it felt contagious. Had his recollections at such times signaled the seed of all his angers, she could not have known, because he would not have told, because he was a type of man who should never have had a family.

Mom, though, had not been so alone. She still had family left in Korea. Two sisters. A couple of nieces and nephews.

Everyone comes from somewhere. But it seemed that something bad had happened, and she stopped talking to them years ago. When Suzy asked Mom why, she was told to stay out of the adults' affairs. Family feud, Suzy later assumed. Probably about money—what else? Couldn't be much money, though. Mom did not come from wealth. Suzy gathered that much.

The subculture of immigrants had nothing much to do with the rest of America. When the girls took sick, Mom would get a concoction from a local Korean pharmacy where they never asked for a prescription. When Dad lost his appetite, he would visit an herbalist in Astoria for a dose of bear's galls. When her parents had some money they could put away, which was hardly ever, they would turn not to a bank but to a *gae*, which was a Korean communal-savings pool where a monthly lottery was drawn to grant the winner a lump sum. It was beyond Suzy's understanding why her parents, like most Korean elders, preferred Maxwell House instant coffee to fresh coffee, or why they wouldn't touch grapefruits or mangoes, though they kept boxes of dried persimmons at home. Had she stayed in just one neighborhood long enough, had she been allowed to build intimacy with one friend, one neighbor, one relative, then perhaps this perpetual Korea, which hovered somewhere in the Far East, might have seemed more relevant. She kept up with the language. She followed the custom. But knowing about a culture was different from feeling it. She would bow to the elders without the traditional respect such bows required. She would bite into the pungent spice of *kimchi* without tasting its sad, sour history. She would bob her head to the drumbeats of the Korean folk songs without commiserating with their melancholy. But how could she? She recalled nothing of the country.

Yet American culture, as Suzy was shocked to discover upon leaving home, was also foreign to her. Thanksgiving dinners. Eggnogs. The *Mary Tyler Moore Show*. Monopoly. Dr. Seuss.

JFK. Such loaded American symbols meant nothing to her. They brought back no dear memory, no pull of nostalgia. Damian hailed her as the ultimate virgin. He laughed when, at one Thanksgiving dinner, he saw Suzy's face brighten as she tried turkey covered in cranberry sauce for the first time. A blessing, he said, to be raised in such a cultural vacuum. But the blessing came with its price. Being bilingual, being multicultural should have brought two worlds into one heart, and yet for Suzy, it meant a persistent hollowness. It seems that she needed to love one culture to be able to love the other. Piling up cultural references led to no further identification. What Damian had called a "blessing" pushed her out of context, always. She was stuck in a vacuum where neither culture moved nor owned her. Deep inside, she felt no connection, which Damian seemed to have understood.

"Nabokov . . . If he hated America so much, does that mean that he loved Russia?" Suzy is fingering the pack of cigarettes in her coat pocket, but this is not a cigarette moment. That would be too close to home. A late-afternoon park in November. A cup of coffee. Jen sitting by her side.

"I don't believe he did. I don't believe he was capable of that kind of love or hate for a country. He was too selfish. You can see that in his writing. He picked each word as though his entire life was at stake. He was notorious for jotting down every thought on three-by-five index cards. His life was a string of exile, from England to Germany to France to America to Switzerland. It was right after renouncing Russian that he threw this verbal masturbation of a novel called *Lolita* at the American public. Here's this Russian guy who's only been living in the U.S. for a decade or so, tripping on English prose like Faulkner on acid! What's worse, just as the American readers can't get enough of him, he skips out to Switzerland. The reason? His obsession with butterflies. Of course he was strange, no doubt about it. But I think Harrison is wrong. Russia versus America would've been too simple for Nabokov. If he'd been tortured, which I believe he was, then it was about something less obvious. The Cold War might have contributed, but his oddness, that something which doesn't quite add up about him, goes way deeper. No, I'm not talking about the sexual perversity of his book, which is hardly relevant, but something else, the neatness, the systematic design of his life, like those index cards. Did you know that he lived exactly twenty years on each continent? Twenty years in Russia, twenty in Western Europe, twenty in America, before his final attempt in the neutral Switzerland, where he ended up dying in his seventeenth year? If he had lived, would he have moved again once he filled his twenty-year quota? Where would he have gone?"

Suzy is hardly listening anymore. *Too selfish for exile.* Was there a bigger reason behind her parents' constant moving? Or had they always been fleeing from one situation to another? Were they skipping out on unpaid rent? Why did they leave Korea?

Once, when Suzy was either seven or eight, she was awoken in the middle of the night. "Get dressed," Mom whispered, shoving the clothes and books into big black garbage bags. Both Suzy and Grace stumbled out of bed and threw on whatever they found, grabbing their favorite dolls before following Mom out. Dad was waiting outside in his dove-gray Oldsmobile. When they stole into the night, both Suzy and Grace fell asleep, only to wake up a few hours later at a roadside motel along Route 4, off the New Jersey Turnpike. The family stayed in a tiny linoleum-floored room for about a week before moving into the studio apartment in Jersey City. Her parents never talked about it afterward, but the silence of the night road stuck with Suzy. The hurried steps of Mom gathering things in their old apartment; the clammed-up face of Dad behind the wheel.

Before Suzy fell asleep in the back seat, she remembers, Mom turned around a few times to look through the rear window. Suzy wanted to look as well, but she felt too sleepy and afraid.

Strangely enough, the weeklong stay at the motel was not so bad. Neither Suzy nor Grace minded much. It didn't happen every day that they could skip school with their parents' permission. It was almost fun to be stranded in a strange room with all their belongings stuffed in bundles. It felt like playing house, to search through the bags for toothbrushes and a matching sock. They amused themselves with whatever they found curious in that motel room. There was an airbrushed painting of Jesus Christ hanging above one of the beds, which Suzy and Grace tried to copy onto a piece of paper. Neither could draw, and their finished sketch revealed a scary-looking, bearded old man. Suzy remembers the drawing vividly, because it belonged to one of the rare moments when Grace laughed with her, when they had no school, no house chores, no Korean-language lesson. Both Mom and Dad would set off each morning, presumably to look for housing and work, leaving them with a bag of food, mostly from the fast-food counters along the highway, a couple of burgers, a bag of potato chips, and a family-sized Coke. It was a treat. McDonald's every day, like eating out for each meal. Grace still ate things like that then. Only later, when she started high school, did she become obsessed with dieting.

Fat was not what concerned Grace, not the way it did other girls. She simply cut out things that she considered extra. No chili-pepper paste, because it contained sugar, which ruled out practically all Korean food except white rice and a few odd dishes. No oil of any kind, which Mom used generously in cooking. No soy sauce, because its black color looked artificial. It did not matter whether the dish contained meat or fish or vegetables as long as it was steamed, poached, or broiled, seasoned only with salt. Grace would blame it on an allergic reaction as she sat picking at a bowl of white rice and not much else. Dad called Grace crazy. Did she realize what he had to do to get that food on the table? Once, he tried to force-feed her a plate of fried dumplings. He sat before her and ordered her to eat. When Grace would not budge, he forced her mouth open and stuffed the dumplings in one by one. Mom sat at the end of the table and did not say a word; Suzy began to cry. Neither intervened, partly because they were afraid to disobey him, and partly because they were both secretly relieved. Grace's food problem had become increasingly noticeable. It seemed to harbor a certain brooding anger, which then manifested into an overwhelming tension around the dinner table. Her silent rebellion broke the code of whatever had held the family together. By rejecting the food they all shared, Grace was declaring herself separate, apart. It was impossible to ignore the weight, the terrible mood of discord that would be cast over the family each time Grace pushed the food away with her chopsticks. As they watched, Grace vomited every mushy bit of meat and dough onto the floor. Finally, Dad slapped her once and stormed out. After that, he never commented on Grace's eating habit. They all learned just to ignore it. That might have been the beginning of their silent dinners.

With each year, Grace became more and more withdrawn from the rest of the family. There was a certain anger Suzy sensed, but nothing palpable enough to put a finger on. The only thing she knew was that if Grace had had a choice she would not have wanted to be her sister, or, more clearly, her parents' daughter, and it was this realization that always came between the sisters. The coldness, or the unassailable distance between them, was in fact a clear desire for separation.

But why, even now, even years later, Suzy cannot say.

"Sorry, I got carried away. Maybe you're right. I could turn forty and still be obsessing over dead writers." Jen is getting up.

It is now past five o'clock. The fax from Harrison might be waiting for her. The day is far from over.

"Thanksgiving. I guess it's Thanksgiving soon." Suzy suddenly recalls the holiday with Damian. He did not believe in it, she knew. He hated holidays. But he seemed to derive a certain oblique pleasure from celebrating this particular American tradition with her, as though he were maneuvering a young woman onto a sordid path. He claimed it an *éducation sentimentale* in the American way. He would fuss over each stage of preparation. The ten-pound turkey that was too big for the two of them, the bread stuffing baked with yellow raisins and macadamia nuts, the cranberry sauce simmered for exactly half an hour, the pumpkin pie he had preordered from Balducci's because he did not bake. He loved watching her eat. He himself hardly touched the food. "Dreadful memories," he said. "You cannot imagine the atrocity of the Midwestern Thanksgiving. Everyone gorges on the feast, because there's nothing else to do. No one has anything to say, because overeating does that to a mind. Remember, it's the core of the American culture, the barest of food, the big slab of what barely qualifies as a bird." No one was more cynical about America than Damian, which must have been why he became fascinated with Asian art. But did it mean that he loved Asia? *He cannot love an Asian woman,* Professor Tamiko had warned her. Yet it took the death of her parents for Suzy to leave him.

"But you don't celebrate Thanksgiving . . ."

Jen is careful. In college, Suzy used to stay behind while everyone went home for Thanksgiving. Jen would come back after a week, grumbling about having gained five pounds. But things are different now. It is no longer a choice. There is no celebration, no family. Holidays always make people feel sorry for Suzy. Even Jen, who should know better.

"No, of course not. I just remembered, that's all."

"Come to Connecticut. I'm going to Colorado first with Stephen, which makes Mom and Dad furious. But with his insane schedule at the hospital, this is probably the only time I'll get to meet all his family. So I promised Mom that I'll fly back early and spend at least three days at home. So come. We can lie around the house and eat leftovers and play Monopoly. They always ask about you."

Colorado with a boyfriend. Connecticut to see Mom and Dad. Suzy cannot help feeling a little envy. She has never had that. Not even when she had parents. Damian was not exactly a boyfriend, the same way Michael isn't. Damian would never have brought her to his childhood home. Suzy was what he chose in order to run from all that, as she did him. The two of them together could never have built a family. How could they, when neither believed in it? But why? Where did her parents go wrong?

"Thank you. I'll think about it."

They both know that Suzy won't come. But it is nice to dream about it anyway. Sitting around the parents' house eating leftovers. Doing nothing for three days except playing Monopoly with Mom and Dad. But in such a dream, the house is in Montauk, and everything appears the same—the pastel house, Mom's brand-new Jeep, Dad's fishing rods, the bag of Korean goodies Suzy has brought from the city—except for someone else, someone standing in the rain against the lighthouse, in so much November rain that for a second it looks as though the person is quietly weeping.

14.

THE 41ST PRECINCT is located on the better part of Gun Hill
Road. The sidewalk is freshly swept. No one honks as though
his mother's honor depends on it. No one fires a shot just for
the hell of it. Even the boom-box blasters stay clear. Any half-
brained crook knows better than to defile its sanctimonious
ground. This is where the mayor's fury takes out its revenge.
This is where his soldiers plot out their games. This is where the
NYPD rules.

Two officers are leaning against the patrol car smoking cigarettes when Suzy approaches the two-story concrete building. Across the trunk of the white car are the big blue letters of
allegiance: *Courtesy. Professionalism. Respect.* One of the officers
skims her over with a whistle, nudging the other with his elbow.
They both appear to be about Suzy's age, maybe even younger,
the local boys who grew up watching way too many episodes of
S.W.A.T., whose sweethearts must be waiting at home with a
couple of toddlers.

"May we help you?" asks Whistle Boy. He is the joker, the one who is not ashamed to ogle any passerby in a skirt.

"Not really." She is not up to this hide-and-seek right now. She is about to enter the station. Hardly any help necessary.

"C'mon. We can't let a lady walk in by herself!" Whistle Boy won't let go. He must be bored. This must be his off-time from ticketing double-parkers. Beneath the uniform and the badge, he is still a mere boy. The sweet dimples. The awkward crew cut. Suzy can't help smiling a little.

"See, I made you laugh. You must let us escort you inside. Let me tell you, it's a jungle in there! Ain't I right, Bill?" He turns to his partner, who laughs along. Bill is the shy one, even handsome. A black man with a clean-shaven head. A set of twinkling brown eyes.

"Sorry. No escorting for me. But maybe you can tell me where I might find Detective Lester in the Homicide Unit."

Then another set of whistles.

"Oh well, she's here to see the boss!" shouts Whistle Boy, turning to Bill, who finally straightens up from the car and says, "Please excuse him; not all of us are like this jerk over here. Follow me inside. I'll take you to Lester."

Suzy is glad that it is the quiet one who is leading her inside. Before following Bill through the door, she turns around once as Whistle Boy hollers after her: "See, I knew it. The bastard always gets the girls!"

Once inside, she is led upstairs, away from the commotion of the general area. Detective Lester is being held up with a real head-case, Bill tells her, motioning her to wait in one of the wooden chairs in front of the door marked "Private."

"A thirteen-year-old, just brought in for blowing some grandpa in the back of his Nissan for twenty bucks," he says, shaking his head. "It's the fifth time we've taken her off the street in the last six months. A kid hooker with her pimp daddy on crack. The city's filled with them, and the juvenile agencies are way too swamped and fucked up, and the kid ends up back out on street in a matter of days. Except this time somebody's popped her daddy." He brings her a can of Coke from the vending machine. Too cold, it is the last thing she wants, but she takes it anyway.

The corridor is curiously designed so that the end appears interminably long, although the distance couldn't be more than thirty yards. There are three rooms on each side of the corridor. Each room is marked "Private," which must mean that inside is where serious questionings take place. She can hear nothing. No noise escapes. It is eerily silent, as if the entire building were soundproof, and bulletproof.

Two bullets total. Not one wasted. Not one straying off its course. Not one missing its target.

"So you here for a case?" Bill is making small talk. He seems reluctant to leave her, or perhaps he is not allowed to leave anyone unattended. After all, this is the inner world of the police station. It is probably not safe for her to be here alone. Who knows, one of those being questioned inside could set himself free and burst out the door. Imagine, to be held as a hostage while waiting for the Bronx detective who's done nothing at all for the past five years.

"Yes, a case," answers Suzy, taking a fuzzy sip from the can.

"Which one? Maybe I know something about it." He is trying to be helpful. He is not being cocky, like most policemen she's met before. But she knows that he could not possibly know anything. Five years ago, he must have only just finished the Police Academy.

"I doubt it. It's an old case." Suzy smiles, not wanting to sound dismissive.

"Unsolved, then. Parents?" he asks placidly. It is the first time, she thinks, someone has mentioned her parents' death without the inevitable gulp of hesitation and stammer.

"Yes, both of them. How did you know?" She is surprised at the casualness with which she answers him.

"We get a hunch in our field. A smart-looking young woman like you showing up here in the middle of the day looking for Lester, it's gotta be serious. Besides, you being Asian helps. Model citizens, hard workers, all that stuff is pretty much true, except for some of those punks out in Queens. You've got no business coming in here unless it's family trouble. Parents most likely, since you don't look married to me."

His voice is soothing, she thinks. A young man of her age. No wedding ring. Polite, straightforward. She never talks to men like him. They remain out of her range, always. Something about them belongs in another world. Something about them suggests a home, a different kind of home from what she knows.

"I'm not trying to impress you, although maybe just a little. But the real clue is your face. I hope you don't mind me saying this . . ." Bill takes a gulp from his can of Coke and says, "You've got the face of a mourner."

Even that does not deter the sudden calm of the moment. Face of a mourner. He is probably right. The years must wear on her face, the five-plus immense years.

"Why, you feel sorry for me?" she asks with a tight smile. Desperation. This must be what desperation is, to beg a stranger for his heart.

"No, I don't. But it's okay to let people feel sorry for you." Then he adds quickly, "But don't get me wrong, I'm not pulling my friend Don Juan out there."

"I know." Suzy nods, to reassure him. She wants him to know that she understands.

"Listen, if you have any questions, or just wanna talk or

something, feel free to call me at the station. Ask for Officer Edwards. Bill Edwards. I'm usually here, unless out there hauling
kid hookers off the street."

He grins bashfully. A nice guy. The sort of guy who probably
won't make a good policeman. Too soft. Too sincere. She will
never call him. It would not be fair to him.

"Hey, sorry to keep you waiting."

Detective Lester emerges from the room, wiping the sweat
off his face. He motions Bill to go inside; Bill waves at Suzy with
a big warm smile before following the order. And just like that,
the momentary calm breaks. She is back here now, back in the
Bronx police station where the record of her dead parents has
been gathering dust among the forgotten files.

"C'mon. We should go into my office for a talk. You look
good. Five years, hah! Long time. I swear, the only thing that
flies is time. How're you doing, married yet? Any kids?"

He is one of those jovial older men who ask several questions
at once, none of which is meant to be a real inquiry. He is
stocky, not quite big, but solid. His balding head is supported
by a remarkably rotund neck. His dark-brown bomber jacket
squeaks each time he moves.

"Good to see you. What you been up to? Are you never
home? We tried you several times last week." He removes a
dusty leather armchair from the corner, filled with stacks of paper and a few gold medals and piles of photographs. Suzy just
smiles in return. She knows that he is not expecting a response.

"I gather you don't know why you're here?" He finally sits
down, facing her across the desk. He looks suddenly more alert.
No more of the avuncular chatter. He means business now.
That's the tricky thing with these guys who work for Uncle Sam.

You never know what they are thinking. You can never be sure which side they are on.

"I know coming here like this isn't exactly a ball game for you. Believe me, I haven't forgotten your parents' case. I know you haven't either." His voice is almost deadpan, as though the speech is already rehearsed, as though he has run these lines before with another sad girl, another heartbroken family member.

"But something funny turned up. Or not funny at all, in fact. About two weeks ago, I got a call from the AOCTF in Queens, that's Asian Organized Crime Task Force, the special unit of the FBI. Supposedly they got a tip about some sort of trafficking and raided a pool hall in Flushing. During the search, they found, hidden underneath a pool table, a bag filled with ice. Twenty kilos, probably the biggest stash of ice they've seen in Queens in years. You know what ice is?"

She shakes her head. A sort of drug, obviously. Cocaine. Heroin. Suzy's never been into that culture. She tried pot once in college and threw up violently. It didn't suit her system. A lucky break, which confirmed nicotine as her only vice.

"Crystal methamphetamine. You might be familiar with its other names. Rock candy. Shabu Shabu. Tina. Krissy. Same thing. Speed, the nineties version. Lethal. Harder than cocaine. Ice has always been the West Coast thing, definitely not the drug of choice around here, which means that those boys in the pool hall were up to something bigger than what we've seen recently, a much higher game than the usual gambling and racketeering. So, right away, the Narcotics Squad goes ape-shit. They round up the suckers and narrow down on three connected to Triad, the international Chinese gang. Except these are Korean. Three former members of Korean Killers, which disbanded in the early nineties. You following all this? You wondering why I'm telling you all this?"

He talks fast, too fast for her. Ice. Triad. None of it rings a bell, except for Korean Killers. They were notorious around Queens high schools, although nobody Suzy knew had ever met one.

"During one of the all-nighters, your father's name popped up." He stares straight into her face. "Got any idea why?"

She stares back, not clear whether he expects an answer. He does not budge. Nothing on his face. No help there. Finally, she breaks: "No."

"Neither do we." He rises suddenly from the chair, as if needing fresh air. "Mind if I smoke?" he says, lighting one of his Lucky Strikes. "What's funny, or I shouldn't say funny, okay, what's peculiar is that one of those KK boys brought up your parents' killing from five years ago. The one called Maddog, the ringleader. Maddog kept saying that they didn't do it. He swore that they had nothing to do with it. He claimed that when they arrived at the store your parents were already dead. He even went on to say that it was a setup, a conspiracy. Then he just clammed up. He realized that he'd slipped up. The squad had no idea about any of this, of course. They knew nothing about your parents' case. Their sole interest was the source of that bucket of ice they found. But now they've got possible murder suspects on their hands for an unsolved five-year-old crime. So I'm the man they turn to, and I go over there and sit up with those assholes for three straight nights, and nothing, none of them will say a goddamn thing, especially Maddog. These are hard boys. Triad. Korean Killers. Any idea what they do to the one who squeals? These boys have been trained to shut their mouths. They'd rather die than betray their honor. Honor, my ass, their monthly paycheck revolves around trafficking either drugs or counterfeits or women. Still, these Asian gangs mean business. They've done their homework. They're even more tightly organized than the Italian mobs. Nothing in the world can get a word out of them at this point, which is why I called you a few days ago." He sucks hard on his Lucky before stubbing it out, as though the monologue has brought him beyond a point of frustration.

"Because?" Suzy is at a loss. Asian gangs. Her parents shot at the store. Anything is possible.

"Because you might know something. Because you might remember if your father had owed the KK a few thousand dollars, or if he'd used their service for one thing or another, or if he had some secret drug habit, or if he'd gotten himself on their bad side for whatever . . ."

"Excuse me, Detective, but I know nothing like that."

Five years of silence, and now a gang connection. Except her father might not have been so innocent.

"Think, though. Was there any point at which you might've seen something or heard something? Did you ever see any strange set of people coming in and out of your house? Did your parents ever talk about a private loan from somewhere?" He is groping for a clue. No more Mr. Deadpan. Each question is a bit more heated. Each question resembles a threat.

"Nothing at all." She can barely contain the anger rising within her.

"Work with me, Suzy. We might've found the answer. These boys vehemently deny any involvement, which can only mean one thing, that they were involved somehow. It's got KK fingerprints all over it. The way they do away with their enemies. The exactness of the shooting. Did they do it? I don't know yet. But I sure am gonna find out. So you've gotta cooperate. Try to remember something, anything." He is turning into the nice uncle again. He is pleading with Suzy. He wants desperately to pin the murder on these boys. Why not? It's the only lead he's got.

"No, I can't help you. I remember nothing." Suzy is tempted just to get up and walk out, but she continues, "What I'm curious about is why you didn't see any of this five years ago. If the shooting method seems so familiar, why didn't you suspect them then? Why did you call it a random shooting and ignore it for five years?"

Turning his back on her, Detective Lester faces the window, a tiny slit between the metal filing shelves which Suzy has not even noticed until now. He stays silent for a while with his arms folded across his chest, and then, without turning around, he says, "I'm not surprised that you're upset. But we're not God here in the Police Department. We're not Sherlock Holmes. We might not always get to do the right thing. Several hundred murders in the borough every year, it's hard to go after each one."

The last bit gets to her. *Hard to go after each one.* So they haven't even tried. It's taken five years to look for a motive. This incompetent detective. This idiot of a man who called the execution random. And the murderer still somewhere loose, still so far from their grip. But nothing is fair. Nothing has been fair for so long. Five years. Why?

"I just don't understand why you're suddenly so interested in finding my parents' murderer. The Asian Organized Crime Task Force. The Narcotics Squad. All of that means nothing to me. Are the stakes bigger now? Now that gangs and drugs spice up what happened five years ago; now that all the higher branches of your police force are having a field day with whoever might've murdered my parents; now that my parents might be more than just a middle-aged Asian couple shot dead in their store? Tell me, Detective, do you get a medal if you score this one? A promotion?"

He must be used to such outbursts. He may even expect them. When he finally turns around and faces her, the furrows between his eyebrows look deeper. He does not like doing this either, she can tell. It is a hard job, to pick up after the most hideous of all crimes. "We didn't ditch them cold, Suzy."

A sudden fatigue washes over her. Nothing more will come out of her. Everything seems to be crashing down at once. Damian, she misses him infinitely. Damian, what happened to Damian? Wasn't he supposed to take her away from all of this? Wasn't that why she lay in his matrimonial bed at twenty, letting the blood trickle down her legs? Wasn't that why she went with him despite everything, despite her youth, despite her then-living parents, despite her Ivy League college, despite all good common sense that had told her to stay still, stay where she was, stay in her rightful spot as the good Korean daughter? Wasn't that what she had wanted after all? To run away from all of this?

"Listen, Suzy, we've gotta work together on this one. Your father, whether you wanna face it or not, must've had some gang connection. It might not even have been a bad one. Many immigrant store-owners pay dues, for protection or whatever. Your father might've just been one of many victims. He might've owed them some money. Maybe business was slow, and he took a loan and couldn't pay. Something as little as that. But we need evidence. We need some concrete motive. You've gotta think, and think hard. You've gotta try to remember everyone your parents knew or had dealings with. Someone somewhere must know something. I've already sent some men over to the Hunts Point Market and the Korean Grocers Association. Something's gotta give. It'll just be faster if you can recall some names, so we can finally resolve your parents' deaths."

He is making sense, of course. He is even convincing. But Suzy is not sure. She still cannot buy into such sudden enthusiasm. Five years is a long time to do nothing. Any evidence must have long been erased.

"I thought you said that Korean Killers disbanded in the early nineties. My parents were shot in 1995. What dues would they have owed? To Triad? I thought they were Chinese. Do they collect dues from Korean stores too?"

He is glad that Suzy seems to be coming around. The shadow of guilt that had clouded his face is gone. He looks almost grateful when he tells her, "No. New York Triad mostly operates within Chinatown. But these ex-KK guys seem to have been sort of working under them for years, at the bottom of the rung since the breakup of their own group. Who knows, there might've been old debts, old scores to settle."

"What about their claim that it was a setup? Isn't it odd that they would bring it up only to deny it? I mean, if they're guilty, why mention it at all, when they weren't even being accused?"

"That's why it was a slip. One of them thought that we'd already linked them to the murder, when in fact we had not a clue. He thought that was why he was taken in for questioning."

"So you're convinced that it was them?"

"I didn't say that. But I'll tell you this, I certainly wouldn't give much weight to their denial."

"And you've known nothing at all about these three guys until now, until they got raided in the pool hall with enough drugs to spread alarm through the entire New York Narcotics Squad?"

"It's like this." He begins pacing around the desk, as if shuffling the bits of information in his head. "KK disbanded nearly a decade ago. We know much more about the other groups, like Korean Power and Green Dragons, who're both still active in the Flushing area. Korean gangs operate differently from either Chinese or Japanese gangs. They tend to keep a lower profile. They often have links to the bigger international groups, like Triad or Yakuza. They might occasionally do some dirty work for the big guys, but mostly they keep to their own. They raid their own Korean communities, who are infamous for never using banks, just hoarding cash in their homes. Easier for them, since Koreans rarely report gang crimes. The AOCTF calls it a 'collective shame.' A sort of responsibility, immigrant guilt for not having properly reared their second generation. You might understand that one better than I can. So, according to the AOCTF, it's always harder to keep track of the Korean gang movements. They don't know much about these ex-KK ones except that all three have done time for fraud, extortion, money laundering, the usual stuff. No murder, though; they've never been charged with murder. One interesting thing is that they used to call themselves the Fearsome Four. They obviously fancied themselves as a bit of legend in their own little-league way. They once each cut off their little fingers to honor their brotherhood, copying that crazy Yakuza ritual. But it seems that's as far as their legend ever got. Other than doing a little time here and there, we've heard nothing about them until two weeks ago."

"What happened to the fourth one?"

"Which fourth?"

"The Fearsome Four. If only three have been arrested, what happened to the fourth one?"

"Oh, he faded out of the picture long ago."

"How?"

"Deported. Gone without a trace. He seemed to have split from his brothers soon after the KK breakup; anyway, it's all hazy, who knows, maybe it was Maddog or one of his many 'brothers' who dropped a dime on him. But somebody reported him, and the INS tracked him down at a motel on Junction Boulevard and packed him home. Turns out the guy never even had a green card. One of those orphans who'd been shipped into the country, probably through the KK's adoption fraud of the early seventies."

"Which was?"

"The typical trick. They'd charge between ten and twenty grand for each Korean orphan adopted by an American couple, and then, once the deal goes through, pocket the money and sneak the kid away."

"Why the kid too?"

"Human resource. Child labor. They usually traded boys over the age of four. I guess the younger ones proved useless. You can't really stick two-year-olds into sweatshops, can you?"

"But why would the orphans be left without a green card? What about the visa that had been issued to them to begin with?"

"*Please*—there never was an orphan, don't you see? The orphans weren't real. Those were just some random kids kidnapped off the streets of Seoul or wherever they were taken from. Whatever papers they had with them were all fake anyway. The visa was only useful to smuggle the kids into America. After that, these kids filtered through the system as nonentities. They truly became the orphans of the world, no name, no nothing, which was exactly what the gang wanted. To pin these kids with nowhere to go. These were the very ones recruited as the next generation of KK. The true brothers. The little boys with no ties in the world except for their gang brothers. Desperation. That's what pulled them together, which is why it's so hard to get any of them to speak."

"When did you say that he was deported?"

"November '95. Roughly five years ago. He was in his twenties. I guess he should be about your age now. Why? You think you've heard of him or something?"

"No, all of this is news to me. What was his name anyway?"

"They all called him DJ. No last name. None of them ever have real names."

An orphan kid smuggled into the country.

No one except for his gang brothers.

She must be getting tired. The day may have dragged on too long.

"Two possibilities, assuming we've got the right boys." Detective Lester suddenly stops pacing. "Either the gang acted on their own, or they were hired by someone. But gangs don't kill for debts. They might threaten or hurt the victims, but they wouldn't just get rid of them. What would be the point? Where would they get the money? So let's assume that they were following someone's order. Then we've gotta start looking around at the people your parents knew. Employees. Other store owners. People with enough reason to want them dead. Can you think of anyone with a grudge against your parents? My men doing rounds among the Korean markets might find something. But Koreans don't tend to trust policemen. They don't wanna tell us anything, which unfortunately doesn't help your parents' case."

Kim Yong Su. And the other witness at the deposition, Mr. Lee. Even Mr. Lim, who'd had a falling-out with her father, who resembles the strange man in Montauk. In fact, the entire Korean community might be filled with people who had hated her parents. Yet no one will talk. No one will cooperate with the investigation. No one wants the murderer to get caught.

"No, I don't know anyone with a reason to kill my parents." She may be like the rest of them. She won't confide in police. She may even be shielding the killer.

"Well, if you remember anything, call me." Detective Lester extends his hand with a smile. If he suspects her of withholding anything, he does not show it. Instead, he asks, "So where's your sister?"

"She's . . . away."

"Vacation?"

"Something like that."

"Funny, she didn't mention it on the phone."

"You spoke to her?"

"Just last week. I told her it was perfect timing."

"*She* called you?"

"Sure, she was just checking in, she's done that before," he muses, as if to say, What about you? "She wasn't much help either. I was hoping to see both of you here today."

So Grace knew about it already. Grace was told.

"When did she call last week?"

"Gee, I don't know. Friday maybe?"

Grace showed up in Montauk the same day. Bob the bartender seemed to think that she then returned to the city. On Sunday, she called Ms. Goldman to say that she was not coming in.

"Well, tell her to stop by when she gets back. She's older, right? Maybe she'll remember more." He shows her to the door. It is not much of a door. A narrow crack, just like the window. The whole building is tightly woven. No sound, no bullet, no room for escape. Before shutting the door, he says, almost in passing, "You look different from how I remembered. I don't know what it is. I can't quite put my finger on it." Then, gazing at her once more, he adds, "Don't worry. It'll come to me."

15.

"ins, may i help you?"

The 800 number was the only viable option. Since eight o'clock this morning, Suzy has kept dialing the local branch, whose computerized operator put her on hold for what seemed like the entire morning only to route the call to the toll-free number. New York City must be one of its busiest chapters. They probably have their hands full, having to answer all the immigrants, whose panicked questions in broken English must get tiresome pretty quickly.

"I'm trying to find out about my status, and that of my parents, who are . . . both deceased."

"Are you a U.S. citizen?"

"I think so."

"Were you born in this country?"

"No, but I'm sure I am a citizen."

"What's your file number?"

"I don't know. But my name is Suzy Park, and my Social
Security number is . . ."

"Miss, I didn't ask for your Social Security number. Do you
have a filing receipt or a certification paper?"

"No."

"Did you file for citizenship yourself?"

"No, I believe my parents did."

"Were they citizens?"

"I think so."

"Miss, I can only help you if you are certain of the situation."

"I'm almost sure that we are all citizens, I mean, that they
were also, until they passed away."

"Miss, I can only help you if you are certain of the situation."

What did she expect? It is the INS, after all. The iron gate of
America, and the gatekeeper is on the other end, not sure if he
wants to let her in.

"Look, if I were certain, I wouldn't be calling you in the first
place. My parents are both dead. They can't tell me a thing.
They never showed me any certification papers. I just want to
know when they might have filed for citizenship and under
which circumstances. You tell me, am I a U.S. citizen or not?"

Then the silence at the other end. For a second, Suzy is
afraid that he may have hung up. She is half expecting the usual
"Let me call the supervisor" move. Instead, the man comes right
back on. Obviously, in his line of work, her level of outrage
must be almost expected.

"Miss, there's nothing I can do for you. It sounds to me like
you need to apply for G639 papers. Freedom of Information
Act. Please hold, while I transfer you."

With that, she is put on hold again. Several minutes later,
when she is put through, it is to a machine telling her to leave

an address to which the G639 application can be sent out. The application will take two to three weeks in the mail.

The INS, not the most open organization, not exactly known for efficiency. It was naïve to think that she could just call and find out anything. Not surprising that no one is jumping to her aid. Looking up a citizenship-status file cannot be as urgent as deporting an illegal immigrant. A few weeks to get her hands on a bunch of papers called G639, a few weeks for them to process, and then who knows when they would get back to her with a response? Freedom of Information Act. Freedom, sure, in the most roundabout way. There must be an easier way.

Her first instinct is to call Detective Lester. He should be able to pull up the record in a second. Aren't they all in league with one another? Would the INS refuse him speedy access when the information might be pertinent to a criminal investigation? *If you remember anything, call me.* He sounded almost chirpy. The police. It is impossible to guess what they know or how much they pretend. Where has he been for the last five years? Why did he declare her parents' deaths random? Why has he ignored the case all this time, until now? Korean Killers. Fearsome Four. On second thought, maybe she shouldn't ask him for help. Why bring him into something that might only be personal?

Grace. Only Grace would know. Grace, the sole evidence of her family.

Without Grace, there remains no trace of her parents. The Woodside brownstone. What did Grace do with all their parents' things? Whenever Suzy pictures Grace sorting through them, she imagines her amidst a pile of blankets in rainbow colors. They each owned thick winter blankets, which Mom called "mink blankets." Fake silky furs with complicated flower designs in pink and orange. They were very warm, but Suzy found them too heavy and flashy. Both Suzy and Grace left the blankets be-

hind when they went off to college. That was one thing Mom
objected to. Although nothing aroused her reaction much, she
seemed hurt when her daughters would not take what she considered to be the family heirlooms. Suzy felt bad when Grace cut
her short with, "Please, Mom, it's not mink and it's not an heirloom."

A few months after the funeral, Grace contacted Suzy once
through the accountant. It should have been handled by a lawyer, but Korean accountants often extended themselves over all
matters, from inheritance rights to tax returns. There was
money, he told Suzy over the phone one morning. Not a whole
lot, but a good enough sum to see her through for a few years.
Suzy refused her share. They had disowned her up until their
death. It seemed unthinkable to take their money. "Sleep on it
for a while," the accountant dismissed her refusal. "Heirs often
react this way. Inheritance evokes guilt. You think you're com-
promising your parents' death. Especially when their death
isn't natural. But believe me, you'll change your mind in a few
months." The accountant was adamant. When Suzy said no for
the third time, he barked, "That won't bring them back, you
know."

What is his name? She had not thought to write it down.
During those few months after the funeral, nothing quite stuck
with her. It is still a wonder how she managed from day to day.
Getting up each morning. Finding a place to live. Finding something to do. Finding ground to stand on. You'll regret it, the accountant warned. But he was wrong. She could not have taken
her parents' money. It did not belong to her, although it might
not have belonged to them either.

*You're so fucking stupid, Suzy, you wouldn't care what kind of
money it is as long as it puts food before you.*

It wouldn't be a bad idea to look up the accountant. The guy
might know something. He had done paperwork for her parents

for a few years. Not for long, he insisted. He made a point of emphasizing "few years," which, for an accountant-client relationship, was not a long period. Later, it occurred to her that he might not have wanted to be associated with her parents' death. At their only meeting, she found him abrasive. But no one seemed to be on her side then. Everyone appeared unsympathetic, unfeeling, including Suzy herself, who remained living while her parents were shot down in a remote corner of the Bronx.

Suzy is about to grab the Yellow Pages when it dawns on her that most Korean accountants would not be advertised in it. What would be the point? No American clients come to them anyway. She would do better with the Korean Business Directory or Korean newspapers, neither of which she has in her apartment. His office had been located in Koreatown, above a restaurant that specialized in bone-marrow soup, 32nd Street in midtown Manhattan. A part of the city she rarely visits. The pervading smell of *kimchi* along the street. The posters on windows displaying jubilant Korean movie stars. Bright neon signs in Korean letters. Too close to home, although her home had never been that festive. Suzy had been to his office once to sign papers. It was a simple procedure. It took five minutes, and all her claims to her parents were over. Afterward, she sat before a bowl of oxtail soup and wept.

She is zipping up her knee-high boots when the phone rings. Ten-thirty on Friday morning. Who else but Michael? His daily phone call. His daily declaration of love, or need. It is good to have a routine. The only problem is that, by the time you get used to it, something inevitably happens to break it. She picks up the phone on its third ring. He should be impressed. He knows she is bending rules for him.

"Michael, I'm on my way out, can you call me later?"

No response. His phone must be acting up again. He must

be out of Germany now. The connection is never a problem from there.

"Michael? Your cell's not connecting. I can't hear you."

He must be calling from Southern Europe. Portugal, maybe Spain, if he is lucky. Michael chuckled when Microsoft announced the downsizing of their Madrid office. "Those hot-blooded Spanish will rock you with their fiestas and siestas. But are they Web-ready? Do they care? They'll be the last civilization to hook up. Why should they, when they actually prefer their world to the virtual one?"

"Michael, it's useless. I'm hanging up."

Then she hears it. The perfect silence. No static. No distance on the connection. This call could be coming from down the block. It is not Michael. It is not Michael on the other end.

"Who is this?" Dropping her bag, she throws a quick glance at the dead irises dried up in the Evian bottle.

"Damian?" Part of her is hoping. Of course it cannot be Damian. He would not be calling her. Not like this anyway.

"I'm going to hang up if you don't speak."

She is about to take the receiver off her ear when the voice stops her. A male voice. Shaky and unnaturally low, with a distinct Korean accent.

"Don't." It is not clear if he just has a feeble voice or is talking in a whisper.

"Who is this? Who are you?" She speaks slowly, strangely calm, as though she has been expecting him.

"I call to tell you . . . No more. Stop. No more talk with people. No police." His English is just barely comprehensible. But he won't speak in Korean. Maybe he is afraid that she will recognize his voice if he speaks with fluency. Maybe he is calling from somewhere not private. She tries anyway and asks in Korean, "Stop what? What're you talking about?"

"Your parents dead. No more. Stop now." He insists on his

broken English. Barely a whisper. She won't recognize his voice even if she hears it again.

"What do you mean? Who are you?"

"No. Nothing. They do not kill your parents. So stop."

He is about to hang up. She can sense it. She cannot let him get away. He is the only clue she's got.

"Wait! Who's they? What did they have to do with my parents' death?"

"Your parents dead. Nothing change. They watch you."

He is gone. She can tell even before she hears the click.

Stop poking around, unless she wants to get hurt.

Is it a warning, or a threat?

Who is watching her?

Who are *they*?

Who is he?

She is slumped on the kitchen floor staring at the phone when it rings again. She snatches the receiver almost instantly. Has he changed his mind? Is there something he forgot to say?

"Wow, what's with you?"

It is Michael. The real Michael this time.

"Babe, what's going on? You been waiting for my call or something? Suzy, are you there? *Suzy, hello?*"

Her heart is beating too fast. She shuts her eyes and counts to three.

"Suzy, what's the matter? You sick or something?" He is not used to a sick mistress. He sounds uncertain suddenly.

"Hi, I . . . I'm just a bit out of sorts."

"Shit, I thought I'd have to jet over, scoop you in my arms, and lick your wounds!"

"Michael, I'm a bit scared." She cannot help it. Sometimes the truth is easier with someone for whom it won't matter much.

"*Christ*, Suzy, what's going on with you?" He sounds more

alert now. He is not used to vulnerable Suzy. He is not sure how to respond.

"Nothing at all. I think it's my period." She quickly changes her mind. It is not fair to dump it on Michael. It is too late for them to be anything but what they are. It is really not his fault.

"*Christ*, sometimes you fucking surprise me." He breaks into nervous laughter. He is relieved.

"I think I better go lie down."

"You do that. But I'm gonna call and check up on you."

"Don't. I'm gonna sleep for a while." She does not want any more calls this morning.

"You need anything? Should I get Sandy to send you a doctor or something?"

Suzy laughs at his suggestion. How absurd, a doctor making a house call to her East Village flat? Michael. He will try anything. He will make anything happen. *Anything.* Of course, why hasn't she thought of it before?

"There is something, actually."

"Just name it." Michael is trying to hide his surprise. Suzy has never asked for anything. She has never had a request for him.

"I need to find out about my citizenship status. And that of my parents. I need to know on what grounds those citizenships were issued, if they were issued. I need them fairly soon."

"Done. Sandy will call you in five minutes and take down the info. I'll tell her to send you a doctor also. What else?" He is a good businessman. Gets the job done. No questions asked.

"Nothing else."

"Sure?"

Suzy is suddenly so grateful that she wants to cry. She must have been alone for too long. She is not used to getting help.

"Michael?"

"What?"

"Thank you."

"Shut up and go get some sleep. And for God's sake, don't act so fucking polite."

From her seat at the window, she can see the bustle on 32nd Street. The same bone-marrow-soup restaurant, just downstairs from the accountant's office. Several tables are occupied already although it is barely noon, not quite lunchtime. Whereas Americans crave eggs and bacon on bleary mornings, Koreans go straight for a steaming bowl of bone soup topped with freshly chopped scallions. They swear that it magically heals the unsettled stomach, the best cure in the world for hangovers. Koreans are known as the Italians of the East. They drink hard and eat to their heart's content. Indeed, the faces bending over the clay bowls appear quite pale, as though they have not yet recovered from the night's triple rounds of *soju* and karaoke. Some of them sneak glances at Suzy sitting alone, hiding behind the *Korea Daily*, which she bought from the dispenser upon entering the restaurant. The sudden flash of Korean letters confuses her for a second. She glares at the print without making sense of it. She stares instead at the row of restaurants across the street. The second-floor windows are plastered with neon signs for hair salons, acupuncturists, even a twenty-four-hour steam bath. The third and fourth floors continue up the same way, cluttered with shops that only Koreans frequent. It is a way of cramming the immigrant life into one tiny block. One could stroll back and forth along this quarter-mile stretch and find anything, from bridal gowns to Xerox toners. Nothing is missing. No craving is hard to fill. It's all here, right on 32nd Street.

The accountant was useless. Mr. Bae was his name. A smallish man with a shocking amount of grease in his neatly parted hair. He barely looked up when Suzy entered. Although she in-

troduced herself three times, he continued to ignore her. Even
his assistant seemed embarrassed by such an outrageously rude
reception. When Suzy started to ask him about her parents' file,
he cut her off in the middle, "First, your sister specifically asked
me not to engage in any talks with you. Second, your sister has
terminated her business with me as of last week, so I'm no
longer working on her case, which naturally includes your parents' file. Third, I told you once that you'll regret giving up your
inheritance rights, but, just like your sister, you thought my advice wasn't worth a dime. Fourth, as you can see, I'm a busy
man, with more than enough work to do for my clients, so I'd
appreciate it if you'd stop wasting my time." Then he turned
back to the stack of files on his desk, leaving Suzy standing there
tongue-tied. His hostility seemed unreasonable and clearly immutable. So Suzy walked out, feeling wounded, as though she
had just been scolded by someone dear, and it wasn't until she
reached downstairs that she remembered bone-marrow soup and
felt suddenly hopeful.

Once she sat down, the smell of brewing bones from the
kitchen tugged at her. A taste from her childhood, although her
mother rarely made such a variety: *sulongtang, komtang, kori-
komtang, doganitang.* From tail bones to knee bones and cartilage to tripe, the choice depends on taste. A true connoisseur
would swear by the subtlety of each, but for Suzy they all taste
somewhat similar. Just a tinge of Korean flavors inevitably
brings her back to Memory Lane. A pinch of garlic, scallion,
ginger would sure enough do the trick, although her house had
never been filled with such culinary extravaganza. The family
usually made do with white rice and a couple of side dishes,
maybe a stew or two, either of tofu or miso. Always *kimchi* on
one side of the table, and on the other, fried anchovies and
salted pollack eggs. They were almost always store-bought.

Mom barely had time for sleep, never mind brewing oxtail bones or marinating *kimchi*.

After Suzy moved out of her parents' house, she often stopped by this neighborhood, whenever she craved Korean food. She would sit alone with a book or a newspaper and order a bowl of *sulongtang*. People would stare at her, because Korean girls rarely ate alone. Back then, there was no way one could get ahold of *kimchi* on 116th Street. Sure, Columbia was filled with students from around the world. Along Broadway, there were a number of Chinese takeouts, as well as a few sushi bars. And if you really wanted to splurge, it wasn't hard to find all kinds of exotic food, from the candlelit Tibetan parlor on Riverside to the hole-in-the-wall Ethiopian takeout near the Law School building. Yet for Korean food you still had to travel down to 32nd Street. It was still the end of the eighties. The *kimchi* trend had not yet begun among students. It soon stopped mattering, though, because things changed almost overnight. First, when Damian happened in her life, she stopped craving anything except him. She would go wherever he suggested. She would skip food all day if that was what he wanted. Besides, they would not have dared entering 32nd Street together, for fear of bumping into anyone they knew. Then, later, with her parents' death, everything lost its color. On certain rainy days, she would wander into this corner of the city, wanting so much, wanting anything on the menu. She would experience such an immense hunger that she wouldn't know which dish to choose. It was as if she was looking to fill a certain longing, a certain desperation. Yet, by the time the food arrived, she no longer had any appetite. In fact, she could not bear the sudden rush of Korean flavors. It was impossible. It hit too close to home. It fell upon her like a sad awakening. Soon she just stopped coming.

But the soup tastes so good today, tangy, with lots of juice. It is a perfect soup for the cool weather, milky white and hot. The lumpy bits must be cartilage, rolling so smoothly on her tongue. She may still be the same girl after all, the one who would skip classes and hop on a subway all the way from 116th Street just for a bowl of soup and a plate of *kimchi*. She is so comforted by this thought that she almost forgets about the mean accountant, and the hushed tone of the caller who seemed afraid for her life. She is about to ask for another plate of *kimchi* when she notices the ad at the bottom of the *Korea Daily*'s front page. "The New Joy Fellowship Church," it reads. "Join us for the Thanksgiving Sermon at our God's House, the largest Korean church in New Jersey! Parking spaces available. Live Broadcasting on www.newjoyfellowship.org."

All Korean churches advertise. The competition is fierce. Sometimes a newspaper is sponsored by a specific church, like an allegiance to a political party. The prime missionary spots are restaurants and airports. At entrances to Korean restaurants, there are often boxes of sermon tapes provided by different churches. At the JFK's KAL lounge, it is not unusual to find Korean missionaries approaching those freshly arriving, like the zealous hostel-owners at tourist islands when the ship comes in. So the ad is nothing new, except that Suzy knows the church. Grace's church, where her parents' funeral was held. Suzy does not remember its being the largest Korean church in New Jersey. Surely it has grown in the last five years. Grace must have worked hard. All those Bible studies. All that hard-earned cash. A safety-deposit for heaven. Maybe someone there will know of Grace's whereabouts. Maybe Grace will even show up, if she has not gone too far away.

It is then that Suzy becomes aware of the face at the window, a young woman peering in as if trying to get a better look at her. She is more like a girl, in fact, twenty at most. A down coat with fur trim and a matching scarf. It is odd that so many Korean girls seem to dress the same. A crushed-velvet ponytail holder, the sure sign of an office girl. Finally, she breaks into an awkward smile and mumbles something. Then she seems to realize the absurdity of speaking through the window and moves toward the entrance.

"Hey, sorry about that," the young woman says, pointing upstairs with her eyes. "He's been like that for days."

Quickly swallowing her mouthful, Suzy stares back, realizing that the girl is Mr. Bae's assistant. Suzy feels compelled to say something, but she is embarrassed at how long it took for her to recognize the young woman.

"Good choice. *Sulongtang*. No other restaurant on this block throws in as much cartilage, and they even marinate their *kimchi* with fresh oysters. For *doganitang*, though, try the place across the street. Ask for ginseng between the knee bones. Costs more, but you won't get cold all winter."

The Asian youth these days are so confident, so full of life. She must be only about ten years younger than Suzy, yet there seems to be a gulf of generations separating the two. Suzy wonders if this girl considers herself 1.5 as well. Suzy has noticed fresh radiance among the NYU kids around her block. The Asian-American hip-hop kids. The petite girls in platform sneakers parading their dreadlocked boyfriends. The goateed boys in bandannas scooting around Tompkins Square Park. Being Asian is no longer embarrassing. Being Asian no longer suggests a high-school chess team. Being Asian might even be hip, trendy, cool.

"What if your boss sees you talking to me?" asks Suzy, cautiously.

"He's in a client meeting. Fuck him. He can't fire me anyway." The young woman plops down opposite her. She then waves at the waitress, raising her index finger to gesture one order of *sulongtang* for herself.

Something about her insolence reminds Suzy of Grace. Young Grace. Suzy feels a sudden rush of affection for the girl.

"Besides, I sort of followed you . . ." Then she blurts out, "By the way, what's up with those glasses?"

Earlier, leaving the apartment in a hurry after the strange phone call, Suzy threw on a pair of black sunglasses and some dark-red lipstick. A clumsy attempt to hide her face. She rarely wears lipstick, especially red. It came out of the last package Michael had sent her. Every possible Chanel beauty product wrapped in the newest Prada. Sandy's choice obviously, although for a second Suzy wondered if the gift might not have been intended for his wife instead. There was a matching nail polish, which she gave away to one of the stenographers on a job. It was silly to think that she would feel less conspicuous behind the shield of glasses and lipstick, but she did feel better as she tumbled onto the N train with the acute sense of someone following her. Apparently, she's kept the glasses on the whole time. No wonder people seemed to be staring at her. A woman alone sitting by the window, slurping soup while wearing dark glasses indoors.

"A hangover?"

Suzy nods, uncertain what to say.

"I can run to the pharmacy next door and get you a bottle of Bacchus. Or maybe they can fix up something even stronger. One shot of it, you'll feel as good as new," says the younger woman, who is now staring at Suzy with concerned eyes despite her tough-girl talk.

Suzy declines, finally taking the glasses off. Bacchus. It's been years since she's heard that name. A sort of miracle cure, like those tiger balms in Chinatown. Except Bacchus is a tiny-bottled drink, used mostly for hangovers or indigestion or anything to do with stomach troubles. Mom used to send Suzy to pick up a box of a dozen on mornings when Dad lay sick from *soju* the night before. Strange, the way Korean pharmacies just give out whatever they consider a cure. Prescriptions are never really an issue there. If you get sick, you just describe your symptoms to the pharmacist, who fixes up a concoction with whatever he has available behind the counter. It is a leftover habit from a Third World country, where prescription drugs were not carefully monitored. Although Korea has long since risen above its Third World status, the people never seem to have gotten over their easy access to antibiotics such as mycin, which, as Suzy recalls, Mom used for everything, from a common cold to a sore. The whole thing sounds dubious, even terrifying, but for Suzy it brings back yet another bit of her childhood. Illogical, yet sadly familiar.

"Hey, now that the glasses are gone, you look less like your sister." Leaning close, the young woman squints her eyes theatrically. "That's funny; if you really look, you don't look like her at all."

The spell of the good soup is over. Suzy asks instead, "So why did you follow me?"

"He was so nasty to you. I felt bad."

"To tell me that?"

"Also, I thought maybe you'd want to know that your sister's in some sort of trouble."

Suzy puts down her spoon.

"She called last week to liquidate her assets. Stocks, real estate, everything. Bae's furious, 'cause he's been playing the market and she pulled out all of a sudden. I don't understand why it's such a letdown, after she did away with all that cash just a month ago. I saw it coming. Between you and me, I smell drugs." The young woman lowers her voice, as if suddenly aware of the people at other tables.

Stocks. Real estate. Was there more money than Suzy knew about? Whose money is this? Her parents'? Has Grace been investing her inheritance? Suzy is not sure what to say, but the young woman makes it easy by talking constantly. She may be one of those people who talk in order to fill the silence.

"She was supposed to come by Monday to sign the papers, but she totally flaked out. Then I find out her phone's been disconnected," she says, shaking her head. "I don't think liquidation's a good idea right now."

Is Grace in some kind of debt? Is that why she has vanished? Selling off everything for cash is what people do when they are planning a drastic move—not a wedding. Last Friday, Grace called Detective Lester out of the blue. Later the same day, Grace showed up in Montauk looking for a boat. Then, on Sunday night, she called Ms. Goldman to say that she was getting married. On Monday, she failed to turn up at the accountant's. If Grace had planned to take the money and run off somewhere with her new husband, why did she not follow it through with the accountant? Was the wedding a sudden decision? What is it that Ms. Goldman said? *A secret from everyone, more like eloping, because they wanted to do it quietly, especially with her parents gone.*

"How much?" Suzy asks, reaching for the glass of water on the table.

"How much what?"

"How much a month ago?"

"A hundred grand. In one shot."

Something must have happened to Grace a month ago. Something changed. The guy. But he didn't sound as if he were in need of money.

"She won't sell the house, though. That, she won't touch."

"Which house?"

"Your parents' house, of course."

"*Grace never sold it?*"

"She won't even charge rent. Maria Sutpen lucked out. I need a friend like your sister!"

Maria Sutpen. Suzy has never heard of that name before, but, then again, she knows virtually nothing about Grace's life.

"Maria's totally useless for an emergency contact. I called like a hundred times this week, but she's never in. I got so frustrated that I almost went there myself. After all, the house is not too far from mine."

"You live in Woodside too?"

"No, in Jackson Heights. But it's just a couple of stops on the Number 7."

Jackson Heights. Woodside. The Queens neighborhoods where the Korean population makes up nearly 50 percent, where a woman named Maria Sutpen has taken over her parents' house.

"How long have you lived in Jackson Heights?"

"Since I was seven; why?" the young woman asks, glancing at the waitress who is heading over with a tray.

"No, nothing, it's just I've lived there too . . ." Suzy mumbles, studying the lipstick smudge on the rim of her glass. She lets a few minutes pass before asking, "So why are you telling me all this?"

" 'Cause I'm an only child, I guess." The young woman shrugs. "I don't get it when sisters don't talk to each other. I think that's like way twisted."

"So you thought to run down here and warn me about Grace's financial problems? So that I might track her down and convince her to keep Mr. Bae managing her money?" Suzy says quietly, meeting the other's eyes.

"No!" the young woman exclaims, her face turning bright pink.

"It's okay, nothing wrong with trying to help your father, or uncle, or whoever he might be for you. He seemed like he could use it," Suzy says with a smile. "Honestly, though, I have no idea where she is. And you're right, it's really twisted that she won't talk to me."

The younger woman looks sullen, pretending to be having difficulty splitting apart her wooden chopsticks.

"Listen, if you don't hear from her by Thanksgiving, call me," says Suzy, writing down her phone number on the girl's napkin.

Give it a few days, she thinks. If Grace turns up to sign the papers, then all must be fine. If she doesn't, Suzy will be notified. That is, unless Suzy finds Grace first. Then, rising from her seat, Suzy asks, "And one more thing, what's the name of that famous pool hall in Jackson Heights? Used to be a big deal in the eighties. Is it still around?"

The young woman looks up, befuddled. "You mean East Billiards on Roosevelt Avenue? Sure, they reopened a couple of years ago. Why? You play pool?"

16.

THERE IS NOTHING REMARKABLE about the brownstone at number 9. A two-story family home. The hexagonal living room protrudes with a fake-Victorian charm. Bright-pink lace hangs across each bay window. The only notable feature is the stoop. Seven steps in total, with newly painted railings. Shiny black layered with white stripes, like a zebra or a snake. It's not a house but a zoo. A miniature animal-farm, right here in the heart of Queens.

It's been half an hour. Late Friday afternoon. No one's home. The adults are at work; the children have gone out to play. This must be the high time for robbery. Where are those Asian gangs? They raid their own people, Detective Lester said. But no gang in sight, hardly anyone on the block. It is not such a terrible neighborhood. Not a bad corner on which to spend your final night.

The sky is turning charcoal gray now. The threat of an imminent shower. She has no umbrella, and it is really not appropriate to get soaked on a stranger's stoop. Her wait is numbered. It is good to have a limit. Otherwise, she might never walk away.

Across the street is a row of identical brownstones. She wonders if her parents knew any of the people there. Neighbors who saw them, who sat across the street while they ate, slept, worked. She wonders if any of them exchanged words on their final morning. Maybe someone's car was parked in their driveway as her father was pulling out. Maybe a jogger waved at her mother walking out the front door. Maybe a newspaper delivery boy on a bicycle saw the light on in her parents' bedroom and wondered who was getting up as early as he.

But no such evidence; it's been five years. When they finally closed on the house, Suzy was long gone. Their first house in America. Their first home. The only evidence of home, although she's never even seen it until now. From the outside, it appears no different from the countless apartments and brownstones in her childhood. A bit nicer, perhaps. A slightly better neighborhood. Woodside, not as bad as Jersey City or Jamaica. Never as bleak as the South Bronx, where her parents worked every day. Except the curtains are wrong. Mom would never have put up such pink frills across the window. Too happy. Too American. Maria Sutpen must be an all-American girl, one of the only whites on the block. A strange neighborhood for such a girl. A strange thing, to choose to be a minority. But, then again, a rent-free house does not come by every day. What does it mean that Grace just let her live here? What was their arrangement exactly? Has Grace always been so generous?

Grace never even let Suzy borrow her clothes when they were growing up. After all, they were only one year apart; it should have been natural for the sisters to share clothes. But Grace would not have it. She said that it creeped her out to see the same jacket, the same skirt on Suzy. Mom did not make it easier.

She would often buy the same clothes for both girls. The same V-neck sweater in different colors, the same Jordache jeans in different sizes. Everything seemed to have been found on a two-for-one sale rack. It never occurred to Suzy to make a fuss. In fact, she could not understand why Grace was so bothered. Sure, they resembled each other, in that general way siblings do, but Grace was the one everyone remembered. On Grace, even the drabbest Woolworth's finds turned into one-of-a-kind. It was like watching Cinderella at a touch of the wand, and Suzy would not have dared to try on her glass slippers. Yet it was Grace who marked her territory with vicious insistence. It was Grace who could not seem to bear the thought of being Suzy's other half. It was always Grace who pushed her away first. So Suzy was completely taken aback when Grace left her most of her wardrobe upon leaving for Smith. When Suzy asked why, she shrugged and said, "Doesn't matter anymore." Not an act of generosity, Suzy thought. The exact opposite. A silent declaration of the end of sisterhood. What Grace wanted was to leave everything behind, including her own clothes, including Suzy in those same clothes. Suzy is still not sure what made her retort so sharply, " 'Cause you're never coming back." Grace was in the middle of packing, the suitcase wide open on the floor. She stopped trying to fit the huge volume of the *American Heritage Dictionary* in between the set of writing pads and looked across at her with what Suzy thought was almost concern. The coldness was gone too. Finally, she said, as if in apology, "Not if I can help it."

Grace had not spoken to the family for a few months by then. Not since the incident. No, not that Keller boy with whom she had once been found naked in the back of his father's car. No, that had happened much earlier and was quickly forgotten once they moved away, soon after. Grace had come up with some story about having been forced by the boy, which Suzy suspected was a lie. The possibility that Grace might have been violated drew the matter to a taboo. It might even have secured Dad's trust, for he no longer seemed to suspect Grace. No, the real thing happened when they were living in Jackson Heights. Suzy never learned what actually triggered such an outburst of violence, but one night, Dad dragged Grace in through the front door, gripping her by the hair. Grace's hair reached down to her waist then; she often wore it in two long braids, like a mean version of Pocahontas, as some girls at school said. But that day, she must have worn it loose, because Suzy can still remember the black silk fluttering through the air as Dad took out the scissors and slashed through it. It had all happened so quickly that neither Suzy nor Mom could stop him. They simply backed against the wall and watched in horror. Grace did not even flinch. When she finally spoke, her voice carried such rage that Suzy felt suddenly afraid. Dad had begun shouting how she was ruining her life, to which Grace shot back, "But you've already made sure of that." Strangely enough, Dad said nothing in return; Mom looked away. Grace turned to leave when she caught her own reflection in the mirror. Her face was all red from Dad's burning hands. Her hair was cropped so close to her head, like a boy's. For a second, Suzy thought she glimpsed a glint of smile on her sister's face. It was a fleeting gesture. A flash of something akin to resignation. But a smile nonetheless.

It had to have been only one thing. Boys. Dad must have found Grace with one of her leather-clad boys. He must finally have stumbled upon the truth. He must have dragged her out of wherever with the fury of a father betrayed. On the surface, Grace had the markings of the perfect daughter. She had just been named the valedictorian. She was off to college on full

scholarship. Even Dad was left with not many grounds on
which to vent his anger. So he did one thing that defied all
words. He took away her hair. Her iridescently black, luscious,
seventeen-year-old hair.

Grace never sneaked out afterward. A point had been made,
it seemed. What that point was, Suzy never knew. Suzy never
asked what really happened that night. It is hard to fathom now
why she didn't. Ironically, Grace looked even more radiant with
her newly cropped hair. A girl monk. An odd transformation.
She would sometimes brush her fingers across her bare neck
while reading. She seemed freer somehow. She seemed ready
now to go out into the world. Dad had done her a favor. For
whatever it was worth, she managed to fool him until the end.

Later, when Suzy heard about Grace taking on the job as an
ESL teacher, she recalled the rage in Grace's voice on that night
many years ago. English as a second language. Fort Lee High
School, whose student body was over 30 percent Korean. Exactly what Dad would have despised. The pursuit of English.
The job of rescuing kids whose Korean language got them
nowhere. The mission of spreading English into all those newly
arrived Korean minds. Grace was still trekking their parents'
wishes, but in the opposite way, in the only way that would hurt
them. Only Suzy knew this, of course. Only Suzy could tell that
Grace was not okay. Only Suzy suspected that whatever Grace
sought in Jesus had nothing to do with God.

No one would have guessed that Grace would go off to a
New England college only to get hooked on the Bible. The
whole thing seemed strange, almost spiteful. Yet church was
what Grace chose, with shockingly fervent enthusiasm. Jesus
Christ—the impostor whom Dad had always rejected as the an-
tithesis of everything Korean, the source of what threatened to
destroy Korea's five-thousand-year-old history, the Western con-

spiracy to colonize Asia and its Buddha and Confucius. Grace
picked Jesus, while Suzy threw herself at Damian, the white
man, the older married man, the one she was not supposed to
love. But Suzy had assumed that Grace would be smarter. She
had always believed that Grace would be freer of their parents.

During one Christmas break, Grace came home and read the
Bible for four straight days. It was the first time Suzy had seen
her since they both went off to college. Suzy assumed that
Grace's Bible-reading was for a paper she had to write. After all,
Grace's major was religion. The only time Grace left the house
was to attend Christmas Eve services. Dad didn't mind, surprisingly. He even suggested that Suzy go as well. He said that, now
that they were both of age, college girls, a church was as good a
place as any for finding decent Korean boys. He believed that
most Koreans, like him, attended church for convenience, for
getting work tips or finding someone to marry. He told Mom to
iron the finest silk dresses for both girls, which were not only
too fancy but also inappropriate for December. But Grace
obliged without as much as a grumble. When they arrived at the
Union Pacific Church on Queens Boulevard, Grace reached over
and held Suzy's hand, which surprised Suzy. Through the entire
service, Grace sat staring elsewhere. She did not seem to be listening to the sermon or the chorus of hymns. Suzy noticed that
at one point, while the pastor was speaking, Grace ripped a page
from the Bible and folded it over the gum she was chewing. It
seemed almost purposeful, as if she wanted Suzy to witness her,
as if she wanted to tell Suzy something. Suzy could not take her
eyes off the Bible with the missing page, which Grace put back
neatly on the shelf as the service came to an end.

On the way home, Grace remained quiet. She looked sad,
Suzy thought. And thin. She had never looked thinner. Her eating habit must have gotten worse at Smith. With her bob that

came down half an inch below her ear, which accentuated her
sharp cheekbones, and her pale face even paler against her dark-
red lips, she looked intensely angular, and yet somehow haunt-
ingly elegant. Then, as they were nearing the house, Grace
turned to Suzy and said in a clear, bright voice, "One day, if you
find yourself alone, will you remember that I am too? Because
you and I, we're like twins."

That was it. Grace never opened up to her again. But for the
first time in years, they had held hands like sisters. Grace seemed
almost concerned for Suzy, almost afraid. What did she mean?
Why twins? Could that be why she hadn't been able to stand
Suzy all along? Because Suzy was the most exact reminder of
home? The next time she saw Grace was at the funeral, and it
was clear that nothing would ever bring them together again. Or
at least that was what Grace indicated.

Strange that all of this should come rushing right now, here
on the stoop of Maria Sutpen's house, the last place her parents
had called home. Still no Grace, no parents. So many afternoons, she had sat like this alone waiting for them. She would
be done with homework by then. She knew no one in the
neighborhood, always the new girl on the block. Sometimes she
wished that she were an avid reader like her sister. She wished
her parents would buy a new TV to replace the one with the
constant buzzing noise. Even the chores would be done in no
time. She was a master at rinsing rice. She'd learned how to vacuum the entire floor in less than ten minutes. Still no one came
home. It would be hours before anyone came home. She was
good at waiting. She was the obedient one. She stood and
watched as Grace's hair fell to the ground. She played mute
while Grace became the designated interpreter. She hid in a corner while Grace got thinner and thinner. She never even wandered off until later, much later, when she could no longer stay.

Looking around, she finds it odd that the block should be so empty, even for a Friday afternoon. The whole world seems to have disappeared to give her this time, to leave her just once more with her parents.

Five years, it has taken her five years to bring herself here. After the funeral, after their ashes were scattered across the Atlantic, Suzy kept imagining her parents' last home. But she could never picture them in such a cookie-cutter brownstone in Woodside. No Flushing, no Jersey City, never the Bronx. In her dream, she wanted to get them out of those immigrant neighborhoods. In her dream, she wanted to rewind their immigrant trekking. So she made up their pastel Montauk house. A shiny Jeep rather than the used Oldsmobile. Sunbathing and fishing instead of peeling-cutting-stocking fruit. TV before bed, like all other aging couples. *Nightline*, *Late Night*, the *Tonight Show*. Thanksgiving dinners. A game of Monopoly. For years, she has stayed away from this house. She has been afraid of shattering their last chance for life.

But a dream remains a dream always. Nothing alters the fact that she never got to see them again. She never held Mom's hands and asked why irises brought a smile to her face. She never let Dad explain what made him leave Korea, why he was so tortured by his old country. She never begged them for time, just a little more time to understand. She never told them that she had to run because she could not see ahead as long as they were there. She could not embrace this place called America while they never forgot to remind her what was not Korea. She could not make sense of her American college, American friends, American lovers, while her parents toiled away twelve hours a day, seven days a week at their Bronx store. She could not become American as long as she remained their daughter. *She betrayed them, so she might live.*

Rain on the brink.

Sky churning.

Empty, gray asphalt in its last light.

There is no such thing as a warning. No gentle first drop. When the rain comes, she crouches on the stoop, her arms hugging her bent knees, her hair now hanging below her waist.

the Graces

17.

"BABE, PICK UP."

Almost noon. She had lain awake most of the night. The rain must have gotten to her. She sure asked for it. Over an hour on that stoop, much of it under the threat of the storm. Maria Sutpen never even showed up. The girl at the accountant's office was right. For an emergency contact, Maria Sutpen was useless. Friday afternoon, silly to think that she would miraculously turn up just to greet Suzy.

"Suzy, pick up already, will you?"

"Hi, I was still in bed."

"You sound like hell. Apparently, you told Sandy to forget about the doctor."

Sandy called right after his phone call yesterday. She took down all the information and promised to get back to Suzy as soon as she finds out anything.

"Michael, I'm fine."

"*Christ*, Suzy, you never listen, do you."

She can hear the tone of disapproval. He does not like things to be out of control. He does not want Suzy sick in bed.

"I'm listening right now, aren't I?"

That puts a little spunk in his voice. "Then where the fuck were you yesterday? Sandy called you all afternoon and you never even picked up!"

"I was asleep. I was out cold." She does not want to get into it. She does not want to rehash the whole business of the anonymous phone call and the accountant on 32nd Street. The house in Woodside. None of it would mean a thing to Michael.

"*Hey*, I was worried sick yesterday."

These are the terms of their relationship. Contrived intimacy. Lots of it. The sort of things a man never says to his wife. The sort of things he can freely admit without sticking to the consequences.

"Well, don't you have other things to worry about over there? Where are you anyway? Frankfurt still?"

"Fucking Germans. Everything's such a goddamn secret. No one tells me a goddamn thing. They think all Americans are out to fleece them, which I might just do so fucking gladly."

Suzy smiles, comforted by Michael's familiar grunt. Suddenly everything seems a bit simpler, easier.

"I swear, babe, the minute they come begging, I'm outta here. The bag's all packed. The chauffeur's getting antsy."

"Then where to?"

"Why, you miss me?"

Typical. He ducks the question again. He never shares his itinerary beforehand. He lets her know where he is each time, but never before getting there.

"Does it matter?" She does miss him, but she won't say.

"Babe, you have no idea."

She is beginning to miss him more. It is all in her body. She must still be dreamy. "So what did Sandy have to say?" She changes the subject.

"Not good, I'm afraid." He is hesitant.

"She didn't find out?" A pang of disappointment. But it is hardly surprising. The INS, not the easiest place to crack.

"Believe me, she tried. Actually, it was some INS stringer who did. But the damnedest thing. It's all blank. Nothing comes up." Michael sounds unconvinced. "Yeah, you're a citizen all right. So were your parents, and your sister. But that's all there is. No past record of green cards or even visas. The guy said that it could be a case of special pardon or amnesty, or even NIW, which means National Interest Waiver, but that's usually for only serious professionals like scientists or academics—you know, the sort of gigs considered to be of 'national interest,' which I assume wasn't your parents' case. But that still doesn't explain why the file draws a blank. Whatever it is, it's all classified. Suzy, take my word, leave it alone."

That Park guy, he had it coming to him . . . He had friends in all sorts of places . . . I knew I didn't want to mess with him. I'd seen what happens to guys who stand up to him.

"Babe, you okay?"

No one is as sharp as Michael. He can estimate any situation to its *n*th degree and react accordingly. A born businessman. A gift. So entirely different from Damian.

"Hey, forget it. It's all in the past, useless."

But the past is all she has.

"Thanks anyway. I appreciate this."

"*Christ*, you sound like you don't even fucking know me."

When she puts the phone down, her first instinct is to grab her notepad to look up Kim Yong Su's phone number. But then she remembers that he did not have a phone number, only a pager, which never picked up. Besides, he is probably not at home right now. There was something in his testimony about working part-time on weekends. Moonlighting as a watchman at a fruit-and-vegetable store. The Hunts Point Market closes on weekends, and he needs the extra cash. She can feel the sudden aches coursing through her body. She puts her coat on, although she cannot remember where Kim claimed that he works on weekends. The Bronx, she vaguely recalls, near Yankee Stadium. That doesn't tell her much. There could be at least twenty Korean markets around there. Korean store-owners generally tend to know each other, especially if they compete in the same neighborhood. Maybe one of them would direct her to him. It would be crazy to roam the streets of the Bronx in this rain, in her state, when she is shivering even here in the warmth of her apartment.

Once outside, she immediately realizes that she has the wrong shoes on. The rain is mixed with something resembling hail. Pelting ice drops. The pavement is a mess, wet and slippery. Hardly anyone on the street, a rare thing on St. Marks Place. Gone are the usual brunch crowds who flock to the East Village on weekends. Some have skipped town altogether for an early Thanksgiving break. Some are holed up in their railroad flats with movies and takeout. Just two more blocks to the Astor Place subway stop. It is then that she remembers she meant to get a bottle of cold medicine. Benadryl, Sudafed, even echinacea, any of them will do.

So, instead of walking straight, she turns north on Second Avenue. There is a Korean market on the east side of the avenue. They sell fruits mostly, but, like all other Korean stores, they also carry almost everything, from candies to cashew nuts to condoms. The prematurely balding man behind the cash register always tries to speak Korean to her, but she never engages. She is not good at small talk, especially not with a stranger from whom she buys fruit almost daily. The storefront reveals a colorful display of clementines, cantaloupes, plums, strawberries, even cherries. New York is the Garden of Eden. Even in such November rain, most tropical fruits are all here, right on Second Avenue. She shuts her umbrella and picks up a few clementines before going inside, where the cashier stands grinning at her. He must have seen her entering in the surveillance mirror on the ceiling.

"*An-nyung-ha-sae-yo*," he greets, as if daring her to answer in Korean.

"Cold medicine, please, anything you think good is fine," Suzy says in English, hoping to discourage him.

"Anything?" he responds in Korean. He is extra-friendly today. Or he is bored, not many customers this afternoon.

"Anything," she repeats in English. Now that she is inside, she can feel cold sweat running down her back. The sure sign of a fever.

"This good?" He grins, handing her a bottle of echinacea. Of course, the East Village's first choice. No one believes in synthetic drugs anymore. She is about to take out her wallet when she notices that the man is still grinning.

"Boyfriend?" As he leans forward, the bald spot on his head catches the ray of the lightbulb.

"Excuse me?" The man's a real pain, she thinks.

"That guy out there, he your boyfriend?" He points his index finger toward the door. Suzy turns, catching a glimpse of someone dashing off.

The clementines tumble to the floor as Suzy runs outside. She looks frantically in both directions, and spots the man under a black umbrella, walking briskly. From the back, he appears to be dragging his right foot slightly, or maybe the ground is so slippery that he is having difficulty running. Even as he crosses First Avenue to head toward Avenue A, he never looks back.

Suzy keeps up at a ten-pace distance, knowing that he will have to stop soon. Ninth Street comes to a dead end at Avenue A, where Tompkins Square Park takes up three blocks in both directions. When he reaches the park, he halts for a few seconds, as if he cannot decide which way to continue. He can either make a ninety-degree turn onto Avenue A or go straight into the park, which is empty except for a few homeless men who've made puddly shelters on benches barely shielded under tentlike coverings.

He quickly enters the tiny fenced-in area between a dog run and a basketball court. He may have decided to give up the charade. He may be planning his next move. From behind, the man is nothing but a collage of a black umbrella and a black raincoat. For a second, she wonders if she is following the right man after all. Maybe the real guy disappeared in a different direction. Maybe he ducked into a cab that had been waiting. Maybe he dodged into the diner next door and watched her follow another man. Anything is possible, as she circles the park for the fourth time, waiting for the guy to make his move.

Suzy is now wondering if she should catch up to him after all. It does not look like he will do anything other than amble through the park. She must be trailing the wrong man. Maybe he's just one of those aimless people who like to meander in parks on rainy Saturdays. As she is contemplating what to do next, he suddenly takes the St. Marks Place exit back at Avenue A. He's decided to leave, obviously, for reasons she cannot tell. He trots along, back toward Second Avenue. The rain is fiercer. She is getting drenched. The umbrella is definitely not strong enough; its spokes keep flipping in whichever direction the wind blows. Already a few of the spines have broken loose, one of them dangling before her eyes at a precarious angle. She might just as well throw it out and take the rain as it comes. Now, suddenly, there are more people on the street. A crowd sweeps past her, which must've poured out of the monstrous Sony Cineplex nearby, or the New Village Theater, where a certain British troupe has been recycling the same sellout number for the past five years. But do shows run this early? Is this the matinee crowd? Then she realizes that it is suddenly impossible to tell which black umbrella belongs to the man. In a mere second, he seems to have gone missing amidst the dancing umbrellas before her eyes. All the strength in her body gives at once, and she is not sure where to turn, what comes next. She knows only how bitterly cold she is suddenly, how wet her clothes are. She is no longer holding the umbrella. What did she do with it? Did it fly off with the wind? She has begun looking around frantically, when something bright and yellow flashes right under her eyes.

It is a flyer, on yellow paper. A club invite. Around here, on weekends, it is not unusual to find kids on street corners passing out flyers. But not now, not in such rain, not when she has just lost someone who's been following her for days. She is about to crinkle it up when a phrase catches her eyes. "HOTTEST PARTY OF THE MILLENIUM"—and underneath it, "COME THIS SATURDAY NOVEMBER 18, D WAVE D RAVE DJ SPOOKY & HIS FRIENDS!!!!!"

It is "DJ" that stops her heart.

DJ. The fourth member of the Fearsome Four. The missing KK. The orphan. The name has stuck with her from the first time she heard it. For no reason, really. It is not even his real name.

Instead of trudging through the rain, she runs for the underground hole less than a block away. She knows exactly where to go. She is almost elated at this sudden direction. And the man she just lost in the rain? Let him catch up with her if he wants to play real hide-and-seek.

18.

BOLTED ACROSS THE TOP WINDOWS of the three-story building is the dilapidated electric sign for EAST BILLIARDS, trimmed
with blinking red lights. A couple of bulbs are broken; the line is
not as smooth as it should be. The floor below is dark, blinds
drawn, no sign of life. On the ground floor, three stores are
jammed together. A Korean market. A nail salon. Santos Pizza,
the third one is called, and Suzy wonders if Santos is as common
a name as Kim.

The rain has not eased. Her clothes are soaked through. The
forty-minute ride here has only made it worse. She can feel the
chill in the core of every bone. She should have grabbed that
bottle of echinacea. She ran out so fast that the bottle just fell
from her hands, along with the clementines. And the gaping
face of the man behind the cash register—probably the last time
he would smile at her.

Climbing the stairs, she is surprised at how quiet it is. Not a
peek coming from the pool hall above. But, then, she has never

been to a pool hall before. Too decadent, where bad kids congregate and dropouts make trouble. What would Dad have said if he saw her here? And Damian? At least they had that in common, she thinks, quickly averting her eyes from the genitalia-shaped graffiti on the cement wall. When she reaches the third floor and opens the door, she finds a spacious room filled with pool tables. Some with solids and stripes dotting their green tops, and others sitting wide and empty. It is dark inside, the only light belonging to the foggy windows, through which the sky is barely visible.

"Hello?" Her voice rings loud, making an echo. Nothing. No one around. "Hello? Anybody here?" she calls out again. Strange, Saturday should be their busiest day. Maybe it is too early. Maybe they don't open until late afternoon, like some restaurants. But, then, why isn't the door locked? "Hello?" Suzy tries once more. No one still. Not much to see. A rickety soda machine by the entrance. A jukebox to its right that's seen better days. A couple of Budweiser cans on the floor, which no one seems to have bothered to pick up. Farther in the distance is a partition; must be an office of sorts.

She is not sure what she expected. What is it that keeps tugging at her? When Detective Lester mentioned the Flushing pool hall where the drugs were found, Suzy remembered another pool hall, in Jackson Heights, which had been a notorious hangout in the mid-eighties. There were always rumors surrounding it, with gory details of gang rapes and drug deals gone sour. Everyone in her high school had heard of it. The kids whispered its name with awe and fear. The KK had still been active then, along with several other minor gangs whose names Suzy cannot remember now. Back then, it was just a rumor. It belonged to the underground world of the underground kids whose lives would never touch hers. That is, until now.

She is turning to leave when she is stopped by a sound behind the partition. "Hello?" she tries again, to no avail. Yet those rustling steps, an unmistakable murmur. Maybe there is more than one person there. Maybe they are in the middle of an important conversation and do not want to be interrupted. Suzy is tempted to turn around and walk out, but then she remembers the rain outside and hesitates. Besides, she is curious. Why wouldn't the person answer her four hellos? What's he doing there behind the wall? From the doorway to the cubicle is about fifty steps. Five rows of pool tables, two in each row, ten total. It is not such a great distance.

When she finally makes her way across the room and stands before the partition, she can hear a sort of humming from the other side. A staccato rumble, oddly youthful and cheery. She knocks before peering in, although the attempt is superfluous. Rocking in the armchair is a young man, with his feet up on the desk. His eyes are shut, his head bobbing to the Discman whose volume is high enough so that she can even make out the lyric. Some kind of rap. Hip-hop, he would insist. Obviously, calling out to him is useless, but she is uneasy about tapping him on the arm. She is standing there mulling over what to do next when, as if in a miracle, he opens his eyes and jumps out of his seat.

"Holy shit! You scared the shit out of me!" the young man screams, peeling the headset off his ears.

"I'm so sorry. I called you a couple of times, but you didn't hear me." Suzy panics as he flinches from her. "I really didn't mean to scare you."

"Fucking hell you didn't; what the hell were you doing creeping up on me like that!"

"I was just . . . I didn't know how to get your attention."

"Yo, let's forget it." His face is turning red, as though he is embarrassed at getting so easily frightened. Then he reaches for the can of Coke on the desk and gulps it down, struck by sudden thirst. "Don't tell my old man. He'll whack me if he finds out I wasn't minding the door."

"It's a deal, my lips are sealed," she says in a conspiring whisper. His father must be the owner. Family business, not unusual.

"So what do you want? A table?" he says, looking her over once, not without a hint of amusement. He is barely twenty. Boys of his age, they have just one thing on their minds. Even when the woman is old enough to be their aunt.

"Are you open? Looks pretty dead to me," she says, surveying the empty room.

"Sure, we're open. I just haven't bothered turning on all the lights yet. Too early, and no one's here these days anyway. Why waste electricity?" He shrugs, strutting over to the wall to flick the switch. In an instant, the room turns fluorescent.

"Why no one these days?" Suzy asks, squinting her eyes as the white balls beam under sudden artificial bliss.

"Some trouble out in Flushing; the guys're laying low," he says, clicking the "Stop" button on his Discman.

"Can't be good for business?"

"We're used to it. It happens once in a while. Everyone crawls back sooner or later. This time, the deal's bigger, so it's taking longer," he says with a purposeful toss of his hair, which is moussed into a ball of stiff spikes.

"How long has your father owned the place?" she asks cautiously.

"What's up with twenty questions? What're you, a cop or something?" he fires back, then stares hard at her for a minute or two before shaking his head. "Nope, you're not a cop."

"How can you tell?" She asks, half amused.

"Too fine to be one," he says with a wink. "Lady cops are butt-ugly. No Charlie's Angels around here. So you're not one, not a chance. So why twenty questions?" The boy is sharp, doesn't miss a thing. He knows how to use a compliment to get what he wants.

"I used to live around here, long time ago. Went to Astoria High for a while, and then Lincoln High, over on Queens Boulevard." She wants him to know he can trust her. No funny business.

"Fucking hell, Lincoln High? I went there too! Well, didn't quite graduate, but still . . . when did you go there?" the boy asks with a wide grin, as though he now considers her okay.

"You were just a kid."

"No way, you don't look much older than me." He smiles slyly.

"I'm ancient; I was around when the KK was around." She takes the risk.

"That's *old*," he exclaims, teasingly.

"Told you!" Glancing at the room, she says, "Those guys, do they come around still?"

"Who? The KK?"

"Yeah. I know it's been too long, but I was in the neighborhood and thought it'd be nice to see an old face or two," she says, running her index finger along the edge of the table. It is easy to believe this. The familiar place of her youth. The friends long gone. Nostalgia is a powerful thing, even when made up.

"Not really, especially not since Flushing. The trail's still hot. No one wants to get mixed up with a drug mess, you know. The cops are jumping on any Korean kids with a record, which is just about everyone who hangs out here." He chuckles. "Even the room salon downstairs is slow these days. Mina's bumming, she only took over the place not so long ago. Fucking hell, all those booties pining away."

"Room salon?" A call-girl joint. The sort of establishment where hostesses sit around with clients and pour drinks. But "hostess" is really a code word for a prostitute. Implicit in the exorbitant entrance fee are girls as part of the deal.

" 'Seven Stars,' right downstairs, didn't you see it coming up? I guess it's kinda easy to miss, they try to keep a low profile."

"Seven Stars?"

"Don't you remember?" the boy asks incredulously. "Used to be a major KK hangout, long before my old man's time here."

Seven Stars. Why does that sound familiar?

"So you here for old times' sake? Why, the rain get to you?" he asks, as if noticing her wet clothes for the first time.

"The rain, yeah . . ." And the yellow flyer, she remembers, yes, the flyer. "Have you heard of a guy named DJ?" A long shot; the boy's too young.

"DJ? What does he look like?"

Of course she has no idea. An orphan. The last one of the Fearsome Four. The one deported to Korea five years ago, the same month as her parents' murder.

"Doesn't matter, I guess. He got deported."

"Deported? That's fucked up. Fuck those INS assholes!" he says, shaking his head.

Whatever happened, happened too long ago. Whatever evidence has long been erased.

"So where's your father?" Suzy asks, walking to the door.

"A dumb fight, a couple of weeks ago. He should've known better than trying to break up those punks," he answers with feigned indifference. "He got shot."

Suzy pauses, turning around.

"Yo, it's no big deal. He's not dead or anything, besides, he's got me." The boy puts on a tough voice, suddenly looking even younger than his baby face.

It is not until she is halfway down the stairs that she notices the silver dots engraved on the metal door on the second floor. Seven tiny stars in the shape of a loop. A logo. No letters next to it. No explanation. Just a plain circular arrangement of seven stars. She tries the intercom, a neon-green button to the right of the door frame. No answer. Not surprising. If it's too early for a pool hall, definitely sleeptime for a bar. The door will not budge. The video camera glares down like a hawk, patrolling from a corner of the ceiling. The security system is no joke. With the sort of guys who frequent here, everything would have to be bulletproof.

A loop of seven stars. Common enough, not particularly memorable. Yet Suzy is sure she has seen it before. *But where?*

She lingers for a while. The staircase is mute, fully cemented, and dim. Not much use standing here. She makes her way down the steps slowly, hoping that someone will emerge. She keeps looking back at the door, but no one is there. Then she is outside again. Out in the torrential rain.

No umbrella. She is about to run into the Korean market to get one when she notices the warm glow from Santos Pizza. It is inviting, this pizzeria in deepest Queens, right below the pool hall. Like a candlelit cottage in a fairy tale, made of cakes. She could be one of the lost siblings, Hansel or Gretel, following the bread crumbs through the haunted forest.

Inside are a couple of empty booths, and a sleepy man in red and white stripes, kneading the dough. He hardly reacts when he sees her. Maybe he can tell that she does not really want pizza. Maybe he is afraid of the abyss of wanting in her eyes. Maybe she is not the first of the lost children to end up here.

"Coffee, please."

"That's it?" he asks grumpily, as if saying, "Hey lady, this ain't a café, you order pizza at a pizzeria."

"And a slice," she adds, to appease him.

He makes no response, cutting a slab from the congealed pie on the table and flinging it into the oven with hardly a glance.

When the slice finally comes back out, nothing about it signals magic. Drippy yellow on an extra-thick crust. The cottage in the forest was a phantom. No wicked witch. Not a single crumb.

The mushy cheese tastes like fat, a lukewarm chunk, moist and chewy. It instantly turns her stomach, and she washes it down with a sip of coffee, which is so hot that it burns her tongue. She puts down the cup and glances out the window instead. The rain does not seem too bad now, at least more promising than the rancid-fat smell. As she is about to get up, she notices a car pulling up outside. A BMW, too fancy for this neighborhood. From the door on the driver's side, a woman pops out and runs in with her hand on her forehead, covering her face from the rain.

A whiff of candy-sick perfume. The flaring red raincoat gleams too shiny against her yellowed skin. Her copper curls look burnt, in need of a fresh dye job or a perm. With her chapped lips and blotted mascara, she seems to have just rolled out of bed. Someone else's bed, most likely.

The sleepy man, though, perks up. "*Ciao, bellissima,*" he greets her with a wide grin.

The woman blows him a kiss, brushing her coat noisily, shaking the water out. "Hey handsome, did you miss me?" she says with a wink.

All gooey now, he asks, "What you doing here so early, Mina?"

"Johnny hasn't come by, has he?" she asks.

The man doesn't look happy when he answers, "Still no news?"

The woman shrugs, glancing at Suzy, as if suddenly aware of her gaze. Suzy quickly looks away.

Mina, the new owner of Seven Stars.

Perched on a stool by the counter, chatting with the no-longer-sleepy man, the woman tackles her pizza and Coke with much gusto. Suzy remains in her booth, trying to listen to their conversation, which is oddly muffled now. Suzy cannot make out anything except the occasional giggle and something about the lack of customers. Then, suddenly, the woman rises, blowing another kiss at her fan behind the counter. Suzy also rises, quickly trashing her pizza. Rather than hopping back in the car, the woman dashes next door. Suzy follows, only to be ambushed by her waiting inside.

"What's the idea?" Mina hollers huskily, squinting as though she forgot to put her contact lenses on this morning.

Suzy is not sure what to say. She has no business following this woman. She can play innocent and keep on walking, or she can make up something, anything that may open doors. Doors to what, though? What is she looking for, why is she here?

Say something about the KK—a voice in her head. *Be an insider.*

"Those guys . . . Have you heard anything new?"

Glaring at Suzy, Mina asks sharply, "Who are you?" Then she adds, almost as an afterthought, "I don't know what you're talking about."

"I've been told to come here for the scoop." Suzy comes up with the first thing that sounds plausible.

"Who told you that?" Mina asks suspiciously.

Recalling one of the names Detective Lester mentioned, Suzy takes a chance. "My man's in trouble . . . Maddog."

"You're Maddog's girl?" Mina then steps back a little, contemplating Suzy in her plain dark coat, black scarf, and matching hat. Her eyes pore over Suzy's face, free of makeup except a touch of rosy lip gloss, most of which has faded by now. It is obvious that Suzy does not belong here. Women like Suzy do not belong to a gangster named Maddog. Finally, Mina snaps, "I've never seen you before."

"I've never seen *you* either," Suzy retorts with purposeful terseness. It works. Mina looks stumped and says uncertainly,

"What's come over Maddog? He likes his girls with a bit more meat on their bones."

"He likes me fine," Suzy says with what she hopes is the right tone of arrogance.

"I don't know who told you to come here," says Mina, shaking her head. "Johnny's got nothing to do with it. Tell Maddog it's not Johnny."

So there must have been some sort of infighting. According to Detective Lester, the AOCTF busted the gang on an anonymous tip. It seems that Maddog believes a guy named Johnny was involved.

"Girl, it's none of my business." She clicks her tongue with a pitying look at Suzy. "But if I were you, I'd wash my hands now. Maddog's a goner." She begins climbing up the steps, then halts suddenly and turns around, leaning closer. Suzy moves away instinctively. Something about the woman's sallow skin makes her cringe, as though its secret is contagious. Scrunching up her face, Mina says slowly, "Wait a minute. I'll be damned."

Suzy stands still, her heart thumping.

A long, cool gaze. Mina cocks her head, muttering to herself, "No . . . she wouldn't dare." Scanning Suzy's face once more, she whispers, "It's not Mariana who sent you, is it?"

"Hey, I told you I'm here for my man . . ." Suzy is about to protest when she remembers.

Mariana.

Grace's code name for marijuana.

May I be excused? I promised my friend Mariana that we'll do our homework together.

"Who's this Mariana?" Suzy stammers. "Maybe . . . I know her."

Mina purses her lips, as if in distaste, and spits out, "Boy-killer, we all called her. She used to hang out here back in the old days."

Suzy tries to keep her composure, to stop herself from lunging at this woman with questions. This aging call girl in blinding red. Suzy swallows hard before asking, "And this Mariana—how old was she?" A faint voice, feeble almost.

"Not the legal age, if that's what you're asking," Mina says derisively. "A schoolgirl gone wild. She thought she was something special 'cause she only screwed big shots. That was her thing, she chose her own guys, no money was ever good enough. Johnny should've ditched her when her father took her away."

"Her father?" Suzy repeats, feeling the height of the stairs suddenly.

"I'm sure she put on the whole show just to get caught." Mina rolls her eyes.

"Her father . . . came here?"

"You sure you're Maddog's girl?" Mina says, studying Suzy with a puzzled smile. "Listen, I don't care who you are, but if you see Mariana, tell her to leave Johnny alone." Then, fixing Suzy with a nearly pleading look, she adds, "He's no KK's bell-boy. Those days are over."

"Johnny, was he her lover?"

"Lover?" she retorts with a sneering laugh. "More like a chauffeur, the way she always made him drive her home so early. She never gave him the time of the day."

"Because?"

"Because she was a bitch," Mina blurts out bitterly. "If it hadn't been for her, he would've never crossed Maddog all those years ago and . . ." She pauses, as if trying to shake off her anger. "Doesn't matter, 'cause he's come back to be with me now. He won't crawl back to her," she mumbles unconvincingly. "Definitely a changed man."

May I be excused? I promised my friend Mariana that we'll do our homework together.

The girl who used to hang out at the KK's bar.

The troubled one who couldn't wait to get caught by her father.

The boykiller face who slept with the gang for money, and yet picked her own guys.

"Look, I don't want you coming around here again." Mina suddenly lowers her voice, her eyes darting nervously, as though she is afraid that Johnny may show up any minute. She seems to ponder something for a few seconds, then says, "If you run into her, tell her to deal with me instead," quickly scribbling a pager number on a piece of paper and handing it to Suzy. She adds in a softer tone, "Girl, about your Maddog, forget it. Do yourself a favor, get yourself a new man."

The cold sweat running down her back is an icy shock. Suzy becomes aware that her body is trembling. Leaning her right arm against the wall, she tilts her face a little, as though burrowing under a shadow. "And this Mariana—she looked like me?"

A wry smile crinkling the corner of her mouth, Mina repeats, "Weird, the more I look at you, the more you remind me of her." Then she adds, as if in vengeance, "Really, you could be the same girl."

19.

THE HAND ON HER RIGHT SHOULDER is a gentle one. Must be Mom, or Dad finally home. She must have fallen asleep at the doorstep. She must have forgotten her key, and school must have let out early, and Grace must have sneaked out again. So she must have sat here and waited with her homework spread out, and still, when the homework was done, still no one came home, and she must have lain down for a while thinking she was hungry and it was getting darker and the draft from the hallway window sharper, and she was afraid that no one would remember, that no one would find her here, and then sleep must have overtaken her, taken her breath away to an even darker place, where she saw the seven stars in a circle like the misshapen Big Dipper that came loose to join hands to finally surround her, who lay weeping because she remembered where she had seen them before.

But neither Mom nor Dad. Can't be, they've been shot. They

will never come home again. When Suzy opens her eyes, her face still wet with tears, it is Mr. Kim stooping over her.

"I tried to wake you, but you were crying in your sleep," he says.

"Oh," she mutters, blinking slowly.

"How long have you been waiting?" he asks, turning the key in the door lock.

"I don't know, what time is it?" she says, making a feeble attempt to get up; the ground beneath feels strangely muddy.

"Six-thirty," he says, glancing at his watch. "You're lucky I'm home early today."

Following him inside, she recognizes the bareness. The white walls. The single sofa. The single bed. The familiar absence.

"I've got nothing here. I can heat up some water, or maybe *boricha*?" he says, putting a kettle on the stove.

Her body feels numb from the cold concrete corridor. The sleep was a blackout, leaving her spent, hollow, confused. "*Boricha*," she answers. My favorite, she is about to add, and then realizes that it's been years since she had it last. Mom used to keep it refrigerated and serve it instead of water. But it had never tasted like water. It was light brown. It smelled of corn, like an autumn harvest. She seems to have forgotten about it one day. Odd how that happens. You swear by certain things— that particular sundress he first saw you in, or that rose lipstick you wore every day, or that barley tea you once declared you couldn't live without. But then, one day, someone, perhaps a stranger, in a bare, bleak apartment far from home, asks, without a hint of history, "Water or *boricha*?," and you suddenly remember that it's been years since you've even thought of it. But how is that possible? How is it that you could go on fine without what had once been so essential, that you haven't even been aware of its absence? How is it then you could declare, without hesitation, that it is your favorite? Shouldn't love require more? Isn't love a responsibility?

"It'll warm you up," he says, taking a mug from the shelf. Suzy realizes how fatigued she feels, and how cold. For hours, she wandered through the streets of Queens. For hours, she could not get rid of the one thought circling in her head—her parents. What did they do to bring on such hatred? And then there was a girl named Mariana.

"Someone's been following me," she says, surprised that she is telling him.

"Have you told the police?" His eyes are on the kettle, which is taking a long time to boil.

"No," she says, leaning on the cushion, glancing at the ashtray on the table. It is filled to the brim. The butts are smoked to their last skin. The sofa faces the opposite direction from the kitchenette. She cannot see him when she says, "I don't think many people are too upset that my parents are dead, including the police."

Finally, a hissing noise.

"I'm not interested in your parents' death," he says.

Now a shrill from the kettle, but he won't turn it off, as though he is grateful for its shield.

She waits. The final pitch of the boiling water, but she is patient. It's been a long day. It's been a long, long five years.

When he stands before her with a cup of *boricha*, which he promptly puts on the table, he says nothing. He merely sits opposite her, waiting for her to finish. After tea, you may go. He does not have to say it. She knows she is not welcome. He is doing her a favor. A sobbing girl, frozen out of her mind, who can turn her out?

"Someone's been sending me a bouquet of irises, someone's been hanging up on the phone, someone's even called with a threat," she says, holding the mug between her cold palms. "What do you think it all means?"

He lights a cigarette. His hands are restless. A chain-smoker.

"The murderer wants to be found," she says, taking a sip. The tea is instantly familiar, clean and hot as it rolls down her throat. "Not by Detective Lester, but by me."

He won't meet her eyes. He does not want any part of this conversation. The furrows between his eyebrows grow deeper as he inhales harder.

"You told me last time that having children didn't really save my parents. You're right, it didn't." Suzy takes a deep breath before continuing. "I need to know why they couldn't be saved, what it is that they did to you. I guess I'm asking you to tell me before you tell the police, because the police will come sooner or later."

He takes a long drag, longer than necessary. "Is that a threat?"

"No, a plea . . . because I think you understand what it means to try living while circling death again and again," she says quietly, glancing at the photo of his wife, the dead woman guarding his bedside.

The frigid stillness, except for the clock ticking nearby. Her hands around the mug tighten, as though their hold steadies her. When he finally meets her eyes, she lets out a sigh, realizing that she has been holding her breath.

"Your father had enemies. Many, in fact. 'Enemies' might not be the right word. People who held deep grudges against him, let's say. I was one of them. So I can't blame you if you were to discredit everything I say. The ones who know the truth are both dead. So who's to argue over what really happened? . . ." He pauses, his eyes wavering between her face and the rest of the room. He seems to be trying to find the right words, the right place to begin. His face clouds with something indefinite, something akin to resignation.

"When we met your father, we were working at a store on Tremont Avenue. My wife was at the cash register. I was doing the setup work around the store. We were both too old for the job, but we tried to make up for it by working hard, getting the freshest produce, opening the store before anyone else. One day the owner called me in. He was moving back to Korea. He offered me the store at a bargain. I'd saved some money by then, not a whole lot, but enough for a down payment. There was just one problem. We were both still illegal, my wife and I. We had no green cards, and definitely no right to own anything. That's where your father came in."

She recognizes the accent in his Korean from his deposition. Each syllable drags into the next without any inflection. It is kind to the ears. From central Korea, where people speak slowly in a quiet murmur. She was told that its land borders no water, anomalous on a peninsula. The only province kept hidden in the hills. The people there must be full of longing, searching the sky for a glimpse of blue. Their gentleness might belie what is unrequited, and perhaps broken.

"He'd done deliveries for us in the past. My wife remembered how he'd wanted to buy a store but didn't have enough cash. He had once offered to invest some money for renovation in exchange for a part ownership. So we sought out your father, made a partner deal, put his name on the lease."

Who would do that? Why would they trust a stranger? How would they know that he wouldn't put the store under his name and run away with it? But Suzy also knows that the world of immigrants has its own rules. Every man is guide to every other man. They don't speak English, or read English. They don't know the American laws. They might even break them without knowing. They are forever guilty before the customers, the policemen, the inspectors, the district attorneys, the IRS agents, the INS agents. Sure, America is the land of opportunity, and yet they wouldn't recognize an opportunity even if it is waved in front of them. Only another immigrant can show them, in their language, in ways they can understand. A fellow countryman who might understand America better, who might be less afraid, who might be legal.

"Soon his wife joined us. Your mother. She wasn't much of a talker. I hold no grudge against your mother. I only say that because I do believe that, deep inside, she was good. I saw her smile once, a real full smile. She was looking at a truck passing by. When I asked her what she was smiling at, she blushed and said there was a load of irises in the back of the truck, and the irises brought back some old memories. I never saw that smile again. Maybe it was too late by then. She seemed tired of life. Numb. 'Dead inside,' is what my wife said. She always did what was required of her. She wouldn't work too hard or too little. She just did her duty with a minimum of fuss. She never talked back to your father. He'd sometimes call her names, bad insulting names in front of me and my wife. They were both well into their forties. It really wasn't right to do that."

What Suzy experiences is dread. The absolute dread of what is to come. It will only get worse, she thinks. *This is not a good story. This is what I have come for.*

"The business began to pick up after the renovation, although your father put down only a fraction of the money he'd promised. He also stopped doing the delivery work and hired someone instead. He was now practically running the whole store. Both our wives were behind the cash registers, since your father installed a second one for the night shift. I told him it was a bad idea. It'd only exhaust everyone. Seven days a week is one thing, but twenty-four hours? A couple of nights later, he called

to say that our partnership wasn't working, exactly what I'd been
thinking, and that it'd be better if my wife and I were to stop
showing up. I was flabbergasted. I thought he must've gone insane. It was my store, I mean our store, although he hadn't ful-
filled his end of the deal. What did he mean, stop showing up at
my own store! That's when he laid it on me—'I could get you
deported within twenty-four hours.' "

Sometimes the answer is there even before you are told. You
may have suspected it all along. It has only been a matter of
time.

"My wife overheard. She snatched the phone and started
yelling. She told him he was a traitor, the lowest of the low. I'd
never seen her lose control like that. All that work, those sleepless
hours behind the register hadn't been kind to her. She was tired,
the way your mother had been tired. My wife still had some fire
left in her. She wanted to fight out the battle. She didn't want to
give up. Your father threatened to report us if we showed up at
the store just once more, but we ran there anyway. It's so long ago
now, but still so vivid. The ugliest, the saddest day of my life."
He takes another cigarette out of the pack. His fingers on the
lighter are unsteady. It takes him a couple of tries to get a flame.
He can only keep his eyes on the cigarette. Anywhere else will be
her face, the girl's face, which is too reminiscent.

"Your father called the INS right in front of us. He reported
us while we stood there in our own house. It was like he'd done
it before. He knew the number right off the top of his head. He
didn't even raise his voice. He looked calm through the whole
thing. I saw your mother weeping in the corner. She was silent,
even in crying. She didn't want him to hear her cry."

The informers.

No record of green cards or visa.

How many people did her parents sacrifice to obtain their
citizenship? How many did they turn in for rewards?

Suzy never questioned why they moved each year. She did not think it odd when they could suddenly afford two bedrooms. She never thought twice when her parents bought a store, a house. She believed that it was the result of their hard work. But hard work, did it really pay off for all immigrants? Reporting an illegal immigrant is a vicious act, an immoral act. No immigrant can do it to another, knowing the fear, the absolutely mind-numbing fright, that a mere mention of the INS brings to those whose underground existence in the forgotten patches of Lefrak City is a source of a collective paranoia. Could her parents have been capable of such a betrayal? Was it out of greed? Could greed be enough motivation for turning on their own people? Why is Suzy not surprised?

"We ran. We shoved our bags into a car and drove to the first place we could think of that was far away. We ended up hiding out at a church member's house on Long Island. That's where my wife fell ill. All that fire inside of her suddenly went out. She kept blaming herself for what happened, for trusting your father. She kept saying that she was useless, that she was a burden to me, and that she was too old to start over. A few weeks later, while I was out looking for work, she took a whole bottle of sleeping pills. She was dead before we even reached the hospital. I buried her out there, in a town we'd never been to before. She was only forty-eight." His voice is small and strained. He is relieved that his story is almost over. "She left me a note, begging me to go back to Korea. But I'm still here, and the only thing I have to show for the past thirteen years is this wretched age, and burying my wife, who wasn't old enough to die. But how could I go back to Korea? Who would look after her? Who would lie beside her out on Long Island?"

From the minute Suzy set foot in this dark, desiccated corner, she might have known that it was her parents who drove him here, who called her here, who wanted her to hear everything, who are now asking her to make judgment on their lives, which, she is finally convinced, could not have been saved.

The tea is tepid. The barley flakes have sunken to the bottom. *Boricha.* It may be years before she tastes it again. Will she like it still? Will she then recall this room, where a dejected man has finally revealed to her what might have been at the root of her parents' murder?

"But I had nothing to do with your parents' death," he says quietly. "That wouldn't have brought my wife back."

What about others? He mentioned that there were many with grudges against her parents. None of them could have gone to the police. How could they? Illegal immigrants, the cheapest target before the law. If her parents had stolen this man's store right under his eyes and driven his wife to suicide, what else had they been capable of? Could her parents have confided to the police as well? Could they have traded information for some sort of protection?

Even Suzy knew that many Korean fruit-and-vegetable stores crumbled in the early nineties. Especially after the Los Angeles riots of '92, relations between Koreans and blacks were at their worst. Over eight hundred Korean stores were destroyed in South Central. Many were torched in Flatbush and Bedford-Stuyvesant. Back then, it was not unusual to find a circle of picketers outside a Korean market, which inevitably drove a store out of business. It was also around then that the Labor Department began cracking down on Korean markets for breaking minimum-wage laws or hiring illegal immigrants, which Suzy learned later through her interpreting. As one wisecracking lawyer put it, "Everyone feeds off the illegals until they get an urge to scratch." Yet, from what she recalls, her parents had never suffered from the upheaval. They thrived, in fact, even bought a house during that time. How did they manage when so many others collapsed? The INS alone would not have guar-

anteed their lucky fortune. It is possible that the police might
have had something to do with it. They could have left her parents alone, in exchange for the names of store owners guilty
of breaking labor laws. It would not have taken much. A few
names. A few handshakes. And how would the police have reacted when two of their snitches were found dead one morning
in their South Bronx store? Would they have rushed to track
down the murderer? Or would they have feared the exposure of
their involvement? Why had the police been so quick to dismiss
her parents' murder as random? *We didn't ditch them cold*, Detective Lester told her. Then why so eager now to pin the murder on those ex–KK members? The gang denied the killing.
They insisted that her parents were already dead when they got
to the store. Who had sent them there? Whose order were they
following on that morning of November 1995?

"What about Mr. Lee of Grand Concourse? And Mr. Lim? I
saw him after the last time I came here. He might've been following me. He certainly hated my father. What do you know
about them? What did they have to do with any of this?" Suzy is
surprised at her relentlessness. Leave the man alone, she thinks.
Hasn't he been through enough?

"I don't know," he says curtly. "I'm not like your parents. I
don't squeal on my fellow men."

Of course not. Not many would side with the INS against
their own people. Suzy lowers her eyes, suddenly stumped. It is
then that she notices the full ashtray again. A black plastic ashtray, the kind that belongs in a bar rather than a home. She carefully picks it up and empties it in the garbage can underneath
the table. Immediately she is struck by the haze of stale ashes,
and a pang of disappointment. Nothing, the ashtray reveals
nothing. Just a common circular shape. What did she expect?

"Have you heard of a bar called Seven Stars?" The question

comes out abruptly. Useless—the man will tell her nothing more.

"Never heard of it."

"And the Korean Killers? The gang that broke up almost ten years ago?"

"Like I said, I'm not like your parents," he mumbles, avoiding her gaze. Yet, from the way his face tenses for a second, it is obvious that he is holding back something.

"No, of course not, you weren't shot in cold blood." She cannot help saying it, although she quickly regrets it, remembering his wife buried in Montauk.

"You think it was me who sent the KK to kill your parents?" he retorts sharply. "I don't have that kind of money, and even if I had, I'm too old to get involved with a gang."

So he is aware of the KK's arrest. Who would have told him? Mr. Lee? Mr. Lim? Someone else? What was it that the mysterious caller had said?

They do not kill your parents . . . They watch you.

Was there more than one person behind it all? Was there a group of them who had hired the gang? Who are *they*?

"Is that what you told them? When they came to you?" She is jumping the gun. But there is no other way. Nothing to lose.

"I told them it was a foolish idea," he says wearily. "I told them they shouldn't get the gang involved."

So it is true. There was more than one. Many who'd been wronged by her parents, who might have plotted the murder together.

"Your parents had both the INS and the police behind them. They were basically invincible. Each time someone got deported, someone's store got shut down, someone's life savings got stolen, all anyone could do was just look on and hope that it wouldn't happen to him next. Your parents left them no choice," he says, staring vacantly at nowhere particular, as though he has reached the end of his defense. "Except the gang wasn't supposed to kill . . ."

Maybe they didn't. Maybe her parents were already dead by the time the KK arrived at the scene, just as the gang claimed.

"That's as much as I know," he says, stubbing out the cigarette. "I can't give you their names. I won't do that. Besides, I don't know exactly who was involved. All I know is that some of them got together to come up with ways to stop your parents. The KK must've been their only option. You can get the police to question me if you want, but my answer won't change. The police, the INS—they got all they could out of your parents anyway. They went after so many Korean stores for whatever violation they managed to squeeze from your parents. It's all politics, white politics. The police will only be glad to wrap up the case now. How perfect that it should be the pack of Korean grocers getting rid of their snitch, who'd gotten past their usefulness! Koreans killing each other, it only proves their theory that immigrants are parasites." Then he fixes her a long gaze and adds, "Whoever killed your parents were victims. They were desperate, even more desperate than me."

So the end of the story.

So that's how her parents came to their end, she tells herself. A bunch of Korean grocers who'd hired the three ex–KK members to threaten her parents, except their plan didn't go as intended: the shots were fired inadvertently, such shots, such final shots. Except she is feeling no relief.

Nothing remains except for the smoke, thicker than the night. The air is hot, moist, stale. The rain outside, she can hear its knocking. Its relentless knocking. She wants to say something, anything that will ease the pain, for him, for herself. But there are no words. Instead, she glances at the photo once more. The unchanging face of the middle-aged woman who never had a child, who breathed her last breath somewhere in Montauk, whose cry still fills this room after thirteen years.

Suzy finally rises. She is afraid, suddenly terribly afraid of stepping outside.

"Take this," he says, holding out an umbrella.

His loneliness is permanent, she realizes. That must be why she noticed him over a week ago at McDonald's. Recognition among the same kind.

Avoiding his gaze, she says hesitantly, "When my sister came to you . . . how much did she know about our parents?"

He contemplates her for a while before saying, "Your sister— I'd never seen a young woman so haunted by grief." Then he asks quietly, "Who do you think interpreted for your parents all those times with the INS?"

20.

FIRST IS THE HEAT. The unshakable heat inside her bones. The darkness is there as well. Then the wetness. The soaked sheets. The body curling into itself. The eyes are shut. The mouth is so stiff that she must be dying of thirst. Where's the water? Is anyone there? Will anyone find her? Will anyone know if she disappears? The last thought frightens her. It is not death that makes her squirm, but a death with no witness, a death with no explanation.

Before her are the rolling hills. Each one appears so smooth that she wants to reach out and brush her fingers across its surface. She imagines plunging her body between the folds. She thinks if only she could get there she wouldn't come back. She keeps wiggling her arms and feet. But the hills are far away, and she cannot reach them. Her body seems to be stuck to a gigantic futon, mixed in sticky breath. She tries to open her eyes, but the weight is impossible, as though a giant thumb is pressing on her eyelids. It is unclear how long she's been lying here. Hours, even days.

Between the hills emerges a face. An exquisite face behind a chunk of hair. The eyes seem familiar, such sad eyes, they bring tears to her own. The lips are painted in red, so opulent that it hurts to look at them. The fingers between the strands are painfully delicate; she wants to gather them in her palms and kiss each fingertip. Such a luminous face that there must be night surrounding it.

What remains is the heat that will not let go. What remains is the girl who will not lie still. The girl who remembers nothing.

Four rings.

The phone's been ringing all night.

On the wooden floor, next to the futon, are several banana peels and an empty bottle of water. Someone must have carried her up the stairs. Someone must have found the key in her coat pocket. Someone must have laid her feverish body on the futon. Someone must have put the hot towel on her forehead and watched her fall asleep before slipping out the door. Bananas and water. Enough to keep her afloat for days. Bananas; she has no recollection of chewing through their yellow meat.

Who was it?

Damian?

Grace?

It's been days, she is sure of it. A flood of sunlight poured in through the cracks between the blinds, only to slide away several hours later. A clock radio clanged with the familiar 1010-WINS chime. Doors have slammed at consistent intervals, as though the neighbors leave for work at the same time only to return exactly eight hours later. Cats meowed just around midnight, serenading the moon. Even in her deepest exhaustion, she was surprised that such things signaled the passing of time with an astounding accuracy.

But the heat is insufferable.

Now comes another face. The same black hair. The same heartbreaking eyes. The same pursed lips, across which a finger makes a cross to say hush. Now two where there was one. Two identical faces floating parallel. It is not clear which one was first. Upon a closer look, they no longer seem identical. A slight incongruence, although it is impossible to pinpoint what. She thinks she recognizes the one on the left. She is almost certain that one of them is her own, but which? She keeps turning from one to the other. What could be more terrifying than failing to identify one's own face?

White is the color of sadness.

A premonition.

A creepy joke.

Each dried-up bulb is her mother watching.

Dead inside.

Like fucking a ghost, Michael grunted after their first night.

The phone startles her again. The exactly four rings, beckoning her from the world outside. Michael is there. So is Damian. Detective Lester. Kim Yong Su. All those Korean immigrants whom her parents had betrayed, who gathered together one morning to plot their murder. The only way they can get to her now is by dialing the seven-digit number. Instead of whispering her name, instead of kissing her face so gently, they must dial the number first. They must keep on dialing to catch her. She is no longer nineteen. She's learned a trick or two. She's buried herself between the hills from which the faces look on a girl drowning. No one will find her here. A perfect hideout.

But wait, there's someone else. Who's over there by the lighthouse, reading a book? What's she reading? The one book in the world to ward off the dead? Suzy runs up to her to break the

news. Look, she's about to say. Look what I've found out, look
what I know now. Look who killed Mom and Dad!

When Suzy opens her eyes, her breath catches at the stillness of
the room. The radiator has been banging through the night,
steaming in excess. Outside is the creeping blue, the first shade
of dawn. She can feel her stomach pulling at her with shocking
emptiness, the sort of hunger so raw that it has nothing to do
with food. She does not bother switching the light on when she
stands before the kitchen sink. Turning the faucet, she puts her
hands under the running water. She stands still for a minute or
two as her fingers get cold. She lowers her face to drink from the
tap before reaching for the glass on the shelf. Just then, as she is
turning, the glass slips from her grip. Shards bounce off in all directions, over her bare legs. It is then that she becomes aware of
the wrenching noise coming from her throat. All air has been
choked out of her. Neither the heat nor the hunger, but an un-
controllable sob from the inside. She crumbles onto the floor,
burying her face in her hands, lowering her forehead onto her
drawn-up knees. It's been years since she cried last. It's been so
long that she cannot seem to stop at all.

21.

SUNDAY MORNING IN NOVEMBER. The third Sunday of the month. The Sunday before Thanksgiving. FORT LEE NEW JOY FELLOWSHIP CHURCH. The sign outside looks almost garish, the sweeping gold strokes befitting its status as the largest Korean denomination in New Jersey. Unlike others, who rent their service time from American churches, they actually own their three-story building. It's been five years since she was here last, or in any church, for that matter. Not since her parents' funeral. Not since they took away the coffins to the crematorium. Suzy would have preferred open caskets. The decision had already been made when she arrived at the church. Gunshot wounds. Must not have been easy to clean up. Yet she would have liked to see her parents one last time. She would have wanted nothing more, even though the thought scared her. How could she have faced them? What would she have said to them? Grace might have been wise to block the last viewing.

The church appears different somehow. The altar behind

which the two coffins had been placed five years ago is now empty, with only the towering candelabra flanking the pillars. The vaulted ceiling scoops high in an uneven angle, as though displaying the relic of an ancient cathedral. The stained-glass windows do not reflect sufficient light; their reds and blues seem to have faded in time. The mahogany pews on either side are filled with faces, mostly young, about Suzy's age or younger.

The service is in full swing when she finds an empty seat in the back. Three young women are standing on the pulpit singing a hymn. An easy-to-follow tune that seems to repeat the magic words: worship, praise, seek, follow. People all around begin singing along, some clapping, some muttering "amen" over and over. Suzy cannot bring herself to join them, although the words are right there on the hanging screen behind the singing trio. Glancing around the room, she wonders why everyone seems so young. It must be the youth hour. Grace is supposed to be in charge of the Youth Bible Study. Although the oldest members appear to be no more than in their late twenties, many are couples with toddlers. Koreans marry early. A woman is expected to choose her match right out of college. By the time she hits twenty-five, the "old maid" label sticks fast. Over thirty, the best she can hope for is a much older man on the lookout for a second wife.

Now the song seems to be reaching its climax, or just the high-pitched refrain: "Lord, you're my all, Lord, you're my joy, Lord, you're my righteousness." Suzy cannot recall when she ever believed in anything with such conviction. Damian, she once followed him blindly. But it was love, or at least she thought it was. This church, the Bible—*this is all Grace had.*

As the choir takes a bow, a short, chubby guy in his early twenties strides up to the pulpit. He introduces himself as Presider Kang. "In charge of this segment of service," he shouts into the microphone as though he were Phil Donahue following cues from the audience. He reminds her of the Korean boys at Columbia who roamed the engineering building at all hours, carrying bulging bags on their back and dragging their feet as if sleepwalking. They always wore a set of black plastic eyeglass frames and a pair of white Adidas sneakers. As a literature major, Suzy was never brought anywhere near their circle. Yet, each time she saw one of them, she felt such a desperate need to run, as though their heavily accented English, their awkward disposition, their palpable loneliness threatened her own faltering position on that American campus. Their unmistakable Koreanness seemed to spin her right back home.

Presider Kang commands a prayer for everyone, three full minutes during which he hails the blessing of Jesus. "Without you, Lord, we're nothing," he recites into the microphone with his eyes shut, inspired by the singing trio's lyric. "Without you, Lord, we have no home. Without you, Lord, we have no father. Without you, Lord, we are orphans."

Your sister—I'd never seen a young woman so haunted by grief.

"Now please walk around and introduce yourself to at least five new brothers and sisters. Give them a hug and a warm handshake. We are all family, under the name of our Lord." Presider Kang struts down the nave and puts his arms around each one; their faces light up as though Jesus himself has just descended. Suzy has no choice but to rise and attempt a half-hearted gesture of looking around. She is farthest back, away from the majority, huddled in the middle rows. But churchgoers are not shy. A few are already making their way toward Suzy with beaming faces, as though they have just found their long-lost sister.

"Hi, I am Kyung Hee, welcome!"

"Hi, I'm Maria, what's your name?"

"Hi, I am Paul, so happy to meet you!"

Suzy would never recognize any of them if she were to run into one on the street. No glimpse of family bonding. Family, from what she knows, has nothing to do with handshakes and hugs.

Finally, there's the pastor, who is by far the oldest man in the room. With the sleekness of a pro, he quickly embarks on a heartfelt tale about how scarce the food had been when he was a kid in Korea, and how a mere apple would fill him with tears, as it struck him what wonder God had given us. He is recalling the spirit of Thanksgiving, although most Koreans do not celebrate the American tradition. She has heard it all before, the stories that begin and end with Korea, although here Jesus seems to be the preferred antidote. She rises quietly as the pastor starts reading scripture from the Bible: "The light shines in the darkness, but the darkness has not understood it."

Outside, in the oversized vestibule, Suzy finds a couple of tall wooden chairs lined up against the wall under a large portrait of Jesus on a crucifix. In one of them is a little girl of about four or five sitting with her feet dangling in the air. Like an angel, Suzy thinks, the way the whispery curls frame her face. Odd that a mother would give a perm to hair so young and naturally straight.

"Hi," says Suzy, sitting by her side.

"Is the service over?" The girl turns with a sullen face.

"No, not yet," answers Suzy, leaning back against the green velvet cushion.

"When will it be over?" The girl keeps crossing and uncrossing her legs, in the manner of a lady in distress.

"Why? You waiting for someone?" asks Suzy, amused by the little girl's precociousness.

The girl rolls her eyes, as if she finds adults dull. "It's so boring here. I should've brought my little Suzie with me."

"Who's Suzie?" asks Suzy, surprised at such a coincidence.

"My daughter. I'm a terrible mom, leaving her home alone to hang out in this dump!"

"So where's the father, may I ask?" Suzy puts on a concerned face, pretending to commiserate with the girl's maternal worries for her doll.

"There's no father, of course!" The girl looks appalled by Suzy's cluelessness.

"Oh?" Suzy plays along.

"Okay, promise not to tell anyone," whispers the girl, looking around once to make sure no one is listening. "I'm not Suzie's real mom. The real mom's dead. Poor Suzie's an orphan."

Suzy studies the little girl a bit more closely before asking, "How do you know that?"

"I just know, 'cause she's mine now."

Then, suddenly, the girl's face breaks into a bright smile. From the door emerges a petite woman in a yellow turtleneck and a calf-length navy skirt. The most distinct feature about her strikingly pale face is the freckles that sprout so mercilessly over her tiny button nose. Her dark-brown chin-length bob drapes her face in such stiff angles that it resembles a wig. Something about her seems unmistakably foreign, as though she could be of another origin, half Korean even. Suzy recognizes her as one of those who shook her hand inside.

"Grace, honey, have you been bothering the lady?" The woman bends down to kiss the girl several times before turning to Suzy. "The sermon's not over yet, but I had to check on her."

A daughter named Grace with a doll named Suzie. Too bizarre for chance, too clever for a plan. Then it occurs to Suzy that during the handshake the woman had introduced herself as Maria. *Could it be?* Suzy asks hesitantly, "What's your name again?"

"Maria. Maria Sutpen. And you are . . . Suzy, right?" the woman answers with sisterly familiarity, just as Presider Kang had prescribed.

"Suzy Park," she mutters; the girl does not miss a beat and exclaims, "Like my poor Suzie!"

"Sweetheart, why don't you go downstairs and play with the other children? They have cookies and hot chocolate down there. Mommy will come right down after the sermon." Maria points to the stairs that lead to the Bible-study room, which also serves as a recreation corner for kids.

"I *hate* hot chocolate!" The girl is pouting now, realizing that she will not be going home anytime soon.

"Don't be a baby, now; you love hot chocolate, and if you don't get down there fast, I bet the other kids will drink it all!" It is obvious that she is a good mother. Firm but with enough sense of fun. Loving in the way that she cannot seem to stop gazing at her daughter. Something about her adoring eyes spells a single mother. It has never occurred to Suzy that Maria Sutpen might be half Korean. With a name like that, who would expect an Asian face?

"All right, I'm going, and I'm not a baby!" The girl nods proudly in Suzy's direction, acknowledging her once before taking her leave.

"Both Mommy and Miss Suzy know you're not a baby!" With a wink in Suzy's direction, Maria kisses her daughter once more before letting her go. The girl runs down the stairs, out of their sight. Turning to Suzy, Maria shakes her head. "For a four-year-old, she's a handful."

"Quite a kid," Suzy agrees, still looking in the direction in which Grace disappeared. "Her name, is that . . . after my sister? Grace Park?"

"A sister?" Maria exclaims, staring at Suzy. "Grace's sister?"

"A younger sister," Suzy asserts.

"I didn't know Grace had a sister," Maria repeats incredulously.

"We haven't been too close," Suzy mumbles. "But I was hoping to find her here today."

Maria's face tenses. "I'm looking for her too. I drove here all the way from Queens."

Suzy is relieved that there is finally someone concerned about Grace's whereabouts. Nothing is scarier than an absence that is never noticed.

"I tried her at home, but she's moved." Maria sighs. "She never misses the sermon. I've asked around, but no one's seen her, and Grace is here almost every day."

"Has something happened?" Suzy asks uncertainly.

"Something odd came in my mail," Maria answers nervously. "A letter from her, which at first didn't alarm me, because it was more like a greeting card, except that it contained another letter inside."

"A second letter?"

"She wrote that I should only open it if I don't hear from her by her birthday. The whole thing sounded so strange, although with Grace I never try to second-guess."

Back in two weeks—Grace had asked Ms. Goldman to cover for her. That phone call happened last Sunday, a week ago. Now there's one week left until her birthday.

"Can I see the letter? When did you receive it?"

"It must've been sitting in my mailbox for a while. I was out of town until yesterday." Then Maria adds with an awkward face, "But I don't have it with me . . . Besides, Grace didn't want it opened."

No wonder the girl from the accountant's office could not find Maria. No one had been home when Suzy sat on her stoop in the rain.

Why is this woman living at her parents' house?

The first friend to appear from Grace's life. Perhaps the only friend. "How do you know my sister?" asks Suzy, contemplating the woman.

"From Smith, a swimming class in freshman year. One of those silly phys-ed requirements," Maria says with a smile in her eyes, as though she suddenly recalls the indoor pool where the class used to be held. "On the first day, the instructor, this rather large white woman, turned to both of us and said how some bodies just won't float. She was talking about body fat, of course, how thin girls don't float as well as bigger girls. But what she was really pointing at was the fact that we were the only two Asian girls in the class, that we were different. Strange, I'm not even completely Korean, as you can see, but in white people's eyes, I'm as Asian as they come."

Suzy tries to distinguish the Asian features in Maria's face, although, the more she searches, the whiter Maria looks.

"I bet I don't look so Korean to you either," Maria muses, reading Suzy's thoughts. "Don't worry, I'm used to it. Even Charlie, my daughter's father, left me because I wasn't Korean enough for him; he told me after seven years together . . . Anyway, thank God no one can tell my white blood in my little Grace, although her hair isn't as straight as other Korean girls'. Genes are weird, don't you think? They pop up in the oddest places." Maria sighs, tucking a piece of hair behind her ear. Suzy wonders why she did not notice before that her hair's been heavily blow-dried to appear straight.

"What a useless class; more than ten years later, I still can't swim!" she says laughingly. "It wasn't until after graduation that I started hearing from Grace regularly. She'd send me a letter every six months or so, always with nice little gifts. The odd thing was we weren't even that close. I guess I still can't say I really know her. I didn't even know she had a sister." Maria seems flustered by the discovery.

"What kind of gifts?"

"Oh, random stuff, like an antique jade ring or a pair of fancy sunglasses. Really nice, except they were all hers, clearly things she'd owned for a while. The letters weren't much, though. Just brief updates of her life. I thought maybe she was lonely."

A jade ring? Mom used to wear one on her middle finger. For good luck, she would say, twirling it seven times before whispering a prayer. Did Mom give it to Grace at some point? Why would Grace pass it on to a friend?

"Then, when I was down and out, right after Charlie left me, I was four months pregnant with no job, it was Grace who saved me. She took me in, and later even set me up in a house that used to belong to her parents." Maria pauses, realizing that they were also Suzy's parents. "I owe so much to Grace. I think she felt sorry for me, because . . . maybe she thought I was a bit like her, a misfit, a Korean girl with a name like Sutpen."

"A misfit?"

"She could never stick to a job, temped for years, strange for a girl who graduated Phi Beta Kappa. It's like she was allergic to a permanent situation—until the teaching job, that is."

Like me, Suzy thinks. A waste of college education.

Who do you think interpreted for your parents all those times with the INS?

Grace had never let Suzy know. Grace never let Suzy in. If Grace did not speak to Suzy, then Suzy could remain innocent. But is Suzy innocent?

Even at Smith, Grace was completely alone. Even at Fort Lee High School. No one seems to have gotten through, not even Maria Sutpen, with whom her friendship still feels guarded. Perhaps Grace was freer with the man who she claimed was alone, orphaned, just like her.

"What about her boyfriend?"

"What boyfriend?"

"It seems that she went off somewhere to get married, although—"

"Married? That's ridiculous," Maria cuts her short, looking dismayed. "Grace is appalled by anything remotely domestic. It's a stretch for her to even be my baby's godmother. I pretty much had to force it on her. She certainly wouldn't be getting married overnight!"

How peculiar that the whole school seems to be aware of his existence when her only friend has no clue.

"She's never mentioned a guy she was seeing?"

"Back in college, boys from U. Mass. and Amherst were always after her. She never went out with anyone, though. Boys used to say that she was a lesbian. But she had someone from home, some guy who used to come and see her every few weeks."

"A guy from home?"

"I never met him, but I've heard people say he was bad news."

"Why?"

"He picked fights with strangers because he thought they were checking her out. Right on King Street. I remember hearing about it, because in downtown Northampton pretty much everyone belongs to one of the Five Colleges." Maria pauses. "Why, you think she's still with him?"

"I don't know."

"That's over."

"How do you know?"

"She told me," answers Maria, squinting her eyes as if reaching back to a remote past. "She mentioned something about him finally giving up on her. She said that he was better off without her, because he knew too much about her. She looked so lonely when she said it, though. That's when it occurred to me that she might've had some feelings for him after all. I thought he was just some freak stalking her, but maybe they had a real thing. She hasn't been with anyone since. Especially after what happened to her . . . your parents."

"Why do you think she couldn't?" Suzy mutters, as though posing the question to herself.

"Something in her died with them. She seemed permanently lost without them. Years ago, when she moved back home after college, she used to write to me about how great her parents were, how much she loved them. I remember being envious. My mother died when I was five, and I never even met my father. I know what it's like to lose parents, but I can't imagine the pain when you've been so close . . ." Maria stops abruptly, realizing that the pain also belongs to Suzy.

Did Grace really use those words?

That they were *great*?

Something begins collapsing inside her.

A quiet sinking.

Grace hadn't even begun facing the truth, Suzy realizes. Moving back home might have been her attempt to bury the truth. Just as Suzy had invented the oceanfront house in her dreams, Grace might have told herself that none of it had happened, that her parents had never used her for their crimes, that they had never violated her conscience.

One day, if you find yourself alone, will you remember that I am too?

"What was his name?"

"I don't know. She never talked about him except that one time."

"When was the last time you saw her?"

"About a month ago, she dropped by suddenly. She said that she was in the neighborhood, which was unusual."

"Why unusual?"

"Because she never comes to Queens. It's almost like she avoids it. But that day, she said she was looking around to buy a store. When I asked her what kind of store, she said she'll tell me later."

A hundred grand, in one shot. A month ago.

Suddenly, pealing laughter halts the two.

"Mommy!" It is the tiny bundle of mess climbing up the stairs, smiling triumphantly, her mouth smudged in chocolate, and opening her palms to reveal a fistful of crushed cookie crumbs. "Look what I got for you!"

Bursting into laughter, Maria gushes, "Sweetie, thank you so much, that was so nice of you to think of Mommy and Miss Suzy." She throws one of the bigger crumbs into her mouth and then exclaims, "Yumm, it's really yummy, but now we've got to get you to the ladies' room to clean up!"

Maria Sutpen seems oblivious, which must be why Grace was drawn to her. Too ordinary, made to be a girlfriend, a mother. She even looks natural in a blow-dried bob. She takes whatever's given without much ado, even something as odd as a used ring or an entire house. The sort of woman you would find anywhere, whom you would never notice or remember, because, despite her mixed colors and name, she is your average all-American girl.

Finally, Maria looks up, her eyes glazed, as though her world has now ceased but for the little girl in her arms. "Please let me know if you hear from her. I'm worried about Grace. And about the letter, maybe we better wait."

Suzy makes no response. She barely hears Maria saying, "Since Grace specifically told me not to open it. I mean, she might have left me a message at home by now . . ." Without letting her finish, Suzy mutters finally, "Was it Grace who gave her the doll, the one named Suzie?"

"My fairy godmother did!" It is little Grace who jumps at the question. "She made me promise to take good care of her, because Suzie's all alone in the whole wide world!"

22.

ALL SHE CAN SEE ARE LINES. Lines to the entrance, lines for applications, lines for registration, lines for interviews, lines for hearings, lines to public bathrooms which are locked with "Out of Service" signs on all forty-two floors except three. She is not sure what made her come here. Everyone under the sun is here. The fluorescent blue makes everyone look sick. Or perhaps it is the perpetual wait that turns golden skin ashen. Men in stiff black uniforms trot back and forth with patriotic salutes. The objects of surveillance are aliens. Because here, at 26 Federal Plaza, "aliens" is the preferred name for immigrants. Ten-thirty on Monday morning, anywhere in the world would be better than here.

She could have said no. The call came at the last minute. The court's interpreter went home sick, and they needed a replacement. Immigrant hearings are rare. The court sticks to its own certified interpreters, and the agency mostly handles depositions that pay much higher fees. Even the voice sounded reluctant when it left the assignment on her machine. But the minute Suzy heard "26 Federal Plaza," she grabbed the phone. It seemed unthinkable not to take the job.

26 Federal Plaza.

The largest civilian federal building in the country.

The home of the Immigration and Naturalization Service.

Returning to the scene of the crime.

Passing the metal detector, Suzy wonders if her parents were summoned here regularly, if they were led through some secret corridor, if they sold off their fellow Koreans in this very corner. Suzy imagines little Grace next to them, her face lowered, her eyes filled with tears. She surveys the crowd in the sprawling lobby, searching for the INS employee who might have lured her parents, who might have given the final order, who might have turned his face away when they got shot. But nothing. Not a trace. The INS is never clumsy in its tracks.

There are thirty-two courtrooms spread over three floors. Courtroom 30 is located on the twelfth floor. By the door is a young woman in a navy suit pacing the floor and whispering into a cell phone, "No, it's not gonna take long. Just a formality, really. Williams never grants relief." She takes no notice of Suzy, who is now entering the room marked "Judge Jack Williams." There are three wooden pews on either side, with two booths and desks in front. Hanging behind the judge's bench is a circular bronze plaque that reads "*Qui Pro Domina Justitia Sequitur,*" with an eagle perched in its center. It is a plain room, clean and deeply worn. Yet enough to set one's nerves on edge.

Squatting in the right booth is a gray-suited man with his nose buried in a pile of papers on the desk. All Suzy can see is the wrinkled forehead and the drooping chin. But all too familiar. One thing she has noticed through the months of interpreting is how lawyers resemble their clients. They begin wearing the same look. The same optimism, the same despondency. A quick glance, and she can usually surmise the situation. Whatever today's case is, there's not much hope.

Next to him is the defendant. Either she's been crying up until the point when she was summoned here, or her eyes are naturally swollen with dark circles. Her gauntness is alarming, the brown cardigan falling shapelessly over her bony shoulders. Her wizened face carries the yellowish hue of someone who hasn't breathed fresh air for a long time. It is hard to guess her age. Somewhere in her late fifties, although with immigrant workers one can never tell. She looks vaguely familiar, though, and Suzy leans for a better look. But unlike most witnesses, whose faces light up at the entrance of the interpreter, the woman does not even stir when Suzy slides into the seat next to her.

"Hi, I'm the interpreter assigned to the case," Suzy attempts. The woman seems not to hear her, muttering instead a few indistinguishable sounds under her breath. The lawyer barely acknowledges her. Occasionally Suzy has run into lawyers who don't address interpreters or stenographers directly. Some even snicker when she stumbles on a word and turns to a dictionary. They might sigh noisily or make a point of shaking their heads. Oddly enough, Korean lawyers are the worst. It might come from the country's long history of class hierarchy. Once, an attorney turned to her during a break and asked her to bring him a cup of coffee. Suzy collected her things instead and walked out. Sometimes bullying is a legal tactic to prevent a witness from being questioned: get the interpreter mad and bust the deposition. A cheap trick, but it works. Most depositions never get rescheduled. They cost too much. Before the second try, the case gets settled.

But no such play at an immigration court. No cocky lawyer, no tempestuous interpreter. There is a grimness here she cannot shake off. Silence infused with doom. Like the end of a civilization, she thinks, peering at the woman, who still won't raise her face.

Then, almost simultaneously, the young woman with a cell phone strides in, and a lanky man in a black robe with bifocals precariously perched on his nose emerges from the side entrance by the bench. The new presence does nothing to lift the ominous air. The defendant recoils slightly.

"Let the record reflect that we are now commencing the removal hearing of Jung Soon Choi," the man with bifocals, who turns out to be Judge Jack Williams, says, turning on the tape recorder. At immigrant hearings, stenographers are rarely used. The court does not have the budget. Facing both lawyers, Judge Williams asks, "Do you, Counsels, wish to present your exhibits?"

Right away, the young woman and the morose lawyer strut to the bench. While the three are poring over the documents, Suzy studies the defendant more closely. A creeping sense of familiarity; what is it? Why does her heart give at every frail motion of this woman?

When both return to their seats, Suzy rises and takes the oath, as does the woman. As if on cue, Judge Williams pounds and says, "For the record, please state your name." Suzy translates in a louder voice than usual, for fear that the woman might not hear.

In a surprisingly clear and coherent tone, the woman answers, "Choi Jung Soon."

"Is that your lawyer sitting next to you?"

Mrs. Choi nods, at which Judge Williams orders her to answer verbally.

"Although I believe that the respondent is not even entitled to a hearing, upon the request of the respondent's counsel, I am

willing to hear her side before making a decision. You may begin, Counsel."

Suzy translates, leaving out the part about her not being
entitled to a hearing. Why drain the woman of her last hope?

"When were you born, madam?" Her lawyer wastes no time.

"Nineteen forty-two. January 7."

Nineteen forty-two. The year her mother was born. The year
of the horse. Mom once said that no one wanted a girl born in
the year of the horse, because she was fated to die far from
home. The stars never lie, she whispered, as though imparting
an ancient wisdom. Suzy thought she was making it up.

"So you are fifty-eight years old."

If her mother had lived, she would have been fifty-eight. Still
a good age. Still young. The ripe age for a parent. It is not right
for a parent to disappear before.

"Where were you born?"

"Korea."

"When did you come to the United States?"

"Nineteen seventy-two."

"Do you speak or read English?"

"Little."

"What is the highest level of education you completed?"

"Objection!" the INS attorney lashes. "The counsel's wasting
everyone's time, Your Honor. His attempt to establish her background at this point serves no purpose."

"Sustained," Judge Williams rules. Get to the point, he
means. This is just a formality, the woman's as good as gone.

Surprisingly, Mrs. Choi replies anyway. "Graduate school,"
she says. "I received an M.A. in music from Ehwa Women's
University."

Not unusual. Many Korean immigrants are college graduates. It is a country with a nearly 100 percent literacy rate. Kore-

ans pride themselves on education. A man who owns a dry cleaner's might have once been an architect, or a pedicurist at a local nail salon might be a trained pharmacist. Their Confucian tradition dictates that learning is the basis of self-worth. But it also backfires. The difference between professionals and merchants is sharp. Most of them never get over the shame of being relegated to the working class. Thus a woman who's been a cashier at a deli for over twenty years will still hold on to her former life as a music scholar.

A momentary silence washes over the courtroom. Nothing about the woman suggests a music degree. The mass of gray hair gathered into a bun at the back of her head. The sallow face in desperate need of Maybelline or Lancôme or whichever product adds color. Then her cracked fingers, caked with dead skin, the nails chipped, which she quietly hides under her sleeves as though she too is surprised at her own revelation.

"Mrs. Choi, what is your status in the United States?"

"I am a permanent resident."

"Under what circumstances did you come to the United States from Korea?"

"I came on a student visa."

"Affiliated with any school?"

"Juilliard."

"And did you study there?"

"No."

"What happened?"

"My parents went bankrupt and could no longer send me money."

"So what did you do?"

"I got a job as a cashier at a Korean deli. I was planning on saving up and going back to school."

"And were you able to?"

"Objection! How is her education history relevant to any of

this?" The INS attorney looks exasperated. Suzy has seen this
before, many times. Lawyers are always acting frantic. They are
perpetually frustrated or running out of time. It must be the
first lesson they teach at law schools: act like an asshole if the
case is not going your way.

"Sustained," Judge Williams drones. Come on, his murky
eyes suggest, do we really have to go through all this?

"Mrs. Choi, are you currently married?"

"Yes."

"Do you live with your husband?"

"I did."

"What do you mean?"

"I did until I was arrested."

"Any children?"

No answer. Suzy pauses as Mrs. Choi clams up. A silent response is the hardest for an interpreter. A pause signals difficulty.
Sometimes the witness is confused or does not know the answer.
Sometimes it is a ploy to avoid the question. But most times the
witness is stuck because the answer is too painful.

"Mrs. Choi, do you have any children?

"Mrs. Choi, according to the record, you have one daughter,
is that correct?

"Mrs. Choi, is your daughter's name Sue Choi?"

Leave her alone, Suzy pleads silently. Can't you see the sadness on her face?

"Okay, Mrs. Choi, let's move on to another topic." The
lawyer relents, or puts the daughter on hold for now. "Where
were you employed last?"

"Together Market."

"Where was Together Market located?"

"Between 125th Street and Lenox Avenue."

"What kind of business was Together Market?"

"A fruit-and-vegetable store."

"Who owned it?"

"My husband."

"What was your job or duty?"

"A cashier during daytime, and in the evenings I prepared food for the salad bar and made fruit cups."

Mom did that too, Suzy recalls. Although Dad never let Suzy, she saw Mom making fruit cups once. Long before they bought the Tremont Avenue shop. It was Grace who took her there. The store was in Manhattan, very far from Queens. It took nearly an hour on the Number 7 train, and at Grand Central, they got out and walked a few blocks. The woman at the cash register had the deepest double folds on her eyelids. Plastic surgery is common among Korean women to make their eyes bigger, like Meg Ryan's. Except the folds on this woman looked too fake, and her eyes seemed to pop out of their sockets, the skin around them pulled too tightly. The woman languidly pointed to the kitchen in the back, where Mom was squatting on a milk crate facing a cutting board and boxes of cantaloupes. She was carving melons into moon-shaped pieces before putting them into a plastic container, which she would tie with a rubber band. Then the process would begin again. And again. She was like Cinderella, with a mountain of chores, except the mountain was made up of cantaloupes and the midnight ball never took place. Suzy cannot remember what came next. Did Mom finally turn around and see them there? Or is it possible that before Mom could find them Grace pulled Suzy's arm with a sudden burst of anger and stormed out? How often had Grace gone there? Did she go back to watch Mom from the doorway? Why had Grace brought her there anyway? Suzy couldn't stand cantaloupes after that. Or Grand Central, for that matter.

For a while now, the questions have been circling around the store called Together Market—when did her husband purchase the store, how many hours per week did she work there, how much was her annual income. Then he finally zeroes in: "Let's go back to the night you got arrested, that would be December 2, 1997. Can you, in your own words, explain to the court what happened?"

For a second, Suzy notices Mrs. Choi's fingers clutching the edge of the seat. Then a curt response: "I stabbed a girl." Suzy hesitates before translating. She tries to think of a softer word for "stab" in English, but there is no such thing. Mrs. Choi did not mean it softly.

The lawyer seems frustrated by her response. He wants descriptions. Details. Whatever it would take to clarify the picture.

"Let me rephrase the question; please tell us the circumstances surrounding the incident in question."

"She was a customer, and I stabbed her," Mrs. Choi answers with not much feeling. And definitely no regret.

"I understand. But could you tell us how the situation specifically arose, or what exchange you had with this customer whom you claim to have stabbed?" He is losing patience. He knew that she would not be an easy witness. Legal Aid had warned him. Despite the language barrier, it is not hard to see that the woman has little interest in saving herself.

Suzy is also losing patience, adding at end of the lawyer's question, *Please say more. This might be your last chance.*

"I was making fruit cups and I saw the girl stealing."

"And then what happened?"

"I stabbed her in her shoulder with the knife I was using to cut fruit."

"Mrs. Choi, isn't it true that the girl punched you repeatedly before you pulled out the knife?"

"Objection!" the INS attorney barks. "The counsel is leading the respondent. Besides, the respondent has already served her sentence. The respondent is not summoned to this court for her crime; she's here because she is deportable!"

"Your Honor, it is very relevant. Her crime is exactly why she has been deemed deportable."

"Overruled, but, Counsel, I will not allow these types of questions for much longer." A warning. Judge Williams wants this show to be over with. Three more cases to go today: two asylum petitions, one status adjustment. Pardon them one year, detention centers get jammed tenfold in the following year. Is America up for grabs? Judge Williams adjusts his glasses, which slide down again almost immediately.

"Thank you, Your Honor. Mrs. Choi, did the girl you claimed to have stabbed provoke you in any way? Such as insulting you with racial slurs or attacking you physically?"

"I don't remember."

"Mrs. Choi, if you would please look at Exhibit A, in front of you, which is the transcript of your testimony from the criminal hearing that took place on January 30, 1998, you will find that you testified that the sixteen-year-old victim had stolen a six-pack of beer and a case of cherries and then called you 'Fucking Chink' several times, among other racial slurs, and then proceeded to punch you repeatedly in the face. Is that correct?"

It is then that Suzy remembers the headline from a few years back. "KOREAN WOMAN STABS BLACK TEENAGE GIRL FOR CHERRIES." It was all over the papers. The girl was out of the hospital in a few weeks, but boycotts spread like wildfire against Korean fruit-and-vegetable stores in Harlem and the Bronx. The *New York Post* called it the "Return of Rodney King"; Reverend Al Sharpton exhorted his people to fight back; 1010-WINS updated the news every half-hour. Suzy remembers the photograph of the distraught woman surrounded by a mob of reporters. Is that why she seems familiar? Where are those reporters now? Do people forget so quickly?

"Mrs. Choi, your silence is not helping," Judge Williams interrupts finally. "You do realize that, in the case of a green-card holder, an aggravated felony is grounds for removal?"

Without a glance at the bench, Mrs. Choi responds, "I've served almost three years in jail. I've lost everything. My husband, my daughter, my store. If that didn't kill me, nothing else will." It is the most she's spoken so far. But self-destructive. No use confessing her heart to a judge who never grants relief, or to the trial attorney sent by the INS. Yet Suzy has no choice but to translate.

Her lawyer then puts the cap back on his pen with an obvious look of irritation and fatigue. "I have no further questions," he sighs. Pointless trying to establish her as the victim, as the one who's lived here for a quarter of a century, whose husband and daughter are still very much alive in this country, for whom being removed permanently means being torn away from a home.

Then the INS attorney perks up, grabbing her notes: "I have a few questions." Suzy winces as she translates her words—the trial attorney from the INS, the source of everything that had gone wrong with her parents. "Madam, where is your daughter?"

Mrs. Choi then raises her eyes for the very first time. Dead eyes. Nothing there, Suzy notices. Nothing left over.

"Isn't it true that she ran away from home when she was seventeen?"

The question shoots out of nowhere and sticks. Suzy stumbles, as though it is her mother being examined, accused, sentenced. *Isn't it true that your daughter abandoned you because she couldn't stand you?*

"Isn't it also true that, before she left home, she had filed a complaint against your husband, Mr. Choi, for physical abuse, in which she alleged that he beat you as well?"

Mrs. Choi's face reveals nothing. Theirs was not a happy home, obviously, which is exactly what the INS attorney wants Judge Williams to consider. No one's breaking their home. They did that for themselves. Green cards were never meant for such undesirables.

"And isn't it also true that you have not once seen your husband, Mr. Choi, since the day you stabbed the girl in your store, almost three years ago?" The INS attorney fixes her gaze on Mrs. Choi for a few seconds, and then turns to Judge Williams. "Your Honor, I have no further questions."

The INS attorney spoke the truth on her cell phone earlier. Judge Williams's ruling is only a formality. Relief was never a possibility. Deportation had begun the minute she stabbed that girl. She should've known better. Immigrants are not Americans. Permanent residency is never permanent. Anything can happen. A teenage thief on one unlucky night. A pair of INS informers eyeing your store. A secret murder that is not so secret anymore. And Suzy, sitting across from the INS attorney on the twelfth floor of the INS building, about to translate a deportation sentence for a Korean woman exactly her mother's age.

When Judge Williams announces the removal date, Suzy chokes. Her voice is suddenly gone. She inhales deeply and then swallows once, twice. All faces are on her. Then she hears it again. The quiet murmur from Mrs. Choi.

Namuamitabul Kuansaeumbosal.

It's the Buddhist chant Mom used to utter when Suzy got sick. It always made her feel better. A lullaby. A dead woman's song.

23.

"HELLO, this is the Interpreter Hotline Services."

"Hello, this is a message for Korean interpreter Suzy Park."

"Hello, Suzy Park, please report to Job Number 009."

She presses "Delete" after each message. It is no longer possible. An interpreter cannot pick sides. Once she does, something slips, a certain fine cord that connects English to Korean and Korean to English without hesitation, or a hint of anger.

For the past three days, the phone kept ringing while she lay in bed. Michael, pleading into her machine. Even in her deepest dreams, she heard his sighs. He would fume, demand that she answer. Then, half an hour later, a softer, sweeter, *Suzy, please.* His calls stopped overnight, which could mean only one thing. He must be back in Connecticut. Even Michael would not dare calling his mistress during a Thanksgiving dinner.

A half-dozen messages have been left by Detective Lester. Suddenly he is eager to get to the bottom of the case. With each call, he seems increasingly confident that he is closing in, although the three ex-KK suspects are still claiming that it was a setup. He has no doubt that he could convict the gang of first-degree murder, although he seems unaware of their link to the Korean grocers. He never lets Suzy in on her parents' back-dealings with the INS, or with the police.

The girl from the accountant's office has called more than once. "Grace is missing," she squealed into the machine. "Grace still hasn't come by to sign the papers. Please call us back as soon as possible."

What is curious is how unmoved Suzy is, how unmotivated she is to pick up the phone. Instead, she is overcome by sleep. Her insomnia seems to have been miraculously cured. All she does now is sleep. No cigarette break. No water break. In between come those voices trailing off into the machine, voices from far away, voices belonging to dreams. The dream of the interpreter who no longer remembers her language.

"Hello, Miss Park?"

A woman, with a Jersey accent.

"Hi, this is Rose Goldman. I'm not sure if I have the right number."

Ms. Goldman. The English teacher subbing for Grace. Suzy reaches for the receiver.

"I hope I'm not calling at a bad time. I thought I'd just leave a message. I was sure you'd be gone for Thanksgiving." She must realize that Suzy, like Grace, has no family. "Oh, Koreans don't celebrate our Thanksgiving, please pardon me. I have so many Korean students, I should know." Ms. Goldman seems embarrassed at having been caught alone on Thanksgiving, although she is the one who called.

"Have you . . . heard from Grace?" Suzy asks, unable to shake off the persistent fatigue.

"No, not yet. But with Thanksgiving and all, the school's out until next week anyway."

Suzy is not sure why she is relieved. No news must be good news. Or is it?

"But yesterday, I remembered something. It's really nothing, but it bothered me. I don't know why, just a silly little thing."

"Yes?"

"Do you remember how I told you that I found it odd that her boyfriend was in the music business?" Rose Goldman sounds almost bubbly now, like a suburban housewife flipping through her copy of *Redbook*. "I finally remembered why. I remembered some kids saying that he was missing a finger on his right hand. And being a musician—although, now that I think about it, he could be a producer or something—but a musician with a missing finger is a bit strange, don't you think?"

They once each cut off their little fingers to honor their brotherhood, copying that crazy Yakuza ritual.

Closing her eyes, Suzy counts to three before firing the question: "Was it the little finger he was missing?"

"How did you know? Yes, that's what the kids said, like those famous gangsters in Hong Kong movies!"

DJ.

The last member of the Fearsome Four.

The one who split on his own after the gang's breakup.

The one smuggled into the country through the KK's adoption fraud.

An orphan, with no ties in the world but for Grace.

DJ was supposed to have been deported in November 1995, right around the time of her parents' shooting. Perfect timing, being sent back to Korea right after the crime. But, then, how is it possible that an ex–gang member who'd been deported reappears five years later, flaunting his BMW, picking up Grace after school? Why would Grace disappear with him? Why did Grace call Detective Lester out of the blue?

What was it that Detective Lester had said? *It's got KK finger-*

*prints all over it. The way they do away with their enemies. The
exactness of the shooting.*

But the gang claimed that they were set up. They said that
her parents were already dead when they arrived at the scene.
According to Kim Yong Su, the grocers had never ordered KK to
kill. If neither the ones who hired the gang nor the gang themselves had murder on their minds, is it possible that the murder
might have been committed by someone else, with an entirely
different motive? Someone intimate with the gang, who knew
about their mission on that morning in 1995, who was not afraid
to frame them? Yet who would have been clever enough to come
up with such a plan?

*The brave one. Someone so righteous that eliminating them
would've been a necessity.*

Suzy recalls the other clever setup. Maria Sutpen and her
daughter, Grace, and a doll, Suzie, a cozy family portrait in her
parents' final house. The little girl seemed happy, as neither
Grace nor Suzy had ever been. It is an odd way for things to
turn out. Their final house in America given away to a stranger.
A half-blooded Korean woman, Dad would have balked. *Since
when do you care about their wishes?* But what they had wanted
was not Montauk, not Damian, not Michael, not mistress Suzy,
not Christian Grace, definitely not a gang member with a missing finger.

Suzy begins pacing the floor. The cigarette smells of gasoline.
She stubs it out instantly. She glances at the ashtray filled with
barely smoked cigarettes. Then it comes back to her.

He won't crawl back to her. Definitely a changed man.

Grabbing her bag from the kitchen table, she pulls out a thin
volume of stapled sheets, *1.5 Generation*, the student magazine
from Fort Lee High School. She flips the pages and finds the
photo of the car that belongs to the "dude rich enough for Miss
Park," BMW M5, the same kind she'd seen parked outside San-

tos Pizza this past Saturday. Running to the closet, she rifles
through the coats on the rack. Which one did she wear on that
rainy day? Then, in one of the pockets, her fingers close on a
crumpled piece of paper. She beeps the number and waits by
the phone. It takes no more than a few minutes. These women
waste no time getting back to clients. Even on Thanksgiving
Day, which means absolutely nothing to an aging Korean prostitute.

"Mina here, someone beep me?" Her voice sounds notice-
ably husky, which must be her professional tone.

"Hi, I met you the other day," Suzy stammers.

"Hey," the woman cajoles in a low whisper, "don't be shy.
We've got girls for all kinds of clients."

"No, no, no, that's not it." Then, hesitantly, "This is . . .
Maddog's girl."

"Who? Oh, I remember now." Her voice sinks.

"Johnny . . ." Suzy says nervously. "When you said that he
was a changed man, did he, by any chance, also change his
name?"

"Jesus, is that why you beeped me?"

"Sorry, it's important."

"What does this have to do with you?" She sounds irritated,
yawning loudly into the receiver before answering: "Of course
Johnny's not the real name, no one in this business uses a real
name, you think 'Maddog' is real?"

The BMW. The gang connection. The room salon in
Queens. She does not even have to ask the next question.

"Did he use to call himself DJ?"

"So why you bothering me if you know the answer?" She is
about to hang up when Suzy jumps in.

"What did Johnny do to cross Maddog years ago?"

No response. Silence at the end.

"Did Johnny tip off the cops this time?"

Anything to provoke an answer.

"Where is he now? Did he run off with Mariana?"

"*Mariana with Johnny?*" The woman lunges. "She would never! That bitch treats him like a dog." The woman is seething. She seems to have been holding back for years. Over a decade of unrequited love. "He wouldn't dare go running off to her now. What more does he want? I give him the car, I give him his Armani suit. He's a fucking fool. Always Mariana, Mariana, even after I packed him off to Korea to get him away from her. All he talks about is how she's the victim, how she needs to be saved, how she's all alone. But what about me? What does he think I've been doing all these years?"

Suzy stands motionless, feeling the blood suddenly draining from her face. She is still holding on to the receiver, long after the woman hangs up. It takes a while for her to walk to the futon and climb between the sheets, facing the wall.

DJ, or Johnny, whatever he calls himself.

Was it him? Was it all for Grace?

And Grace?

What did she know?

How much did she know?

Why did she run away with him?

"Fuck them," her sister chortles from the top bunk, sucking on a Marlboro. She is terrified, watching the door through which Dad might storm in at any second. "They'll never catch me, 'cause they don't want to." She wants to sneak one of her sister's cigarettes too, but she is only fifteen, still the younger one, still the one who never breaks rules. "Do me a favor, empty this for me, would you?" Her sister pokes her head from above, carefully handing her the full ashtray. A black plastic ashtray, which, upon emptying, reveals a cluster of white dots on its bottom.

Seven stars in a circle. A secret code. A girl by the name of
Mariana.

Through the metal window-guards is the rain, the relentless
rain. And the red tip of the cigarette.

*One day, if you find yourself alone, will you remember that I am
too? Because you and I, we're like twins.*

24.

"MEET ME BY *SUNFLOWERS*."

A thirtieth birthday, suicide to spend it alone, Caleb insisted. "It'll be tattooed on your calendar, like the stupid sweet sixteen or the last date of your virginity!" Suzy had been inclined to stay home. She could not get out of bed. A celebration seemed impossible.

November 24th. The day after Thanksgiving. The Metropolitan Museum seems even more crowded than usual. It's been years since she was here last. The Met had always been Damian's territory. He had been a consultant for its East Asian Wing. He would come here whenever the mood struck, would retreat into one of its myriad rooms and disappear from Suzy. She would never accompany him. This was the world he kept separate from her.

She did not mind. He had thrown away everything for her, she thought. It seemed enough that they were together. It seemed enough to know that he would be with her from now

on. She had jumped at the chance to play his young bride. She
sat patiently and waited for him all day. She cooked elaborate
Korean dishes. She threw on skimpy red lace and moaned
harder each time she felt his attention drifting. Yet, once the initial shock of their escapade wore out, interminable silence hung
in its place. Four years. It took her parents' murder. It took their
death for the two of them to finally give up.

Damian contacted her just once after she moved out. It came
during the second year of her living alone. "Suzy, enough," he
commanded quietly into the machine. She did not pick up the
phone. "Isn't this what you wanted after all, to be free?" He had
no doubt that she would come back to him in time. He knew
that she had nothing else. And she would have if she could. She
wanted to, more than anything in the world. But on nights
when she cried in her sleep, on mornings when she woke missing his arms around her, she heard gunshots, the tumultuous explosion of two exact shots.

Now the police have behind bars suspects who might have
pulled the trigger, who might have wanted to pull the trigger,
who might be filling in for the real murderer.

The guard points to the second floor. European Paintings.
It's the nineteenth century she is looking for. Past the Grand
Staircase, buried among the glorious pastels of Cézanne, Renoir,
Seurat, Monet, are van Gogh's mad strokes against the wall.
From the crowd gathering in front, it is easy to spot *Sunflowers*.

"Hey, birthday girl, you look not a day older than twenty-
five!" Caleb exclaims from the wooden bench in the middle of
the room. Twenty-five, Suzy's age when she first met him.

"Hi, how was home?" Suzy slides by his side, kissing him
once.

"Rick told me we're finished if I ever bring him home again."

"Oh no, was it that bad?"

"Brutal. The funny thing is, they actually liked him. My

mom even went on to say that she thought he was *prettier* than Boy George. It was Rick who couldn't stand her. He said that she reminded him of Sally Jesse Raphael. I guess it was the glasses."

Suzy smiles, picturing Caleb's mother with her oversized red plastic frames.

"I had to rush back anyway to get ready for the opening. The artist is the newest British import. The next generation of the Sensation kids. He gobbles up classics and whips out blasphemous installations. A mannequin replica of one of Ingres's ladies that slowly turns into Princess Diana puking. A Botticelli painting where all the boys are sucking the Pope's dick. This time he's on to *Sunflowers*." Caleb turns to Suzy, rolling his eyes. "Personally, I don't see the appeal. I'm *so bored* by blasphemy."

Van Gogh's sunflowers look almost morbid. Not the usual perky, happy yellow faces, but a close-up of two withering heads, as if in torment. Beautiful, yet haunting. The madman's last reach for the sun.

"In Chelsea, no one gives a shit about the real thing. Everyone's just dying to know what new offense is about to be committed against the masterpiece. Except Vincent practically invented blasphemy. Look at his strokes, look how he twisted Impressionism senseless!" Glancing at the group of Japanese couples who are now following their tour guide to the next painting, Caleb continues, "In college, I was the only art major totally obsessed with Vincent. Everyone thought I was so passé. You fall in love with van Gogh, you study him in Painting 101, you copy *Starry Night* for your first assignment, but you don't obsess over him. While they all moved on to Mondrian, Beuys, Duchamp, I stuck loyal. Even now, *Starry Night* blows my mind. His cypresses make me weep. I used to read his letters every night before going to bed."

Suzy is suddenly struck by the image of the sky-blue bowling jacket Caleb always wore when they lived together. It had "Vince" stitched above its right pocket. She had assumed that it belonged to a former boyfriend. Strange how long it takes to know a person. Yet somehow reassuring that a person could have so many secrets.

"His letters? So that's what you were doing when you used to keep your lights on until dawn?" Suzy asks, half laughing.

"No, honey, I did other things too." Caleb winks before continuing. "But I used to read his letters religiously. They're painful. He was so damn alone. He wrote to his brother Theo almost every day. He told him every single detail of his life, down to the exact color of the sunset he'd seen that evening, the price of the paper he was writing on, the angle of his fingers gripping the pen. He was so needy. He begged women for love. He latched on to Gauguin for friendship. He threw himself into a painting frenzy. He even turned to God."

"God?"

"Vincent covered the whole nine yards. Studied theology, did the Evangelical bit, taught the Bible. But he didn't quite make it. He didn't fit. His loneliness was too deep, it really couldn't be helped."

So alone, so incredibly, desperately alone.

Something begins to break down inside Suzy. Something she has known almost from the beginning.

"Why was he so lonely?"

But the answer is there already. They are like twins. Suzy and Grace.

"Who knows? He was mad for sure. But there were other things, like his family, for example. His parents, his uncles, his siblings, including Theo. They sheltered him. They found him jobs, paid his rent, sent him paper and brushes. They had a strong hold on him, and Vincent was dependent and hated himself for it, although his family was by no means at the core of his problems."

"Then why write to Theo?"

"That's what makes those letters so fascinating. He felt suffocated by his family's love, and yet he couldn't help being a part of it. He choked Theo with his daily reports. There was a certain boundary he never learned. The suffocation he felt might've had something to do with it. No boundary with anything, with his family, with himself, even with something as common as sunflowers. Look at how he paints nature! His flowers are unique because there's absolutely no distance from the artist. For him, they're all the same, the self-portrait, the local postman, the sunflower. It's fun for us to sit back and analyze them, but for Vincent it must've been hell. You can only drive yourself crazy if you have no distance from the world."

Her face feels cold, as cold as her right hand against her cheek now, the curled fingers, the hollow of her palm. It is not clear which part emanates the chill, the hand or the face. It is the chill inside breaking loose. It is impossible to recall how long it's been there, this knowledge, this anger.

"Oddly enough, Theo died only six months after Vincent shot himself. They were connected by some desperate blood, like twins." Caleb shakes his head, still gazing at the painting. "Vincent paid for his genius, while Theo suffered for being sane."

Except that Suzy and Grace are not twins. Suzy's guilt is still tucked inside her unspoken. Suzy will continue to live.

"C'mon, enough culture for turning thirty. Let's go to Barney's to find you a dress. Your biological clock is seriously ticking, darling!"

Caleb is pulling her by the arm when Suzy notices a painting in the corner. A lime-green vase of violet petals against a pale-pink background. It is a tame still-life. Quiet, almost dejected, as if the artist has reached the requiem of his madness.

"Oh, *Irises*," says Caleb, following her gaze. "I'm not a big fan of his irises. They're a bit strange, tense. He painted that one at the mental asylum. It's like witnessing his death."

Irises.

It had to have been Grace who sent her irises each November. It was a letter to Suzy. A confession. A bouquet of Mom's last kiss. Because Suzy is the only one in the world who understood. The only one Grace could have reached out to. Where could she be now? Where has she disappeared to?

It is then that Suzy panics. Leaving Caleb frowning in confusion, she breaks into a run. She is flying past Cézanne, Renoir, Seurat, Monet. She is leaping through the narrow corridor of Rembrandt drawings. She skips down the Grand Staircase in double steps. People turn to look at her. Some move out of her way. A few guards even step forward to stop her. But Suzy sees nothing. All she knows is that something terrible is about to happen to her sister, if it hasn't already.

Then, running toward the coat check, Suzy stops suddenly at the sight of a man at the front of the line squatting before a bright-red stroller. With his back to her, the man seems to be adjusting straps across the infant's waist. His hair is dove gray, the color of Dad's Oldsmobile. His shoulders droop much lower than she remembers.

Damian, here on the ground floor of the Met, in the same line even, hunched over a baby. But it couldn't be. He couldn't ever be a father, ever deserve a home, ever own anyone in the world but her.

He does not see her. He does not sense her nearness. He is much too occupied with the baby's seat belt. The heavy black sweater is wrong on him. He never wore black. Too easy, he claimed, too young. Nothing else is recognizable to her. It is winter. He is covered under the layers. Nothing visible, not even his hands, buried in the stroller. Not even the back of his neck, wrapped in a scarf. She knows the scarf. She picked it out for him. The cream beige to suit his blue eyes. It looks different on him now, on that implausibly aged man in a black sweater bending over a baby, which might even be his.

But Damian could not be a father. He would have flinched at the thought. He would never have allowed it.

Then Suzy notices the woman standing next to him. Handing him a matching black coat, the woman is now stooping as well. It is hard to see her face, beneath the cascading blond hair. She is not much older than Suzy, late thirties maybe. Damian with a white woman. Suzy would never have believed it. He was too adept at caressing her olive skin, too skilled at kissing her black hair, too addicted to her Asian face. Suzy can almost hear the echo of Professor Tamiko's laughter—*He could never love an Asian woman.* How could he? His whole life had been about running from his whiteness. His purpose was searching the other. He couldn't even love his own kind. She was the antidote for his inability to love.

He raises his upper body, slides his arms through the coat sleeves. Turning around, he faces Suzy's direction for a second. Damian. She has not seen that face for so long. It has been so heartlessly long. Her first impulse is to jump the length of people in line, past the woman and the baby, and explode into his arms. But then she is suddenly not sure if it is indeed him. Perhaps another man who looks much like him. Perhaps her mind is playing tricks. All she can do is to stand still and stare straight at him. All she can do is stay where she is, continue standing. It is not clear if he saw her, although, from where he is standing, he must have. Then, before she can meet his eyes, before he can react, his face is blocked from Suzy as the woman lifts the crying baby from the stroller and dumps it in his arms.

Snatching her coat, Suzy starts running.

Before she can stop and catch her breath, before she can break into tears, she is already out of Damian's life.

25.

SUZY IS NOT SURE how she got here. She could have run the entire forty blocks. She could have hopped in a taxi. She knew she had to get out of the Met, although she had no idea where she was headed. But now that she is here, standing before a woman with a neat bob and a buttoned-up blouse surrounded by empty desks, it all makes perfect sense. Of course, this is where she had to come. From the moment she saw *Irises*, from the moment she realized that it had been Grace who sent her the bouquet, the next destination was clear. The New York Public Library. The only place to find facts, fast.

"I need to look up newspapers within the last two weeks."

She must appear strange to the woman, charging in like this, breathless, soaked in sweat despite the post-Thanksgiving chill outside. But the woman does not flinch. Anything can happen here. Free service. An open door to all New Yorkers. She must be used to all kinds of visitors. In a calm, friendly voice, she asks, "That would be in the periodical section. Is it local information?"

"Long Island. Montauk, actually." Her voice is strained, sounding almost foreign to her own ears.

"The best thing would be to look it up on Nexis, the online news search." The woman studies Suzy's face for a little longer and then adds, "But you need a library-membership number to access it. Do you have your card with you?"

No, she doesn't. Of course she doesn't. Even if she did, she could not remember where it might be.

"You okay?" The woman leans forward, as though alarmed by the look in Suzy's eyes. Such sad eyes, such immense sorrow. "I'll set you up at Terminal A. Better yet, I'll look it up for you if it's a quick one, there's hardly anyone here anyway."

"A boating accident, off Montauk coast," Suzy states numbly. She watches the woman's nimble fingers punching the keyboard. It is odd how calm she feels. This must be resignation. This must be the final relinquishment. She must have been afraid of such an end.

"That was easy!" The woman's face brightens with the researcher's delight at the correct answer. "Here are a few lines from the *Long Island Weekly*, dated November 19th, five days ago.

A couple disappeared when a boat sank off the Montauk coast. The cause of the accident is not known, police say. The body of an unidentified Asian male in his thirties has been recovered. The only distinct mark is the missing finger on his right hand. According to Sam Kelly, the boat's owner, the accompanying Asian woman could not swim. The police are continuing their search for her body.

26.

THE FACE ON THE WINDOWPANE must be a lie. Dark eyes in which lights flash, splitting her in two. When did she grow into such a beauty? Little clueless Suzy? Little innocent Suzy? But Grace had been the beauty. She was the brave one. She was the first interpreter. Which one is she? Whose face is this? As she leans closer, the mirror shuts with a heartless snap.

A boat in November.

Montauk, a sure sign of trouble.

What's in that water?

Except the ashes of her parents, the tears of the woman who died childless, the blood of the man who'd chased the wrong girl.

Before boarding the train, Suzy made two phone calls.

Open the letter, she asked point-blank. *I don't give a shit about your loyalty crap. Open the goddamn letter before I throw you out of my parents' house.*

A will, whispered Maria Sutpen. *It's a will, in case she doesn't come back. A will leaving everything to my little Grace, except for a title to a store, a Korean market; it says you'll know what to do with it.*

Now the real question. What happened in that class? You never learned how to swim. What about Grace, what happened to Grace?

Grace? No, not Grace. Grace passed with flying colors. She even cocaptained the swim team. She could swim through any waters.

There is no such thing as an accident.

Grace must have suspected him all along. She must have known that he would do anything to save her. She must have prayed never to find out. Except DJ must have crawled back somehow, must have confessed to her at the parking lot of Fort Lee High School. She would never have let him get away with it. She would never have forgiven him. Since when does a good Korean girl marry the one who's shot her parents, even if it had all been for her? Love? Bury him in the same water, that would be Grace's revenge. Never messy. No evidence. Not a chance of suspicion. She would've fooled them all. Fuck KK boys. Fuck grocers who hated her parents. Fuck INS. Fuck the Bronx DA. And most of all, fuck Detective Lester.

Only Suzy would be spared. The silent witness. The bouquet of white irises. A title to a Korean market—what's she supposed to do with that? Give it to Kim Yong Su as an apology? A piece of the American Dream? A family heirloom? What the hell's an interpreter if she can't even interpret her own sister?

Tell us, Suzy!

Stop lying, Suzy!

Dear Suzy, my only family, this is your dream come true!

The pastel house by the shore. The sunlit faces of her parents. Not guilty, never guilty, never having crossed the line between what is family and what is not, what is right and what is deadly wrong, what is Korea and what is not home. The line was always there. The line had been marked from the beginning,

tightly woven around the two girls who couldn't find their way
no matter how they tried, how hard they studied, how many
boys they seduced, how many husbands they stole, which god
they worshipped, unless their parents went away, unless their
parents sailed a boat never to return, unless their parents drove
to work one morning and never came back.

In the phone booth at Penn Station, Suzy made the final call,
relieved that it was only the machine at the other end.

*Detective Lester, this is Suzy Park. I know who killed my par-
ents. I know it was the Korean grocers; a group of them had sent the
gang that morning. I've got their names. Start with Kim Yong Su,
and he'll tell you the rest.*

Outside is no longer the city. No more Bronx, no more
Queens, not even downtown Manhattan. The swaying is kind
to her heart, to its beats of one, two, back to one. The sun is setting. The night is surging. The train is carrying her far, far away.
At the end will be the lighthouse. At the end will be a new
country.

She could swim through any waters.

Leaning back, Suzy closes her eyes. There is enough time until the arrival. Plenty for sleep. Soon it will be tomorrow. The
end of Suzy's birthday. One more day until Grace's. For now,
they will remain the same. Two girls with no parents, such fine
American beauties.

ACKNOWLEDGMENTS

MY GRATITUDE to Suzanne Gluck and John Glusman. Thanks to my first readers: David France, Lisa Hamilton, Sean Kim, Kathryn Maris, Dara Mayers, and Amy Peterson. And to my sister, Sunny Kim, whose painting graces the cover.

IT'S ALL IN THE BOOKS . . .
New York Times **bestselling author**
JOHN DUNNING is
". . . a master yarn-spinner whose prose is so
mesmerizing that you hate to come to the end
of the tale" (*Chicago Sun-Times*),
and his thrillers are
". . . mad, fantastical, and darkly original"
(*Kirkus Reviews*)!

THE SIGN OF THE BOOK

"It's great fun thumbing the pages with Cliff
Janeway, who knows his business and takes a
keen, almost sensual pleasure in a virgin edition."
—*The New York Times*

"[A] compelling whodunit. . . . Compulsively
readable."
—*Publishers Weekly*

"You're in for a smart literary surprise."
—*Bookmarks Magazine*

"Dunning's dialogue is at its snappy best."
—*Rocky Mountain News* (Denver)

"An intriguing insider's look at the business of au-
thenticating collectible autographs, and plenty of
smart, funny dialogue from an appealing and
thoroughly human main character."
—*The Boston Globe*

THE BOOKMAN'S PROMISE

"A thorough delight. . . . No crime writer has
ever written more knowledgeably or more enter-
tainingly about the world of rare books than John

Dunning. . . . Impeccably plotted, with characters who spring to life."

—Otto Penzler, *The New York Sun*

"[A] compelling mix of hard-boiled action and exquisitely musty book lore. . . . The combination of Burton the adventurer-author and Janeway the cop-bookseller is a match made in crime-fiction heaven."

—*Booklist*

"Exciting. . . . Remarkable."

—*The New York Times Book Review*

"A fascinating contemporary mystery. . . . Original and entertaining."

—*Chicago Sun-Times*

"A delicious read. . . . Dunning writes with reverence and passion."

—*St. Louis Post-Dispatch*

"A guaranteed high-five moment for suspense lovers."

—*Miami Herald*

"Endlessly inventive, exhilarating, and literate. Quite a knockout punch."

—*Kirkus Reviews*

THE BOOKMAN'S WAKE
A **New York Times** *Notable Book of the Year*

"Nail-biting suspense."

—*The Denver Post*

"Stunning."

—Associated Press

"Bookbinding has never been so compelling."

—Kirkus Reviews

"[Dunning] immerses the reader in this intriguing, little-known milieu without losing sight of the page-turning yarn he's spinning."

—People

"[A] 'don't miss' mystery."

—The Kansas City Star

BOOKED TO DIE
Winner of the Nero Wolfe Award

"No one . . . can fail to be delighted by [Janeway's] folkloric advice."

—Boston Sunday Globe

"[A] whodunit in the classic mode."

—The New York Times Book Review

"Intelligently written, bafflingly logical . . . [with] a sucker punch of a finale."

—St. Petersburg Times (FL)

"[A] meticulously detailed page-turner."

—Publishers Weekly (starred review)

"Book lovers will be fascinated."

—Houston Chronicle

ALSO BY JOHN DUNNING

FICTION

The Bookwoman's Last Fling
The Bookman's Promise
Two O'Clock, Eastern Wartime
The Bookman's Wake
Booked to Die
Deadline
Denver
Looking for Ginger North
The Holland Suggestions

NONFICTION

On the Air: The Encyclopedia of Old-Time Radio
Tune in Yesterday

JOHN DUNNING

THE SIGN OF THE BOOK

POCKET BOOKS
New York London Toronto Sydney

POCKET BOOKS, a division of Simon & Schuster, Inc.
1230 Avenue of the Americas, New York, NY 10020

This book is a work of fiction. Names, characters, places and
incidents are products of the author's imagination or are used
fictitiously. Any resemblance to actual events or locales or persons,
living or dead, is entirely coincidental.

Copyright © 2005 by John Dunning

Originally published in hardcover in 2005 by Scribner

All rights reserved, including the right to reproduce
this book or portions thereof in any form whatsoever.
For information address Scribner, 1230 Avenue
of the Americas, New York, NY 10020

ISBN-13: 978-0-7434-8247-9
ISBN-10:   0-7434-8247-6

This Pocket Books paperback edition April 2006

10 9 8 7 6 5 4 3 2 1

POCKET and colophon are registered trademarks
of Simon & Schuster, Inc.

Cover design by Carlos Beltran

Manufactured in the United States of America

For information regarding special discounts for bulk purchases,
please contact Simon & Schuster Special Sales at 1-800-456-6798
or business@simonandschuster.com.

To Susanne Kirk of Scribner.

Without you there would be no Janeway.

ACKNOWLEDGMENTS

Thanks yet again and a tip of the fedora to Wick Downing for heroic and persistent advice on legal and practical matters. If I made mistakes, they weren't his doing—just my own dogged determination to get things wrong.

And to Sarah Knight, the world's best assistant editor, for her good cheer, her rapier wit, her frightening intelligence. I trust her with my life.

Book I Death of
an Old Flame

Two years had passed and I knew Erin well. I knew her moods: I knew what she liked and didn't like, what would bore her to tears or light up her face with mischief. I knew what would send her into fits of helpless laughter, what would make her angry, thoughtful, witty, playful, or loving. It takes time to learn someone, but after two years I could say with some real confidence, I know this woman well.

I knew before she said a word that something had messed up her day. She arrived at our bookstore wearing her casual autumn garb, jeans and an untucked flannel shirt.

"What's wrong with you?"

"I am riding on the horns of a dilemma."

I knew she would tell me when she had thought about it. I would add my two cents' worth, she would toss in some wherefores, to which I would add a few interrogatories and lots of footnotes. I am good with footnotes. And after two years I was very good at leaving her alone when all the signs said *let her be*.

She picked up the duster and disappeared into the back room. That was another bad sign: in troubled times, Erin liked to dust. So I let her ponder her dilemma and dust her way through it in peace. Since she now owned part of my store, she had unlimited dusting privileges. She could dust all day long if she wanted to.

Two customers came and went and one of them made my week, picking up a $1,500 Edward Abbey and a *Crusade in Europe* that Eisenhower had signed and dated here in Denver during his 1955 heart-attack convalescence. Suddenly I was in high cotton: the day, which had begun so modestly ($14 to the good till then), had now dropped three grand in my pocket. I called The Broker and made reservations for two at seven.

At five o'clock I locked the place up and sidled back to check on Erin. She was sitting on a stool with the duster in her hand, staring at the wall. I pulled up the other stool and put an arm over her shoulder. "This is turning into some dilemma, kid."

"Oh, wow. What time is it?"

"Ten after five. I thought you'd have half the world dusted off by now."

"How's the day been?"

I told her and she brightened. I told her about The Broker and she brightened another notch.

We went up front and I waved to the neighborhood hooker as she trolled up East Colfax in the first sortie of her worknight. "Honestly," Erin said, "we've got to get out of here. How do you ever expect to get any business with that going on?"

"She's just a working professional, plying her trade. A gal's gotta do something."

"Hey, *I'm* a *gal*," she said testily. "I don't gotta do that."

"Maybe that lady hasn't had your advantages."

The unsavory truth was, I liked it on East Colfax. Since Larimer Street went all respectable and touristy in the early seventies, this had become one of the most entertaining streets in America. City officials, accepting millions in federal urban renewal money, had promised a crackdown on vice, but it took the heart of a cop to know exactly what would happen. The hookers and bums from that part of town had simply migrated to this part of town, and nothing had changed at all: city officials said wow, look what we did, now people can walk up Larimer Street without stumbling over drunks and whores, but here they still were. I could sit on my stool and watch the passing parade through my storefront window all day long: humanity of all kinds walked, drove, skateboarded, and sometimes ran past like bats out of hell. In the few years since I had opened shop on this corner, I had seen a runaway car, a gunfight, half a dozen fistfights, and this lone whore, who had a haunting smile and the world's saddest eyes.

"You are the managing partner," Erin said. "That was our deal and I'm sticking to it. But if my vote meant anything, we would move out of this place tomorrow."

"Of course your vote means something, but you just don't up and move a bookstore. First you've got to have a precise location in mind. Not just Cherry Creek in general or some empty hole in West Denver, but an actual place with traffic and pizzazz. A block or two in any direction can make all the difference."

She looked around. "So this has pizzazz? This has traffic?"

"No, but I've got tenure. I've been here long enough, people two thousand miles away know where I am. And not to gloat, but I did take in three thousand bucks today."

"Yes, you did. I stand completely defeated in the face of such an argument."

I went on, unfazed by her defeat. "There's also the matter of help. If I moved to Cherry Creek, I'd need staff. My overhead would quadruple before I ever got my shingle out, so I'd better not guess wrong. Here I can run it with one employee, who makes herself available around the clock if I need her. What more could a bookseller want? But you know all this, we've had this discussion how many times before?"

"Admit it, you'll never move." Erin sat on the stool and looked at me across the counter. "Would it bother you if we didn't do The Broker tonight? I don't feel like dressing up."

"Say no more."

I called and canceled.

"So where do you want to eat?"

"Oh, next door's fine."

I shivered. Next door was a Mexican restaurant, the third eatery to occupy that spot since I had turned the space on the corner into my version of an East Denver fine books emporium. In fact, half a dozen restaurants had opened and closed there in the past ten years, and I knew that because I had been a young cop when this block had been known as hooker heaven. Gradually the vice squad had turned up the heat, the topless places and the hustlers had kept moving east, and a series of restaurants had come and gone next door. Various chefs had tried Moroccan, Indian, Chinese, and American cuisine, but none had been able to overcome the street's reputation for harlots and occasional violence. Some people with money just didn't want to come out here, no matter how good the books were.

We settled into a table in the little side room and I ordered from a speckled menu: two Roadrunner burritos, which seemed like pleasant alternatives to the infamous East Colfax dogburger. "What's in this thing we're about to eat?" Erin asked.

"You'll like it better if you don't know."

The waitress brought our Mexican beers and drifted away. Erin reached across the table and squeezed my hand. "Hi," she said.

"Hey. Was that an endearment?"

"Yeah, it was."

I still didn't ask about her trouble. I gave her a friendly squeeze in return and she said, "How're you doing, old man? You still like the book life?"

It was a question she asked periodically. "Some days are better than others," I said. "Today was a really good one on both ends of it. Sold two, bought one—a nice ratio."

"What did you buy?" she said, putting things in their proper importance.

"The nicest copy you'll ever see of *Phantom Lady*—Cornell Woolrich in his William Irish motif. Very pricey, very scarce in this condition. I may put two grand on it. That wartime paper just didn't hold up for the long haul, so you never see it this nice."

"You're getting pretty good at this, aren't you?"

"It doesn't take much skill to recognize that baby as a good one."

"But even after all this time you still miss police work."

"Oh, sure. Everything has its high spots. When I was a cop, I loved those high spots like crazy, I guess because I was good at it. You get a certain rush when suddenly you know *exactly* what happened. Then you go out and prove it. I can point out half a dozen cases that never would've been solved except for me and my squirrelly logic. There may be dozens of others."

"I'd have guessed thousands."

"That might be stretching it by one or two hundred. A dozen I could dredge up with no effort at all." I took a sip of my beer. "Why do you ask, lovely one? Is this leading somewhere? It's getting fairly egotistical on my part."

"I know, but I asked for it. Please continue, for I am fascinated."

"I was *really* good at it," I said with no apologies. "You never want to give up something you have that much juice for. When I lost it, I missed the hell out of it. You know all this, there's no use lying, I *really* missed it, I always will."

I thought of my police career and the whole story played in my head in an instant, from that idealistic cherry-faced beginning to the end, when I had taken on a brute, used his face for a punching bag, and lost my job in the process. "But I was lucky, wasn't I? The book trade came along and it was just what I needed: very different, lots of room to grow, interesting work, good people. I figured I'd be in it forever."

"And indeed, you may well be. But nothing's perfect."

I mustered as much sadness as I could dredge up on a $3,000 day. "Alas, no."

"If you had to give this up, how would you feel about it?"

"Devastated. You mean I get lucky enough to find two true callings in one lifetime and then I lose them both? Might as well lie down in front of a bus. What else would I do? Be a PI? It's not the same after you've been the real thing."

"How would you know? You've never done it: not for any kind of a living."

"I know as a shamus you've got no authority. You don't have the weight of the department behind you, and where's the fun in that? You're just another great pretender."

A moment later, I looked at her and said, "So why are you here on a workday? How come you're not in your lawyer's uniform? What's going on with your case? And after all is said and done, am I finally allowed to ask what this problem is all about?"

"The judge adjourned for the afternoon so he could do some research. I think we're gonna win, but of course you never know. Right now it's just a hunch. So I've got the rest of the day off. And let's see, what was that other question? What's this all about? I need your help."

"Say no more."

"Something's come up. I want you to go to Paradise for me."

"You mean the town in western Colorado or just some blissful state of mind?"

"The town. Maybe the other thing too, if you can be civilized."

"Tough assignment. But speaking of the town, why me?"

"You're still the best cop I know. I trust your

instincts. Maybe I'm just showing you that if you did want to do cases, you'd have more work than you've got time for."

"The great *if*. Listen, being a dealer in so-called rare books leaves me no time for anything else anyway. Why do you keep trying to get me out of the book business?"

"I'm not! Why would I do that? You could do both, as you have already so nimbly demonstrated."

Our food came. The waitress asked if there was anything else and went away. Erin took a small bite, then looked up and smiled almost virginly.

"Let's say I want you to go to Paradise and look at some books. You should be able to do that. Look at some books and see if they might be worth anything. Because if they're not, the defendant may lose her house paying for her defense."

"It would be damned unusual for any collection of books to pay for the exorbitant fees you lawyers charge. Is there any reason to think these might be anything special? What did she say when she called you?"

"She didn't call, her attorney did. Fine time to be calling, her preliminary hearing's set for tomorrow."

She didn't have to elaborate. The most critical hours in any investigation are always the ones immediately after the crime's been committed. "Her attorney says she mentioned selling her husband's book collection," she said. "But she's afraid they aren't worth much."

"Trust her, they aren't. I can smell them from here, I don't even have to look, I can't tell you how many of these things I've gone out on. They never pan out."

"I'm sure you're right. Do this for me anyway."

I looked dubious. "Do I actually get to touch these books?"

"Take your surgical gloves along and maybe. You did keep some rubber gloves from your police days?"

"No, but they're cheap and easy to get."

"Kinda like the women you used to run with, before me."

"That's it, I'm outta here."

She touched my hand and squeezed gently. "Poor Cliff."

She took another bite of the Roadrunner. "This really isn't half-bad, is it?"

I shook my head and slugged some beer. "Oh, Erin, you've got to get out more, you're working too hard, your taste buds are dying from neglect. I'll volunteer for the restaurant detail. I promise I'll find us a place that'll thrill your innards."

"When you get back from Paradise."

I ate, putty in her hands, but at some point I had to ask the salient question. "So do you ever plan to tell me about this thing?"

She didn't want to, by now that was almost painfully clear. "Take your time," I said soothingly. "I've got nothing on my plate, we could sit here for days."

"The defendant's name . . ." She swallowed hard, as if the name alone could hurt. "Laura Marshall. Her name is Laura. She's accused of killing her husband. She wants me to defend her, but I've got two cases coming up back-to-back. Even if I took her on, which is far from certain anyway, I couldn't get out there until sometime next month. That's it in a nutshell."

"I thought you said she had an attorney."

"He's her attorney of the moment. He sounds very competent, but he's never done a case like this."

She gave me a look that said, *That's it, Janeway, that's all there is.*

"Well," I said cautiously, "can we break open that nutshell just a little?"

I waited and finally I gave her my stupid look. "What is it you want me to *do*, Erin? This isn't just an appraisal job. I get the feeling it's something else."

"Maybe you could talk to her while you're there. Take a look at her case."

"I could do that. I'm sure you don't want me to advise her. The last time I looked, my law degree was damned near nonexistent."

"Go down, talk to her, report back to me. You don't need a law degree for that. Just lots of attitude."

"That, I can muster. In fact I'm getting some right now. So tell me more."

"I'd rather have you discover it as you go along."

A long, ripe moment followed that declaration.

"She'll tell you the details," Erin said. "And by the way, I pay top rates."

"So now you're bribing me. Is this what we've come to?" I gave her a small headshake. "Something's going on here. This isn't just some yahoo case that dropped on your head. It's more than that."

She stonewalled me across the table.

"Isn't it?" I said.

"She was my best friend in college. In fact, we go back to childhood."

"And . . . ?"

"We haven't seen each other in years . . ."

"*Because . . . ?*"

"That's irrelevant."

"No, Counselor, what that is, is bad-lawyer bafflegab. Tommyrot, bushwa, caca, bunkum, and a cheap oil change. Not to mention piffle and baloney."

She stared.

"Old oil sludge," I said. "Remember those ads? Dirty sludge, gummy rings, sticky valves, blackie carbon. And a bad Roadrunner burrito."

She laughed. "Are you all through?"

"Hell no I'm not through. Help me out just a little here. Make at least some sorry stab at giving me a straight answer."

"Marshall was the first great love of my life. Is that straight enough for you?"

"Ah," I said, mildly crushed. My pain was slightly mitigated by the word *first*.

"He can't compare to you," she said. "Never could've, never would've, though I had no way of knowing that back then. Remember two years ago just after we met? I told you then I had known another guy long ago who collected books. I guess I've always been attracted to book people. I couldn't imagine I'd wind up with Tarzan of the Bookmen, swinging from one bookstore to another on vines attached to telephone poles."

"It was written in the stars."

"I'm not complaining. But that was then, this is now. He was my first real love and she was my best friend. More than that. She was closer than a sister to me, we marched to the same heartbeat. I would have trusted either of them with my life. And they had an affair behind my back."

I said "Ah" again and I squeezed her hand. "Jesus, why would *any*body do that to you?"

She shrugged. "It was a long time ago."

"And people do things," I ventured.

"Not things like that."

"So how'd you find out about it? He break down and tell you?"

"She did. Her conscience was killing her and she had to make it right between us."

I took another guess. "So when did you find it in your heart to forgive her?"

"You're assuming facts not in evidence, Janeway." She looked at me across the table, and out of that superserious moment came the steely voice I knew so well. "I'll never forgive her."

"Then why . . ."

"Why doesn't matter. Look, will you do this for me or not?"

I really didn't need to think about it. The answer would have been the same with or without the particulars. All I needed to know was that it was important to her.

"Sure," I said.

2

I left my bookstore in the hands of Millie, my gal Friday, and by dawn the next morning I was well out on the road to Fairplay. I heard reports of scattered snow in the mountains as I headed west, but they didn't bother me much. People who worry about scattered snow are afraid of everything.

I figured I'd stop at the Fairplay Griddle to eat, gas up, and take a leak: one short pit stop and straight through from there. Paradise is in a tiny, out-of-the-way county, in the mountains just west of the Continental Divide. This is almost as remote as a traveler can safely go without backpacks and mules. You don't just stumble into Paradise: you go there only with a purpose. There are two or three small, unincorporated towns and then, at the end of the one paved road, Paradise, the county seat. A dirt road does go south from there, which I had heard was a helluva spectacular ride. In a Jeep, a truck, or with lots of moxie in a car, you can eventually hook up with U.S. Highway 160, the main east-west route across southern Colorado. But you must go over some of the state's most rugged mountains and it's closed in the winter anyway. Practically speaking, the road to Paradise is also the only way out, a hundred-mile round-trip from anywhere.

It was nearly a six-hour drive from Denver, giving me time to brood over my life with Erin and the questions she had raised about my life in books. "The problem is you, sweetheart," she had said on another occasion. "You're letting yourself become too static in your book world. But I'll make you a deal: I promise I'll be happy if you will."

She had sensed my drift toward boredom long before I put it into words. "It's not the books," I told her then, "it's what money and greed are doing to them. The books are still what they always were, some of them are wonderful, exciting, spectacular, and on the good days I believe I could do this forever. But soon all the best ones will be in the hands of Whoopi Goldberg and a few rich men, who will pay too much because they can. They'll drive the market upward till they chase out everybody else."

I cocked my head back and forth and said, "I don't know if I want to do that."

I had seen this coming. The book trade was then just beginning to peek into the computer world; what has since become an indispensable part of the business was getting itself timidly into gear, and I knew almost chapter and verse how it would turn out. I am certainly no clairvoyant: sometimes, in fact, I can be incredibly dense, but that day I saw the demise of the open bookshop. I saw the downturn at book fairs. Wiser heads scoffed—the trade had always weathered storms, they said—but I feared that soon we'd be in a time when all anyone would need to reach the higher levels of the book world was enough money. Erin had brought money into my business, but my commitment continued to lag. I told her about it one night and she had understood it at once. I said, "When you take the best parts of any business away from the masses and hand it over to the rich, you can't be too surprised when it starts dying on the inside." There had been a time, just a year or two earlier, when this had all seemed so exciting. The thought of dealing in books worth $50,000, of flying off to book fairs here and abroad, had been thrilling as hell. The trade offered unlimited opportunity for growth, so I thought, but one night in a dream I saw where it would end. "I don't think I want to do that," I told her again.

The next day I made some bold predictions.

In a few years much of the romance would disappear from the book trade forever.

The burgeoning Internet, as it would later be called, would bring in sweeping change. There would be incredible ease, instant knowledge available to everyone: even those who have no idea how to use it would become "experts." Books would become just another word for money, and that would bring out the hucksters and fast-buck artists.

No bookseller would own anything outright in this brave new book world. One incredibly expensive book would have half a dozen dealers in partnership, with the money divvied six ways or more when it sold. "I might as well be selling cars," I said.

Strangely, I still loved the nickel-and-dime stuff. But that would change as well as bookstores closed and people became more cautious about what they were willing to sell. The ability to buy huge libraries would diminish and then disappear. Moving to a higher level would mean bigger headaches. The computer would tell us where all the great books were, and the thrill of the hunt would quickly diminish.

That's when Erin first floated her PI idea. "You know what you need to do?" she said.

"You need to find the bad people of the book world and put them in jail."

I laughed at the thought. A detective agency specializing in book fraud? There was no way anyone could take such a thing seriously. But then fate took a hand. *The Boston Globe* had covered my first major acquisition, a mysteriously signed copy of the most famous work by Richard Francis Burton, and that story had been sent everywhere in an AP rewrite. Luck, pure luck. But it had led me to two book shysters in Texas, and another case had sent me to Florida. The trade press had taken note and suddenly in the world of rare books I had a name. I didn't need to hang out a shingle, didn't run even one advertisement. Today more than ever, books are money. When the inevitable disputes arose, people came to me, and now I was more inclined to listen. When some unwashed schlemiel called from afar and said, "Are you the book cop?" I said yes and resisted the urge to laugh in his face. Yeah, I was the book cop. As far as I knew, no one else could make that claim.

My original plan with Erin had been a fifty-fifty partnership. Almost forty days after the Burton affair she had called and we had had a hot, sweaty tumble, our first, on the cot in the back room of my bookstore. We laughed and shared a postcoital pizza on the front counter. Everything seemed poised for a great new beginning, but even that first night Erin could sense my growing discontent. "You need to get out more," she said. "I get the feeling that the book business is not treating you as well as it once did." I leaned down and kissed her hand and said, "Hey, I'm fine, the book business is great," but that didn't count because she didn't believe it. "I think under the circumstances," she mused a few weeks later, "we'd better put our active partnership on hold." She still wanted in: she anted thirty thousand to make that point and said there was more where that came from. For now she'd be a silent partner and go back to practicing law to keep off the streets.

She joined a new law firm on Seventeenth Street, a dream job she said, if she had to have a job. "It dropped in my lap all of a sudden, it gives me everything I always thought I wanted. What's really great is how much *they* wanted *me.*" Why wouldn't they be enthused, I asked: she had been a brilliant student in law school and a tireless workhorse at Waterford, Brownwell; she had worked on two big water rights cases as part of a team and had won three murder cases on her own. She had built a splendid reputation for herself, there had never been any doubt of her ability to get back into law on the fast track whenever and if ever she wanted, so why wouldn't they jump at the chance to hire her?

We went out to lunch that week. She took me to a fine lawyers' hangout not far from her new office downtown. I shoehorned myself into a jacket and tie and we walked up the street together, chitchatting our way along. The waiter remembered her well from her days at Waterford. "Ms. D'Angelo, how nice to see you again . . . yes, I have your table ready," he said, and we were ushered past the gathering crowd to what looked like the best table in the place. It was set up far away from everything, in a dark world of its own, framed by indoor trees with our own private Ansel Adams nightscape on the wall between us. "So tell me," she said, "was I right or wrong to take this job?"

"I don't know, Erin. How does it feel?"

"I'm a hired gun again. But listen and believe this: I am totally at your beck and call. Say the secret word and I shall give notice that same day and join you in whatever comes of your book world."

"God, what power I have over you."

"Yep. You could join the Antiquarian Booksellers Association and travel to real book fairs everywhere. I'd go along, of course, as your apprentice and eager sex slave."

"I like the sound of that. Especially the last part."

"I would reply with sarcasm, except I remember who raped whom that night."

"I think we were concurrent rapes, as you legal types like to say. We each had a simultaneous leap at the other."

"I had half my clothes off by the time you got the front door open."

"Really? I never noticed. Which half did you leave on the street?"

"Panties in the gutter, bra tossed over the fireplug. Stockings, shoes, and other accessories strewn down the sidewalk."

"*That's* why I never noticed. You blended right into the habitat."

"And now here we are."

Impulsively she kissed my hand. "Nothing is forever," she said. "I don't know where I'll be in two years, or five, but somehow I don't think I'll be practicing law. Right now it's my strength, it's what I know. And I'm making good money at it."

"Then it's good."

"For now it'll do."

Snow began to fall just before I reached Fairplay. The Griddle was a typical country place, full of smoke and packed with locals talking about winter, politics, and the hunting season. I lingered over coffee and the *Rocky Mountain News* I had brought from Denver. Outside, through a dingy storefront, I could see the snow beginning to stick, and a swirl of it danced across the road like a white dust devil and disappeared into nothing. I watched the gaunt old faces hunched over their ham and eggs and I wondered what it would be like to live here. I thought about Erin and the young woman, still faceless, who awaited my arrival in Paradise.

I left the paper unread and headed on south. The snow thickened, but I got past Poncha Springs, over Monarch Pass and the Continental Divide, and the worst seemed to be behind me. The snow stopped and I came into one of those spectacular midmorning sun-showers that made me glad I live in Colorado, and beyond that was nothing but blue skies and sunshine. A good omen, I thought, knowing better. In this business, in matters of life and death, there are no good omens.

Highway 50 took me straight into Gunnison. It was still only half past ten, and Paradise was due south. I got out of the car and walked the streets till I found a drugstore. If the Marshall case had made the Denver papers, I hadn't seen it, but I imagined to the local weekly press it was a

much bigger deal. I stopped at the newspaper office and looked back two issues. On the front
page, just below the fold, were two pictures of
Laura Marshall, and suddenly the lady without a
face had one. The headline said WOMAN CHARGED
IN HUSBAND'S MURDER. In the first picture she
looked like any other felony suspect: grim, lonely,
guilty as hell. She was in handcuffs, being led by
some gruff-looking lawman through a rainstorm
into what was probably the county jail. Her hair
streamed down across her face and her eyes were
the only memorable features. The arresting officer
was identified as sheriff's deputy Lennie Walsh. I
wrote that down in my notebook, and I also
noted the tiny agate name of the photographer
under the cutline. *Photo by Hugh Gilstrap.*

The second picture was a posed head shot,
obviously taken under more favorable conditions. Again I was drawn to her eyes. Just a
bunch of dots on newsprint, but as I pulled back
from it, a woman appeared. She smiled slightly,
looking warm and innocent. In fact, she looked a
little like Erin. At some point Erin herself had
said that. They were the same age, they grew up
together, they might have been sisters. I sat over
coffee in the first café I found and read the story
twice. It was more headline than substance: a few
paragraphs below and around the bold type did

tell me somewhat more than I already knew, mainly because what I knew was almost nothing.

This was the story. On Monday three weeks ago, Robert Charles Marshall, thirty-three, of Paradise, had been shot dead in his home. His wife, Laura, thirty-two, had called the sheriff's office and reported his death. The sheriff's deputy, after investigating at the home and interviewing the widow, had concluded that enough evidence existed to charge Mrs. Marshall with murder. There was nothing in the paper about the evidence—no indication whether Mrs. Marshall had said something incriminating or had been Mirandized or when—but newspapers don't usually have information like that. It did say that the Marshalls' three children were now in the care of the victim's parents, who had arrived in Paradise at the end of the week. Marshall and his wife had lived in the area for eight years, moving there from Denver, where they had met. They had been somewhat reclusive and apparently had few friends. The suspect had been arraigned and the preliminary hearing had been scheduled Friday—today—at 1:30 P.M. before District Judge Harold Adamson.

I looked at the clock on the wall: it was 10:43.

I got in my car and headed south. Ninety minutes later I arrived in Paradise.

3

It was a sleepy-looking town, one main street and half a dozen side streets. An old, imposing brick building could be seen from the highway: it squatted on a street a block over and I guessed it was the hall of justice, probably a combination of courthouse, county offices, and, in a connected wing, the county jail. The barred windows were dead giveaways and the two cop cars parked outside were additional clues. I pulled into the lot between them and sat there for a minute thinking. While I sat, the deputy came out and got in his car, giving me the evil eye. I recognized him as the same guy who had booked Laura Marshall. He sat there staring, and a moment later he got out of his car and came around to my window. I ran it down a crack, enough to talk to him, and he leaned over.

"Can I help you with something?"

"I don't know, maybe. I was just about to come inside and ask how I could find the lawyer representing Laura Marshall."

"What's your interest in that?"

"Her attorney called Denver about retaining another lawyer."

He didn't like that. Hotshot city-slicker mouthpiece, I read in his face.

"You the lawyer?"

"I work for her."

"Doing what?"

At that point I opened the door, forcing him to step back against his own passenger door. I got out and we looked at each other. He was lean and lanky, about half a head shorter than I was and thirty pounds lighter. I warned myself not to pop off or start anything dumb, but cops like him bring out the absolute worst in me.

"I asked what you've got to do with this case," he repeated.

Answer the man's question, Janeway, my inner voice warned. *Be civil.* But the same voice asked, *Why, oh why, do I attract these pricks like a magnet?*

"I was sent by Ms. Erin D'Angelo, Denver attorney, to investigate the circumstances of Mr. Marshall's demise," I said. Most civil: almost cordial.

"I thought that was my job."

"C'mon, Deputy, it's cold out here."

"What's that supposed to mean?"

"Just that I'm freezing my ass off. If you want to jack me around, let's do it inside. Either that or I'll break out my heavy coat from the trunk and we can build us a campfire and send out for Chinese food."

"Funny guy. You musta done stand-up comedy somewhere. What's your name?"

"Janeway. Onstage I was known as the Merry Mulligan."

"You saying you're a cop?"

"I used to be."

This didn't impress him. It never does wow a real cop.

"So, what'd you do, direct Denver traffic?"

"Yeah. I directed a few badasses right onto death row."

He still didn't look as if he was buying it. "You got a license to investigate?"

"Nooo . . . I wasn't aware I needed one."

He didn't like my singsong, wiseass tone. He said, "Maybe you'd better get aware," and I said, "Well, I sure will do that, Mr. Deputy Walsh."

He looked surprised that I knew his name. While basking in this advantage, I said, "And I'd appreciate it if you could show me the statute that requires me to have a license to ask questions in Colorado."

We sized each other up again. I said, "Look, I really didn't come down here to cause trouble. All I want to do is to see Mrs. Marshall and her lawyer for a few minutes."

"Well, you can't," he said smugly. "They're meeting upstairs now, so I guess you'll have to wait till after her hearing."

"Thank you, Mr. Walsh, sir," I said, and I got back in my car.

I drove out of the lot and two minutes later Walsh eased in behind me and turned on his flashing red lights. I pulled over and again he came to my window. I cracked the window and he leaned over and looked at me.

"May I see your driver's license, sir?"

This was said deadpan, as if we had never seen each other before that moment. I fished out my wallet and took the license out of its plastic sleeve. Walsh walked away and got in his car. In my mirror I could see him talking on his radio. This went on for some time, longer than it had to: then he broke out his clipboard and began writing. A ticket . . . the son of a bitch was giving me a ticket for something, I couldn't imagine what. I simmered while he wrote out the equivalent of the Magna Carta on his clipboard. I may have fallen asleep waiting, but eventually he got out and ambled back to me.

"Sir, the reason I stopped you was your failure to observe the four-way stop sign at the intersection you just went through."

"I did stop, Officer."

"Well, sir, that may have seemed like a stop to you, but out here the word *stop* means you come to a complete stop and look both ways before proceeding across the intersection. This is a family community and schoolchildren use that crossing all the time. I don't want to see stops like that in my town."

He tore off the ticket and passed it through the window. "Have a nice day, sir."

I knew better than to argue with a cop like that. I had done my arguing in the parking lot and this was what it got me. I was on his turf—argue now and failure to stop could easily become careless or even reckless driving, with no witnesses to take my side of it. I had two choices, neither of them happy: shut up and pay my fine, take my three-point violation and lump it, or protest the tactics of Deputy Walsh in some local kangaroo court where the judge might be no better than the law enforcement. A bigger question had suddenly become Walsh's connection to Laura Marshall. That's when he'd first gotten his back up, when I had mentioned her name. He pulled around me and drove off and I sat there for another long moment, thinking about it.

4

At one-fifteen sharp I arrived at the county courtroom. I knew, because of the remoteness of the county, that District Judge Harold Adamson probably didn't live here, and in fact his judicial district might sprawl across half a dozen counties. In some of the smallest counties, the county court judge might not even be a lawyer: he could be an ex-cop, a highway patrolman, a businessman, or any respected member of the community. Not surprisingly, the DA had filed this case directly in the district court and Adamson had had jurisdiction from the start. The sheriff would be a county officer based in Paradise. Lennie Walsh, the deputy, might live here or in one of the smaller towns and would be a roving badge, patrolling wherever he was needed or saw fit. These were the characters as the hearing began.

The room was crowded for a workday: lots of interest was being shown in the plight of a good-looking young woman charged with killing her husband. They probably got just one murder case each century down here, and a sexy one like this had filled the seats early. I sat near the door, best seat I could get, surrounded by gawkers and the endlessly curious. At one-thirty a door opened to the far right of the bench and Deputy Walsh escorted Laura Marshall into the courtroom. She wore the plain orange jailhouse garb and kept her eyes straight ahead as she came in. Her hands were uncuffed, as if at some point someone had decided that she was not a high risk to grab the deputy's gun and start blazing away. I thought she looked good under the circumstances. Walsh looked like Walsh—see Janeway's *Prick by Any Other Name* rule. They were met at the defendant's table by an old man with white hair who was well decked-out in a three-piece suit, and Walsh turned Mrs. Marshall over to him. At the opposite table two attorneypeople were locked in earnest conversation. One was a young woman whose looks rivaled the accused's—a surprise to find someone such as she in a small county like this—and the other was a man in his midforties. A shark, I guessed from the look of him.

Almost before I had registered these impressions, the door behind the bench opened and the judge came in. He was on the upper end of the age scale, a stern-looking geezer with a beak like a hawk. His bailiff did the *Hear ye* honors, announcing that District Judge Harold Adamson was presiding, and we all sat down.

"*The People versus Laura Marshall,*" the judge announced. "The parties will enter their appearances for the record. Mr. McNamara?"

The old man rose at the defense table. "Parley S. McNamara for the defendant, Laura Marshall, who is also present. I would also state for the record that my client has contacted another attorney, and—"

"What are you talking about? Are you the lawyer for the defendant or not?"

"I am her attorney, sir, but—"

"But nothing. If you want to bring in someone else at a later time, file a motion and I'll consider it. But as of now, you are her lawyer. Is that clear?"

"As the court knows, criminal law is not my specialty."

"Then why did the defendant engage you? We do have one or two attorneys in this district who have some experience in criminal law."

"Mrs. Marshall wanted someone she knows—"

"Never mind that, you still haven't answered my first question. Do you understand that as of this moment, and until you are relieved by me, you are the attorney of record for Mrs. Marshall?"

"Yes, Your Honor."

"Mrs. Marshall, under the circumstances I must ask you the same question. Do you understand what we just said?"

She looked up at the judge and nodded.

"Speak up for the record, Mrs. Marshall. That man over there is a court reporter: he can't record gestures or nods of the head. You have to answer so he can hear you. Now, do you understand that Mr. McNamara is your attorney until he's relieved, and I don't care whether criminal law is his specialty. He has been a lawyer in this county for many years and I know him to be highly competent. I will not tolerate unnecessary delays in the speedy dispatch of this case. Have I made myself clear?"

The sound of her name had brought the defendant's head up, and she said something so softly the reporter had to ask her to repeat it.

"Mrs. Marshall," the judge said with exaggerated patience, "do you understand what we've just said here?"

"Yes."

"Good. Mr. McNamara, your appearance is noted. For the people?"

The two lawyers stood at the other table.

"Leonard Gill, district attorney, Your Honor."

"Ann Bailey, assistant district attorney, if it please the court."

"Then let's get started."

The judge read the information, and said that the defendant had been advised of her rights and had requested a preliminary hearing. He said the people had the burden of proving that the crime of first-degree murder had been committed and there was probable cause to believe that the defendant had committed it. Gill took his seat and the judge said, "Are you ready to proceed, Miss Bailey?"

"Yes, Your Honor."

"Then call your first witness."

She moved out to the lectern. "Deputy Lennie Walsh."

Walsh testified that on Monday at 3:09 P.M. he had been dispatched to the Marshall home on a code red, a reported shooting.

"When you arrived at the house, what did you find?"

"The front door was open."

"You mean wide open?"

"Yes, ma'am. And it was raining, which made it—"

"Just tell us what you saw, please."

"I went to the door and banged on it."

"You didn't cross the threshold?"

"No, not then. I knocked loudly and called inside."

"Did you identify yourself at that time?"

"Oh, yes. I yelled my name and said I was from the sheriff's office."

"Then what happened?"

"Nothing for a minute. I yelled again and rapped on the door with the butt of my gun—"

"You had your gun out?"

"Well, yeah. I didn't know what was in there."

"Then what happened?"

"Nothing. I had a real bad feeling about it, so I went into the hall. In the front room I could see somebody slumped over the table. I came closer and I saw that it was Mrs. Marshall."

"The defendant."

"Yes."

"What was her appearance then?"

"She was dazed, like she didn't—"

"How did she *look*, Deputy?"

"She was all bloody. I mean, she had blood everywhere. Her dress was torn, just drenched in blood."

"Did she say anything?"

"Yes, ma'am. She said, 'I shot Bobby.'"

"Just like that."

"Yes, ma'am, just like that."

"Then what?"

"I came on into the room and saw the victim on the floor."

"Did you then advise the defendant?"

"I didn't have time. All this happened in, like, twenty seconds. What she said she just looked up and said."

McNamara stirred in his chair. "Your Honor . . ."

The judge furrowed his brow and said, "All right, this isn't the trial, let's hear it."

"She said, 'Bobby's dead, I shot Bobby.' Then she leaned over and fainted."

A look of skepticism spread over Miss Bailey's face. "I see. She fainted. And what did you do?"

"Went over and examined the victim."

"Describe his condition, please."

"He didn't have any condition. Had his face blown half away and another one in the area of the heart. I checked his pulse, and found none."

"What did you do then?"

"I found the weapon and bagged it."

McNamara rose from his chair. "We don't know what weapon he found."

"He found *a* weapon, then," Miss Bailey said.

"Now the prosecutor is giving testimony," McNamara said.

"What kind of weapon was it and where did you find it?" Miss Bailey said.

"A .38 revolver, on the floor by the table."

"Your Honor," McNamara said. "May I please get a word in edgewise?"

"Slow down, Miss Bailey," the judge said.

"Sorry, Your Honor." She looked at McNamara. "You have an objection, Counselor?"

"I could give you a whole laundry list of objections. You assume facts not in evidence, his answer is vague and unclear, we don't know what gun he found, whose it might have been or how it got there—"

"Sustained, sustained," the judge said impatiently. "Let's try to get things in their proper sequence."

Miss Bailey nodded crisply. "So you found a gun on the floor, correct?"

"Yes, ma'am. That's when I tried to advise Mrs. Marshall of her rights but she was still pretty much out of it. I tried several times. Then I went outside and called the coroner. I secured the scene as best I could, got Mrs. Marshall up, and put her under arrest."

For a moment it seemed there might be more. The two prosecutors looked at each other and Gill shook his head. "Your witness," Miss Bailey said.

McNamara rose slowly and came across the room.

"Deputy Walsh. When you went into the house, did you take any photographs?"

"No, sir."

"Isn't that standard procedure? Don't you have a camera in your car?"

"Sure, most of the time. It got broke last month."

"Well, is that the only camera in the entire Sheriff's Department?"

"There's one in the sheriff's car."

"So you've been without a camera now for a whole month."

"Three weeks is closer to it. I've been meaning to get it fixed, or put in for a new one."

"Do you still have that camera, Deputy Walsh?"

"It's at home."

"How'd it get broken?"

"I knocked it out of the car one night. It fell on the pavement and got smashed."

Miss Bailey rose from her chair. "What difference does that make now?"

"If he'd had it, we'd have more than his word about the scene."

"But he didn't have it. We do, however, have some excellent pictures, which you can see when we call the coroner."

"Not exactly the same, though, is it?" McNamara said. He turned again to the witness. "Did you conduct any gunshot-residue tests on Mrs. Marshall's hands?"

Walsh looked away for just an instant. Then he looked back at McNamara and said, "Sure I did."

"Where were these tests conducted?"

"Down at the jail."

"And what did you do with them?"

"Sent 'em over to Montrose, along with her dress and the gun."

"Montrose meaning the CBI lab in that town, correct?"

"That's right."

"And that's where they conducted the gunshot-residue tests. Were you told the results of those tests?"

Walsh looked at Miss Bailey, who said nothing.

"Deputy?"

"I was told they were inconclusive."

"Inconclusive. Meaning it couldn't be shown that Mrs. Marshall had fired a gun."

"She had washed her hands. She had blood all over them and she scrubbed 'em almost red at the kitchen sink."

"Were you there when she did this? You seem to know a lot about what she did."

"I asked her. You know, how her hands—"

"When did you ask her that?"

"This was after. After I read her her rights."

"So she had been almost incoherent, and then suddenly she upped and described in detail how she had scrubbed the blood off her hands. Is that what you're saying?"

"I didn't say in detail. She told me she'd washed her hands. I could see from the condition of 'em—"

"That's fine, Deputy." McNamara came around the table and leaned over it, spreading his hands on the edge. "What was Mrs. Marshall's condition when you first saw her?"

"Well, like I said, she was almost incoherent, in shock . . ."

"Which would be understandable, wouldn't it, under the circumstances? How about her clothes? Was she wet? Dry?"

"Her dress was damp, as if—"

"Don't guess what she was doing, please, just tell what you saw."

"I'd say damp."

"But you don't know for sure."

"Well, if you'd let me finish my answer . . . I didn't exactly take her temperature, I had a dead man on the floor, but she looked to be in some kind of deep sweat."

"Or had been outside. You've already testified about the weather, that it was raining, right?"

"Yes, sir."

"Where were Mrs. Marshall's children when all this happened?"

"When I got there they were asleep in one of the bedrooms."

"They had slept right on through this, is that what you're saying?"

"They were taking a nap when I arrived, that's all I know."

"Did you question them at all about what had happened?"

"No, sir. The oldest one, you know, he can't talk. And the other two . . . I didn't want to disturb them, they're so young. At that point I had Mrs. Marshall's statement that she had shot her husband, so why upset the kids?"

"What did you do with them?"

"Got 'em back to town and called Social Services. Standard procedure. They have a family in Paradise who took 'em in till they made other arrangements."

"Which were what?"

"My understanding is that the grandparents came out a few days later to take care of them."

"The deceased's parents."

"Yes. They've rented a place out on Waters Road."

McNamara cleared his throat and asked his next question almost reluctantly, I thought. "When did you call the coroner, Deputy?"

"As soon as I had secured the scene and made sure there was no further danger."

"Which was approximately how long after you got to the house?"

"No more than a few minutes. Ten minutes at the outside."

"Where'd you make this call?"

"On my car radio."

"You didn't use the phone in the house?"

"No way. I didn't want to touch things in there."

"And the coroner's office has a radio that's monitored constantly, is that right?"

"I can't say about that."

"Did you ever get through to him?"

"No, sir."

It turned out that the county had never had a full-time coroner—a local undertaker named

Lew Tatters had served in that capacity for forty years—and aside from the occasional auto accident and a few deaths by natural causes, he had had little to do. He had arrived about three hours later, Walsh said, had taken photographs and examined the body. McNamara looked over at an old man sitting behind the prosecution table and I thought I saw a look of regret pass between them. They knew each other well, that's how I read it; they might even be old fishing buddies, and now McNamara had to put his friend in a hot seat.

"Isn't the coroner supposed to be on call around the clock?"

"Yes, sir. Somebody's supposed to know where he is."

"But nobody did."

"His wife said she could find him."

"But that took a while."

"About three hours, like I said."

"You don't know exactly?"

"Not exactly, no. I didn't make a note of when he came."

"And what did you do with the defendant all that time?"

"Took her down to the jail."

"You left the scene unattended and took her down to the jail."

"Sometimes you gotta make a judgment call. I didn't want to leave the house but she looked like she might be going into shock."

"So you secured the house . . ."

"Ran tape around the doors and locked it up."

"With Mrs. Marshall's key."

"That's right. Listen, I know better than to leave the house. But sometimes—"

"You gotta make a judgment call," Mc-Namara said dryly.

They looked at each other for a long ten seconds. "That's all for now," McNamara said.

This was followed by technical testimony. The coroner was called and McNamara asked him a few soft questions. He had gone on an errand for his wife, who had been feeling ill, but it had taken the drugstore longer than expected to fill her prescription. Then he had met some old pals and they had visited for a few minutes . . . not long, but by the time he did arrive at the house there was no way he could pinpoint a time of death. He had no rectal thermometer and no means of measuring the victim's liver temperature. Lividity was present and rigor mortis had begun. The body had cooled and was no longer warm to the touch. "Could you have been longer than three hours?" McNamara asked, and the undertaker allowed that he might have been as much as an hour more than that.

The DA had had the body shipped to Montrose for autopsy. There, a forensic pathologist had chopped it to pieces and now offered his opinion on the time of death, probably between 1 and 3 P.M. But this was a guess, he said, subject to a wide margin of error. The coroner fidgeted—he should have done more. A CBI agent, who had examined a .38 revolver and the bullets, gave testimony on that, on Mrs. Marshall's dress, and the fingerprints on the gun. The prints belonged to the defendant and the blood to the victim. The gun was established as the victim's. Lots of detail, little to challenge. At the end of it, the judge said there was probable cause to believe that a murder had been committed and that the defendant had done it. "The defendant is remanded to the custody of the sheriff, and the arraignment will be next Thursday at one-thirty." McNamara said, "Your Honor, I'm gonna move for bail, and I'd like to have that hearing at the arraignment if possible." The judge nodded inconclusively, got up, and walked out. I watched the deputy lead Laura Marshall out through the side door, and I sat there till the crowd thinned out.

At a pay phone outside the courthouse I called Erin's office in Denver. She was in court and unavailable till tomorrow. I called her home phone and left a message on her machine, a succinct report of what had happened. I stood in the cold for a moment, thinking it over. Deputy Walsh came out of the sheriff's office, lit up a smoke, and stared at me across the lot. I took a deep breath and headed his way.

5

He blew a smoke ring as I approached. I walked past him, close enough to reach out and knock him on his ass. This, in a masterpiece of restraint, I did not do. His smoke swirled around us. I pushed my way through it, went into the office, and worked my way around an old man sweeping the floor. He looked like Walter Brennan in his later years, with a gap-toothed face and a name, FREEMAN, sewn across the pocket of his coveralls. Across the way a woman in her sixties sat at a desk, writing in what looked like a ledger. She gave me a pleasant smile, the first decent thing that had happened since I'd arrived in this one-horse town.

"Yes, sir, what can I do for you?"

"I'd like to see Laura Marshall and her lawyer, please."

"Are you connected with her case?"

"Not yet. I represent the Denver attorney she has asked for advice."

She got on an intercom and talked to a Sheriff Gains. A moment later a stocky, gray man of about fifty years came out from a back office. He didn't look friendly or unfriendly. He did look formidable, far more a presence than his underling, who was still outside, smoking.

"You want to see Laura?"

"Yes, sir."

"She's up in the conference room with her lawyer right now."

"If you would tell them I'm here, I'd like to see them both."

He took my name and disappeared up a circular flight of stairs. At the same moment Deputy Walsh came in, reeking of smoke and wearing his attitude like a battering ram. I looked at him and gave him a smile, not a friendly one, and he said, "What the hell're you looking at, cowboy?" I saw the receptionist frown, but Walsh didn't seem to care what she thought. By then he had pushed one button too many and I said, "I don't know what I'm looking at, Deputy. Based on our short mutual experience, I'd guess a crummy little pissant with a badge."

He came straight up, as if I'd just shoved a

hot steel poker up his ass. I looked at the lady and apologized for the tone of my voice, but to Walsh I said, "Just so you know, Lennie, that cute little business with the ticket has been recorded and sent off to Denver with a copy of the ticket and my notes. I'll pay my fine and give you that one, just to show my goodwill and stuff. But if you try anything like that again, I'll have a team of state investigators all over this office. By the time they get through with you, you'll be lucky if the sheriff lets you pick up his lunch at the Main Street café."

"Oh, you're *really* asking for it."

"Yes, I am," I agreed earnestly.

There was a bump at that moment from the top of the stairs. "Come on up," the sheriff called. Deputy Walsh moved to escort me but I turned to him and said, "I think I can find the top of the staircase."

"Don't tell me how to do my job."

"Somebody needs to."

Before he could react to that, I said, "I'll tell you one more time, Walsh, stay away from me." He stood his ground and the woman at the desk saw and heard it all.

I went up alone.

Upstairs, the sheriff led me along a corridor, past what I figured was the jail, and down to an oblong conference room at the end. He opened the door and backed away diplomatically, leaving the three of us alone. "Take whatever time you need," he said. "Press the buzzer near the door when you're through."

The door locked behind him.

The room was airy and white. Laura Marshall was sitting at the end of the table. McNamara had been in the chair to her immediate left, and now he stood as I came across the room and we shook hands. He looked to be around seventy but his hand was firm and strong. He introduced me to Mrs. Marshall and I shook her hand, which felt fragile and cool in mine. They motioned me to the chair on Laura's right and the two of them sat expectantly, waiting for me to speak. I said, "Erin sent me," an unnecessary opening since they both knew who had sent me, but I hoped it would get the ice broken. Instead, Laura shivered, covered her face, and wept quietly into her hands.

McNamara looked at me and shrugged. His look said, *Maybe somebody could tell me what's going on,* but I returned his shrug and left it to Mrs. Marshall to tell us. She had now turned away from us, facing the barred window. We could see she was still crying, and it took a while for her to get her control back.

"Laura?" the old man said. "Are you okay now?"

She nodded, but she didn't look okay. Tears welled up again; she said, "I'm sorry," and turned away.

"It's okay," I said. "I've got plenty of time."

I gave the lawyer a questioning look and he nodded. "The sheriff's all right with it. Like he said, he'll let us have whatever we need. He's a decent guy."

"His deputy sure is a piece of work," I said, and McNamara rolled his eyes.

After a while Mrs. Marshall got herself together. I didn't know how long that might last, so I plunged right in. "I guess we need to know what happened. Where you were when it happened. Your version of that Monday's events."

"Just a minute there," McNamara said. "I don't want her answering that question yet."

I said, "Why not?" but I knew just enough law to be dangerous and I could see why not. He didn't want me to know too much, not yet: he didn't want to be limited in what defenses he might mount on her behalf. As an officer of the court, he couldn't use any defense that he knew to be based on false or misleading information. Sometimes it's better not to know. "Let's just leave it at that for now," he said.

But suddenly it was a moot point. Laura reached over and touched the old man's hand. He shook his head as if he had just read her mind but couldn't stop her. "I shot him," she said. She looked at the floor. "I shot Bobby."

She took a deep breath, as if she was relieved at getting it said.

"I did it," she said, stronger now. "I killed him."

6

McNamara said, "Oh, Jesus," got up, walked away from the table, and stood looking down into the yard. Laura and I sat quietly, each waiting for the other to say something. "I got the gun out of his room and I waited for him to come home," she said after a long time. "When he did, I shot him."

"Why'd you do it?"

McNamara turned away from the window with *objection* written all over his face. He settled instead for a slight headshake, then he turned back again.

"Mrs. Marshall?"

She blinked as if she had lost her train of thought.

"Why?" I asked again.

"Does it matter?"

"It sure can."

"I'm just . . . I don't know . . . if I have any defense."

"You're not in the best position to know that. As I think your lawyer will tell you."

A long moment passed. I said, "Why'd you ask your lawyer to call Erin?" and she teared up again.

"Oh, God," she said to the wall. "I must've been out of my mind."

"Well, at least you may have a defense there."

"Not when I shot Bobby. I was very clear-headed then. I'm talking about later, when I asked Mr. McNamara to call Erin."

McNamara turned growling from the window. "Laura, for God's sake, you're making this worse every time you open your mouth."

She didn't seem to hear him. "I guess I just wanted to see her again."

Another stretch of time danced away.

"Did she tell you?" she asked. "About us?"

"Some. She's not exactly a fountain of information about it."

"No, I don't imagine she is."

"Neither are you, so far."

McNamara moved around the table, into her line of vision. "Laura, have you heard anything I've been telling you? Did you understand it when I explained what the defenses to murder are, and what limitations are put on each? Are you deliberately trying to put a noose around your own neck?"

She shook her head. "Of course not."

But then she said, "I just don't think it matters much."

McNamara bristled. "What are we gonna do with her, Mr. Janeway? You see how she is?"

"Mrs. Marshall," I said softly, "you really should listen to your lawyer."

"What does that mean?" she said. "Are you walking out?"

"No," I said. "Just don't tell me anything yet that might get pried out of me and used against you on the witness stand. Erin is not your lawyer, I'm not sure this is privileged information."

"I want you to stay."

"In that case maybe I should leave," McNamara said.

She and I said, "Don't," at the same time.

"Stay," I said. "At least long enough to tell her what her risks are."

"What good will that do if she doesn't listen to my advice?"

But Laura said, "Please," and he sat in his chair and watched us.

"Mrs. Marshall, why do you want Erin to represent you?"

"I want to see her again."

McNamara leaned over the table and made an imploring gesture. "Laura, you can't pick your lawyer for something like this on the basis of a childhood friendship! Mr. Janeway, please! Get her to use her head."

"He's right," I said to Laura.

To both of them I said, "Erin is a very good lawyer. You'd be in good hands. But at this point I'm not even sure she'll do this. I'm not sure she can, legally."

"What's that about?" McNamara said.

"There'd be a conflict of interest. Ms. D'Angelo was once involved with the deceased." I gave McNamara a knowing look, hoping he would pick it up.

"Before we were married, Bobby and I had an affair," Laura said. "He had been Erin's . . . but that's private business. Surely a judge can't dictate who will represent me."

"Mr. Janeway is right," McNamara said. "It's a potential conflict of interest."

"Is that some insurmountable thing?"

"You may have to sign a waiver saying you understand it and want her anyway."

"Then I will. I've got to talk to her. I've got to tell her . . ."

"Tell her what, Mrs. Marshall?" I said.

"How sorry I am."

"I'll tell her that."

"You can't possibly, there's too much between us."

"Then I'll tell her that."

"And what then? Will she come?"

I shrugged. "I have no idea what that lady will do from one day to the next."

"I still love her."

We talked about her childhood with Erin. They had lived as next-door neighbors when they were very young kids; they had always been such great friends. "We were so different, and yet there was a kinship between us that I've never known with anyone else. We never had a cross word, not once that I can remember."

A few minutes later, Laura said, "Does she ever talk about me? Those old days?"

"She hasn't yet, not to me."

"So where are we now in the scheme of things?" McNamara said.

"I'd like to go up and see the house," I said. "Erin wants me to look at your books, assuming the sheriff is finished up there."

"Sheriff's been done at least ten days," McNamara said. "I'd better tell him you're going, though, and you'd better have someone with you. I'll go along if you want."

"That's very generous, Mr. McNamara. I'd appreciate it."

We pressed the buzzer and a moment later the sheriff came and let us out. Across the street I made another call to Erin and was surprised to find her in the office. "Our judge is entertaining some motions," she said. "We may go back this afternoon, we may not. What's happening out there?"

I gave her a report. At the end of it, she said, "Not much doubt she did this?"

"She's not denying it. And the evidence looks pretty strong."

"Well, then . . ."

"Well then what?"

"Come on home."

"Erin . . ."

"Yes? Is something wrong?"

"She wants to see you."

"What for?"

"That's between you and her. As far as her case goes, it seems pretty open-and-shut. There may be extenuating circumstances and I think what she mainly needs is advice on how to plead. The old man who's handling her seems to be pretty competent. He's cautious damn near to a fault."

"Sounds like she's well represented."

"I don't know . . ."

"What don't you know?" There was a pause, then she said, "Come on home."

"I'd like to stay another day. I haven't even seen her books yet."

I listened to the phone static between us. Abruptly Erin said, "They're calling us back, I've got to go. Tell her I'll send her some names of lawyers in her neck of the woods."

I said nothing for a moment. Erin said, "Don't waste any more time, Cliff. You said it yourself, the books probably don't matter. Look, I've gotta go."

She hung up and I stood there looking out toward Main Street. Deputy Walsh came out and lit a cigarette and we stared at each other like two old gunfighters in a bad cowboy flick. It would be so easy to pack it in: take my fee, which I knew Erin would make generous, and forget about Laura Marshall and her tragedy. For the moment it would also be damned near impossible.

7

Deputy Walsh met us in the parking lot. "Sheriff says you're going up to the house," he said. "He wants me to take you up."

"I don't think you need to do that," Mc-Namara said. "House is back with us now. We'll find our own way up."

"He'd rather have me go with you."

Parley looked at me. "No way," I said.

"You really are trying to piss me off, aren't you, cowboy?"

"Trying my damnedest, Red Ryder."

"Sheriff Gains said I should *take* you up."

By then I had had more than enough of Sheriff's Deputy Lennie Walsh. "But that was you and this is me," I said. "The sheriff doesn't tell me when to take a leak, either."

He stood there, seething malice.

"Look at it this way," I said. "If you watch

carefully as I pull out of the lot, maybe you can catch me obeying some traffic laws. Then you could give me a ticket for safe driving."

McNamara made a sound that might have been a laugh, maybe only a cough, and I said, "Goddammit, Walsh, I thought the defense had a right to some privacy. Do you really want to make an issue out of this? Where the hell's the sheriff?"

"He went over to Gunnison to see a friend."

"Well, we're going up alone."

Walsh flipped his cigarette into the gutter and managed to flip me off in the same smooth movement. But he got in his car and drove away to the west.

"You boys are off to a great start with each other," McNamara noted wryly.

"Sometimes it happens that way. I do tend to meet more than my share of the world's real sons of bitches."

"Wonder why that is."

"Maybe because they tend to get my back up. I've found that it's best to draw a line with tyrants and let them know right away that there are certain flavors of crap I will not eat."

"I'll bet you've got some kinda blood pressure."

"It tends to stay around one-thirty over eighty-five. How's yours?"

"Mine would be two-fifty over one-twenty if I wasn't on pills." He grunted. "So much for accommodating the world's cheeriest assholes."

The sky had darkened and the mountains were faint outlines in the swirling gray mist. "Looks like it's gettin' mean up there," McNamara said, smoothly changing the subject. Within three minutes we went through a light snow shower into a heavy, wet autumn blizzard. About five miles beyond the town limit the road forked. McNamara motioned me to the right, and almost at once we clattered onto a snow-pocked dirt surface and began to climb. I put the car into four-wheel drive. The dirt road disappeared and fresh snow swirled down from the dark skies. It came in flurries, then in gusts that shook the car. "Looks like Lennie's goin' up anyway," McNamara said. Ahead, the deputy's car swirled through the snow and a stream of smoke poured from his cracked-open window. I could see his head bobbing fiercely from side to side. "He seems to be carrying on quite a conversation with himself," I said.

McNamara nodded. "Watch out for that one, Mr. Janeway. I've known him since he was a kid and he's never been any good."

"Why does it not surprise me to hear that?"

"I don't know if he'd actually do anything,

but he talks a bad show. Struts around flaunting his authority under the guise of protecting the community. Never known him to resort to any brutality, but I don't imagine he'd be the first lawman to shave a point here and there. Just watch your flank, that's all I'm telling you. I'm not one to say he's crooked, but he's always been mean as hell."

"He's crooked too," I said, and I told the old man about my run-in at the stop sign. At the end of the story McNamara was no longer accommodating: he was damned mad.

"That sorry-ass son of a bitch." A moment later he said, "I'll take your case gratis if you want to hang around and bring it to the judge."

"What kind of chance would I have?"

"Hard to say. You'd be in county court, and the county court judge out here is just an old highway patrolman. But he's got a good sense of right and wrong, and he knows Lennie and his ways. I think you'd have a chance."

"What kind of bird is the district court judge?"

He rolled his eyes.

"Oh," I said.

"Yeah. He just got appointed this year. He lives up in Gunnison and has a summer home in Paradise. Used to be a pretty good lawyer, coulda been a real good one, but that's just my

opinion. He represented a couple of corpora-
tions, one or two banks in Gunnison and Montrose, and I hear did a good job. Worked his
way up in the Colorado Bar Association, served
on commissions and ethics committees and was
real diligent. Then we had a sudden vacancy, the
governor picked him, and the appointment went
straight to his head. He likes to pontificate from
the bench, loves to lecture defendants and their
attorneys. He'd be okay, in other words, if he
didn't think he was God. He's got a rude awakening coming when he's got to stand for election
with the voters."

"So he's eccentric and he's got an ego. Is he
fair?"

"He's a political animal is what he is. Out
here that means pretty solidly pro-prosecution: a
conservative law-and-order type with a short attention span and an impatient streak as wide as
the Colorado River. He wears a gun in the
courtroom, underneath that black robe."

"You're kidding."

He laughed. "I never kid about the law, son.
Well, hardly ever. Sometimes it gets so strange
you just can't help it."

"Now I'm tempted to hang around, just to
see him in action."

"You should do that. And while you're here,

give Lennie a run through the county court. It wouldn't be any piece of cake, but you know you need to take Lennie to court over that. You can't let that stand."

"Yeah, but in real life I haven't got days to waste on it, only to lose anyway."

"That's what bastards like Lennie Walsh count on."

He was quiet for another minute but I knew it was still grating on him and I liked him for that. "If you don't mind," he said, "I think I'll walk down the street after we get back tonight and talk to people in the stores on that corner. They all know me. I think there's at least a fair chance somebody saw it happen. We'd have him by the balls then."

"You're a good man, Mr. McNamara."

"Call me Parley. And I'll call you what?"

"Cliff'll be fine."

Snow swirled down from the mountaintop and the road ahead looked increasingly forbidding, dark and socked in. It peaked, dipped, and wound upward again. I couldn't see the bottom of the valley now: it was all fog with occasional dark spots. Suddenly I saw Walsh's car ahead of us, moving fast and half-obliterated in a swirl of white powder. "Wonder what that silly bastard is up to now," Parley said.

"Letting us know who the boss is."

"He must be really haulin' ass up there. If it was us driving like that, he'd give us a ticket."

"Maybe we should make a citizen's arrest."

The old man laughed. "I'm game if you are."

Walsh was now out of sight. I asked how much farther and McNamara said four or five miles. Casually I said, "So what can you tell me about Mrs. Marshall and her late husband?"

"I hope you mean just background. I don't want to get into the specifics of this case yet."

"Background's fine. We can hash over the other stuff if and when we find ourselves working the same side of the street."

"Just for background, then, Laura's a good woman. I always thought so, even if nobody else did."

"Are you saying nobody else did?"

"She didn't suck up to the local yokels. That won't ever get you on lists as the most popular gal in this town."

I was formulating another question when he said, "Sinclair Lewis had it right, and not just about Minnesota, either. Little towns like this are the same everywhere. Friendly people who take real deep offense if all that coziness isn't returned in full, right away."

"And Laura didn't?"

"She's just a private lady. Didn't have time for committees and clubs, coffee-klatching and endless bullshit. She had three kids to raise and a house to run. I think she's got a right to her own life without being expected to do things."

"What about her kids?"

"She and Bob had two: they adopted one, years ago when it seemed she might not be able to have any, then surprised themselves and had two of their own."

"What about Marshall?"

"What do you want to know?"

"What kind of guy was he?"

"He was all right."

I waited but the elaboration didn't come. "All right how?" I finally asked. "You mean he walked in good health, he made no obvious enemies, or he was a jolly good fellow?"

"All of the above, as far as I know. Take that right up there."

I turned in to a narrow, rutted road and bumped my way up a slope toward a wooded crest. Again McNamara had lapsed into silence.

"I really am asking just for background, Parley," I said. "I've got maybe another day at the most to formulate a recommendation and then get out of here. In fact, Erin told me to come on home. I'm not even supposed to be here now."

"Tell me about Erin. What kinda lawyer is she?"

"She practiced in a big Denver firm for several years. Worked on corporate matters and on a big Wyoming water rights case. She's a supercompetent generalist. Was on a fast track to make partner by her midthirties but got restless and quit. She's thirty-two now."

"You say she's a generalist. She ever handle criminal cases?"

"Quite a few, actually. Mostly pro bono."

"Those are the ones you've either got your heart into or not. They show me what kind of lawyer you are."

"She wasn't assigned to do 'em, I'll tell you that. She did a lot more than the company wanted her to do, and she won a helluva lot more than she lost. She's a good trial lawyer, and I'm not just saying that because I like her. If Laura Marshall were my sister, I don't think I could find her anyone better."

"She'd have one strike against her before she even gets her coat off. The judge won't ever say so out loud, but he doesn't like women attorneys."

"Well, the prosecution has one too, so at least they'd start out evenly handicapped."

"Yeah, but he knows that one. Watched her grow up. And she is the prosecutor."

Suddenly I saw the house through the trees. It perched on a hilltop facing a sweeping mountain range and overlooking a valley. It was visible for just a few seconds, then swallowed by the snow-storm, then visible, then gone again. "We're get-tin' there," McNamara said. "You see any sign of Lennie's car?"

"Not yet."

We made a sharp turn and started up a long last incline, coming between two pine trees into the front yard. "Where the hell's Lennie?" Mc-Namara said softly, almost to himself. There was no car anywhere in sight, and no tracks in the fresh snow. "You see anyplace he could've pulled over?"

"Maybe he ran off the road somewhere. He was going way too fast."

"We'da seen him, though, if he'da cracked up. I don't see how we wouldn't see him, wher-ever he went off."

I pulled up in front of the house and we got out. From the front porch a picture-postcard vista of snow peaks stretched across the full horizon and around to the side. "This must've cost the Marshalls plenty," I said. "How much land they got up here?"

"Oh, a hundred acres easy. Enough to keep the bastards at bay, so there won't be any Holiday Inns going up right under their faces."

"Must've cost 'em," I said again.

"Actually, Marshall's grandfather bought this tract back in 1930. You could get land up here for a song then. If you think this is remote now, think how it was then. He picked up the whole thing for next to nothing. They started building this house a few years later. It started as a cabin—that's the main part of it—and later they added more rooms. That's what gives it its rambling look. Different generations added to it."

I walked out to the edge of the porch. "Wow," I said, breathing in the cold air.

"I don't think Laura and Bobby are rich by any means, so don't assume that. I think it's been a struggle the last few years just to keep up the taxes on this place. But that's life in America. Just because you've got something fine like this, that don't mean the bastards'll let you keep it."

We stood there together, listening to the wind whipping across the hill.

"Now where the hell has that silly sumbitch gone?" He jingled a small key ring in his hand.

I figured Lennie was just being Lennie, screwing with our heads. I stood at the top of the steps looking out across the meadow. From there I could see the weather moving in, rolling across the opposite range. I could see the road disappearing as it came, and the trees being consumed along the lower rim, almost at eye level with where we were standing. And suddenly I saw something move.

"There he is."

McNamara squinted, but Lennie, or whatever it had been, had disappeared.

"My eyes ain't what they once were," the old man said.

"He's gone now anyway."

"You sure it was him?"

"Actually, no."

McNamara said, "I'm gettin' damned tired of this," and he turned toward the door. At that moment Lennie stepped out of the woods across the way and stood watching us with a rifle in his hands.

It was almost too dark to make him out: in another five minutes I wouldn't have seen him at all. McNamara got the door open and said, "Come on in," but I stayed there watching Lennie watch me. Lennie lifted the rifle to his shoulder but I didn't move. We stood still, a pair of fools playing chicken, until he lowered the gun and stepped back into the trees. What was he trying to prove, that he could kill me? That he could do it from some vast distance and there was nothing I could do to stop it? That he was crazy enough? What does one fool ever prove to another?

"Come on in," McNamara called out again, and I turned away and went into a dark front hall.

"Just so you know," I said, "I saw Lennie across the way. This time there wasn't any doubt about it. He was pointing a rifle at us."

McNamara turned and faced me. "Why in the *hell* would he do that?"

His face was a pale blur and I couldn't read the silence that followed. His voice had been incredulous, as if even Lennie couldn't be that crazy. What would the natural conclusion of such doubt be? . . . That *I* was the crazy one?

"He *must* be nuts," he said, and I felt better.

He shook his head. "This really makes you wonder, doesn't it?"

He turned and walked ahead of me into the house, putting on lights as he went. The hall stretched straight on back through the house, past another hall that led, I assumed, to the bedrooms. Off to the right was a large room of some kind; to the left, another big room where the tragedy had happened. *The death room,* as the press would probably call it.

McNamara went left and turned on the lights. I came to the door and stood there for a moment looking at the carnage. The carpet had been a light tan—probably lighter than it now seemed, I thought: now the center of it was dominated by an ugly black bloodstain. How many death scenes had I seen like this in my years as a Denver cop? I didn't know what it would tell me this time; maybe nothing, but a cop always had to look, and in that moment I was a cop again. McNamara had gone across the room, stepping gingerly around the blood to stand near an old-style rinky-tink piano. Behind the piano was a pair of French doors, which were curtained with some flimsy lace stuff. I didn't move. McNamara watched me as if he'd seen me work in some past life and knew what to expect. My eyes roved around the room and finally came back to where the old man was.

"Ugly, isn't it?" he said.

"It always is, Parley."

"What're you lookin' for?"

"No idea," I said. "Maybe I'm just hoping the room will speak to me."

"You cops are funny birds."

"Yeah. Some of us are a riot."

Eventually I came into the room, taking care not to touch anything. Yes, it had been three weeks. The sheriff had gone over it and he had had technicians out from the CBI, but to me it was a new scene. I could now see for myself what Parley had just told me: that this house, this cabin, had been built in pieces, with God knew how many add-ons over time, and this main room had probably been here for the full sixty years. There was nothing new-looking anywhere in sight. Straight across the room was a rustic rock fireplace. To the left of that, a glassed-in porch that in good weather would overlook the mountain range. But now darkness had spread beyond the glass, and with the lights on it seemed even darker, as if night had been upon us for hours.

"So what's it tell you?" Parley asked.

"Nothing yet." I shrugged: I really didn't expect much. "It's cold."

My eyes roved back to the left. There, near the fireplace, was a couch and a small circle of chairs with a coffee table in the center. Two floor lamps were placed behind the chairs, making it a cozy little reading circle when the fire was lit. In fact, a small stack of books was on the table and instinctively I moved across the room to see what they were. I looked down at *The Quality of Courage,* a recent book with Mickey Mantle's byline.

"Was Marshall a baseball fan?"

He shrugged. "I really didn't know him that well."

I bent over and touched the book by the edge. "Can I borrow your gloves for a minute?"

"You think they'll fit you?"

"You got big hands, Parley. They'll be good enough."

I pulled the right glove on. It was snug, not quite tight.

"What's the deal?" Parley said. "Sheriff said they were finished in here."

"Maybe, but I don't see any residue on these books."

"You mean fingerprint dust?"

I nodded. "Just call it an old cop's habit. I don't like to touch things where somebody's been killed."

I picked off the Mantle book, holding it by the corners, and laid it flat on the table beside the others. Under it was a novel, *The Ballad of Cat Ballou,* and under that a thing called *How to Be a Bandleader,* by Paul Whiteman. Under that was *The Speeches of Adlai Stevenson,* and at the bottom was a cheap tattered paperback, *Gabby Hayes' Treasure Chest of Tall Tales.*

McNamara seemed to sense my surprise. "Something wrong?"

"I don't know. This is just the strangest damned group of books I ever saw. Way too weird for anybody to be reading them."

"Then why are they here?"

"Exactly."

I looked at them again.

"Are they worth anything?" Parley asked.

"Not so you'd know it. The *Cat Ballou's* got a little sex appeal because of the film, but I don't think it's ever gonna be this century's answer to *War and Peace*." I couldn't help laughing. Singsong, I said, "Adlai *Steven*son and *Ga*bby *Hayes*?"

"It does kinda blow your mind, doesn't it?"

"Best laugh I've had all day."

But then my eyes wandered back to the bloodstain, and that was no laughing matter. We stood transfixed for another moment. A hundred thoughts ran through my head, none of them worth a damn on the face of it. I walked across to the piano, turned, and said, "I'm missing something somewhere."

"Maybe you're trying too hard to make sense out of something that's just . . . you know, happenstance."

"Maybe."

A moment passed.

"It's not happenstance, Parley. Happenstance would be five disparate books, maybe an eclectic mix of fiction and non. But what does this little collection tell you? I mean, Paul *Whiteman*? A history of the Whiteman band maybe, but a book on how to be a bandleader? Were either of the Marshalls fans of band music?"

"You'll have to ask her."

I touched the Mantle, opened the cover.

"It's signed."

"What do you mean signed? Who signed it?"

"Mantle."

"So what does that do for it?"

"Makes it ten times the value is all. It's probably a hundred dollars signed. Maybe a bit more now, I don't know, they keep going up. I haven't had one in a while."

"Still, not exactly a motive for murder."

"No."

But I had a hunch now. I opened the Whiteman. It was signed in Whiteman's distinctive hand. The Gabby Hayes—signed, an uncommon signature from any perspective. I had never even seen one and I guessed it might be as high as two hundred.

"Look at this," I said. "The *Cat Ballou* is signed by Nat King Cole and Lee Marvin from the film. I'll be damned."

I opened the Stevenson. On the half title was a tiny signature, a hand I knew very well.

"John Steinbeck," I said.

"What about Stevenson?"

I shook my head. "Stevenson doesn't matter: his signature's common as dirt and just about as cheap. Steinbeck's name on wallpaper's worth three hundred."

"I don't understand. Why would John Steinbeck sign that?"

"Maybe he gave it to somebody. He admired Stevenson and he wrote the foreword to the paperback of this book."

I looked around the room with a new eye. "Well, damn, Parley, I think we've found something here."

"I'm not sure what. Maybe you should look in the library across the hall."

It was one of those moments, wasn't it? Even before we went there I had a hunch what I'd find: a wall of books, and as I began taking them gingerly off the shelf and opening them, the hunch grew into a certainty. They were all signed, either by their authors or by well-known figures associated with their stories. Leonard Bernstein. Alfred Hitchcock. Wernher von Braun. Duke Ellington. Al Capp. John Wayne.

And on and on.

"Man, Parley, these are worth some money."

"How much money?"

"I don't know. There's gotta be a thousand books here. If all of them are signed, even if the average is only—hell, I don't know, say two hundred—what've you got?"

"Two hundred grand."

"And that's probably wholesale. John Wayne didn't sign many of his books. He's four hundred by himself."

At that moment we heard a bump outside.

"Sounds like Lennie's come home to roost," Parley said.

But when I went to the door, no one was there.

I walked out onto the porch. The night was full, the grounds dark as pitch. I went out to the steps and shouted at the mountains. "Hey, Lennie! You out here?"

He was there. I could feel the slimy bastard all around me.

Suddenly nervous, Parley said, "Come on inside."

"Listen, you prick," I said to the darkness. "If you ever point a gun at me again, I'll take it away from you and shove it and that badge up your ass. You got that?"

I stood there feeling naked. I felt vulnerable and alone, damn foolish, a silly cock framed like a bull's-eye in the door light, but unwilling to move.

"Come on in here," Parley said from somewhere far behind me. "Come on, Janeway, you're giving me the creeps."

Inside, I heard him take a deep breath. "What do you want to do now?"

I thought about it. "I don't know. This changes everything."

"Does it?"

"Sure it does." I thought about what might be done and how to proceed. "We've got to talk to Mrs. Marshall about these books."

"Surely she knows what they are."

"You'd think so, but if they were valuable, wouldn't she say that? This wouldn't be the first time somebody died and left a spouse in the dark."

He didn't seem convinced. I said, "Well, look at it this way. She's sure not handling it like it means anything to her. I've got a feeling she hasn't got a clue what her books might be worth."

I glanced back into the room. "Other than that, let's keep it quiet for now. These books are unprotected in a vacant house, far from any-where. A book thief could clear this room in an hour, so nobody needs to know but her. That in-cludes the sheriff and Lennie, no aspersions on either of those fine gents. Let 'em think these are just what they look like, a bunch of cheap books."

I looked it all over again. "I wouldn't mind spending a day in here, just to go through it and see what she has. I could give her a loose appraisal if she wants it."

"You can ask her in the morning."

I could see he wanted to leave. Outside, the snow was piling up, but damn, I hated to leave those books like that.

"C'mon, Cliff, it's gettin' cold in here. We can't do anything else tonight."

"One more thing. Just give me a few more minutes."

I walked through the room making notes in my notebook. I wrote down where things were and put in my impressions. I jotted down some titles and where they were on the shelves. It wasn't much, just enough that, maybe, I'd know if someone had come in and disturbed them.

We were halfway back to town when suddenly Lennie pulled in behind us. He followed us on in as if he had been there all along, dropping off as we passed the sheriff's parking lot.

8

McNamara was a widower who had lived in the county thirty years. "I eat down to the Paradise Café ever since Martha died," he said. "We never had any children, so that's where I do my socializing, such as it is. You feel like grabbing some supper over there?"

"Sure."

We sat in a corner booth and I learned that his wife had died two years ago. They had been together almost fifty years. I could sense some of his loss when he mentioned her, and maybe I could imagine the rest of it.

"I try to keep busy," he said. "Sometimes I go a little stir-crazy, but most of the time I find enough work to do."

Actually, he said, there wasn't much legal work in a small county like this. "The house keeps me busy. I work in Martha's garden and putz around.

Funny, I never gave a damn about the garden till she was gone, and then it became more important than I'd have believed to keep those green sprouts coming. I feel good watching it bloom in the spring, kinda like she's still here. But there's no gardening this time of the year and now I miss it. I do keep my shingle hung out. If a legal dispute does come up, I usually get it. I'll travel if the case calls for that . . . over to Hinsdale County, up to Gunnison. That's rare, but I keep busy."

He broke some bread. "For a while I thought of moving to Chicago. I was there on a visit to my sister when I met Martha. Christmas, 1939. Now my sister's long gone too. When Martha died, I thought maybe I'd move back there, but in the end what the hell would I do? I'm too old to get a job, even doing legal research, and I think the big city would be worse than living out here in the sticks. At least I know this kind of solitude: the other I can only imagine, but what I imagine is pretty excruciating."

He laughed. "Hey, don't get the wrong idea. I don't feel sorry for myself. I've had a pretty good run at life. Where you staying tonight?"

"Hadn't thought about it." I looked outside at the snowstorm. "I'd better start thinking right after we eat. I'd hate to have to sleep in my car."

"Don't worry. There are only two places, the

Paradise Hotel and a motel back out on the highway, but neither one of 'em ever fills up. I wouldn't wish those places on my worst enemy. The old sheriff used to sometimes let people sleep in the jail. I'd rather sleep there than in either of those fleabags."

The waitress, a buxomy gal named Velma, poured some coffee and flirted with Parley. He watched her ass as she walked away and we smiled foxily at each other. You never get too old to look.

I paid our tab. "Put your money away, I'm on an expense account."

Outside, he huddled into his coat. "You could stay with me if you want to," he said almost shyly. "The room's warm and private, it's free, and the roof don't leak."

"Well, that's generous of you. I wouldn't want to put you out."

"Ah, hell, you'd be doin' me a favor. I'd like the sound of a voice in the house."

"In that case you're on."

"Now let's walk up the street and see if anybody saw your little run-in with Lennie this morning."

His house was at the south edge of town, on a one-acre tract with trees and light underbrush and a clearing in the back that was probably the garden. The house had been built in the twenties and was still solid. "I don't have much to do to it," he said. "I paint it every five years or so and I had it inspected in 1980, but it's solid as Gibraltar. I expect to be here for the duration, however long that is."

Inside it was spotless, with the kind of spit-and-polish attention that made me stop at the door and take off my shoes. He's keeping it that way for her, I thought. He said, "Don't worry about it," but I removed the shoes anyway. He fired up a big fireplace and I got the tour. "This place has always been too big," he said. "Martha wanted it that way, in case her brothers came to visit. They did a few times, but now they're gone too."

We walked back through a hallway and he turned on the lights as he went. "My only complaint about it these days is that it gets so godawful dark in here. I never noticed that before, but now it can be depressing. So if you see a dark corner, feel free to turn on a light. Back here are the bedrooms."

There were three rooms with beds. "You can have your pick," he said. "My room is clear over on the other side of the house, so you can bump around, sing in the shower—you won't bother me a bit. We don't get TV down here. The signals just won't come in over these mountains, so I hope you brought a good book to read."

I stashed my stuff in one of the bedrooms and joined him in the front room for a nightcap. We talked about my case against Lennie if I chose to bring one. Only two of the stores on that corner had still been open, but Parley had collected three names. "I'll talk to the others tomorrow."

At Jenkins' Hardware the proprietor had not only seen it but had discussed it with a customer, who was also willing to talk. Lennie's tactics were well-known in the county. "I think we've got a chance not only to get it dismissed but also to cause Lennie some general embarrassment," Parley said. "That's got to be worth doing."

"You're sure taking a lot of trouble with this."

"It's what I do. You can't let an asshole make a mockery of the law."

"No," I said.

"Does that mean you'll fight it?"

"Hey, how could I not fight it after all your hard work?"

"That's the ticket, boy, no pun intended. If the judge won't listen, I'll appeal the son of a

bitch, I don't care if it is just a traffic dispute."
He laughed suddenly. "I'll get my friend Griff
Edwards to do a piece on justice in Paradise for
the *Paradise Mountaineer*. Embarrass the sons of
bitches, that's language they understand."

We talked about Mrs. Marshall. I asked how
long he had known her and he said, "Just about
as long as she's been here. Eight years or so. But
long don't mean well. She and Marshall kept to
themselves."

"Didn't you tell me you knew her better than
him?"

"When she first came here, she got talked
into being on an old-town preservation committee. That's how she met Martha and that's how I
met her. We had dinner once, the four of us, and
whenever they went out of town, I'd drive up
there and keep an eye on their place. That's
about the extent of it."

"Did they always have a big library like
that?"

"If they did, they had it hidden. I guess the
first time I saw those books was three or four
years ago. And it's grown some since then."

"Did either of 'em ever tell you what it was,
where they got it?"

"No, but I didn't ask. Lots of people have
books."

"You mean you just said, wow, what a lot of books?"

"Something stupid like that. It was just a wall of books to me."

"Did you get any feeling for how they were getting along back in the beginning?"

I didn't think he'd answer that, but he said, "Laura never struck me as a happy woman. I always liked her, but she was . . . private . . . if you know what I mean."

"Secretive?"

"Don't read your own stuff into my words, son. *Private* means *private*: not that she had anything to hide, just stuff she'd rather keep to herself that wasn't anybody else's business anyway."

He poured himself another shot, gestured to me, and I shook my head.

"Right from the start I sensed some tragedy in her life," he said. "That wouldn't have anything to do with your friend the lawyer over in Denver, would it?"

"Could be."

I sipped my brandy. "I'll be talking to Erin in the morning. I'll see if she'll tell us about it."

"Just tell her I'm a curious old bastard. Got nothing to do anymore but poke around in other people's business."

"Yeah, Parley, I'll be sure and tell her that."

The big question was still there between us. At some point I asked it.

"So what do you think happened?"

"I don't know that, do I? I don't know much more than what you heard her say this afternoon. I told her a dozen times not to say anything . . ."

"Well, now that she has . . ."

He shrugged. "Could be any number of things. Maybe Marshall was a womanizer and she got tired of it. Maybe he abused her and she got tired of that. We know it wasn't for any big life insurance claim. The policies they had wouldn't amount to a hill of beans. So far she hasn't shown much willingness to talk about the two of them. I don't know if these things happened, but I will tell you that Laura never struck me as a woman who'd put up with much bullshit. That's why one day she walked out on the preservation committee, right between the crumpets and the tea. Too much bullshit, too many pissy little kingmakers more interested in having their way than getting things done. That seems to be the way of all committees, from the UN all the way out here to West Jesus, Colorado."

He coughed and leaned forward, warming

his hands. "There's another theory, I guess, but so far it's just my own intuition." He grinned like an old fox. "Would you like to hear it?"

"Sure I would."

"I don't think she killed him at all."

9

"Then who did?" Erin said.

"He doesn't know, or isn't telling," I said. "So far it's just a feeling he's got."

I listened to the telephone noise while she mulled it over almost three hundred miles away. I was standing at a downtown Paradise pay phone, basking in the great Colorado autumn morning. The snow had stopped during the night, the sun had cast the valley in a brilliant glow, and all along the street I could hear the scrape of steel on pavement as people dug out and got ready for a new day.

It was Saturday and I had called Erin at home. She listened intently: there was no talk now of come on home or pack it in. I heard her sip her coffee and sniff. Her voice was thick, as if she was getting a cold.

"He doesn't know who did it," she said at

last. "He doesn't know who *might* have done it, or why, or why *she* might be covering up for someone. He doesn't know *her* all that well either. This is just some gut feeling he's got."

This was not said sarcastically or to diminish anything the old man believed. It was just Erin, in her lawyer voice, putting some facts in order.

"Anything else?"

"I asked the same questions you just did," I told her.

"And he had no reason at all for his hunch."

"Nothing he was willing to put to words, let alone take into court."

"Where were the kids when all this went on?"

"In their bedroom, asleep, way over on the other side of the house."

"And the sounds of gunshots didn't wake them?"

"She says not."

"You believe that?"

"I'm just telling you what she told McNamara."

"A .38 makes a lot of noise," Erin said.

"Tell me about it." I touched my shoulder, where I had once been shot by one. "I guess it's possible. There are three big rooms and a hall between the kids' rooms and the front room where Marshall was shot. Maybe, if all the doors were closed."

"I don't suppose you've seen any of the reports yet."

"Not yet. Parley's got the CBI reports and other evidence the DA has."

"What'd the CBI say, did he tell you that?"

"He's not ready to tell us that; not till we know we're either in or out. He did say it was two days before the CBI got out there."

"Jesus! What was that all about?"

"They weren't called right away. A lot of the physical evidence—the bullets, the blood, some fibers, some hair—was collected by the Sheriff's Department and sent over to the lab in Montrose. Parley was pretty disgusted."

"He should be." I knew what she would ask next and she asked it. "How do you read him?"

"He's a solid old guy, sharp under all that folksy stuff. I wouldn't blow him off."

"But you haven't really questioned her yet?"

"Just what I told you about yesterday."

"No idea what the books might mean, if anything?"

"Not yet."

A moment passed. I thought it could go either way. She was making a decision now, and maybe then I'd have my own decision to make. "You said he was into books. Even way back when you knew him."

"Yeah, he was," she said. "I told you about that, remember? . . . That night we met in your bookstore two years ago, I told you my first boyfriend was a book freak like you. But I guess, given the way it all turned out, I didn't know what he was into." She sniffed. "Any reason to think the books might be part of it?"

"Nothing I can put my finger on. They might be a motive for something."

I looked up and saw Lennie Walsh drive past. He turned in to the parking lot at the hall of justice and sat in his car, smoking and talking to himself.

"Go over and see her," Erin said. "This time don't pull any punches. Ask her about the books and see if McNamara will confront her on this confession she's so eager to give him. Make an issue of it. Tell her if she lies, or evades your questions, you're out of there."

"I guess I can do some form of that."

"However you do it, let's get a straight story from her and see where we are."

"One more thing. McNamara wants to know what happened between you two."

"What for?"

"He says he's a nosy old bastard who likes to pry."

"Ha. He asks good questions. That's one I would've asked as well."

She thought about it, then said, "Go ahead and tell him they had an affair behind my back. See what he thinks of my conflict of interest."

Again I was shown into the conference room on the second floor. "You'll have to wait for Parley," said old Freeman, the custodian. "He's down talking to the sheriff about another matter and he doesn't want your lady questioned until he can be here."

It was a half-hour wait. When Parley came in, he said, "They don't want to dismiss your ticket outright. I could have Christ and twenty-six disciples lined up to testify and he'd still want to take Lennie's side of it. They're all down there now hashing it over. Secretly I think the sheriff is pretty damned mad about it. Like I told you, this is not the first time Lennie's done this kinda thing."

Another fifteen minutes passed before Mrs. Marshall was brought in. I couldn't tell from the sheriff's expression how the wind was blowing, but he didn't look happy. He escorted Laura to the same chair and left us there.

I watched Parley, waiting for his lead.

"Laura, we need to talk turkey, you and me."

"Can Mr. Janeway stay?"

"It might be just as well, for right now, if it was just the two of us."

"But he needs to be here," she insisted. "So he can tell Erin what was said."

He looked at me, clearly annoyed. "Dammit, Janeway, is this woman of yours gonna come down here or not?"

"She'll come," Laura said, surprising us both. "I know she'll come."

"I talked to her this morning," I said. "She has not accepted your case, Mrs. Marshall, she certainly can't be considered your attorney at this point. And for what it's worth, I think she'd agree with the advice Parley is giving you."

"This is not a question I'd normally ask," Parley said. "Now I think you've got to tell me what really happened the day Bobby was killed."

"I did tell you."

"So far you've only said that you shot him."

She nodded warily. "What else is there?"

"Was there something remotely like a reason? How'd your dress get torn?"

"It was a private matter between us."

Parley rolled his eyes back and closed them.

"That won't make any difference anyway," she said. "What happened is what's important, not why it happened."

"Is that what you think? Well, missy, where's your law degree?"

I saw two things in her face: a flash of anger

and an immediate look of regret. "I'm sorry," she said. "I know I'm making it harder for you."

"It can't get too much harder than impossible. You'd better come to realize a few things, and right now's not a minute too soon. You're in a bad spot."

"I know that. I know it. What would happen if I just plead guilty and throw myself on the mercy of the court?"

"You could do that. Without any mitigating circumstances, and based on what I know of this judge here, you might get out in time to see your great-grandchildren graduate from college. That's *if* you get out at all, and *if* he doesn't fit you for a hot seat at Cañon City."

"They won't execute me."

"Probably not. This state doesn't have any stomach for its own death penalty statute. The point is, they *could*; that old man downstairs could put you on death row, where you might sit for years before some other old man commuted it to life. Or he could give you life without possibility of parole right out of the gate. Do you know how difficult it can be to even get something like that reconsidered, let alone overturned? Whatever your reason is for not talking about it now, that'll look pale as the years pass. You can trust me on this, Laura, if you don't believe anything else I tell you: the day will come when you'll wish to God you had listened to good advice when you heard it. Then it'll be too late. The very best you can expect to do is twenty years of damned hard time. That's what I want you to think about."

"What do you think I've been doing? If there was anything I could tell you . . ."

"You can start by telling me why you shot him. And don't keep saying it's a private matter. When you shoot somebody dead, there's nothing private about it anymore."

"What difference does it make if you can't use it anyway?"

"Is that what you're saying? There may be mitigating circumstances but you won't let me use them even if I know what they are. Is that what you're telling me?"

"I didn't say there were mitigating circumstances, you did. That's different from the reason why, isn't it?"

"Don't do this to yourself, Laura. Don't play games with your lawyer."

"I just can't get into it," she said, and the room passed into a long, deadly silence.

"Let's try it once more," Parley said. "Look in my face here, not at the floor. I'm your lawyer. That means you can talk to me and nothing you say will ever get out of this room without your permission. If you've got second thoughts about having another party present, Mr. Janeway will leave us in private. This will stay between us. But you've got to tell me what happened."

"I just can't get into it. How many times have I got to say that?"

"Goddammit, you are into it, you're up to your pretty neck into it. Don't look down, look at me and tell me who you're protecting."

"No one. *No* one! Why would you even ask that? I told you I did it."

"I don't believe you. I think you're protecting somebody. Who could that be, Laura? Was it one of the kids?"

Her eyes opened wide. "Don't say that! Don't even *think* that!"

She looked at me and said, "I want another lawyer."

She looked at Parley. "Why won't you do what I want? It's my life, isn't it?"

"Did Bobby abuse you in some way?"

"No!"

"Did he abuse the kids?"

"*No!* Stop this! Stop it, I want another lawyer."

"Well, that's certainly your right. But any lawyer worth a damn will ask these same questions. This stuff won't just go away, Laura. And the truth has a way of getting out, no matter what you want."

"I've told you the truth."

"Yeah, well, I don't think so. You're lying right now, I can see it in your face. And I can't think of anybody you'd lie for except the kids."

She shook her head.

"Was it Jerry?"

The room turned suddenly hot. Her face was flushed.

"Was it Jerry, Laura? Did Jerry shoot Bobby?"

"You must be mad. He's a child. For God's sake, he's only eleven years old!"

"How old do you have to be to pick up a gun?"

"I'm not listening to this. I want to see Erin."

"Well, I'll do my best to get her here. Maybe she can talk sense to you."

He looked to me, I thought for support. I said, "He's right, Mrs. Marshall. Erin would ask exactly the same questions."

"If Jerry did this, you've got to tell me," Parley said.

"*Stop saying that!*"

"As I was *about* to say, he's a minor. That would make it an entirely different ball game with its own set of rules. With a kid that young, they look at treatment rather than punishment. If the circumstances—"

"Mr. McNamara," she said icily, "I think I'm going to ask you to leave."

"I might as well leave, for all the good I'm doing you. If you come to your senses, you call me."

He pressed the buzzer and stood near the door. I pushed back my chair. But suddenly Mrs. Marshall reached over to me and said, "Can you stay?"

"You'd better ask your lawyer. Parley?"

"What have we got to lose? Talk some sense to her. Get her to listen."

The sheriff arrived. Parley said, "Mr. Janeway will remain for a while and talk to Mrs. Marshall as Ms. D'Angelo's representative. Attorney privilege still applies."

"Sure, I guess so," the sheriff said. "On that other matter, I've got a deal for you."

"No deals. I want that citation dismissed. No fine, no points: I want it taken clear off his record."

"Let's go downstairs and talk it over."

"Talk your damn heads off. I'm goin' out and get us some more witnesses."

The door closed. I could hear them arguing their way down the hall. The room became quiet as Laura and I waited for the other to speak. She looked to be on the verge of tears again. I smiled at her, half in sadness, half in hope.

"I looked at your books," I said.

"More junk I'll have to get rid of."

"Don't do that. Not yet."

"Are you telling me they're worth something?"

"They're worth something."

"Bobby always said they were. I never believed him, even though he spent enough money on them. I thought he was just justifying his habit."

"I could make you a rough appraisal if you want one."

She looked as if she wanted to laugh but couldn't. "What good will money do me now?"

"You'll have legal expenses to cover."

"Of course. Of course, what can I be thinking of?"

"I think you could get some real money for those books."

Her eyes opened wide as the first realization came over her. "How much money? Are you saying I could pay my legal expenses with them?"

"Maybe."

"What's so special? They look like ordinary books to me."

"May I ask where they came from?"

"Bobby started buying them way back when we were young. I never paid much attention. We had more money then."

"And you never discussed what they were or what he planned to do with them?"

She shook her head. "He was full of secrets. Even when we were kids, he was like that. Erin thought she knew him but she didn't. She had no idea. God, don't tell her I said that."

"There's no question he owned them?"

"What do you think, he stole them?"

"It's just a question, Mrs. Marshall. You're going to need some money."

"I guess I am."

"And you need to make sure nobody's got any kind of a claim on your books."

"I don't even know where he'd have kept records of that stuff."

"Let's make an effort to find out."

"What if there's nothing?"

"Cross that bridge when you come to it. You've got possession. A third party would need his own proof to show ownership."

"This all seems so trivial now."

"It's not trivial. You're gonna need a lawyer. For what it's worth, I think Parley's a pretty good man."

"I'm sure he is. I know he's trying to do what he thinks is best for me."

"I take it Jerry is your son?"

"Oh, please, don't you start."

"I'm just trying to get it straight."

"There's nothing to get straight. Jerry had nothing to do with this."

"Hey, that's cool. If that's how it was, that's how it was."

Then, after a long, quiet moment: "You say the boy is eleven?"

She stared at me.

"The reason I ask is it's bound to come up again. What McNamara's thinking, others will think. I understand how you'd want to protect him, but it would be smart not to be so touchy about it."

"Wouldn't you be touchy if someone accused your son of murder?"

"I'm sure I would. But when you fly off the handle, that doesn't protect him, it has exactly the opposite effect. When you get defensive, people naturally think you're covering up for somebody. Who would that be but one of your kids? If he didn't do it, just say so, but say it calmly, as if the question itself is too ridiculous to worry about."

"Do you even have any children, Mr. Janeway?"

"No, but I can imagine how fiercely I'd want to protect them. The trouble is, you're going about it the wrong way. If Jerry didn't do this, just say so."

"I thought that's what I was doing."

"You were getting pretty shrill. Try turning down the volume and say it."

"The volume won't matter now. Parley will never believe me."

"If Jerry really didn't do it, you'll have to convince him. My advice would be to tell him the truth. Whatever that is, just get it said."

I let that settle on her. At some point I said into the quiet, "Erin is not leaning toward taking your case. You should know that before you chase a good lawyer away. There's too much old baggage between you, she'd need a waiver, and even then she doesn't think it's a good idea."

"I'll give her a waiver, I said I would. I'll sign anything."

"You're not listening, Mrs. Marshall."

"Please. Call me Laura."

"You're not listening, Laura. You haven't seen her in years. You've got some notion of her from when you were kids together. Maybe there's still some of that left in her, I don't know, but she's been on her own a long time now. Even if she did come, she'll ask the same questions, and I'll tell you right now, you can't stonewall her."

"You don't know how we were. You have no idea."

"That makes no difference now. If she does come to see you, it may be because of how you were, but I can promise you she won't stay for that reason. That was a long time ago and a lot of stuff has happened. She might just want to put something to rest between you."

"She won't do that."

We sat quietly for a full minute. At last she said, "What are you thinking?"

"Right now, just wondering how the hell I can reach you."

"I've *heard* what you're saying."

"I don't think so. Listen, this is what Erin told me to say to you. If you lie, if you stonewall or evade, I'm out of here."

Her eyes filled with tears. "She still hates me."

"Laura. Listen to me. That doesn't matter. It doesn't matter. Nothing matters right now but getting your story straight. If one of your kids . . ."

She shook her head. "Don't say that. Don't say it anymore."

"Laura, listen—"

"I can't let this happen. I can't."

"Just listen for a minute—"

"I can't. I won't."

"Did your son shoot your husband?"

"*No!*" she whispered.

"The only way Erin might come is if you tell me the truth."

"I am."

More time passed. At some point I said, "I was a cop for a long time, did you know that? I was a pretty good cop. I had good juice. That means I knew nine times out of ten when I was being lied to."

"I'm not lying."

"Laura, you are one of the worst liars I've ever seen. Don't take offense, that's actually a virtue. Some people can't lie. I've seen a hundred of 'em try over the years and I imagine old Parley has seen a hundred more. And Erin is better than we are at sniffing out a lie. If you think she'll ride over here and buy into this, think again. The only possible way to get to her is to stop the lies."

"I know that. That's what I'm doing."

I shook my head.

"I am," she said. "I *am*."

"If that's your final word on it, that'll have to be what I'll tell her." I pushed back my chair. "I'm sorry I couldn't be more help."

I was halfway to the door when she said my name: "Mr. Janeway . . ."

"Yes."

"You can't just walk away like this." Her voice cracked. "Please, I need you."

"I know you do."

"Will you help me?"

"I can't if you don't let me."

"I'm afraid. Oh, God, I'm scared."

"I know you are."

"Not for myself," she said, and I knew then we were finally at the truth. "Not for me."

Suddenly she said, "Will you stay?"

"I'll do what I can do. But you've got to talk to me."

"I will, I promise. I trust you."

"That's a good start."

Again I sat in the chair across from her. Tears streamed down her face. She took a deep breath and trembled. "You can't tell anyone I said this. Only Erin."

"Okay."

"You can't tell *anyone* else. Not even Parley."

"I won't, without your okay."

"He'll want to use it. That's why you can't tell him."

The moment stretched till I thought it would

break. When she spoke again, she whispered so softly I had to lip-read her.

"Jerry shot him.

"Jerry shot him," she said again.

"My God," she said. "Oh, God, I still can't believe it.

"Jerry shot Bobby," she said in her disbelief.

She shook her head. "Remember what you said. What you promised. No matter what happens, you can't tell anyone."

Then she broke down and wept uncontrollably on the table.

10

"Are you okay now?"

"I think so."

"Good. Maybe you can start putting things back together."

"Why? What for?"

"For your kids."

"Of course . . . of course. What am I thinking? It's amazing how you have to keep reminding me of what ought to be obvious."

"You're not thinking straight, that's all it is. I've seen it happen before."

"Not like this, you haven't. I betrayed my dearest friend. How could I have done that? She was the only friend who ever mattered to me, and she mattered more than anything. But I betrayed her and my life has never been the same again. I haven't been thinking straight for ten years."

"For what it's worth, I hope she does come."

"But you know she won't. I can see it in your face."

"I don't know that at all. She's not one to play games. If it had been out of the question for her to come, she never would've sent me over here."

"I guess that makes sense. Oh, God, how I want it to. Can I . . ."

"What?"

"Can I tell you what happened between Erin and me?"

"I don't know if—"

"Please, I want to. It was my fault, right from the beginning. No matter how much Bobby pressured me, there's no excuse for what I did. That night we drank too much and got way too silly, but that's no excuse. As long as I could see and hear, as long as I had a coherent thought running through my head, I was responsible. Now there's nothing I can say except I am so, so sorry. Whatever they do to me here, I need to say that to her. Erin and Bobby were so much in love; you'd have to have seen them together: if ever there were soul mates, they were, and I destroyed them. I've thought about her every day, every hour: I see her face everywhere. I've never stopped loving her. But Bobby and me, that one night we got drunk and did it. When you've betrayed someone you love, the hurt never goes away, it defines you. The betrayal becomes what you are, a fair-weather friend who couldn't keep her pants on when she had to."

"Sounds like you've paid for it."

"Oh, yeah. Oh, yeah, oh my God, yes. It'll never end."

"Never's a long time, Laura."

"Tell me about it."

"Maybe after ten years it's time to cut yourself some slack."

"That'll never happen. What I did has consumed me. I know it's unreal, it must sound sick the way I dwell on it. I just can't shake it, and it only gets worse with time. I feel guiltier now than I did right after it happened all those years ago."

"Did Bobby know?"

"What, how miserable I am? Oh, yeah, he lived with me for years, how could he not know? Bobby gave up on me long ago."

"Maybe he shouldn't have. He had to at least share the responsibility for what happened."

"I can't look at it that way. I don't know how to, I just don't know how. All I know is, Bobby and I were never any good together. How could we be? Erin was always there between us. I could feel her walking beside me, she was on the porch where we sat after supper: she was even in our bed. The bed was the worst. I got so frigid Bobby couldn't come near me. We haven't touched each other in four years. That's about when he began seeing other women. You can't blame him, can you?"

"I'm trying to retire from the blame business. That includes you, by the way."

"Thank you. You're a kind man, Mr. Janeway. Are you and Erin lovers? . . . Never mind, that's none of my business. Sorry, I just found myself wishing, you know? She should be with someone like you."

"Mrs. Marshall—"

"Laura."

"Laura . . . do you want to tell me what happened the day your husband was shot?"

"It won't matter. You can't use it."

"Let's take it one step at a time. Right now I'd just like to understand it."

"I'll tell you, then. I've got to tell someone or go crazy."

"Take your time."

"No, I need to get this said now or I'll never say it. Bobby and I were never happy, we never had a moment's peace. I told you why but I know you can't understand it. It was all me, I've been consumed by guilt."

"Then why'd you marry the guy?"

"That was the reason. To try to make the guilt go away. Have the marriage justify the affair, if that makes any sense. But does that really matter now?"

"It might. When you go to trial and bring in issues that the average Joe can't identify with, it helps if you can explain them."

"Surely all this won't come up."

"Don't count on that."

"God, what a nightmare. How can I explain such crazy behavior? If I said that one of us had a terrible conscience and the other did it for spite, would you believe that?"

"Is that what you're saying?"

"I told you it would sound crazy. Jesus, are real lawyers going to be this hard?"

"They can be a lot worse than this. If they can make you look like a fool, they will. You don't want to help them do that."

"I *was* a fool. This sounds like a stupid soap opera. No one will believe it."

"Millions of people watch soap operas and believe them. Just tell the truth and don't worry about melodrama."

"When Bobby said we should get married, it just seemed right. Erin was finished with both of us, we couldn't hurt her any more. Did I love him? I must have, right? Why else could I betray my friend? Marrying Bobby was a way of proving to Erin that what we had done was more than trivial. If it could only be dismissed as a cheap fling, what did that say about us? Does that make sense?"

"If that's your reason, sure. What about his?"

"He said he loved me. He'd been falling in love with me for a year."

"And out of love with Erin?"

"He said he loved us both."

"Do you believe that?"

"How would I know? I never gave him a chance. I think he tried, but I couldn't."

"So what happened?"

"Bobby thought if we had a child it would help, and we did try in those first few years, but no child came. We moved out here and adopted Jerry. He had emotional problems, he was nearly four years old when we got him, and he couldn't talk. He wasn't what they called highly adoptable; he had been horribly abused by his birth parents, that's why getting him was so easy. Jerry has always had problems, he still can't talk, can't or won't. Except with me. He talks to me."

"Has anyone else ever heard him speak?"

"He doesn't talk in words, it comes out in

looks between us, in things he does. It's a very simple level of communication. But I know what he wants, don't ask me how, I just know, and he knows what I expect of him. It's all in the eyes. His eyes are like Erin's were as a child: brown with those flecks of green around the edges. I loved him to death the first time I laid eyes on him. We were like the walking wounded together."

"What did his parents do to him?"

"Do I have to go through that? At one point to stop him from crying his mother put him naked in a cold basement and left him there without food or water for two days . . . stuff like that."

"I get the idea. I assume you had him tested, to see—"

"Oh, sure. There didn't seem to be any real reason why he couldn't speak, but he never has. He's never said a word since we got him, but he's aware of everything around him. If I say, 'Bring in some wood, Jerry,' he'll go right out and get it. I never have to belabor anything, his hearing's extremely sharp. The psychologist ran an intelligence test on him."

"And that showed what?"

"There seemed to be no reason why he couldn't speak. But he won't."

"So he was nearly four when you got him. And then you had two of your own."

"The twins, Little Bob and Susan. What a surprise that was. It must've happened the last time Bobby ever touched me. One of the last times, and we get kids from it."

"How old are they now?"

"Five."

"There's no real reason to ask, but I take it they were both normal."

"Oh, sure. I was the one who wasn't what you'd call normal."

"What does that mean?"

"I can't tell you that. You'll think I'm a monster."

"Let me guess. Your own blood children drove you two farther apart."

"It was Erin again. I know this sounds sick, but they seemed like her children to me. They were the kids she should have had with Bobby. I tried to love them. I did love them. I do, I swear I do. And I've been a good mother. But it was Jerry who had touched my heart, who had nothing to do with Erin or Bobby or me. If there was any light in my life at all then, it came from Jerry."

"You loved him. Don't beat yourself up, I can see how that could happen."

"I loved him more than my own blood children. People will think I'm sick if that comes out. I can't help it: he was my baby, my poor wounded child. The night we brought him home, I swore to Bobby I'd never let anything hurt him again."

"So what happened the day of the shooting?"

"I had gone out for a walk. I was on my way back when I heard a shot from the house. I ran across the field and up onto the porch. Bobby was lying in the front room. Even before I saw him I had this terrible feeling: I could smell the gunpowder, and something else . . . something foul. I knew it was a death smell. I went into the room and there Bobby was. Jerry had the gun in his hand . . ."

"What time was this?"

"I don't know. Suddenly I can't remember times. Middle of the afternoon?"

"What did you do?"

"You mean right then?"

"Yes. That first moment, what did you do?"

"Took the gun away from him and just hugged him."

"Then what?"

"Had him take a bath. Burned his clothes."

"Where did this take place?"

"In the back-room fireplace. Then I opened

the window back there. I didn't want the smell
of it all over the house when the police arrived."

I made a note. "Then what?"

"Sent him back to the bedroom: told him I
wanted him to lie down till I came for him
again. Then I handled the gun and got blood on
my dress. Ripped it up some. Then I called the
sheriff."

"So right from the start you were thinking—"

"—that I would confess, yes, of course, that I
had to protect Jerry no matter what."

"It hadn't surprised you, then, that Jerry had
shot your husband?"

"Of course it shocked me."

"But that's different."

"Yes. I was shocked, not surprised."

"Why not?"

"Jerry knew."

"Knew what?"

"What went on with Bobby and me."

"Did Bobby abuse you?"

"Not physically. Never."

"Did he ever touch Jerry?"

"He knew better. I'd have killed him for real
if he had."

"But there was no love lost between them."

"Jerry never liked Bobby."

"You know that for a fact?"

"Oh, yeah. That child seemed to know everything. He knew how unhappy I was and Bobby was the reason."

"Did you ever tell him that in so many words?"

"That's hardly the kind of thing you tell a child. I would never tell him anything that would undercut Bobby in his eyes."

"But . . ."

"Jerry knew. He just did, I know he did. We talked about it, Bobby and me, how we had made such a mess of things, and sometimes I think Jerry overheard us. There are places in that house where a child can hide and hear everything. I'm telling you, Jerry knew. At night when Bobby would come home with some whore's perfume on his clothes, I'd sleep alone on the couch in the front room. And I'd wake up and Jerry would be there, asleep with his head on my lap, holding my hand."

"So Jerry had a good reason to hate Bobby, is that what you're saying?"

"I don't know what you'd consider a good reason. He killed him, didn't he?"

"I don't know who killed him."

"But I told you—"

"You didn't see him do it, did you?"

"But no one else was there."

"No one you saw."

"What are you saying?"

"How long did it take you to get to the house, after you heard the shot?"

"I was out at the edge of the meadow. Still, not much more than a few minutes."

"Did Bobby have any enemies?"

"Oh, Janeway! What are you thinking?"

"Same thing you're thinking, Mrs. Marshall. Let's go over it again."

11

Erin flew into Paradise International late that afternoon on a single-engine private flight from the Jefferson County Airport. It had taken her less than half an hour to make the arrangements. She had used this pilot on cases for Waterford, Brownwell, when other days were waning and her schedule was tight, when she needed to get to places like Laramie or Rock Springs or Albuquerque and had no time for long car trips. This was a ninety-minute hop over the hills from the Denver suburbs.

Paradise International was a bit of local sarcasm, the name painted on a board and tacked to a tree. It was a long dirt runway nestled in a valley about five miles from town, with two tin hangars, a radio room, and a rustic coffee shop. I waited just inside the coffee shop, my eyes scanning the sky to the east. Erin had said they'd get here by five, and at four-thirty the valley was already in deep shadow. Whatever daylight was left was high above us, wasted on the tops of the mountains.

"Can this guy land in the dark?"

"If he's more than a half-assed pilot he can," said the old fellow on duty. "We'll give him some lights to help bring him down."

He flipped a switch and the airstrip was defined by two long strings of what looked like Christmas lights. "There ye go. Just like the Macy's parade."

A moment later the plane made radio contact. "Your bird's about twenty miles east of here," the old man said. "Be on the ground before you can hawk up a good spit."

I walked nervously into the coming night. I am always nervous when someone I care about is flying, especially over unpredictable mountain air currents in a glorified egg crate with one little engine, a single heartbeat from disaster. But ten minutes later the plane broke over the hills and glided under the sunset into the purple valley. I watched it bump along the runway and come to a stop a hundred yards away.

Erin had dressed for weather: corduroy pants and a flannel shirt, scarf, boots and a heavy coat, a furry Russian-style pillbox hat and gloves. The pilot was a young stud named Todd Williams, who wore a leather cap and let his matching coat flop open in the wind. Erin made the introductions: we shook hands and Todd said he'd take care of his plane and join us in town. "We'll be at the jail for a while," I said. "After that you'll find us in the café on the main drag. You can't miss any of it unless you miss the whole damn town."

In the car I said, "You're looking good."

"I'm getting a cold," she said. "And frankly, my attitude sucks."

She didn't have much time: "I'm supposed to be working on my case this weekend. If I go into court unprepared on Monday, I'm in deep soup. I've got to be back before noon tomorrow."

"Are you nervous?"

"What have I got to be nervous about, she's the one in jail." She cut her eyes at me from the far corner of the car. "Yeah, I am. Did you tell her I was coming?"

"Haven't seen her since this morning. Wouldn't have told her anyway."

"Good. That first few seconds may tell us something." She flipped through some notes. "I want somebody to go up to that house and ex- amine the back-room fireplace."

"I can do that."

"I'd rather have two of you together when you do that."

I had left word with Sheriff Gains that we'd be coming over to the jail sometime before dinner, but the only car on the lot was the deputy's. "Looks like you're about to meet the town charmer. Might as well get it over with."

We walked into the jail. Lennie Walsh was sitting behind the desk, smoking.

"Deputy Walsh," I said. "This is Ms. Erin D'Angelo. We'd like to see Mrs. Marshall for a few minutes."

"Visiting hours are posted on the door."

"That doesn't usually apply to a prisoner and his attorney."

"It does if I'm on duty. It's my call."

"I cleared this with the sheriff this afternoon."

"He didn't say nothin' to me about it."

"So what does that mean? Do we have to wait for him to get back?"

"Be a long wait. He went up to Gunnison, won't come back till Monday noon."

"So what do we do?"

"Come back Monday."

Erin pulled up a chair and leaned across the desk. "Deputy Walsh."

She offered her hand. He looked at it for so

much time before finally taking it that I wanted to reach over and knock him off the chair.

"Help me out here, please. I've come here at great expense to see Mrs. Marshall."

"Shoulda called first."

"Maybe so but there wasn't time. I'm involved in another case in Denver, I'm supposed to be working on it even now. This is the only possible chance I'll have to speak with her for at least two more weeks."

"I appreciate how busy and important you are, Ms. . . . what's your name?"

"D'Angelo."

"Whatever. Like I was saying, I appreciate all that. At the same time, you can't expect us to drop everything when you walk in unannounced like this."

"Am I missing something here? Would it work a vast inconvenience on this department to let me see my client, please, for just a few minutes?"

"No inconvenience at all. Monday at ten."

"Deputy . . ."

He smiled pleasantly. "Yes, ma'am?"

"We're getting nowhere," she said to me. "Does your friend McNamara have a home number where the judge can be reached?"

"What are you callin' the judge for?" Lennie

said. "You wanna piss that old man off, you just call him at home."

She ignored him. "Let's go."

We got up and started for the door.

"I don't know what you think the judge is gonna do," Lennie said.

She stopped at the door and turned. "I'll tell you what he'd better do. If he doesn't get you off your dead ass *right now*, I will delay this trial until next March and have good cause to do it. This is inexcusable. We'll be back in an hour. Deputy whatever."

"That was fun," I said.

"As long as it's my biscuits he's got on the fire, not yours."

"He's had mine."

I told her about my ongoing shitfight with Lennie Walsh.

"God, where do you find these guys? You run afoul of the worst creeps even in the middle of nowhere. You must run ads in the paper looking for them."

"Yeah, but then I find guys like you, and Parley, to pull me out of hot water."

"I like old McNamara better all the time," she said. "Haven't even met him yet and he reminds me of one or two old lawyers I know."

The waitress came. I told her we were waiting for a couple of people and she went away. Todd Williams, the first of our people, arrived a few minutes later. He was a flamboyant, young, blond hot dog but I liked him. He flopped next to Erin and draped his leather cap on her chair.

"Plane's all secured and here we are. I've been in some dead places with you, Miss Erin, but this one's unreal. What the hell are we supposed to do here tonight?"

"Speak for yourself. I've got to work."

"There's not even any TV in this place."

"There's a pool hall up the street," I said.

"Where do the ladies hang out?"

"I haven't found that out yet. The only one I've seen is our client, and she's in jail."

"Maybe we should go ahead and order," Erin said. "McNamara can catch up to us. I don't want to let too much grass grow under my feet, give that idiot at the jail any more excuses."

"You actually intend to call the judge?"

"If I have to. But I'm betting the deputy lets us in without a squawk when we go back." She smiled and clutched her purse. "Five'll get you ten."

"Not me," I said.

"Todd?"

"I don't even know what we're talking about."

I told him while Erin was signaling the waitress. "I'd never bet against this woman," Todd said while Erin was ordering. "You boys would make lousy lawyers," she said between instructions to the waitress. "You bluff too easy." She asked for a bottle of wine, paused when the waitress wondered if she wanted the big bottle or small, and said she'd come over and look at what was available in a minute. "I wonder how big the big bottle is," she said, and the woman told her she could bring half a gallon if we were superthirsty. Erin suppressed a laugh. "You bluff too easily," she said again, looking at me. "I can always bluff Williams out, but I expected more of you, Janeway." To the waitress she said, "Thank you, I'll come look. Put all this on one bill, please."

The waitress went away. "I'll bet it's Gallo," Erin said softly. "Any takers?"

She went away to look.

"She sure is hyper tonight," Todd said. "She tries to seem easy but I could tell the minute I picked her up, she's really uptight about something. This must be a tough case."

Erin came back and flopped. "I took the Gallo," she said. "Don't ask what the other choice was."

"I ate in here last night," I said. "They run a truck up to the window and pump the stuff into fifty-gallon drums."

Parley arrived as the waitress brought our wine: a nice bottle of French merlot, five years old. She uncorked it and poured a thimbleful for Erin to taste. "Lovely, thank you," Erin said, and she smiled at me brilliantly. "You never know, Janeway, you never know. That's five dollars you could've won from me tonight and we haven't even seen the deputy again."

Four glasses killed the bottle. I made the introductions and offered a toast to friendship.

Erin and Parley talked; Todd and I listened. The old man gave her his assessment of the case based on what he knew. "Some new things have come to light," she told him. "I can't go into them until we talk to the client, which I hope will be within the hour. I'll see her again tomorrow morning, and we'll decide at that time if I'm going to represent her. If I'm not, she needs to get someone right away. Cliff tells me he likes what you've done to this point."

"I'll take it if there's nobody else. I'm no criminal lawyer and I've told her that. I'd probably do as well as the public defender, but I'm not way up on her list of favorite people just now."

"What's that about?"

"I think Jerry did it and had the temerity to say so. She flew off the handle when I said that."

"That was then, this is now. But we can't talk about that yet, Janeway's tied our hands till we get her okay. Listen, if I do take this case, would you be willing to help?"

"Yeah, sure. I guess so."

"There's going to be lots of stuff that I can't be here for. It'd be great to have somebody here in town who knows the people and the turf."

"Kind of a second chair, you might say, huh?"

"Yeah, but you'd actually be doing most of the real work till I can get clear. We'll talk every day on the phone. Bill your time at your regular rate and send the bills to me. Once we get the client to understand what our defense is going to be, whatever that is, I think she'll be easier to get along with."

Supper came and we ate it. The wine was the high spot.

"We'll have to get us a place to stay," Erin said.

"You can all stay with me," Parley said.

"Best hotel in town," I said.

"That's good," Erin said nervously. "That's good."

She paid the bill. "Guess we'd better get on over to the jailhouse and see if anything's changed. In case it hasn't, do you have a number where I can reach the judge?"

"Oh, yeah. Wish I could be there when you call him."

Lennie was sitting at the same table, reading an old copy of *Startling Detective*.

"Didn't get any call from the judge," he said.

"I haven't talked to him yet. Do I have to?"

He grinned maliciously. "Naw, go on up. I was yanking your chain. If you hadn't flown off the handle and got all pissy on me, you'd be up there talking to her now."

"Thank you."

"You know the way, don't you, cowboy?"

"Come on," I said to Erin.

"Might take a while for me to get her up there," Lennie said. "Prisoners are eatin' supper now."

Upstairs, we sat in the conference room and waited. An hour passed.

"He's really rubbing it in, isn't he?" Erin said.

"Goddamn little tinhorn asshole."

She laughed. "Why don't you tell me what you really think of him?"

"Little tinhorn turkey-jerk South-Succotash pisswater asshole."

"That's very good. Don't hold back your best stuff on my account."

I filled the air with invective, one long impossible sentence, and we both laughed.

"Prisoners," I said derisively. "If he's got more than one prisoner, I'll be amazed."

"Keep a record of all this," she said. "Write down everything that's happened since you first laid eyes on him. Did he actually point a gun at you?"

"You think I made that up? But I was the only one who saw him. Even Parley found it hard to believe."

"Write it all down anyway, dates and times, everything. He sounds really unstable, but maybe we'll want to give him some grief down the road."

Footsteps came along the corridor. Erin took a deep, shivery breath, her last concession to nerves, and put on her steel face. Lennie held the door open and let Laura come into the room.

She stopped in shock and put her hands over her cheeks. Tears began at once.

Lennie spoke but his voice seemed far away. "So how long's this gonna take?"

"Go away, Deputy," Erin said.

"Hey, I got my own supper to eat sometime tonight."

"Then go away and eat it. I'll try to be brief right now, but I'll want to see her again tomorrow morning."

He grunted and closed the door. Erin waited, listening to his footsteps as he went down the hall. She and Laura looked at each other.

"Don't do that, please," Erin said. "Don't cry."

"I can't help it."

"We don't have time for old tears."

"I'm sorry."

"Sit down here."

Laura sat trembling near her, fighting the tears. "I knew you'd come. I knew it. I've dreamed of this." She broke down and sobbed into her hands.

Erin looked at me and her eyes were a thousand years old. She reached out and touched Laura's back, not an easy thing for her to do, and I winked at her.

"We can't waste time," she said. "You heard what Barney Fife said."

"I'm sorry. God, I'm sorry. I am so sorry for everything."

"Listen to me. Whatever we do here, that old stuff has nothing to do with it."

Of course this was not true: she knew and I knew and probably Laura Marshall knew that the old stuff was the cause of everything, but she went on as if none of us knew, staking out her turf. "I don't want to get into any of that. I'm here to talk about your case, not rake over old times. Can we please be clear on that?"

Laura sniffed and dabbed at her eyes but the flow wouldn't stop.

"I just don't want to talk about it," Erin said.

"Do you hate me?"

"I don't want to talk about it."

"I'm sorry, I'm sorry."

Erin looked at me and said quietly, "Is this place secure? Can we talk?"

"It should be. It would be stupid and very rare for them to bug a witness room." I shrugged. "With a cop like that idiot, who knows?"

"Let's just chat a bit tonight," Erin said.

On a legal pad she jotted a note.

"How've you been?"

"Not so hot," Laura said.

"Are they treating you okay in here?"

"I guess so. I'm going nuts. I've never been in jail before."

Erin wrote something on her pad. Laura said, "Are you going to help me?"

"I'll see if there's anything I can do. But you've got to be straight with us."

"I will, I promise."

"No more evasive stuff."

"I swear."

"That means everything is fair game. You hear what I'm saying? Everything."

"Of course."

"Good."

Erin started to write something, then changed her mind.

"How long were you out on the meadow before you heard the shot?"

"I don't know, maybe fifteen minutes. I wasn't thinking about it."

"Think about it now."

"Fifteen minutes," Laura said. "Twenty at the outside."

"Then you heard the shot."

"And I ran back to the house."

"And you've said that wouldn't have taken more than a few minutes."

She nodded.

"And from then until the deputy arrived, you heard no sounds of anyone or any vehicle coming or leaving."

"I don't know." Laura closed her eyes. "I don't know."

"If you do remember anything like that, tell us at once."

Another half minute passed. Again Erin asked, "Did you see or hear anything that might lead us to believe someone else might have been there?"

Laura looked to be in deep thought.

"This could be important," Erin said. "If you heard anything, either before or after you went into the house, I need to know exactly what you remember."

Laura nodded, her face intense.

"Let's go over a few things again," Erin said. "Why did you tell Mr. Janeway you killed Bobby?"

"I wanted to protect Jerry."

"You thought your son had done it."

"Yes. But now . . ."

"Are you willing to accept it if Jerry did shoot Bobby?"

Laura shook her head and looked away.

"Look at me."

Laura looked up.

"The fact is, we don't know who did it," Erin said.

"That's right. Janeway showed me it might've been someone else."

"But right now we have no other suspects."

"No."

"You see what I'm getting at?"

"I'm not sure."

"We have one version of what happened. Yours. Unless Jerry comes to life and begins talking up a blue streak, yours is the one we're going with."

"But what if that means . . . ?"

"If I take this case, my job is to get you off. That means everything else is up for grabs, everything. If Jerry did it, we'll have to deal with that later."

"Oh, God, Erin . . . oh, Jesus . . ."

"We've got to be clear on this. I will not have my hands tied."

A long moment unrolled. Erin wrote something on her paper.

"Make up your mind," she said.

Laura nodded.

"Be sure."

"Yes."

"Mr. McNamara will be talking to you again in the coming days. I want you to be as straight with him as you will with me. He's to be told everything you remember, as soon as you remember it. If you think of something you'd forgotten about, I want you to call him. Are we clear on that?"

They stared at each other.

"Okay?" Erin said.

Laura looked unhappily at the wall.

"Okay?" Erin said again.

"Okay."

"Okay, then. Don't talk to anybody else. No reporters, no lawyers, especially not that cretin who minds the jail. Talk to nobody but one of us. Can you do that?"

"Yeah, sure."

"Refer anything you're asked to me or Mc-Namara. Try to get some sleep, I'll be back early in the morning."

"So what do you think?" Erin said.

"I like her."

"Yes, she's always been very likable."

"There's a guarded statement if I ever heard one."

I pulled up at Parley's house and we sat there a moment letting the car run and the heater warm us. Erin took a deep breath. "Yeah, it is," she said at last. "I'm trying to figure out what I feel about her after all these years. I may never know."

"There's something about you two," I said. "In some ways you're very much alike; in others—"

"—we could be from different species."

"Yeah. Somehow I can't picture her being you."

"I think when we were kids she was suspicious of my motives. She never seemed to believe I liked her as much as I did; she always had something to prove. She was dirt-poor, her people had nothing: her father literally worked himself to death. When she was a teenager, she took on a full-time job to help them out, going to school the whole time. Man, I admired her spunk. In time I think she knew that and we became good friends, then best friends. If she had any shallowness, it was a certain preoccupation with the rich and famous. Easy for me to say, I was one of the privileged, but I always thought she was too enchanted with stories of wealthy, fabled people. She seems different now. Different and yet I still see flashes of her old ways. In her face. In her eyes."

"Do you still hate her for what happened?"

"I never hated her. I just can't do that. I sure tried to, when the hurt was new and raw: I cursed them both a hundred times a week but I couldn't ever come to hate her. I'm afraid in my youth I bought into the old stereotypes. It was the man's fault. He was much easier to hate. What can you expect from a man, you're all a bunch of randy old goats. But it was different with her. She took my man, but women have lost men forever and lived through it. What he took from me was just as priceless."

"Did he ever try to make it up?"

"Oh, yeah. He called a lot, at first half a dozen times a week. And I did talk to him about it, at least in the beginning. I guess I should say I heard him out. I didn't have much to say, but I thought I owed it to him to hear what he had to say. We had been together for years, we were high school sweethearts, and even before that we were so close. So I felt I should at least listen."

"What did he say?"

"Oh, he tried to blame her. But it takes two to tango, doesn't it? At least she never tried to duck the blame, I've got to give her that. She cried and said how sorry she was, but never once did she say it was his fault."

"Well, I think she's suffered for it."

"Good."

A long moment later, Erin said, "If I did hate her, this would be the perfect opportunity for me to get back at her. Wouldn't it?"

"If you were that mean-hearted. And a good enough lawyer to be just bad enough to lose her case."

"What's your guess about that?"

"You're one of those two things. But only one."

"Thank you, I think."

"I'm not worried about you. You wouldn't do that. I think you already know what you're going to do."

Another moment passed, lost in thought.

"I couldn't even say her name in there. I'll have to get over that."

Suddenly she said, "I've got to get her off, Cliff. I've got to get her off."

12

We sat up past midnight in a three-headed council of war. Erin sent Todd to bed early—"Go read a book," she said, "we have some lawyer stuff to hash out"—and he departed cheerfully for the third bedroom down the hall. Most of our talk until then had been about tomorrow's agenda. "I want to go to the jail as soon as deputy whatever will let me in," Erin said. "I don't think I can count on getting in there much before eight o'clock. And I've got to see that kid before I leave. I know he doesn't speak but I need to spend a few minutes with him anyway."

"What do you want me to do?" Parley said.

"You come with me, if you will. That might make it easier for you to work with her after I've gone. All billable hours now, so keep track."

"Would it be out of line to ask who's paying for this?"

"Nothing's out of line. Until she gets out and decides what to do, I'll pay the bills. Is that a problem?"

"Not for me it isn't."

"Good. I think it'll be best if just the two of us see her tomorrow. You understand that, Cliff . . . just the lawyers and the client this time around?"

"Do I look like I'm getting my feelings hurt?"

"In the afternoon, after I'm gone, Parley can bring you up on what was said."

"I could also put this time to good use. At some point I've got to spend a day with her books. Make a list of what's really there. And we've got to get those books out of that house. I could rent us a U-Haul, go on up there, and spend the day packing 'em up, doing the donkey work while the brain trust does whatever it does down here."

"I don't know. Somehow that strikes me wrong."

"Why, for God's sake? What's the downside in that?"

"I don't know. At the moment, we're the only ones who know about those books."

"That doesn't necessarily change just because we've moved them."

"It tells the other side something I might not want them to know yet. I don't think we should move them without noticing-in the DA on what we know, and I'd like to at least ask our client about them first. I know you mentioned them to her, but let's see what she says when we get more specific."

"Can I at least have the keys so I can go up and take another look?"

"Can you make an inventory just by looking at the titles on a shelf?"

"I can make a *list*. I can do that much, which is a helluva lot more than we've got right now."

"A list, then. If you need to take something off the shelf, fine, but then put it back where it was."

Parley handed me the keys.

"Erin," I said in my pleading voice, "we are going to feel mighty stupid if anything happens . . ."

"I know . . . I know. Let me think about it, how to proceed. You go on up early tomorrow and make your list, then we'll talk again."

"We could be fairly inconspicuous, if you want to move 'em," Parley said. "Let Cliff inventory and box 'em up and then we go up there after dark and load up the truck."

"And put 'em where?" I said.

"What's wrong with right here? I've got a room that's not being used."

We looked at each other for half a minute. Then Erin said, "I'm just not comfortable with us going in there at night and stripping the library. I know we *can,* that's not the question: legally the house is back with us, we've got the keys, we can *do* what we want with it. But that kind of thing can come back to haunt us. If you're right about the books and they're worth real money, that becomes a potential motive."

"Against our client," Parley said drily.

"It could cut both ways. This could be a motive for anybody."

"So if this anybody killed Bobby, who and where is he and why hasn't he made some attempt to get the books?"

"That's what we don't know," Erin said. "Maybe he's afraid to go up there now. Maybe he's afraid of a trap."

"You could almost make that feasible, if we had some other name to work with."

"Who else might benefit from the victim's death?"

"Well, I've been all through the DA's file," Parley said. "I've looked at every scrap of evidence they've got, and I don't see anybody there who'd fill that bill. They're going with a fairly simple and straightforward case. The blood was all over her dress, and most damning of all, she confessed. Never mind that she might've had second thoughts about the confession later, she still confessed. Where's Mr. Anybody figure into all that?"

"I don't know. Look, the books have been there three weeks now and nobody's touched them. It's possible that they'll only be in jeopardy if you call attention to them. That's the wonderful thing about books, isn't it? They never look valuable to an unwashed second-story man."

I sighed with exaggerated patience. "Erin, we've got to get them out of there. We might as well take out a STEAL THESE BOOKS ad in the newspaper."

"But what's likely to happen when we do that? More to the point, what happens to the books as evidence in some future action we may take, based on facts we don't yet know?"

"Right now we don't know what the hell's in there. My opinion is based on a ten-minute walk-through. Do you have any idea how unprofessional that is?"

"No, but I'll bet you'll tell us." She smiled sweetly and made a short list of notes, structuring the next day. "I'll bet Parley will tell us his opinion as well."

"Jerry shot Bobby, just like Miss Laura said."

"As theories go, that's not bad. I'm certainly

not above using it if we have to, even though it'll make our defendant very unhappy."

Erin shuffled through her pad. "I guess we need to talk about a change of venue."

"I can't see any downside to getting it out of here," Parley said. "This county is way too small, not to mention small-minded."

"But if we move for a change of venue, that would delay the trial. Adamson's almost certain to want to continue it, and I don't think he would grant it anyway. We'd have to appeal the delay, waive our right to a speedy trial, and how will our defendant like being locked up an extra two to four months while all this is going on? She's strung out as it is."

"I sure don't like the idea of trying it here."

"Neither do I, but it may be the lesser of two evils. We need to get things moving, especially if we think they've got a weak case."

"I don't know," Parley said. "I'm glad you're here to make that call."

Erin pondered what we had said. "Look, their case starts with that stupid deputy. I've only had the briefest pleasure of his company but I think he'll be a weak link right out of the gate. From what I've seen so far, the investigation is pathetic."

"The DA thinks it's in the bag."

"Let him think that. I'd like to hold his feet to the fire and see what evidence he's actually got; we may find out he's not as well prepared as he thinks he is. We know they have no written confession. Their investigating officer is a certified wild hare, and he did everything during that first critical hour by himself. I'd like you to file a boilerplate motion to suppress everything he did and found up there. Let's push for an early trial date, hold their feet to the fire before they realize there are all kinds of holes in their case; before they have a chance to prepare."

She studied her notes. "Cliff, it would help if you can find out anything new about our friend Lennie—what his movements were that day, what he did, who he talked to and what was said, where he was when he got the call, whether he took a leak at the scene and where—you know the routine. Make a chart showing all that. Give us anything that shows him as a wild man. And you'll need to interview him as well."

"That'll be fun."

"Parley, you could set up the interview, then take Cliff with you when you go."

"Ambush the bastard."

Again the room went suddenly quiet. Then Erin said, "I don't know how you work, Parley, but I like to start with my own theory of what really happened. Even if it's early, even though this'll all change as new facts come to light. Puts the onus on us and gives me a focal point to carry into the next day's work."

"So what's your current theory for this one, as if I didn't know."

"The victim was killed by an unknown assailant. The alternate suspect theory. That gives us an excellent place to dig around."

"Some third party did it. Great defense if we can sell it."

"You know how the alternate suspect idea works. I don't have to name names or prove it, but if I can get it planted that Bobby had enemies and that someone else might have been at or near the house that day, they'll have to deal with it." She looked at me. "Let's see if we can find who might have done this, who might have had a reason to shoot Bobby. That would be a fine use of your spare time. And if you actually find such a creature, I will swoon into your arms with delight."

"Now you know why I work so cheap," I said to Parley.

He shook his head. "I don't think we've got diddly-squat along those lines."

"Not yet," Erin said. "But we do need to find

out if anyone had a motive and opportunity, and who that might be."

She wrote some notes. "Maybe a jealous husband, someone who lost his shirt in a business deal with Bobby, maybe some real estate venture that went sour." And at last she said, "And the books could be a motive."

"Wow, the books could be a motive," I said. "Why didn't I think of that?"

"Because you're too busy being a wise guy."

"So if the books are a potential motive, we need to find out where Bobby got them," I said. "Who'd he buy them from? Why? Was he buying them to resell? If so, where was his market?"

"Whatever you can find that backs up the alternate suspect theory. If we can do that, we've got something to work with."

"And if we can't," Parley said, "then we're back to Jerry."

"But for today let's believe somebody else was in that room before Jerry came in and picked up the gun."

"Jerry and Laura . . . they're both innocent."

"They're both innocent."

"Lots of luck."

BOOK II THE PREACHER AND THE MUTE

13

It was a long/short night: long on worry, short on sleep. I thought about those books almost constantly and I fell asleep sometime after midnight. I awoke three hours later dreaming of a vast library, all signed and inscribed books stretching in neat rows for miles, as far as the eye could see. For another half hour I lay in bed hoping for sleep, which I slowly realized would not return. Eventually I managed to get out of bed without disturbing Erin, dressed, and sat in Parley's big front room. I stared into the black nothing until, driven by some inner demon, I got on my coat and went out.

I didn't know where I was going: at that time of night I'd have to drive at least sixty miles to find even a trace of life. I cruised through the town, hoping for an all-night coffee shop, knowing there could be no such animal on this far-flung planet. Not a light shone anywhere at four o'clock in the morning—not a movement, not a hope, not a living soul.

Understanding comes slowly at that time of day, but as I drove along the abandoned streets, I recalled the dream of the endlessly inscribed books. I passed the courthouse for the third time, turned around abruptly, and headed out of town. A few minutes later I reached the dirt road heading up into the hills.

I was halfway up the mountain when I finally realized that I was going up to the house. At that early hour I had no plan or reason, beyond what we had discussed the night before. I sure didn't expect the real killers to be hard at work stealing Mrs. Marshall's books at the exact moment when I happened to show up: it was only profound restlessness that drove me on. Friday's snow had melted away, but I remembered the terrain fairly well and my headlights picked out some landmarks that were vaguely familiar. I was pretty sure that just ahead was where Lennie and his car had disappeared into the swirling snow. I slowed to a crawl and alternated my headlights between dims and brights, stopping wherever I saw a nook or a break. Occasionally I got out and walked along the road, staring at nothing across the deep black infinity until I ran out of light and had to pick my way back to the car.

I had driven all the way over the crest when I found a rocky-looking trail on my left. It meandered precariously down into the void, one of those places that looks bad anytime but just reeks of peril to a stranger on a black morning. Maybe this was it, maybe not: I wasn't about to drive in there in the hope I'd be able to turn around: I'd have to walk down. I found a place where I could hide my car off the road. Then I put on my heavy coat and hood, got out my flashlight, fixed my beam on dim, and started along the trail.

I found a place no more than forty yards down: a wide spot where his car could have been parked and easily turned around. A foot-path went on from there, around the gulch and along the face of the hill. Instinctively I knew Lennie had been here. I sensed it, I smelled him as I got closer. I couldn't see a damn thing, only what was straight ahead in the beam of my light and no more than three feet of that. The path was okay: not many rocks or sudden dips to send a silly hiker careening off to break a leg or worse, and I kept at it slowly. In recent years I had made a startling discovery, that when you're going nowhere anyway, there's no real hurry to get there.

And I knew something else. If this was where Lennie had been, he had probably left me a few clues. I moved ahead with my light on the ground, and ten minutes later I saw a small rocky recess, protected from the weather and just big enough for a man to stand in. There was the inevitable pile of cigarette butts, soggy from snow runoff, but a clear enough sign that I had arrived.

Good old reliable Lennie, the son of a bitch.

I stopped and sat on the ground to wait for the new day.

Dawn doesn't even think of cracking in the Colorado mountains before six at that time of year. Six couldn't be too far away, but as I sat and the dawn didn't break, I lost track of the time. Soon I slipped easily into my own personal brand of Zen. The minutes passed . . . it might've been an hour, might've been two weeks, it didn't matter because I wasn't thinking about it now. I had no goal beyond the number ten, staring at the black wall and counting to ten, starting over, doing it again and again with only an empty mind to keep me company. This is how a moment passed, then an eternity, and the dawn finally cracked. November in the Rockies: I was aware of it without ever seeing the crack, which would be somewhere slightly aft and off to port. I didn't turn my head but there was some suggestive thing, just the slightest hint of firmament across the way, though I couldn't really see it yet. I counted to ten and counted again, and at one point I wished I'd known about this Zen tool years ago when I had been a cop on stakeouts.

So that's what this was then, a stakeout. I hadn't thought of it that way until this moment, but, yes, I had come here to watch the house with only a hunch that if nothing had happened by now, something might just be overdue. Slowly the day brightened, gradually I saw the road on the opposite hillside, and suddenly the house took shape in the trees across the gulch. I made a small adjustment and burrowed deeper into the underbrush, drawing my coat up around my face so seeing me would be difficult and maybe impossible from there. I imagined all kinds of evil afoot, I pictured someone standing just inside the Marshall living room scanning my hill with binoculars. But I sat still, staring at the house. I counted to ten a hundred times, I stared and I counted, and in this way the time passed.

At some point I came fully alert and looked around. For the first time I took note of the day.

The dawn never did have any real crack to it; the sky was gray and snow was swirling over my head, blowing down the gulch and around the house and over the mountaintop. I thought of all the stakeouts I had done and how Jesus-Christ-boring they had all been. I had been here now five hours—I looked at my watch—but the day was still early and at that point I didn't even allow myself the luxury of feeling like a fool. I counted to ten and cleared my mind.

I counted to ten and the snow piled up on my hood, on my shoulders, and settled in a deepening mound around my ass. Trickles of water ran down from my head and across my cheeks from my eyes.

I counted to ten.

Much later I thought of Erin.

Looked at my watch. It was half past eleven.

She'd be finished interviewing Laura Marshall by now; she and Parley would have seen the mute boy. She had taken the case, I had no doubt, and she'd be getting ready to fly back to Denver. She'd be pretty well pissed: this I knew. Briefly I wished I had written her a note of some kind, but how could I know at four o'clock in the morning that I would lose my mind and disappear? What would I have said? *Don't worry if*

I lose my mind. Don't fret if I disappear for a while. I'm on the case, love, Janeway.

Yeah, right. What does "for a while" mean? All day? All week?

How long would this madness continue? How long before I packed it in?

Not yet, came the quick answer. At some point, obviously, but not yet.

I counted to ten and the hours passed.

I had been there more than ten hours. Ten hours of counting to ten. My watch told me so, but it didn't seem to matter. If I left now and something happened to the books, what kind of idiot would that make me? I was becoming a captive to my own mad fears.

Did this mean I was prepared to sit through the night? The snow had fallen throughout the day and I knew I must look like some stupid abominable snowman sitting here alone. Erin would be back in Denver by now. She knew me well enough not to worry, I hoped. She would know I was off somewhere on the case, she'd know I would never do anything to screw it up. But that knowledge might be starting to pale by now.

Oh, yeah, Erin would be pissed.

Too bad for her. She should've taken me more seriously about the books.

I looked at my watch. Four o'clock. I'd had nothing to eat since last night, and only the snow for water. Strangely, it seemed like enough. My hunch was stronger now than it had been this morning, and that's what kept me here. I sucked on a snowball and laughed as that silly bumper sticker DON'T EAT YELLOW SNOW wafted through my head. I made sure to pee downhill so as not to foul up the water supply.

At four-thirty I finally took a break and hiked out to my car. The road was now tightly snowpacked and I made good time to the edge of town. There I stopped at the café, got something to take out, and called Denver from the pay phone while they were cooking it.

Erin wasn't home. I left a message on her machine, told her I was alive and well, apologized, and told her to look for me when she saw me. Then I took my lukewarm sandwich and a bottle of beer and headed back uphill. I had a fresh new commitment and a crazy, growing sense of urgency. I didn't like being away even for half an hour.

How can I describe the twenty-four hours that followed? To say I ate my food, I sat and I waited: these things have no meaning in a surrealistic world of silence and white flutter. The snow fluttered and the darkness fell, and sometime after that I hiked back out to the road and got my bag from the car. From there the hike to the top was arduous: the snow was deep and I didn't want to take a chance on it, even with four-wheel drive, and I didn't want to leave deep furrows showing that a car had been here. So I made the climb, finally reaching the house at nine-thirty by my watch.

I stood on the porch for a time, watching the snow fall, seeing nothing beyond my reach. At some point I let myself in.

I took off my shoes. Followed my light down the hallway to the library. Took a deep breath of relief as my light revealed the tall shelves of books, apparently undisturbed since I had last seen them.

I unrolled my sleeping bag on the floor, got out my notebook, propped my flashlight, and started the long job of making a list. I made it in order, as the books were shelved, and after a while I got into a rhythm. I used my own crude shorthand and things went faster after that. Still, it was after midnight when I finished.

A check of Bobby's office revealed nothing. His desk contained only the insurance policies— life, house, and car.

I walked through the house to the back room, bent down, and looked at the fireplace.

The grate looked undisturbed, still full of ash, and I stood there for a full minute looking at it in the soft glow of my light before judgment reared its head and told me to leave it alone.

I was bone-tired now. I put my sleeping bag at the end of the hall and crawled inside it. In less than five minutes I was sound asleep.

The hours blended together: blended, fused, became a single black unit of time.

I don't remember waking up. Sometime before dawn, I rolled my bag by the dim glow of my flashlight, locked the house, and trudged back down the hill.

I don't know why, I just felt better from the vantage point across the gulch. I took up the vigil again, sitting in the trees, counting to ten, staring across the way as the land went gray, then pink, and the sun came out.

The sun . . . what a crazy, happy sight that was. Strangely, it didn't matter after a while. The sun shone bright but at midmorning clouds blew out of the west and made the world gray again. I remember two thoughts from that second day: *This has got to stop* and *Just a little longer*. A little longer and surely I'd be ready to pack it in. Thus did the hours pass: I counted to ten, 10 trillion times I counted, and in the late afternoon a gentle snow-flutter blew down from the mountain.

Again I walked out to the car. Drove into town for my fast-food dinner. Called Erin, got her machine, decided to go back for one last look.

Good thing, too. The two men were there when I got back.

14

They were sitting in a pickup truck. If they had been there awhile, it had been a very little while. They sat in the cab with the motor running—I could see the exhaust even across the gulch—and they appeared to be in earnest conversation at the deserted look of the place. Two guys in a picture of indecision. They hadn't come up here to steal Laura's books: they'd had another purpose and now they were stymied at what they had found. This was all speculation on my part, but moments passed and they still didn't move. What else could have stopped them? Suddenly the horn blew. It echoed across the meadow and down the gulch, and when no one came from the house to greet them, they turned the truck around and got the hell out of there.

I ran now: slipped and slid back along the trail to the road, arriving just in time to get a good look at the truck as it came past. It was a late-model GMC two-seater, green with a black, waterproof tarp covering the open bed, licensed by the state of Oklahoma. It roared by in a blizzard of snow: I was crouched in a ditch and I cursed when I could read only the last three plate numbers. Five-six-three, I thought, five-six-three. I was still committing it to memory as I got my own car and rolled down the mountain behind them. At the juncture of the main highway, I got lucky: I saw their taillights through the trees just before I blundered upon them.

I eased up to the bend, got out, and walked to the edge of the trees. They were parked at the stop sign facing the main road not twenty yards away. I got the rest of the license plate number and committed it to memory.

They were talking earnestly again about something. More indecision, this time perhaps over which way to go. To the left just a few miles away was the town, a warm bed, and supper: to the right, nothing but seventy-five miles of bad road, high mountain passes, and snow.

They turned right. I got back in my car, pulled up to the stop sign, and sat for a moment watching their taillights recede in the distance.

It was five o'clock: night was quickly coming on and I had lived in Colorado long enough to

know better. To dare the remote high country in
wintertime with a truck was bad enough. To
take the same road alone in a car, even with
four-wheel drive, was irresponsible and damned
dangerous. There are easier ways to commit suicide.

But I knew I was going. I looked at my gas
gauge—three-quarters of a tank—and I gave the
books a final wave and headed south.

C'est la vie.

I had gone no more than five miles, just past the
so-called airport, when I passed an open road
barrier. The sign said ROAD CLOSED NOV 15–APR
15. They should've closed it last week, not next,
I thought grimly . . . they might've just saved
three lives by doing that. But a fool will always
find some way to kill himself, and I thought
other optimistic things as the road began to
climb. This is when a book thief will choose to
show up at the house, I thought. He'll empty out
that room in a heartbeat and nobody will see
him, nobody will know which way he or the
books went, or what it was all about. In the
spring, when the highway department clears this
road, they'll find Janeway's leathery corpse perfectly preserved like the two-thousand-year-old
man, his car half-buried under a snowdrift. This

was not funny: there was too good a chance of something just like that happening. Turn around, kid, I thought, the hell with those guys: go back and babysit the books. But then I could see their taillights again, climbing toward some unseen summit, and that drew me on. Those boys hadn't just materialized at the house, and I wanted to know what they knew. I could always turn around if it got bad. So I thought. I could always turn around.

They were maybe a quarter mile ahead, rolling along at a pretty good clip. I was able to make good time as well. The snow had been drifting during the day, but there had been no traffic across the pass to pack it down and my tires got good traction on the gravel. The road was dark and getting darker by the minute: the snow seemed suddenly heavier, at last I had to use my lights, and I knew that far ahead the two guys would be well aware of my presence. I imagined them saying, *Who is that crazy bastard back there?*

Such is life, I thought. *Such is life and death.*

My mind was a jumble of thoughts, none of them good, as I climbed toward the great Continental Divide. In another week this drive would be impossible. This road should already be closed, I thought again. What are the highway people thinking?

There comes a point on such a journey when final thoughts of turning back are cast aside and forgotten. I had reached a summit, and for a while I rode along at the top of the world with swirling mists on either side. The effect was bizarre, almost grotesque in its dark beauty. There was a dense cloud cover and yet a full moon broke through almost continuously, lighting up a road that seemed like a silver ribbon around the universe with spiraling galaxies on either side. I couldn't see the truck at all now, which only increased my paranoia, and ahead was a fearsome-looking storm-thing that almost turned me back even then. That was my point of no return . . . if I went into that cold hell, I was in effect giving myself up for dead anyway, I was going all the way. The snow hit like some kind of battering ram. I felt the car shiver in a fierce crossing wind. Oh, baby, this was nuts. But then the car pushed through it, the moon broke through, and for that moment I could see forever. Again I could see the road running on and on: I could see another mountain range in the far distance, and down the road, at least a mile away, I saw the truck.

I stopped for a moment and sat watching, idling. Something wasn't right.

The truck didn't seem to be moving, that was the strange thing. There was no movement at all to the picture ahead: it was as if the two guys had stopped to talk it over yet again. I knew, having driven these mountain roads for years, that the downslope is the dangerous part. I could feel the ice under my wheels: even at a crawl and with four-wheel drive, if I hit the brakes the car would slip. Suddenly I knew something else. Those guys weren't moving because they had lost control going down. They had run off the road and got stuck. Here they were, miles from anywhere, and unless they had a radio, I was their only hope.

I sat there and the moon went south, the world went dark, and blowing gusts obliterated everything. There was no question now about what to do: I had to go check on those guys, had to roll up and introduce myself and pretend to be a hail-fellow-damned-well-met, just an unwashed slob as crazy as they were, and see if they bought that. I had an uneasy feeling about it, but I no longer had a choice. I got out of the car and opened the trunk, fished around in the far back, and took out my gun. Made the unnecessary checks (it was always loaded, always ready for some ugly job) and put it under the seat, just a long stretch from my left hand.

"Let's go get 'em, Danno," I said out loud.

I took my time getting there. For a few minutes the blizzard was horrendous. I couldn't see more than a foot of road ahead, and I crawled along at the speed of nothing. I took heart in the occasional pockets of clarity, but it was a long time, at least twenty minutes, before I saw the truck's lights again. When I did, the effect was startling: I came across a flat spot and the snow whipped past, just before the ground dipped precariously, deeper into the valley. I stopped at the edge. This is where he lost it, I thought, and at the same instant my vision cleared and the truck was there, not fifty yards away. He had slipped easily off the road—I could see his mistake from the distance: he had taken way too much liberty on the flat, and then when the sudden downgrade began, he had not been ready for it. I started down slowly, and as I did one of the men ran frantically into the roadway, waving his arms. Here we go, I thought.

I rolled down the window and a coarsely bearded face filled it.

"Jesus Christ," he said, almost out of breath.

"God bless America, brother, am I glad to see you! Whoever the hell you are, you sure look good to me right now."

"Run off the road, did you?" I said stupidly.

"Yeah. My goddamn brother and his balls of steel. If he doesn't kill us yet with his daredevil bullshit, I'll be one surprised mother."

"That looks like a pretty ugly crack-up from back here. I got a rope, if you'd like to try pulling it out."

"No way, pardner. He wrapped it around a tree while he was at it. We'll have to send a wrecker back after it when we can. Will you give us a lift out of here?"

"Sure. Where you headed?"

"You mean I got a choice?"

I laughed. "Straight ahead seems to be it for the moment."

"Wherever there's warm and something to eat. We know a fellow in Monte Vista."

"I'm going right through there."

He went back to the truck and I sat idling. So far, so good. I didn't know them, they didn't know me. A minute later the other one arrived: a spitting image of the first, except that his beard had a few streaks of gray. "Howdy, stranger," he said. "I guess Willie already told you, we're damned glad you came."

"You guys hop in. With luck, maybe we'll all survive."

"That's fine. If you don't mind, we've got some merchandise we've got to carry with us."

"Sure. Will it fit in the backseat?"

"Oh, yeah, long as the three of us can sit up front."

That was fine with me: I remembered what Jack McCall had done to Wild Bill Hickok and I wasn't partial to having either of them at my back the rest of the way down. I asked if they needed any help and the guy said no, they could get it. In fact, what came out of the truck took them each four loads to carry out of there: eight cardboard boxes a foot deep and about two feet square. I turned on the overhead light and saw the name *Daedalus* printed boldly on the sides of each box. I knew it well: Daedalus Books was one of the better remainder houses of the book trade. I bought remainders myself about twice a year, and I had half a dozen identical boxes in the back room of my store. They were ideal for shipping or for transporting books to book fairs.

I decided not to comment on any of this yet: there would be time enough later, if the situation felt right at some point. The two guys slammed the back doors and got in the front beside me.

"You guys must be twins," I said, offering a hand. "Cliff Janeway."

If I had earned any kind of name in the book trade, these boys hadn't heard it. I had been thinking about giving them a phony name: the book world is so small and insular. Sometimes it seems as if everybody knows everybody, but they showed no reaction to my name. This, I thought, was good.

"Wally Keeler," said the reckless one.

"Willie Keeler," said the other, from shotgun.

I didn't recognize their names either. If they were accomplished grafters, I might expect to, again because book people love to talk and word gets around. We shook firmly and I backed out onto the road. "You sure that's everything?"

"Everything we can carry tonight."

I started down. "Man, we've all got to be a little crazy to be out here tonight."

I said this in my self-deprecating, no-offense-intended voice and Willie gave a dry, humorless laugh. "You got that right."

"Don't start, Will," said his brother. "It wasn't just my say-so."

The tone was far from cordial. Willie gave a derisive grunt and the atmosphere in the car was poisoned by sibling discord.

"So what're you doing out here?" said Wally.

"Made a hot date with a waitress over in Alamosa," I said.

Willie laughed. "That must *really* be a hot date."

"It ain't that hot." I looked at them in the reflection of the odometer. "Never woulda started across that pass if I'd known what was ahead of me."

"Good thing for us you did, pal."

"Then it got to a point where it seemed just as easy to keep going as to go back."

"That's all I was saying," Wally said. "Didn't hear any fuss about it till things turned ugly."

"Maybe if you tried staying on the goddamn road, things wouldn't turn ugly. Oh, no, not you. Every fuckin' highway is the goddamn Indianapolis 500."

"Listen, you son of a bitch—"

"Hey, fellas," I said. "You boys wanna fight, at least wait'll I get us out of here."

"Yeah," Willie said sourly. "Show some manners, asshole."

Nothing more was said for a while, but the air simmered with their anger. We bottomed out in the valley and started up again. I thought about asking them what their business was: nothing too inquisitive, just making-conversation-type conversation, but it didn't feel right yet. Ahead the road looked better: I could see the moon clearly now, and I had high hopes that the worst was behind us. We wound our way upward and upward, and then, at the peak, another mountain range loomed ahead.

"Goddamn brand-new truck," Willie said suddenly.

"I'm not gonna tell you again, Willie—"

"Looks like better weather ahead," I said in my jolly-boys voice.

"Couldn't get much worse."

"Where you boys from?"

Willie said, "Raton," and Wally said, "Tulsa."

"He lives in Tulsa," Willie said quickly. "What about you?"

"Denver."

"What're you doing out here?"

"Just a little R and R."

I let a moment pass, then asked the question. "How about yourselves?"

"Same answer," Willie said. "We came over to see a fellow we know."

I took another moment, then: "What line of work you boys in?"

This time the pause gave them time enough to concoct some serious fiction. Apparently

Willie was not a stupid man: he figured I had seen the Daedalus imprint on the boxes. So I thought in the ten seconds it took him to answer.

"We're book wholesalers," he said.

"You mean like traveling salesmen?"

"Yeah, something like that. We represent a book dealer who sells remainders. We've got a five-state region where we market our stuff."

I knew this was fiction. In fact, remainder-house reps never carried boxes of books: instead they arrived with half a dozen briefcases full of dust jackets. I had spent more than one afternoon sitting across the counter from remainder salesmen, looking at jackets one after another, saying, "Three of these," "Five of these, please," and so on. But to Willie I was polite and ignorant. "That sounds interesting."

"It's all right. What do you do?"

"I play the ponies," I said in a masterpiece of my own spontaneous bullshit.

"You're a gambler?"

"It's not exactly gambling," I said.

"Aw, c'mon. You tellin' me you play the horses for a living and it's not gambling?"

"Not in the long run. Not if you're careful and know your business."

"What the hell, then . . . are the races fixed?"

"Not at all. I've just worked out a formula."

"Damn, I could use some of that formula."

"I'm not saying I never lose," I said easily. "When I do lose, I take it big in the shorts. But I win a lot more than I lose, just by knowing when certain horses are miles better than the competition. I play small fields, no more than half a dozen in a race, so a good horse doesn't get screwed in traffic jams. I bet big, and I put it all on the nose."

"You must get no odds at all."

"You never do with a sure thing, but it's better than you'd imagine. I average four-to-five. Eighty cents on the dollar. That's fine if you've put down ten grand to win eight, and you win nine out of ten."

"Jesus Christ," Wally said. "Man, I wouldn't have the balls to do that."

"You've got to know how to pick the right horse, that's for sure. Can't just play every four-to-five shot that steps on the racetrack."

"Deep pockets probably don't hurt either."

"Don't kid yourself; my pockets aren't that deep. I've got a little money in the bank, but there've been times when I came this close to looking for a job. Once I was down to my last grubstake. Then I won fifteen in a row and was back on top again."

"Jesus. How long've you been doing this?"

"Ten years."

"Jesus! You never know who the hell you're gonna meet."

I almost wanted to laugh. This all sounded real because it was real. Once I had known a guy who had lived just that way. He had a powerhouse system and he had put two kids through school with it. He had won fifteen in a row many times and once had a fabulous win streak of twenty-three. But then came the day he hit the inevitable skids, lost six big ones, and died in the stretch. The last I heard he was working in a gas station, but I knew enough about his good years to make the story fascinating to a pair of wannabe fast-buck artists.

We talked our way up the pass and across it: they asked naive questions and I gave them sophisticated answers that sounded legit even to me. It kept them away from each other's throat long enough to get us into relatively flat country, then across that on the swing into Monte Vista.

"Looks like we survived," I said.

"Yeah," Willie said. "We can drop our goods and get home from here. Pal, you sure came along at the right time. Don't know what the hell we'da done without you."

"Happy to oblige," I said.

"We need to get together sometime. We could maybe go racing and you could show us that magic system you've got."

Ahead the lights of Monte Vista stretched across the horizon. It was a small town, no more than four or five thousand people: strange place for a book drop, I thought.

"Turn left up there," Wally said. "That gray building in the middle of the block."

I pulled up in front. "Lemme give you boys a hand with that stuff."

"Oh, we're fine now."

"I could use a stretch about now, if you don't mind."

"Hell, then come on in. The least we can do is give you a cup of coffee."

There were no signs anywhere on the building: just a plain warehouse of some kind. In the front was a small room that looked like an office. A light was shining in the window and another somewhere back in the building itself. Willie climbed a ramp and rang a bell. An outer light came on and a door went up. I saw a man standing there in silhouette. There was my third alternate suspect.

He loomed over the Keeler boys like a giant. Behind him I could see a long row of bookshelves, and beyond that another. Books on the shelves, books on the floor: I had been in a hundred places like that, but those had been bookstores, open for business.

The three of them looked at me down the ramp. "Come on in," one of them said.

15

I climbed up the ramp and met a thin, towering creature. "This is Mr. Kevin Simms," Willie said, and Simms shook my hand warily, limply. He was at least six-ten, a beanpole with a severe look on his face. "What's going on?" he said, and immediately the bickering began again. Willie said, "A. J. fuckin' Foyt here lost the goddamn truck is all," and for most of the next minute Simms had to stand between them to prevent what each tried to sell as true mayhem for the other. They screamed insults and I stood back and watched it all and tried not to laugh. In fact it was no laughing matter. Even before I stepped into that room I had a hunch, it wasn't a good one, and I was already planning my exit strategy in case something went suddenly, desperately wrong. Simms seemed to be the authority here, and above all the screaming I had sensed his distrust. This was more than a look I picked up over the bickering brothers, I was getting powerful vibes even with nothing to back it up. But I had learned long ago to always, always trust my own juice. I was still alive because I had listened to that inner voice at least three times when it counted.

Simms would be the dangerous one. I could feel his suspicion rippling across the gap between us: I could see it in his eyes. If something happened, I would take him down first and fast. I would get him with a sucker punch if I had to: a hard shot under the sternum should take out what wind he had. I didn't figure the brothers as patsies, but I liked my odds against the two of them without the severe-looking giant in the mix. At last Simms shouted, "All right, knock it off!" and the Keelers immediately pushed away from each other and stood apart, seething. "What's the matter with you two?" Simms yelled. "Are you both crazy?"

"It was an accident," Wally sulked. "That's all it was, a goddamn accident, and now he's trying to make out like it was some kinda diabolical thing I did on purpose."

"We can do without the language," Simms said. "I hope I don't need to tell you boys again, I don't like having the Lord's name taken in vain."

"Sorry," Wally said.

"You too, Willie."

"*Me?* What did I say?"

"Just . . ." Simms closed his eyes. "Just . . . *watch your mouth.*"

He opened his eyes wide and they stared straight at me: the coldest, bluest eyes I had ever seen. "So, sir, I take it you came along and pulled these two out of trouble."

"I was coming over the pass and I was able to give them a ride," I said. "I was in the right place at the right time."

"You can say that again," Willie said. "Tell you what, Preacher, if it wasn't for Clint here, we'd still be back in that snowbank."

The blue eyes fastened on me. "Your name is Clint?"

"Cliff."

"Then it's good indeed that you came along . . . Cliff."

He didn't seem much interested in last names and that was fine with me. Willie said, "I told him to come in and have some coffee," and the Preacher said, "That's good. You'll have to make some."

"Y'know what?" I said. "Maybe I should move on down the highway. I'm meeting somebody in Alamosa."

"He's got a hot date," Wally said.

I saw Simms react again with distaste.

"When're you meeting this dish?" Wally said.

"She gets off at eleven."

"Alamosa's just up the road," the Preacher said. "Let us extend you some courtesy: warm yourself, and then you can be on your way."

He rolled down the ramp door and locked it. Not a good sign.

I smiled, Mr. All-Easy America. "You ever play basketball?"

"I never had time for games."

"I guess maybe it's just the name, Kevin. You remind me of Kevin McHale."

"I don't know who Kevin McHale is."

"Great basketball player for the Celtics."

"Preacher probably never heard of the Celtics either," Wally said.

Simms gave him a cold look but Wally said, "Preacher'd blanch if I told him what you do for a living."

Simms looked at me. "And what might that be?"

"He's a gambler," Wally said, enjoying the moment. "An honest-to-gosh hossplayer, Preach."

"Hey, you," Willie said from some distance. "How about remembering that this guy saved your butt back there."

"Well, I am most extremely sorry, sir," Wally said, grinning at me. "I certainly had no intention to offend."

"That'll be the damned day," Willie muttered.

"How's the coffee doing?" Simms asked.

"It's getting there," Willie said.

I looked at Simms and said, "You guys mind if I look around?"

"You interested in books?" Simms said.

"Sure, isn't everybody?" I said, knowing full well how few people really are, how pitifully few ever read anything more than the morning newspaper.

"I do read a lot," I said. "And I've got a small collection of first editions."

"What kind of first editions?"

"Mostly modern stuff. Literature . . . you know, fiction. It's nothing special, just books I liked reading and wanted my own copies. Nice stuff in nice jackets, all since around 1945. With a few exceptions."

"Then do by all means, look."

I moved away from them and wandered along the first row. It was all modern, a mix of fiction and fact but all firsts, very nice, and no remainder marks. "Any of this stuff for sale?" I called.

"Everything's for sale," Simms said.

"No prices on any of it, so I just wondered."

"Make yourself a stack, I'll be reasonable."

I found my first signed one: *The Philosophy of Andy Warhol,* with his drawing of the Campbell's tomato soup can. I knew some dealers were asking big money for that book, but even signed it was far from uncommon. I had sold it several times for around three bills.

"Just so's we know we're on the same page, what do you want for the Warhol?"

"That's signed, you know, with a drawing. But I'd take two hundred for it."

"Okay." I began to stack up some stuff. "I could be in here all night."

"Take your time," Simms said. "I happen to have all night."

"Unfortunately, I've got to be in Alamosa."

"Yes," he said, the distaste still evident on his face. "I almost forgot."

"Coffee's ready," Willie said.

"Never mind the coffee, we're doing business now." Simms tried smiling to blunt the harsh tone of his voice, but his smile, like the rest of him, was ice-cold. To me he said, "I'd have him bring it back to you, except—"

"—books and coffee don't mix."

"Exactly."

I browsed for another twenty minutes and had what I estimated would be eight hundred retail. "I really do have to go."

"Well, have your coffee while the Preacher tallies you up," Willie said.

I took a cup and shot the breeze with Willie. Simms shuffled through the stack and said, "How about five hundred?"

"That'll work." I fished five bills out of my wallet.

The money disappeared into a thin hand. Wally laughed and said, "The hoss racket must be pretty good, hey, Preach?"

I sipped at my coffee. "You a real preacher?"

"Oh, yes, indeed," he said, and in that moment a kind of fever lit up his eyes and I could see the face of zealots everywhere. In that moment a collage of righteous oppressors swirled through my head and I saw our Preacher in medieval days, sentencing harlots to be stoned. I saw his face behind the judge's bench in the modern Middle East, condemning a woman for showing her face in public. I watched him deny help to a sick child, ordering parents to pray and leaving them with their guilt when help failed to arrive. Somehow the failing was theirs, their son was dead because they weren't good enough, they hadn't prayed hard enough, and the Lord wouldn't hear them. Modern medicine would have saved the child but damned his soul. The Preacher moves on and finds another sick kid and keeps on preaching. Jesus, Muhammad, and Moses, he is everywhere. I saw him on the stage, sending the farmer to death in *The Crucible* for refusing to confess, and he was that preacher's real-life role model, Senator Joe McCarthy, damning by innuendo, wrecking lives and getting away with it by preaching to the fear of a gutless majority. I hated zealots, and in the moment he knew that, he saw me as clearly as I had seen him. We spoke cordially but he knew me well. I was the enemy.

He said, "So how are you with the Lord, stranger?"

"Well, Preacher, I do the best I can. You know how it is."

"I know very well how it is. And it may be that you think you do the best you can, that's what a lot of people think. But deep inside you must know that gambling and women are not the way."

"Then I'll have to try and do better." I looked around and said, "Maybe I'll give it all up and become a bookseller."

"That would depend on whether you have a greater goal and what that is. Books can be a simple means to an end. Whatever I make here, for example, goes directly into the service of the Lord."

I wanted to get away from his Lord and my own inevitable damnation. "I bet you'd sell a lot of stuff here if you'd hang out a sign and open it up."

"Undoubtedly. But then I'd have . . . *people* . . . pawing over it. It doesn't take long for *people* to mess things up. People have no idea what's coming."

I looked around: there were still dark corners crammed with books, places that I hadn't even seen yet. "You've been collecting this stuff quite a while I'll bet," I said. "You must have twenty thousand books in here."

"Oh, at least that."

"I get down this way occasionally. I really would like to spend some time here."

"I'm sure that could be arranged, if I'm here. You'd have to take a chance. Just pull up and ring the bell. Now that we've done business together, I'll let you in."

"Maybe I could call ahead."

"I don't have a telephone," he said.

That seemed to settle it, but at that exact moment a phone rang somewhere. I looked at him and he looked at me. I tried not to react, but there are times when no reaction says more than an outcry. I was dying to say, *Thou shall not lie, Preacher,* but instead I picked up my books and sidled toward the door. He moved across the room, surprisingly quick for a big man. I shouldn't have been so surprised: Kevin McHale was pretty quick, too.

He was standing in my way at the ramp door, and in that half moment I wasn't at all certain how it would go. I was right on the verge of throwing that punch but I waited. I looked down at the lock and said, "Well, Preacher, it's been real."

He had about two seconds to get out of my way. He may have sensed that, because he moved aside and flipped open the lock, bent down, and pulled up the door.

"Have a good time in Alamosa," he said, but his tone said the opposite. His tone said, *Get syphilis, go blind, and die in agony, whoremonger.*

"Night, boys," I said to the Keelers.

I hurried down the ramp, got in the car, and backed out into the street.

16

I drove around the block and parked; got out, drew my heavy coat tight, and pulled the hood over my head. I walked back to the corner and stood in the shadows watching the book warehouse. I'd give a thousand dollars to be in there now, I thought: an invisible man or a mouse in the corner. I'd give a hundred if the Preacher had provoked me just a little more. I wished to hell I could've thrown that punch. But that was crazy.

Time passed. Was this going to be another marathon stakeout? I didn't think Zen would help me much this time: I needed to be awake and alert now till something happened. I had slept only a few hours last night, and I knew that soon I'd begin paying a stiff price for that. At the moment I seemed to be okay: I was still in the grip of a heavy blood rush, drawn on by the excitement that always comes with sudden discovery, and I was in no immediate danger of falling asleep on my feet. I might be good through the night, if I had to be.

But within minutes I felt the most crushing fatigue. When that comes on, it comes so damned quickly . . . one minute you're fine, the next you feel your blood beginning to thicken and you're dead on your feet. I toyed with the idea of getting closer. I needed any kind of movement: if I could wiggle under that ramp, better yet crawl under the floor of that room, I might be able to hear something. At least that would keep me going.

I struggled against it for ten minutes and felt myself losing the battle. That relentless light from the office window was having a mesmerizing effect.

Gotta move. Can't stay here. Gotta move now.

I crossed the street and walked boldly up to the ramp. Nothing was going on anywhere. No sound from inside, not even a muffled voice beyond that rolling tin door. I knew I couldn't stand there long . . . one or all of them might come out anytime now, but the crawl space under the warehouse looked so cold and dark that I hated the thought of going there.

I heard a bump and that opened my eyes wide.

A footstep: not inside, but somewhere much more immediate. The sound of a boot on gravel and a smoke being lit.

Now a voice. "That goddamn Preacher better stop talkin' to me like that."

Wally. Apparently they had come out through a door on the other side of the building and were standing just a few feet away. Willie said, "Yeah? What're you gonna do about it?"

"Maybe I'm gonna quit this shit."

"Do I look like I'm stoppin' you? You wanna quit, quit. Soon as we get the truck out and see what the insurance will fix for us, you can go wherever the hell you want."

"You can have the fuckin' truck."

"Big deal. Don't do me no favors, okay?"

"Man, this's bullshit."

"Then quit. You see anybody out here stoppin' you?"

"Nobody anywhere's about to stop *me* if I want to quit. The money ain't that good, and it's a pain in the ass when you gotta watch what you say around the sumbitch *all* the fuckin' time."

"Then fuckin' quit and for Christ's sake stop talkin' about it."

"If I do quit, it'll be my own choice, and I'll do it in my own good time."

"You ain't gonna do a goddamn thing. Just gonna talk, just like always. Talk-talk-talk-talk-talk."

"You're gonna push me one time too many, Willie."

"Talk-talk-taaaaaalk," Willie said in a croaky parrot voice.

"Listen, you son of a bitch—"

"Let's just shut the hell up about it, that's all."

They stood smoking for a while.

"Where the hell is that Preacher?" Wally said.

"He's on the phone," Willie said with exaggerated patience. "Didn't he just tell you he was gettin' on the goddamn telephone?"

"What's he gonna be, on the telephone all damn night? It's colder than a witch's tit out here."

"You'll be warm enough when you get to California."

"You gonna stay here and take care of the truck?"

"Somebody's got to. You'd just fuck that up too."

"Willie, I've really had enough of you and your bullshit."

Willie yawned loudly as the lights went out

and a door slammed. I eased down below the ramp level and the Preacher's gaunt silhouette came around the corner. The three of them crossed the street and got into a car. I waited till they were half a block away, then I ran back for my own car. As I pulled onto the highway, I could see them stopped two blocks away at a red light. Easy to follow in a small town, as long as I stayed back far enough and they didn't see my car. But in the next block I had to run a red when they were on the verge of disappearing around a corner.

I had a flashing vision of Lennie Walsh hiding in the weeds with his ticket pad.

I hoped they weren't going straight on to California now.

I felt new waves of weariness and I knew I'd never make it.

They drove out to the edge of town and turned into a long dirt driveway that led back to a house surrounded by trees. I parked and waited till I could see some lights: then I walked back through the underbrush, keeping low as I approached the house and taking it slow as I went. I reached the edge of the trees. I could see them going back and forth between the house and a garage off to one side. I stood still, hiding myself

behind a big ponderosa, and at some point they
finished whatever they'd been doing in the house
and moved out to the garage. A long open space
was between my tree and the house, a gap where
I'd be a sitting duck if anyone walked out
through that half-opened door. I took it anyway:
walked across as if I'd been born there and flattened against the dark outer wall. I eased down
to the edge, peeped around, and froze.

I was looking down the length of a Ford station wagon, a dozen years old and sporting current Oklahoma plates. Around and beyond it
were several dozen bookshelves, all packed with
books, most draped with sheets of plastic, I assumed to protect against blowing wind and
snow when the door was up. The station wagon
had been backed into the garage, the tailgate
was up, and the three of them were loading
boxes into it: Daedalus boxes, I could see
through the windshield and across the front
seat. They were being stacked three across, four
down and three high, making a solid block, un-
likely to shift even on a long ride. Thirty-six
boxes, ideal for shipping: I did the math. Four
stacks of octavo-sized books could fit in each
box: ten books per stack . . . fourteen hundred
books, give or take a dozen or two.

"Here's your big list," Preacher said, handing

a sheet of paper to one of the Keeler boys. "Study it tonight."

"What time do you want to leave?"

"If we can get out of here by seven, we can be in Salt Lake City tomorrow night. That'll give us plenty of time to work the bookstores the next day."

"Salt Lake's always pretty good," Wally said.

"That's because nobody else thinks it is," Preacher said. "People don't know what to look for."

"Maybe *we're* gettin' better too," Wally said. "Don't you think we're getting better, Preach? Bet you never thought us yokels would ever learn this stuff."

"Don't brag on yourself too much. Vanity is a sin in the eyes of the Lord."

"I'm goin' to bed," Willie said.

Wally laughed. "You gettin' up in the morning to see us off?"

"Not if I can help it. I'm sayin' adios right now. Don't shake me unless the world's ending."

"Don't speak too lightly of that," Preacher said.

He reached up and slammed the tailgate shut. Wally began turning out the lights and I moved away, back into the darkness.

I could still hear them when they came out.

Preacher was telling Willie to call him once they had some idea about the damages to the truck. "We'll be in the Motel 6 in Salt Lake. After that I can't say. We'll probably go south across Nevada. You know I don't like to stay in Las Vegas."

"No books there anyway."

"You can catch us in Burbank at the Motel 6, but probably not before next Thursday or Friday, just before the fair sets up."

They walked in the shadows across the yard. "I think this is gonna be a good year," Preacher said. "Good all around. We got some nice things that ought to move fast at the prices I put on 'em. Next year maybe we'll go back East."

They went inside. I waited till the lights went out, then I backtracked out to the highway, picked up my car, and checked into a motel.

I took a shower and called Erin. She answered on the first ring.

"By God, it's good to hear your voice," I said.

"Well, listen to this. Should I be relieved, angry, or something in between?"

"I was hoping for overjoyed. Maybe even sexually aroused?"

"I've never been interested in phone sex.

Mildly overjoyed might be the best I can do on such short notice."

"How the hell can anybody be *mildly* overjoyed?"

"I have superb control of my emotions. Where are you?"

"Motel in Monte Vista. I may be going to California."

I told her what had happened. I talked for ten minutes.

"Wow. I should pay more attention when you talk to me, shouldn't I?"

"Yes, you should. That's why you sent me out here, or so I thought."

"And now you want to go to California."

"I'm on the fence about it. It may be a colossal waste of time and money. But on the other hand . . ."

"You don't want to lose them."

A long silence spread out between us.

"I think you should go to California," she said. "Aside from having fun at the book fair, you can do a little work to shore up our alternate suspect theory."

"Have we really got a chance with that?"

"Colorado isn't very clear on it. But if you can find enough evidence to raise a reasonable doubt, that someone else may have killed Bobby, we'd have a real chance to raise it. Those books could be the key. We're moving them out of the house tomorrow."

"Good. Who's moving them?"

"A fellow from town will do the lifting and toting. Parley will be there to watch, along with somebody from the DA's office."

There was a pause, then she said, "We thought about it, talked it over, and there seemed to be more reasons to notice the DA in now than there were not to tell them. If these books do become evidence, which looks increasingly likely with your discoveries, we can't spring their significance on them at the last minute, as much as I'd like to. I'd like to have Parley examine that fireplace ash while the DA's there, but there's a possible downside to that. I don't want them finding something we didn't expect. Laura still seems determined to protect Jerry no matter what, and it would be nice if she didn't incriminate herself any more than she has in her effort to do that."

"So we need to know first if there's a chance of anything else in there."

"Yep. This is actually a good test of her story. But let's talk to her again and make sure before we do something we can't undo. If she waffles, we do nothing with the grate, we keep it to ourselves and leave whatever's there alone."

"Are you okay with that?"

"Sure. My first duty is to defend my client."

"Good. I'll stick with the books for now. Where are they being stored?"

"There's a room they use for an evidence locker just off the sheriff's office. Parley's going to examine each book for signatures and anything else he thinks you might find interesting."

"He seems pretty diligent."

"I think he's great. A good old country lawyer. I can trust him to do things right the first time."

"Unlike some people you know."

I asked about strategy and she said, "As of this moment, paint Bobby as a shadow man who knew strange people and was into things his wife didn't know about. But we've got a lot of work to do there. We'll need to know a lot more about him."

I listened to the telephone noise. At some point she said, "He must've changed a lot since I knew him. I remember him as a happy-go-lucky kid, always laughing, always so open about everything. He wore his feelings on his sleeve."

More time passed. "I'm lining up some good expert witnesses," she said. "I'm getting a psychologist to come talk to our client. We've got to bring him in from Chicago, but he's really superb in the fields of coercion and mental stress. I'm hoping he'll help us construct a good case for why our client lied."

I noticed she still couldn't say her client's name.

She had seen all of the DA's evidence. "I've got copies of the deputy's report, the autopsy, the fingerprints and ballistics from the CBI. If necessary we'll get our own experts to go over it and put our spin on it. We'll see how it goes. They're putting a lot of stock into her confession. And there's no question she handled the gun."

"And the gunshot residue is inconclusive."

"She admits she washed her hands, scrubbed 'em red, in fact, trying to get the blood off. If we can get her confession suppressed, I'll feel a lot better."

"How'd your second interview go?"

"It was okay. Easier somehow than the first. I stayed cool and so did she, for the most part. She cried once; other than that, she was almost like any other client. Of course we both knew better. I explained what we're going to do and how, all subject to change. And I interviewed her at some length about what happened that morning."

"Any surprises?"

"We'll have to comb through it all and talk to her again. I'm having my notes typed up this morning and I'll send a copy to McNamara. You can see the report when he gets it."

"Did you see Jerry while you were in Paradise?"

"Only for a moment. As you can imagine, Bobby's parents are not real eager to help our case. They used 'going to church' as an excuse."

"How did they wind up with the kids?"

"They came out and offered, and that's what Social Services decided."

"And Laura has no say at all in it."

"She's not in a real good position, Cliff. They tend to look at what's right for the kids, not what the defendant wants. And they'd always rather place children with family."

"So what's gonna happen to Jerry?"

"That's not clear yet. His mother was schooling him at home. Old Mrs. Marshall used to be a teacher, long ago, so they may just leave him there till the trial's over. None of this is set in stone. Social Services still has it under advisement. There's a lawyer in the county who's been assigned as guardian ad litem—protector of the children. My guess is they'll leave them there till we all see how the wind blows."

"You've been busy."

Softly she said, "Yeah. And it's never too early to begin preparing for the possibility that we'll lose."

"Did the old folks remember you?"

"Oh, sure. I think they blame me for letting Bobby get charmed away from me. Because I wasn't forgiving enough, somehow I caused his eventual death."

"There's logic for you."

"I'd like you to try talking to Jerry, if you ever stop wandering in the wilderness."

"Why me?"

"Because, in addition to being good with thugs and killers, you're pretty good with kids, kittens, and other furry creatures."

"I'm good with women too," I said, and I heard her cough.

"The old Marshalls," I said. "What kind of people are they?"

"I always thought she was a really sweet woman. He's a bit cold, but you can't have everything. So what are you going to do now? You'll have a fine time trying to follow those guys across nine hundred miles of open country, if that's what you have in mind. They've seen your car, you know."

"I don't need to follow them. I know where they're going."

17

I got almost eight hours' sleep and was back on the road by nine. I wasn't about to go over that pass again, even in daylight. The weather forecast was for slippery conditions at the top of the world, with gale-force winds and blowing snow. Instead I went up 285, connected with 50, and stayed with the main highways on the longer, saner loop back through Gunnison and on south to Paradise. I had ten days until the Burbank Book Fair opened in north L.A. It was a two-hour flight from Denver. I could put the time to good use and catch up with my book suspects later. I still had no idea what I'd learn from them; this was nothing more than a grand hunch. But if all else failed, I could buy something great at the fair. I could schmooze with old pals and write off the whole trip as a booking expense. There are worse ways to spend one's time and money.

I arrived in Paradise in the early afternoon and went looking for Parley. I checked at his house and the café, then went on up to the Marshall place. At the top of the hill I saw his car among several others: Lennie Walsh's police cruiser, two black sedans, and a medium-sized, closed-bed truck with a ramp that extended onto the front porch. I pulled into the yard, got out, and started across the yard. Suddenly the judge was standing in the doorway in a plain black business suit, a matching hat, and a red tie, a picture of authority even without his robe. I was astounded to see him there.

"So who're you?"

"I'm with Mr. McNamara, Judge."

"Let me guess. You would be Janeway, the one that started all this goddamn trouble."

"That could be one way of looking at it. I'll be glad to apologize if that makes any difference."

"Don't get smart with me, son. Where'd you get to know so much?"

"I'm a book dealer."

"And I'm Whistler's great-grandfather. Where've you been all day?"

"I had to go down to Alamosa."

"What for?"

"Personal business."

"What personal business would you have in Alamosa?"

"Well, Judge, I can't exactly talk about it. That's what makes it personal."

He bristled. "If it had anything to do with this case, I've got news for you, it ain't personal. Are you a lawyer?"

"No, sir, I'm not."

"Then how about getting the hell out of here? We've been doing just fine without you, and you can see McNamara later on in town."

"I'd rather stay, if it's all the same to you."

"If it was all the same to me, I wouldn't have said get lost just now, would I?"

I put on my appeaser's face. "Judge, may I please make a point?"

"Let me make one first. How'd you like to spend the night in jail?"

Suddenly Lennie appeared in the doorway, his timing too perfect for coincidence. He stood smiling malignantly behind the judge, just out of the old man's sight.

"I came up to assist Mr. McNamara," I said. "That's really all I'm doing."

"What makes you think Mr. McNamara needs your help?"

"Because I know books. And he doesn't."

"This boy thinks a lot of himself, Judge," Lennie said. "He's a real piss-ripper."

"Where the hell did you come from, Deputy? Don't you know better than to walk up behind me like that?"

"Heard your voices. Sounded like you might need me for one thing or another."

"I need you for anything, I'll call you. Goddammit, make yourself useful. Go tell Miss Bailey this Janeway fellow's finally out here."

"Yessir."

A moment later the young prosecutor came out. She was sharp-looking in her own dark suit with amusement showing around the corners of her mouth. "Well, if it isn't the elusive Mr. Janeway," she said. "Ann Bailey."

We shook hands. "Okay if I take him in, Your Honor?"

Inside, I spoke to her in a whisper. "What the hell's the judge doing up here?"

She took a moment to answer. "Maybe he's just unorthodox."

"How does he think he can preside over a case if he gets involved in it?"

"That would be his problem. And maybe yours."

"Maybe yours in the long run."

"We'll see. I guess His Honor felt an irresistible impulse." She took a deep breath. "This is a very big deal you dumped on us, Mr. Janeway."

"Makes you want to rush right back to town and dismiss the charges, doesn't it?"

"Yeah, right. I was thinking more along the lines of, it gives her a great motive we didn't even know about."

"I see. She killed him for his books, is that what we're thinking now?"

"People have been killed for less than that. How solid are your notions of the values of these things?"

"I didn't know I had given out any solid values."

"They might be quite valuable: Wasn't that how McNamara put it?"

"I don't know, I wasn't there when he said it. Anything could be quite valuable."

"You're cute, aren't you? Nimble too. Have you ever done any fencing?"

"You mean for real?"

"Sure, for real. It's a great sport."

"I'll take your word for that. I usually confine myself to verbal jousts."

"I was on a fencing team in college. We even got to the national finals. I bet I could stick you just full of holes."

We had reached the door to the book room. She stopped and turned: she must've been looking straight up at me but I couldn't see her face in the darkness. "I am told you were a Denver cop," she said.

"A long time ago, in a galaxy far, far away."

"You are much too modest, Mr. Janeway. You're not that old and it wasn't that long ago. You left some deep tracks when you stomped out of the department."

"Easy to find, if all you care about are the newspaper accounts."

"So shoot me at sunrise. I did have a colleague in Denver dig them out and fax them to me. But I always knew you'd have your own version of it, which I would be only too delighted to hear. I might even buy you a cup of coffee for the privilege."

"By the way," I said, rather obviously changing the subject, "what's the judge really doing up here?"

"Whatever I said, it would just be an opinion, and just between us girls."

"I'm all ears."

"He's bored, he's got a gap in his schedule, maybe he just finds the idea of all these valuable books in a house on a remote mountaintop fascinating. As we all do, Janeway, as we all do.

But, hey, I agree with you. You could move to have him recuse himself from the case, you'd certainly have grounds. If you wanted to go that route."

"I don't make those decisions."

"Whatever you do, please remember: nothing I've said here is to be repeated."

I heard Parley's voice from the other room. Miss Bailey said, "Don't do anything without telling us first. Don't pick up anything, don't move stuff around—you know the routine. I know you were in here the other day, but it's different now. We're treating this room like a whole fresh crime scene. Got it?"

"Yes, ma'am."

"Then let's go in."

The room indeed looked different today. They had set strobe lights along the perimeter and the scene was harsh-looking, the ceiling garishly white. The bookshelves still looked full of books: on second look I could see that the top shelf had partially been cleared, but at that rate we'd all be here till next Easter.

Parley came over and said, "Am I glad to see you. We're gettin' nowhere fast." Another man was kneeling near the fireplace, looking at something. "Leonard Gill, the DA," Parley said in a whisper. "He's going over everything with a fine-tooth comb. He's trying to establish some kind of rough value for these things, and none of us has a clue. So far he's only allowed two boxes of books to be loaded in the truck. Maybe you can speed things up."

"I don't think so. Let 'em get their own expert, if that's how the wind's going to blow. I didn't come up here to make their case for them."

"God, we'll be here all week."

"He'll get tired after a while."

"You don't know this boy. Come on, I'll introduce you."

We approached the fireplace. The DA was looking at a book. I craned my neck and saw the distinct handwriting on the title page: *Martin Luther King*.

"Hey, Leonard," Parley said. "This is Cliff Janeway."

His handshake was abrupt, like everything else about him. On balance, I knew I was going to like dealing with Miss Bailey a lot better.

"This book worth any money?" he said as if the world owed him a living.

"Maybe."

"What does that mean?"

"It means maybe it is, maybe it isn't. This is some circus you've got going here."

"I thought you were supposed to help us move things along."

"What do you want from me, a signed affidavit? This isn't an exact science; you don't just prop up a signature and put an ironclad price on it. That's not how it works."

"Then how does it work?"

"It takes research. It takes time. You can't do it here."

"Then where can you do it?"

"If I were doing it, I'd have to bring a ton of reference books out from Denver."

"Then let's get 'em out here."

I laughed; couldn't help myself. "Mr. Gill, I don't work for you. Whatever values I might eventually put on these books is between me, Mr. McNamara, Ms. D'Angelo, and our client."

This snapped him back to reality. "I'm going to have to hire somebody, is that what you're saying?"

"I would think so, yes."

"Under the circumstances, then, maybe you should leave. You're doing nothing but cluttering up the process."

"And what'll you do after I'm gone? Assign some whimsical values based on your own vast knowledge?"

"What exactly are you saying?"

"It's you who's wasting the time. You can be up here for a month of Sundays and you won't have any better idea than you've got right now. Our idea was simply to get the books secured. Get 'em inventoried, get 'em down to the evidence locker, and get a lock on that door. Worry later about what you've got. And by the way, you shouldn't stack books in the box edges-up like that, they'll get cocked."

"Which means what?"

"The spines will get bent out of shape. To put it in basic terms, you're damaging the hell out of Mrs. Marshall's books. I'd advise you to lay 'em flat instead."

He motioned to Miss Bailey and they moved away for a confab. Parley and I walked discreetly out into the hall and talked in low voices.

"Has everything you've seen been signed?"

"So far."

"Jesus Christ," I said. "Martin Luther King."

"Is that worth some money?"

"Hell, *yes*." I laughed. "Try fifteen hundred and you won't be too far off on the high end. But it's a tricky signature. King is like Kennedy, other people signed for him and left no way for an untrained eye to tell the difference. Secretaries got very good at signing his name."

"Why would he let 'em do that?"

"Because people like King were pestered to death by autograph hounds and book collectors. They allowed their secretaries to sign without worrying about the havoc they might be causing. Evelyn Lincoln signed for Kennedy all the time. Somebody from the campaign brings in a book, it disappears into a back room and comes out signed. Compare it to a facsimile and most times it takes an expert to know the difference."

"Man, that doesn't seem right somehow."

"It isn't right, but it happened anyway. Depended on the nature of the guy in office. Lyndon Johnson signed almost nothing himself; unless it was shoved right under his face, it's all secretarial and autopen stuff. But anything with Harry Truman's name on it is probably real."

I told him about the burning of Jerry's clothes in the back-room grate. "Erin wants to keep that quiet for now." He nodded and we waited some more. In a while Miss Bailey came out and said, "Look, we're willing to cooperate if you will. Let's get the books out of here. Make a list and if you're willing to give us a copy, maybe we can do this reasonably quickly."

Parley looked at me.

"Sure, we'll share the list," I said.

Ten minutes later we were moving books off the shelves as fast as I could check them off against what I had written in my notebook. The money began adding up in my head, a ballpark figure, to be sure. There'd be some surprises, there always are. But at least now the books were safe. At least now I'd have a starting point.

18

I got my first disturbing look at Jerry late that afternoon. The victim's parents had rented a house near the edge of town, not far from where Parley lived. They had taken what they could get on short notice, and the house had no telephone as yet, so Parley said it would be a drop-in-and-take-your-chances affair. I walked over: two blocks up the main road from Parley's place, then right on a dirt road for another half mile. Parley had given me a verbal road map and I knew the house when I came to it. It was well back from the road at the bottom of a hill near the creek, barely visible through the woods.

Jerry was sitting alone in the front yard, watching keenly from a swing as I stopped on the road: a typical kid with a mop of dark hair, wearing corduroy pants and a sweater. Even from that distance I could see awareness in his face, as if somehow he sensed who I was and why I was there. I knew this was impossible but the feeling wouldn't shake. I came into the yard and said, "Hi, Jerry," but I knew better than to approach him before going to the house and announcing my presence. I said, "Is your grandma home?" but if he comprehended, he gave no sign of it. I came up through the trees and moved past him, up the path to the front door.

A woman in her sixties came out as I knocked. "I hope you're not selling anything."

"Erin sent me. My name's Cliff Janeway and I'd like to talk to your grandson for a few minutes."

"What for? He can't talk."

"Yes, ma'am, I'm aware of that. But we thought it might be helpful . . ."

"Helpful to who? She killed my son. Why should we help her?"

"It's not a question of why, Mrs. Marshall. We just want to know what really happened."

"Isn't that fairly obvious?"

"What's obvious isn't always what's true. That's why we have courts, to sift what people think happened from what really did happen."

This could go either way, I thought. I watched her agonize over it for half a minute. "We don't think she did it," I said at last.

"Lawyers always say that. I heard this was cut-and-dried."

"Prosecutors like to say that. And newspapers always make it seem that way."

"Well," she said as if momentarily confused, "if she didn't do it . . ."

Her eyes wandered out to the yard, where Jerry hadn't moved, and I saw a slow-creeping awareness come over her.

"My God, are you suggesting—"

"No," I said quickly. "That's not even a hint of what I'm saying."

"Well, if it wasn't her, who else could it be?"

"That's what I'm trying to find out."

She shook her head. I had an urge to tell her that there had been time for a third party to be in that room and her son may have known some shady characters. But I couldn't say that at this point.

"Look, Mrs. Marshall, I know this is difficult. I don't want to make it harder than it already is. I'm hoping you'll understand the difficulty on our side. We just want to find out what happened."

Her eyes narrowed. "You're going to make out like the boy did it."

"Don't do that, Mrs. Marshall. That's not fair to anybody at this point."

"Then what am I supposed to think?"

"Nothing, yet. Just let the facts come out."

"I understood she was going to plead guilty . . ."

"I don't know who could've told you that, but it's just not true."

"She was going to plead guilty. Then you lawyers came, and—"

I felt the interview getting away from me, spinning out of control before it got started. "None of that is true," I said in a slightly pleading voice. "Look, I know you wouldn't want to send her to prison if she's innocent. Even if there are hard feelings, nobody would do that."

I let that settle on her for a minute. Then she said, "What do you think this child can tell you? . . . This little boy who can't even speak his mother's name?"

"I don't know."

She thought about it. "Am I required to allow this?"

"Not at this moment."

"What happens if I say no?"

"I could ask for a court order. They'd probably want to videotape it and do it in the courthouse. They might have some psychologist brought in from Denver to ask the questions. I'd rather not do that now, unless it's necessary."

She thought about that and took her time.

"If I did let you talk to him, I'd have to be there."

"Absolutely."

"I'd want to know what questions you're going to ask him."

"That depends on him, I don't have anything written out. Maybe I'd just want to say hello for now."

"I don't know what good you think that'll do."

"I don't know either. Maybe none."

"If you upset him, if you start asking questions I don't like—"

"I'll leave. I promise."

Again she wavered. She was curious now but suddenly a little afraid as well. I could see the fear in her eyes as she stared out at Jerry on the swing. She turned and looked up at me and I could almost read the fear in her face—*What if he's right? What if that kid murdered Bobby, and if he did do that, what's to stop him from killing us all in our sleep?* I wished I could reverse the clock and take back everything that might have put that idea in her head. I wanted to go back a few hours and rethink the wisdom of coming out here in the first place, but there was no going back: there never is.

"Come on," she said abruptly, and I followed her out into the yard. Jerry sat up straighter at our approach, like a bird watching an animal it has never seen before. His eyes never left my face: he seemed wary, not afraid, and as we came closer, I noticed a splash of freckles across both cheeks and his nose. He looked like a kid I might have known in my own childhood.

"Jerry," Mrs. Marshall said. "This is Mr. Janeway. He just wants to say hello."

I sat on the ground across from him and looked into his blue eyes. "Hi, Jerry," I said. He looked so familiar to me: it was almost spooky, till suddenly I realized that his face was the spitting image of Alfalfa from the old *Our Gang* comedy shorts.

"You look like one of the Little Rascals," I said. "Anybody ever tell you that?"

I asked if he had ever seen those comedies on TV.

"They don't have TV here," Mrs. Marshall said. "Just as well, judging from what's on it."

"It doesn't matter," I said. "For what it's worth, you look like Alfalfa. He was a great movie star, long before I was born."

I said, "He's the one I always liked as a kid."

I reached out my hand. "It's good to know you."

"Shake the gentleman's hand, Jerry," Mrs. Marshall said.

Reluctantly Jerry put his hand in mine and I squeezed it and held it for a moment. There was something about this kid: even if he couldn't show his feelings, I could almost sense the hurt in him. I felt him tremble and I thought, *Oh, kid, if there's any way I can take some of that pain on my shoulders, let me have it, I'll take it all if you'll just give it to me.* "Don't be afraid," I said. "I'd like to be your friend."

I reached out to touch his shoulder but he drew back sharply. "It's okay," I said.

I was about to say I was a friend of his mother's when Mrs. Marshall said, "I told you. Didn't I tell you you couldn't talk to him?"

"His arm seems to be hurt," I said.

"It's fine."

But I had a hunch, as strong as any I could remember. Before she could object, I had touched his shoulder and peeled down the sweater, revealing an ugly bruise.

"How'd he get that?"

"He fell off the swing. It's fine, it's nothing to worry about, leave him alone. You had no right to touch him."

I backed quickly away. "Can I ask him about what happened that day?"

"I don't think that's wise."

"Only if he saw it. If that bothers him, I'll leave."

"It makes no sense. Why ask the question when you know he can't answer you?"

"If I just asked him . . . what happened to his dad."

"You're going to upset him."

"Jerry," I said.

"I think you should leave now," Mrs. Marshall said.

"Okay." I was good and goddamned frustrated, but a deal is a deal.

"It's been good meeting you, Jerry."

Suddenly he grabbed my hand and held me tight. Mrs. Marshall said, "Jerry, you stop that," but I looked back at her and told her it was okay. "It is *not* okay," she said. "How do you expect us to teach him any manners if you come behind me and say that's okay?" I offered a sad little apology but I was looking at Jerry when I said it. His mouth opened and I had the crazy thought that he was about to speak, and that once he did, all the mysteries of his universe would roll out in a deep, bassy voice. But Mrs. Marshall said, "I think that's enough," and I got up slowly and followed her back to the house, giving Jerry a wink over my shoulder. At the door I turned and waved to him.

Inside, Mrs. Marshall fidgeted nervously. "What did that prove?"

I just looked at her, which made her more fidgety.

"You had no right to touch him. You shouldn't have done that."

"I'm sorry it upset you," I said. But I didn't apologize for touching him.

"What'll happen now?" she said.

"That'll be up to Erin. I'm sure she'd like to keep him out of it but I don't know if that'll be possible."

"Did he really see what happened?"

"He might have."

"Oh, God. God, what a thing," she said, and her voice was thick. "Do you actually think he could've done this himself?"

"No," I said, as earnestly as I could. "Nobody thinks that, Mrs. Marshall, I promise you."

In fact, I didn't know what to think. All I could go by was my gut.

I looked around at the sparse furnishings. She said, "We had to move in here on a moment's notice. Good thing we're retired."

"What about the other two kids?"

"My husband has them. They went downtown for some ice cream." She looked at the clock. "They'll be back any minute."

She sensed an unasked question and said, "Jerry certainly would've been welcome to go with them, if that's what you're thinking, but he didn't seem to care. I'm sure they'll bring him back some."

I nodded a *That's good* motion and again she looked around uneasily.

"Mrs. Marshall, may I ask you a few more questions?"

She looked wary but she didn't say no so I pushed ahead.

"Has Jerry shown any unusual behavior since he's been with you?"

"What do you mean? I haven't been around him long enough to know what's usual. All his behavior is unusual, wouldn't you say?"

"Nightmares. Does he ever scream in the night?"

"If that child has ever uttered a sound, nobody I know has heard it."

"What about nightmares? You can have those even if you don't scream."

She didn't answer for a minute, long enough to be an answer in itself. "Sure, he's been troubled," she finally said. "God help him, who wouldn't be?"

"How can you tell?"

"I'll wake up and find him standing beside my bed. Just standing there trembling." She looked worried, as if suddenly the thought frightened her.

"Does he do this every night?"

"I've only had him for two weeks. But, yes, so far he's not had a night when he's slept all the way through."

"What do you do when you find him like that?"

"Put him back to bed. What else is there?"

"Does he ever resist that?"

"Just that first night."

"What did he do then?"

"Struggled a little. Got away from me and ran outside."

"Where outside?"

"Back to the shed, that ramshackle old thing behind the house."

"Was he trying to hide?"

"Who knows what's in that child's head? Whatever's troubling him, I couldn't leave him there in the middle of the night."

We looked at each other.

"Well, could I?"

"No," I said. "Of course you couldn't."

"Don't be judgmental, please don't do that.

We're really doing the best we can here. We're trying to help, but this isn't the greatest situation in the world, either."

I wasn't aware I had looked judgmental and said so. "I'm sure it isn't easy for you, Mrs. Marshall."

I thought hard about my next question before I asked it: I didn't want to scare her more than I already had, but it had to be asked.

"Have there been any signs of anybody around the house?"

"What signs? You mean like a prowler?"

"No, I didn't mean that. Never mind, it's a silly thought."

But it wasn't a silly thought and, yes, it had frightened her. Something had certainly scared Jerry. Maybe it was just a nightmare after all: God knew the kid was entitled to a bad dream if he had seen something.

"What is it you're trying to find out? What do you want from us?"

Perhaps I hadn't known until that moment, but hearing the question hurled at me in that tense voice, suddenly I did know. *I want to know he's safe,* I thought, but could not quite bring myself to say. I didn't like that bruise on his shoulder and I didn't like the old woman's evasive eyes. To call his safety into question would disrupt them all, maybe for no good reason. But the fact remained: if Jerry hadn't killed Marshall, somebody else had. I looked across the road at the gathering dusk, at the trees now deep in gloom. Somebody, I thought: maybe someone he saw, maybe someone who saw him.

19

I walked back to town and ate in the Main Street café. I didn't want to go back to Parley's; didn't want to talk to anybody about what I had seen or what its significance might be; most of all I didn't want to be talked out of what I knew I was about to do. After a mediocre meal I walked out to the edge of town where I had seen a bar called the Red Horse Tavern. I went in, blended with the dark, and sat in a corner nursing a beer.

Two hours later there I was again, hiking back on the road to the grandparents' house. My feet made soft crunching noises in the frozen snow and I felt the stinging air around my eyes and nose. I had just a trace of a low moon lighting my way around a thin, circular cloud that hung in my face like a halo. This wasn't much help: the tall hills on both sides blotted out most

of the deeper countryside and I could only see
the road, and nothing past the ditch, for thirty
yards ahead. Beyond that it was all hope-and-
grope, a shadow world broken by the dim and
very occasional light of a cabin off in the trees.
In the woods away from the road the night was
as black as I had ever seen it, murk that couldn't
be penetrated without a light.

I had bought a penlight at the five-and-dime
and this I clutched in my fist as I walked, keeping my hands in my pockets and letting the
moon show me the way for as long as it would.
I could think of a thousand places I'd rather be
than out here tonight, but I had a hunch and I
couldn't shake it. I psyched myself up for another long watch.

I trudged over a rise, vaguely remembering the
terrain from my trek up here a few hours before.
The night was bleak and a wind whistled down
through the pines, chilling even through my heavy
coat. I started down the long incline to the arroyo
at the bottom where the creek ran through. The
air wasn't yet cold enough to freeze the creek over,
and I could hear the trickle about sixty yards
away, so much louder here in the pitch-dark night
than it had been in the daytime. I remembered a
small bridge where the creek curled around from
the foot of the mountain and darted across the

road. Beyond that, far back in the trees, was the house. I still couldn't see the place: it was fairly early yet, nine o'clock would be a good guess, but there were no lights anywhere.

I crossed the bridge and a few minutes later reached the driveway, a long, looping dirt road where I could finally see a faint light from the front room. It flickered through the trees. No *Tonight Show* back there. No TV to lull them into some nightly catatonic state of mind. I had a feeling that the old Marshalls would be going stir-crazy after less than two weeks of it. I stood on the road, lost in the shadows of the trees around me, and I stared at the light from the cabin and wondered what to do next.

I did nothing for a while. At some point I stepped into the drive and groped my way along it. The sound of the creek got louder as the house emerged in a tiny ring of light. I could see a partial outline of the porch, only from the front door to the living room window, but it was hard to get better bearings in the deep mountain night. How close did I dare go, what would I say if someone popped up and demanded answers, what was I looking for anyway?—these were questions that defied easy answers. I stood there for at least another ten minutes and nothing got any clearer.

The answer I wanted was inside the house, not out here.

I didn't trust the Marshalls with that kid's welfare.

There it was: I didn't trust them. I had only that bruise to hang this on, a strange place, I thought, for a bruise to be, from a fall off the swing.

As if anything is ever that plain and that simple in this life. I hadn't yet met the old man but there was something about the old woman, some kind of fear of her own. For the moment that was plain and simple enough, and that's why I was out here tonight.

Oh, God, Erin: Am I about to screw your case beyond redemption? I hoped not, but I remembered Jerry's Alfalfa face and I couldn't just walk away from him.

I was now no more than twenty yards from the front porch. The house was deadly quiet. Nothing moved except that rushing stream somewhere beyond the shed in the backyard. I felt desolate. It boggled my mind that anyone would consign three children to this after what had just happened to their father. Those kids needed music and light and whatever good cheer there might be in the world. But this was what they got from a system that never had enough time, never enough people.

I stood just outside the tiny circle of light cast by the living room lamp. I stood there for another twenty minutes. Didn't move at all until I saw a shadow pass across the front room window.

It was the grandfather. He had turned and was now standing with a drink in his hand staring out at the yard. I dropped back a step and saw him look over his shoulder and say something. He took a deep hit from his drink, emptying the glass, then he poured another. I could see the Seagram's label clearly in the lamplight, and he was taking it straight-up from a tall highball glass, enough to put him on the short list for a liver transplant if he wasn't there already.

I stood in the dark and watched him drink.

I stood in the dark.

After a while he moved across the room. There was a narrow side window and I eased over that way, one step at a time. The light was dimmer there, probably all of it coming from the one lamp near the front of the room. Here we go, I thought.

Here we go.

I walked boldly across the lighted space and slipped around the edge. Flattened myself against the dark wall, as I'd done at the Preacher's place, and felt my way along until I could take a quick look inside.

The two of them sat facing each other. He was slumped on the sofa, a big man with slate gray hair and mean eyes. Okay, now I had seen him. Now I could be fair about it and say I had seen the bastard and I didn't like him. Good objective judgment. I didn't like his ass. I had the uneasy feeling that either of them would gladly sell Laura Marshall down the river, guilty or not.

She was in a chair staring beyond him at the wall: a picture of two people going mad, just as I had imagined it. She said something but I couldn't make out what. He took another swig of whiskey and that was his response. She said something else or perhaps again and his head snapped up. He yelled, "Shut up, goddammit, shut up!" His booming voice carried easily through the wall. The kids would sleep well through that, I thought. He leaned forward with his elbows on his knees, his head down and the drink in his hands, and what he said then was inaudible, but when he looked up, I could fry an egg in the hate on his face.

There's trouble in Paradise, I thought. These were not happy campers.

Not happy with the kids. Not happy with each other or themselves.

Then why are they here?

Why face three months in hell if it wasn't for the love of the children?

I backtracked into the woods, away from the light, and stood watching. I stood there thinking. Brooding.

I circled the house, carefully getting the lay of the land. A back porch opened from the kitchen, and I could see through the screen, on through the room into a short hallway. I saw the light from the front reflecting off a stove and a refrigerator, and on either side were the two bedrooms. One for the old folks, one for all three kids. I moved away from the porch and looked into a window, pale with the distant light. Again the door was open and there was enough light from the front to make out a few objects. I saw what was probably a dresser with a mirror and a small table and a double bed, empty. This was where the old people slept. I didn't dare look in the other window: I had a vision of Jerry lying in that room, staring at the glass, ready to be scared out of his wits if a face suddenly popped up.

At least I knew where things were. I circled the house and stood in the dark.

Time passed and the light from the window was hypnotic.

Eventually it went out and I stood trapped by

the night, sealed in a drippy world of uncertain blindness.

This was infinitely more depressing than the stakeout on the ridge. Then I knew that dawn could not be far off: now I had no faith that the sun would ever come up again. Now I couldn't see the house, I couldn't use my light. I couldn't see the trees or even a hint of anything out there in the black. I knew from my police days how these stakeouts could weigh down the spirit. Too many nights just sitting and watching got to everybody eventually. Even in the old days, with a partner to talk to, with food and light and the steady chatter of the police radio, the negative effects tended to accumulate. Too much of it made reality slip away. But I stood leaning against a tree, hanging in there, struggling to count to ten but seldom making it past four.

I don't know when the shock came—it was well after midnight, maybe much later. Suddenly a light went on in the kids' room. I must have been asleep on my feet. I felt it first—sight came later, like an exploding galaxy—and I jerked back, lost my balance, and fell facedown on the rocky earth. I rolled over and the vision of that yellow-white window hit me again. My heart leaped into fast-forward and I felt my hands, slick with blood. I felt a stinging pain where I had tried to break my fall and had hit the rocks. I rolled over and got to my feet, pressed my hands against my pants, and held them there just as Jerry appeared in the window. With a jerky, frantic look he pushed up the sash and stuck his hand through the crack, flailing at the cold air. I heard a child's voice from inside the house: "Gramma, Jerry's being bad again!" Jerry leaped back from the window. Almost immediately the door flew open and he came running out wearing only his pajamas. He rushed across the yard and into the trees toward the road.

A minute later the woman appeared on the porch, dressed in a nightie with a coat thrown over her shoulders. In another minute the man loomed up beside her. "I am getting *god*damn tired of this shit!" he bellowed at the darkness.

He screamed at the night: "*Jerry!* Goddammit, you get back in here!"

"Ralph," the old woman said.

"Don't Ralph me." He came to the edge of the porch. "Boy, you better knock this off! If I've gotta come find you again, it'll be too damn bad!" He waited a moment, then yelled, "*Jerry!* I'm not kiddin', you get your ass back in here, *right now!*"

Nothing happened: no sounds above the constant noise of the creek, no movement in the woods where Jerry had disappeared.

"That goddamn little fucker!" the old man said. "I oughta leave him out there."

"You can't do that," the woman said. "Jesus, Ralph, he'll freeze to death."

"Let him freeze, the little bastard. I didn't sign on here to put up with this."

"Ralph, stop this and go find that boy before something awful happens to him."

"I'll find him, all right."

"Don't you hit him again."

"Don't you hit him again," he mimicked.

Ralph disappeared into the house and a minute later he came out fully dressed. He charged off the wrong way into the woods, yelling and kicking at the undergrowth.

Gradually his voice began to fade as he went back toward the creek.

I headed down the other way, toward the road. A path cut through the trees and at the end of it I found the kid shivering and huddled in the ditch. I reached out my hand to him and he cringed.

"Hey, Jerry. You don't want to stay down there, kid." I opened my coat and held out my hand to him. "Come on up here. Come get warm."

I shined the little light in my own face. "I met you this afternoon, remember? Come here, I won't hurt you."

I got down on my knees and handed him the light.

"You musta been having a bad dream, son."

Yeah, a dream called life.

I knew he was cold, I could hear his teeth chattering, but I didn't try to rush him. I sat on the ground and let him touch my hand, and after a while he did crawl into my lap and I pulled the coat tight and held him against me till he stopped shivering. I could feel his heartbeat, his breath against my neck, both hands clutching my shirt.

"It's okay, kid." I touched his head. "It's okay now."

This was something to say and it filled the moment. But in real life I had no idea what was okay, and in that moment I couldn't imagine what to do next.

Follow your heart, Janeway. That's what got you here.

My heart was full of anger.

I didn't know what Ralph's problem was and didn't care. Right now, at this moment, I only wanted to kick him a new asshole.

Do that and explain it to the judge.

Ralph had custody and I had only a bad attitude, which grew worse every minute.

But in the heat of that moment I didn't care about the judge or the old man's custody. I sat on the edge of the ditch and Ralph's voice got louder as his search widened. In the same time my own choices winnowed downward from almost nothing.

I could take the kid home with me, the riskiest and craziest thing to do.

I could give him up, which I hated.

I could confront the old man here in the dark woods.

Intimidate the bastard. I was good at that, I knew how it was done. It had failed to work once, with a brutal thug who finally had to be convinced the hard way.

I heard footsteps. He was coming now, tearing through the underbrush. "Jerry," I said into my coat. "You've got to go back."

His fists tightened on my shirt and his head burrowed under my chin. Something about this kid, something other than the obvious, touched me deep, but here and now I couldn't find a handle for it.

"I'm sorry, kid."

I couldn't elaborate: I was out of time. The old man loomed up not twenty yards away, a shadow talking furiously to himself. "I'll kill that little bastard," he said.

I felt my own fury rise up to meet him.

"I'll kill him," he said, and in the same heart-beat I got up close, right in his face. "How'd you like to try that with somebody your own size?"

He cried out, spun away, dropped his light.

I kicked it out of his reach and he fell trying to get it.

For God's sake don't touch him, I thought.

I didn't need to, he scared easy enough. I could taste this old man's fear and I liked the taste of it. Killer-soft, with snakelike malice, I said, "How'd you like to try that with me, Ralph?"

I had truly scared the hell out of him. He wheezed, hyperventilating, and finally managed to croak, "Who the f-f . . ."

I covered Jerry's ears and said, "I am your worst fuckin' nightmare, old man."

I heard him struggling to his feet.

"Who're . . . y-y . . . who'r . . ."

"You touch this kid again and you'll find out who I am."

"How'd . . . d'you know . . . m-m-n . . . ame?"

"I know everything about you, Ralph. I know how you like to beat up little kids."

"That's a-g-g-od-amn-l . . . lie."

I let the moment pass in ominous silence.

"I didn-n't mean that. Some-omebody's t-t-ellin' you lies, tha's all . . . I . . . meant."

"You must think I'm playing around with you, grandpa. Is that what you think?"

"No . . . G-g-od, n-o . . ."

"Because if it is, you are making a monster mistake."

He tried to speak but his voice quaked and he couldn't get it out.

"Have you been listening to me at all, old man?"

He tried a single watery word but sucked air in through his nose and lost it.

"Was that a yes, Ralph?"

"Y . . . y . . ."

"That's good. Maybe you just don't realize how soft the human body is. Maybe that's your problem. You don't know how easy a body can be broken or torn up. How easy an arm can be pulled out of its socket, or a skull fractured . . ."

"Oh Christ . . . oh Christ . . . please J-es-s . . . on't do that . . ."

"I'm not talking about me, Ralph, I'm talking about you. You push a kid around, you can mess him up bad."

"I nev . . . n-n-n, uh, n-never hurt him . . . he just gets wild . . . n . . . eeds d-d-dis-pline."

"Maybe you're the one who needs the discipline."

I felt him cringe back into the dark, a typical coward. "Please . . . don't do that . . . p-p-lease don't . . ."

A moment passed. In the distance I could hear the old woman calling Ralph's name. Ralph tried to say *please* again but couldn't quite get it out.

"That's much better. *Please* is a good, kind word. You should use it more often."

I picked up his light and tried to give it to him, but it fell short and I left it there. I wanted to brush off his coat for effect but didn't.

Don't touch the old fucker, I thought. *Not even a finger. Don't touch him at all.*

"Your grandson is cold, Ralph. Take him inside and warm him up. Give him some hot chocolate. And do yourself a helluva big favor. Remember what I said."

The night has a thousand eyes and I told him that.

"You so much as touch him again and I'll know."

I uncovered Jerry's ears and let the quiet night surround us all.

"I'll know, Ralph," I said.

I am in deep shit, I thought. But if anything had felt right in a long time, that had.

I turned away and left Jerry in the woods with his so-called grandfather.

20

A judge is the ruler of his kingdom. He sits on his throne and makes decisions that affect people profoundly and change their lives. If he's a good judge, his decisions are not only good law, they are made with conscience and rooted in humility. If he's not a good judge, he comes to his throne steeped in arrogance and concerned mainly with his own ego. If he's a bad judge, he combines the arrogance and the ego with bellicose intolerance, and, in the worst cases, ignorance.

Sometimes he may go too far and get overturned. Occasionally he is reprimanded or removed from the bench, but all too often he's left alone and his bad decisions stand for years, maybe decades, till the principals die or just don't care anymore. The law has many soft spots where there is no black-and-white and the judge's discretion is broad. A capital offense in one kingdom has far fewer dire consequences a few miles away, in the land across the river where laws are different. This is not a job for ego, yet the job nurtures and in fact demands it. The job cries out for wisdom and compassion and anger, and half a dozen other qualities that are incompatible or almost impossible to find beating in a single heart. In the country of the law the one-eyed judge is king. Contempt of court is a potent weapon and it too is a sword with a wide blade. The judge can be lenient, understanding, or an absolute tyrant. Mess with the judge and you can go to jail.

I had met all kinds of judges in my police career: I remembered bleeding-heart liberals who wore their politics into the courtroom and mean-spirited old bastards who suffered no slight, real or imagined, to their dignity. I had known a judge who had ruthlessly punished defendants because of a dislike for their attorneys, and another who was a notorious woman-hater, finding any flimsy excuse to let vicious rapists back on the street. A lot of judges hold a cop's balls to the fire: such are the times we live in. One judge I knew had the memory of an elephant, had been quick to form a bias and quicker yet to take offense. He had wielded his power heavily and had been known to remind attorneys years later of small incidents he had found offensive. Most judges I had met were at least okay; a few had been superb, and one on the lowest end of the spectrum was a moron who had barely eked out a passing grade on his fourth try at the bar exam. Amazingly, he survived on his suburban-Denver-county court bench for almost twenty years and finally died there.

The Honorable Harold Adamson seemed to possess at least some of the bad traits. I knew he was eccentric: I couldn't think of any other judge in all my days on the fringes of Denver law who'd have gone up to the scene of a case he'd be hearing. The judge wouldn't want to get that close; judges just didn't do that. Still, Parley considered his knowledge of law sound, his understanding of due process at least okay. It was his ego that got in the way, overruling knowledge and dismissing due process when it suited him. Since his appointment to the bench a year ago, he had become like a new cock in a barnyard, and that night I had a hunch I was about to fall directly into his crosshairs.

In the best of all worlds old Marshall would have accepted the heartfelt advice I had left with him and would suddenly have become endowed

with infinite kindness and the spirit of grand-
fatherly love. He had seemed thoroughly frightened, but I knew that, like the judge, I had
stepped over a line and my own comeuppance
was a phone call away. I opened my eyes in the
morning as a car door slammed, and when I
went to the window, Lennie was standing in the
front yard smoking. He finished his weed, tossed
the butt in the snow, and headed up the walk to
the front door. I met him there.

"Mr. Janeway?" His official voice: the ticket-
writer, as if we had never met.

I stared at him and he said, "Wonder if I
might have a word with you."

I stared some more. This wasn't my house, it
wasn't my place to invite him in.

"We had a complaint last night from a Mr.
Ralph Marshall. Are you familiar with that gentleman?"

"I know who he is."

"I thought maybe you would. Apparently
some skulker came out to his house in the middle of the night, threatened and terrorized himself, his wife, and the children who have been
put under his care. You wouldn't know anything
about that, would you, sir?"

"Did he say I did?"

"What Mr. Marshall said or did not say is

between himself and our office. Right now, would it be too much trouble for you to answer my question? *Now*, sir. It's really a simple question. Did you threaten Mr. Marshall last night?"

"Mr. Marshall wrenched his grandson's arm damn near out of its socket. I told him not to do that anymore."

"You didn't knock him to the ground?"

"I never touched him."

"That's not what he says. And he's got scrapes and bruises all over his face. Any idea how those would've gotten there?"

"Mr. Marshall was drunk. He fell in the dark woods."

"So you say. Doesn't sound like you're denying it was you out in the woods."

Behind me I heard Parley come into the hall. "What's goin' on here?"

"It's nothing," I said. "The deputy wants to ask me a few questions."

"About what?"

Lennie handed me a piece of paper. I recognized the look of it.

"This is a summons ordering you to appear later this morning at a hearing in Judge Adamson's court."

"Hold on, what's this about?" Parley said. "We haven't had notice of any hearing."

"It's a summons to appear at a hearing on a temporary restraining order against your client."

Parley laughed. "You call this notice? What the hell's going on here?"

"Look, I came out here to serve him and now he's been served."

Lennie turned and walked away.

Parley stared at me. "Jesus H. Christ."

"All I did was talk to him, Parley."

"Well, goddammit, that's enough. Tell me exactly what happened."

We sat at the kitchen table and I told him.

"God almighty," he said. "Haven't you got any sense at all?"

"Apparently not. I didn't have a lot of time to think about it."

"Christ in a hot-air balloon."

"Look," I said, "I want you to stay away from this. For the sake of your client, consider me resigned from your case, as of six o'clock last night."

"So now what, you're gonna be your own lawyer? You really are losing your marbles, kid."

"Yeah, I know. What can I say, I screwed up. I want to stay away from your case as much as possible from here on out. Don't bail me out, don't put in any appearances. If you want to do something, call Social Services and get that kid out of there."

"You're outta your goddamn mind. Erin's gonna love this."

A few hours later I met the judge in his arena.

The courtroom was empty, except for the judge, the deputy, and a reporter. The hearing was announced and the judge peered down from on high.

"Well, you're just like Charlie Chaplin, aren't you? You seem to pop up when I least expect you, and when I do expect you, you're not there. Would you explain to me, please, what the hell you were doing out at the Marshalls' last night?"

"I went to see the kid. I had visited with him that afternoon and I was concerned for his safety."

"What about his safety?"

"He's being abused by his grandfather."

"What does that mean? You don't mean to insinuate he's . . ." He made an obscene gesture with his hands.

"Not that kind of abuse."

"What, then?"

"He beats the kid."

"Is that all? Listen, a little birching never hurt a kid yet, and from what I've heard, that one's a handful."

"He can't *speak*, Your Honor, and I'm not talking about a little birching. I'm talking about a *beating*, Judge, a beating bad enough to leave his whole shoulder black."

"In case you hadn't heard, Mr. Janeway, there's a system in this state. Social Services is in charge of the kids. There's a guardian ad litem who's been appointed—"

"I know all that, Your Honor . . ."

"Then why didn't you report all this to the guardian?"

"There wasn't time."

"So you thought you could ride in there and rescue this kid yourself. Is that about what happened?"

The hell with it: I launched into the tale. I told him about my interview with the grandmother and my growing sense that something was wrong. Call it an old cop's instinct: call it a feeling, a hunch. I told him about the bruise on Jerry's shoulder and how I had found it. I told him about the grandfather and how he had chased the kid through the woods, threatening him with more violence. "That's a toxic old man the kid's been put with, Judge; he's already been slapped around at least once and would have been again if I hadn't been there. The old man drinks like a fish and talks like a drunken sailor. Maybe he loves the hell out of his real, blood grandchildren and hates this one, I don't know. Last night Jerry ran away and hid freezing in a ditch, wearing nothing but a pair of pajamas, while the old man thrashed drunkenly through the bushes, cursing and threatening to kill him. I'm afraid for his safety, and if somebody doesn't take him out of there, whatever happens to him is on all your heads, all of you, I don't care who's got jurisdiction or who wants to pass the buck to some other department. I'm going to make it a personal cause to see that everybody in the state of Colorado knows about it."

Stunned silence. For long seconds the judge stared as if he couldn't believe what he'd just heard. Then he leaned over his bench and said, "You *dare* come in here and talk to me like that. My courtroom is not a soapbox. You must want to go to jail, fella."

"Lock me up, I don't give a damn, but somebody's got to do something for that boy. This is a kid who may have witnessed the bloody murder of the only father he knew, and now the *system*'s got him sentenced to a dark house that's no better than some prison camp, with an alcoholic who seems to resent the hell out of him, and I can't get you to care. If that kid doesn't get help soon, he may go off his rocker for good, so put me in jail if that's your only answer."

"Is this your doing, Mr. McNamara? Is this how you're going to try this case?"

I turned and saw Parley sitting behind me. "Well, Judge—"

"Don't blame McNamara for what I say. This has nothing to do with his case."

The judge rapped his gavel. "You're in contempt of court. Five-hundred-dollar fine."

"I won't pay it."

The judge laughed. "You are a piece of work, aren't you? You waltz in here and expect who?—me, I guess—to take those children away from their grandparents, who have relocated from Denver, gone to a helluva lot of trouble, and you expect me to do this on your say-so."

"In the first place, they are not the grandparents of the older boy. They came out here to take care of their dead son's blood children. There's no reason to assume that they care at all about—"

"You're wasting my time. What the hell is wrong with you?"

"I must be stupid, I guess. With all due respect, sir, one of us seems to be."

"Why, you arrogant young snot. How'd you like to double that fine?"

"Judge, at this point I don't care."

"Then go ahead, sit in jail and think about it. On Friday I'm leaving to hear a case next week in another county. If you haven't had a drastic change of attitude by then, you can sit there for three weeks till I get back again."

He shuffled through some notes on his bench. He looked up and said, "Jail this bastard."

"Yes, *sir.*" Lennie approached the bench and said, "Put out your hands, cowboy."

Behind me, Parley said, "Your *Honor,* I don't think the handcuffs are necessary."

"I don't tell the deputy how to handle his prisoners. You break the law, you might just get humiliated."

Out in the yard, Lennie gave me a shove. I crossed the lot in shackles and people watched from the sidewalk.

"Step lively, dickhead," Lennie said. "Your ass belongs to me now."

"You belong in a circus, Lennie," I said.

21

I was almost a model prisoner. The sheriff asked what had happened and the deputy told him he had brought me in for contempt, trespassing, menacing, and half a dozen other possible charges. The sheriff nodded and said, "Thank you, sir. It always helps to know why we have people in our hotel here. Did he give you any idea how long you're to be a guest of our county?" I told him it seemed to be open-ended, probably till I had a change of heart. The sheriff said, "Any idea when that might be?" and I said, "Sometime between tomorrow morning and whenever hell freezes over." The two of us laughed while Lennie stood apart and found it all unhappily unamusing. The sheriff said, "Goddammit, Lennie, get them handcuffs off this man," and I was taken, uncuffed, back to the cellblock, which consisted of half a dozen cells and one big barred room, the bull pen.

Three of the cells were occupied: two Indians and a mean-looking white guy, all of them, I later learned, being held for drunk-and-disorderly. I was put across from the bull pen, away from the others, where we could all look across and see each other. There's not much privacy in jail. The cell consisted of a four-by-eight barred room with a bed and a toilet. I figured the doors were opened during the middle of the day and the men were allowed to stretch themselves in the relative expanse of the bull pen. I sat on my cot and stared at the wall.

Parley came in within the hour. We met upstairs in the conference room.

"Janeway, did I have a mental lapse in there or did you really call the judge a moron?"

"I called him stupid. There's a difference. A moron can't help what he does. A stupid man can, but does it anyway. That's what makes him stupid."

"Look, I'm trying to get you out of here, but unless you crawl up there and kiss his ass in open court, it's gonna take some serious finagling. At least I think you got his attention about the kid."

"Then my living has not been in vain. What's happening?"

"We called the guardian ad litem, who's having the kids picked up today. He's going to talk to them away from the grandparents. Even if Jerry can't talk, the little ones might know what happened to him."

"That's a start. If that doesn't work, I may have another ace up my sleeve."

He closed his eyes. "Dare I ask?"

"There's a fellow I know at *The Denver Post*. I did him a few favors when I was a cop. He specializes in tearjerkers and knows how to write 'em. I think he'd love this story. Former Denver cop jailed by Podunk County judge, who won't give kids an even break. I think he'd walk all the way out here for that. I'd be disappointed if it didn't make page one, under the fold. Streamed across the top if I get lucky. Read by everybody in the state and rewritten for every local newscast."

"You really are crazy."

"Tell the judge you're trying to talk me out of going to my very good friends in the Denver press. Tell him I'm a wild hair, hard to control."

"I think he already knows that."

I looked at him across the table. "A tyrant can survive for years in his own dark world, Parley, but he can't live long in the sunshine. And I think this one knows that."

I pondered the mess I had created and it still felt right. "You need to call Erin."

"Already did. Caught her at home and gave her a full account."

"And what was the word from she-who-must-be-obeyed, the prisoner asked in fear and trembling."

"She sighed mightily. I think you actually might've done her proud, which only goes to show she's as crazy as you are. She did tell me to bail you out."

"No way, Parley. Not yet."

The morning dragged by. I sat in the cell and marked time, a room away from where Laura Marshall also sat marking time. I stared at the wall and counted to ten.

At noon, more or less, the sheriff came in and let the two Indians out. "You boys behave yourselves or next time you're goin' to court."

He stopped at my cell. "How you doin'?"

"Lovely."

"I gotta be gone till tomorrow. You and Lennie try to be good to each other."

"If he comes near me, I'll rip his heart out."

He leaned close, looking for some sign I was kidding.

"Sheriff, I think you're a decent man. But Lennie would rape his own mother and then tell her what a lousy lay she is. Tell him to stay away from me."

"Freeman's gone till Friday. Lennie'll have to bring you your food."

"If he brings me anything, he'll wear it out of here."

Lennie came in at three o'clock. I could see he had been told something because he did a cell check or a head count, proving he could count to two, without ever coming near my side of the jail. He opened the other prisoner's cell door and said, "Okay, Brady, get the hell out of here. Sheriff's orders. If it was up to me, you'd sit here for another week." I heard them shuffling down the hall together.

The jail was on the east side of the building, so darkness came fast and early. I sat and stewed, alone. By five the whole cellblock was in deep shadow. I assumed there was a light somewhere, which Lennie had apparently decided I could do without, and in fact I was just as happy without it. Now I could lie back on my cot and pass the hours in my vacuum, dreaming of happier times and better places. Occasionally thoughts darker and more worldly forced their way into my space, but I met them all knowing that, hell, tomorrow was another day.

I fell asleep. When I opened my eyes, the darkness was everywhere, the silence deafening, and I knew someone was standing out in the cellblock.

Guess who.

I couldn't hear him, couldn't see him, but I knew he was there.

"Hi, Lennie," I said. "You come in here to play mind games?"

Nothing moved.

"I like mind games," I said. "It's hard matching wits with a half-wit, but I'll see if I can crawl down in the slime, somewhere near your level."

There in that darkness, seconds were eternal. The clock ticked in my head.

"You are laughable," I said. "You are all the Keystone Kops rolled into one sad little twisted man. A sorry, strutting, self-important fool."

I told him other things between tickings of the clock and he never fired back.

"You're a goofball. Everybody here knows it.

"You are beneath contempt," I said.

"You drag that noble word *asshole* down to new depths. Next to you an asshole is an icon. You are the apex of assholery, Lennie. You even understand what I'm saying?"

Under all that bluster, I had him figured for a coward. I told him so and dared him to prove me wrong.

"I know you're ignorant," I said. "That's a given. You make lousy decisions and then hide behind your badge, and that's the worst kind of cop.

"You couldn't find your ass with both hands and the Hubble telescope.

"You're a cockroach, Lennie.

"A maggot.

"Whichever's worse, that's you."

This went on for a while: me talking to the darkness; him out there listening.

Listening . . .

. . . till suddenly, at some point, I knew he had slithered away.

22

The next face I saw was the sheriff's. I could see the morning sun on the trees through the jailhouse window and I sat up on the bed, amazed I had slept so well. The outer door clanged open and he unlocked my cell. "Get up, Janeway, your lawyer's here."

We walked up the steps together. "What'd you say to Lennie last night?"

"Me? I never saw the guy after it got dark."

"He's actin' funny, like he doesn't want to come near you. I thought you two might've had some words."

"Damn, I thought we were getting along just fine."

"You hungry yet?"

"Yeah, actually."

"I'll bring you some grub, if there's time."

Parley was waiting, as usual, in the conference room. As soon as the sheriff left us, he said, "You ready to get out of here?"

"What have I got to do?"

He told me. At six-thirty this morning, the judge had called him at home. After a visit late yesterday afternoon with the guardian ad litem and a Social Services caseworker, the kids had been taken to Denver and were in safe hands. The grandparents had already left town and the grandfather had suddenly declined to press charges. "You can walk out of this if you'll just apologize and eat some crow," Parley said. "I think he's motivated to dispose of it."

"And the kids are okay?"

"Yep. I talked to the social worker myself, just before they left. They won't be coming back here again. So what do you say?"

"Sure, I'll apologize."

"Make it good. If we don't get this done this morning, you may sit in here till sometime next month. He's willing to see you at eight-thirty."

"Then by all means."

"I'll come for you in an hour. And Cliff, please, be contrite. This isn't according to Hoyle and it'll be hard for you to choke down, but he wants it on the record, in open court. You okay with that?"

"Sure. I'll eat everything he puts on my plate."

Lennie was nowhere in sight in the jail. I had a pretty good breakfast, the sheriff released me in the care of my attorney, and we walked together across the parking lot to the courthouse entrance. The judge was already on his bench. The only people in the courtroom at that hour were Himself, his reporter, Parley, and me.

"The prisoner will face the bar," he said.

I stood before him and the lecture began. I had shown crass indifference to Himself personally, to his position, to the Court and the Law. I had been insulting, degrading, disrespectful, contemptuous, and foul. I deserved to be jailed and to sit there for however long it took until I realized the error of my ways. But he had bigger fish to fry. "Have you had enough time yet to reflect upon what you said?"

"Yes, Your Honor."

He shook his head. Not good enough. "Do you *beg* the Court's forgiveness?"

"Yes, I do. Yes, sir, Your Honor."

"Do you realize how out of line you were in both your choice of words and in the tone of your voice?"

"Yes, Your Honor."

"Then *say* so!"

"I was wrong. I know that now. I was disrespectful and insulting, I got swept up in the moment and said things that never should have been said. For any insult I may have given the Court or Your Honor personally, I am truly, deeply sorry, and I humbly beg the Court's pardon."

He looked down as if he didn't believe a word of it. But he had run out of groveling exercises to put me through, and all that remained was his decision.

"Fine reduced to one hundred dollars," he said. "Get the hell out of here."

23

It was now midmorning, the arraignment was just three hours away, and Parley and I had a short telephone conference call with Erin to plot strategy and deal with the likelihoods of the day. At the arraignment, Laura would enter her plea and would request bail. This was a formality: the judge wasn't about to grant it, and Erin had chosen to push for the earliest trial date she could get. Now she was convinced that the prosecution would be going to trial with a weak case. "I don't think they know how weak it actually is, and I don't want to give them time to find out. We don't want our client to sit in jail any longer than she has to."

First, she said, there should be no more talk of the books to anyone. "They may bring out their own book expert from somewhere, but that'll be costly. If it doesn't seem to be an issue to us whether they're valuable or not, maybe they won't. Unless we can tie those three book guys to Bobby, and put them in the area on that day, the books only cloud the case. At some point, probably after Cliff gets back from Burbank, we'll have to make that call, maybe list them as witnesses, and get them subpoenaed."

After the arraignment, Parley would file our motion to suppress evidence. This would be based on our contention that the deputy had acted unlawfully from the beginning; that Laura's verbal confession was illegally obtained, and evidence from the house had been improperly seized. "I smell blood," Erin said.

Parley and I went upstairs and sat in the conference room waiting for our client to go over some last-minute details before arraignment. The sheriff brought Laura into the room and left us, and we talked through the lunch hour. Laura listened intently to Parley's account of my adventure with the in-laws and the judge, and now the room was quiet except for the periodic hissing of the radiator. She was suddenly giddy over the kids and there was a feeling of hope on her side of the table. Parley's next words brought her down to earth. "It won't be enough to show that there was this two- or three-minute gap from the time you heard the shot to when you got up the meadow to the house and found Bobby dead on the floor. Even if we accept the theory that Jerry might've done it—"

"*I* don't accept that."

"You did readily enough, before Janeway talked to you."

"Please," she said, looking away from him. "Let's not start this again."

Her roving eyes stopped on me. "Listen to the man, Mrs. Marshall," I said. "That was the deal, remember."

"He still thinks it was Jerry."

"I think it's a strong possibility," Parley said. "I haven't seen any facts to counter that theory."

"There could've been somebody there."

"Sure, it coulda been the Godfather or the ghost of Alferd E. Packer, but it's up to you now to tell me who it was."

"I don't know." She shook her head. "I don't know."

"So you want us to build a defense based on the premise that some unknown party, neither you nor Jerry, did this. Even allowing for the fifteen minutes you were walking, that's not much time for a third party to have been there and shot Bobby and got away before you could see him."

"But it could have happened."

"Anything's possible, but right now we've

got nothing to hang that on. I may have asked you this before, but tell me again. Did Bobby associate with any unsavory people?"

"Well, sure, there were some women . . ."

"Any specific women you can think of? I'm not talking about hookers, Laura, I mean women of the town, people who might be the cause of a jealous rage by a third party."

"I can't think of any."

"Did he gamble?"

"Not that I know."

"Did he owe any big debts?"

"I don't think so. In recent years, I haven't known much about his business."

"Did he have any enemies?"

She shrugged.

"Can you think of anybody else who might want to harm Bobby, or any reason that someone unknown might want to?"

"No," she said softly.

"Nobody?"

"No."

"Then it's back to you and Jerry."

A silence settled over the room.

"We know he didn't kill himself," Parley said. "Either of those shots would have been instantly lethal, so he couldn't likely have fired the second one, could he?"

"I'm not helping you much."

"No, and you didn't help yourself when you had Jerry bathe and then burned his clothes."

"I told you why I did that."

"Why doesn't matter. What does matter is that any evidence from the shooting that was on his hands or in his clothes may be long gone now."

"I was stupid. It never occurred to me that I was destroying evidence which might've proved his innocence."

"Or the other way around. And if you did prove his innocence, where does that leave you?"

"As the only suspect," she said.

Almost a minute passed while we sat and Parley drummed his fingers on the table. "I've got to tell you something, miss," he said. "Your friend Erin might have a few ideas, but if she does, she's more than just a good attorney, she's a damn genius. As it stands now, you have only one defense."

"Jerry did it," she said glumly.

"No, you *thought* Jerry did it. That was your first reaction, that explains everything. People will *understand* that, Laura, it gives you at least a fighting chance, so that's got to be your defense. You thought what anybody would think under the circumstances, and you reacted and did what any mother would do. You tell 'em exactly what happened, tell the truth, then describe what you thought and what you did. You came up the hill and into the house, and there was Jerry with the gun in his hand."

"For Christ's sake, I *can't* say that."

"You'd better say it and forget about Christ, say it for your own sake."

She watched him drum his fingers. "What if I said . . ."

"What? What if you said what?"

"Can't I say I thought someone else might have been there?"

"No, you can't, because you *didn't* think that. You never gave that a thought till much later, it never crossed your mind in that room on that day. You've already told both your attorneys and Janeway here what you were thinking, and we can't put on testimony that we know to be false. Now do you understand what I've been trying to tell you from the first day? How what you say to us limits what we can do?"

He leaned over and engaged her with his eyes. "Get used to this fact, Laura. We can't defend both of you. It's impossible."

"What would happen to Jerry? If I did tell what happened, what would they do to him?"

"Nothing compared with what they'd do to you."

"Could I be involved . . . have a say . . . in what kind of treatment he gets?"

"I'm not the one to ask about that. My only job here is to help Erin get you acquitted. I'm not a social worker or a child psychologist. I'm not Jerry's lawyer, I'm your lawyer, and my job is to defend you in court."

"Damn, I just hate this."

"I know you do. But think what happens if you go to prison. What happens to Jerry then? Whatever that is, you won't have a damn thing to say about it, ever. By the time you get out, he'll be a middle-aged man and you'll be lucky if he even remembers you. You've got at least a decent chance to beat this, Laura, and that's my honest opinion. Get this legal crap behind you. Stop fighting us at every turn. Let us do our jobs."

They hemmed and hawed some more, but this was the story she would take into court. She was not a stupid woman and she saw that now.

Parley pushed back his chair. "Cliff?"

"Yeah, I've got a few questions . . . if that's okay."

I didn't have any notes: all the time they had been talking I had silently been ticking off questions on my fingers, my own crude way of putting things in order. "Mrs. Marshall," I said, "where were the guns kept?"

"Bobby kept two rifles and the shotgun in a cabinet behind his desk. The handgun in a holster over his chair."

"None of them under lock and key?"

"No. They were much too easy to get at."

"Did anyone know about the handgun?"

"Other than me, sure, all the kids have seen it at one time or another. I told Bobby I didn't like having it in the house. I hate guns. We used to fight about it . . . when we still cared enough to fight. When we moved into separate bedrooms, I just gave up. What he had in his room was his own business."

"Then you never went in there at all."

"Well, you know . . . there were occasions. Bobby wasn't a neat man, and there were times when things just had to be picked up. I couldn't stand to live like that."

"So you went in the room, what? Once a week?"

"Less than that. He left the door open when he wasn't there, and when I could see green mold growing across his desk . . . maybe I shouldn't exaggerate, but he was so annoying. When it got too bad, I went in and straightened it up."

"Did you ever see his gun when you went in the room?"

"You couldn't really miss it. It was always in that holster."

"In plain view?"

"As you got close to the desk, you couldn't miss it. You couldn't see it from the door, or out in the hall."

"He never took the gun with him when he went out?"

"He had another one in his truck."

"But this gun in the bedroom might've been seen by anybody who came calling."

"Sure, if anybody ever did. We didn't entertain or have casual callers."

"Have you ever heard Bobby say anything about a man called Preacher? Tall, skinny guy, his real name's Kevin Simms."

"I never knew his name. But, yeah, now that you mention it, someone like that did come up to see him occasionally."

"What about?"

"I have no idea."

"What about two brothers named Willie and Wally Keeler? They may just be grunts. Muscles with beards."

"I never saw those two guys," Laura said. "I know the tall one, or some very tall man, came up to the house a few times to see Bobby."

"When was this?"

"Oh, gosh, I don't know. Quite a while back. Maybe as much as a year ago."

"And you never found out even in a general way what it was about?"

"Never cared, never gave it another thought till you asked me just now."

"Did he either leave or pick up anything while he was there?"

She shook her head. "I don't know."

"Did you hear anything that was said? Anything at all?"

She shook her head. "I just wasn't interested. I'm sorry, I'm no help at all. God, I feel so stupid. Is this important?"

"We don't know what it is yet, Mrs. Marshall."

"I wish you'd call me Laura."

"When he came up there—how long did he stay?"

"Less than an hour. They went into Bobby's room and talked, then he left."

"And Bobby never mentioned it, what they might've been talking about?"

"Like I said, we weren't sharing much by then."

"That's fine. Just a few more questions."

She was on edge now, as if she had failed some crucial test and dreaded the next one. I told her it was okay, she had done well, but she looked doubtful.

"When you burned Jerry's clothes, had you been using the fireplace that day?"

"No, none of the fireplaces. I had the furnace on to warm the house."

"So you lit the fire only to burn Jerry's things."

"That's right."

"What exactly did you put in the fire?"

"Oh, gosh. His shirt was drenched with blood, and his pants. I think that's all."

"Underwear?"

"I didn't see any blood there, so I put those things through the wash."

"What about his shoes?"

"They seemed fine."

"Are those the shoes he's wearing now?"

"They were his everyday shoes. I suppose he's still wearing them."

"What about the fire? How long did you let it burn?"

"I poured coal oil all over his things, then doused and lit 'em again when the fire died down. I didn't want to leave any trace."

"And that's when you called the sheriff."

"When the fire was pretty well done and I had aired the place out."

"You opened the windows?"

"Yes, just long enough to get the smell of kerosene out of there."

"And that would be the last time that fireplace has been touched or looked at."

"Yes, but I'm sure there couldn't be anything left."

"And there'd be nothing else in there that could hurt your case."

"No, how could there be?"

"Be very sure of that. The DA will probably have to be in on the discovery if we find anything. So if there's anything else in that grate . . ."

There was nothing, she said again.

After the arraignment we called Erin from Parley's house. Now we had a trial date: it would start in the last week of January. "Okay," Erin said, "let's go look in the fireplace tomorrow. And she'd better be telling us the truth."

The next morning Parley and I went up to the house and checked the grate in the back room. Parley stood back while I prodded gently among the ashes. "There's something," he said, and I held it up with the poker: a significant piece of plaid shirt that had separated and dropped behind the grate. It had been hidden for weeks under the ash and had been thoroughly soaked, presumably in the victim's blood. We also found a photograph of Jerry wearing that shirt, framed on the mantel in the front room. It had been taken last June and still had the photo lab markings on it, including the date.

I called Erin from the telephone in the house and told her what was there.

"Are you sure there's nothing else in that grate?"

"I can't be absolutely sure without sifting through it and disturbing everything."

"Don't do that. Give me your best guess."

"If there's anything there, we can't see it."

"Don't move anything. Leave the shirt fragment right where you found it, then call the DA and have them come up and get it."

24

I arrived home with a week to spare before Burbank. I spent a day on a grand tour of my own turf. I hit every bookstore in Denver: I talked to people and no one had ever sold the Preacher a book or seen him in action. That night I took Erin out to eat and caught her up on everything that had happened. She had won her trial and was heading into another next week. After that she had a clear schedule and had already given notice that she would be out of town for a while. Her best estimate for joining us full-time was early December.

I caught up on business—researching and pricing books, returning overdue phone calls, paying bills, giving my employee some time off. On Monday I went out to Social Services to see what I could learn about the kids. I finally spoke to a woman in her fifties who knew about the case. She had a fairly complete report, including my own role in getting the kids away from the Marshalls. The nameplate on her desk said Rosemary Brenner.

"I can't tell you much of anything you don't already know," she said. "The two young ones are in foster care here. They are in a good home and are doing well. The older boy is also here in Denver."

"That sounds like they've been separated."

"For the moment. Maybe you can tell me a few things about him."

"I can't imagine but I'll try."

"Do you know anything about his birth parents?"

"Not much. They didn't do him any favors in life."

"I'm aware of the abuse. Right now I'm more interested in his ancestry."

"Why does that matter? Do you think he's retarded?"

"I didn't say that."

"No, but with a question like that, it figures."

We each waited for the other to say something. She said, "We really haven't had him very long yet. It's hard to tell at such an early stage what he might be."

"I can ask Laura, but I'm going out of town. I won't be seeing her again till next week."

"I'm interested in who the parents were, where they went, who their parents might have been. Maybe I can find out on my own if I know the agency that handled the adoption."

She smiled like someone who knows something and wants to say it, but can't because of rules and procedures. I said, "You probably know this. That kid may be a witness to the murder of his adoptive dad over in Paradise."

"That's what I understand. And if that's true, it only adds to his problems. But I really can't tell you anything else at this point."

"Not even whether he's retarded."

Again the enigmatic smile, this time with a slight headshake. "From what we've seen so far, Mr. Janeway, that boy is far from retarded."

She took note of my surprise and said, "That's really all I can tell you now."

"Will he ever be able to talk?"

"Can't say yet."

"Can I check back with you?"

"Call me next week if you want to. We'll see where we are then."

25

The Burbank Book Fair was held twice a year in the Burbank Airport Hilton Hotel. Erin and I had done this fair ourselves a year ago, setting up our booth in the far corner of the sprawling room. That had been our year of discovery, traveling to book fairs and sales, sampling the life, meeting the people. A book fair resembles a book sale only in that books are sold at both; in other ways they are as different as a fine uptown bookshop is from a Goodwill store. At the vast Planned Parenthood sale in Des Moines, bookscouts begin gathering before dawn. They will wait all day, some bringing lunches and lounge chairs, decks of cards, dominoes, even miniature TV sets, to ward off boredom. They will travel hundreds of miles and wait more than eight hours just to get a thirty-second jump over the serious competition when the doors open. In that thirty seconds a good scout, if he's also lucky, can slurp up ten serious first editions at fifty cents each, stash them under a table, and toss his jacket over the pile, his eyes warning predators of split lips, severed arms, and death, while he scouts the tables again. When the doors open, it can resemble the Oklahoma land rush.

A book fair is a different animal. There's not much land-rush mentality here: everybody knows these books will all be priced more or less at retail. No $500 treasures will be lingering in some $2 pile of dreck: there are no $2 books anywhere on the book fair floor. Twenty dollars is about the lowest price, even for dreck. Occasionally there's a legitimate $500 title priced at $300, and if it hasn't already been sold to a dealer before the sale, chances are it'll still be there by the time the second or third wave of customers gets around to it. If the cheapskate customer comes back on Saturday and the book's still there—a chancier prospect—the dealer may be motivated to give a slight additional discount, and on Sunday, if the book has somehow slipped through all these cracks, the motivation may go up another notch. The cheapskate customer might not even have to ask: just fondling it lovingly might bring a comment, "I can do better than that if you need it."

A bookman who has not had a good fair may be willing to deal on Sunday, to help cover his overhead, for the costs of doing a book fair only begin with booth fees that seem to go up every year. For a major fair put on by the Antiquarian Booksellers Association of America the fee can be $4,000, and even for a smaller fair like Burbank it can run a grand. There is also transportation for the dealer and his help if he brings someone; there is airfare, often from one distant planet to another; there are lodgings and meals and, finally, the rental of glass cases for items held truly dear, for the oddly precious or the true sweetheart that, the dealer will be happy to tell you, is rarer than a chicken's lips. And the books are supposed to pay for it all, on markups that are often just double their cost, and sometimes, for expensive items, quite a bit less.

I didn't remember the Preacher from my earlier trip here and there wasn't much chance I'd have missed him, even in a hall with more than two hundred booths. A man like that stands out like a white buffalo, as Marshal Dillon once said, and I had visited every booth and talked to every dealer before the gates opened to the public. This is a large part of the book fair culture. People schmooze, they go out to dinner in crowds, they drink and talk. Dealers come to

buy books as much as sell them, and I have
known bookmen who happily break even on the
fair circuit year after year and come for the buying opportunities. It is something of an open secret in the book trade: the most important hours
of a book fair weekend are those before the fair
opens to the unwashed public at four o'clock on
Friday.

One incident last year had burned itself into
my memory. I had set up my booth at 8 A.M., as
soon as the committee got the tables up and the
tablecloths spread. The public may think it gets
first dibs on books being displayed by dealers
from all parts of the nation, but in fact by the
time the gate opens, those books have vora-
ciously been picked over by the other dealers for
six or eight hours. From the moment the boxes
are opened and the books come out on the tables, there is wheeling and dealing all across the
floor.

I had drifted into a booth that day, where the
dealer had just unloaded his boxes from the
truck. Nothing had been put on display yet: just
a sign propped against the table announcing the
fellow as a specialist in modern first editions. As
he opened his stash, a small crowd gathered.
The first book out was a pristine copy of *Laura*,
the 1943 mystery novel that had become such a

memorable movie the following year. Gene Tierney, Dana Andrews, Clifton Webb, and Vincent Price had lit up the screens for those wartime crowds, making the single name of the title a household word and giving the author, Vera Caspary, a brief day in the sun. As a mystery it wasn't a bad story, but its real story as a collectible book has been phenomenal. Two factors made the literary quality of the novel almost incidental. It had a reputation as a great film of its time, and the book was impossible to find, anywhere, at any price.

It was a book so scarce that no one in the crowd had ever seen one. No one in a roomful of fairly sophisticated book people had any idea what its value might be or what the demand was. There had been no recent pricing history, unheard of for such a modern book, and as I looked down at the pulpy jacket, I thought how unusual that was, for a major American house like Houghton Mifflin to have issued this and nothing was ever seen of it anywhere. They must've printed all of ten copies, I thought then. The book as I remember it was far from pretty: the jacket showed just the simple face of the heroine, who has allegedly been murdered as the story starts, painted against a bland background. I didn't know it then, but a few dealers with contacts to rich collectors had been searching for that book for years, keeping its name a deep secret in the hope that one would pop out of the woodwork.

I remember the stir that went around that circle as the book made its sudden appearance: not quite a sigh, certainly no more to give it away than the eyes of a cunning gambler might reveal in a high-stakes card game. It was a feeling I got, some invisible, inaudible chemistry that had spread from one man to the next. "What do you want for *Laura*?" said the man to my left. The dealer opened the cover and the boards creaked, it was so fresh. Tucked in was a review slip, sweetening the deal for whoever bought it. "How much for *Laura*?" the guy asked again, but it was clear by then that the dealer had heard him, he just didn't know what to put on it. "Six hundred," he finally said, and in a heartbeat the guy said, "I'll take it," and began writing his check. Six other guys stood by, suffering for their good manners.

The fellow picked up his book and walked out of the booth. A small trickle of dealers followed him and I went along for the ride. "What're you gonna sell that for?" someone asked, and the man turned and faced the little circle of colleagues. He pondered it a moment, said, "Fifteen," and the second dealer wrote a check in the middle of the aisle, using a friend's back for a desk. A smaller group followed him into the next aisle, where again the book changed hands, this time for three grand. It traveled back the other way now, halfway across the hall, before the question was asked again. "Six thousand net to you, soldier," the man said, and it sold again, for the fourth time, without ever reaching the booth that would finally handle it. I think of that book when sleep is elusive and the parade of books begins in my head. I am a bookman. When the hour is late, I count books, not sheep, and I learned something that day.

Another thing I had learned: Los Angeles had not been a regular pit stop for the Preacher and his boys. I had spent all day Thursday and Friday morning drifting across the vast LA bookscape in my rental car, and no one I met knew anything about a lanky bookseller and his two bellicose sidekicks. I had a hunch the Preacher was new, not only to Burbank but to Colorado and the West as well. His facility in Monte Vista had a temporary look to it, despite the thousands of books he had stored there.

I got out to the gate at three-thirty, half an hour before the doors opened. A line had already formed and was growing. Wherever there are books, there are early birds, but this was a much quieter bunch than I had seen in Des Moines. The line was sprinkled with lawyer types, doctors, stockbrokers: collectors looking for a perfect copy of a long-cherished book had a good chance to find it at a book fair. "On these three days," one of the fair organizers was fond of saying, "this is the best bookstore in America."

The doors opened at four sharp and I wandered up the aisle nearest the west wall, pausing to chat with people I knew and pick up a few things along the way. I bought a nice second-state Richard Burton for three grand net and a couple of early Steinbecks. I wavered on a Jim Cain and finally passed because of a slight problem with the jacket; then I found the same title, *Mildred Pierce*, in a booth not twenty yards away, a perfect copy that ended up costing me almost twice as much but made my good day better. I love to buy books I love, and I am in no hurry to sell them.

I talked to some people I knew from Santa Barbara and during a lull I described the Preacher and asked if they had seen such a man. "Yeah, he's over in the middle row, about halfway back," my friend Jim Pepper said. "A really weird guy but he's got some interesting stuff."

There were five long rows of booths, at least forty book and autograph dealers in each row. I knew it could take all night to work my way across that floor, but I wasn't in any hurry: the Preacher was here for the duration. In fact, there were moments when I almost forgot him as I strolled along chatting. But not many moments and not very long.

I was tempted by a nice mixed-state *Huckleberry Finn*. I should buy this and sit on it, I thought. In five years it'll double, and go up from there. But I passed.

I bought a lovely *In Cold Blood*, signed by Capote: not too common signed, thus slightly pricey in the here and now. I bought it for my futures shelf.

Enough, I thought. I left my stash under Pepper's table and moseyed over to the middle of the floor. It was well after six when I saw the Preacher looming above the crowd. I had no idea where this was going, but I had not made the trip only to view him from afar and turn away. I zigzagged my way across the aisle and back, looking in one booth after another, a picture I hoped of book-browsing nonchalance. Now I could see Wally Keeler in the corner of their booth, showing someone a book. I came closer, and some unseen force, maybe the same kind of thing in the gambler's steady eyes or the bookseller's bluff, drew the Preacher slightly, momentarily away from his customer.

He looked straight at me.

There were no nods between us: almost immediately he looked past me, as if he had missed the connection, as if I wouldn't know better. I turned in to a booth two down from his and browsed the merchandise. The books all blurred now: my mind had shifted into its cop mode, and my juice was flowing like sixty. In the end there was no way to plan this. As that great philosopher Doris Day would say, what will be will be.

I walked into their booth.

"Hi, guys."

I didn't expect sudden warmth to break out from the Preacher: the man had none to give, but Wally's unfriendly face immediately told me something: *They know who I am.* It had been a stupid mistake, giving them my name. The Preacher turned away from his customer and a faint smile crossed his face. "What are you doing here, gambler?" he said. I went along with the charade, seeing how far it would go. "Came out for the racing season," I said, lying affably.

"How's the fair treating you?" He nodded and said it was early yet, things were just getting started. "Buying much?" I said casually, and I didn't need to wait for the answer that never came. These boys had come to sell books, not to buy them. I made a point of looking at Wally. "How you doing, Wally?" I said easily. "Where's your brother, still back in Colorado, trying to get that truck out of the hills?" He muttered something and turned away, and I thought, *Oh, yeah, they have learned a lot about my big stupid ass since I saw them last.*

I looked over their books: a mix of things with some common stuff out front and the high spots on a shelf that had been set up at the back of the table. Some of their books were signed, some weren't. I picked up every one and looked them over, and the night waned while I stood in their booth. The hell with them, my cat was out of the bag now.

It was nearing eight when the real hostility began to show. The crowd had thinned in this part of the hall, and I could sense their rapt attention to whatever I was doing. I could feel their annoyance, especially Wally's. An old gentleman came into the booth and engaged the Preacher in conversation about a signed Robert Frost. While they were talking, Wally eased into the back of the booth and said in a low voice, "What the fuck do you want, Janeway? What the hell are you doing here?"

"I'm looking at books, Wally, what's it look like?"

"Yeah, well, why don't you do it somewhere else?"

"I like it here. You guys are so friendly and stuff. I like friendly people."

"Lemme tell you something, pal. Don't fuck with us."

I smiled. "Wally, I've fucked with guys who could tear your head off."

He moved away and fiddled with some books in the opposite corner. I eased out closer to the Preacher and without being too obvious, I hoped, listened to his conversation with the Frost collector. It was a common, cheap book, *In the Clearing*, with a black state jacket with white lettering, issued in the last year of Frost's life. I heard the collector say, "The jacket's pretty rough on that," and the Preacher said, "I'm not selling it as a pristine copy, friend. You know the signature's worth the seventy-five I've got on it, and if you want it pretty, you can find a jacket for that book anywhere." The Preacher wasn't motivated to deal and the collector cluck-clucked and moved away. I watched over the top of a book as the Preacher reshelved it and turned his attention to someone at the front of the booth who seemed to be more serious. I moseyed over under Wally's watchful eyes and picked the Frost off the shelf. Then something happened that changed the course of everything. Wally came across and reached for the book. "That's not for sale."

I had no intention of buying it, but now I drew the book protectively back under my arm. "It's on an open shelf, it's gotta be for sale," I said.

He took a step closer. "Maybe it's not for sale to *you*."

I got my back up and reached for my checkbook.

"I don't think you hear so goddamned good, Janeway."

"You don't think, period. What are you, some bush leaguer? That's a good way to get bounced out of here, not to mention blackballed at any legitimate book fair that hears about it. You really wanna push this? I've got a good grapevine and I can spread news fast."

Suddenly the Preacher loomed over us. "What's going on here?"

"Your caveman doesn't want to sell me this book. It's marked seventy-five, here's my check for it."

He looked disdainfully at the book and said, "Why would you want that?"

"Maybe 'cause I've got a jacket, maybe 'cause I'm crazy. But I'm a customer who's just written you a check after standing in your booth for an hour. Now the question is, are you going to sell me this book or do I really have to get annoyed over a stupid thing like this?"

The Preacher gave Wally one of his seriously frigid looks. "For gosh sakes, Wally, don't you know better than that? Of course we'll sell him the book."

He took my check, bagged and sealed the book for clearance through security, and deposited it in my hands. "Enjoy it," he said coldly.

Then suddenly he made a mighty effort to warm up. He smiled and said, "Wally's just annoyed, that's all. It's probably because you didn't tell us the truth back in Colorado. He'll get over it. We don't want any hard feelings."

"Hey, that's cool, Preacher, I don't hold grudges."

"That was quite a story you fed us back there. I don't know why you thought it was necessary, but people do things for all kinds of reasons. If we gave you any grief, let me apologize for both of us."

"No need at all, we got it resolved, everybody's happy."

Wally didn't look happy, and his unhappiness doubled when the Preacher said, "Will you be here till closing? Let us buy you a late dinner and make up for any annoyance we might have put you through."

I wouldn't eat with these snakes for my pick of his books, but I didn't come twelve hundred miles to play it safe. I clapped Wally on the shoulder and said, "That's real decent of you boys. You don't have to do that, but if you insist, I'll be back."

I drifted over to Pepper's booth. He was curious, as usual.

"So'd you buy anything from that tall guy?"

"I'll show you if you don't bug me about it."

We opened the bag and he looked at the Frost. "Not much margin in this."

"I know, I know. You're bugging me about it."

"So what's the story?"

"His factotum got my dander up. Tried not to sell it to me before I even told them I wanted to buy it."

"Now why would he do that?"

"Good question."

He looked at it carefully now. "The signature doesn't look right."

I looked at it over his shoulder. I had seen Frost's signature many times, not nearly as often as Pepper had, but it looked okay to me.

"There's something wrong with it," he said more definitively. "You gonna leave it here for a while?"

"I can leave it all night if you want to read it."

"Yeah, right. I was thinking more along the lines of, I take it to an autograph dealer I know over in Row Four. He can tell us right away if there's a problem with it."

"I'd appreciate that, Jim."

I drifted across the floor again. It was now well after eight and I still had most of two rows that I hadn't yet seen. But I worked them quickly, my mind no longer on books but on something far more serious. At ten minutes to nine I circled the room and returned to Pepper's booth.

"We think it's a fake," he said. "It's a very good fake, but I'd take it back to him before we close up tonight and get that check back."

"You hang on to it for me. I'll see you tomorrow, and thanks."

He dropped the book in the bag, resealed it with his own sticker, and I drifted back toward the middle aisle again. I knew I'd have to watch my flank now. I was going unarmed into a hostile meeting, however friendly they might want it to seem at the moment; the odds were two to one, and there was a dead man in Colorado. At least I went knowing these things. I hadn't just fallen off the Kiowa County Bookmobile.

26

They were rolling a cloth covering over their books when I arrived. Wally had brightened his act, no doubt on orders from his boss: he gave me his signature grin, one of those crap-eaters that only his mother could have loved. "Hey, Cliff," he said, "no hard feelings, huh?" I said no, hell no, we were fine, and he went into his charm mode, as charming as lung cancer. "I'm glad the Preach talked you into coming with us. Sometimes I forget my manners when I've got a hard-on for somebody else. I'm still pissed at Willie over the truck, that's all it is."

He yakked it up and I asked politely about the truck. Willie was trying to get it towed into Alamosa, where the repair shop told him the tariff could amount to seven grand. "Might as well take the bastard out and shoot it," he said, and I avoided saying the obvious, that he was the one who'd been driving that night.

The Preacher was busy with a last-minute customer, who surprised him and bought a $250 book. I could see it was signed and I eased closer to see what it might be. Wally kept talking, his voice droning like that of some perp trying to draw attention away from what really goes on, but I just nodded dumbly and kept moving slowly to the front. I saw a name, Larry McMurtry, and recognized the graphics: the guy was buying a copy of *The Desert Rose,* a common book unless signed, and this one had the impatient, almost-unreadable scrawl that McMurtry's signature was becoming. The Preacher bagged the book and sealed it. Behind me Wally chuckled, a halfhearted guffaw that telegraphs deep annoyance under false camaraderie. "I swear to God, Janeway," he said, still forcing the silly laugh, "goddamned if you aren't the world's nosiest bastard."

The Preacher looked back at me as he finished his deal, the guy walked away, and we three headed for the gates. "So what're you in the mood for?" the Preacher asked affably. "There's a good Moroccan restaurant I know of, but it's off the beaten trail and a bit of a drive."

"Sounds great," I said.

"You can ride in front with me. Plenty of room for those long legs of yours."

This time I wouldn't even consider getting in a car with Wally at my back. I said, "I'll follow you," but he tried to insist. "I'll bring you back," he said, but I told him no, I wanted to go straight to my hotel after dinner. There was an awkward pause: we all stood indecisively in the parking lot as Pepper walked out with a couple of bookpals and came past, giving us no more than a brief glance. He moved on without saying a word.

"I'll follow you," I said again, with no room for argument in my voice.

"Let's go then," the Preacher said under that snaky smile.

My simmering suspicion came to a boil as we drove. Twice he stopped and reversed his direction as if he had lost his way. I bet myself a dollar that there was no Moroccan restaurant: *none that he knows about,* I thought. We were now in a grim part of town, dark and close, not at all typical of any part of Los Angeles I had ever seen. We had been driving almost haphazardly for twenty minutes when he pulled to the sidewalk and stopped. I could see in the glare of an oncoming car that they were talking earnestly. The car passed us and the block fell again into deep blackness, with only a dim and distant streetlight revealing the outlines of their heads through the glass.

They started off again but the same thing happened, down into some dim ghetto where the likelihood of any good restaurant diminished with each block. He stopped again and I pulled up behind him, wishing I had my gun.

He opened his door, got out, and came back to me. I rolled down my window and he leaned way over and looked in. "We seem to be lost. I've only been there once, thought I could find it again."

"Do you remember the name of this place?"

He shook his head. "I'd know it if I saw it again, but I have no idea where we're at now. I think we'll have to find someplace else."

"Well, I'm not particular, let's grope around. I don't know the town any better than you do, but I'll take what comes."

He got back in the car but didn't move for another moment. They were still talking up a storm, and I'd bet myself another dollar it wasn't about the neighborhood, restaurants, or the kind of food we'd eat. We headed off to the west, and eventually we hit something that looked like it might lead to a main drag. The Preacher turned south and I stayed close on his tail. In one place he almost lost me—a traffic light that he took speeding up on a late yellow. Two cars were approaching the intersection on the crossing street and I had to stop. By then the Preacher was almost a block ahead.

I went across on the red but now I had a new hunch, that whatever he had planned for me, he was losing his nerve. Too much indecision, too much talk: his backbone's starting to ooze a little, I thought, maybe his taste for what had seemed good to him at a distance didn't look so good now. Maybe Mr. Kevin Simms would be just as happy to shake me and write it off with an apology tomorrow.

I closed the gap between us and we came to a wide boulevard with lights and motels and gas stations. He went past a couple of restaurants and I flashed my lights in his mirror. "Time to eat, boys," I said to the back of their car. "Let's do something or get off the pot." He turned around the block and came through the neighborhood again, stopping at the place with the deep, dark parking lot.

He pulled into the shadows at the far corner of the lot and I parked beside him.

"This wasn't what I had in mind," he said when we stepped out.

I'll bet it wasn't.

But they were stuck with me now. The Preacher said, "Well, let's make the best of it," and we started around the building to the front entrance. Inside, the place was about what I expected—a hash house, with an ancient cashier who doubled as the hostess and two harried-looking waitresses. The cashier said, "Be with you in a minute," but she couldn't seem to unlock the cash drawer and she didn't seem to care. Meanwhile, people were standing in a growing line to pay their checks, we stood at a sign that said PLEASE WAIT TO BE SEATED, and I could see that the Preacher was getting impatient.

The old cashier had called one of the waitresses over and was getting detailed advice for working the till, repeating everything that was said to her and still not comprehending. "Say, can we ever get some help here?" the Preacher said loudly, and the people waiting in line stared at him darkly. At last the other waitress came and seated us. She was young, was having a bad night, looked strung out and near tears. The Preacher's opening salvo, "I hope the food in this place is better than the service," brought the tears closer. "I am very sorry, sir," she said softly. "Please, what can I get for you?" She had her order pad out and her pencil poised, and he stared at her in that cold way he had and said, "Would it be too much to ask for some napkins and place settings, a few of the niceties of civilization? What is this, your first night on this job?"

"I'm sorry, I'm sorry." She turned away and he shouted after her, loud enough for the cook to hear, "This table is dirty too."

By then I was getting damned tired of the Preacher. I said, "You really shouldn't do that, you know."

"Do what, demand just a modicum of decent service?"

"Abuse the waitress. You should never abuse a waitress, Preacher, that's not in sync with the Golden Rule. Imagine if she were your daughter."

Before he could reply, I said, "How old do you think she is, seventeen? Maybe she's not very good but this is probably her first job, so let's cut her some slack."

I pushed his buttons again. "And maybe you can tell me before things truly go to hell why we're really here."

"What on earth is that supposed to mean?"

"It means, what do you guys really want from me? Why bring me way out here when there's obviously no Moroccan restaurant closer than Rick's Café in Casablanca? Why the hail-fellow routine all of a sudden until now, when your real colors begin to come through? I'm really curious about that, Preacher, why the pretense of a night on the town when the fact is you don't like me any more than I like you?"

The waitress returned with the table settings and a steaming towel to wash off the tabletop. "I'm sorry," she whispered again. "I'm very sorry."

"Don't worry about it," I said. "We're probably not going to stay, but that's not your fault."

She left us and the Preacher said, "I was right about you the first time I saw you."

"You probably were."

"A troublemaker. I knew it then and I can see it now."

"Yeah, but I was right about you too."

"And what might that bold assessment have been?"

"Not a preacher at all, just a crooked two-bit book shyster who'd better hope there really isn't any God."

"Man, you better watch your mouth," Wally seethed.

"Oh, yeah, I wouldn't want to get *you* mad at me. Jesus, I quake at the thought."

"I'll make you quake, pal. You wanna step outside?"

I laughed and said, "No," still laughing.

"I didn't think so. C'mon, Preacher, let's get out of here. I told you this guy was bad news."

"Oh, Wally, I'm much worse news than you know. I'll tell you what bad news I am, I am wise to your book scam. I know the Frost I bought had a fake signature, probably that McMurtry as well, and I can't help wondering how many more fakes you're selling as the real thing."

The Preacher paled. "I have no idea what you're talking about."

"Then try this. How well did you know Bobby Marshall? Well enough to kill him, maybe? Did you boys have a falling-out over the money?"

"You're crazy. You really are a crazy man. I don't know any Bobby Marshall. If there's something wrong with that book, bring it by in the morning and I'll give you your money back, no questions asked. *No* questions asked."

"I might do that. Maybe I'll have a few questions for you while I'm there."

"Never mind your questions, you bring that book back. In fact I insist on it."

"You can't insist on anything, Preacher, it's my book now. That means I can keep it, give it to the cops for evidence, or run it through a paper shredder."

"Evidence of what? What cops are you talking about?"

"Keep on playing that role. I'll call ahead to Cañon City and tell 'em to have their tailor make a set of jailhouse threads, extra tall."

They got up and left, slamming their way through the door.

I sat there, and in a while the waitress came timidly by. I apologized for my companions and said, "On second thought, miss, I think I will eat. I've just been working up an appetite."

The food was actually worse than the service, but I had survived the East Colfax Roadrunner and I still believed I could eat anything. I left the waitress a sawbuck, the second-best thing about this lousy night. That look on the Preacher's face had been the best. That had been worth the trip.

I walked casually across the blacker-than-hell parking lot, aware of a growing unease that might have nothing to do with the Preacher or his lowlife sidekick. I was thinking about the case now, about dead Bobby Marshall and his guns, his loner ways and his books. As much as I wanted it to make sense, it didn't.

I had to go almost to the wall before I could see my car. The Preacher's car was gone, but I remained on full alert. I scanned the area and made my approach slowly, looking first to star-board, then to port, whistling softly, jingling my keys in my pocket. I didn't expect any real trouble now but I was ready for it. That was Wally's bad luck when he leaped out of the shadows and came at me with a pipe wrench in his hand.

His first swing grazed my shoulder as I ducked under it. His second grazed nothing but air. He never got off the third swing.

I belly-punched him hard and he flopped on the ground with a pathetic whooshing sound, a sorry grunt, and a little cry of pure misery. I heard the wrench hit the pavement.

"Hi, Wally," I said. "I think you dropped your wallet."

He managed to croak out three words. I thought they were "Oh, you asshole," but I couldn't be sure. He wavered for a moment on the cheeks of his ass, listed sideways, and toppled on his back. He looked up briefly at the terrible swirling universe, then he rolled over and tried to suck up all the gravel in the parking lot.

I got in my car and picked my way back to Burbank.

27

I was out at the book fair again in the morning. I wanted to touch their books, see what was signed, what was not, and just be a continuing irritant. I wanted to stare up the Preacher's nose and see if he'd tell me something new. Sometimes it happens that way: a jolt like I had given him last night takes time to work through the brain and get a guy talking. Even if he lies, you learn something.

By the time I went through admissions and got out to the middle of the hall, it was nine-fifteen. His booth was empty, his books were gone, his tablecloth rumpled and thrown on the floor.

It was the talk of the fair. When a dealer signs on at a book fair, he commits himself for the entire weekend, but sometime in the hour before the doors had opened, the Preacher and Wally had come in, and in fifteen minutes they had dismantled their booth and hustled themselves out to the back ramp. There had been a strenuous argument with the fair organizers. The Preacher had offered no excuse, not even a hint of a family emergency: "The only thing he said was, 'I've got to go, get out of my way,'" said the dealer directly across the aisle. "In the end, what can you do about it? They're his books, it's a free country, all you can do is tell him to go to hell if he ever tries to sign up for a fair around here again."

I sat in the makeshift cafeteria and drank some serious coffee. By now they're in San Bernardino heading east, I thought. They'd be in Monte Vista for at least a day, clearing out that facility. They wouldn't move those books in fifteen minutes.

I called United Airlines and got on a noonday flight to Denver. Picked up my books, said adios to everybody, and headed for the gates.

I knew it would take them thirteen hours for the return trip to Colorado: that's if they drove straight through, spelling each other at the wheel. They'd be there sometime late tonight, not in any great shape to move twenty thousand books, but well motivated. There'd be three of them by then, but even at that it seemed like an all-day job.

They couldn't do anything about the road time: it takes as long as it takes to drive nine hundred miles. Figure half a day to get a rental truck and move the books if they were true supermen: the only way it could be done, even in that time, was to hire some help. Assume that. Assume they would get home bushed after thirteen hours on the road and start loading immediately. Figure they'd be out of there before noon tomorrow.

Meanwhile, my flight would touch down in Denver a little before four o'clock. Just about the time Wally and the Preacher would be streaking across Arizona, I'd be in the air. When they reached Four Corners, I'd be heading down I-25. I had time, unless they called ahead and had Willie start breaking down the warehouse now . . . which of course they would do.

I called Erin from a phone booth. Got her machine.

I tried her again from my hotel.

Tried her again at the airport and got lucky. I explained things fast, with my flight being announced in the background.

"I can get you down there," she said. "There's an airfield in Alamosa: you could use Todd and we could have a rental car waiting for you. The question is, what are you going to do when you get there? Leaving a book fair early isn't against any law I've ever heard of. You can't have them arrested, you have no proof of anything, so what are you going to do about it?"

"What I always do. Grope, hope, wander in the wilderness, play it by ear."

29

"There she is," Todd said, nodding toward a string of lights in the distance. "We'll be on the ground in a few minutes. Then what?"

"Then I get in my rental car and drive to Monte Vista and you get to go home."

He banked low over the hills and started his approach into Alamosa. We had said nothing about my purpose on the trip down, and now I read more into his question than the usual small talk. "I don't know," he said at last. "What if I ride along with you instead? Just to keep you company."

"It's only twenty miles, Todd."

"Twenty miles on the ground can be a long, lonely trip."

"This sounds like a put-up job," I said. "Erin's handiwork is hard to miss."

"It's nothing she said. I just got a feeling."

"Uh-huh. So what didn't she say?"

"Just that there's a warehouse full of books that might be evidence in this case you're working on for her. Might be some bad apples guarding it."

He talked to someone on the ground and eased the plane into a landing pattern.

"It's just a thought," he said.

"Did she tell you there's a remote chance it might get ugly?"

"I can handle ugly."

"There's also a question of the law. We don't know yet whether the guys who get arrested, if anybody does, will be them or us."

"I guess that's why we've got us a good lawyer."

We bumped twice on the landing strip and he taxied us in.

Twenty minutes later we were in a rental car heading west on U.S. 160. It was just after seven-thirty: by my best guess, Wally and the Preacher were out on the same highway, somewhere in Colorado, heading our way through Cortez and Durango.

We got into Monte Vista a little before eight. It was a cold, clear night and the streets were almost empty. I drove past the Preacher's house first, only because it was on the way. It was locked and dark. We moved on across town, easing into the narrow lane where the warehouse was. "There he is," I said. "Looks like he's all by himself."

Willie had the door up and had pulled a large U-Haul truck up to the ramp. I could see him working feverishly around the edges of the truck, loading boxes as fast as he could carry them. From that limited vantage point, I could also see one long row of bookshelves and part of a crossing shelf, both empty. Todd said, "If he's been working like that all day, he won't have much fight left in him." I said, "Let's hope," but just in case I got my gun out of the backseat. Todd stared at it as I gave it a check and snapped the holster on my belt.

"Why don't you sit here and be the lookout?" I said.

"Are you trying to insult me?"

I reached over and squeezed his shoulder. "Yeah, I was; glad you didn't take it personally. What I really want you to do is hang back in the dark and don't let him know you're there till we see how the wind blows."

"I'm not a bad guy in a fight, you know."

"If it comes to that. The idea here is *not* to fight unless we absolutely have to. If these books do turn out to be evidence, the last thing we want is to taint it with some gestapo tactic."

I flicked off the interior lights and we got out. "Easy with that door," I said, and we pushed them almost shut and left them that way, making no noise. I walked as quietly as I could along the graveled path, and I could see Todd's shadow moving forward across the driveway. To the left of the ramp was a small steel stairway, and I took the steps carefully, two at a time, coming only to the edge of the door.

I could hear him now, rummaging somewhere in the back. From there I could look into the room and see how much work he had done. He had to be well motivated to rent the truck, box those books, clear out this room and the shelves well into the back, all alone. The Preacher must have called him early, maybe before they even went to the hall and broke down their booth. If I had put some fear in all of them, that's what I wanted, that's what I hoped.

I heard him grunt: a tired man struggling with the endless parade of boxes. He came into the room and we stared at each other for the smallest time, a second maybe, before he dropped the box of books on his foot.

"Willie," I said softly. "Looks like you've been at this awhile. You need some help?"

He sat on the floor beside the box, which had

split open on two corners and was spilling books on the floor.

"You shouldn't be doing this alone," I said. "You'll get a hernia."

I still hadn't crossed his threshold yet. "Really, I'd be happy to help if you need it. Just say the word."

Just say hi, you son of a bitch, and invite me in.

"Who the hell *are* you?"

I told him my name, knowing full well that's not what he meant. I had my coat pushed back so he could see the gun on my belt, not much of it but enough. All legal, all kosher: I had a proper, legal permit for my nonthreatening gun.

"May I come in, Willie?"

"Yeah, sure," he said numbly, and I stepped into the light.

"Looks like you guys are clearing out fast. What's the deal?"

He still looked stunned, as if I had just hit him between the eyes with a two-by-four. "Who are you?" he said again.

"I hate to say this, but I'm the guy who's about to send your big ugly ass to jail."

"You gotta be kidding."

"Do I look like I'm kidding? And by the way, in case you've got any crazy ideas, do I look like

I'm stupid enough to come here alone?" I called out through the crack, "How's it look out there?" and Todd, giving it both balls and a bucket of octane, said, "Everything's fine, boss."

"So where are we in the scheme of things, Willie? The Preacher and that idiot brother of yours will be here in a couple of hours. Question is, where will you be?"

"I don't understand."

"Come on, Willie, don't play stupid. Maybe you're just trying to buy some time, but your choices at this point are pretty well limited. You can stay there on the floor and we can all wait for those boys to arrive. You can keep loading your books. You can decide to cooperate. I guess you could start a fight, but that would be disappointing and unfortunate. If you get my drift."

He shook his head, like a man still in some kind of shock.

"How much more have you got to do back there?"

"Oh, Jesus," he said. His look said, *Oh, God, tons.*

"I think it's only fair to tell you," I said: "you can load them, but don't count on leaving here with them."

"Then what's the point?"

"Exactly."

He leaned forward and massaged his foot, still trying to buy time.

"Willie?"

"I'll wait for the Preacher."

"That's fine. You can all go together when you go."

"Go where?"

"I think you know where."

He got up slowly. I moved a step closer.

"No sudden moves," I said. "If you've decided to wait, you can sit in that chair against the wall. That would be my advice."

"What if I don't take your advice? What if I just walk on out of here?"

"That would be your choice. The wrong one, I think."

"But you're not gonna stop me, are you?"

He was beginning to get the drift of things now. He knew I had no authority except force, which as things now stood would be illegal.

"What if I get in that truck and just drive off?"

"I'm afraid I will have to stop you then."

"But not if I walk off."

"We'll have to see about that."

He started to move toward the door. I was standing in his way and I could see the fear on his face and in his eyes. He took another step. One more and he'd be in my face.

He took the step.

I moved aside.

He walked out the door.

I came out on the ramp and saw him hobbling down the steps.

"You're making a mistake," I said.

He flipped me off and kept going, past the truck and on down the road.

"Follow him," I told Todd. "Keep well back, try not to let him see you. When you find out where he's going, come on back here and let me know."

I sat in my rental car and watched the warehouse. An hour passed.

So far, so good, I hoped. I hadn't touched anything. Hadn't searched, seized, stormed the gates, roughed up anybody; hadn't really threatened except that one warning about stopping him if he tried to take the truck. I didn't know how a court might interpret that if it ever came out; maybe I hadn't done anything wrong, but I wished now I hadn't said it. At least I had left us with a fighting chance, but so far it was a moot point. We still had no case against them for anything.

I saw Todd come into the road. He opened the door and got in beside me.

"He went to the bus station. He's there now:

looks like he's waiting for a bus out of town."

"Okay. Take the car and drive out to a phone booth. Call Erin and tell her what's going on. Tell her the warehouse is wide open, the truck's sitting here full of books, the Preacher might pull up in another hour or two and I'd be interested in her advice."

I was painfully aware how thin my legal situation was. *Christ, we've got nothing on these guys,* I thought again, but I said, "Tell Erin I tried not to compromise things too much."

I stood off in a small grove of trees. This time Todd was gone ten minutes.

"She says hang loose and call her yourself when you can. If they take off, get their plate numbers so we can find them if she wants to subpoena them down the road. And don't do anything she wouldn't do."

Yeah, like I'm supposed to know what that is.

"She says she trusts you."

I fought back a laugh. "Damnedest thing I ever saw. Hard to tell which side of the street I'm working on. It almost seems like I'm making their case for them."

He had brought some coffee. I took one of the two steaming cups, said, "Bless you, my son," and tried to lighten the moment.

Ten o'clock came and went. The truck filled

my vision, blocking the interior lights like some solar eclipse where only the glow around the edges is visible. At ten-thirty I stirred restlessly. "Time they were getting here."

Almost in the same breath I saw the Preacher's station wagon turn in to the road. *Uncanny,* I thought. *Maybe it's a sign, maybe a harbinger. But of what?*

We slumped below the dashboard. They had pulled up beside the U-Haul and now got wearily out of the wagon. I had my window cracked; I heard the Preacher say, "Something's wrong." They stood in indecision; then the Preacher walked warily around the U-Haul and looked inside. "He left the keys in it."

He went to the little iron staircase and I heard him call Willie's name. "Something's not right here," he said.

For a moment I thought they might make some kind of run for it—jump in the wagon and leave it all here. But he overcame his fear and went up the steps to the ramp.

"Willie?" he called softly.

Wally was still standing at the bottom of the steps. But he climbed to the ramp as the Preacher disappeared inside.

"I'm going in," I said.

"Let's go, then."

"Same as before. You be the backup out here."

I got up the steps to the door and Todd stood in the shadows at the front of the truck. I heard the Preacher say, "Let's get the truck and get out of here."

"What about the rest of the stuff?"

"Leave it."

"God, Preach, there's five thousand books left back there."

"You want to go to jail over five thousand cheap books? Now come on, let's get these lights off and get the place locked up."

I stepped up to the doorway. They were standing just across the room, about fifteen feet away. The Preacher's eyes narrowed to slits as he saw me.

"I knew it would be you," he said. "I knew it the minute I got out of the wagon."

"You're a smart man, Preacher."

"Not smart enough, apparently."

We looked at each other. Wally stood limply and stared at nothing. The Preacher said, "You're trespassing. I could have you arrested."

"Willie invited me in."

"Willie doesn't pay the rent here. He has no authority."

"Hey, you weren't here, Willie's your authorized agent."

"We could argue that all night. Where has Willie gone?"

"I really think he's leaving town, Preacher. Last time I saw him he was walking down to the bus station."

The moment ripened. "So what happens now?" he said.

"I guess we wait for those cops you were about to call."

"I don't think so."

I could see his attitude changing by the moment. From fear he had become antagonistic. I had nothing on him and he was beginning to know it: If I had any proof of anything, where were the cops? A slimy smile now spread across his face. "You're not gonna do a thing, are you?"

"We'll see."

"Wally, get in the car and go get your brother."

"Listen, Preach—"

"Will you just shut up for once in your life and do as you're told? This guy's got nothing on us, nothing. If he tries to stop us, I'll sue his socks off. Go get Willie."

Wally came toward me. "Move, Janeway."

"Or what?"

"Or I'll move you."

"You tried that in California, fatso."

He kept coming and I backed out onto the ramp. I eased down the iron staircase and around the truck, till I could see Todd standing at the driver's door. How easy to grab the keys: easy and so illegal. But I was out of options.

"I'm not gonna tell you again, Janeway, get out of here. If we go at it again, it'll have a different ending this time."

I moved out of his way and he grinned. "That's better," he said, easing stealthily around the truck toward the station wagon. He looked like he was about to hyperventilate with fear. I could've nailed him then: he was a sucker for a punch of almost any kind, but I let him go past to the station wagon and watched him drive away. When I looked up the ramp, the Preacher was in shadow, but I sensed that a deeper change had come over him. "Go ahead, stand out there all night," he said. "You've got nothing on anybody." He backed into the warehouse and left me out in the dark.

30

We sat in the car, watching the building from a grove of trees down the road. Wally returned with Willie in half an hour. Willie looked pretty despondent. He stood outside for a moment, then trudged up the ramp and disappeared inside. We sat in the car, in plain sight for anyone who looked our way. Wally hadn't bothered to look but the Preacher knew we were still here: he had come to the door once and given us a long, hard look down the length of the rutted dirt road in the light of the distant streetlamps.

"What's he gonna do?" Todd said at one point.

"He's gonna finish loading those books and then they'll all drive away."

"You gonna stop him?"

I laughed drily. What did I know? The Preacher had visited the murder victim at least a few times during the past year. Nothing illegal in that. They had talked in the victim's home, and that, for all we knew, had been the extent of their dealings with each other. The only witness who could place them together at all was the dead man's wife, who wasn't paying attention and barely remembered the Preacher visiting.

Of course they might have met any number of times in town, in Chicago, Rio, or in Cape Town. Perhaps they were hatching the second coming of Hitler, or maybe they were old pals from way back, who were just catching up with each other.

So what did I know? Nothing. What did I think? I figured Marshall and the Preacher were involved in a book scam together. The Preacher had scouted the books and Marshall was able to get them signed. What mattered was that they be cheap books, easily found for a few bucks in junk shops and bookstores. The Preacher made up a list, a roster of authors to look for. He and his boys traveled and found the books and Marshall got them signed—by a bunch of people who were dead by then.

Pretty good work if you can do it.

These books were by or about people whose signatures were worth something on the face of it. Personalities, not just your average

Joe–schmuck writer types. At some point the Preacher or his boys would come back and pick up the signed books from Marshall's mountaintop. They'd leave him some more, take away the old ones, and peddle them. So they were involved on both ends of it and Marshall was the man in the middle, who talked to God and had John Wayne's name appear by some kind of immaculate inscription on his book. *Presto!* A $30 book becomes $400, and the signature was good enough that nobody questioned it when it was offered for sale.

That's what I thought. I should've thought it earlier.

Too much goes down on faith in the book trade, I thought.

We go by experience. If something looks good and we've got no reason to doubt it, we buy it. Then we sell it, and it passes—perhaps forever—into the vast book world.

Except for extremely valuable signatures, this is how it's always been.

Maybe that'll have to change now.

This still didn't begin to solve Laura Marshall's problem. I kept remembering something the Preacher had said to Wally in that moment just before they had seen me standing on the ramp—

You want to go to jail over five thousand cheap books? Nobody but a grafter talks like that. So the Preacher and the Keelers were grafters, I knew that much, but how did that tie in to Bobby Marshall's murder? Wally and Willie had gone up to see Marshall on the mountain that day, bringing him a new load of books. They didn't know he had been killed. *They didn't know.*

Jerry did it. I kept coming back to that thought. The real motivation had nothing to do with the Preacher or his books. As much as I wanted to make a murder case against these birds, I couldn't.

They rested on the loading dock. For a time they seemed to be sleeping.

"They're rubbing our noses in it," Todd said.

"And they're just plain tired."

They started at it again around three o'clock. I could see Wally and the Preacher working around the edges of the truck, and every so often the Preacher would stop and peer down the road. Once he came out and sat on the ramp, taking another obvious break with his legs dangling off the edge.

"He's undecided," I said. "We all are."

Todd took a deep breath. I said, "They're afraid to finish. Scared we'll follow them right on across the country."

At six o'clock Wally left on a breakfast run, returning thirty minutes later with three cold-looking McDonald's bags. I looked at Todd sadly and shrugged. "This won't get any easier. It may be a huge waste of time."

"But you don't want to leave yet."

"No, but you can. I'll get back to Denver okay on my own."

"I'm in no hurry. Just making conversation."

We sat, and Wally, on one of his smoke breaks, gave us a look that even Todd, half-asleep on the seat beside me, picked up. "They're laughing at us," he said. "Cocky bastards."

That's when I gave voice to a notion that had begun stirring around in my head. "How'd you like to sit here and watch while I go over to the house and see what I can find there."

He sat up and opened his eyes wide. "I hope you don't mean what I think you mean."

"Just a look around is all I'm thinking."

"Outside the house or inside?"

I said nothing and felt him squirm on the seat beside me. "Jesus Christ, Janeway, you're not gonna burglarize their house?"

I wished he hadn't said that. All I could do now to keep him from being an accomplice was deny it.

"I'm not burglarizing anything, Todd. Whatever I do, we'll find that out when I get there. All you've got to do is sit here and watch."

"That's all. Just sit here and watch."

"That's all. If it starts to look like they're wrapping things up here, you might drive over to the house and blow the horn. If you feel like it."

"Just blow the horn."

"Three times. Just drive past and give it three quick blasts. Then you drive on back here and park in this same place. If I don't come in ten minutes, you take off and go back to Alamosa. You turn in the car, get in your airplane, and haul ass for Denver."

A long, sober moment passed. I drew him a crude map from here to there.

"Naturally, you don't have to do any of this," I said.

I saw his backbone stiffen. "Hey, don't worry about me, I'll be there."

I got out and took a small leather tool pouch from my suitcase in the trunk. I hadn't used it in years, but it was like my gun and my credit card: *Don't leave home without it.* It slipped easily into my coat pocket. I waved cheerfully at Todd through the glass and started up the road.

31

It was a ten-minute walk to the Preacher's house. I made it in eight. My heart quickened as I walked into the long dirt road and saw the grove of trees looming ahead. This would hardly be the first time I had stepped over the line, and the risk always came with a rush. I knew how quickly and badly it could all go wrong. In the old days I worried only about covering my ass and dismissed the ethical argument too easily. Occasionally I had debated it with my lawyer friend Moses, who passionately believed that the end never justifies the means. "Once you step outside the law," Mose said, "your whole cause sinks right down to the perp's level. Even if you think you're right, the end can't justify the means." The trouble with that notion, I said to him then, is that it worries too much about rules and not enough about protecting one terrified, flesh-and-blood victim. Look, the system's never going to be perfect anyway, I said loftily, so why not bend it a little if you can put away a true badass who might otherwise slide and could still do great damage? "If you really believe that, why don't you just go out and shoot him?" Mose said. I grinned wickedly but he wasn't worried, he knew what my limits were. I had a strong unwritten code. In it was everything I knew in my heart about right and wrong. Moses knew I wouldn't abuse a suspect. I'd never lie under oath. I wouldn't trump up a case or manufacture evidence. I might open a locked door, but to purists like Moses even that went too far. He wanted the game played according to Hoyle, but Hoyle never had to work three months on a case only to see it disappear because some judge was having a bad-hair day or an essential witness had been intimidated. Hoyle had no idea how much real evil there is in the world: he didn't even know how many rotten lawyers there are, eager to earn a dirty fee by putting some baby-killer back on the street. "Listen to yourself, Cliff," Moses said. "Can you imagine what would happen if every cop went by the law of the streets? Just do whatever you want, as long as *you* think your cause is right. Jesus Christ, we'd have absolute chaos." I couldn't speak for other cops: all I could do was counter chaos and Christ with my own logic, earned in the heat of battle. Rules can't cover every situation, I said: sooner or later some decent soul gets the shaft. There are times when the *only* way to get a very bad guy is to play by his rules.

The rush came stronger and faster than I remembered it. This situation was different from anything I had done in the old days. I wasn't just a wild-hair cop, putting nobody but myself at risk. Today I represented Laura Marshall, and what I did might have serious consequences for her case. I probably wouldn't be able to use anything I found except for my own information, but sometimes that's enough. A fact discovered illegitimately can lead to a bigger fact, which might suggest a more legitimate path to its so-called discovery. What's the bigger risk, ignorance or jimmying a door? This was what I told myself as I walked up through the trees. In another few hours, whatever was in that house would be gone, maybe forever: maybe burned, maybe shredded, maybe trashed. The Preacher would be gone, the Keeler boys, gone. For all their sudden nonchalance, they were about to disappear, and they might be hell to find again.

I knew how it was to justify an act. But I had

a weird feeling this time. I had the creeps but I pushed ahead anyway.

Slowly the garage emerged through the trees, then the house. The place looked as bleak and uninhabited as it would soon be. I took a pair of rubber gloves from my inside coat pocket, ripped open the package, and stuffed the wrapper back in the same pocket. Stepped up to the door. Knocked loudly and stood back.

Nothing.

I looked around at the trees. Peered down the road as far as I could see. Took out my picks and in less than a minute I was inside.

I closed the door. Locked it. Crossed the room. Opened the window, just a crack. Enough, I hoped, that I might hear a horn blow from the road.

I looked in the living room.

Back in the bedroom.

No books, just a pair of unmade beds and a TV set. This would be where the Keeler boys slept.

On the other side, the Preacher's room. No books here either.

I eased into the room. The Preacher's bed, also unmade. But less disorder here.

A bathroom, off to my right. The door open, with sunlight shining in through a window, giving the bedroom a dusty kind of haze: I could see dust swimming in the air, as if something had just disturbed it.

I looked into the bathroom, which was musty and basic. Washbasin, toilet, shower stall in the corner. Dark over there . . . dingy . . . the shower curtain scummy, not even a hint of what I assumed was its former opaqueness.

Mold everywhere. These boys were slobs.

Across the bedroom, a filing cabinet. Locked. A wooden cabinet with a tough old-style lock.

It took a while but I got it open.

Files.

Dozens of folders in each drawer. I would never have time to go through it all.

Sift . . . skim . . . separate the wheat from the chaff.

Each of the files was labeled with a small, circular tab.

Names of people I didn't know.

Names of companies. Subjects . . .

Publicity . . .

Sermon topics . . .

Clippings . . .

World catastrophe . . .

Day of Reckoning . . .

More of the same in the second drawer.

Miracles . . .

Events . . .

Biblical prophesy . . .

And on and on.

The third drawer looked more promising. A dozen fat files.

Books . . .

Keeler . . .

Marshall . . .

Personal . . .

I began there, in his personal file. Touched its top pages almost timidly, then leafed quickly through it, and out of the mass of paper the real man emerged.

His name wasn't Kevin Simms, for starters. He was Earl Chaplin of Jonesboro, Arkansas, thirty-six years old last November.

And he wasn't a preacher, except in the most unsavory sense. He had a certificate from some biblical diploma mill and apparently aspired to do his work on television, where he could fleece a flock more effectively and rake in money with both hands. He was the kind of preacher who makes real ministers cringe.

He had an address in Oklahoma, where he intended to establish the roots of his so-called ministry. I took out my notebook and wrote it down.

There was something else about Earl Chaplin. He was a racist.

I leafed through papers from the John Birch Society and the Ku Klux Klan. He had been a kleagle in Alabama, but had resigned five years ago. I could guess why, and it had nothing to do with any sudden change of heart. The kind of ministry he envisioned didn't thrive on a pulpit of open racism, but he still got letters from Klansmen around the country, with references to mud people, sheenys, and right-handed Jesus-lovers.

God was alive, he loved money, and he was all-white. I had only been in the Preacher's house a few minutes and I had already learned these valuable lessons.

He was a compulsive file-keeper. He kept everything, including his grade-school report cards. He had been a mediocre student, a misfit. Notes from a fourth-grade teacher to a parent or guardian: *Earl needs to apply himself. He can do much better.*

Why would he keep this kind of stuff? The only answer is no answer at all. There's no accounting for people and what they do.

Quickly now I took down everything I could get about him: all his vitals, everywhere he'd been, everywhere he'd lived, every church where he had held a membership. I had his address in Alabama, his car registration, affiliations, blood type. I had his army deferment. They don't take giants.

From the Keeler file I took down an address in Oklahoma. The brothers had been nickel-and-dime booksellers for years and had known Kevin Simms since his Earl Chaplin days in Arkansas.

Quickly I skimmed some of the Preacher's personal letters. He railed against Democrats and thought even Republicans were communists. What this country needs is some backbone, he wrote. We needed to invade Cuba for real, not pussyfoot around like Kennedy had done. The old John Birch line, with a few world-wide twists. Get Castro, then take care of the Middle East: Iraq, Iran, and Syria. Knock off those three mongrels, cock our guns, and dare any turban-topped gook nation to look at us crosswise.

Time to move on. I had enough stats to find him wherever he tried to hide.

I looked in the *Marshall* file and one thing was immediately clear. He had known Bobby Marshall for several years and they had had a much deeper relationship than Laura knew. There were typewritten, signed letters from 1986, referring to meetings in Denver and on the East Coast. They had gone bookhunting together in New York, sometime last year from the look of it, and the books they talked about were exactly the kind that had recently come into question. Cheap books, common, easy to find, but books that would take a sharp rise in value if signed: nothing too splashy, nothing that might get noticed. Literature if the author was reclusive, thus scarce. But mostly sports figures, film stars, personalities.

The letters were formal throughout: *Dear Mr. Marshall . . . Dear Mr. Simms.* Marshall had signed his full name, *Robert Charles Marshall,* in light blue ink, fountain pen not ballpoint, and the Preacher had typed his phony initials, *KS,* at the end of his. Marshall's letters were all originals on his letterhead; the Preacher's were carbon or Xerox copies with no signatures.

They were strictly business. A relationship powered by money.

I went through the whole file. This took far more time than I wanted it to.

At some point I looked up, gripped again by that creepy feeling I had brought into the house. Nothing specific: no noises inside or out, not even a chirping bird or a scurrying squirrel outside the window. It was the wrong season for chirping birds, but I was spooked anyway.

I walked to the window and looked down the

drive. It looked like some still-life painting. Not even a breeze to flutter the dead leaves.

I watched and I waited. I had enough now, I could button it up, lock everything back the way it had been, and get the hell out. But I couldn't pull myself away.

The thing that bothered me as I dipped back into the file was that the deal between Bobby and the Preacher had no beginning. The earliest letter just appeared, as if their acquaintance had begun in a vacuum, telling nothing of any prior contact. It spoke of a meeting they would have in Gunnison, but there was no indication that they had had others before it. The letter dealt with books as if each knew perfectly well what the other was talking about, yet there had been no foundation to indicate that this was so. One day they might have been strangers, the next day they were partners in crime. Why? Where had this begun? Whose idea had it been? None of those questions, or any of a dozen others I might ask, had even a hint of an answer.

I am bringing some books out next month, the Preacher wrote at one point.

Don't come out to the house, Bobby had written. *I will meet you in Gunnison.*

A time and a date was mentioned.

I want to keep our transactions strictly be-

tween us, Marshall wrote. And yet the Keeler boys had come driving up to the house, bold as brass, three weeks after the murder. What did that mean? Had they changed their plans by telephone? I looked at more letters but could find no evidence that they had ever spoken on the phone.

Four large book exchanges were discussed in the letters I saw. These spanned two years, and Marshall, in an early letter, insisted that no record be kept of the money that changed hands. But the Preacher had cheated: he was a compulsive record-keeper and a born-again cheat, so he had these crude notes tucked away, chicken scratches on common loose-leaf paper. He had paid Marshall $15,000, cash in a suitcase, for delivery of five hundred books. No mention was made whether this was a full or partial payment. I did the arithmetic and guessed it had been paid in full. Five hundred times two hundred was a hundred grand. The books had probably cost an average of $10— $5,000 for basic seed money—still an $80,000 profit. My best guess was that $200 each would be a very low retail average. And they'd want to keep it low retail to move 'em fast.

Suddenly I saw how I would do it if I were running this scam. I would pay Marshall as little as possible and blow the books out as cheaply as I could. If I went to a book fair with John Wayne's book signed, I'd have a reasonable chance to sell it for four bills. Price it at half that and it would fly out the door. I would want to move them fast without selling much to other dealers. No matter how good the forgeries were, there would be talk if too many turned up at once, so I wouldn't put these out at all before the gates opened. I'd wait until the unwashed public got in, then I'd slip them onto my table two or three or half a dozen at a time. Maybe I'd also have a far-flung little network of dealers I could sell to around the country, dealers who didn't do book fairs and wouldn't think twice about buying a signed book that looked real. As long as I didn't get too greedy in any one place, I'd be fine. Spread the stuff around, let it get absorbed into the vast wasteland, and if the signatures were good enough, they'd never be questioned by anyone. Once they were out there, strewn across the country like manure in a garden, who would know where they had come from? Who would ever see them again?

Many would disappear for years, till the collector died and his widow liquidated his estate. Then they would pass, again largely unnoticed, into some other collector's hands. If they had been good enough to pass muster once, why not again?

A forger is like any other con man: he counts on the greed of his customer. The buyer wants it to be real, and if it quacks like a duck and waddles like a duck and has webbed feet and a duck face, well, damn, it's probably a duck. If the price is way down near wholesale, why wouldn't he buy it? Why wouldn't the next generation of collectors buy it as well?

Provenance? Forget it, we weren't talking about Hemingways or signed Salingers here. Who asks at this level?

The more I read the more I believed that the Preacher was following my own game plan almost to the letter. Five hundred books sounds like a bunch, but I could sell these like hotcakes.

Marshall was a good forger. None of the signatures I had seen looked in any way suspicious. The Robert Frost I had bought looked real enough to fool me, until a question arose and I looked closer. Even then a specialist had to tell us for sure. It was a damned good fake.

Either Marshall himself had been that good or he'd had access to a good forger.

I stood at the file, trying to imagine who that might be.

I was still standing there when the horn blew.

32

Everything I did in the next few minutes was driven by instinct. First I lifted one of Marshall's letters, a one-pager that did nothing but confirm a meeting. I folded it carefully along the original folds and slipped it into my pocket.

Insignificant . . . small enough, I hoped, that they wouldn't miss it.

Almost in the same motion I pushed the file back into the cabinet. I slammed the drawer shut and shoved in the long steel rod that was supposed to lock it.

The lock wouldn't catch.

I shoved it again and banged it with my palm. Finally had to leave it that way.

I faced the open window. I heard a bump.

Another bump, closer now. I was out of time.

I heard the squeak of a loose board on the porch and a soft breath from the breathless room next door. Footsteps came in through the kitchen. There was a pause, then the unmistakable ratcheting noise of a shell being jacked into the chamber of a gun.

"I knew it." The Preacher's voice had a soft, steely edge that I hadn't heard from him before. "He's been in here."

Wally grunted. "Everything looks the same to me."

"How would you know?"

"I got eyes, Preacher. Maybe I'm not as dumb as you think I am."

The footsteps came closer. I flattened myself against the wall.

"I think you're just lettin' him spook you," Wally said.

"A lot you know. Every time I turn around, he's there. I can't even take a leak without running into that guy in the same stall."

"You got him on the brain is all."

"Don't tell me what I've got. Go look back in your room. I'll stand here where I can see both doors."

I heard Wally move down the short hallway. They'd be in here next. I stepped back into the bathroom and eased my way around the toilet.

The floor creaked under my foot.

"What was that?"

"Jesus, Preacher, it's just me. That guy's gonna give you a nervous breakdown."

I stepped into the shower stall and carefully, noiselessly, pulled the scummy curtain tight. A moment later I heard Wally say, "Well, he ain't back there."

"Never mind the sarcasm. You go look around outside. I'll check in my room and we can bring over the truck and load this stuff up and get out of here. The sooner we clear this town, the better I'll feel."

I heard his footsteps coming close. In the distance a door closed as Wally went out. The Preacher started across the bedroom and stopped. I heard the filing cabinet open and close.

"Wally! Get in here! He's been here! He's broken into my filing cabinet."

"Maybe you just left it that way."

"Shut up, Jesus, shut up. Just get out there and find him. I need to look through these files and see if anything's missing."

"You think he might still be out there?"

"How do I know where he is, he's like some phantom, he turns up everywhere."

"Look, Preacher—"

"Just shut up and get him."

"Yeah? What am I supposed to do if I do see him?"

The Preacher said something in a low voice. Wally said, "Yeah, right," but he clumped out anyway. I heard him a minute later, walking through the weeds outside the bathroom window. In the other room the Preacher had begun talking to himself.

"God *damn* it."

A moment later, barely audible: "Oh, that fucking bastard."

I heard the rustle of papers, a quick shuffle through the mound of files. This went on for some time, until Wally came in again.

"Anything missing?"

"Doesn't seem to be."

"There you go, then."

"There you go *what*? For God's sake, just go! Go *find* him!"

I heard him slam the cabinet drawer.

Footsteps, coming my way. Very close now . . . he was in the bathroom, a few feet away. The toilet seat banged up. The Preacher broke wind loudly as he peed.

He stood back, breathing hard. I could see his shape in the light coming in from the window. I thought he had turned and was facing the shower but couldn't be sure. I put my hand on my gun and waited. I heard him breathe. I lifted my gun to my side.

Suddenly his shadow filled the shower curtain like the image of that old-woman figure in *Psycho*. He jerked it back, we stood looking at each other with guns ready, and in that second all the worst consequences of my breaking and entering were there in my face. This was why I had been spooked, that half-formed hunch that I would not help Laura but would ruin her case. He could have shot me then and been legally justified: he had the law on his side and if I shot him, I'd be up the creek. I thought he must know that. If I thought anything in that wild, crazy instant, that would probably be it, but who can tell whether instinct in the heat of a moment is the same as thought?

He must know that. He knows it, but he's no killer.

He can't kill me. It takes a certain kind of man to do that and he's no killer.

He didn't move for what seemed like a long time. In fact it was all part of the same few seconds. The sun coming through the window broke over his shoulder and fell on my face. I felt his eyes burning out of the shadows. Neither of us spoke: there was no outrage or fear or anything else. But what I did then may have saved one or both of us. I grinned at him . . . and I winked.

I heard a little cry come up from his throat. He shook his head and closed his eyes as if he could blink me away, then he took a step back and lost his balance. He almost fell, almost lost the gun as he grabbed frantically for something to hold. The gun went off and blew a hole in the roof. He kept flailing and finally grabbed the shower curtain and it ripped halfway off its rod, then the whole rod came loose and he fell back against the sink, tangled in the scummy plastic. I heard him cry out as he struggled like a live fish in Saran Wrap. "Ah!" he yelled. "Ah! . . . Ah!" . . . and he rolled over and fell again, this time through the open doorway and flat on his back in the middle of the bedroom. He scrambled up and crawled out into the hall. I couldn't see him now but I could hear him, running through the house and out onto the porch.

I heard the car start as I went cautiously into the bedroom. His tires sent gravel flying into the air, and from the doorway I saw Wally, running along the road, yelling for him to stop.

I looked back just once. The filing cabinet was still wide open with the files in plain sight, and in that last crazy instant I was tempted to go at them again. Common sense said, *What are you, out of your mind?* I had pushed luck far past its limit, and Prudence, that cautious old whore, wanted me to get the hell gone. I hustled out the back way and across the yard, around the garage, and into the trees, on through the thick underbrush in the general direction of town. The day felt suddenly warm in the wake of my near disaster, and again I thought, *Damn, I've gotta change my ways,* even as I knew I probably wouldn't. If I had ever listened to Prudence, I wouldn't be here now, shooting my own case full of holes. I'd still be a career cop. Laura Marshall would sink or swim without my help. I wouldn't have become a bookseller or made these discoveries, wouldn't have met Erin in the first place.

I turned back up toward the warehouse. It never crossed my mind that Todd might be gone: it was the kind of day when no one does what he's supposed to and nothing quite happens according to Hoyle. I got in the car beside him and he drove us away without a word. It was clear enough what had happened here: the Preacher had come roaring up and he and Willie had taken the truck and vanished in about two minutes. I didn't need a crazy man's Baedeker to figure that out, and Todd didn't want to talk about it. We drove past the open ramp door and I glanced into the room. I could see books scattered across the floor, out onto the loading dock, and down the ramp. A few had fallen into the tall grass across the yard and their pages billowed at us in the wind. I had a sudden hollow feeling and a strong premonition that I would never see the Preacher again.

So is this where it ends? Does it just fizzle away with disappearing perps and me with no good answers?

This was the damnedest case. We had a crazy judge and a crazier deputy, at least two hundred grand of worthless books, and none of our suspects or their motives made any sense at all. I thought of Lennie and the Preacher, linked only by their arrogance and in the similar ways I had backed them down, and I wanted to laugh.

We passed Wally, trudging along and muttering under his breath. He glared at us as we sped by but I looked straight ahead as if he didn't exist. An hour later we were in the air, banking north-northeast toward Denver. It was a quiet ride, almost stilted. Todd asked me no questions and I told him no lies. He was a smart guy, Todd, and he understood that the less he knew the better. Better for himself, better for Laura Marshall's prospects, better for Erin, and most of all for me. I had nothing to say to any of them. Soon enough I'd reflect on what it all might mean, but for the moment I was happy just to be alive. Moses had been right, and one day over a deep highball I would tell him so. But I wouldn't take any pride in my sudden enlightenment or how I got that way.

BOOK III CHRISTMAS IN PARADISE

33

Erin made plans to move over to Paradise in early December and we prepared for the hearing on our motion to suppress. Now I was wary of my involvement in the case and warier yet of telling Erin why. I would have to, of course, but not now and not by telephone. She sounded unusually optimistic as November winnowed down: "Apparently Lennie never heard of the Constitution," she said. "Their investigation sucks. All their evidence is tainted." I thought of my own potentially tainted evidence, if we should ever get that preacher on the stand as an alternate suspect. "The DA has no idea how badly his witness may have screwed things up," she said. *And you, sweetheart, have no idea how I have screwed up,* I thought. In my mind, Lennie and I faced each other in a titanic battle of morons. *Gunfight at the Dipshit Corral.*

I tried to redeem myself in legitimate work. The books were in limbo in the sheriff's evidence room and I had spent three days examining them. I was certainly no handwriting expert, but I was reasonably certain that the majority and perhaps all were forgeries. Too many seemed signed with the same kind of pen, the same ballpoint ink. Erin was thinking of hiring an outside handwriting expert and was still mulling it over as December approached.

She considered the usual battalion of expert witnesses, who would testify if needed about things they hadn't seen based on textbook science and likelihoods and their own professional experience. I have never quite trusted professional witnesses: I understand the need for them in this day and age, but in the end they are hired guns lined up to discredit the same witnesses for the other side. An expert is impressive as hell until suddenly the opposite truth comes out. They are trained to know things, yet we have seen even the best of them make mistakes. I remembered the handwriting experts with impeccable credentials who got hoodwinked by that ingenious murderous forger, Mark Hofmann. The experts knew everything about paper and inks, they knew all the tricks, while Hofmann was nothing but a self-taught madman. And he fooled them.

Our witnesses would talk about everything from the condition of the house to the condition of our defendant's mind. Our psychologist, an expert on coercion and mental stress, had interviewed Laura twice and could buttress her story of why she had initially lied. He was a solid guy Erin had used before, a young dynamo who had testified in dozens of cases and presented an unshakable demeanor, she said, in court. In Denver, Erin had spent a lot of time with Jerry and his guardian ad litem, trying to communicate with the kid and figure out what he might have seen, whether he could somehow give testimony in writing and what this testimony might reveal. She had found an expert on juvenile witnesses, but at this point none of us knew what Jerry had actually seen or done, or what we might want him to testify to. He was a risky wild card at best, and Laura was still trying to insist that he be left out of it.

At the end of this parade Erin had her book expert, me. The DA had contacted his own rare-book authority, a dealer named Roger Lester, who had recently moved to Denver from New York. Lester had opened a shop downtown, on Seventeenth Street, and had taken out one of those splashy quarter-page phone-book ads, putting my own modest one-inch ad to shame. *International book searches,* it said. I didn't do that. *Expert appraisals,* it offered. I did do that, at least well enough to know that one man's expert is another man's idiot. *Highest prices paid for good books,* it blared. Yeah, well, people could say whatever they wanted in the yellow pages, and in fact Lester might be very good. I fought back my drift toward reverse snobbery and prepared to like the guy.

He would arrive in Paradise the second week in December to do his appraisal for the state. "They still don't know that our own assessment of the books has changed," I told Erin on the telephone. "They have no idea yet that any of them are forgeries, and unless he figures that out on his own, they're going to assign the values as if they're real." I sensed Erin's amusement and read between the lines. Gill was going on the old sucker's assumption that one out-of-town expert was worth ten local guys, and Lester after all was from New *York*!—Jesus, he must know *lots* of good stuff. Let him come, I thought. Let him make his appraisal and we'd see then how good he was.

All these witnesses and more, at $100 per hour and up, travel time extra. The DA would

try to show that our experts were simple merce-
naries, bought and paid for.

After that I was crushingly restless in the little
town. I had begun a search for the Preacher and
the Keeler boys, in case something turned up
suddenly that focused new attention their way. I
had called the president of the ABAA as well as
the officers of several regional booksellers
groups from Texas to Minnesota; I had described the Preacher and what kind of scam he
had tried to pull in Colorado. If everybody
called just five book friends and had them look
for new booksellers in their towns that fit the
description, maybe we'd hear something, maybe
we wouldn't. In the case of the ABAA alone, the
night had more than eight hundred eyes, and the
Preacher would be an easy man to spot.

I bird-dogged Lennie's movements the day of
the murder, but all he had done was play check-
ers with Freeman until the call came in at 3:09. I
had still not interviewed the photographer who
had taken that first-day picture of Laura being
booked. His mother had had a heart attack
somewhere in Florida and he had gone out of
town.

I left a note on his door and checked it every
day.

But there was a feeling as winter settled in that the town was deader than Bobby Marshall's moldering carcass; that whatever might have been here was long gone. Paradise was a spent force, a crime scene sucked dry. If the Preacher had been a compulsive record-keeper, Bobby had been his polar opposite. "Bobby burned everything," Laura told us. "He was secretive, I told you that, he didn't want old letters around to tell people what he had done in life." The Preacher had left no visible tracks in Paradise, I could find no one who remembered him, and this in itself was troubling. If he had passed any time here with Bobby, even if their meetings had been few and far between, someone should have seen him. People in small towns talk and they notice and remember a stranger, especially one as unusual as the Preacher. But in the days I spent talking to people, I picked up nothing.

The one line in the Preacher's files that troubled me more as time went on might in fact have been meaningless. *We'll meet downtown,* Marshall had written, but now I had to figure that this might not mean in Paradise at all, it might mean Gunnison or Denver. I drove over to Gunnison to poke around, ask about the Preacher and show pictures of Bobby Marshall. It was a futile, frustrating morning. I went on to Alamosa and Monte Vista; I checked the garages and found no evidence that the truck had been towed in or repaired. I checked the Preacher's house and found it empty with a FOR RENT sign up in the yard. I wasn't surprised, but again I knew I couldn't have stopped him. There was no criminal charge outstanding against this man, Parley said: "All we've got is your suspicion."

Erin took this news calmly, as if she had expected it. Never discussed in those critical days was what I knew and how I had come to know it. That's the trouble with burglary as an investigative tool: you can't testify without being willing to say where your facts come from, and an attorney can't put on testimony that she knows to be false. I could imagine what she might've heard from Todd, but I didn't ask that either and she didn't say. "I've got some things to tell you when you get here," I said.

We were all touching base daily by telephone. I gave her full reports on what I was doing, but it amounted to little more than wheel-spinning. Again I spoke with everyone I saw—on the streets, in the bars, in the stores—and all I picked up was what I already knew. Laura and Bobby Marshall had been rich topics of gossip for years. Occasionally they had been seen in the town, but always apart. She shopped alone and

he drank and schmoozed occasionally with locals at the High Country Tavern. After her early
stint on the town preservation committee, Laura
had kept to herself, a trait that always encour-
ages talk in a small town. Bobby had been more
outgoing, which had become their saving grace
as a couple. He bought drinks and laughed; he
told good stories. But none of his drinking acquaintances was more than that: none could remotely be elevated to the status of pal, and no
one knew any reasons why anyone would kill
Bobby.

"I've been thinking about how we'll work together if it does go to trial," Erin told Parley one
night. "I'd like you to carry the brunt of this
case. I'll be the second chair, at least as far as the
world can see."

"Uh-huh. And the reason for that would
be . . . ?"

"Obvious. My relationship with the defendant and the appearance here that I'm a carpet-
bagger. The judge knows you. And there's
a third reason. I think you're a real solid
lawyer."

"You'll still be calling the shots, I hope."

"We'll call 'em together."

On December 3, Hugh Gilstrap, the newspaper photographer, returned to town and left a

message. My hunch about him suddenly grew stronger: again I sensed a fellow who had been in a position to know something and was maybe just waiting out there to be asked. I made arrangements to see him late that morning.

34

He lived alone in a small house about five miles from town, a slate-gray man in his fifties who liked to fish and shoot pictures. We sat over a pot of the blackest coffee I ever had, straddling our chairs at the potbellied stove in his rustic front room.

"I don't actually work for the paper," he said. "I might freelance if something comes up that strikes my fancy. That's pretty rare in a quiet county like this. They pay almost nothing but it keeps my hand in, you might say."

He was putting together a collection of artsy and idyllic high-country photographs, he hoped for a book. He had moved to Paradise ten years ago after a stint at *The Denver Post*. "That was a real photographer's newspaper in those days," he said, pouring coffee. "Best in the country back then, bar none. Every day the entire back page was given over to us photogs, the whole page was nothing but pictures, with maybe one little graph of text. We always resented the hell out of every word they made us use. If a picture was good enough, it ought to explain itself. That was my philosophy as a photojournalist. It's what we all pushed for—two or three pictures and no words on that great big page."

His mother had died. "Best thing all around. She was pushing ninety and had already had a stroke, a year or so ago. But I had to stay with her, you know what I'm saying?"

"Sure I do."

"That's why I've been gone so long," he said by way of apology.

We sat and talked about mothers, the weather, the high country, and the nightmare that Florida was becoming. I didn't push him. I had a hunch and I had learned in my police career to let guys like him get at things in their own way.

"Too many people today, that's what's happening to Florida," he said. "They're getting at us here too; the goddamn Texans are already pouring in here like a bunch of crazy people."

In a hopeful tone of voice, I said, "Maybe we won't be around to see it," and he smiled and said, "Maybe, but it's happening faster than you can believe."

I knew we were getting along when he asked if I wanted some lunch. I said sure, if he'd let me buy him a beer in town sometime. "I remember you, you know," he said. "You worked a downtown homicide I covered for the *Post* years ago. I can't remember the guy's name now, some skid row nobody, but I remember you. You were damned helpful and I got a picture page out of it."

Good, I thought: another strike against the no-good-deed-goes-unpunished rule.

"A great page," he said. "Dark and moody, in one of those dingy old upper Larimer Street hotels. Just the body, sprawled out on the floor in that big empty room, wearing nothing but a pair of dungarees."

"His name was Jason," I said, remembering. "That's what he went by. Nobody knew his real name. They kept him on ice for a month and finally buried him in an unmarked potter's field grave."

"Yeah, I covered that too."

It was almost two o'clock when he said, "I take it you want to know about Lennie and what happened that day." I nodded and he said, "In case you hadn't noticed, Lennie Walsh is a nickel-plated asshole. Just imagine the most screwed-up possibility in any situation and that's what Lennie'll do. That's the short version."

The long version was more interesting. There had been nothing on the police radio that day: "There's usually nothing out here anyway, but sometimes I leave it on back in the shop . . . turn it up loud so I'll hear it if anything does happen and play soft classical music on the phonograph. I get the itch, you know, to be out there again. Late that afternoon I went out to the grocery store, just for a few minutes, but that doesn't matter, I got a radio in my car. So I just happened to be in the right place when Lennie drove by like a bat out of hell. I knew right away that something unusual had happened. Whatever it was, he didn't want it out on the radio for anybody to hear. He came by real close and I could see he had a prisoner in the backseat. A woman. I put it together pretty quick; it was Ms. Marshall."

"You knew her?"

"Oh, yeah, I worked with her on the preservation committee a few years back. We both got disgusted and quit about the same time. Who's got time for all that bullshit?"

"So your opinion of her was . . ."

"A real straight shooter. She says what she thinks and I like that."

"So what happened then?"

"I followed them on back to the jail. By the time we got there the rain was really pouring down. This was just before the season turned. Still, we don't get many rains like that, it tends to be snow. But it rained like hell for at least twenty minutes and they sat there for a while in the car. The windows were all fogged over and Lennie seemed pretty damned engrossed in whatever he was saying to her."

"No idea what that might've been?"

"That's how he is."

"That's his notion of technique," I said.

He nodded. "All these years of struttin' around and he's finally got himself a real case. Nobody even remembers when they last had a killing here. So this is a big deal."

He sipped coffee. "So I got out of my own car and draped two cameras around my neck. I don't think either one of 'em saw me. I know he didn't, 'cause when he pulled her out of the car—"

"She was cuffed then, right?"

"Yeah, he had her hands cuffed in front of her and another set of cuffs holding her tight against the door. He had to fumble around for the keys to get her loose from the door handle, and all that time both of 'em getting wet as hell in this freezing rain. I shot 'em three or four times through the lens, him groping around for the keys and her standing there looking like the world had just ended."

"But he didn't see you then . . ."

"No, he had his attention on her, and she looked to be in real bad shock. Even when he came my way, he didn't see me. He had an arm over her shoulder with a good grip on her like he was afraid she'd crumple and fall over. The wind was blowing, made him pull his hat way down and walk like this. He was surprised as hell when he walked her up to the door, looked up, and my flash went off in his face."

I savored the moment vicariously. He could tell and he laughed thinking about it.

"Then you shot more than the one they printed."

"Oh, hell, yes, shot 'em half a dozen times with each camera. I got a good one of him yanking her out of the car by her hair."

"Jesus Christ, you're kidding."

"Not so you can tell it. He was pretty damn rough with her, like he'd been frustrated questioning her."

"Did you give that one to the paper?"

"Yeah, but I knew when I did it they'd never use it. They don't want to make local law enforcement look bad . . . as if Lennie doesn't do that all by himself."

"And you've still got these pictures?"

"What kinda photog would I be if I didn't have? Lemme tell you something, Janeway, you always shoot way more than you'll ever use. Then you pick the two or three best ones and send them in. The paper will still print the weakest one every time."

"I guess management's the same all over. It doesn't matter whether you're a photographer or a cop or a junior vice president at General Motors. So what happened when your camera went off in his face?"

"Well, he got belligerent: got his ass right up on his shoulders like he always does. One thing you can say for Lennie, he finds so many ways to be consistently ignorant. So he comes at me like this . . . like he's gonna rip my camera off my neck. Just leaves his prisoner standing there in the cold rain and says, 'Gimme that goddamn thing, you son of a bitch.'"

I laughed out loud and he joined me in undisguised mirth.

"What a flaming ignorant hemorrhoid he is. So I just said, 'Touch my camera and I'll sue you and this county clear into the next century.' He blinked and stood there, musta been all of half a minute, and this whole time Ms. Marshall, who could still barely stand up, was left shivering there in the rain."

I covered my face in near helpless laughter. "Jesus, what a jackoff."

"Oh, yeah. Oh, yeah! Like the silly sumbitch never heard of freedom of the press or the rights of prisoners—he thinks that dumb badge of his gives him license to be the county's official Nazi storm trooper or something. Didn't she tell you about this?"

I shook my head.

"I shot her three or four times over Lennie's shoulder while he was standing there trying to decide what he could do about it. But that's nothing—what happens next is just ungoddamn real. He takes her in and books her. They go into the back office, but I had come on in the front. Hell, I ain't about to let a turkey turd like Lennie Walsh push me around, and this was a public building so screw him. I could see him through the glass, talking, probably reading her her rights, I thought then. She looks just stunned, like she's got no clue what's happening to her or why. Then Lennie glances up and sees me standing out in the office watching them, and it's like he don't have a clue whether to come throw me out or cut me some real wide space. Suddenly Laura sits up and says something and it hits him like a slap. He spins around and says something back at her but I can't see what it is. Whatever she said, it really knocks him for a loop. Suddenly he gets the old man down, the old jailer, and they haul her upstairs to that little holding cell off the bull pen. He comes out into the office and I say to him, 'What're you bookin' her for?' He starts to brush on past me and I repeat the question. 'What's the charge, Lennie?' I say. But all he says is, 'Get away from me. Get away if you know what's good for you.'

"Out he goes, into the lot. I'm right behind him, and as he gets into his car, I say to him, 'Are you puttin' that woman in jail in those wet clothes? Because if you do and if she catches pneumonia, I'm here to tell you, I'm a witness to how she was treated.' He slams the door and yells at the top of his lungs, 'Get away from me, goddammit!' and I've got to backpedal fast to get out of the way when he rips out of there. He heads back out of town, it looks like up to her place again. Back I go into the jail. The office is pretty well deserted by then, but I make enough of a fuss to bring old Freeman down. 'What's he holding her for?' I ask, but the old man knows nothing, or if he does, he's not telling. 'Where's the sheriff?' I ask. Well, the sheriff's gone to Gunnison of course, he's a good enough guy but he's always off in Gunnison chasing nooky, he's got some widow woman there he goes to see every chance he gets. 'Listen, Freeman,' I say. 'Ain't that woman got any warm clothes?' I can see by the old man's face what the answer is, he don't even know, so off I go, downtown to the old five-and-dime down on the main street. I get her a robe and a blanket and I beat it on back to the jailhouse.

"I've got to bully that silly Freeman to take me up to her, and all he can say all the way up the stairs and the whole time I'm talking to her is, 'Jesus, Hugh, Lennie ain't gonna like this.' So we get up there and I look at her and she still seems stunned: at first she don't seem to know who I am, she's just sitting on the cot shivering. Then she says my name, just, 'Hullo, Mr. Gilstrap,' and by God my heart goes out to her. So I hand her the robe through the bars and then the blanket and I tell her to get those wet clothes off. When I see that she comprehends what I'm saying, Freeman and I leave her alone to change. Five minutes later I go back in there and she's sittin' in her robe, wrapped in the blanket, still cold and shivering but at least not wet. So I bully some more blankets out of Freeman and we hand 'em to her through the bars. Then Freeman says, 'Dammit, Hugh, you really got to leave now.'

"'In a pig's eye,' I tell him. 'This woman is entitled to counsel and I'm gonna see that she gets it.' So I look at Laura through the bars and I say, 'What did they book you for?' Then she says, right in front of me, Freeman, God, and everybody, 'Bobby's dead. I shot Bobby.'"

He shrugged and looked dire. "I know that's not what you want to hear."

"No," I said. At least it's consistent, I thought.

I looked at Gilstrap and he had a wide grin on his face, and in that moment I knew my hunch was still alive and kicking. "So you wanna hear what happened next?" he said.

"Sure I do."

"I talked to her through the bars for a minute. 'If I were you,' I said to her, 'I wouldn't say another thing till I see a lawyer first.' She says, 'I don't have a lawyer,' and I offered to call old McNamara for her. That's how he got into the case."

"Didn't Parley ever ask you about any of this?"

"Why should he? We just talked briefly on the phone that first day. I told him Mrs. Marshall had been booked and had asked for him. I figured she'd tell him. Then I went out of town and I've been gone ever since."

A long moment passed, but I knew there was more, I knew it the way a cop sometimes knows these things, and in the few seconds before he spoke again my own common sense told me what it was. I didn't dare believe it till he sank back in his chair and spoke. "I was about to leave when she said, 'Where are my children?'"

I took in a sudden deep breath. "Oh, man."

"Yeah. 'Where are my kids?' And I had to tell her I didn't know, and she got real upset. I told her not to worry, I was sure they were okay. But even then I knew."

"Lennie left them up there."

He laughed. "That stupid bastard. He's so anxious to clear the case solo he forgets about the kids. Seals up the crime scene with them still inside it, gets all the way down here and never gives the kids a thought till she asks where they are."

"Oh, *man*," I said again.

"Yeah. Naturally I can't prove any of that last part. But what else do you think could've happened?"

"I think we'll find out. Will you testify to what you just told me?"

"The facts of it, sure. That's my civic duty."

"We'll need your pictures too. A contact sheet would be nice for now."

He thought about it for a moment and said, "It won't surprise you to know that I've already been called by the DA."

I wasn't surprised: I would have been surprised if he hadn't.

"I don't think they'll be real anxious for me to be a witness." He laughed again. "Lennie's gonna shit a screaming green worm when he finds out you talked to me."

"Yeah, he is." I looked at him and tried not to laugh. "Hugh, that's the least of what he'll shit."

35

"I don't remember any of that," Laura said.

"What exactly *do* you remember after the deputy arrived?"

She shook her head.

"It's just that your memory is so clear and specific until then," Parley said.

"Yes, it is."

"So what happened to you?"

"I don't know, I must've fainted."

"Had you ever done that before?"

"Never. God, I've never fainted in my life. I don't believe in women who faint."

"Then what—"

I put a hand on his knee. Laura had closed her eyes, as if she might faint here in the jail. But suddenly she said, "You're right, everything was crystal clear up to that point. As long as I was moving, as long as I had a purpose, I was fine. I didn't look at Bobby at all, I just did what I had to do. It was afterward, when I had called the sheriff's office, that's when I remember looking over at Bobby on the floor. What an awful sight, just . . . it was just, Jesus, horrible. He had no face. The whole back of his head . . ."

"Take your time, hon," Parley said.

"I remember I had to hold on to something to keep my balance, even sitting down. I was sitting at the table and it was like this wave of nausea and—what's the word?—dizziness, vertigo, whatever you call it, came over me. I put my head down on the table and closed my eyes. I do remember that."

"Where were the kids all this time?"

"I had sent them to their bedroom at the far side of the house. I told Jerry not to let them out, and not to come out himself, until I came back for them."

"Did they know what had happened?"

"Jerry certainly did. I tried to keep it from the little ones."

"So you laid your head down on the table. What's the next thing you remember?"

"Being in jail."

"You don't remember the deputy arriving?"

"No. I think I had left the front door unlocked and I guess he just came on in."

"You don't remember him knocking or calling out?"

"No."

"You don't remember anything about what the deputy might've said to you, or what he might've done while he was there?"

She shook her head and shrugged.

"Nothing of the ride down?"

"I remember his smoke," she said suddenly. "Oh, God, I'll never forget that. It was stifling in that car, and he smoked till I thought I was gonna throw up."

"But you didn't?"

"Didn't what?"

"Puke in his car."

She shook her head. "I don't know."

"And that's all you remember?"

She nodded yes. Then she said, "I remember a voice, I guess it was his."

"Do you remember what it said?"

"He called Jerry a . . . he called Jerry a *retard*."

"I thought he didn't see Jerry."

"I don't know. Must've been later, in the jail, when I asked where my kids were."

"You remember anything else he might've said?"

"No. Just the voice in all that smoke."

"Okay. So you were in jail, then what?"

"It was cold. I was wet and it was very cold. I thought all this must be a dream. But I remember someone giving me some blankets and a bathrobe."

"Do you remember who it was?"

"Mr. Gilstrap," she said after a moment. "He's a photographer. You remember, we were all on a committee together a few years ago."

Parley made some notes. Again with that suddenness, Laura said, "I remember . . ."

"What?"

"I don't even know if this is real."

"Tell me anyway."

"It feels like a dream. But I remember a voice saying, 'You might as well sign a confession right now, honey, it'll go easier on you if you do.'"

Again she closed her eyes. "'You might as well tell old dad all about it.' I seem to remember somebody saying that. 'C'mon, sweetie pie, write it down for daddy.'"

"But you don't remember who it was."

"I couldn't say for sure. Couldn't tell whether he was my friend or my enemy. He was a sweet-talker one minute, angry the next." She shook her head. "Does any of this matter now?"

"Yeah, it matters." Parley made some notes.

"What did the deputy finally have to say about your kids?"

"He came in later and said they were fine. Said I could see them, in fact. I had a few minutes with them right here in this room."

"You say he came in later. How much later?"

"I have no idea. But it wasn't right away. I don't know. My whole sense of time that day was shot."

"When you saw the kids, did you ask them where they'd been?"

"No. I was too anxious to calm them down for anything like that. I knew I must look a fright and I wanted them to know I was okay."

He looked at me. "Janeway?"

I leaned over toward Laura. "Do you know anything about Jerry's birth parents?"

"No, nothing. Why is that important now?"

"I promised the caseworker I'd ask. No idea who they were?"

"No."

"Do you have the name of the adoption agency?"

"Somewhere, I think. I haven't looked at any of those records in years."

"What about the books? Did you ever hear any talk that maybe they weren't real?"

She looked puzzled at that and I said, "Like maybe the signatures were fakes?"

"No, I would have told you that. I didn't even know they were signed." She watched Parley gather his notes. "Does this mean they're worthless?"

"It sure would knock 'em for a loop," I said. "Without those signatures most of them are just used books."

"Let's not worry about that yet," Parley said. "Right now you just worry about remembering what happened. If you think of anything else, you call me pronto. Don't tell anybody else what we were talking about. Nobody, Laura. Not a word."

Out in the parking lot, he said, "It really doesn't matter about the books anymore, does it? If we get our motion to suppress, they won't have a case. A lot depends on the only other witnesses in that house that day—the kids—and what, if anything, we can get from 'em."

We called Erin that night. She was remarkably calm about the developments of the day. The news was good but we hadn't won yet. On her end her juvenile expert had interviewed the children several times. "It looks more and more like the little ones didn't see anything. And so far we've had no luck with Jerry, who may have seen everything."

I could almost hear her thinking. "Cliff," she said. "You were going to call that social worker back about Jerry."

"I had good vibes from her. Like she had something to tell me but couldn't."

"So call her. If she'll see you, come on back to Denver."

36

I met Rosemary Brenner for the second time the next afternoon, at the main office of Denver Social Services. She was eating lunch at her desk: an apple and a banana.

"How's Jerry doing?" I said.

"Surprisingly well. Have you found out anything for me?"

"Laura doesn't know anything about his parents. What's happening on your end?"

"Quite a bit, actually. We've had a number of meetings since I saw you, and your name has come up several times. It may surprise you to hear this, you've tried so hard to put people off, but it seems you do still have one or two advocates in this town. I've even heard it mentioned in passing that you've got a certain code of honor."

"Don't let that get around. It almost sounds like a certain strain of clap."

She smiled and dropped her banana peel into the trash can. "I'm only saying I like what I've seen of you and I do tend to trust you. But you must know we have rules and procedures, and people who forget that soon find themselves standing in unemployment lines. I'm not quite ready to retire from here in disgrace."

"I hear you."

"I would like nothing better than to have this charge against Mrs. Marshall resolved, however it goes. But if you want me to help you, I need to know that this kid's life won't be turned into some circus."

"At the same time—"

"He's a possible witness in your homicide case. I know."

"Some of this is going to be out of our control, Rosemary. We'll all do the best we can do, but surely it's in that kid's best interest for us to clear this case."

"I think we'd all agree with that. And there have been new developments. I was told I could show some of them to you, if you ask." She smiled foxily. "Are you asking?"

"Sure."

"We have an unusual situation here, something I've never encountered in all the years I've been doing this. On the one hand we have the interests of justice; on the other, the welfare of this child. That in itself isn't an unheard-of conflict, it's the way the pieces of it fit together this time that's unusual. The interests of the child may be vitally linked to the outcome of your case, but we don't yet know how, or what that outcome ought to be, at this point in time."

"We think she's innocent."

"I'm sure you do. If you're right, winning your case becomes urgent for both sides. Ideally, then, we'd like both sides to be served. But the child's interests have to be my top priority."

"I understand that."

"Let's make sure you do before we go any further. If I can get your word of honor that you'll try not to make a spectacle of this, I'll show you something that may enlighten you. At this point it's my call."

I felt the warning bells in my head. "I don't know what you're asking me to do."

She liked that: I hadn't just leaped at her with a rash promise, and I could see the approval on her face. She said, "Don't run right out and leak this to the press. It's all going to come out anyway, we know that. But I'm hoping maybe you can help us understand it better before that happens."

"I won't give anything to the press. But what could I possibly—"

"Think about it a minute. We're still discovering things. It changes almost daily, sometimes by the hour."

A moment passed. She said, "I'd do this if I were you."

"Then I will."

She leaned slightly over her desk and said, "Are you familiar with the term *savant*?"

"You mean like in idiot savant?"

She made a face. "That's an old expression, Janeway, well out of favor today. I would have hoped you'd know better."

"Oh, Rosemary, I have *deep* pockets of ignorance. But I'm always open to enlightenment."

She smiled. "Today we call them autistic savants."

"Is that what Jerry is?"

I saw her hand tremble. "He may be far more than that."

She leaned over the desk and said, "Did you see the movie *Rain Man*?"

"Sure. Great film."

"Remember how the Dustin Hoffman character was?"

I remembered Hoffman talking incessantly, often to himself: how he could cite endless sports statistics and instantly do unbelievable square roots in his head, but could barely function in what we think of as a normal world. "That's one example of an autistic savant," she said. "There aren't many of them in the world, and within that small group there are smaller groups, some so brilliant in their one field that they leave what we think of as normal minds in the dust. A mathematical savant may need help tying his shoelaces, but he can tell you in a second what day Christmas fell on in the year 1432. A musical savant can hear a classical piece one time and play it perfectly. Some of them have hundreds of scores in their heads and can do them flawlessly even years later. Just mention a name and out it comes."

She opened her desk and took out what looked like a small, detailed pencil sketch. "Recognize that?"

"Sure. It's the room where Marshall was killed." I held it up to the light. "This isn't a police sketch."

"No," she said, and again I felt the chills, the hair rising on my neck.

She took out another. "Ever seen that?"

"It's Marshall's study. That's his desk in the foreground, and behind the desk is the cabinet for his guns. There's the shotgun, leaning against the wall."

"How about this?"

"The library across the hall from the room where the murder happened. Look at those *books*, the definitions are incredible. You can actually read some of the spines. If you know the books, you can picture the jackets from the little piece that's visible here."

"Take a closer look."

She handed me a large magnifying glass and I went straight to the books. What the glass revealed was nothing less than a photograph would show. This was better than a photo: it had detail beyond clarity, far past the ability of a camera except in perfect, extraordinary light with the best equipment and a master photographer. In the sketch the drapes were open: you couldn't see them, but a stream of sunlight poured in, hitting the floor in front of the bookcases and lighting up the corners of the room. My eyes went back to the books. The titles had been filled in with the steadiest hand, his pencils razor-sharp, his eye missing nothing even in recall. I saw a title, *America, Why I Love Her.* "That's the John Wayne book," I said, and Rosemary leaned over to look. "Look at this," I said, "he's even got a hint of the publisher's name at the bottom." I touched it with my finger, careful not to smudge the delicate pencil markings as I pointed out the name, Simon &

Schuster, at the bottom of the spine. "We wondered about that," Rosemary said, "whether he got that kind of detail correct. But where would it have come from except from what he actually saw? I wouldn't imagine he has any idea what a Simon & Schuster is."

"I held this book in my hands," I said. "It's now in the sheriff's evidence room. This copy has a chip on the bottom edge of the jacket and he's even put that in." I went on down the bookshelf and it was almost as if I had stepped back into that house.

"He put in pieces of publishers' names on many of them," Rosemary said. "Harper & Row, Random House, Doubleday, on and on."

"Yeah," I said, "and all of them are right."

I ventured an opinion. "It must've taken him days just to do this one."

"Most of these sketches took less than an hour. The library took half a day."

I didn't know what to say, an extremely rare occurrence.

She rustled through some papers. "Here's one that's different."

Everything about it was shadowy, misty as in a dream: the room, the furniture, and even the brightly sunlit porch were indistinct. I could see a figure outside on the porch, but nothing, not even the sex of the subject, could be told. He, she, or it stood about five feet from the window, apparently trying to look in, but I couldn't be sure of that, either.

Rosemary said, "What do you make of that?"

"I don't know."

"No idea who that might be?"

"No."

"He was almost in a trancelike state when he made this. Later, when we tried to talk to him about it, he got upset."

"Upset how?"

"Cringed on the floor. I don't have to tell you, we didn't show that to him again."

A moment later she said, "I was wondering if this could be his way of getting at whatever happened."

"I don't know. If you're thinking it's a literal interpretation, a few things don't work. The sunlight, for example. It rained the day Marshall was killed."

She handed me another sheet: the same scene only darker. This time the porch was so shrouded that the figure was all but invisible, less than a shadow, present only by suggestion in the slightest human-sized darkening of the background. I stared at the two pictures. "What are the little pencil numbers at the top corner?"

"That's ours. That's how we kept track of what order they came out."

"He did it in sunlight first."

"Yes, in about twenty minutes. I wasn't there, but I hear he was totally absorbed. Finished it, then ripped it off the pad and threw it down on the floor and started the dark one immediately."

"You didn't show him the dark one?"

"God no, not after the first reaction we had."

"How'd you learn he could do this?"

"He was sitting quietly in the counselor's office and there was a magazine on the table. On the back cover was one of those *Draw Me* ads for an art school correspondence class. Suddenly he reached over and took up a yellow pad and drew the model. Then he put in the headline, in almost perfect block type, then he started on the text. We got him a sketchpad and some pencils, then an easel, then a *lot* of pencils and somebody to keep them sharp. He's been doing it nonstop ever since."

"Have you talked to the DA about this?"

"Not yet. We'll have to, of course."

"Of course," I said.

"A young woman from the district attorney's office made a few attempts to talk to him. We haven't seen much of her lately."

I looked at number 54 in the upper corner. "I take it you've got more of these."

"Dozens."

"Could I see them?"

"They aren't all here, but sure, at some point. Here's another one." She opened her drawer and handed me another sheet, numbered 85.

"That would be the twins," I said. "Little Bob and Susan. Damn, their faces are so real."

"Notice the loving looks he was able to put on them. You can almost see the affection he has for them. And I understand *that's* highly unusual. You don't often get feelings like this . . . usually it's just what he saw."

The twins were sitting in a room that I hadn't seen: probably their bedroom at the house. Behind them were two bunk-style beds, and on the wall a picture, a mountain scene that Jerry had also rendered in detail, a picture within a picture. Beside it was a calendar with its days marked off and a clock showing that it was one o'clock in the afternoon. Light could be seen shining in from some window off to the left.

"He did another one like that," she said.

I stared at the second picture. "It's not exactly alike."

"The clock's different. It seems to be later the

same afternoon. The twins are gone and the light's not as good."

"And the picture's been moved on the wall."

"A little, yes. A foot or so to the right. Maybe he's correcting something. That might be the whole reason for the second picture. He drew some of you."

"Really?"

"Several, actually. In all of them you're in a wooded place at night. Maybe you'll see those at some point. For now—"

"I know where they came from and I know what I look like."

"He seems to like you. Like the twins."

"I helped him out of a little problem he was having."

I knew she wouldn't be satisfied with that, so I told her what had happened in the woods that night. I told her about my subsequent run-in with the judge and my night in the Paradise hoosegow, and this was followed by a moment of near total silence. Slowly the sounds of life returned: someone talking in the hall, the ticking of the clock on her wall. We made eye contact again and something had changed between us.

"Did Jerry put words to any of these?"

"He can't write," she said. "Here, I've got a

couple more to show you. Do you recognize this man? He looks like a cop."

"Lennie Walsh. He was the arresting officer. A real bastard."

"Only part of the scene is shown . . . just that slash down the middle of the page. What do you make of that?"

Lennie stood in the death room, radiating anger. He had a notepad in his hand and his mouth was open.

"He looks like he's screaming at somebody," she said.

"Laura, no doubt."

"Is he allowed to talk to her like this?"

"Depends, I guess. He shouldn't, if he is."

"He looks like an ugly man. I don't mean necessarily in the physical sense."

"I know how you mean it, and you're right." I looked up at her. "This guy's a caveman, Rosemary. He shouldn't be allowed to talk to anybody."

"I wonder why there's only that little slice of picture. Just on this one."

"The kid was probably seeing them through a crack in the door. Didn't want them to see him." I looked up at her and smiled. "But I think you knew that."

"I imagine I could've figured it out."

I went through all the pictures slowly, trying to burn them into my mind. A full minute later she said, in that same too obvious voice, "So I take it this is important."

"Oh, please." I held my hand over my heart.

A big piece of another minute passed. "Please," I said again.

"I've got one more to show you."

She had saved the best for last. When she showed it to me, I felt light-headed, almost faint at the implications. Again we were in the murder room. In the seconds after I had looked at it, I looked again and saw all the little things that didn't matter. I could see on through the front porch to the fierce rain falling on the meadow. I could see, half-lost in that mist, the fence where Laura had been standing when she heard the shot. I could see a hint of the hill across the way, where I had staked out the place and watched the Keeler boys drive up to the front door. None of this mattered as I looked again at what the picture really showed: the broken police tape that Lennie, that incomparable moron, had used to seal the room as a crime scene. I could only read part of it clearly but I knew what it said, I knew the words POLICE LINE DO NOT CROSS by heart: I could see that image almost any night in my dreams. This one had been partly crushed and tossed over the table.

There was blood on the wall, bloody little handprints, fingerprints on the tape, smears everywhere. None of this had been mentioned in the evidence.

Be still my raging heart. First the stupid bastard had left the kids inside, then he had gone back up there and washed off the walls in an effort to hide what the kids had done. He had committed a crime and a second fatal error trying to cover up the first.

Rosemary smiled sadly. "Just be careful, Janeway. Let's do this right."

37

Erin and I finally talked about the case after supper. She listened in stony silence as I told her about my adventure with the Preacher, my burglary of his house, and what I had found there. Gradually her eyes narrowed to slits, she suffered through the account to the sorry end of it, and then, in a masterpiece of brevity, said, "Okay, let's move on." This was fine with me: she knew now and if she didn't want to beat it to death with too much talk, I figured there was a reason for that. She was much more upbeat about my conversation with Rosemary Brenner. The savant discovery was exciting but it had a troubling edge to it. Why had Laura failed to tell us about this? Could she possibly not have known? "I think it's reasonable that she never associated it with Bobby's murder," I said. "She didn't know Jerry's abilities would suddenly become important." Still, Erin said, now we had to ask her these things. The hearing on our motion to suppress was two days away. "I'm going over tomorrow anyway, so I can do that." She had to tie up some loose ends here in the morning and she should be in Paradise sometime after noon. "I think I'm going on ahead," I said. "I want to look at the house again."

If she suspected anything, she didn't ask. I hadn't told her about the picture in the kids' room. If the picture had in fact been moved, there was probably a reason, and I didn't want to make that discovery openly on my own. I didn't want it to come from me at all. We went to bed at eleven; I got three hours of restless sleep and was on the road in the dark early morning. I turned in to Paradise just as the sun was breaking over the mountains. Parley was already up when I arrived at his house. "Just in time for some flapjacks and eggs."

We sat at his table, eating a breakfast guaranteed to shorten any life span.

"I take it Erin called you," I said.

He nodded and offered more pancakes, which I waved off with an appreciative gesture. "So where are we in the scheme of things?" he said. "Do I want to ask you what really happened between you and that preacher man?"

"Probably not." A strained moment passed. "I think I should stay out of the court's way as much as possible from here on out. Not be an obvious part of the team, so to speak. Just between you and me, though, I'd sure like to go back up to the house before the world finds out about Jerry."

"That's no problem. The DA turned the house back over to us. I've got the keys."

He noticed my surprise. "Mainly what they cared about was getting those books out. The house had already been gone over, hadn't it?"

"That's what I understand," I said. "Miss Bailey did say they were treating it as a whole new crime scene."

"I guess Gill overruled her on that. Probably figured there wasn't much to be gained by doing it all over again, not after Lennie'd been plowing ass-first through it. And they didn't know what we know. If you still want to go up, leave those dishes and let's go do it."

Twenty minutes later we came up the rise to the meadow. It looked different, peaceful now in the warm sunlight. We stood on the porch for a moment, gazing over the distant mountain range; then Parley unlocked the door and the dark interior pulled us in where death was still part of the air. I stared down at the black bloodstain.

"What is it you're lookin' for?"

"Just looking. Can I wander a bit?"

"Sure. Long as you don't mind me wandering with you."

I wandered into the library, where long rows of empty shelves now faced the two doors. "Not much to see here anymore," Parley said.

I went on back into a dark hall. I could feel his scrutiny and hear his footsteps just a couple of feet behind my own. At the end of the hallway was a closed door. I got down on my knees and looked at the doorknob.

"Is it possible to have some light in here?"

He turned on a dim hall light. "That's not much, I'm afraid."

"I think there's something here. You got a flashlight in the car?"

"In the glove compartment."

"I'll come with," I said before he could ask.

We retrieved the light together; then, again in the hallway, I lay on my back and lit up the bottom of the doorknob.

"There is something here," I said. "It's black now, but I think it's old blood."

He lay down on the floor beside me.

"Don't touch it, Parley. I think it may be a fingerprint."

"Damned small one if it is." He shook his old head.

"Can I open this door? I'll be careful."

The door opened into the kids' room. I rolled to my feet and gave Parley a hand, and he got up with a grunt. The room looked exactly as Jerry had pictured it: the calendar frozen on that day, the clock still going, the picture there on the wall where, perhaps, someone had moved it. I walked through the room looking at the walls. I looked out the window.

"You see something out there?"

"I don't know, I thought I did."

He went to the window and just that quickly I touched the edge of the picture and tilted it slightly off-center.

"Nothing out there. You sure get jumpy when you come up here, Janeway. Must be something about the thin air."

I laughed politely and waited for him to notice the picture, even though I had no way of knowing what, if anything, might be there. Parley looked up.

He sees it, I thought. But he turned away and said, "You finished in here?"

"I don't know yet. Let's look some more."

Goddammit, Parley, look at the friggin' picture!

He stared out the window, his mind obviously in neutral. To him the case was in good shape and I was spinning my wheels. Annoyed, I said, "It takes you a while to wake up in the morning, doesn't it?"

He looked at me curiously. "Why, am I missing something?"

"Hell, how would we know, you're in such a helluva hurry to get out of here."

"There can't be much left to it after that mob's been through here, can it?"

"I wouldn't say that. Didn't we just find a print on the door?"

"That could be an old Popsicle smear for all you know. What do you want to do, toss the place again?"

"As a matter of fact, yeah. I sure would like to give it more than just a casual once-over. Look, we know Lennie locked the kids in the house. We've already found what may be blood or Popsicle residue on the doorknob. Whatever it is, you should be excited about it, not walking around in some stupefied state."

A flash of anger spread across his face, replaced by embarrassment. "Okay, so it takes me a while to get goin' in the morning. What do you want me to do?"

"You look on one side of the room, I'll look on the other."

"What'm I looking for, more blood?"

"Hell, anything. Look under the bunk beds with the flashlight. Let's be careful, so we don't contaminate it any more than it already has been."

"Hey, I'm awake now, you don't need to belabor the obvious. What're you gonna be doing while I'm crawling around over here?"

"I'll look in the closet and around the dressers."

I tried to forget him then: just let him be, I thought; let him find it in his own way and in his own time. But as time passed I found my patience wearing thin. *What the hell are you doing over there?* I wanted to shout. *Does something have to rise up and bite you between the legs before you—*

Then he said, "Cliff," and I knew by his tone that whatever was there, he had found it. I leaned out of the closet. He had the picture off the wall and was holding it by its corners. On the wall was a full black palm print with four partial fingers.

38

By midafternoon the house was again crowded with people. Erin and Parley had agreed that the DA would have to be informed, *noticed-in* in legal jargon, and people began arriving just after one o'clock. For the third time there was a full-court press by the prosecution with cameras and lights and people coming in and out. Erin came in at two. Ann Bailey arrived a moment later, looking furious. She and Erin nodded crisply to each other. Meanwhile we began building our record of what we had found there. "We'll need our own photographer," Parley said, but the only one in town was Hugh Gilstrap, who would also be our witness. "I don't think that'll hurt his credibility," Erin said. "Let's hire him if he'll come up, deal with him like any other professional, and keep our distance otherwise." Then she stood back and watched the circus, saying nothing in that first hour while the lab man shot his photos of the wall.

Gilstrap arrived and duplicated the scene for us, and in the late afternoon we conferred with Miss Bailey.

"We'll want to send this palm-print over to the CBI in Montrose," she said.

"We'd have no objection to that," Erin said.

"It does mean we'll have to cut this piece of wall out. I don't think we could lift that print off without destroying it."

"Ann, it's pretty clear that one of the kids made that mark," Parley said.

"Yeah, well, let's find out for sure this time."

"You'll at least agree that it's not Laura's print."

"I'm not agreeing to anything at this point."

"Ann," Parley said patiently. "You've gotta know—"

"What, that our deputy screwed up? Even if that's so, that's all we know at the moment. You want me to what, dismiss this case on the basis of that?"

"This case is bullshit."

"Is it? Do I have to remind you that she confessed? She confessed, Mr. McNamara. The first words out of her mouth to your own witness were 'I shot Bobby.' She said it at least twice after that, and we have witnesses."

"This isn't getting us anywhere," Erin said. "We'll see what happens at the hearing tomorrow."

"We'll see," Miss Bailey said. She sounded confident but Erin met her eyes and put on that enigmatic face and Miss Bailey looked away. Was that my imagination or was it the real crack in the wall of ice she showed to the world? She had to be seriously worried about Lennie at this point. What she might not know was how worried she ought to be and why. She spoke to Parley. "Can we agree on taking out that piece of wall? Or does that have to go through an act of God like everything else in this case?"

Erin nodded and Parley said, "The defendant gives you her blessing to desecrate her house."

"Then let's get it done. I *had* a dinner date tonight."

A technician came in with a drill and a small saw. "Take that whole square, everything the picture was hiding," Miss Bailey said, and five minutes later the piece of wall was free and bagged. "I want the doorknob too," Miss Bailey said, and it was carefully removed from the door and bagged.

Gilstrap shot pictures of the whole process.

Miss Bailey said, "We're going to seal the house again, I'll need your keys, please," and Parley turned them over.

They wrapped up their work in the early evening. Miss Bailey stayed until the end and Erin stood off to the side and watched her. Again the house was locked and sealed with crime tape and we all moved outside to the cars.

"Tomorrow, then," Miss Bailey said.

Erin nodded. "See you then."

That night we had a two-hour meeting with our defendant in the jail. Laura's defense, simple and old as time, would be that she hadn't done it. If she had confessed to anyone, she had done it under stress, out of fear for her eldest son.

This was it, then: the murder of Robert Charles Marshall had been the work of some unknown party, for reasons unknown and perhaps ever unknowable. This fit somewhat with the shadowy figure Bobby had become, and the burden of proving otherwise would belong to the state. In death no one could pin him down: there were no files in his cabinet, no letters from the Preacher or anyone else. "He burned a lot of stuff," Laura said. "He was always burning stuff in the yard. As he got older, he seemed to be slipping deeper into paranoia. He had become obsessed with his privacy."

Erin took lengthy notes. She couldn't imagine Bobby that way, she said: he had always been so outgoing when they were young. "He was like a different person then," Laura agreed. "You can't imagine how he'd changed. I lived with him for years, and there were times at the end when I barely knew him."

She had thought seriously of divorce, especially in the last three years. "But then I considered the children and I couldn't do it. The little ones loved Bobby."

"He was good to his own children?" Erin asked.

"Oh, yeah. He loved them and they loved him. I have no doubt of that. And he tried with Jerry too, I'm not saying he didn't try. In his own way Bobby was a good man and he sure didn't deserve what happened to him."

"How did he try? What did he do?"

"Oh, he'd take Jerry for walks . . . not real often, but sometimes they'd walk down the road and Bobby would try to talk to him. Then when they came back, he'd take Jerry into his room and they'd . . ."

"What? What did they do?"

"Talk. I don't know, they'd be in there for maybe an hour. I couldn't make out his words but I could hear Bobby talking through the door."

"Not angry, though."

"No, I'd have gone in and stopped that. Bobby's voice was always very soft."

"Did he sound like he might be trying to teach Jerry something?"

She almost laughed at that. "God, no! Bobby was no teacher, that's for sure."

"I don't mean teach like in schooling."

"Then I guess I don't understand you."

"Persuasion," Erin said. "Like maybe he was trying to persuade Jerry to do something."

"If he was, he never got anywhere. Jerry just didn't like Bobby, I told you that."

Laura watched Erin writing in the long silence that followed.

"Did you ever suspect that Bobby had any improper relations with Jerry?"

Laura's eyes opened wide. "My God, what are you suggesting?"

"I'm just asking questions. What are you thinking?"

"But you can't mean anything like that. Jesus, Erin, you knew Bobby, you know he'd never do anything like that to a child."

"As it turned out, I didn't know Bobby at all, did I?"

Laura stared at the wall. "I've told you before, you've got a right to be angry with both of us. But you can't believe that."

"Look," Erin said, "let me put it in very straight terms, okay? Did Bobby ever abuse Jerry, any of your kids, sexually?"

"That's offensive."

"That's what I get paid for," Erin said. She smiled slightly, perhaps at the fact that she wasn't getting paid yet for anything. "I get paid to ask offensive questions."

Laura took a long time to answer; too long, I thought. At last she gave us a slight head-shake.

"Did Bobby ever molest Jerry?" Erin asked.

"Of course not."

"Pardon me for lingering on this, but you don't deny it with any real conviction."

"What do you want me to do, scream?"

"Damn it, I want you to tell the truth."

"No," Laura said. "No, no, no."

"No what? No, he didn't, or no, you won't tell me the truth?"

"He didn't. Of course he didn't." But then, into the silence, Laura said, "What are you going to do? What are you thinking?"

"I'm asking you a question. Which you are doing your best to avoid."

"What if I said . . ."

Erin arched her eyebrow.

"I never actually saw anything, but once or twice I wondered. That's all." Her face was flushed as she stared at Erin. "That's all! There's nothing else to say! It's just something you think in an odd moment. Surely this won't come out."

"Not tomorrow. But if it goes to trial, we'll have to see what's there."

"It would give me a great motive for shooting Bobby."

Erin said nothing, but I saw awareness light up Laura's face. It was also a sudden new motive for Jerry.

"You have any questions, Cliff?" Erin said.

"Yeah, I do. I want to ask a few more things about Jerry."

"Oh, Christ, will this never end?"

"It's just that he seems to have an amazing talent."

The silence stretched and became awkward.

"Laura?"

"What do you want me to say?"

I shrugged. "Just a reaction would be a start. Some kind of acknowledgment that we're on the same page."

"He's an artist," Laura said at last. "Jerry is a great natural artist."

Clearly annoyed now, Erin said, "You never told us about that before."

"You never asked me. Is it important?"

Parley gave a little laugh and looked away.

"Is this important?" Laura asked again. "What's it got to do with what happened?"

"You've *got* to stop making those judgments," Parley said. "If I can only do one thing on this earth, I would like to get you to stop playing lawyer. Do you think you could possibly do that?"

"What don't you understand about what I did? I didn't want him to be involved in any of this, is that so hard to understand? I didn't want everybody probing him like he's some kind of guinea pig, like you're doing right now . . . upsetting him with all this terrible stuff. Anyway, how is it important?"

"Jerry's been drawing almost nonstop all week," I said. "Scenes of the crime. Pictures of that day—"

"Jesus Christ, this is *exactly* what I was afraid of! It's not enough that he had to go through it, now you're all going to drive him crazy worrying about it."

"Nobody's asked him to draw anything.

From what I understand it was a spontaneous thing."

"What difference does it make how it started? Now they've got him started, it doesn't matter how, and they're going to keep after him till they break him down. Jesus, hasn't he had enough trouble in his life?"

She looked at Erin. "I knew I shouldn't have tried to fight this, I knew Jerry would be dragged into it, and now here he is; he should be drawing pictures of the mountains and the streams, and instead they've got him reliving all this terrible stuff."

The room went suddenly quiet. Then Erin said in her hard voice, "Get used to it. Jerry's a material witness in a murder case. The questions are just getting started."

Laura shook her head. "I should never have agreed to this."

"Agreed to what?"

"Any of this. You knew from the start I didn't want to do this."

"Then tell me, please, what *do* you want to do?"

"What I should've done all along."

"You'll have to say it."

They looked at each other.

"Well?"

"I've got to change what I . . ."

Erin gave a dry little laugh. "Change what? Your plea?"

"If I have to, yes."

"Then you can do it without me." Erin began gathering her papers.

Laura, with a sudden look of alarm, said, "Where are you going?"

"Where do you think I'm going? I do have one or two other things to do in my life."

"You're angry. I could always tell when you were angry. Still can."

"It doesn't matter what I am. I told you before, I haven't got time for this."

"Wait a minute—"

"What for? So I can watch you throw yourself to the wolves? I don't think so."

Laura looked at Parley. "Can she do this? Can she just walk out on me?"

"I can do whatever I want," Erin said. "I'm not your attorney of record. He is."

"Wait a minute. Please, Erin, *please*! You've got to understand something."

"No, *you* understand. What is your case? Did you kill your husband or not?"

They looked at each other.

"Did you?"

Laura shook her head.

"Then that's how you'll plead. Not guilty. Not maybe not guilty with footnotes for unanticipated contingencies. You will not even think of offering yourself as a sacrifice for Jerry or anybody else. No extenuating circumstances, no waffling. You are not guilty. Once and for all, can we at least be clear on that?"

"All right, yes . . . yes, okay . . . okay."

"Get that apology out of your voice. You aren't maybe not guilty, you will not plead guilty if suspicion falls on someone else, you are flat-out not guilty. That's what we go with, wherever it leads."

"You don't understand. You can't understand."

"Here we go again. Please listen carefully. I don't *care* why you think you've got to lie. I can't care about stuff like that. The only thing I need to understand or care about is what this case is, not why you want to cloud it up with other issues. You're going to kill yourself with that argument." Erin pulled her chair closer. "Do you want me to help you or not?"

"You know I do."

"Then stop worrying about Jerry and get your own story straight. Let's go over it again . . . what you'll say if we go to trial and how you'll say it."

Because much of the doubt we would cast over the state's case had to come from Laura herself, she would have to testify at the trial. Parley was clearly nervous about this. He still considered her too unpredictable, too easily shaken when the inevitable questions about Jerry arose, but Jerry was in it now and nothing could be done about that. The ashes from the back-room fireplace were part of the evidence. The sheriff had bagged and taken the entire grate, and he had noted a charred smear of blood on it, and traces of blood scattered throughout the ashes. The shirt fragment looked identical to Jerry's shirt, just as Laura had said. "I think we have a reasonable doubt," Erin said. "But Laura can't escape it, it's coming in, what she did with Jerry's clothes is not going away. Now we've got to make them understand why."

I knew Erin considered Jerry one of our strong suits. She liked our chances but she retreated from optimism if we tried too hard to agree with her. "They're pushing a weak case, and that's always a reason to worry. Like they've got something we don't know about." She considered Gill easily capable of pushing it for political reasons. This was the county's first murder case in forty years, and he didn't want to back away and he sure didn't want to lose it.

It was late when we left the jail. The town was dark and the café about to close, but Parley turned on the charm and coaxed three simple hamburger steaks out of them. We sat at a table in the far corner of the room and went over tactics and where Lennie's lies would take him next. "This guy is a worm," Erin said. "I have no sympathy for creeps like him."

She ticked off his offenses on her fingers.

"First he messes up the crime scene. Then he panics and he's got to manufacture a cover-up, so he destroys evidence. He's not guilty of perjury yet, but he will be if I give him a little bit of rope. What else can he do now but keep up the lie?"

She stared into the dark place under the table. "I'm gonna destroy that bastard."

"They'll never sit still for that," Parley said. "Not in a hearing to suppress."

"You can bet me. Whatever else he is, Gill's a political animal and he doesn't want to go to trial on Lennie's flimsy shoulders. I've got a hunch we can win this thing right there in the hearing."

She looked up at me. "I'd like you to go in with us. You don't need to say a word, just sit behind me in the courtroom and give Lennie the evil eye. I think you've got his number."

I was uneasy even in that role, but she lifted her wineglass. "Here's to tomorrow. And the beginning of the end for deputy whatever."

39

Lennie was sitting sullenly in the courtroom when we arrived that morning. The judge's court reporter was leaning over his box looking bored. We were all early; no one else was yet in the room, but Lennie squared his shoulders, filling out his police jacket, and looked back at us. "What's he doing here?" he said gruffly, and the court reporter smiled playfully and took down his words.

"Mr. Janeway is my investigator," Erin said. I faced them all and smiled.

"I didn't ask you that, I know who he is. What's he need to *investigate* in here?"

"You never know." Erin smiled pleasantly.

"You never know *what*?"

"When some great lie that needs investigating will surface."

"Are you trying to fuck with me, sister?"

"No way. I wouldn't do that for a hundred million dollars."

Two doors opened suddenly. The bailiff came in from chambers, and from the hall I heard Ann Bailey's voice. She and Gill came down, nodded crisply, and sat on the bench across from us. Our witness, Hugh Gilstrap, was right behind them, and he took a seat in the row behind us.

Lennie stared back at the photographer and he looked pale. He jerked his thumb my way. "I don't want him here."

"I'm sure you don't want any of us here, including yourself," Erin said. "Too bad you don't get to pick and choose."

Lennie pointed a trembling finger. "Listen, sister, don't you screw around with me. You hear what I'm saying?"

"My goodness, Deputy, that sounds like a threat."

"Lennie, please," Miss Bailey said, wincing.

"I don't know what the hell these people think they're gonna prove. Everything I did was by the book. *Ev-ry*thing."

"Then you won't mind telling us about it," Erin said.

"It's all in my report. This hearing is bullshit."

"That may be, but it's one of the trials of life, you'll just have to put up with it."

"Lennie," Miss Bailey said softly. "Remember what we discussed."

"Some people you just can't coach," Erin said. "They are the great uncoachables. No matter what you tell them, they're always going to be a wild hair."

"Listen to that shit," Lennie said. "That's exactly what I'm talking about."

Now Gill leaned forward and looked Lennie in the eyes. He spoke so softly that only Lennie could hear him, but he was intense, and when he was finished, Lennie sat glumly and silently. Erin was right, I thought: he's a loose cannon, ready to blow up.

I heard another shuffle and the sheriff arrived with Laura. She sat with us and he joined the prosecutors. The bailiff said, "All rise," and the judge came in.

The judge sat, then we sat, and he looked over at the prosecution's side of the bench. "Where are your witnesses, Mr. Gill?"

"Mr. McNamara is only interested in Deputy Walsh, Your Honor. If we brought them all in, this hearing could run half a day. We could have done that, but the testimony from the preliminary hearing won't change. We're trying to save the court's time."

"Mr. McNamara?"

"That's fine with us, Your Honor."

"All right then. Let's get going."

Miss Bailey rose and called Lennie, who raised his hand over the Bible and was sworn.

What followed was ten minutes of routine, almost pedantic questioning: *Where were you when you first got the call? Where was the sheriff and why wasn't he in the office?* Lennie lied about that, covering the sheriff's ass by saying he wasn't sure.

What did you do right after the call came in? How long did it take you to get up the hill to Mrs. Marshall's house? Did you knock on the door? When did you decide it would be proper for you to enter the premises?

"I looked in through the open door," Lennie said. "I could see that something bad had happened. Mrs. Marshall was sitting at the table with blood on her dress. There was a gun on the floor."

Gill leaned over and whispered something to Miss Bailey. She furrowed her brow, obviously annoyed. "One minute, please, Your Honor."

The judge looked away and drummed his fingers on the bench. Miss Bailey and Gill were locked in some kind of disagreement for most of a minute. In the end, Gill made his point more forcefully and Miss Bailey, frustrated, said, "Okay, tell us what you did next."

The remainder of Lennie's testimony was almost to the letter what I remembered from the preliminary hearing. Everything sounded proper to hear him tell it. He had gone step by step, discovering things in their correct order. Miss Bailey gave Gill another look and said, "That's all."

Erin rose slowly and came forward. "You say you looked in through the open door and saw Mrs. Marshall at the table with blood on her dress. You say there was a gun on the floor. And you could see all that from the front doorstep?"

"Most of it, yes."

"How much of it?"

"Enough of it."

"What specifically does that *mean*, Deputy? Keep in mind, please, that we have all been up there, we have all looked in through that front door. If you'd rather do this the hard way, we can all go up there right now and see just what's visible from the front door."

Lennie seethed in his hotbox.

"Isn't it true that you went inside without seeing anything?"

"I sure didn't go up there on a blind. I knew something bad had happened."

"How did you know that?"

"Because of the *phone* call, isn't that obvious? She didn't call the sheriff's office to find out the time of day or directions down the mountain. What would you think?"

"What I'd think isn't the point here, I didn't enter the Marshalls' house." Erin moved around the room, looked out the window, and came back to her spot. "What did she say when she called?"

"Her husband had been murdered."

"Is that what she said?"

I saw Miss Bailey give a slight headshake across the table. Lennie turned and we stared at each other for a few seconds. "Make him stop that, Judge," Lennie said.

The judge gave me a stern look. But he said, "Just answer the questions, Deputy."

"The question was," Erin said, "did she say her husband had been murdered?"

"Maybe that wasn't it exactly."

"It doesn't have to be exact, here and now. Just the true gist of it. There's a tape, as you know. We can get the exact wording later if you can't remember it now."

"I'm trying to recollect."

"Take your time."

"She said there'd been a shooting. Her husband had been shot."

"Yes, that's what the tape will show. There

had been a shooting. For all you knew at that moment, it had been an accident. Isn't that right, Deputy?"

"I knew it hadn't been any accident."

"From what, just the sound of her voice?"

"That's right."

"From your vast experience and the sound of her voice."

"Don't you belittle me," Lennie said, and Miss Bailey closed her eyes.

Erin smiled. "I certainly don't mean to, Deputy."

Miss Bailey came up from her chair. "Your Honor, these personal attacks—"

"Just ask the questions, Ms. d'Angelo."

"How many shootings have you investigated in your career, Deputy?"

"I know what guilty people sound like."

"That must be a great talent in your line of work. So the answer to my question is what? Fifty? . . . Ten? . . . Two?"

"You know we haven't had many shootings here."

"The answer then is none. Is that right?"

"The woman was hysterical."

"I'm sure she was. Her husband had just been killed." Erin looked at her notes. "All right, you got up there, the door was open, you went inside and found Mrs. Marshall at the table. Is that it?"

"Something like that."

"Well, if it wasn't *exactly* like that, Deputy, would you please tell us what was different about it?"

"I'll have to refer to my report."

"I have a copy of it here. Do you want to look at it?"

"No, I remember now."

"Then tell us, please."

"I called in through the open door. Nobody answered, so I went in. Hell, for all I knew Marshall might still be alive, bleeding to death in there."

"So you went on in. Were you armed? Did you take out your weapon?"

"You better believe it. It's easy for you to ask sarcastic questions here in this nice warm courthouse. You try going out alone to a scene like that and see how you like it."

"So you walked in on Mrs. Marshall with your gun drawn."

"And I was right, wasn't I? Her husband was dead at her feet and there wasn't any ifs or maybes about it."

"No, there weren't. And you immediately assumed that she had done it."

"Well, he had two lethal wounds, so I knew right off he didn't do it to himself. Nobody else was there."

"Nobody you saw. Tell us what happened then."

"I spoke to her. She looked up and said, 'I shot Bobby.'"

He said this smugly, with a smirk of victory, as if he had just put the biggity-ass, hotshot lawyer in her place. Erin nodded and said, "I understand you spent some time down at the station trying to get her to confess. Now you're telling us she'd already confessed, is that correct?"

I glanced at the prosecution table, expecting an objection that never came.

"She gave me a verbal confession, first words out of her mouth."

"And at the station you were trying to . . ."

"Get her to sign it, what do you think?"

"Without a lawyer present to protect her interests."

"I had already read her her rights—twice, in fact. Once up at the house, once in the jail."

"Which no one but yourself saw or heard."

"Freeman was there when I gave her her rights the second time."

"Freeman being the old jailer."

"That's right."

"So she gave you this spontaneous confession at the house. Did she repeat that at the jail?"

"Yeah. Not to me, but—"

"Why do you suppose not?"

"Someone had arrived and told her not to."

"Ah. Who might that have been?"

"You know who it was."

"You mean the photographer, Mr. Gilstrap, is that correct?"

"Yeah," Lennie said with obvious reluctance.

"Good thing he was there, wasn't it?"

"Good for you maybe; it gives you something to chew on. But lemme tell you something, lady, what he did was totally off-base. He was interfering with an officer of the law in an official duty. Whatever he says, I'd take with a grain of salt if I were you."

"Thank you, officer. He'll give us his version shortly."

"He'll say I'm lying. Are you calling me a liar?"

Miss Bailey leaned forward. "Lennie —"

"Goddammit, I don't have to sit still for that shit."

"Let's assume somebody was lying," Erin said. "You're saying it was Gilstrap, is that correct?"

"I'm saying what I just said. Nothing more, nothing less."

"I think you're saying a good deal more than that, Deputy. In fact you know exactly what Mr. Gilstrap observed that day."

"I know what he *thinks*."

"He's here to testify to what he saw. Under oath, sir, as you are."

"Don't talk to me that way. I don't lie."

"He thinks you sealed up the house and left—"

"Now *that* is bullshit."

The judge picked up his gavel. "Sir, you will not use gutter language in my courtroom."

Lennie stared ahead as if he had heard none of this. Erin leaned over into his line of vision, and in that moment there were just the two of them locked in a battle as old as time. "Are you going to tell us you did not seal up the crime scene and leave Mrs. Marshall's children inside?"

"That's a fuckin' lie."

The gavel rapped; the judge roared something about contempt. Lennie said, "It's a lie, it's a lie, it's a goddamned lie. Read my lips and go to hell." Erin said, "Your Honor, may the record reflect that the witness appears to be enraged by this line of questioning and that his attitude toward me is one of extreme hostility."

"So ordered."

"You've gone a bit pale, Deputy," Erin said. "Would you like some water?"

"You just go to hell." He looked at Gill, then at Miss Bailey, and finally, at last, at the judge. In a watery voice, he said, "Your Honor . . ."

Softly, Erin said, "May I just ask a few more questions, Your Honor?"

And the judge, in his steely voice, said, "Go on."

Go on, fry the bastard.

"Are you people gonna sit still for this shit?"

Miss Bailey rose from her chair. "Your Honor . . ."

"Hey," the judge said, motioning her down. "He rigged his own sail."

"Did you seal up the house," Erin said, "and *then* go back up there—"

"*No!* . . . No, I did not!"

"—and while you were there the second time, did you destroy every blood trace that that kid had put on the walls *after* you left them in there—"

"You . . . are . . . outta . . . your . . . fuckin' . . . mind."

"All the bloody little fingerprints—"

"No, goddammit, *no!*"

"All the smears on the wall—"

"I'm not saying another word to this bitch."

"What did you do with the bloody police tape with the fingerprints all over it?"

"You looked at the crime scene photos. You see any tape with blood on it?"

"I'm talking about the other tape, Officer Walsh. The original tape you used to seal the room before the kid got in there and messed it all up."

"That never happened."

"Let me suggest, Deputy, that you did return to the Marshall house. And at that time you discovered that the children had smeared blood on the walls and had even handled the police tape with their bloody hands. And let me also suggest that when you saw what they had done, you destroyed that police tape and replaced it with a fresh one, and that you also washed all the smeared blood and handprints off the walls. Isn't it true that this is in fact what you did."

Lennie looked at the DA. "She's gone crazy. She's gone fuckin' nuts."

Erin smiled at him, not unkindly.

Lennie looked imploringly at Miss Bailey. "What the hell are you doing to me? We're supposed to be on the same side, for Christ's sake! How can you let her do this?"

"Better now than at the trial," Erin said. "Right, Miss Bailey?"

"I wasn't *talking* to you, goddammit! Can't you understand English?"

"Your honor, I would once again ask that the record reflect—"

"Fuck you! Fuck you all!"

Suddenly he got up and pulled open his jacket, and for just a moment his hand came to rest on his gun. Everyone in the room tensed. Miss Bailey said, "*Jesus* Christ, Lennie, what are you doing with that gun in here?" Lennie whirled, kicked over the chair, shattered it against the wall, and stalked out. We all sat and stared at one another, and for a moment no one knew what to say.

The judge recovered first. "I want a warrant sworn out for that man's arrest," he said to the sheriff. "Then you get out there and find him."

"Yes, sir."

He looked at the two sides. "Is there any reason why I shouldn't rule right now on the motion to suppress?"

Gill stood and said, "Well, Your Honor, I would respectfully request a continuance until Deputy Walsh is found and we have a chance to assess his bizarre behavior here today."

"What's to assess?" Erin said. "It's clear that his entire investigation is tainted and his testimony has been full of lies from the beginning.

So while they're assessing things, our client continues to sit in jail based largely on the word of a man who did everything but pull a gun on us all."

"I'm inclined to agree," the judge said.

"At least, let us find him, Judge," Gill said.

"I'll give you till the middle of next week," the judge said. "I'll be out of town till next Wednesday. If Deputy Walsh has not been produced by then and brought in here as a prisoner, unarmed, I will suppress his entire testimony."

"Thank you, Your Honor."

The judge got up and went into his chambers.

Gill cleared his throat. "I think we might be willing to look at a lesser charge. What would you say to man one?"

"She killed him in the heat of an argument," Miss Bailey said.

"Whoever killed him might've done that," Parley said in a soft, corrective tone.

Whoever it was had killed him, then shot him again for good measure. Miss Bailey was right about one thing: that was indeed hot blood at work. Erin smiled, gracious now, and said, "Of course we're obligated to take your offer to our client. But there's no way I could advise her to accept such a thing."

Of course they knew that too. No one asked what the defense would suggest, but at some point Erin, in her softest voice, told them anyway: "C'mon, guys. How about dropping these charges and letting her get back to her children?"

40

We headed toward the Christmas season on a high note. Lennie had disappeared. The Wednesday deadline came and went; the judge threw out all of Lennie's testimony, and there was a mood of celebration at lunch that day. "Essentially this leaves them with no case," Erin said.

She hoped that afternoon for word from the district attorney that the charges were being dropped, but it didn't come. "It's starting to look like they intend to string us along till the fat lady sings," she said for my ears only. "I still think they've got to dismiss, but until they do I've got to prepare for trial." In mid-December Miss Bailey was conspicuously everywhere. She personally conducted all the interviews yet again in her rugged determination to salvage their case. We saw her in the stores and hustling across the street from the saloon where Bobby

Marshall occasionally drank and bought the boys a beer. I ran into Hugh Gilstrap downtown and learned that she had been out to see him twice that week. But the case was as cold as the high mountain passes, and with every passing day it got colder.

Erin spent long hours alone, reading case law and making notes, and at night she and Parley went over and over the people's case. At least once a day she went to the jail and visited with her client for an hour or more. "Mostly we go over the same stuff," she told me. "Occasionally she remembers something new, but never very much and nothing of any value." I asked if they had ever been able to talk about their old days, and Erin said yes, they had finally broken through that ice. "So how are you with her now?" I asked, but she shrugged and said, "I still don't know. I'm still uneasy. She's eager and I'm distant, and I guess that's how it's going to be, at least for a while." But I could see that she wanted something, some final answer to an enigma that had been on her mind for more than ten years.

I passed my time covering the same ground Miss Bailey was raking over: I talked to people, I went over the scene, I combed through the town and called Rosemary in Social Services and wandered in the hills above Laura Marshall's house. I made out-of-state phone checks daily, trying to pin down where the Preacher and the Keeler boys might have run. I called booksellers cold: dealers in Arkansas and other places where Kevin Simms, also known as Earl Chaplin, had been known to live, and in Oklahoma, which the Keelers had once mentioned was their home base. I figured they had gone to ground. The Preacher would open a bookstore somewhere well off the beaten track; he'd sell off what stock he had and he'd dream of bigger things. Maybe somewhere, someday, he'd try another scam.

Near the end of the week the answer popped up from an ABAA bookseller, some man I had never seen or heard of in far-flung Texas. The elusive Kevin Simms had come into his bookstore yesterday, asking questions about the walk-in traffic in that part of town. "He says his name's William Carroll. He's looking at a vacant store about a block away," the fellow said. "He talks like he's already made up his mind." I thanked him and left him with a warning: "Don't buy any of his signed stuff, no matter how cheap he makes it. And please, whatever you do, don't tell him we had this conversation. He may be a witness in a murder investigation."

I reported this to Erin and she made notes, taking down the fellow's name, address, and phone number. The way the case looked now, Kevin Simms and the whole issue of signed books was irrelevant. But she had a subpoena prepared for Earl Chaplin, aka Kevin Simms or William Carroll, perhaps doing business in Huntsville, Texas. She wasn't sure yet whether or how to use this. "We'll have to spring it on him fast to keep him from taking off again, and we'll need grounds for his arrest if we want to assure his appearance. And those two buffoons who worked for him: God knows where they are now."

If they weren't with him in Texas, I had their addresses in Oklahoma and the plate number for that truck. I had found the name of their insurance company—there was no claim on file as of last week. "I can't find any evidence that they actually towed the truck in—I think they may have just left it up there, in which case it'll sit there at least till the road opens again in the spring, and maybe forever."

"If we can keep it simple, we'll be better off," Erin said. "They've got to prove she did it and we've got to counter whatever evidence they put on. Her confession is their big enchilada. That's it in a nutshell, and Lennie's the unshakable millstone around their necks. If they can't find him and they can't get past that, what do they do?"

They asked for a continuance, a move Erin vigorously opposed. There was a hearing in the judge's chambers and His Honor came down with unexpected grit on our side. The woman had been sitting in jail, for God's sake, separated from her children since October. Fish or cut bait.

They dropped the charges a week before Christmas.

Erin's law firm had given her a long leash and she wasn't expected back in the office till mid-February. "You can go on back to Denver if you want to," she told me. "I know you've been itching to get away from here and I don't blame you. But I think I'll stay around for a few days."

Laura had asked her to, she said: "There are some things we need to tidy up, a bunch of legal odds and ends and money matters. She's only now beginning to realize how much this thing may wind up costing her."

And there was still the old stuff between them, all the things that Erin had avoided and now needed to face. "I didn't just come out here to get her off, I've always known that, even when I wouldn't say so. It's hard for me to make even you understand why she was so important

to me in those old days. Have you ever had a
friend like that? . . . She's just never been out of
my mind. I believe there's an answer to us,
somewhere in that head and heart of hers, and
now I want to find out what that is, for my own
peace of mind."

Sure, I understood that. "I'll stick around
too, if it's all the same to you; give you something to warm your feet on at night. And my
store's doing fine; Millie says I should take off
more often. Denver'll still be there when we get
back."

By Christmas week the streams had frozen over
and the kids were out skating, building snow-
men and ice forts. At one house south of town, a
row of tiny igloos was going up on each side of
a long driveway. The snow that year was just
short of sensational. There hadn't been much
recorded in Denver so far, but here in the mountains, and particularly in Paradise, there were
drifts as high as a car, a wonderland for kids and
even for old duffers who appreciated a good
snowball fight. Back-country skiers were flood-
ing into town.

Within a day of her release, Laura rented a
house in town for herself and the kids. She
planned to have her place recarpeted and re-

modeled so that maybe they'd be able to go up there again without those constant reminders of what had happened. But when all was said and done, she thought she would sell the place, pay her legal bills, take the kids and move somewhere out of state.

"I think I need to get a new start," she said more than once after her release. "Paradise just has too much old baggage attached to it."

I thought her words contained a hint, a hope that perhaps she wanted Erin to say, "Why don't you move back to Denver?" But that invitation didn't come quickly or easily, and at the moment Laura took pleasure in what she had avoided when Bobby had been alive. She pushed back her reclusive nature and was seen almost every day on the streets, wandering into shops, talking to people, walking with her children. "She's taking the pulse of the town," Erin said, "trying to see whether people are suspicious, and how they are with her." In the afternoons she and Erin walked the town together: Laura would come by, and Parley or I, sometimes both of us, would babysit the kids while she and Erin went out alone and tried to rediscover themselves in a free world. I never asked what they talked about: it was Erin's business, but at night, when we were alone, she volunteered glimpses of it. "We haven't talked much about the old days yet. It just doesn't come up. I think she wants to have some kind of ongoing relationship but I'm not sure yet what that might be. Today she talked again about moving back to Denver."

Score one for the old Janeway and his hunches. But where it would go from there was anybody's guess.

For her part, Erin still didn't know what she wanted. "Maybe I still love her," she said one night. "But I've pushed her away for so long, I denied not only her existence but her right to exist in my mind. And yet she was always there. Even after all these years I'd find myself suddenly thinking of her. I'd be in court and I'd have a momentary lapse in my concentration, like a cat had just crossed my path, and I'd stop and think about it and it was always her. Her face would come floating up out of nowhere, and sometimes I was almost certain she was back there in the crowd, watching me."

"Do you think you could be friends again?"

"I don't know. Not like we were, I don't think. But life is strange, who knows how the ball bounces? Suddenly out of the blue she'll say something that makes me laugh, and we'll almost be like those long-lost sisters we were."

I had still not heard her say Laura's name: it

had always been "her" or "she" when we talked, "Mrs. Marshall" in court. But I didn't mention it again.

As the holiday approached, Laura was looking radiant: she had had her hair done up and had splurged on some new clothes for herself and the kids. There was almost an air of freedom about her but not quite. "She understands that murder charges are dropped without prejudice," Parley told me one evening. "They can still refile them, and I think they intend to, somewhere down the road. They'll always have the Lennie problem to deal with. They'll need new evidence, a stronger case than they have right now. But I know they're not satisfied the way it is."

The judge was fairly well pissed at the way the case was frittered away, Parley said. "He wants Lennie in his court." Gill remained his usual distant self, but Parley knew after talking to Miss Bailey that he had been right, that they were trying to gather information for a case down the road. "Ann's like a lot of women I've known," he said, "she's stubborn to a fault."

Parley's best guess was that Lennie had left the state: "That damn fool has gone as far away as his truck will take him." Me, I wasn't so sure of that. I had a hunch Lennie was still around, and every day I walked the streets and talked to people in gas stations and shops, the waitress in the café, the old people who sat bundled in the park on the strangely warm snowy days and watched the kids at play. I asked everyone I saw: I left Parley's phone number and asked them to call me there if they saw or heard anything.

We had planned an old-fashioned afternoon dinner at Parley's house on Christmas Day. Erin would cook it, Laura and the kids would come over around noon, and we'd spend the afternoon watching *It's a Wonderful Life* on video and listening to Christmas music. "This'll be the first time I've had a Christmas tree since Martha died," Parley said. "I should always do this at Christmas; I ought to have one every year, even if there's nobody but me to enjoy it." Erin smiled and said, "Yeah, you should," but later, in the kitchen, she told me he never would. "There's nothing worse than trying to fake good cheer when you're really alone. A tree would drive me crazy if I were him, getting old alone, with nobody really close around me." A little later she said, "I've been considering asking him if he'd like to move into Denver. I think I could get him a job in the firm. I know I could. We always need help, and he could work as little or much as he wanted to."

That afternoon the three of them went for a walk while the turkey cooked. Erin had pointedly invited Parley to join them, leaving me alone to watch the kids. The big front room was full of toys, which delighted the twins even as they went through them all for the tenth time. Jerry and I sat alone watching them. Laura had bought him some new clothes and a fine-looking watch, which alternately seemed to fascinate and bore him. He and I drank eggnog, which he loved coated with cinnamon and spices, and I talked about the world that, so far, he had seen only in movies. I watched his face as I talked and I thought I saw real comprehension there. His eyes were soft and doelike, and at some point I put on *Hondo,* another of the films we had rented, and watched him as it began to play. He sat transfixed in front of the set, and when the credits came up, I said, "You like John Wayne, Jerry?" Instantly he took up a paper and began to write. I let him do this undisturbed until he had filled the page, then I asked if I might see what he had written. He handed it to me without expression, and it was line after line of John Wayne's signature, all perfect replicas as if the man's ghost had floated into the room and done it himself. I handed him another sheet and said, "Can you do Alfred Hitchcock, Jerry?"

and in an instant he had scrawled Hitchcock's signature, with the little Hitchcockian fat-man caricature attached to the end of the name. "That's fine," I said, "that's great. Let's see what you can do with a few more." I thought of the books, which had been released by the DA and were now stacked in Parley's back bedroom; but I didn't want to get up or disturb anything, so I scanned them in my mind and softly said the names of the authors I remembered—Leonard Bernstein, Paul Whiteman, Robert Frost—and with each name I instantly got back what looked like a perfect signature on the paper. I remembered some of the Preacher's books and said the names, and some of them worked and some of them didn't. "What about Andy Warhol, Jerry?" I said, and almost before I got the name out he had scrawled Warhol's name and had added the famous tomato soup can. He had begun to go down the page, line after line of the same signature, but then I heard a laugh outside and a bump on the porch and I said, "That's enough for today," and I reached for the paper and took it gently when he handed it to me. I folded it and put it away as the door opened and Erin came in.

"Well," Laura said, "what've you two been doing all afternoon?"

"Just hangin' out, watchin' movies."

I nodded at Jerry and said, "This is a good kid you've got here."

"He sure is." She tousled his head. "He's my boy."

The turkey came out of the oven at four o'clock and we ate at the big dining table in a room that had been dark for years. Erin offered a toast, "To new beginnings," and four glasses clinked lightly. Outside, the snow had begun again: we could see it fluttering past the windows as darkness fell over the town. Parley had lit the fireplace and it roared mightily as we ate and talked and shared an occasional laugh. "Parley's considering moving to Denver," Erin said at one point, and Parley shrugged. "I will admit that it sounds exciting," he said. Laura said she had already made her decision: "I can't live here anymore. This was never my place." She didn't mention her dead husband by name, but we all got the point. It had been his house, his town, his choice to live here. "I'm going to put the house up for sale next week," she said. "The kids'll be better off in the city, with real schools and others their own age. I think they've had enough of me as a homeschool teacher."

She was motivated to sell it, she would be

willing to dicker the price, she wanted to be far away from Paradise and its little minds before the season turned.

"At the same time, don't be foolish," Erin said. "This land alone will be worth a fortune in a few years, and you don't want to give it away."

"I know that. But I can't live my life based on what may be, either. Besides, as I think you all know, I've got some pretty steep legal bills."

Erin said nothing.

"I may move somewhere I've never been before," Laura said a few moments later. "Seattle maybe. I've always liked the rain."

Erin nodded and they looked at each other across the enormous gulf of that tabletop. Laura said, "You think that's a good idea?"

"I think what makes you happy is what's good."

"I don't know what happy is," Laura said.

"Then maybe it's time you found out."

There was a moment just after dinner: Erin and Parley had cleared away the dishes and taken them into the kitchen, and the kids were playing in the far hallway. Laura and I moved past each other at the end of the table, and suddenly she reached over and hugged me tight. "Thank you," she whispered. "I know how much work you did for me. God knows where I'd be without you."

Even more suddenly, she stood on her toes and kissed me hard on the mouth. I felt her tongue and I pulled back instinctively and stammered, "Uh, Laura . . ."

"Mistletoe," she said, pointing over my head. "But I guess I'd better leave you alone before Erin comes in here and gets the wrong idea."

The evening passed uneasily. I had the feeling of something afoot that hadn't been there before. At nine o'clock, late by Paradise standards, the telephone rang.

"It's for you," Parley said.

I went into the hall and picked it up.

"Mr. Janeway?" A woman's voice.

"Hi, who's this?"

"It doesn't matter who I am. You've been going around town, asking about Lennie Walsh. You still interested?"

"Sure I am."

"Well, he's still here. I saw him night before last."

"Where?"

"Up at the end of Main Street, right on the edge of town. He was talking to old Freeman Willis . . . you know, the jailer."

"You're sure it was him."

"Oh, yeah. Listen, I've got my reasons for wanting that son of a bitch to get whatever's coming to him. He hasn't made many friends in this town. But I'd rather not get directly involved in whatever happens. Just a word to the wise."

"Thank you," I said, but she had already hung up.

41

Erin sat still and said nothing while I put on my coat. "I'll be back in a little while," I told her, and I hurried out before any of them had a chance to ask any questions.

One thing about a jail: Christmas, Easter, or the Fourth of July, it never closes.

Freeman was sitting behind the big desk with his feet up, playing sheriff. He jumped when I came in, as if I had caught him robbing a poor box, and his feet clattered on the floor.

"Oh, it's you."

"Hi, Freeman."

He came around the desk and sat in the perp's chair looking guilty.

"I thought maybe you and I could have a little talk."

"I got nuthin' to say to you."

"That's okay. You can tell it to the DA instead."

"Tell what to the DA?"

"How a good country boy like you became an accessory to a crime."

"The hell you talkin' about?"

I sat across from him and looked into his face. "Hey, Freeman, no matter what you think, I am not your enemy. I have no wish to see you go to jail."

Alarmed now, he said, "Why would I go to jail?"

"Aiding and abetting a criminal was a crime itself, last time I looked."

"You talkin' about Lennie?"

I nodded solemnly, avoiding the temptation to be sarcastic. "Lennie's got himself into a mess, Freeman. And you two were seen together two nights ago, here in town."

We stared at each other and I smiled, not unkindly.

"I know you don't think he ran in here and quit his job just because he suddenly got bored with it," I said. "I know you're smarter than that, Freeman," but in fact I knew nothing of the kind.

"Who said he quit his job?"

"Then where is he?"

A long moment passed. Freeman rubbed his grizzled chin and tried to look away. I did look away, striking a pose of infinite patience. I read the WANTED circulars on the wall and avoided saying the obvious: that soon Lennie would be up there in the rogues' gallery with Elmer Trigger Adams and Henry Scott, notorious flasher and tit-tweaker, who had moved on to buggery, child molestation, kiddie porn, and other monkey business. *I wonder how you'd look up there in that company, Freeman.*

"Lennie says you're trying to sandbag him."

"That's about what I'd expect Lennie to say. In fact, I don't care anything at all about Lennie. You can believe that or not, Freeman, it's no skin off my nose, but if you crawl into bed with Lennie Walsh, you'll live to regret it."

I waited. "You were seen the other night, talking to Lennie," I told him again.

"Who says?"

"Never mind that. Somebody reliable, I'll tell you that much. What'd you boys have to talk about so seriously?"

"Nothin'. He just wanted me to give somebody a message."

"Who might that be?"

"I can't tell you that."

"What was the message?"

"I don't know." He looked into my doubtful eyes. "I'm tellin' ya, I don't know. It was a sealed-up letter."

"I see. Did you deliver it?"

"Why wouldn't I? Lennie never did me no harm."

I shrugged. "I'm looking for a killer, Freeman. If that happens to be Lennie, and you go down with him . . ."

I let that settle on him. Softly I said, "Murder's serious business."

"What's it got to do with me?"

"I think Lennie knows something about it."

"Well, he didn't tell me where he was going."

"I see."

"He didn't. I'm not lyin' to ya."

"I think you know where he went anyway."

I pushed back as if to leave.

"Wait a minute," Freeman said. "Listen."

I pulled in close again and I listened.

42

Fourteen hours later I was rolling gingerly along what looked like a rutted turn-of-the-century logging road. It had taken most of the morning to rent the Jeep; I had to wait till the guy decided to open and do the paperwork, and now as I went higher, I felt the tension growing like a knot in my belly. There was a feeling of death in the air: it's always that way when a standoff is in the works and you don't know what the other guy is capable of. The way so far was just as Freeman had said: a nearly impossible road unfit even for horse and mule teams, with deep holes in both ruts that kept me rocking back and forth and in the worst places tilting precariously to one side and then the other over yawning rocky valleys. The cabin was just below timberline, surrounded by a few scrawny, mutant-looking trees and some hardy underbrush. Far below I could see the remains of an old mining town, a collection of ruins that twisted around smaller mountains along what was probably a snow-covered dirt road. Beyond the range was Paradise, socked in now as a storm system moved in from the west. I could see it coming seventy miles away, a swirling gathering of black clouds and snow moving slowly across the rugged landscape. I came over a crest and saw a higher mountain just ahead, and one to the north beyond it. *You'll know you're gettin' close when you see them two peaks,* Freeman said. *You follow the road on up the ridge, past what's left of an old mine, and right after that you'll come on the cabin all-of-a-sudden-like. You'll have to walk or crawl them last two hundred yards. You could make it in a Jeep, but he'd see you comin' and I wouldn't wanna be you if he does. Lennie is a crack shot with that deer rifle.*

He looked worried. *Don't let 'im know it was me you got this from. He'll know anyways; he ain't stupid, and he ain't talked to nobody else.*

I'll cover for you, Freeman, I said. I tried to mean it, but he wouldn't say more than that; he froze and shook his head, afraid he had already put himself in jeopardy, probably wishing that he'd said nothing at all.

Before starting out, I had retrieved my own gun and it was snug under my left arm. But I knew Lennie's deer rifle would beat it at a distance hands down, and there was a good chance he'd be watching.

I stopped and got out; looked over the terrain and imagined Lennie out there, cunningly hidden. No fooling around now, no silly games as we'd done on the slope across from the Marshall place. In plain fact I didn't know what to expect from Lennie. He had talked a bad show, but I had met others like him, dozens of badass hoods who had talked and were dead now because they had messed with the wrong guy or hesitated at the wrong time. Three of them were in the ground by my own hand, and I wasn't anxious to add to that dark tally. But here the odds were on Lennie's side and I knew that as well. That fact alone made me too ready to shoot first and ask questions later, and I still couldn't pin him with anything more than intentionally screwing up a crime scene and lying about it.

I still didn't know. I had had one quick glimmer and a growing hunch that whatever had happened, for better or worse, the answer went through Lennie.

Hunches, instincts, glimmers: all converging in a game of life and death.

But it was more than a hunch now. I moved on, keeping my head below what his line of sight would be from the ridge, and I skirted it with the gun in my right hand, held down at the ground as I walked. There was a path, but it was rugged, cutting across the face of the hill, apparently to the top of the mountain a mile downrange. Much farther than I wanted to go on my belly. For now I picked my way along, dropping off the path whenever I sensed too much open space across the gulch. I knew there would come a time, and it was coming up quickly, when I'd have to dare the hundred-yard final approach across what was essentially open terrain or lie down and wait for the darkness, many hours away. My sense of things told me I didn't want to do that. The storm that was coming would be wicked, especially here at the top.

I had almost reached the ridge when I saw the roof of the cabin peeking above the hill. I stuck my gun hand inside my coat and started on a perpendicular path across the face of the mountain. Ten minutes later I eased up the ridge and saw the cabin just below. Parked behind it was Lennie's truck, and beside that, two freshly cut stacks of firewood.

I sat on the ground and thought about everything, starting long before the murder of Laura Marshall's husband and going right up through this morning. And I looked over the ridge and watched for any sign of life.

There was no life.

The truck sat cold and untouched.

There was no smoke coming from the chimney. Nothing.

I stood and surveyed the cabin from the top of the ridge. I watched every window for a glimmer of the rifle and there was nothing.

I faced my fear and sucked it up. Started across the open ground. My feet went noiselessly in the fresh, uncrusted snow, which gathered in the wind and whipped across the rocky mountaintop like tiny white dervishes. Once I had decided to go, I went: didn't stop or slow down; just walked straight to the edge of the cabin and stood there getting my breath.

Maybe he's sleeping, I thought. But slowly the truth dawned.

The cabin had a cold, empty feeling to it. No cheery windows steamed warm from his fire.

No fire. Not a sound from inside; only the wind out here.

He wasn't there.

Could be a trap.

I eased around the corner. The door facing

the range was open, billowing gently in the wind. From there I could hear the rhythmic squeaking of the hinges. I went to the door and peered inside.

Nothing.

It was a simple hunter's cabin; crude, one big room with a smaller room off to the right and a bathroom on the left; both doors open, light shining in from windows beyond.

I moved quickly now, sensing the worst. Went into the bedroom and rifled through his closet, rummaged through his dresser, such as it was, looked in the desk/table that had been pushed aside in some kind of haste.

A few papers; nothing current, nothing valuable. Lennie wasn't much of a writer, letters or otherwise.

On a whim I tossed his bed; I slapped down the pillows and then turned the mattress. Under it was a sealed yellow business envelope.

I sensed its importance; I could feel it burning through the paper. I tucked it under my arm and moved back out into the big room, went to the doorway, looked out over the distant mountain range.

The door to Lennie's truck was open, like the cabin. Not a good sign.

I moved across what yard there was. Came

around the edge of the truck, and there was Lennie, sprawled grotesquely across a seat drenched black with his blood. He stared up in disbelief. One shot had ripped his throat out. The other had got him between his wide-open eyes.

Suddenly I knew what had happened, should've known all along. I tore open the envelope and looked inside and felt a sudden deep chill. It went from my gut up my backbone to my numbing brain. I had made a horrible misjudgment at the start of this case. I thought of Erin and I trembled, and I felt my knees buckle in fear as I slipped quickly down the ridge to the Jeep. I dropped the keys in the snow and roared my anguish at the dark sky as I scrambled frantically to find them.

43

The fear doubled as I rolled dangerously down from the mountain. It doubled again before I reached the edge of town.

I fishtailed into Parley's street thinking, *Oh, God, please, pleeeeease let them be here.* But Parley came out on the porch, looking anxious.

"You seen the ladies?"

"They left here almost four hours ago. I thought they were just goin' for a drive."

He came down from the porch and looked in through my open window. "This is a bad storm coming. All the stores downtown are closing early. This town's gonna be socked in good tonight."

"Where are the kids?"

"I got 'em inside."

"Good. I'll go out and see what I can find."

"Laura knows this country. She knows what can happen when it turns ugly."

"It's probably fine, Parley."

I watched him in my rearview mirror till the swirling snow blotted him out.

The sky over the town was already black; only a few people were on the streets, shopkeepers hurrying home. The snow had just begun, but in the time it took me to sit at a stoplight, it welled up and crusted on my windshield.

I stopped at the house Laura had rented. One quick look around the empty building and I headed out of town.

I started uphill to the Marshall house. If they weren't there, then what? Sit down in the snow and go slowly crazy. Run around in circles chasing my tail.

There was nowhere else to look.

Of course she would know that. She knew everything.

I sensed her cool mind. I felt her tongue, heard her laugh.

Mistletoe.

And there was my own smug voice in the afternoon darkness. *Laura, you are the worst liar I've ever seen.* With those words, barely knowing her, I had pronounced her innocent. *You are the worst liar.* But what if she had been the best?

What if she had coldly decided to kill Bobby

and blame Jerry? What if she had killed Bobby in a sudden rage, then confessed and manufactured evidence of her own cover-up; what if she had played that dangerous game, putting herself in the crosshairs of a murder probe and rolling the dice on her ability to lie her way out?

Jerry did it, she whispered at last to that dumb klutz Janeway. *Jerry shot Bobby.*

I had dragged it out of her and so I was ready to believe her.

The land went white and the sky turned black. An almost garish look had come over the earth, like nothing I had ever seen. Not quite day, not yet night. My worried mind had begun to drift and I found myself thinking of that line about Cathy in *East of Eden*. I think of it in troubled moments like this one. I revisit all the crimson-streaked crime scenes in my head, the bloody walls, the throats slashed open, the brains blasted into a door; and all I see is carnage done for nothing more than the hell of it. It took a writer, not a cop, to bring the answer into its clearest focus. Steinbeck said, *I believe there are monsters born in the world to human parents,* and that line has stayed with me all these years. Now it seems to define my old life. I was the guy who tracked down the monsters. Experts, pundits, social scientists—whatever they call themselves today, those boys don't ever want to admit there's such a thing as pure mean-as-hell evil, but I know better, I've seen its grim handiwork. There are in fact monsters. Sometimes they can snooker and charm us and that makes them even more monstrous. As a cop I was supposed to counter them in court with nothing more than the facts of a case. No ivory-tower textbook opinions, no attitude, no mumbo-jumbo psychobabble; I wasn't the one with the $800 suit and the PhD in Everything: I couldn't coolly analyze from afar and then fly in, a hired gun on expense account, and snipe at the truth. My own testimony must be limited to the physical evidence—what I had seen, what I had found, what I knew and had meticulously recorded; what I could prove. I'm probably hopeless, stuck in my cop mode till the day I die, but I will never understand how we can pardon an animal who rapes, then cuts off his victim's hand and sits calmly smoking, watching her bleed to death. How can we say he was crazy then but now he's well, what kind of doctorate covers wisdom like that, and who cares if he is? Who cares if his mother beat him every day with an ironing cord when he was five? I'll grieve for the child he was and lock up forever the monster he has become. All I know is I will never trust his sorry ass on the street again.

These were the cheery thoughts that chased me up the hill.

The hill was a nightmare of blowing snow . . .

So easy to get disoriented and go off the road, especially hurrying with fear in my heart. I passed the turnoff where Lennie had gone that day to watch me from the far slope, and my Jeep sloshed and skidded uphill into the last half mile.

No tread in the snow, no tracks. There wouldn't be, of course, if they had come up hours ago. It didn't mean a thing, it didn't mean anything, it meant nothing, nada, nothing, zip . . .

I turned in to the road leading back through the trees to the house. I could see a hint of it now: the house, materializing through the trees and the blowing snow.

Looks deserted.

My heart sank.

But this means nothing.

Means nothing how it looks.

Lying to myself, maybe just warning myself to be careful. *As if I need it.*

I got as close as I dared in the Jeep.

Stopped, got out, snuggled the gun inside my coat. Began to move, just off the road: through the trees, up the hill into the teeth of the storm. The house became clearer, more sharply defined.

Looks dead.

Lousy choice of words.

How it actually looked was abandoned. Except for the wildly blowing snow, it would have looked like a still painting.

Then I saw the faint light . . . half a breath later, a wisp of smoke from some room on the far side of the house. *Somebody's here, all right . . . somebody . . .*

I know everything that happened . . . don't know why but that doesn't matter now . . .

I felt a chill in my heart. *Doesn't matter why. Doesn't matter . . .*

Now there was no thought of stop, be careful, wait awhile. I crouched low and zigzagged like a foot soldier in enemy territory, up the slope to the road. I hurried along it to the yard.

Around the porch I went . . .

. . . quickly, carefully . . .

Around another corner to the lighted window.

Laura stood in the kitchen, not five feet away. She was alone, humming some melody to herself. I couldn't hear it through the thick winterized walls; I got just a sense that she was humming and that was enough. She had a soft, idyllic, almost dreamy look on her face. She looked peaceful and contented . . . happy . . . almost frighteningly calm.

No sign of Erin.

No time to plan or worry about it. Just go.

I went quietly up the back-porch steps, crossed the porch to the back door, looked inside through the door glass.

Nothing.

The room was just as I'd seen it through the window. Everything shipshape, everything cool, except there was no Erin and now there was no Laura.

Fresh coffee dripped from the percolator.

The coffee dripped and the clock ticked. I could see the pendulum hacking away at the pieces of life and the black liquid dripping like blood into the pot.

I tried the door. It eased open with a slight creak.

Quickly I crossed the room, heels down first to minimize noise. I left pools of water on the floor from my shoes.

The hell with it; nothing's perfect.

I flattened myself against the wall. Listened.

Nothing. Not a sound anywhere in that big house.

I had an urge to call out their names.

Stupid . . . stupid . . .

. . . no noise . . .

. . . not a sound . . .

But I was already vulnerable. She knew I was there.

She had seen me or heard me; one way or another she knew. Why else would she do such a quick disappearing act?

She had stood in her kitchen singing softly, knowing I was there as if she had eyes in the side of her head. I relived that moment and saw her eyes shift slightly my way and a small smile tremble upward at the corners of her mouth.

Christ, I was demonizing her.

What if I kill her and none of this is true? She walks into the room and before she can say, "Hi, Cliff, what're you doing up here?" I blow her away. She's innocent, it's all in my mind, she's done nothing and I kill her. She reaches for something in her apron and I kill her where she stands. Then it turns out to be nothing, her hands were wet and she's drying them and I killed her. How could I live with that? I've killed men but she's a woman and that makes it worse. So I'm a flaming sexist idiot asshole; it damn well is worse that she's a woman, just thinking about it makes my skin crawl. I never shot a woman but of course I won't just blaze away like some stupid Rambo clone, my training and instincts are strong and I know better. But what if I hesitate and she kills me instead? Remember Lennie. Remember Bobby Marshall. And where oh where is Erin?

I eased around the door and into the hall. Almost pitch-dark from here on: a faint gray light at the doorway to the death room. I flattened myself against the wall and inched my way along it, feeling in the dark for unseen things.

My leg touched something and it fell in the hallway. A clatter went up and I froze there. I scrunched down and felt for whatever it was.

A poker.

Damned strange place for it. No fireplace within two rooms of here.

She had left it for me to knock over.

I waited.

Nothing.

Waited.

Nothing.

I moved across the hallway in the dim gray light and sank into the darkness on the other side. Felt my way toward the light, carefully now . . . carefully.

I heard a bump. One . . . dull . . . bump . . . somewhere ahead.

I tensed against the wall. My gun had come up instinctively, the barrel cold against my cheek. I watched the light for a full minute but there was no movement, no break in the solid gray square, no more noise . . . until, suddenly, I saw her.

She had darted noiselessly across the hall: I saw her silhouette against the window for just that instant, but it was a moment quickly frozen and then gone. A moment when she stopped and turned and I swear she was looking straight at me.

She scurried back into the dark places like a cockroach.

Should've gone after her; now the moment was lost.

Can't hurry, can't get careless. She knows this house far better than I do; she knows every part of it and can pop up anywhere—behind me in a doorway I didn't know existed and can't see in the dark; or ahead, where I expect her but not where she really is. I try to remember but it's spotty . . . didn't know about this alcove I'm passing, didn't see it till I was almost abreast of it: she could easily have slipped in there, might be hiding there even now in the darkest part of it.

Got to assume she's armed. No room for mistakes.

I moved slowly down the hall.

Slowly, carefully, easy . . . the best thing I can do for Erin is not get myself killed looking for her.

I eased past the crossing hall to the door of the library, now stripped and empty of books. I stood almost flush with the doorway, looking into the death room with peripheral vision, unwilling to risk my head in a full frontal view. I could see on through from there, the same scene I had come upon that first night with Parley but now so enormously changed. Everything beyond the house was going from deep purple to coal black with fierce flecks of white snow swirling across it. I turned my head and glanced back into the library. Nothing there but the black. I eased around the corner into the death room, keeping my back flat against the wall and the gun ready. Somewhere I could see a light, like a candle or a lantern a room away. It was on the side porch, I saw as I came closer, a flickering candle on the glassed-in porch. I knew I was in the greatest danger here: one false step, getting lured by the light, stepping away from the shadows, any mistake would be fatal. How could I not go? But the only way was straight ahead.

It's a trap.

It's a trap.

But I've got to take the chance.

Go fast! . . . Be a moving target.

I lurched onto the porch, crouching against the wall.

Erin lay on a cot a few feet away. Between us was a small table with two candles lighting the room. I scrambled across to her, blew out the candles, and threw my arm across her body.

She was strapped down and covered with heavy blankets.

I felt her face. It was hot, sweaty. I felt the pulse beating in her neck. I put my face against hers and softly said her name. I fumbled with the ropes and got them loose.

Then I felt another, and another . . .

Half a dozen knots on top, more underneath. I picked at them and slowly worked them free.

Erin moaned softly as if she'd been drugged. I thought of the coffee, dripping in the pot. *We were sitting in the kitchen having coffee,* she said in my mind. *That's the last thing I remember.* This wasn't rocket science. Now I had to get her out of there.

"Laura." At last she had said her old friend's

name. I felt her take a deep breath and I heard her say it again. "Laura . . ."

"Don't talk."

"Cliff . . ."

"Shhh."

I had to get her off the cot. She was a sitting duck.

"Come on," I whispered. "Try to sit up."

The cot squeaked. I squeezed her arm. "No noise now. Quiet . . . quiet . . ."

Slowly I got to my feet. I stood in a crouch. At some point I thought I could see beyond the porch. On three sides the swirling snow; on the other the interior of the house, a black place made only slightly less black by the indirect light trickling through from the kitchen. I could make out where the doorway was, I could almost see the room and the hall beyond it wrapped in pitch-blackness; I could see the black hall, which must mean I was seeing the light, as faint as it was. I could see across the porch and somewhat into the house. I knew I could see a little better, I was sure I could, as my eyes adjusted more to the dark.

I could see the hall, definitely a lighter shade of black, I thought. But what was definite; what was real?

The corners of the room seemed to emerge murkily. I crouched absolutely still till my muscles began to ache. Then I moved, slightly; I stood up straighter and convinced myself that, wherever Laura was, she wasn't in this room.

I waited. Watched.

Nothing.

She wasn't in this room. So I believed, after an eternity of crouching.

I got my arm around Erin and pulled her off the cot . . . an inch at a time.

Now we were against the wall, deep in a pocket of darkness, and we huddled together in the black corner. The wind howled around the house and there was an occasional bump from somewhere. Might be a limb blowing down on the roof . . . maybe a load of snow falling and hitting something . . . or was *that* noise just now something closer, inside the house, a room away? The building creaked in the wind. The glass above my head seemed to be rattling in its sash, and beyond it the snow whirled past like a giant white cyclone.

I knew one thing: the house was getting colder. No heat had been turned on; whatever we had was coming from that one distant fireplace. By morning, if we were still here, the fire would be out and the house would be like an icebox. I had worn my heavy winter overcoat and I drew Erin inside it. She squeezed my hand and we moved along the wall.

One . . . step . . . at a . . . time.

I heard another bump. Erin hitting the wall, probably with a heel or an elbow.

Hush, I thought. *Oh, please, hush.*

I heard her sigh and I said it was okay. But it wasn't okay, it would never be okay till we were out of there.

"Can you run?"

"I don't know . . . I don't . . ."

"When we get outside, we'll have to make a run for the car."

"I feel sick."

"Hold tight to my arm."

"I'm sorry, I just . . ."

"Don't worry, I'll wait for you. As long as you need me."

"Where're we going now?"

"Out of here. Down the slope to the car. Is there a door out of this porch?"

"I don't know. It would probably be locked."

"Did you come in this way?"

"No . . . no. Oh, God, I feel sick."

"I'll wait for you. However long it takes I'll be here."

I felt her sag against me. An ice age passed. At some point she said, "It's not going to get any better. Let's go."

The shortest way was out the front door. We moved slowly into the hall and turned right. Backs against the wall we went to the end. "Hold still," I whispered, and I tried the door. It was locked.

"We'll have to go back through the house."

I gripped her arm and eased down the wall toward the kitchen. *No noise now, no noise.* "Stay behind me," I whispered.

I peered into the house.

O black night. Blacker than black.

Now I saw why. The light had been turned off down in the kitchen, plunging the whole interior into this blacker-than-hell midnight.

I couldn't see anything, not even the blowing snow beyond the windows. This was how it would be from now on, groping along an inch at a time, going by feel and memory. I inched down the wall, holding Erin with my right hand and my gun with my left, easing along it toward the kitchen. A sudden slight change in the air told me I had reached the crossing hall. I felt for the opening with my hand and there it was, yawning into eternity. *She's there,* I thought: *that's where she'll be,* and we stood for another eon trying to wait her out. But nothing moved, nothing changed, nothing happened.

"Come on," I whispered, and we hurried across, again sinking against the wall on the other side.

I stopped for a breather. "Almost there," I said, but in plain fact I didn't know what we almost were. I took a step and that goddamned poker fell again, clattering like ten ghosts screwing on a tin roof.

So. She repropped it.

Clever, diabolical, while all I had been was blind, stupid, unthinking, stupid.

I stood somewhere south of the kitchen, feeling stupid and alone.

Gotta go.

I squeezed Erin's hand and took a step. Another. Another . . .

In this way we reached the threshold of the kitchen.

One more room to cross. But then I heard a noise: not behind me . . . ahead . . .

Something bumped.

"That wasn't me," Erin said in my ear.

"Mmm-hmm."

A footstep.

She's getting impatient.

This time the noise was softer, closer.

She's coming.

She's coming.

She's here.

She's in the next room over from the kitchen.

She's here, just across the room.

She's here in the kitchen with us . . .

"Hi," she said.

44

"I know you're in here," she said.

She crossed the room and disappeared into the far side of it, but for those few seconds I could see her shape and track her movements. I could have shot her then, but of course I couldn't and of course she would know that. The advantage of the moment was hers. She had taken off her shoes; she made no sound as she walked, but then she disappeared again into the murk and the house settled back into that eerie quiet, broken only by the pounding of the wind. She'll go crazy after just a little of this, I thought, I can outlast her. But time passed and nothing happened.

Had she gone farther back into the house or was she still nearby in some black hole of her own? I squeezed Erin's hand. *No noise now ... not even a soft sigh to give her a hint that we are together or where we might be ...*

I pictured vast sheets of ice moving across the land, thousands of years apart. I saw asteroids pounding the earth, sending tidal waves rolling toward us.

I thought about what I knew and tried to imagine why.

She's insane. That's the easy answer.

Too easy. Far too simple, much too pat.

If she's a monster, she's not like Steinbeck's monster. No, and she's not like those real-life monsters, Bundy and Gacy and Dahmer, either; there are so few women like that, it's not worth the time it takes to think about them. Serial savagery is like poaching, it's almost exclusively a male sport. Unless she's some kind of freak with bodies buried all over this mountaintop, she is far more typical of women who kill than any of those monsters. There's a strong personal motive for what she does, I'd bet four of my best books on it: the two sweetheart Raymond Chandlers, my cherry Grapes of Wrath, and the signed Richard Burton. If she kills once, others may follow, but they too are personal, not random. She has no inherent bloodlust; if no one offends her, we may never hear of her again. Bobby had been personal, an accumulation of long resentment; maybe it hadn't even been premeditated. Lennie too was personal, though we don't yet know

THE SIGN OF THE BOOK 493

how. Something he said, perhaps, in that angry moment captured on Jerry's sketchpad as he looked through the doorway. Erin would also be personal, maybe a grudge of such long standing that even she can't understand it anymore. I don't want to kill her but I have a bad feeling about any probable outcome.

Erin's voice, close now: "Let's talk to her."

"No way."

"What can it hurt?"

Are you kidding? You must still be under the influence of that dope she gave you if you can even ask such a thing. "Not a word," I whispered. "Not a sound."

Let her stew.

Suddenly, somewhere out in the void, she sneezed and laughed irrationally. "This is ridiculous," she said, just above a whisper. "What's wrong with you two?"

She sneezed again. Sneezes come in twos, but this time there was no laugh and her voice was louder. "What's the matter? You're treating me like some kind of leper."

A long, quiet moment passed.

"What's wrong? What's going on here? Can't we even talk?"

She's beginning to crack.

"Talk to me.

"Talk to me," she said again, some time later. But she was the one who talked.

"None of this would've happened if it hadn't been for that stupid deputy. Trust me, Erin, you'd have killed Bobby long ago if you'd had to live with him, you'd have shot him dead, fed him rat poison, cut his throat in his sleep. I thought about it a hundred times over the years. At first it was a shock that I could even think such a thing. But I saw the whole thing one morning in a vision over my cornflakes and bananas. I remember thinking, *What if Jerry killed him?* What if Jerry did it? They wouldn't do anything to him, we'd both be home scot-free.

"When it finally happened, it was over so quickly I couldn't believe it. I shot him in an argument that flared up before either of us saw it coming, it was just, oh, *Christ*, it was an accumulation of stuff that had been building up for years until finally I had had it. There was his gun on the chair; I picked it up and, *wow!* Bobby Marshall was the most surprised fellow in the state."

She laughed, a crazy schoolgirl giggle. "So what the hell, I did it, there he was. But that deputy was such an idiot, then McNamara came, and after a while everything was unreal, and it almost seemed like I hadn't done anything at all.

"Jerry did it."

I heard her breathe, a deep shivery sound just across the room. Her voice in the void was like velvet.

"Jerry did it."

She sniffed. "I am the victim here, not Bobby."

She sighed. "You were always my idol, Erin. Still are. I'll bet you didn't know that. You need to know how I've been quietly admiring your life and career for years. Anytime you won a big case, I kept the press accounts, I cut them out and put them in a scrapbook. Would you like to see it? I can get it out for you and turn on the lights. Just say the word. I know you'd be as impressed with yourself as I've been; how could you not be? I know you would never collect your own press accounts, you'd never stoop to such vanity. You've always been better than that, but not me, hey, I'm not above it. I loved seeing you excel and accomplish things. I know her, I would say to myself; she's a very good friend of mine. I'll bet I know things about you that you yourself don't know, or have forgotten. I'll bet you don't know how I've watched you at work. I can make myself up to look like an old woman and I've done that; maybe a million times I've driven to Denver and sat in the back row of some courtroom, watching you work. I drove all the way to Rock Springs for that water case you were on. And I always think, *Damn, she is so good, she's so smooth and quick,* and I'm so proud to have you for my friend. I've always been proud of you, Erin. I've been waiting for years just to tell you that."

She coughed. "One day in Rock Springs you looked straight at me. Our eyes met and I thought, *She sees me, she knows, in a minute she'll come over here and say, 'Don't we know each other?' and I'll say, 'Of course we do, dear,' and everything'll be all right again.* But it never was, was it?

"Does it matter to you, what I've just said? Do you care? You must not or you'd say something. I know you're awake, I heard your voice back here. I didn't give you that much sugar in your coffee, just enough when you started to realize what had really happened here, when I could see it in your face.

"I was only trying to *explain* something to you, but I could see that you . . .

"I could see it . . . I saw it in your face."

She moved and something bumped. "I wouldn't hurt you, Erin. You can't believe I'd do you any harm. All I wanted was to find something I thought I had lost forever."

I heard her move. Again I saw her shadow

against the windows; again she dropped low and disappeared into the dark places.

"Jesus, I wish you'd talk to me. Don't shut me out like this. You've been doing that for so long, how long do I have to pay for that silly thing I did all those years ago? I wish you'd talk to me about it. I know I could get you to understand if you'd just . . .

"Talk to me . . .

"*Talk* to me.

"*Please.*"

I heard her tremble in the dark. Her breath came out in a shivery gush.

Now a touch of anger rippled through her voice. "It wasn't all me, you know. It wasn't like I set a trap for Bobby just to hurt you. You know I would never do that. He's got to have some responsibility in what happened. Takes two to tango, but you, you could never forgive either of us. Just a word from you would've made all the difference in my life. Just something easy like 'Hey, I understand' or 'It's okay.' Is that asking so much? You could do that now. It would be easy just to say you understand. Then we'd be okay again. Just like old times. Just like old times, Erin. Just . . ."

I squeezed Erin's arm. *Not a word . . . not a sound.*

"I love you, Erin. I always have."

She sniffed.

"You were so good to me when we were kids. Remember that day we met, when those brats were jeering at me at recess? How you stood up to them all and told them off? You didn't care if they ostracized you, you didn't need those creeps. I always admired that. Still do. And I've been waiting years to tell you.

"Years . . .

"A lifetime.

"You were so much better off without Bobby. Actually I did you a favor if you only knew it. You have no idea how maddening he was, like some pissy old woman, he picked and fussed over everything. I couldn't cook, couldn't make love, there was always you; you were always there between us; there were always those subtle little reminders, and some not so subtle. Someone like me finds that pret-ty hard to take. It would've been so easy to resent you . . ."

She sighed. "If I just hadn't loved you so much."

Her voice broke. "Oh, Erin, I've always loved you. Why won't you believe me?"

A long silence.

"Men," she said contemptuously. "They mess up everything. You think that one you've got now is such great shakes, but don't bet your farm on it. He kissed me, you know. Right there in McNamara's dining room he kissed me hard on the mouth. I'll tell you something, Erin, you cut to the heart of it and your precious Janeway is no better than Bobby was. They all think with their cocks."

I squeezed Erin's arm. I heard Laura sniff and saw her move opaquely across the room. Suddenly she screamed. "God *damn* you, SAY something! *Say something!* Don't just sit there in the dark and judge me with that superior silence! Who in the *hell* do you think you are?"

I felt Erin tremble against me. I squeezed her tight.

"I'm sorry. God, I'm sorry, I didn't mean that. Of course I didn't mean it. I can never stay mad at you. But now you've got to talk to me, that's why I brought you up here. Just a few words to say you understand and it's all okay. I'll tell you how it was with Bobby and me and you'll thank your lucky stars I took him away from you.

"That's what I'll do, I'll tell you about Bobby. And you'll be surprised. You may've thought he was God's gift to women . . ."

She laughed without humor, a dry chuckle. "He was a nightmare to live with. All he cared about was those *God . . . DAMN . . .* books!

"From the moment he found out what Jerry could do, he had a one-track mind. We laughed at first when this little boy could sign all this stuff and it looked so real."

Again she laughed. "It was fascinating to watch him. All he had to do was see a signature and it rolled out of him. You should see what he does with Beethoven and Mozart. But Bobby wasn't stupid enough to fool with that. Bobby said, *We'll stick to the new stuff, the stuff nobody questions.* You don't have to know about papers and inks to put some movie star's name in a book. Jerry could do it with a modern pen, and we laughed, God, how we laughed. But then Bobby began selling this stuff and it wasn't funny anymore. He knew this bookseller from Arkansas and they made this alliance. The guy would bring up some books, give us a lot of money, and take away the signed ones, no questions asked. We could live forever out here on the money they brought us.

"But we fought. We fought all the time. I'm telling you, he'd have driven you nuts. He was so *damned* controlling. It was his way or the highway.

"He asked me for a divorce. Fine by me. But then he said, 'I'm taking Jerry,' and everything unraveled.

"*I'm taking Jerry.* Of all the nerve. Where was he when that kid was nothing but trouble and hard work? Where was he then?

"Jerry meant nothing to him except as a money machine. So we fought. And it got worse and worse . . . kept getting worse until that day in a fit of anger I had to kill him.

"Tell *me* he's gonna take Jerry!"

Softly, a moment later: "He got what he asked for."

Her voice settled into a quiet drone. "So I killed him. I killed Bobby."

I heard her move. The floor creaked.

"I killed him and here was Jerry, waiting to help me like some gift from heaven. Jerry's always been so anxious to help me. He always wants me to be pleased with what he does.

"This is what you've got to understand. Jerry *wanted* to help me.

"He seemed to be speaking to me. *Say I did it,* he said to me. Nobody will know.

"Hey, don't sit out there in silent judgment like that. I told you Jerry talks to me, didn't I tell you that? So what if he doesn't speak? I know what he wants; I know what he's trying to say.

"*Tell them I did it.* That's what Jerry wanted.

"But then I thought, nobody will believe it. So I would confess instead, let my lawyer discover on his own what Jerry had done. Everybody goes home happy.

"Was that clever? Only that deputy knew what really happened. Another one who got what he asked for. He wanted me to pay him to get out of town—ten thousand dollars so he could run away and not be an . . . not be . . . not . . .

". . . an embarrassment."

She sighed. "So he wouldn't embarrass me in front of you.

"Actually it was cheap at ten grand. I've still got Bobby's book money, all the money he got from that preacher, it's hidden away where I can get at it. You know I'd never kill anybody for money, not even that stupid deputy. When I tell you, you'll understand. Just say yes. Erin? Just say you want to hear it and you want to understand. That's all that matters to me now, that you understand what happened."

More time passed. Suddenly she said, "I want you to know everything. That's all I want, then. you'll understand it. I know you'd have done exactly what I did, there's never been any real differences between us. Just understanding."

So this was Laura's story of Lennie's sorry death. When he went back up to the house to get the kids that day, he had found Jerry in the bedroom with the twins, shivering and clutching a sketchpad. It never occurred to Lennie to look at what Jerry had drawn. He found it much later, under the backseat of his police car. Jerry had drawn two pictures of the shooting: Bobby in his last living moment, his face showing realization and sudden terror . . . and the killing itself . . .

"Me shooting Bobby," she said.

But Lennie wasn't happy with his ten thousand. "He took my money and then said, 'Oh, hey, didn't I tell you, that was just the down payment.' If I wanted what he had to sell, I had to ante up a lot more money. So fuck it, I killed him and took my money back. You should've seen his face when he knew what was coming. What a surprise. He begged and whined for his miserable life, he said the pictures were out in the truck. So we went out there and guess what, no pictures. And I shot him just like Bobby, on the spur of the moment."

She coughed. "Tell me he's gonna take Jerry."

I heard her moving again. She had come closer and now she faded back. I could see her melting into the inky woodwork.

"Erin? . . . Talk to me . . . where've you gone?

"Where've you gone?

"Where are you? Damn, I need you now more than ever. Say something."

What happened next was almost unbearable. The room melted into nothingness and for ten thousand years there was only the sound of the wind. I felt Erin trembling under my coat and I drew her as tight as I could. Laura made no more moves, no sound until the last minute, when she cracked wide open.

"Erin?

"Say something. Say something. Talk to me.

"*Erin . . .*

"*Talk to me.*

"*Talk to me!*

"*Erin? . . . Erin! God damn you, Erin, you fucking TALK TO ME!*

"*You better talk to me. If you know what's good for you . . .*

"*What makes you so fine? What makes you better than me? You've always thought you were better than me.*

"*Say something!*

"*SAY SOMETHING!*

"*YOU TALK TO ME RIGHT NOW!*"

Suddenly the lights went on: she had reached the wall and the room flashed yellow-white like dynamite had gone off in her hand. She was standing about five feet away. I saw the gun for perhaps three seconds. She said, "I'll always love you, Erin," and, "Good-bye," and I remember thinking in that moment, *She's going to kill herself.* But when she brought up the gun, it wasn't herself she shot. I heard the explosion and felt the incredible violence as the slug ripped into me. It flattened me against the wall and took my breath away. I knew right away it was a bad one, it had gone through most of me and hit my spine, I could feel the sensation going out of my hands and feet, and in the same half second she fired again and I felt Erin jerk over backward with the pain; she groaned out three words, "My God, Cliff," and rolled out of my arms. Laura took three giant steps and loomed over us; I heard her gun click and at last then I shot her, knocking her backward across the room, into the glass door, shattering it in the gale of blowing snow.

45

I saw red. I opened my eyes and the flashing red lights told me we were heading down the hill in an ambulance.

When I opened them again, I was in a white room, and the doctor standing over me looked grave. I heard him say I had lost all my blood, every drop of it had leaked out in the snow. But that had to be a dream because nobody can live any time at all without at least some blood.

A young nurse peered over my bed and said hello.

"Where am I?"

"You are in intensive care at CU Medical Center in Denver."

I didn't ask how I'd gotten there. I flexed my fingers . . . moved my toes, then my head. "It's all there," the nurse said. "A little stiff but all apparently in working order."

"Where's Erin?"

"Lie still," said the nurse.

"What about the woman who was with me?"

"She's here too."

Again I said Erin's name and the nurse went for a doctor, who came in a few minutes later. "You're a lucky man. A fraction of an inch to the left and you'd be paralyzed."

"How's Erin?"

"Your friend is doing as well as can be expected."

"Don't bullshit me, Doctor . . ."

There was a moment when I thought the worst. He's not answering my question because he doesn't want me to know the truth, I thought. I gripped the sides of the bed and tried to pull myself up.

"He's getting upset," the nurse said. "Maybe we should . . ."

"Should what?" I said. "All you people need to do is just be straight with me."

The doctor leaned over my bed. "Lie down there and listen to me. Your friend is in grave condition. We almost lost her twice last night. She is very serious."

She had been shot above the left breast. The shot had missed her heart by the same thin whisker, almost exactly the margin as the one that had missed my spine. Two blood transfusions had temporarily improved her outlook, but she was still critical. "We are doing everything we can for her," the doctor said.

I asked if I could see her. "Maybe in a while," the doctor said. "We'd have to roll your bed down the hall, and right now she's unconscious; she wouldn't know you're there anyway."

I couldn't help thinking of Hemingway and his death scene in *A Farewell to Arms*. This was going to be like that. She was dying and there was nothing I could do for her. I had used up all my luck that other time with Trish, and now there was none to call up for Erin. I looked over at the window and it was raining like that scene in the book. Rain, the symbol of all things bad.

"I'm going in to see her," I said.

"You can't yet."

"I'm going. You can either help me or get out of my way."

The doctor called an orderly and they decided not to restrain me. They wheeled my bed down the hall and into her room.

She looked dead to me. Her face was pale and she had tubes running everywhere. Her eyes were shut tightly, her breathing . . .

"She's not breathing," I said. "Do something, for Christ's sake, she's not breathing."

"She's very weak," the doctor said.

"She's not breathing."

"This is why I didn't want you to come in yet. The fact is, we don't know what's going to happen with her. We're doing everything we can."

"Can you save her?"

"I don't know. I wish I could tell you that but I can't."

They've got to save her, I thought. They've got to.

They will save her.

But the Hemingway illusion would not go away. I kept seeing that rain falling on the window and I couldn't shake the notion that I had used up all my luck that night years ago with Trish.

"You should go back to your room now," the doctor said.

"No, I want to be here."

I had a good grip on the foot of Erin's bed. He couldn't make me let go so they left me there and I watched over her till she died.

I jerked out of the dream. Across the way her eyes blinked open . . . just slits . . . enough to know I was there and who I was. I raised my finger in a *Hi there* motion and she saw it and she knew.

The next face I saw was Parley's. He sat and we talked for a few minutes.

They had found Bobby's autograph books—*hundreds* of dealer catalogs with vivid facsimiles—but no one ever found the money Laura claimed to be hiding.

"This was the most screwed-up case anybody could imagine," he said. "I feel like it was my fault as much as anybody's. I was the one she snookered."

"So was I."

"But I was the one that led to all the others. Then mistakes were made and made again on every level. I don't think we ever *could've* resolved this in a courtroom."

It was Erin who had called him that night from the house . . . Erin who had saved us. All I could do was roll over and play dead, but somehow, through some massive gut-check and a deep well of strength, she had crawled over and got the phone off the hook. "I thought you were both goners when I got up there with the doctor," Parley said.

But I have tough genes and so, apparently, does she.

Evening came and she was hanging tough. I ate my chicken soup stuff in her room and Parley sat with me, talking. I could feel myself gaining strength almost by the hour.

The sheriff had found Laura in a snowdrift behind the house. She had crawled down the back steps and died there, her hand sticking grotesquely out of the snow, still clutching the gun.

Laura is my cross to bear and I carry it alone.

At the Rocky Mountain Antiquarian Book Fair the following summer a dealer from Kansas came up with the novel *Laura,* so scarce it might almost legitimately be called rare. The book was hardly a perfect copy, but at twelve hundred it was a steal. I knew I could blow it out of my shop in a few hours. I stared at the jacket, and in the heroine's face I saw what I could not have seen in Burbank. She looks almost like the real Laura, I thought: the hair is different, the mouth, the eyes . . . all different. Everything was different, and yet there was something about that pulpy dust jacket that reminded me of what I'd rather forget. The Laura of the book was heroic; I knew with one phone call I could double my money on her. But I didn't want her in my store, not even for a little while.

I felt an arm on my shoulder. Erin said, "Is that a good one?"

"No."

"Must be at least pretty good at that price."

She didn't say anything more about it, but she did touch the paper where the title was, and in her fingers I sensed a wave of feeling. Too many people she had cared about had betrayed her, and all I could do was make sure that I would never be one of them. The dealer saw us looking at the book and he drifted over and asked if we could use it. "I could do a little better," he said, but I thanked him and moved on.

I saw a signed Cormac McCarthy, priced right and thus scarce. The reclusive McCarthy signs little and his early books get a premium, but I passed on that as well. I have a different feeling about signed books now, and I have quit dealing in them unless I know the dealer well or witness the signature myself.

That afternoon I ran a slow mile and vowed to burn a candle until I could do it again, double-time, without pain. That night Erin and I went out for our long-delayed dinner at The Broker.

The days and weeks passed.

Time is our mortal enemy but it's also the great healer. We never talk about Laura, never mention her name, though we do keep tabs on the kids. They are now in good foster homes and the twins are being adopted. Jerry remains an enigma even to the experts. He had combinations of abilities that none of them had ever seen in a single subject, and later that year, with diligent encouragement and coaching from a young teacher, he began to talk. He has a good, rich voice, but almost as soon as he said his first words, his savant skills went into a slow fade. This is what sometimes happens when a mute savant learns to talk. So I read. So they say.

Don't ask why. Might as well ask why they are in the first place. One door swings open; another closes forever.

Today Jerry can talk but he can't draw a straight line or write his own name.

The mysteries of the human mind are far beyond my comprehension.

SCRIBNER BOOKS
PROUDLY PRESENTS

THE BOOKWOMAN'S LAST FLING

Coming soon from
Scribner Books

Turn the page for a preview of
The Bookwoman's Last Fling. . . .

1

THE MORNING was angry but I was cool. The rain rolled in from the west like a harbinger of some vast evil brewing, but I had the man's money in my bank account—it was mine, he couldn't get it back unless I went nuts and decided to give it to him, and that made me cool. I had followed his orders almost to the letter, varying them just enough to satisfy my own persnickety nature. Long before the first faint light broke through the black clouds, I got up, dressed, got out of my motel room, and drove out toward the edge of town.

I found the all-night diner without a hitch; parked at the side and sat in my cold car with the motor idling. I was early. I had been told to come at five o'clock, no more or less, but I tend to ignore advice like that, especially when it comes with an attitude. I waited ten minutes and the appointed hour came and went. I could sense his presence off to my left beyond the parking lot: if I looked hard at that patch of darkness I could make out the vaguest shape of a car or truck, a vehicle of some kind in a small grove of trees. At 5:05 by the clock in my car I got out and went inside. The waiter took my order, a slam-bang something with eggs and pancakes: enough cholesterol to power the whole state of Idaho. I consoled myself. I seldom eat like that any more unless I am on the road, and apparently I am one of the lucky ones: I have great good genes and my so-called good cholesterol readings are always sensational. No matter how much fat I eat, my system burns it. To my knowledge, no one in my family tree has ever died of a heart attack, which only means that I have a fine opportunity to be the first one.

The waiter tried to make the cook under-stand what I wanted through a serious language barrier. The cook looked illegal as hell: he spoke a kind of Spanglish through the window and the waiter struggled with that. I sat through two cups of coffee and no one came out of the lot beyond parking. My breakfast was surprisingly tasty and hot; I ate it slowly and looked up occasionally for some sign of life in the parking lot. When I looked at my watch again, it was five-thirty. The man was half an hour late.

I stretched out my legs and waited some more. If he didn't come at all it was truly his loss. I had five thousand of his American big ones and that usually guaranteed good faith. I could buy a fairly nice book with that. It was my rock-bottom minimum these days, the least it took for a stranger like him to get me off my dead ass in Denver and on the road to some distant locale. I got the money up front for just such contingencies as this one: a client with guff to match my own. That's one thing people had said about Harold Ray Geiger in all the newspaper accounts I had read of his life and death. He was abrupt, and so was the guy who had called me.

Geiger's man was also mysterious, enigmatic to a fault. He had sent me a cashier's check, so I still didn't know his full name. "My name is Willis," he had said on the phone. "I am Mr. Geiger's representative in Idaho." Normally I wouldn't touch a job like this: I certainly wouldn't leave home and make such a drive without knowing certain salient details. What had sold me on the case were the books. Geiger had died last month with a vast library of great first editions, the estate had a problem with them, and that was partly what I did now. I didn't do appraisal work: I found that boring and there were others who could do it faster and at least as well. There can be huge differences between honest appraisers, and I tend to be too condition-conscious for people who, for reasons of their own, want their appraisals high. But I would help recover stolen books, I would try to unravel a delicate book mystery, I would do things, and not always for money, that got me out in the sunshine, away from my bookstore in Denver and into another man's world. It all depended on the man, and the voice on the phone seemed to belong to a five-grand kind of guy.

Six o'clock came and went. I rolled with it, prepared to sit here half the morning. The man deserved no less than that for five thousand dollars.

At some point I saw the truck move out of the shadows and bump its way into the parking lot. It was one of those big bastards with wheels half the size of Rhode Island. The sky was still quite dark and the rain drummed relentlessly on the roof of the truck. I could see his knuckles gripping the wheel: nothing of his face yet, just that white-knuckle grip beyond the glass. I knew he had a clear look at me through the windshield, and at one point I smiled at him and tried to look pleasant. But I had a come-if-you-want-to, don't-if-you-don't attitude of my own. The ball was in his court.

Eventually he must have realized this, for I saw the unmistakable signs of life. A light went on in the truck and a man in a hat and dark glasses materialized. He climbed down and came inside.

"You Janeway?"

I recognized his voice from that cryptic phone call a week ago. I said, "Yep. And you would perhaps be representing the estate of Mr. Harold Ray Geiger?"

"I'm Willis. I was Mr. Geiger's right-hand man for more than thirty years."

He sat in the booth and sent up a signal for coffee. He didn't offer his hand and I didn't take it. There was another moment when I might have taken it by force, but then he had moved both hands into his lap and I figured groping around between his legs might cast us both in a bad light. From the kitchen the Mexican cook was watching us.

The mystery man sat sipping his coffee.

"Do you have a first name, Mr. Willis?"

"Yes, I have a first name." He said this with dripping sarcasm, a tone you use with a moron if you are that kind of guy. Already I didn't like him; we were off to a bad start.

"Should I try to guess it? You look like somebody named Clyde, or maybe Junior."

I said this in a spirit of lighthearted banter, I hoped, but he bristled. "My first name doesn't matter. I am the man who will either take you out to Mr. Geiger's ranch or leave you to wonder for the rest of your life what this might have been."

Now it was my turn to stifle a laugh.

"Are you making light of this?" I sensed a blink behind his dark shades. "Are you trying to annoy me?"

"Actually, Mr. Willis, I was starting to think it was the other way around."

"You've got a helluva nerve, coming out here with an attitude."

"I wasn't aware I had one."

"Keep it up and you can just climb right back in that car and get the hell out of here."

I stared at him for a long moment. I was suddenly glad I had been paid by cashier's check: his money was now firmly in my bank.

"I want it established right from the start," he said: "You are working for me. You will appraise Mr. Geiger's books and do it ASAP. If it turns out that books are missing and lost forever, I want you to give me a document to that effect, something that will satisfy God, the executor of Mr. Geiger's will, and any other interested party who happens to ask. Is that clear enough?"

"I wasn't told I had to satisfy God as well as all those other people."

"I am not paying you for that kind of wiseass commentary. I was told you are a reliable professional and that's what I want from you. That's all I want."

"Well, let's see if I understand it so far. You want me to look at some books. Supposedly there are some missing titles. I'm to give you a written appraisal and do it on the quickstep. I'm to tell you what's missing based on your assertion that these missing books were ever there in the first place. I'm to do all this in a cheerless environment; I'm not allowed to ever crack a joke or even smile once in a while for comic relief. Twice a day you send a gnome up with bread and water and he hands it to me through the bars. I get to go pee occasionally, as long as I don't abuse this privilege; otherwise it's pucker-up-and-hold-it time. Is that about it?"

"I don't like your attitude."

"We've already established that." I slipped into my Popeye voice. "But I yam what I yam,

Mr. Willis. That's what you get for your money, which by the way isn't all that great. And it's looking less great the more we talk."

"Then leave," he said in an *I dare you* tone.

I slid out of the booth, picked up the check and started toward the counter. I sensed his disbelief as I paid the tab and sidled back to the booth to leave the waiter a tip.

"Thanks for the call. Give my regards to Idaho Falls."

I was halfway across the parking lot when I heard the door open. He said my name, just "Janeway," and I stopped and turned politely.

"What are you, crazy? You haven't even heard what this is about."

"Believe me, I would still love to be told."

"Then stop acting so goddamn superior."

"It's not an act, Clyde. I don't have any act. This may surprise you, but I have lived all these years without any of Mr. Geiger's money. I've gotten wherever I am with no help at all from you guys, and I'm willing to bet I can go the rest of the way on my own as well. I do appreciate the business, however."

"Wait a minute."

We looked at each other.

"What do you think, I brought you out here just for the hell of it?"

"I have no idea why you do what you do. If you want to talk, let's go. Your five grand has already bought you that privilege."

He stood there for another moment as if, with enough time, he could reclaim some of the high ground he had lost. "You're a slick piece of change, aren't you?"

"Yes sir, I am. I may not be much of many things, but I am slick. Two things before we go. First take off those glasses, please. I like to see who I'm talking to."

He took them off slowly, and in that act the authority passed all the way from him to me. His eyes were gray, like a timber wolf or a very old man.

"Thank you. Now tell me, please, who you are. Is Willis your first name or last?"

"Last."

"What's your first?"

He stared at me for a long moment. Then he said, "Junior," I swear he did, and that confession made the whole trip worthwhile.

2

I CALLED him Mr. Willis after that. I try to be polite unless people deliberately piss me off, the man was older than me by at least twenty years, and respecting my elders is part of my code. He could have been any age between an old fifty-five and a well-preserved seventy. I parked my car on the street and we drove out of town in his Sherman tank. The city lights fell away and the rain came hard again. I could now see a faint streak of light in the east, but it was still too faint to matter. He drove about ten miles and turned into a dirt road posted KEEP OUT, fenced on both sides with the distinctive wooden slats of a horse ranch.

That was the other thing I knew about Geiger from his obit: in addition to his book collection he had been a horse-racing man. But I'd soon found out that I had this chronology backward. In addition to being a lifelong horseman, Geiger had a book collection. Horses were his life and books were now part of it, a combination I found irresistible. I had always been partial to the horse, a nobler, wiser, much gentler and far more majestic creature than man. I had been an enthusiastic customer at Centennial Race Track in Littleton, just south of Denver, until it closed for good in 1983. I was one of those daring young kids who got in as soon as the law allowed and maybe a little sooner than that. This was years before my police career began. I had been drawn to the turf by the spectacle, not so much as the lure of fast money. Before I was ten I had read all of Walter Farley's wonderful *Black Stallion* novels, and for a year I pictured myself as an impossible cross between Alec Ramsey and Eddie Arcaro. Of course, I could never have been a jockey—I was still a growing boy and already pushing 175 pounds, but at eighteen I could spend entire afternoons watching the races. I talked to the grooms over the rail and I quickly learned their lingo. They were called ginneys, a term going back to old racing days in England, when winning owners tipped their grooms a guinea. Today, I had heard, well-heeled owners passed out bills, not coins, featuring Jackson and Grant, occasionally a Franklin if the winning pot had been good enough. I knew these things, though I had never crossed that magical line between the grandstand and the backside. I knew where the class raced, at Hialeah and Gulfstream in Florida, at Aqueduct, Belmont, and Jamaica in New York, and on the west coast at Santa Anita and Hollywood Park, among other fabled places. I struggled with algebra but I knew the difference between allowance races and claimers. Claiming races were the guts of almost any racing program. Here a horse's true grit could be calculated, scientifically some said, against others of similar company. In a claiming race, each owner was putting a price on his horse, and the horse could be bought—claimed—by any other owner at the meet who was willing to pay the claiming price. At the same time, the price was a measure of a horse's class. How I loved those hazy, distant Saturdays at Centennial. I was caught up in the majesty of the post parade and the drama of the race, and I didn't care whether I had the two bucks for a bet.

Willis clattered and splashed us along the dirt road for a good quarter-mile. The country here was mostly a gently rolling plain. Occasionally there were trees; I could see them now as the black sky became reluctantly gray; nestled among them were some barns and beyond it all was the house. We turned in among the barns and came up to a small training track. There I got my first look at a man who might have been Geiger in earlier times. He stood at the rail watching an exercise boy work a horse in the slop: a stoop-shouldered figure in silhouette, lonely as hell, by the look of him. He wasn't wearing a GEIGER sign on his heavy black slicker; I just figured he was one of the old man's three sons the way you sometimes figure things out. He glanced over his shoulder as we went past and that's how he took note of us: no wave of the hand, no other movement at all. He wore a hood that showed nothing of his face. He just stood there like some grim reaper in a bad dream; then he turned away as the boy galloped his horse around the track again to complete the mile.

Willis didn't stop and I didn't ask. We didn't exchange any wisdom or wit; he didn't pull up under the big old tree and start showing me pictures of his grandchildren or his prizewinning roses. Sudden camaraderie was not about to break out between us, so my best bet was to keep my mouth shut and not annoy him more than I already had. This I did while he drove along the track and around it, turning up the road to the house, which now loomed before us in the rain. It was an old two-story house, old when Geiger had bought it would be my guess, built here sometime well before the nineteen-twenties for another old sodbuster now long dead. None of that mattered now. Willis pulled around to the side and parked under a long overhang. A set of steps went straight up from there. We got out of the car; he gestured me sullenly and I went up ahead of him, emerging onto a wide wraparound porch. I stood at the railing looking out at the farm, which was just coming to life in the gray morning. I could see up to the track where the horse was being led back through the gap. The groom held him while the hooded man stood apart, and the boy sat straight in the saddle. On the road he hopped off and they all walked down to the barn, where a black man stood waiting with a bucket of hot water. They were a hundred yards away but my eyes were good. The ginney washed the mud off his horse and then skimmed off the water with a scraper. Steam floated off the horse like the bubbling ponds around Old Faithful, but I still couldn't see anything of the hooded man's face. His hood kept him dark and mysterious.

I heard Willis cough behind me. He said, "You comin'?" and I said yeah, sure. His tone remained surly while I tried to keep mine evenly pleasant. I followed him into the house through a side door. He said, "Wait here," and for once I did as I was told as he disappeared along a totally black corridor. A moment later a light came on, far down at the end of the hallway on the other side of the house. He motioned me with his hand and turned into the room. Almost at once I was aware of another light beaming out into the hall, and when I reached it I saw Willis sitting behind an enormous desk. My eyes also took in two dozen horse pictures on the far wall, winner's circle pictures with an oil painting in the center. The centerpiece was a great painting of a magnificent red stallion. The caption said *Man o' War, 1921.*

"I've got a few chores to do before we talk," Willis said. This was okay. For the moment I was at the man's beck and call; if I computed what he was paying me on a per-hour basis, I would be way ahead of the game for the seeable future. I had never made anything close to this kind of money when I was a cop, so if he wanted me to sit I could sit here all week. At some point I would hear his story, I'd tell him what if anything I could do or try to do for him and maybe, if the answer was nothing and his demeanor was civilized, I'd consider giving him a chunk of his money back. For the moment I didn't want to drop even a hint of that possibility. Willis asked if I wanted coffee. I didn't; I had had my quota in the restaurant but I said sure, I'd take a cup, I'd be sociable. Who knows, it might help us break some ice, I thought. Willis disappeared and I was left to give the room another inspection alone.

The first thing I noticed was, there were no books anywhere.

The second thing, which took me slightly longer to determine, was that Geiger himself appeared in none of the winner's circle pictures. I got up and walked along the wall looking at them.

A winner's circle picture, in addition to being a quality professional photograph, gives some good information in three or four lines. First there is the name of the winning horse. Then it tells the racetrack where the win occurred; then the date, the name of the winning jockey, the horses that ran second and third, the distance, the winner's time, and the names of the owner and trainer. In all of these, H. R. Geiger was named as the owner and trainer, but the only men who had come down to stand with the winner were Willis and the groom. There was no gang of celebrants in any of them and this, maybe, told me a little more about Geiger. Even in cheap claiming races a crowd often assembles around the winning horse. The groom must be there to hold the horse; the jockey, of course, still seated in the saddle, and a whole bunch of people dressed in suits and ties, flowery dresses or plain shirts and jeans, all friends of the winning owner. I had seen winner's circle pictures that had twenty grinning people crowded together as if they personally had pushed the hapless nag the entire six furlongs. But here was a whole wall showing only four faces in each: Willis and the groom, the jockey and the horse. Willis wore his western attire, boots, the hat and a string tie tight at his neck. The pictures were in chronological order. The oldest was from April 1962, the most recent from March 1975. Geiger's winner in that first shot had been a dark filly named Miss Ginny, who had gone to the post with all four legs wrapped. Willis was a slender young man in those days; he stood almost timidly, the jockey wore a look of authority as if he, not Willis, had been running things, and the groom was a serious black kid who looked straight into the camera. The picture had been taken at Hot Springs, Arkansas: a bright, sunny day, from the look of it. Miss Ginny had won handily, beating the place horse by five lengths.

I moved along the wall looking at each individual picture until, at some point, I felt uneasy. I didn't know why then: If I had thought about it at all I might have attributed it to the almost unnatural sameness of the people in the circle. From year to year they never changed places: it was always Willis standing alone on the far left, then a broad gap, then the groom, the horse and rider. The jockey was the same skinny white kid for that first half-year; then a series of jocks had replaced him, each riding for the old man for a year, more or less. The ginney was mostly the same black kid; he had been in the first picture and was in the last, with three white kids taking turns with him, holding the horse in the sixties. What was so unusual about that? I finally decided it must be Willis. He wasn't the owner or the trainer; he didn't hold the horse; he had no real purpose in the picture, as far as I could see, and yet there he was, standing far apart, staring into the camera with that same eerie way he had. Expressionless—that's how I would describe him. He looked almost like a mannequin, a man with no soul.

"Here's your coffee," he said suddenly from the doorway.